Simon Andrew Stubbs

THE TRADE

Also by Simon Andrew Stubbs
and available in paperback or
for Kindle:

Envy
Bodies
Jackson Hope

FOR JOSEPH

Your light blows the darkness away

PROLOGUE

Scrunching his toes on the thick office carpet Martin took one last look at the papers on his desk then slipped them back in the manila envelope and placed them in his drawer. Outside Canary Wharf jostled like a writhing claw out of the horse shoe shaped land that clung to the embankment of the Thames. From his huge double-sided picture window he had a fantastic view of both the gherkin and the shard, though by comparison his own offices were a little more modest they were however here on merit, and unlike some of his close neighbours would still be here for time to come. The Empire, for the time being at least, was stable.

"They're waiting for you sir." The man at the door said, clasping his hands comfortably in front of him.

"How many times have I asked you to simply call me Martin?" The man at the desk asked with a warm smile.

The man at the door smiled in return.

"Many, many times. I don't know, I guess I'm old school, I just like it, gives the whole shebang a kind of upstairs, downstairs feel wouldn't you say?"

"I would, that's why I don't like it, sometimes I think you know that and do it anyway, just to spite me."

"I do, I'm hoping one day you'll get so worked up you'll have a huge heart attack and the Empire will all be mine." The man at the door said with a grin, not knowing that in just a few minutes time his words would return to haunt him.

Martin let out a huge belly laugh and fished under the huge mahogany desk for his shoes; he slipped them on and pushed back his chair with his feet.

"How do I look?" He asked, adjusting his tie in the mirror.

"Like a man that's eaten his fair share of late suppers...sir."

Martin laughed again, then grabbed his jacket from the hook next to the mirror.

Peter Werth-Duncan had been the direct understudy, assistant, right-hand man and friend of the CEO of Sapient Trans Global for the last seven and a half years. He was credited by Martin Rooley as the man responsible for lifting Sapient into the FTSE top 100 two years ago, and if his shrewd understanding of the market continued to deliver the net growth it had this last six months Martin was sure he would lead them there again.

He was a thin man with a balding head, always immaculately dressed, but at forty-two had never married, he was the classic business bachelor. Martin had liked him from the go, there was something about him, a prissy charm if you like, and if you watched him efficiently ghost about the floors of the Brans-Turner building, orchestrating the continued success of this long time haulage company, it was impossible not to be impressed with his ambition and ability.

Martin loved his business too, had hand reared it from a one truck courier service in the Lancashire city of Bolton some forty-odd years ago, but at sixty-seven had started taking more of a back seat, watching in wonder as his young understudy continued to linchpin the operation, taking it to places Martin wouldn't have dared to dream, and in such a short space of time. Martin had created the business, in his mid forties had grown it into a huge global colossus, but was in no doubt that this young man was the future of Sapient Trans Global, and deservedly so.

Peter opened the door and Martin stepped out into the PA's quarter, known to all at Sapient as the green room, adjusting his collar as he walked. The secretary's desk was empty as he had hoped it would be; he had practically demanded Sheila join the party, there would be time to pick up the paper trail on the 27th.

As he walked through the door and out into the short corridor that led to the atrium he could hear the commotion coming from downstairs. He smiled as he ambled towards the noise; the annual Christmas address was as much a part of the festive season at Sapient as mistletoe and mince pies, and this year there was nothing but good news to share. He stepped out onto the gantry with Peter close behind and looked down at the mass of people gathered in the foyer below. He loved this time of year, everybody all relaxed and ready for the holiday period, no matter what the working day threw at you it never seemed to stick, there was January just around the corner for that, but for now you could almost taste the joy in the air.

The party was in full swing, and it looked like the workers were enjoying the free champagne and canapés that were being banded about, why not, they deserved it; this year alone their hard work had earned Sapient an annual turnover of almost sixty-three million pounds, eighteen million of which could be boasted as profit at the annual general meeting that coming May. In the forty two years since Martin Rooley had laid out a hundred and sixty seven pounds for that all important first less than reliable delivery van, Sapient Trans Global had earned the unassuming entrepreneur a net worth of over four hundred million pounds, all assets considered.

He gazed down at the people happily milling about, laughing in their groups, gathered under the huge Christmas tree decorated in resplendent silver and gold, sipping at their champagne flutes, some talking shop, some talking up the latest game, some talking nonsense from the countless glasses of free bubbly. He could see Tina Spoyles from Admin desperately chasing a rather harassed looking Nigel Crow from HR with a sprig of mistletoe and a young couple sat kissing on the grey leather couch in the corner of reception, he smiled, remembering what it was like to be young and in love.

Yes he loved this time of year, and always enjoyed milling about at the annual Christmas party, trying to get to know some of the people a little better that were the true driving force behind his hugely successful business. He almost wished he didn't have to make his address, he was enjoying just watching the fun unfold down below, but it was expected of him, and he knew for some bizarre reason that if he didn't it would be missed. Why this was the case would always remain a mystery to him; why would they want to break off their Christmas celebrations for five or ten minutes to listen to an old fart like him? He didn't know, but they seemed to like it, and secretly he liked it too, it made him feel fatherly and having never had any children of his own - Rose had simply never taken on - he always looked on his work force with a fatherly care.

"I think it's time." Peter said at his side. Martin nodded and leant slightly over the rail.

The thin man passed him the megaphone, a gift from Sheila two Christmases' before – adorned at the time with a hideously large silver bow - after workers had complained they hadn't been able to hear his address, and he clicked the switch on the side.

"I hate this blasted thing." He whined to Peter as it let out a howl of feedback.

"Oh come on, where's that famous Christmas spirit?" Peter said with a grin.

Martin shook his head in mock frustration, then raised the mouthpiece to his lips.

"Ladies and gentlemen, ladies and gentlemen, if I could have your attention please."

Slowly the revellers turned their attention up to the gantry, tapping one another on the shoulder or arm and gesturing up to their popular leader. Little by little the commotion died down until only a few murmurings from some of the more intoxicated members of staff remained; he had their attention now as good as he was going to get it.

"Thank you for giving an old man an opportunity to break up your festivities and drone on as men of a certain age seem to have a habit of doing."

There was laughter from below, and it wasn't simply to be polite, these people genuinely liked their CEO, a rare occurrence in this day and age and in a blue chip organisation the size and scale of Sapient.

"I promise not to take up too much of your time, you all have better things to do and besides I wouldn't want to ruin Tina's chances with Nigel."

More laughter erupted at this and the mortified woman reddened at the cheeks, quickly hiding the mistletoe behind her back.

"I'm sorry Tina that was a cheap laugh," the CEO continued with a wry smile, "but at my age if I tried to tell a proper joke I'd probably jumble up the punch-line. Anyway I digress, as is the custom at this time of year, before this little haulage company shuts down for the holiday period and you good people get a well deserved rest with your loved ones, albeit children or kittens, it is time for our annual Christmas shindig and this sad old tradition of me mumbling on at you for a few minutes."

Down below a group of well dressed sales executives, their ties slightly askew and their cheeks a little rosy, started chanting his name, as though he were the latest teenage sensation at Stamford Bridge rather than an over weight, wispy haired businessman.

Martin settled them by raising his hand, feeling a little embarrassed but far from annoyed, they were just letting off steam after all, and it was Christmas.

"It's been another fantastic year for us at Sapient, in a difficult Economic climate when we have seen some huge corporations fold and well known brands disappear from the high street, we have continued to stay strong, to turn a profit and to grow as an organisation. In this age of uncertainty let me tell you that is no mean feat, and that success is down to the hard work and commitment of the best and most loyal workforce in Great Britain."

A huge roar of approval met this and down below every pair of hands applauded the sentiment.

Martin let them applaud for a few moments; they were applauding their own achievements after all, then slowly brought them under control with a small gesture of his hands.

"I would like to pay particular heed to my second in command," martin continued, gesturing towards a modest looking Peter, "it's true that he's about as full of the Christmas spirit as Jacob Marley, but he's a good man, and his commitment, drive and leadership have driven us in a direction that will make our countless share holders very happy over their turkey dinners this Christmas. We owe him an awful lot, and I for one am very grateful, ladies and gentlemen please give a warm hand for your head of corporate strategy Mister Peter Werth-Duncan."

The crowd below applauded again, but a little less enthusiastically this time, it was hard to celebrate the man that cracked the whip, Peter understood this but didn't seem to mind.

Martin smiled at his right hand man, his nod of acknowledgment both warm and genuine, then turned back to face the gathered throng.

"The coming year holds many challenges for us, in order to simply stay afloat we need to be brave, but we at Sapient do not want to simply stay afloat, we want continue this positive glide path, we want to continue to grow, in order to grow we need to diversify, but if we continue in the manner that we have this year then we have nothing to fear, and whatever challenges come our way we will face them head on, with the guts and glory that have got us where we are today.

Thank you again for your hard work and commitment, may I be the first to wish you all a very Merry Christmas, and a happy new, a happy new, a…. a…."

Peter Werth-Duncan, who had been absently thinking about the calls he had to make before closing down his own office for the Christmas period and smiling politely while his colleague and friend gave his address, was quickly brought back into the here and now. He looked to his left and saw the ashen look on Martin's face. The mans eyes were huge orbs and his bottom lip was trembling, Peter had time to think that the old guy looked absolutely terrified before he dropped the megaphone to the corrugated steel floor of the gantry where it let out a shrill screech.

Down below gasps of horror could be heard as onlookers watched the drama unfold.

"What is it?" Peter asked, clearly very worried.

"Heart!" Martin hissed, his face turning purple, his hand coming up to clutch his chest.

Peter froze for a couple of seconds, but to him it felt like a lifetime, he had never felt so small and unworldly in all his life. Then as the old man slid down the side of the banister with his eyes pleading up at his friend, the middle aged man snapped into action.

"Ambulance, somebody call an ambulance!" He called down to the crowd below. A huge din erupted now as people slipped into an inevitable mode of panic, but thank God Sheila was on hand to grab the phone from the reception desk and make the necessary call.

When he saw that the situation was reasonably under control Peter dropped down to his friends side and lay a comforting hand on his shoulder.

"An ambulance is coming; you're going to be alright."

Martin let out an agonised moan, his hands were shaking very badly and he was afraid that he had wet himself.

"Try not to talk." Peter continued. "Everything's going to be ok, everything…"

But Martin's eyelids were starting to flicker, he was no longer aware of what was happening around him.

"Martin, Martin God damn it stay with me." Peter pleaded as footsteps were heard racing up the stairs. "An ambulance is on its way, you stay with me now."

The sixty-seven year old man, who had considered retirement after making his first million at forty-two, felt the room disappear into a deep but not unpleasant fog. At one moment he was looking up into the harried face of his friend, the next he was drifting away, the sights and sounds of the office Christmas party a vague memory. His eyelids fluttered a little quicker, then stilled, then slowly winked shut, a deep breath escaping his throat that came right from the pit of his stomach.

Now it was Peter's turn to look ashen, fearing that the old man was dead, his mouth a small o as revellers from the party below made it onto the gangway and hurried towards them.

But the old man wasn't dead, he had suffered a massive cardiac arrest, and as the panic continued to unfold about him had slipped gracelessly into unconsciousness.

PART ONE:
THE WAITING GAME

1

His eyes blinked open and the first thing he became aware of was the glare from the sunlight coming through the gap in the thin curtains. He closed his eyes again and his world was filled with the tinge of red light that you only get after looking directly into the sun. Something was blipping away at his side, he let out a huge breath and ran a hand that felt attached to a sluggish left arm up to his cheek. There was a days worth of growth on his chin, his hand traced the contours beneath the rough surface hair and then dropped lazily back to his side.

Slowly he peeked his left eye open again, being careful not to look in the direction of the almost blinding white light, he blinked a couple of times against the glare and when he was comfortable opened it fully, taking a first tentative look around the room.

He was lying on a bed that was pushed with its plastic headboard back to the soft peach coloured wall. The linen was crisp white and plain and was pulled up to his waist, he could feel that beneath here he was wearing pyjama bottoms of some kind; he didn't think they were his own. His right eye crept open to join the left on its exploration of the room, it too blinked a couple of times before it adjusted to the light. With a stiff neck he raised his heavy head slightly off the pillow and peered down at his naked chest. It was covered with pads and wires, electrodes that were hooked up to the noisy machinery at his side. He looked at this now; he had seen enough hospital dramas in his time to recognise a heart monitor when he saw one. He gazed at the small green blip on the screen as it bounced rhythmically up and down to the beat of his unseen internal organ. Was it this organ that had landed him in this mess? Martin suspected it may well be the case.

He could vaguely remember being at the office Christmas party; he was either about to give his annual speech or part way through it when the pain had gripped him, squeezing his chest like a boa constrictor. Everything after that was a blank, but he guessed that at some point in between he had landed here, in what appeared to be a private hospital bed, no doubt fully covered by his BUPA health insurance.

His throat felt very dry and his whole body was wracked with a deep exhaustion, the like of which he had not endured even in his younger days when he had been given to wild weekends with his golfing buddies up at St. Andrews or at the private club for which he was a member in Hampshire. His head also throbbed; it felt as though he had been struck on the cranium with an iron bar and though he knew this not to be true it was hard to ignore that pulsing, living pain.

With his fingers tingling and the muscles in his upper arm dancing back to life he traced his fingers morosely over the pads on his chest. He wanted to rip them off; they felt intrusive against the grey curly hair beneath and he felt exposed with his pot belly out for all to see. He hoped his nurse wasn't pretty.

Martin sighed and rested his head back against the soft pillow. A heart attack; that was the likely cause of his misery, and he only had himself to blame. He wasn't a smoker, but he liked a cigar every once in a while, and his drinking had become heavier ever since he turned sixty, feeling he deserved it now he had reached his twilight years, when most men of his age were starting to consider retirement. Again it wasn't excessive, but a day rarely went by without at least one scotch, and this could be two or three if the mood grabbed him. He was under no illusion as to the real culprit behind this crime though, and he lifted his head again and looked down at it now; his stomach. Just looking at it made him feel queasy, it was as white as the sheets that draped around his waist and the skin was pulled tight around a formidable gut, a gut he had created through years of excess.

The Rooley's could afford a chef if they so pleased, but Rose enjoyed cooking for her man, always had, and Martin had always enjoyed being her chief taster, why not, she was one hell of a cook, he doubted if any paid help could rustle up a Sunday roast or deliver a piping hot pie from the oven half as good as hers. There was a standing joke at meal times that the Rooley's had enjoyed for at least thirty of their forty-odd years together; as Rose served up whatever mealtime treat was on offer that evening she would ask Martin how much he would like, and his reply was always the same, 'just a lot Rose dear, just a lot.' And now it would seem that the years of dedication to his stomach were finally catching up with him, for he lay in this hospital bed feeling frightened and alone, wondering how being a man who liked his food could have possibly landed him in such a mess?

The door crept open and Rose walked in with a cardboard cup from Costa coffee in her hand, she slunk across the room and slumped down in the soft chair in the far corner. Martin watched as she took a sip from the plastic lid and placed the coffee down on the table. He had never understood those blasted lids, where had that fad come from? Years and years and years people had been drinking coffee, tea, hot chocolate, Ovaltine or any damn hot drink they liked without needing a lid like some over sized child's Tommee Tippee cup, and now it seemed impossible for grown up's to swallow a drop unless it came from a hole in a round plastic lid the size of a twenty pence piece. The whole world had gone mad. He blamed 'Friends', that infuriating programme Rose always watched on repeat on those late night comedy channels, until that damned programme came along you got your coffee from a local café and it came in one variety; coffee bean. Now there was every damn flavour under the sun; latte, grande, mochaccino, cappuccino, caramel latte, espresso, it was enough to make your head hurt, but Rose like so many others had bought into the whole Starbuck's, Costa, Café Nero experience, where you could enjoy your over priced drink in a large cup with a slice of something on the side with about as much personality as a dog chewed slipper. Greggs the bakers was Martin's vice of choice, where you could get a decent cup of normal coffee and a sticky bun for a little over a pound; it wasn't the money (he had plenty of that) it was the principle. Oh well as Rose was often fond of saying, you can take the boy out of Bolton but you can never take the Bolton out of the boy.

She hadn't noticed he was awake and sat staring into the corner of the room, her eyes looking tired and forlorn. Martin looked at her, the curly grey hair on the top of her head which had once been a silky auburn and the pallid skin of her cheeks that hid the model like bone structure beneath. Time may have aged her, may have added pounds to her hips and an arch to her back, but he loved her all the same, to Martin Rooley he still saw the shy young girl he had courted at the Picture-dome in Bolton back in nineteen sixty-nine. The years could take away a lot of things, but they could never fade his love. As he looked at her now he felt a deep sadness inside, she looked so lost and vulnerable, sat there in that ill coloured seat with the steaming cup of nonsense at her side, her eyes tired and grey, she looked this way because of him, and because of what he had so badly gotten wrong. He just hoped it was not too late to undo some of the damage he had undoubtedly done.

Martin closed his eyes again and waited for the beating in his chest to calm, the last thing he needed right now was to get himself all excited, then when he felt he was fully under control, he opened his eyes and lifted his head from his pillow once more.

"Rose." He tried to say but his voice came out all hoarse, barely a whisper. It was so low that his wife of all these years didn't even notice. He flopped his head back on the pillow and tried to clear his throat; it was this that caught Rose's attention. She looked over from her place in the corner of the room with wide, hopeful eyes; when Martin lifted his head from the pillow once more she let out a startled breath, then hurried over to the bed, with the soft skin of her upper arms flapping beneath the thin cotton blouse she wore.

"My God, Martin, you're awake! Thank God!" She said, tears prickling at the corners of her eyes. She reached out and grasped his hand between two of hers and brought it up to her chest where she planted a small kiss on the freckles next to his wedding band, this sent the muscles in his arm jangling again but he tried not to let it show, she was smiling and he didn't want to spoil that. "Wait here," she said, her breath coming in short sharp gasps, "I'll go get the doctor."

"Where else am I going to go?" Martin whispered as she shuffled out of the room, but he was smiling as he relaxed the tired muscles in his neck and rested back down on the soft hospital pillow. He could hear her outside talking excitedly to whoever would listen, and waited for the expected fuss that was likely to follow. He gazed up to the suspended ceiling with its un-turning fan and the small patch of damp in one corner; it seemed even private hospital facilities could use a little upkeep, and wondered absently if he'd missed Christmas. Just how long had he been asleep? He had no way of telling, but the growth on his chin suggested it hadn't been long.

Footsteps were coming up the corridor now, Martin sighed and rested his eyes for a few seconds before the door opened and a tall man with thinning black hair and bifocal lenses stepped into the room, his tie slightly askew, with Rose following close behind, her hands clasped together in front of her ample chest.

"Mister Rooley, you gave your share holders quite a fright." The tall man said as he stepped into the room and strolled quite casually up to the bed.

"I'll bet." Martin croaked through his parched lips. "I bet they were rubbing their greedy little hands together."

The tall man smiled. "My name is Doctor Crowley, I'm the duty Doctor this morning, do you know where you are?"

"In hospital." Martin whispered.

"That's right, you're in St. Cuthbert's, and you're in good hands. How are you feeling?"

"A little woozy, my throat is dry."

The doctor nodded, then turned and poured a plastic cup of water from the jug on the bed stand.

"I'll do it." Rose said, taking the cup from the doctor, Martin figured she needed to do something, anything to ease her nerves. She placed a hand under his neck to support his head then placed the cup to his lips. The first cool taste of water burned his parched throat, then the soft mineral taste filled his mouth and he was greedy for more, he sucked at the lip of the cup, lapping it up like a thirsty dog, enjoying the sensation as the cool liquid lubricated the desert like contours of his tongue.

"Not so fast." Doctor Crowley chided.

Rose pulled the cup away from Martin and placed it back on the bed stand; he eyed it greedily but didn't ask for more.

There was a pause while Martin caught his breath, the doctor had perched down on the edge of the bed and Rose stood slightly behind him, rubbing her hands together, the anxiety on her face more than Martin could bear. It was the doctor who again broke the quiet.

"Do you know why you're here Martin?"

The successful businessman thought for a couple of seconds before answering, he was thinking of some wise crack that would lighten the mood a little, but one more glance at his stress fuelled wife told him this wasn't the time or the place for the funnies. In the end he settled for the most basic response he could muster.

"Heart."

"That's right." Crowley said, nodding. "You've been through a turbulent time Mister Rooley, you suffered what's known as a myocardial infarction, more commonly known as a heart attack. I won't bore you with the details but it was pretty serious there for a while. Now you're not out of the woods yet, but you're stable, and you're talking, that's a good sign. You'll be under careful observation here in ICU for the next few days while we run a few tests to determine just what type of damage you've sustained and what was the cause."

I can tell you the cause right away, Martin thought, his eyes flickering down to his naked stomach, but chose for now to keep the thought to himself. "How long am I going to be in here?" He asked instead.

"I'm afraid you're going to be here over Christmas, it's disappointing I know but under the circumstances it's for the best."

"So I haven't missed it."

"It's Christmas Eve Marty." Rose said with a small smile.

"So I was asleep..."

"Not long." Crowley said. "Not long at all under the circumstances, a little over sixteen hours."

Martin nodded slowly.

"More than anything right now you need to rest, no excitement, that pretty much counts Christmas out I'm afraid. Like I say there are a few tests we need to run to find out just what we're dealing with here, and we'd like to get on with that as soon as possible, it pays to be hasty in these situations."

"What type of tests?" Rose asked, looking more anxious than ever.

"Well, we need to perform a physical exam, listen to your chest with a stethoscope; we'd be listening here for murmurs from the heart or crackles in the lungs, tell-tale signs of a problem. We'll test your blood pressure and your pulse. You'll need to go for an electrocardiogram, an ECG, to look for heart damage, and a troponin blood test would be standard as well. Once we're comfortable that you've been stable for long enough we'll most likely perform a coronary angiography as well, this is where we use x-ray and a special dye to test the blood flow through your heart. There are other tests you may need to have in time, echocardiography, exercise stress test, but for now I think the ones I've mentioned will give us a pretty good idea of what's going on in there."

"Sounds like it's a fun Christmas ahead." Martin grumbled.

"The important thing is that you're here to see Christmas at all, and it's our job to ensure you have many more Christmases to come."

"Thanks doc." Martin said humbly.

"Get some rest, I'll be back in a little while to check on you, if you need anything there's the buzzer at your bed side, there's always a nurse manning the station. You have nothing to fear, we'll get you right." The doctor smiled and stood up, brushing down his pants with the palms of his hands. He re-adjusted his tie and head for the door.

Martin watched him leave, the door closed and he was left in the room with his wife.

"Oh Martin I was so scared." Rose whispered.

Suddenly the enormity of what had happened broke the paralysis that had kept Martin's emotions in check since coming round from his lengthy slumber and his bottom lip started to tremble. He didn't want to cry but he couldn't help it; his whole body wracked with uncontrollable shakes and then the dam broke and the tears spilled from his eyes, coursing down his cheeks and dripping from the corners of his jaw onto the pillow.

"Oh Martin." Rose said again, her face a picture of perfect misery, then she was cradling him in her arms, trying to comfort him as best she could as the sunlight continued to pour through the hospital window.

Outside England prepared itself for the festivities ahead.

2

What followed was the strangest Christmas Day of Martin Rooley's life. He was awoken at four-thirty am by a fat nurse in a uniform bursting at the seams, wanting to check his pulse and take his blood pressure. She left advising him to get more sleep, easy for her to say; when you're awoken in the small hours of Christmas morning by anyone other than Santa Claus it's never easy to rest, especially when your day ahead consisted of tests that could very well change the entire course of your life.

He lay staring at the ceiling for a couple of hours, wondering if he watched for long enough if he would see the damp patch in the corner creeping out into the room. It didn't and a little before seven am a Filipino porter with spiky black hair and a perfectly round head marched into the room, whipped open the curtains and shrilled "wakey wakey rise and shi-ine!"

"Merry Christmas." Martin replied, and the rotund man marched back out of the room with a smile pasted on his face that could not be attributed to any natural cause.

He was allowed breakfast but could only manage half a grapefruit, his mind wasn't with it and his chest ached like a bastard. He pushed the rest of the fruit around with his fork for a while before the nice lady with the curly blonde hair took it away.

Rose arrived a little after nine and she came bearing gifts; literally, she had brought a couple of the presents she had picked out for Martin, neatly wrapped, their tips poking out of the top of the Harrod's bag she carried. But it didn't feel right opening them here, not when they usually opened their presents in front of the fire in the comfort of their own home, he realised he had missed out on his favorite pastime the previous evening of waiting until Rose had gone to bed and then ducking under the tree to have a good feel of the parcels, something he had done ever since childhood and which unlike him never seemed to grow old. With these thoughts in mind he thanked his wife for her kindness but asked her to return the gifts back home until a time when he was well enough to enjoy them.

At nine thirty the doctor did his rounds; this time a small man with enormous sideburns, the name tag labeling him Dr. Stephen Matthews. He gave Martin a breakdown of the festive celebrations ahead including that stalwart of Christmases since the introduction of popular music 'rockin' around the coronary angiography' and that old classic for which Christmas just wouldn't be the same 'we wish you a merry electrocardiogram'.

And the festive cheer didn't end there; Martin wouldn't be tucking into a delicious turkey dinner with the rest of the patients; today he could enjoy his pigs in blankets, Brussels sprouts and brandy infused Christmas pudding direct into his blood stream, courtesy of a soluble drip bag, surely the yummiest way to really enjoy the holiday period.

A little after eleven everybody's favorite cheery Filipino porter returned with a wheel chair to take Martin away for a series of tests. Rose cried when her husband left and tried to remember if she had ever suffered such a miserable Christmas day.

As the wheelchair took him on a journey around the hospital Martin smiled despite himself, the halls had been adorned with colourful paper decorations and there was a poorly decorated Christmas tree next to the nurse's station, the lights twinkling, the star atop stuck out at a rather jaunty angle. It wasn't much but the staff had made an effort and he reminded himself that they were stuck here on Christmas Day too, not just the patients.

His ECG was first, followed by the troponin blood test. He had never had an ECG before but had seen the procedure many times on T.V., but when the pads were being attached to your own body it was hard to see the connection. He was surprised at how quickly the test was performed and in a little over five minutes there was a document being produced by the machine that detailed how fast his heart was beating, whether the rhythm of his heartbeat was steady or irregular and the strength and timing of electrical signals that passed through each part of the heart.

When this was done the nurse on duty, a line of silver tinsel coiled about her head, conducted his troponin blood test; it was simple enough, a tourniquet first placed around his upper arm and then samples of blood for two separate tubes drawn from his vein with a hypodermic needle. All things considered this morning's tests were not too testing which prevented Martin from being too testy.

He was wheeled back to his room a little after twelve thirty just in time for his drip bag of nutritional Christmas lunch. Rose was eating a sandwich when he was rolled in but she stood up as soon as he entered eager to hear how the tests had gone. He reassured her that everything was fine and allowed the nurse to hook him up to the drip, eyeing Rose's club sandwich with notable envy.

In the middle of the afternoon Peter arrived looking troubled and sheepish, a huge bunch of flowers in his hands that literally blocked his skinny frame from view. He wasn't allowed to visit with Martin still being in ICU but Martin sent a message out via Rose thanking him for the kind thought and chastising him for heading down to the hospital on Christmas day. When the balding man left the hospital he looked a lot happier than when he had arrived.

Five o'clock rolled around and the Filipino porter had been replaced by a big man with a heavy set beard and even thicker hair on his well toned arms. He announced he had a surprise for Martin and wheeled him down to the recreation room at the end of the hall where the other poor souls on J ward were gathered, waiting for whatever surprise was about to occur.

After five minutes of waiting the staff of J ward; nurses, matrons, porters and one slightly harassed looking doctor appeared wearing Santa hats and proceeded to belt out a few carols, out of key but full of gusto. It wasn't exactly Carols from King's but Martin was pretty sure it was still the best carol concert he had attended in all of his sixty-seven years on this earth and was for him the highlight of his day. As one lady sang a solo of Silent Night the white haired man felt his wife's hand on his shoulder and took it in his own, he couldn't see her but he knew instinctively that she was crying again.

It was funny how filling the drip bags were, he was due another at six pm and felt over faced when he was hooked up to it; this from a man who would normally reload his plate with extra turkey and roast potato's, always have double helpings of Christmas pud and then spend the rest of the afternoon gorging on tins of Roses and Quality Street, not to mention the traditional nine o'clock turkey sandwich.

The staff on the ward had dwindled down now, with the maximum possible leave being granted on this most sought after of holiday days, and those that remained laughed and joked in the nurses station, sharing chocolates and slices of cake, Rose said she had seen a couple sharing a glass of wine and hoped they weren't tending to Martin!

Despite the skeleton crew Martin's tests couldn't wait, and after his blood pressure and pulse were checked again he was wheeled once more off the ward to conduct a coronary angiography, the most invasive procedure that he was to endure that day. A catheter was inserted into his neck and threaded into his coronary artery. Dye was released into his arteries to make them visible via x-ray and as such allow the doctor to see if there were any blockages that could have caused the initial attack. The whole procedure lasted a little over thirty minutes and when it was over his blood vessel where the catheter had been inserted was a little sore, but compared to the heart attack it was a stroll in the park.

He made it back onto the ward by quarter to nine and by now both he and Rose were looking tired. She didn't want to leave him on Christmas Day but he reassured her he was fine and reluctantly she agreed to leave, it was a good job, another five minutes and the matron would have been ejecting her from the building anyway.

Martin settled in for the night, able to watch the Queens speech from earlier on catch up Sky T.V., one of the many perks of going private, before drifting into a silent slumber. He was awoken just before midnight for his pulse and blood pressure to be checked once more, but was so tired from an activity filled day shortly after a traumatic life changing event that he easily drifted back to sleep again afterwards.

The moon crept through the gap in the curtains and Martin slept on as the heart monitor continued to blip away at his side.

And that was Christmas.

3

Boxing Day. Martin sat on the soft cushioned seat in the consultation room looking at the various charts and graphs on the wall, wondering just how anybody had the capacity to learn so much about the human body. Rose sat at his side, her Chloe handbag clasped tightly on her lap, her knuckles white around the handle.

She had arrived early that morning, wanting to spend the day once more with her husband, and they had received the news around mid-day that they had discovered the cause of Martin's myocardial infarction. Now they were here, waiting in this consultation room like death row in-mates, only dressed in a hospital gown and Gucci slippers rather than an orange jump suit.

Martin was quietly confident, he felt a lot better today than he had yesterday and was sure that whatever the problem he was on the mend. He was prepared for the lecture that was bound to come and would nod his head and agree his faults in all the necessary places. He would agree to exercise more, to eat healthier, to cut down on his alcohol consumption and to cut out the cigars for good. What's more he meant it; the terrible scare of the twenty-third had shaken him badly, and made him realise just how fragile he was. He would take a step back at work, give Peter a little more control, join a gym, go swimming, take evening strolls around the park, see a dietician.

He would agree that he had been a naughty boy, that he had abused a gift that should have been respected and that he should have known better at his age, he would possibly be on some form of medication for a while, maybe even for the rest of his life, probably for blood thinning or something to do with angina, but that was ok too, he had Rose to act the role of the factory foreman and ensure he didn't forget his responsibilities.

Yes sir boss, he was a changed man, and was willing to put in the necessary work to get his tired old frame back in shape. He had already made this commitment to himself and relished the opportunity to get started; he just hoped he would be getting out of here tonight. The hospital was ok but he missed his home comforts, and wanted to get back into a normal everyday routine.

He looked across at Rose, her lips pressed so tightly together that they looked like thin white lines. "Will you try and relax?" He said, placing his hand gently on her arm.

"Relax, how can I possibly relax?" She said, her face racked with misery.

"Everything's going to be fine." He said in his most reassuring voice.

"Oh you know nothing of the sort." She replied. "I must have been taking a nap while you slaved away at those seven years of medical school Doctor Rooley."

Martin sighed and placed his hand back in his lap, he considered what else he could say but before he had chance to say anything else the door opened and a tall late middle aged man walked in dressed in a nice suit, his brown hair combed into a side parting.

"Sorry for keeping you waiting, my name is Mister David Purefoy and I'm the consultant heart surgeon assigned to your case."

Surgeon, why do I need a surgeon? Martin thought with a sudden surge of panic as the tall man sat down at his desk and opened Martin's case file.

"How are you feeling?" Purefoy asked when he had made himself comfortable.

"A lot better thank you." Martin replied honestly enough. "In fact I was hoping I may be able to go home today."

"Uh-huh, uh-huh." Purefoy nodded slowly, but his eyes were not filled with reassurance. "You've been through a very traumatic experience Mister Rooley..."

"Oh please call me Martin."

"Of course, you've been through a very traumatic experience Martin, I imagine one of the scariest experiences you can have as an adult male, and it's important we reflect on that and what this means for you both as a family."

Martin didn't know why, but he felt as though the consultant was building up to something here, he was trying to stay positive but there was that look in the surgeons eyes that had not gone un-noticed, and now this slowly creeping conversation; Martin felt like a zebra out in the plains of Africa, being slowly and meticulously tracked by a lion. "I understand I'm going to have to make a lot of changes, I've already been thinking about joining a gym and talking to a dietician."

"I'm afraid it's a little more complicated than that." Purefoy spoke slowly.

There it was, out in the open, suddenly Martin's mouth felt very dry, and he had thought he was on the mend. To his side Rose clutched all the tighter to the handles of her expensive bag, her lips had now all but disappeared.

"Ok." Martin said after a moment's consideration. "This doesn't sound like good news."

Purefoy didn't respond in words, he pulled a couple of acetates from Martin's case file and started to rifle through the paper work that remained; it was all the answer that Martin needed. It was Rose who finally broke the silence.

"Is he going to die?" She almost wailed, the look of misery on her face enough to bring a lump to Martin's throat.

"Not if I have anything to do with it." Purefoy responded, reassuring and frightening the couple in equal measure. "These are the results of your tests yesterday; they were mixed to say the least. Your coronary angiography showed no visible signs of blockages to any of your coronary arteries, meaning the blood is flowing to and from your heart just fine."

"That's good." Rose said, though the statement came out more as a question, she was clearly fishing for more reassurance.

"It is, but the results of the ECG were not so positive." Purefoy let the statement hang in the air; Martin could feel the flesh creep on his bones and a cold shudder ran the length of his spine; he fought hard not to let it show. He tried to respond but found he was incapable; Rose was suffering a similar affliction to his side. When Purefoy felt they had suffered enough he continued, but not before Martin realised something that made the lump in his throat grow to the size of a golf ball; the consultant was actually enjoying this.

"I mentioned that there were no blockages to the coronary arteries so blood is flowing to and from the heart just fine, normally the cause of a heart attack is a build up of plaque in the arteries, this prevents the blood from flowing to the heart, and essentially starves it. Your case is different, the blood is flowing to and from the heart just fine, but the heart is not functioning as it should, you see the hearts purpose is to pump blood that delivers life sustaining oxygen and nutrients to trillions of different cells that operate your body. The average heart will expand and contract, or beat if you prefer around a hundred thousand times a day, yours is struggling to do two thirds of that, frankly I'm amazed it took as long as it did to send a distress signal that something was very seriously wrong."

Martin swallowed hard, there was a very audible click and he hated himself for it. "What are you saying?"

"I'm telling you that your heart is incapable of performing the required duties that your body needs for sustained life." Purefoy replied matter-of-factly.

Martin rubbed his mouth with the palm of his hand; at his side Rose had gone very white.

"Level with me doc am I dying?"

"Your heart is dying."

"Forgive me for being impudent, but if the heart dies doesn't the body die with it?"

"That's correct." Purefoy nodded slowly, clearly not used to being challenged. "But we aren't going to allow the heart to die."

"What are we talking about, a transplant?" Rose asked, a horrified expression on her face.

"That's correct." The surgeon nodded, his swept over hair un-moving on his head.

Martin let out a deep sigh. "Isn't there an alternative? Medication maybe."

"Medication is a given, but it isn't a cure, if we were to leave the heart untended, eventually it would die, and take you with it. This is a lot to take in right now and I know how frightening it must be, but be assured you are paying for the absolute best treatment and care, you're in safe hands, nothing is going to happen to you."

There was a long pause whilst the surgeons words slowly filtered through to the terrified couple; Martin was shocked but he could see that Rose was close to hysteria, he clasped her left hand in his right one, giving it a gentle squeeze to try and keep her in check.

"So what do I get added to a waiting list?"

"Yes, you'll be added to the UNOS or United Network for Organ Sharing waiting list as a category two patient. Category one patients are those that are hospital bound or need permanent intervention to keep their heart working; you don't fall into that category because you're reasonably stable. This increases your wait time. The good news is your blood group is O which is the most common; this means there are more hearts that become available under this blood group than any other. Having said that we can never say for sure exactly the length of the wait, given the very nature of donor organs it's impossible to ever know for sure when a heart will become available."

"Does it speed things up us being private?" Rose asked, her grip on Martin's hand very firm now.

"I'm afraid not, but it does improve the level of after care you receive and of course it means you get me as your surgeon. I know this has all been a big shock to you and I'm sure you have a hundred and one questions you want to ask, but I'd like to give you a little time to come to terms with the news I've just given you. I'm going to leave you for a while, I'm going to have the porters wheel you back down to the ward, but I'll be back a little later to answer any questions you may have.

Try not to panic, you're in good hands, and we will get you right."

Martin nodded slowly, watching as the consultant surgeon stood up to leave.

"It's important that you get some rest, I'm afraid we need to observe you for a few days yet, but we'll get you home soon." Purefoy nodded slowly, showing he had closed the conversation, then left.

As the door closed behind him Rose turned to Martin, her bottom lip trembling violently.

"Oh Marty!" She managed before the tears started to flow.

"Hey, hey, its ok, its ok." He said, taking her in his arms and cradling her head against his chest, but in his mind he felt far from ok, in fact he didn't feel ok at all.

4

It was on the second of January, when his haulers would resume their lengthy tours of the country after the Christmas break, that Martin was finally discharged from hospital. Despite his vast fortune he had never been one to be chauffeured around, preferring to drive his Aston Martin to the office himself, so today it was Rose who was behind the wheel and Martin was squashed into the passenger seat of the Mini Cooper, she steadfastly refused to drive anything bigger.

He had been back on solid food for just under a week, and had received his paper work and medication in a huge sealed plastic container just after breakfast. He wouldn't have believed it to be true a week ago but today he was actually nervous to leave. It was easy here; there were people to look after him, at home there was only Rose, and what could she do if his dickey ticker decided today was the day that it finally quit its roles and responsibilities for good?

The last week had passed by in a blur; an endless spiral of monitoring and counseling to help him come to terms with the devastating news. He was poked and prodded, jabbed and tested, and kept up to date on his ongoing prognosis on the daily rounds by the on duty doctor and Purefoy, who grew smarmier and less likeable to Martin with every visit. He had been assured that all that could possibly be done to find him a new heart was being done and to try and relax in the meantime and wait with whatever patience he could for the heart to arrive. He was given a beeper that he was assured would beep the second a new heart became available and was advised to keep it on him at all times. As predicted he was visited by a dietician who explained at great length the focus he was going to have to apply to his diet; Rose took particular note here and Martin sighed as he considered Rose's legendary treacle sponge being usurped by an elderflower compote. He was given a program of exercises which again as predicted included regular walks and swimming and he made a promise to himself that he would stick to it as best as he could. Finally he had received the news that for now at least he was stable and was to be discharged from care.

Now he was here, sat bunched up in the front of Rose's electric blue Mini Cooper while Radio Two played in the background. He had his bag of medicines in his lap and scrunched the plastic container with his hands as the car slowly ambled along, to Rose the speed limits were there for a reason, and to Martin that reason had always seemed to understand the restrictions of the road then drive five to ten miles per hour under them.

"What do you think it will be like?" She asked as she pulled off the duel carriageway.

Martin had been concentrating on his wife's inability to recognise any kind of traffic signal and had been gripping his meds bag tighter and tighter.

"What?" He said, cringing as she cut up an old Volvo estate.

"What do you think it will be like, having a new heart?"

"I don't know." He answered honestly.

She thought again for a while, Martin could practically see the cogs turning behind her eyes.

"I mean, do you think you'll feel different?"

"I expect that's the whole point." He answered with a wry smile.

His wife's tears had finally dried up by the twenty-eighth, and what had replaced them was a kind of brooding silence, as she slowly came to terms with what had happened in her own unique way. Now she was communicating again, and though it was a typically Rose like turn of conversation it was better than the sad withdrawn woman that had pottered about the hospital like a harbinger of doom.

"I mean," she continued, clearly still deep in thought as she turned the roundabout and drove the car into the suburbs, "what if you say, got the heart of a runner, would that make you fitter? Or what if you got the heart of a really mean person, would that make you mean as well?"

"I expect I'd still be me."

"Hmm." She replied, clearly unconvinced.

Martin settled back and listened to the radio. Soon the car was winding down a country lane, the houses that dotted the side of the road growing with stature the further they ventured. After a couple of minutes they turned onto a private road and the car pulled up to a huge iron gate. Rose punched in the four digit code on the keypad attached to her dashboard and the sensor picked up the signal; the gate slowly started to open. When it was wide enough she drove through and pulled the car up in front of the triple garage unit to the side of the house.

The red brick mansion was modest by the standards of Martins net worth, when some of his contemporaries were practically living in castles, but compared to the average British household it was definitely a cut above, and had been home to the Rooley's for the last fifteen years. Seven bedrooms, five bathrooms, a huge kitchen, two reception rooms, an indoor swimming pool and five acres of gardens out back that were tended by a contractor that worked the whole year round.

Martin stepped out onto the gravel driveway and pulled the collar of his coat up against the cold; it was mild for the time of year but when you had been stuck inside a ridiculously over heated hospital for the last week and a bit anything under twenty-two degrees felt practically Baltic. He sighed, leaned back into the car and grabbed his med bag.

"Home sweet home." Rose said with a smile.

"Home sweet home." Martin replied.

"It's good to have you back; the bed has seemed really cold without you."

They started walking up to the front door via the little path that split the lawn.

"I haven't missed you warming your cold feet on my legs I'll be honest."

Rose laughed and stepped up to the keypad next to the pine front door. She punched in the same code she had used for the gate (something the security firm had implored them not to do, but they were getting on in years and didn't need the hassle of numerous security codes) and the internal bolts slid back. She opened the door and Martin stepped into the warmth of the entrance hall. He sighed and looked around, why was it whenever you had been away for a little while you expected everything to have changed when you got home? But no, everything was the same; the same pictures on the wall of family and friends, the same nook that led into the living room with the entertainment system on the wall, the same curved stairway that led to the first floor and the Christmas tree beneath it that twinkled as it had on the day he had been admitted to hospital.

"Everything's the same." He muttered, feeling low and vulnerable all of a sudden.

"What?" Rose enquired.

"Nothing." Martin replied and walked into the living room where he plonked down on the huge leather sofa.

"I'll make some tea." Rose said and walked through to the kitchen. "Earl Grey, no sugar. I'm going to support you and have the same."

"The treats just keep on coming." He replied, then placed his head back in his hands and looked up towards the ceiling.

He had been ordered to take it easy, to let work take care of itself and concentrate instead on getting himself as fit as he could. He could take a walk, yes, he could go for a swim, yes, that was great, but what the hell was he going to do with the rest of the day?

"I don't think this is going to work." He said to nobody in particular, and before he knew it the tears were rolling down his cheeks again.

5

There was a pile of dead leaves the colour of used sandpaper next to the gutter; Martin took the brush from the shed at the top of the garden and a green hessian waste bag and started sweeping them in. When he got near the end of the pile he took a hand shovel and swept the leaves onto the shovel before dropping them into the bag. It was January fourth, and though it was crisp and cool outside the sun shone brightly and the air tasted good, full of ozone.

Rose had been watching this show of bravado from the kitchen window and opened the conservatory door now to speak to her man.

"We pay Horne brothers a good fee to do those jobs for us."

"Say what you really mean." He said without getting up.

"You're supposed to be resting."

"There it is." He said with a sigh. "I watched two repeats of 'Only fools and horses' on Gold this morning, sat there on the couch right in front of you with my feet propped up on a nice fat cushion. I'm bored of resting; I can't do it any more."

"You're a fidget, always have been."

"I don't disagree, but I'm ok I promise."

"Well you're going to catch a cold."

"I doubt it, under all these layers I'm sweating buckets."

"Well no more, come in as soon as you've done."

"I promise." He said.

Rose regarded him with her best school ma'am expression, and then walked back inside, closing the conservatory door behind her.

Martin sighed and finished sweeping the leaves into the waste bag. Is this what his life had come to? He wasn't even allowed to do a simple household chore without getting the third degree. He couldn't blame Rose, she was only looking after his best interests, but he was just so damn frustrated. In truth doing the sweeping was little more than childish rebellion on his part; before his episode the thought of a little work in the garden would never have entered his mind; like Rose said they paid a company to do these tasks so they didn't have to, but now, knowing that he was not expected to do anything out of the ordinary for fear of upsetting his ill behaved organ was all the motivation he needed to push his luck.

He was bored. Now into his third day of being house bound other than the occasional walk on the town common he was already losing his patience with the quiet life. He wasn't used to it; Martin was a workaholic, had been since he was in his early twenties and the business had started to flourish, and all this sitting around at home trying to rest just wasn't in his nature.

What were they doing now? Right this instant, what was happening in the corridors of power at Sapient Trans Global? Was Peter brokering a new deal that would open doors in some remote country? Was there a meeting to discuss the plans to start shipping from Portsmouth instead of Southampton? Had Tina been successful in her pre-Christmas pursuit of Nigel? Were they discussing at great length the new toilet paper that had been ordered for the lavatories? He didn't know because he wasn't there, and it was killing him.

At his request Peter had called with a daily mission update but it wasn't the same as being there in person. He missed the people, he missed the work, he missed the view from his desk, more than anything he missed the buzz of trying to maintain the company's success in an ever more difficult financial climate.

Rose just didn't understand; she had never worked, had never needed to, so for her taking the time to rest should have been easy. But it wasn't, not to Martin. He had risen at five and set off for the office at six ever since they moved their headquarters into the city, and now that he didn't have to be there he was still up at the crack of dawn, staring out the window, wondering what he was going to do with his day. Wondering jus how in the hell was he going to make it through until bedtime.

He would rise at five, eat a little breakfast and wait for the morning paper to arrive. When it finally came he would read the news and the business section and do what he could of the crossword and then check the stocks on the news channels. This done and his breakfast settled he could go for a swim, only five or six laps at first; the pool had been installed before they moved in but neither he nor Rose ever really used it. He was out of shape as he well knew and after several laps would be utterly exhausted. Lunch would roll around and he could look forward to some yummy Ryvita slices, thin strips of cucumber on top of the heart healthy margarine. Martin thought he would have been better off eating the packaging; it would have tasted less like cardboard. In the afternoon he would try and find something to watch on the television but all they seemed to show were property programmes or chat shows full of fat people with bad teeth shouting at each other. If this was the state of the television he felt it prudent to send back his license. His evening meal was usually better than his lunch, with Rose trying her skills at any of the new recipes in her healthy eating cook book, but it was still a far cry from the days of glory; pies, pastries and puddings to make your heart melt, sadly for him this had been quite literal. A slow walk around the common and either a little more television or a few pages of the latest Tom Clancy and that was his day. It certainly wasn't anything to write home about, which would have been a little daft too as he was already there.

There had been no further complications from his heart, in fact in an uncanny sense he felt better than he had in years; but then his diet had improved, he'd cut out the booze and smokes and was even doing a little exercise now, he was bound to feel better. He had lost half a stone since Christmas and had gone one notch tighter on his belt. Yet despite all this his heart was dying, exercise and a healthy diet may help with regards to his general fitness but there was nothing it could do about that. But what was he to do, mope around all day worrying that his dodgy ticker was going to pack in at any moment? That the vice like grip was going to wrap again around his chest, squeezing until he could bear it no more? He couldn't live like that, what's more he wouldn't live like that, life had to go on.

He had made a decision; he was going to go back to work. If he took it slowly, didn't get involved in too much, didn't have any heated confrontations or stress inducing stakeholder meetings he would be fine. The toughest thing would be convincing Rose; as far as she was concerned he should be covered in bubble wrap and placed under the stairs until his new heart arrived. There was no way she would understand his need to be back, to be doing something useful, anything. But at the same time he knew that he was going to have to convince her; he just couldn't keep going on like this.

The company was in great hands with Peter at the helm, but he just wanted to be there, to be back to normal, surely she would be able to understand that?

He finished sweeping up the leaves and carried the refuse sack out to the wheelie bins where he placed it down and then head back to the shed with the tools. He left the gardening gloves by the door and then head back to the house.

Rose was in the kitchen baking bread, she smiled at him as he entered. Was now the time to break the news? He didn't think so. Instead he walked through to the living room and plopped down on the couch. He grabbed the remote and switched on the television. 'Homes under the hammer' was on, and that was all he needed to convince him that enough was enough.

6

In the end Martin decided the best policy was to not discuss his decision with Rose at all. His body clock woke him at five as it always did, he crept out of bed and wandered along the hall to one of the guest bathrooms, figuring if he didn't use the en-suite he probably wouldn't wake her. He showered, dressed and head downstairs. It felt good to be back in a suit; all he ever seemed to wear these days was pyjamas and that was no way to carry on. The huge Samsung fridge was bare of actual goodies; no packet of bacon rashers, no box of eggs, no string of sausages from Giuseppe's the butchers in the village, Rose had got rid of it all following his episode. Instead he took out a carton of fresh orange juice and poured himself a glass. He looked at the cereal in the cupboard and turned his nose up at the muesli, he was poorly, that didn't make him a damn rabbit. He plumped for the Weetabix instead and took a couple from the box, smothering them in semi skimmed milk.

His breakfast finished he quickly cleaned his teeth, combed the thin strands of his white hair into a more dignified shape and crept from the house.

There would be hell to pay when Rose realised what he had done, but he would cross that bridge when he came to it. He opened the garage and got into his Aston Martin; two minutes later he was through the electric gate and starting the forty mile journey to London's financial district.

It felt good to just be behind the wheel again; he was a man in control of his destiny, at least for as long as his heart would allow. He had remembered to grab the beeper from the bureau on his way out of the house, it wouldn't pay for a new heart to be ready and he wasn't around to answer the call. He switched on the radio and listened to one of the talk shows as he made his way towards the city.

It was nearly six thirty when he pulled the car into his private parking space and head towards the plus shaped glass building, feeling the adrenaline start to flow as he stepped through the sliding doors and into the huge foyer. The Christmas tree was still standing, it would be taken down with tradition the very next day, and this led him to look up to the mezzanine level, where all this sorry mess had started.

"Good morning Martin, welcome back sir, we weren't expecting you."

The voice startled Martin from the unpleasant thought and he was glad.

"Hi Lithgow." He said to the burly security guard.

"It's good to have you back sir, we were worried about you."

"It's good to be back Lithgow." He said as he crossed the foyer to the lift. A couple of cleaners were polishing the floor and he tipped them a wave as he punched the key to call the lift. It arrived and he journeyed up to the fifth floor, where he walked down the corridor, through the green room that would be empty for another hour or so until Sheila arrived, ready to organise his life for another day. He stepped into his office and put his coat on the stand, then he placed his briefcase under his desk and stepped up to the huge picture window.

"I've missed you London." He said, gazing out at the high rise buildings that surrounded them at Sapient. The sun was just coming up over the horizon and it glinted on the glass of the shard, casting an orange glow over the streets below. When the huge orange globe crept further into the sky London would explode into life, he always enjoyed watching it happen.

"Well well well, look what the cat dragged in." He was startled from his thoughts for the second time in a matter of minutes; he hadn't heard the thin man enter the room. He turned and regarded him kindly.

"I see you're still burning the candle at both ends too." Martin said with a smile.

"What choice do I have? The CEO of this tin-pot organisation has been shirking his responsibilities; someone had to step up to the plate."

Martin laughed and stepped forward; he wrapped his arms around his friend and pulled him close. "It's so good to see you Peter."

"Trust me it's nothing compared to how good it is to see you, for a while there..."

"Don't finish that sentence."

The thin man nodded slowly. "Look I'm not saying it's not great to have you back, but should you really be here?"

"Don't you start; I get enough of the pampering from Rose."

"Talking of which I'm surprised she let you out of the house."

"Yes well, as of this moment she doesn't know."

Peter's jaw dropped open. "You're kidding me; you mean you haven't told her?"

Martin's lips pursed, but there was humour behind his eyes.

"She'll find out soon enough."

Peter chuckled, then rubbed his mouth with his hand. "Oh you are in so much shit."

Martin laughed again, a big belly laugh, and it felt good, he knew he had been right coming back, Peter always knew the right things to say, even if it was just his own innate ability to find Martin's funny bone and give it a good pull every once in a while.

"Seriously though are you sure this isn't too much too soon, we don't want any repeats of what happened at Christmas."

"I'm going to take it easy, I've earned the right to kick back a little and watch you sweat for me, I'm sure I'll be fine."

"As long as you're sure. How are you anyway?"

"Fit as a fiddle." Martin said with a smile, but it looked strained.

"Martin please."

"You called me Martin, not sir." The CEO said with a raised eyebrow.

"Well I've held you in my arms when I thought you were going to croak it on me, I think I've done enough to deserve first name basis now."

"Trust me you'd done enough five years ago." Martin replied earnestly.

"Seriously how is your heart?"

"That's the most frustrating thing, I feel fine in myself, as good as I have in years, but the quacks insist it has to go. Listen, you haven't told anyone have you?"

"God no." Peter replied, looking hurt at the very thought. "No this is just between us. Is there any news on when you'll receive the new heart?

"Nothing yet, it may take some time I guess."

"Yeah I suppose."

Both men were quiet for awhile, pondering on what had been said. Eventually Peter spoke again.

"Well if you insist on coming back here so early I insist on you taking more of a back seat, for the time being at least, I don't want you in any stressful situations, I can handle it."

"Oh I know you can, and I have no desire to be putting myself in the danger zone so to speak, I'm happy enough to just sit back, watch you doing all the work that makes me a little bit richer."

"What else is new there then?" Peter asked with a smile.

Martin laughed and turned to look out of the window once more.

The thin man's brow furrowed as he chewed over something that had been bothering him. He looked nervously at his employer, dropped his gaze, chewed on his lip a bit more and then continued.

"Listen Martin, about what I said before, the Christmas party, you know, if I'd have known…"

Martin turned and looked at Peter, genuinely confused. "I don't understand."

"Come on Martin don't make this harder than it already is,. I get it, I'm an asshole."

"I honestly don't know what you're talking about."

"Genuinely?"

"Genuinely, what's got the ice man Peter Werth-Duncan all worked up?"

"You mean you don't remember?"

"Will you just spit it out?" Martin said.

"Oh boy this is even worse than I could have imagined. Before the incident, we were in here, in this room, and I made a joke, and that's all it was, a joke, about wishing you'd have a heart attack so the business would be mine, listen, you need to know I would never…"

Peter's honest and heart felt apology was cut short by Martin's wild laughter; the CEO gripped his ample belly in both hands and tilted his head back as the noise erupted from him. Peter looked at him in hurt disbelief, he was bearing his heart and soul here and it had been met with the usual; child like mirth he had come to expect of his employer.

"Is that all?" Martin managed when he had gotten himself under some form of control.

"What do you mean is that all, I've been working myself up to this conversation for the last two weeks and you laugh in my face." Peter said, clearly taken aback by the proceedings.

Martin laughed again, he couldn't help it, just looking at Peter's sad puppy dog expression was enough to get him going again. This was a man that brought corporate leaders to their knees, completely unfazed by high stake negotiations, a strict disciplinarian that led with a steely determination and yet he had been completely undone by a flippant comment he had made in jest to a friend.

"I, I'm sorry for laughing." Martin said, the tears rolling down his cheeks. "But you should see your face."

Peter crossed his arms in front of his chest, his lips pressed tightly together; he was still struggling to see the funny side.

"Ok, ok." Martin said. He let out a huge sigh and then bent over to catch his breath. "I have no idea whether a good belly laugh like that is good or bad for me in my condition but I can tell you it certainly felt good."

"I'm pleased for you." Peter replied, his expression showing he was anything but.

"Will you relax?" Martin said, finally getting himself under control. "I know you didn't mean what you said, you may be my employee but you're also my friend, and frankly if it wasn't for your quick thinking in getting an ambulance out to me when you did I may not be here at all, so stop giving yourself a hard time, if anything I'm indebted to you."

Peter did as he was bid and visibly relaxed, his shoulders dropping as though they had been bearing a huge weight that had just been unexpectedly lifted.

"You don't know how pleased I am to hear that." He said earnestly. "I thought, well you know…"

"What?"

"That I was going to lose my job."

Martin shook his head slowly. "Peter I could catch you in bed with my wife and you wouldn't lose your job, you're integral to the success of this operation. You know that. That wasn't a green light to jump into bed with Rose by the way."

"Thank you sir, I appreciate that." Peter said with a reassured smile.

"There it is again, that damn upstairs downstairs word."

Peters smile broadened.

"I don't think you realise just how good you are." Martin said honestly. "I want to thank you Peter, I was never in any doubt that Sapient would be in safe hands, and I know that if this damn ticker of mine means I have to push back a little over the coming months then I know I have the right man in place to steer the ship in my absence. You're a good man Peter, and I thank you."

"Thank you for the vote of confidence." Peter said happily. "I'll leave you to get settled in, you know where I am if you need anything."

Martin nodded his understanding and watched as his friend shuffled out of the room, with the compliment he had received Martin was surprised he could still fit through the door. Now he was alone in the room, and he sat down in his well cushioned chair and swivelled around to look at the orange skyline about Canary Wharf. He sat like that for a while, feeling content as the sun slowly rose on a bitterly cold morning over London.

Then his mobile was vibrating in his pocket, he pulled it free and looked at the screen; Rose. Well, the good mood had to end at some time.

7

Time moved on as time always does; if there is anything that can be relied upon in a world full of uncertainty it is that.

Martin did indeed receive a fair amount of heat from Rose for his decision to go back to work, and for not discussing it with her beforehand of course, but by the fourth day she could see that her protestations were falling on deaf ears and decided instead to give him the silent, sullen treatment. Martin found this even worse than the constant badgering, but it still didn't deter him. By the middle of the following week his long suffering wife had decided that her illogical husband was too pig headed to ever see sense and dropped her campaign to get him to rest for good.

It wasn't easy, but where changes were needed Martin was good to his word; every night he would go for a stroll around the common, and as the weeks progressed so did his pace, with a little help from his personal assistant Sheila who had always been technically savvy he even downloaded an application to his phone that told him how far he had walked, at what speed and how many calories he had burnt. He found the robotic American voice quite motivating, and not wanting to disappoint her he worked hard on his distance and pace. On a weekend he would make use of the indoor pool, swimming five lengths at first and feeling exhausted, then working up to fifteen, twenty and finally thirty-five lengths by the time the summer rolled around. The toughest part was the meal times. He missed his food, and though he knew the celery and broccoli bake that was now on the menu would serve him better than the deep fried goodness that he was accustomed to, he just couldn't help missing some of his favourite dishes. He was allowed a treat meal every Friday night and seemed to count the minutes away until he could have some chips or some Yorkshire pudding or a nice juicy steak. The will power that was required to keep walking as he passed Greggs was phenomenal and though he had strayed on a couple of occasions, unable to resist the call of a chicken bake and a sticky bun, as a general rule he had been good, walking right past with his eyes to the pavement and heading next door to grab an Innocent smoothie from the organic deli to satisfy his sweet tooth.

His perseverance paid off, he could see the results on his waist line, going from a size forty-two to a very respectable thirty-six in just a matter of weeks. He felt better too, fitter, little jobs like taking out the rubbish or changing a light bulb no longer left him gasping for breath, in fact they didn't affect him at all. His wardrobe had to change with his new improved look, and all at the offices of Sapient commented on the dashing new CEO with the new line of Armani suits.

He wasn't the only one to benefit from the changes; Rose too had lost nearly three stone in the time between Christmas and early summer and had a new lease of life because of it. She was the envy of her bridge club friends for a start, who all wanted to know her secret; 'try being on the BUPA health scare diet and shed pounds in days' she wanted to say, but instead just enjoyed the compliments she received and the green eyed looks form Rhonda Harvey, her oldest friend, who had tried every diet under the sun and still shopped at Faith and Evans. She had joined a dance class and a lawn tennis club and now filled the days while Martin was at work practicing her back hand or learning to line dance to Billy Ray Cyrus rather than eating cakes in front of the soaps.

Martin loved the change in his wife; not so much her appearance, he had always loved that, but in her demeanour, there was a glow about her now that he hadn't seen since their early days back in Bolton.

Snow fall covered London come February and stayed until March, causing chaos on the roads as it always did in Britain, but by the time the first daffodils started to appear all that was left was the exhaust blackened drifts at the side of the road.

In April Sapient went up against one of its biggest rivals in a bidding war over a new shipping contract and lost out by only fifteen thousand pounds, a blow to the company and damaging for a little while on the stock exchange, but as always good faith and a clear head steered them through and by May shares were slowly on the rise again.

In early June Rose's dance class came third in a regional competition for the over fifties; Martin was in attendance and watched the enthusiastic routine to that old classic 'Achy Breaky Heart' and the beaming smile on his wife's face as her instructor, the unfortunately named Joan Maggot collected the twenty-five pound cheque and the bunch of flowers.

June brought its own problems to a Britain that had never been able to cope with anything other than light drizzle; it had been incredibly warm for several weeks now so naturally there was talk of potential hose-pipe bans in Yorkshire and the Home Counties.

Throughout this time Martin had regular check-up's at the outpatients department at St. Cuthbert's, having his blood and his pulse checked and being hooked up to the ECG once more to get the latest news from his dodgy organ. Each time the news was more damning than the last, and there was still no sign of a replacement heart. Martin played the news down for Rose on the first couple of trips, but with her panic growing with each visit he attended his appointments on his own as spring time led into summer, preferring to keep the worrying truth to himself for the time being at least; the fact was if he didn't get a new heart soon he may not make it to Christmas.

On June thirteenth Martin sat in his office looking out at the baking heat of London, thankful for the air conditioning that was keeping everyone at Sapient cool during this unusually hot period. There had been a meeting of the key stake holders that morning where the marketing department had delivered their strategy for the final quarter, but Martin's mind had been elsewhere, he kept pulling the match box sized beeper from his pocket and checking the battery light was still on.

The last couple of months had been tough on the CEO, when he had received the news that he needed a major heart transplant he had known there would be a bit of a wait before a new organ became available, but as winter turned to spring and spring to summer, and the news form his continued trips to St. Cuthbert's became graver, he had slipped into a deep foreboding the like of which he had never before been accustomed.

He hid it as well as he could from Rose and Peter and Sheila and his golfing buddies, of whom he saw less and less these days, but the truth was as the wait grew longer the deeper grew his anxiety. He would wake in a morning covered in sweat, fresh from a nightmare where he was being buried alive; he could see his friends and family at his graveside but his chest was clutched tight in that old vice like grip and barely a breath escaped his parched throat, let alone a cry for help. The soil would bear down on his rigid body as his mind frantically begged for mercy, trapping him in this early grave. The dream would always end the same, with Rose turning and walking away, sometimes rubbing at her eyes with a hankie, sometimes just looking off into the distance; the grounds-man would lean over the grave, look Martin straight in the eye end say 'you did this, you did this to yourself!'

The dream could come at any time of the night, sometimes just before his body clock was due to wake him, sometimes in the early hours of the morning, but the dream was always the same. One thing was for certain, whenever the dream was to come he could be sure that when he woke that was it, there would be no more sleep that night. Shaken and afraid he would creep downstairs, boil a pan of warm milk and sit in front of the fire, trying to shake the creeping realism of this relentless and horrible dream.

And the dreams weren't the only thing that was causing his anxiety; for the last month or so he had started having pains in his chest, dull at first but sharper as of late. He would be working at his desk or out walking on the common and all of a sudden the left side of his chest was alive with pain. He would break out in a sweat that lathered his entire body and his left arm would start to tingle. Panic would seize him and he was sure each time that this was it, he had reached the end of the road; he would sit or stand perfectly still, his eyes huge orbs that stared into nothing. But each time, so far at least, the pain had abated and after a few moments the pressure on his chest would release.

It was terrifying, absolutely terrifying, and he had no choice but to face it alone. He couldn't tell Rose, she deserved better than to spend her days in a permanent state of worry. There were no children to turn to and he wouldn't have turned to them if there had been. There was Sheila and Peter of course, but he felt it would be extending the boundaries of a working relationship to burden them with his problems, friends or not. So instead he faced his fears alone, crying in silence at his desk or staring out of his huge picture window at the city below, not really seeing a single thing.

Now he sat here again, enjoying the cool manufactured air that drifted down from the air conditioning and staring hopelessly at his beeper. There was a stack of papers on his desk that needed his attention, but even work couldn't motivate him today. Instead he stood up, placed his shoes back on his feet and head to the door.

"I'm just popping out for a while, will you manage my calls?" He said to Sheila on his way to the lift.

Of course she would, that was her job after all, but Sheila took her role more seriously than that of a standard PA, she was proud to work for Sapient and a true and loyal servant of Martin's. Her simple polite response sent him on his way and he journeyed down in the lift not really sure what he was doing or where he was going.

He said a couple of hello's in reception and then stepped out into the brilliant early afternoon sunshine. He walked with his hands in the pockets of his suit trousers under the shade of the high rise buildings that poked out of Canary Wharf like searching glass fingers, down through streets that were lined with money to the embankment of the Thames. From here he could see Tower Bridge, which he had always found a wonderful feat of engineering and beyond it the Tower of London.

The sun was hot on his neck as he strolled along the side of the river, looking at the ducks that paddled around the embankment and avoiding the constant stream of tourists that posed for photos and jostled for souvenirs at the roadside stands.

There was a bench at the side of the river that was shaded by the overhanging branches of an elm, Martin wandered over to it and plonked down. He sat gazing out at the river, thinking once more about his dodgy heart and wondering if his cursed beeper would ever do just that; beep.

A small boy passed by, no more than four years old, he was carrying an ice cream cone twice the size of his tiny hand and strawberry sauce was dripping down to the pavement from his sticky fingers. The bottom half of his face was literally covered in ice cream and he turned to Martin as he passed and gave him the biggest, goofiest grin the businessman thought he had ever seen. The little boy hurried to catch up with his mother who had wandered several yards ahead and Martin watched him go.

Suddenly the tears were rolling down Martin's face; thinking in his head how he wished they had tried a little harder for children of their own. He seemed to be always in tears these days. He lowered his head and clasped it in his hands and allowed his body to rack with the uncontrollable sobs.

An elderly lady was passing by and noticed him sat there enveloped in misery. She sat with him and placed a comforting arm around his shoulders, trying to soothe him as best as she could. Martin let her, feeling embarrassed that he had regressed into such a childlike state, but seeming completely incapable of controlling his emotions anymore.

8

The cook book was open on the kitchen counter, as Martin placed his briefcase down on the breakfast bar he had a quick glance at the open page; cauliflower and leak pie, which didn't sound too bad, though they'd neglected to mention the pastry had been replaced with wholemeal pasta strips. Martin didn't know how they had the cheek to call it a pie, and wrinkled his nose at the prospect. Rose was stood at the sink with her back to him; he would try his best to look appreciative of the effort she was clearly making when she turned around.

"Hey honey I'm home." He called out as he always did; hoping that how flat he felt wasn't noticeable in his voice.

If Rose noticed the lack of gusto she kept it to herself, she turned around partway through chopping leeks and gave her husband a warm smile.

"Dinner will be about forty minutes, have you taken off your shoes?"

Martin always seemed to be in trouble for wearing his shoes in the house.

"I was just about to change into my slippers." He lied.

"Yes of course you were."

He stepped back out into the hall and slipped his shoes off by the door. His ridiculous slippers were in the shoe rack; he took them out and slipped them on. They were a joke present from Rose from the previous Christmas; each one was a giant Mr Burns head from the Simpson's, a reference she found hilarious given his own position of power. They were comfortable he had to admit, but God help him if any of his golfing buddies ever saw him in them.

"Jean called today, her and Alan want to have us over for supper, I said I'd check the calendar and get back to them."

"That's nice." Martin replied distractedly, flicking through the mail.

"You could have it as your treat night, whatever night we go." Rose continued as she finished with the leeks and dropped them into a pan of simmering water. "I didn't want to go into all the in's and out's of your dietary requirements."

"No I guess not." Martin placed the envelopes back on the nook table and wandered back into the kitchen. Rose turned to face him as he came into the room, lining strips of pasta in a casserole dish on the island unit.

"You'll never guess who I bumped into today?" She said excitedly.

"Steve McQueen?"

"Hardly. Though that would be nice."

"Not that nice he's been dead for over thirty five years."

"Jilly Cooper." Rose continued as if he hadn't spoken. "I was coming out of the tennis club as she was just going in, she was driving that new Jag that Daisy had seen her in and she had a tan like she'd just got back from abroad."

Martin had to smile; his wife was always at her most animated when delivering the latest gossip. In late April Martin and Rose's long term friends Sebastian and Jilly Cooper had split amicably; their hundred million pound estate being divided straight down the middle. Since then the ladies of the blue chip wives bridge club had been desperate to dig the dirt on whatever seedy little deeds had caused the break-up. So far information had been pretty hard to come by, but this was a turn of events that had set tongues wagging all over again.

"Think about it Marty, why would Jilly Cooper be visiting the tennis club? She's about as sporty as Boris Johnson. It's because she's seeing that tennis coach, the Norwegian one with the funny name, Mags or Migs or something."

"Well to be fair no-one would have expected you to take up tennis either six months ago." Martin countered. As he spoke a sudden pain shot into the left hand side of his chest, it seized him like a steel claw and forced him into an uncomfortable stoop. Luckily Rose had her eyes down looking at the recipe book and didn't notice.

"Oh come on Martin don't be naïve, you've always been naïve. She's having it away with the tennis coach, Queenie said she saw the two of them walking hand in hand around Kensington market, can you believe it? He must be half her age."

But Martin wasn't listening anymore, the pain was excruciating, he turned his back on his wife and stumbled into the hall, not wanting her to see him like this, not again. His right hand clutched at his chest for comfort but his entire left arm was going numb, a bad sign for sure.

"Anyway while all this has been going on Queenie heard from a friend of Michael's that works with Sebastian at the office that he's been seeing his secretary, and apparently she's young enough to be his grand daughter!" Rose continued, completely unaware of her husband's current situation. "The dirty old dog, and she's no better, I mean she's hardly with him for his looks is she? Probably likes driving round in his Porsche, I bet he's always buying her gifts and taking her off on fancy weekends, he'll be like a sugar daddy to her."

Martin screwed his eyes shut tight and leant back against the under stairs cupboard, sweat was pouring down his face and he was battling to stay conscious. Not again, this couldn't be happening again!

"Anyway I was thinking, it's been a while since you last had a round of golf with Sebastian, why don't you arrange one for this Saturday, you never know, he might open up to you about his little trollop in the city, what do you think?"

Suddenly, as quickly as it had come the grip on Martin's heart released, his arm stayed numb but his lungs were filled with sweet air and he sucked it in, thankful that he wasn't going to slip into unconsciousness again.

"Did you hear me? I said I thought you could give Sebastian a call, maybe go for a round of golf, you could call him tonight."

Martin mopped sweat from his forehead and looked down at his shaking hands.

"Yes, yes could do." He managed.

"Are you ok?" Rose asked, her face etched with concern, she started walking around the island unit and Martin was quick to stop her.

"I'm fine, I'm fine. Just tired, too many late nights and early mornings." He said between gasps.

"What did I tell you, I said you needed to take a step back at work, and the hours you do, in your condition you're going to work yourself into an early grave, and what will become of me then?"

"I'm going to go for a lie down." He said, slowly shuffling towards the foot of the stairs.

"Ok, I'll call you when supper's ready, you need to take it easy Martin, please think about it."

"I will." He replied, and for the first time he actually meant it.

Martin crept up the stairs still clutching his chest, the sweat dripping from his chin and landing on the stair carpet. He made it into the master bedroom and closed the door behind him. He suddenly felt utterly exhausted. He ambled over to the bed and lay down with his head on the pillow. His chest still ached but the most shocking pain had subsided and he was pretty sure he was in the clear again, for the time being at least.

But he was scared, badly scared. This was the worst pain he had suffered since the initial attack, and being so close to unconsciousness had unnerved him badly. He wasn't on the mend, he wasn't getting better, his heart was dying and there wasn't a damn thing he could do about it.

Martin placed his hands over his face and waited for his body to stop shaking, wondering as he did just how long he had left.

9

Martin and Peter stepped through the sliding glass door and up to Peter's BMW which was parked in one of the five private parking bays at Sapient. He pressed the key fob and the doors unlocked. Martin climbed into the passenger seat and placed his briefcase at his feet. Peter used the same key fob to ignite the engine and a couple of moments later they were manoeuvring the turning circle and heading to the fly lane that ran parallel to the Thames.

They were heading to the Greenwich offices of Fisher Warner Marcus to meet CEO and founding partner James Warner to discuss a possible contract involving the haulage of their overseas pipe line; a lucrative deal that would give Sapient a direct link to the Crimea for the next five years. It was a huge deal for Martin and Peter both financially and in terms of foreign relations and if they were successful in their negotiations it would give Sapient some much needed stability following the loss of the Magruder shipping contract in April.

This was a part of the business for which Martin had always struggled, and he was happy to have Peter by his side. The younger man was an expert negotiator and had secured most of the major contracts from which Sapient had benefitted in the last five or six years. He was unfazed by stature and would always open negotiations clearly and concisely, with a confident reassuring manner that regularly sealed the deal. Now they were ready to start negotiations again and Martin felt confident that if his head of corporate strategy was on form they would have moved Sapient Trans-Global one step closer to its first major contract in a Soviet state by five-thirty.

"So we're definitely agreed on the terms," Peter said as he pulled the car up to the lights, "we're looking for a minimum five year contract with the flexibility to use sub-contractors in order to meet shifting SLA's."

"From what I know of James Warner he's very particular over whom he does business with, so the sub-contracting could be a sticking point."

"And that's where I'll turn on the charm offensive to reassure him that Sapient holds full responsibility for anyone who is working under our flag, and we'll agree to all penalty clauses for failure to meet the demands of our client, focusing of course on the fact that we haven't failed an SLA since 1996 and that was due to adverse weather conditions that closed off the Scottish highlands."

The lights turned to green and Peter crept forwards behind a black London taxi cab and a Blue Citroën C4. They turned right towards Tower Bridge and Peter manoeuvred around them onto the straight.

"Do you think it will be enough?" Martin asked earnestly.

"You never can tell, I hope so, we need this contract."

"Oh we'll survive just fine without it, but it certainly would be a damn fine scoop."

"That it would." Peter said, nodding his head slowly. "Just being mentioned in the same sentence as a giant like Fisher would give us some real clout when the FTSE opens tomorrow."

Martin nodded, he could empathise with his friend's ambition; he wanted to see the firm continue its steady growth too, but it was just so hard to concentrate on anything other than his damn heart at the minute.

Peter took the A102 and crossed the Thames via the Blackwall tunnel, coming out by the O2 Arena, then took the roundabout that led to Blackwall lane. Martin looked out at the huge Dome that had lain empty for years until the mobile giant had gone into partnership with AEG to save the colossal structure and turn it into one of the biggest and most sought after entertainment venues in Europe. Thank God, Martin had thought at the time, without them it would have remained a constant reminder of the government's blasé and foolhardy use of public funding.

As the BMW stopped at the traffic lights on Blackwall lane Martin felt a vibration in his pants pocket; it was his mobile phone. He pulled it out and looked at the screen; a withheld number. He considered closing the call, then thought better of it.

"Hello." He said, holding the iPhone up to his ear.

"Is that Martin Rooley?" The female voice asked at the other end of the line.

"Speaking."

"Hi this is Claire from Outpatients at St. Cuthbert's, I have an urgent message from Mister Purefoy, he has requested to see you at the hospital immediately."

"Immediately." Martin repeated, feeling a little shaken. Waiting at the lights with his hand on the wheel Peter turned and looked at his boss.

"Yes please Mister Rooley, the information I have been given is that he needs to speak with you immediately."

Martin sighed, thinking of the importance of the meeting they were about to attend.

"I'm going to need to get back to you." He said eventually.

"If you could get back as quickly as possible Mister Rooley, it would be appreciated."

"I will, thank you." Martin closed the call and put his hand over his eyes, rubbing at his forehead with his fingers.

"What is it?" Peter asked as the lights turned green, he slowly edged forwards towards Greenwich.

"It was the hospital; they want to see me immediately."

"Really?" Peter replied, his eyes wide.

"Really, what the hell am I supposed to do?"

Peter thought for a couple of seconds, nodding his head slowly and staring off into the distance. When he had finished contemplating he leant forwards and tapped a couple of buttons on his dashboard.

"Maria."

"Yes Peter." The computerised female voice spoke through the sound system.

"Get me Fisher Warner Marcus."

Martin looked at his friend in confusion.

There was a sequence of blips as the number was dialled, then the line was ringing.

"Fisher Warner Marcus, you're through to Samantha today." The voice answered after a couple of rings.

"Hi Samantha, this is Peter Werth-Duncan from Sapient Trans-Global, my colleague and I mister Martin Rooley have an appointment this afternoon with Mister Warner at three o'clock, I'm calling because we're sadly going to have to postpone the appointment."

"What are you doing?" Martin asked, astonished, his face a mask of concern.

Peter waved him to be quiet with his hand and continued talking. "If you could please get the message to Mister Warner we'd be truly grateful."

"I will Mister Werth-Duncan, was there anything else?"

"Just please offer our sincerest apologies, we will be in contact soon."

"Thank you Mister Werth-Duncan."

"Thank you Samantha."

The call closed and Martin buried his head in his hands as Maria's synthetic voice returned through the cars speaker system.

"Call closed. Call duration forty-seven seconds. Do you require any further services?"

"That will be all." Peter replied and the computer fell silent."

"What the hell have you done?" Martin asked, raising his head from his hands and looking at his friend.

"The right thing." Peter replied.

"You do know this will probably cost us the Fisher contract, James Warner is not a man who likes to be messed around."

"There'll be other contracts; you may only get one shot at a new heart."

Martin looked at his friend in stunned silence. If you had told him just that morning that Peter Werth-Duncan was capable of sentiment over business he would have scoffed at the idea, but as the middle aged man signalled to turn the car back around in the direction of the A102 Martin found himself slightly choked, a lump in his throat the size of a golf ball.

"I don't know what to say." Was all he could manage.

"Don't say anything, not to me anyway, but get on the phone to St. Cuthbert's and tell them we're on our way."

Fifty minutes later, after battling with the traffic on the M25, the BMW pulled into the car park outside the Outpatients wing of St. Cuthbert's. Martin looked at the double glass front door of the hospital with worry lines stretched right the way across his face.

"This could be it, this could actually be it." He mumbled, his hands were shaking so he clasped them together to save face in front of his friend.

Peter, who never missed a thing was well aware of Martin's anxiety. "Do you want me to come in with you?" He asked.

"What? No." Martin replied quickly, but there was something in his eyes that again was shrewdly picked up by the thin, balding man.

"Come on, let's go inside."

"Are you sure? I mean, you don't have to do that."

"What you think I'm going to just sit out in the car here like a chauffer, you wish. Come on." Peter opened his door and prepared to leave, but before he could Martin grasped his arm.

"Thank you Peter." He said earnestly. "Really, I'm just so damn scared."

"Don't mention it." The younger man said, and nodded his head reassuringly.

Martin nodded in return, having to fight back the tears once more; if he could connect a pipeline to his tear ducts he reckoned he could give Thames Water a run for their money at the moment.

The two men climbed out of the BMW and looked up at the white walls of the hospital.

"You go get registered, I'll pay for the car park, I'll be through in a minute." Peter said.

"Ok." Martin replied.

Ten minutes later they had been guided through to a waiting area that Martin was now well accustomed to. Though he had spoken to David Purefoy several times on the phone he had not actually laid eyes on the man since his stay at the hospital last Christmas. Surely if he wanted to see him in person it could only be news about his new heart.

"Try to relax." Peter said, flipping through a copy of GQ.

"I am relaxed." Martin replied stuffily.

"Well tell that to your feet, they're tapping away like Michael Flatley down there."

Martin stilled his feet immediately, he hadn't even been aware they were moving.

A couple of minutes passed and then a door opened and Purefoy leant out.

"Martin, come on through." He said, and stepped back inside.

"Well, this is it." Martin said. "Do or die right?"

"You want me to wait here?" Peter asked.

"Yeah, yeah I'll be ok from here." Martin nodded solemnly.

"Well good luck, I hope it's the heart of an athlete." Peter said with a reassuring smile.

Martin stood up and walked into Purefoy's office. He closed the door behind him leaving his friend to peruse the clothes he would never wear and the aftershaves he wouldn't buy.

"Take a seat." Purefoy said, gesturing to the chair in front of his desk. Martin sat down and the cushion let out a huge farting sound.

"God..." He said quickly, reddening at the cheeks.

"Sorry about that, damn thing does it all the time." Purefoy said with a sly smile.

Well, he may be a dick but it gave me something else to worry about for a second or two, Martin thought, trying to relax.

Purefoy rustled a couple of papers on his desk, found what he was looking for and placed it to one side, then he looked up at Martin gravely.

"Thank you for coming at such short notice."

"Not a problem." Martin replied, trying not to let his frazzled nerves show all over his face. "Is it news on a heart?" He asked hopefully.

"Of a sort." Purefoy replied. He paused for a second, seemingly gathering his thoughts, when he continued he looked very serious, Martin could feel his stomach start to tighten. "I've been looking at the results of your latest ECG, I'm afraid it's not good news."

"Oh." Was all Martin could say, he suddenly felt very short of breath but fought to keep his composure.

"Basically to put it in layman's terms the blood that is being pumped around your body by your heart is on the decrease, and it seems to be slowing at an alarming rate."

"Wasn't this always the case?" Martin asked, his mouth was very dry.

"It was, but not to this level. When we first diagnosed the problem with your heart there was time to find a suitable replacement. But the deterioration is happening now at such an alarming rate I'm no longer certain it will buy us the time we need. Have you noticed any further physical symptoms yourself?"

"Some yes, err just go back to the part about not having enough time."

"Well," Purefoy said with a sigh, "there have been hearts that have come in that would have been suitable for your blood group, but they went to either category one patients or children, who always take precedent. We're going through a bit of a barren spell I'm afraid, there just aren't enough hearts to go round."

Martin was silent for a while, mulling over the damning news the surgeon had just delivered. When he spoke again his voice sounded very quiet in the room.

"So what does this mean for me?"

"Well I think I can bump you up to a category one patient now, especially with your standing in the community, and we will monitor you more regularly to ensure we're doing all we can to maintain stability."

"That's not what I mean." Martin replied meekly. "I'm asking how long I have."

Purefoy was quiet for a very long time. Martin could hear the clock ticking away at the back of the room, listening to its slow, rhythmic pace, not unlike the beating of a heart.

"Not long." He replied, and then fell silent again. When it became apparent that he wasn't going to elaborate Martin stepped in, needing to bury his agitation before he said something he would later regret.

"Well how long is not long?"

Purefoy sighed. "An estimate, I'd say no more than six weeks."

A chill ran through Martin from his head to his toes, creeping down his spine and making the small hairs on the back of his neck spring to attention.

"Six weeks." He repeated quietly.

"That's only an estimate, but like I say the damage you have sustained is quite severe, and it's deteriorating rapidly. If it continues at this pace pretty soon your vital organs are going to start shutting down, now depending on the organ we have ways and means to keep them going, but if your heart stops pumping all together, which is my biggest concern, it's going to starve your body of the blood and nutrients it needs to survive."

Martin stared at the man before him with eyes that no longer knew how to blink; he felt very cold and was struggling to breathe. Purefoy noticed his distress and tried too late to ease his suffering.

"Trust me Martin we're doing all we can to find you a new heart, if I bump you to a category one patient it will certainly help our chances, and we're going to do everything in our power to keep you comfortable. I'm sure all is going to turn out fine, but I just wanted you to be aware of what was happening so you had all the information, I don't believe in keeping my patients in the dark."

"Oh I appreciate that." Martin replied, feeling like he was having an out of body experience. "So the bottom line is if I don't get a new heart in six weeks I'm going to be dead."

"It won't come to that." Purefoy tried to reassure.

"That's ok; I appreciate you not treating me like a child Mr Purefoy." Martin stood up to leave.

"Err are you leaving?" Purefoy asked in a panic.

"Well I think I have all the information that I need." Martin smiled and turned to the door.

"We're going to need to make an appointment, this week; we want to monitor you closely like I say and…"

"Oh have your admin team contact me at home; I'll be free whenever it is."

"But I…"

"Goodbye Doctor, thank you for your time today." Martin said, turning back to face the surgeon. "Do I call you Doctor? I've never known that."

"Err no, it's mister for a surgeon."

"Oh, ok." Martin said, then he continued out of the office and closed the door behind him.

Peter had moved on to Chat magazine and when the office door opened he quickly dropped it back into the magazine rack shame-facedly.

"Come on Peter let's get out of here." Martin said, briskly walking past his friend towards reception and the hospital exit.

Peter stood and followed him out, there was a strange look on his friends face, was it joy? Had the old man finally had some good news?

"Well?" He said when it became apparent Martin wasn't going to be forthcoming with the news.

"Outside." Was the brisk response.

"Ok." Peter mumbled, feeling on edge.

They stepped out into the mid afternoon sunshine and crossed the car park to the spot where Peter had left his BMW. He pressed the key fob and the doors unlocked. Martin climbed in without saying a word. Peter climbed into the driver's side. He leant over and checked his briefcase was still under the seat well, satisfied that it was he turned back and started the engine.

"Will you please tell me what's going on? The suspense is killing me." He said with a grin, but when he turned back to face his friend the smile quickly faded from his lips. Martin was crying, rivulets of tears dripping down his cheeks, and his face was a picture of absolute misery, Peter didn't think he had ever seen such raw emotion from a man before.

Martin slowly turned to face his friend, and what he said next made Peter's breath catch in his throat.

"It's over Peter, I'm going to die."

10

Standing outside the closed office door Peter took a moment to gather his thoughts. It was the day after the fateful trip to St. Cuthbert's and there were too many thoughts troubling his tired mind. He wanted to talk to Martin, reassure him if he could that everything was going to be ok, but how could he do that when he was so unsure himself?

The journey back from the hospital had been a quiet one; once Martin had overcome his initial reaction to the terrible news he sat in contemplative silence, mulling over his situation. Peter had tried to engage him but the old man wasn't in the mood to open up; he had given his friend a basic rundown of what Purefoy had told him and then decided to brood for a while, uncommunicative and vacant.

Now Peter wanted, no, needed reassurance for himself, and to provide some in return if that was at all possible, but first he needed to gather his courage. He drew in a deep breath, let it out and then knocked at the door.

"Come in." The voice responded from the other side.

When Peter walked in Martin was stood up at his desk, packing up his belongings and placing them in a plastic box that was perched on top. Just seeing the old man resigning himself to his fate in such a simple way made the skin crawl on Peter's arms.

"I've never known you to knock before." Martin said with a smile as Peter walked over.

"I guess I've finally found my manners." The balding man replied. "What are you doing?"

"What does it look like?" Martin asked, picking up the framed photograph of he and Rose in Malibu, looking at it affectionately for a couple of seconds and then placing it with the rest of his belongings in the box.

"It looks ill advised is what I think, you're not really thinking about leaving are you?"

"I'm not thinking about it no, I'm doing it. I'm leaving the business Peter, for the time being at least. The truth is I should never have come back, my heart isn't in it anymore if you'll excuse the pun."

"You can't be serious, come on, you're the heart and soul of this place, if you'll excuse a pun of my own, there is no Sapient without you."

"Oh I'm sure it will muddle on." Martin said with a faraway look on his face. "Besides it's about time I gave a little more attention to my backswing and let the financial Empire take care of my coffers like most fat cats."

"Well that's one thing you couldn't be accused of any more, you look like you've just been released from Auschwitz."

Martin smiled, though his eyes were still distant and sad. "What can I do you for Peter? You after the proposals for the Maplethorpe consortium? If so I asked Sheila to have them delivered to your office."

"No I'm not here about the Maplethorpe consortium," Peter said with a sigh, "I'm here checking up on you is all."

"You worried about me?" Martin asked, still smiling.

"Would it be so strange if I was?"

"Well let me tell you that there's no need. I'm fine. I'm sorry I had a wobble on you yesterday; it was just a shock you know, hearing it like that. But I had a revelation last night, I was lying in bed staring at the ceiling and waiting for the sun to make an appearance when I realised I'd be crazy to waste my time; if I do only have around six weeks to live then I don't want to spend them moping around the office making everyone feel uncomfortable, Sheila's going to find me a suitable excuse and I'm going to go and spend some time with the people who'll miss me the most, and you can bet your bottom dollar that isn't my damn shareholders."

"I don't know what to say." Peter said honestly.

"Don't say anything; just give me a hand with these boxes if you like."

Peter shuffled around the side of the desk and grabbed the plastic box, carrying it over to a pile of boxes that were already stacked in the corner.

"I don't like seeing you do this, it all seems very final." Peter said as he ensured the boxes were stacked safely. "Besides you're going to have it all to undo when you come back."

"Come on Peter, let's not be naïve, we both know I won't be coming back."

"Don't say that; don't even think that, anything can happen in six weeks, anything."

Martin sighed. "Peter you're a sweet boy, and I thank you for your well-meaning words, but if I don't face the facts and start dealing with them soon I'm likely never to, and that won't help me. I need to be true to myself, yes a new heart could come through, but by the time it does I could be too sick to operate. Who knows, anyway, it's time I started preparing for what I deem to be the inevitable."

Peter was quiet for some time; the colour had drained from his face, when he spoke again there was a small tremble in his voice.

"I just can't believe this is happening."

"You and me both Peter, you and me both."

"What have you told Rose?"

"Nothing yet, I know I need to, but I can't seem to find the words to say."

"I know its hard Martin, but she has a right to know, she'd want to know."

"You're right, you are, you're right. It's just going to set her back again you know, when she was starting to turn a corner. But you're right, I need to tell her, I'll tell her tonight."

Peter looked to the floor, he found he couldn't meet his friends gaze and it made him feel ashamed.

"What can I do?" He asked, finally looking up with the saddest expression Martin had ever seen on another man's face.

"What do you mean?" Martin asked.

"I just feel so useless." Peter said, his voice sounding terribly naked to his ears.

Martin sighed, he didn't like seeing his friend so out of sorts, and felt even worse knowing that he was the cause.

"Peter, my friend Peter, you can't punish yourself over this, it is what it is. Listen to me and listen close." Martin stepped forward and placed a hand on Peter's shoulder. "You've already far outstretched your remit. This company is where it is today because of you, because of your hard work, and it will go where it goes because of your dedication and leadership. You're the future of Sapient now, and it's in damn safe hands. But more than that you've been a true friend, you've cared for me and looked out for me, you've had my back more times than I care to admit. When you came to the hospital with me…that type of thing, I won't forget it let me tell you that. As long as I'm on this earth I will not forget it. So stop beating yourself up, cos frankly Peter I couldn't ask for a better friend."

Peter nodded slowly; he had gone a little pink in the cheeks at the speech but looked a lot happier despite this. They were both quiet for a moment, when the silence became uncomfortable Martin turned back to his desk and continued packing his things. Peter watched him, knowing what he had to ask but feeling decidedly uncomfortable about it. He twiddled his thumbs for a few moments and looked down at his immaculately polished Gucci loafers. Then he found the courage he needed and dived on in.

"Listen Martin, I feel a real asshole even asking this but…"

"Asking what?" Martin said when Peter paused.

"I don't think anything's going to happen to you, you know that right? I think you're going to get a new heart in plenty of time and everything's going to be just fine. But saying that isn't the case, saying I'm wrong, are all your affairs in order?"

Now the middle aged man really did redden at the cheeks, and it wasn't just a little pink like before but a deep scarlet, it turned his whole head into a stress filled ball and made Martin smile at the sight.

"No, no my affairs aren't in order. I haven't changed my will since the mid nineties."

"Don't you think you should get onto it?" Peter said a little sharper than he had intended.

"And I thought I was going to be alright." Martin said with a grin.

Peter looked embarrassed. "You know I think that, but you also know that I believe in preparing for any scenario, even when that scenario is too horrible to comprehend."

"I'll get to it." Martin said quietly.

A look passed Peter's face, it could have been agitation, and Martin could understand this, his old friend didn't like loose ends, especially not where business was concerned.

"Don't worry Peter." Martin tried to reassure. "Sometime in the coming days I'll get round to it, you're right it does need my attention, you were right to bring it up."

"I'm sorry, I feel like a major asswipe for even mentioning it."

"Well you shouldn't." Martin said briskly. "I need to keep my responsibilities in mind, there re a lot of people that are reliant on me."

"Ok." Peter said quietly. Another uncomfortable silence descended and Peter took it as his cue to leave. "Listen I understand why you feel you need to be around your loved ones right now, and I respect it I do, but don't be a stranger around here ok?"

"I won't." Martin said with a strained smile.

Peter walked to the door, as he opened it he turned back around.

"Everything really is going to be ok you know, I guarantee it."

Martin thought it an unusual thing to say under the circumstances but he let it go. He nodded slowly and held Peter's gaze for a moment, then the middle aged man was gone.

When the door closed Martin sat down in his leather chair, he swivelled round and gazed once more at Canary Wharf through his picture window. That was the most difficult goodbye to take care of, there was only Sheila left, after that the excuse she had prepared would be enough.

The sky was a brilliant pastel blue, the sun glinted off the windows of the high rise buildings that surrounded his office and cast brilliant rays that shimmered like diamonds. Out of everything he loved about his work, he was going to miss this view the most.

11

Martin was sat in the living room reading that evenings paper when Rose came in from her dance class; he folded the paper, placed it on the chair side table and waited patiently for her to sort herself out. He heard a jangle of keys being placed in the pot by the door and then she was in the room.

He couldn't help but smile, seeing his soon to be sixty-four year old wife in leggings, a pink leotard and matching head band would be something for which he would never grow tired.

"Hi." She said with a huge smile as she entered the room, it was almost enough to sway Martin from his course, but he gritted his teeth and held firm. "You'll never guess what Joan's got us dancing to now, Ricky Martin, a samba song. Well it was all legs and arms you should have seen the state of us."

"I can imagine." Martin replied with a thoughtful smile.

"What's the matter?" Rose said, her face suddenly dropping and the colour draining instantly from her cheeks. He couldn't hide anything from Rose; she had always had an uncanny ability to read him like the Bible, no matter how hard he tried to keep his feelings to himself if there was something troubling him Rose would sniff it out like a border collie at a Cuban baggage control.

"Sit down Rose." He said gently. She did as she was told, perching on the edge of the sofa, her hands clasped tightly in her lap and her eyes huge and expectant.

Martin couldn't leave her like this, he stood from his seat and crossed the living room, sitting down on the sofa next to her and taking both of her now trembling hands in both of his.

"Do you remember our first date dear one?" He said with a warming smile.

"Of course." She replied, the memory causing a mixture of emotions under the harsh circumstances.

"I was twenty years old, you were only sixteen. Your daddy didn't like me courting you he thought there was too much of an age difference and he wanted you to step out with that boy who was an apprentice at his paper factory."

"Lance Peters." Rose said, smiling softly at the memory.

"But I knew, I knew as soon as I saw you." Martin continued, happy in the flow of the memory. "You were all big round eyes and wavy auburn hair. I'd seen you a couple of times at the ice rink, I was with my boys and you were serving ice drinks in the café bar. My gosh I was smitten from the start."

Rose smiled and cast her gaze down, she was blushing and Martin was pleased, she deserved to feel special; she was special, to him she always would be, no matter how long his forever turned out to be.

"Laurence Pettifer was going to ask you out first; I was mortified, I knew what Laurie was like, he had a way with the ladies, they'd fall in love with him and then he'd move on to the next, leaving them heartbroken. I couldn't let that happen, so I plucked up the courage and cornered you by the changing rooms, you remember?"

"You never told me old Laurie was on the cards." Rose said with a cheeky smile, more relaxed now.

"I wouldn't would I, if I let on that old dog was interested I'd have stood no chance."

"Oh you'd have done better than you think."

Martin smiled; it was his turn to avert his gaze. "I was so nervous."

"You could hardly get your words out." Rose added. "I thought at first that you must suffer from a terrible stutter."

Martin chuckled. "But despite this you agreed to let me take you to the Picture Dome that Saturday night. They were showing an old John Wayne western."

"Not a western, a war film,' The Undefeated'." Rose corrected.

"That's right, it was 'The Undefeated' wasn't it." Martin smiled. "You wanted to see something girly."

"And you took me to that old war film. At least you bought me popcorn."

"But I was so nervous and my hands were shaking so badly that I spilled it all over the balcony, it dropped all over the people in the floor seats below do you remember?"

This time Rose chuckled. "I do. I remember."

"I didn't think I'd ever get a second date after that, but here we are today."

"Yes, here we are." Rose's smile thinned, she removed her hands from Martin's and stroked him gently on the back of his hand.

"I'm dying Rose." He said suddenly.

Rose looked up at him slowly, her eyes met his and he saw that she was racked with a number of different emotions, but the biggest of these was confusion.

"I know that Martin, that's why you need the new heart."

"You don't understand." He said, feeling a sinking in his stomach like lead. "I saw Purefoy this week, there's still no news on a new heart, nothing. And my heart, well it's..."

He couldn't finish the sentence, didn't know how to, so he let it hang, hoping she had understood enough to be able to read between the lines.

She didn't say anything, but she leant forward and pulled him close, holding him against her as he trembled in her arms. He would have stayed like that all night if she had let him, but after a while she peeled away from him and held him at arms length, looking deep into his ageing eyes. There was a look on her face that Martin couldn't place at first but after a while he got it, she was trying to stay strong.

"I don't want to lose you Martin; my God I don't want to lose you. But I know there's nothing more anybody can do."

Martin looked down at his knees, feeling very tired and very weak.

"How long?" She asked next.

Martin thought for a few seconds about how to respond, he realised in this time that the truth was really the only option.

"Not long."

Rose nodded solemnly.

"I won't give up on you Martin, not while there's a chance that things could still turn out alright."

"Rose, we have to start facing the facts, I'm going to die."

"No." Rose shook her head defiantly from side to side. "Don't you ask me to think like that, I won't do it I tell you, I won't. I don't care if the odds are a million to one, if there's still that one to cling on to then by God let me cling on to it Martin, please. It's the only way I can cope with all of this. Without hope I have nothing."

"Ok." Martin nodded slowly.

"We'll fight, with every tooth and every nail we'll fight. We'll fight this thing and in my heart I believe we'll win, I believe you'll win. I have to believe."

Martin nodded again, but it was clear that he didn't share his wife's optimism.

Rose was quiet for a while; she dropped her hands back to her lap and sat in contemplation. When she spoke again there was a small smile on her lips.

"If this is it Martin, if this really is it, then we need to make the most of what time we have left."

"What do you have in mind?"

"I don't know, we always liked Rome, we could take a trip."

"I can't, they'd never let me fly. Besides I shouldn't leave the country, just in case you know, long shot or not I could do with being around just in case there was some good news."

"Ok, so we'll go to the country, somewhere nice, spend some time just for us."

Martin nodded, warming to the idea. "I'd like that."

"I'd like that too." Rose said.

They were quiet for a while, both lost in their own thoughts. Martin was pleased that Rose hadn't broken down as he had thought she would, it was good for him that she remained strong wherever she could. He was looking down at the living room carpet when he felt her take his hands in hers.

"A million to one Martin." She whispered. "Even at a million to one, there's still hope."

Martin wished that he shared his wife's enthusiasm for the odds, but he gave her the moment as he sat in the ever growing certainty of his impending doom.

12

They found a cottage in the Cotswolds and spent three nights enjoying each others company as best as they could under the difficult circumstances. In the day Martin would fish in the little stream at the end of the meadow while Rose read a book on the sun deck. At night they would sit out in the cool summer air, enjoying a nice meal and a bottle of wine. Rose had relaxed her dietary regime since learning of her husbands remaining time and now he would enjoy a little more of what he liked to eat and drink, though never to the excesses of his past, she wasn't the only one who had changed and as much as he still loved his food he was no longer a glutton.

They would take a walk in the fields, listening to the chatter of the birds and enjoying the smells of the honeysuckle and wild aspidistras. Sometimes they would wander into the nearest village to buy bread and cheeses and sometimes they would enjoy long leisurely lie-in's. But whatever they did they did in the knowledge that time was precious and each moment a thing to be cherished.

When they returned home to London three days later they each felt it had been one of the best holiday's they had ever taken, even with the threat of death hanging over their heads. It was funny really; their wealth had provided many opportunities over the years and allowed them to see things that most people only dreamed of, they had holidayed in Monaco, stayed at the best hotels in Dubai, had a guided tour of the valley of the Kings in Egypt and visited the Great Barrier Reef off the East coast of Australia, but they had never really appreciated any of it. They had thought they had at the time, but looking back now it wasn't the case, those three nights in their little cottage home in the Cotswolds proved that.

They vowed on their return that things would not change just because they were home, they would continue as though they were still in that holiday mode, and make the best of every day with which they were blessed, and they did for a while. Martin would spend more time with his friends working on his back swing and at night he would go with Rose to her dance class or her book club, wanting to be close to her as the days thinned out.

It was a strangely happy time, but it all came to an end whilst trying to improve his handicap on the seventh hole of the private golf club of which he was a member. He was there with Davey Flannigan, a long time friend he had known since moving his business to the capital, Bill Syers, who owned a chain of quality restaurants in London's west end, and Sebastian Cooper, with whom Rose was still desperate to dig the dirt following the breakdown of his marriage to Jilly Cooper of the ex-tennis pro fame.

Bill was lining up his shot, three behind Sebastian who had the best handicap of the old friends, and Martin could see that his fat old friend thought today was the day he might actually get one over the silver fox. Martin, who had the worst handicap in the group was not as competitive but liked to watch his friends desperately try to get one over Cooper, who seemed to play with an almost absent-minded grace, brilliant at the sport without even trying; which of course frustrated Bill and Davey all the more.

Bill was sweating, it was a hot day but his clammy condition was nothing to do with the heat. Sebastian was currently in the rough and Bill was on the green, this shot could potentially bring him level. He pulled back his putter, steadied, looked again at the hole then tapped the ball and watched as it careered a foot wide of its target.

"Son of a bitch!" He muttered, knowing that the pressure had gotten the better of him but unable to do anything about it now, he watched on desperately as the ball rolled away from the seventh hole and disappeared off the green.

"So," Davey Flannigan said, quickly trying to draw attention away from Bill who looked fit to burst. "What's the latest with you and that tricky little piece of candy in the city?"

Sebastian, who always seemed oblivious to his friend's desperate need to beat him at anything, looked just as undiscerning now.

"Nothing to tell." He said with a small smile.

"Come on, the girls half your age, and I'm being generous, are you really trying to tell me there are no tales to tell?" Davey countered with notable frustration.

Martin reckoned the old guy wanted all the sordid details to try and kick-start his own waning sex drive, but he also wanted Sebastian to spill the beans, and listened on intently, though his agenda was a little different to Davey's, he just wanted to give Rose and her bridge club buddies some gossip to keep them going for another couple of weeks.

Sebastian walked over to the ankle deep grass by the tree-line ten foot from the green and steadied himself next to his ball. "Well, I'll tell you this much, she may be less than half my age but she could still learn a thing or two from Jilly." The tall man hunkered a little, looked over to the hole and with a deft flick of his wrist sent the ball up a couple of feet into the air where it landed on the green and rolled to within a couple of inches of the hole.

Martin let out a splutter of laughter and had to stifle it with the back of his hand. He couldn't help it, he had seen the look on poor old Bill's face as the almost perfect shot was made, the big man was utterly crestfallen.

"Come on," Davey said, not wanting to leave it there, "you're honestly trying to tell me this isn't the best thing that ever happened to you?"

"Oh please," Sebastian said with a shake of his head, "you can't compare a firm bosom and a tight ass with twenty years of marriage."

"I know which I'd choose." Bill said, cooling down from his moment of misery.

Martin stepped up to his own ball which was still a good eight foot from the hole and started to line up his angles.

"Seriously." Sebastian continued, trying to make his case. "I'd give it up in a shot to have what you guys have."

"What's that? Expanding waist lines and type two diabetes." Bill said huffily.

"Successful marriages." Sebastian countered.

"Aw bullshit." Davey shot straight back. "You just don't want to dish the dirt."

Martin looked up from his ball at his ludicrously handsome friend, curious as to what his response would be, but the enigmatic man just smiled and went back to polishing his clubs.

"This is horse shit, play the damn ball will you Martin I need a drink." Bill grumbled.

Martin leant back over his ball, but as he gazed down at the green a sudden wave of nausea overcame him, he felt short of breath and dizzy and his brow had broken out into a thin sheen of sweat, he knew the signs and panic coursed through his body.

In the background his friends continued to chat, unaware of his plight.

"There's still another eleven holes to play." Davey was saying to Bill, whose interest in the game had died around the time of Sebastian's superb putt.

"If I want a dink I want a drink what can I tell you?"

Martin wheezed, there was a dagger wound pain in his chest and he was certain at that point that this was it, his time had come. He clutched his chest and put his full weight down on the handle of his putter.

"You ok Martin?" Sebastian asked, noticing his friend's unusual stature.

"Jesus his face is purple!" Bill said with clear exposed shock in his voice.

Martin dropped to his knees, his putter flopping down to the green at his side with a dull thump. The vice like grip was back on his chest and this time it was squeezing even harder. He dropped onto his face on the grass, his body wracked with spasms.

It had been Martin's decision to keep his condition from his friends, and although the extent of the problem was still unknown to them, they knew enough now to cause panic amongst the group.

"He's having a heart attack, Jesus! Someone call a doctor!" Bill cried.

It was Sebastian who was first to grab his mobile from his pocket and dial for assistance. Davy crouched down next to Martin and placed a hand on his shoulder, unsure of what to do as Bill watched on with wide unbelieving eyes.

Martin lay on the freshly cut grass of the seventh hole, dirt on his cheek, gasping for breath, and as his brain was starved of oxygen he slipped into unconsciousness once more, leaving his terrified friends thinking he had died.

13

This time the hospital room was magnolia, but it had the same standard furniture as the room he had occupied at Christmas. The same monitors were blipping away at his side as well. But the room colour wasn't the only difference, when he had been a guest of the hospital before he had been a victim of the misguided notion that everything was going to be alright. This time there was no such luxury.

The good feeling that had filled him for the last week was gone, replaced by a deep feeling of foreboding, it would seem that he would not be enjoying his final days on this earth as he had hoped, consigned instead to this hospital bed, hooked up to an oxygen mask to help him breathe, another new factor in this swiftly spiralling story that he had hoped could be avoided.

Rose was once again at his side, this latest setback had seen a change in her too; for she no longer held onto the vain one in a million hopes she had naively clung on to when he had delivered the news of his quickly deteriorating condition; now she was ashen and forlorn, the hope no longer evident in her eyes. She had sat for hours in the softly cushioned chair at the side of his bed barely saying a word, and without her having the desire to lead the conversation they had sat in silence for the majority of the day.

Now it was real, now it was something that they had to face head on and grow accustomed to, for this problem was not going away, it would grow and grow like a tumour until it reached the point where his heart could no longer perform its most basic of functions. One by one his other vital organs were going to shut down, and when they did he was going to die. The only question that was left was when exactly was this likely to happen?

He sucked again at the oxygen mask, liking the feeling of the air rushing into his lungs, but it made him nervous at the same time, how was he to cope with the reality of not being able to breathe by himself? It was alien to him, for sixty-seven years he had opened his mouth and filled his lungs and now this was no longer a possibility, not if he wanted to live anyway, for whatever semblance of life he still had to live.

Rose cast her eyes down to the floor and feigned indifference, but Martin knew that the sound was starting to grate on her, and the fact that it was grating on her was starting to grate on him, after all, he was the one stuck in this bed, sucking at a plastic mask to make his tired old lungs work, hopeless in the knowledge that his days on this earth were numbered, really what did she have to be upset about?

He tried to think a little better of his wife but with the departure of what little optimism he had left came a cloud of darkness that was making him bitter and distant, lost in feelings of self pity and remorse.

The door opened and a nurse walked in; the same nurse who had already checked his pulse and his blood pressure three times that day, he bit back his frustration at the constant poking and prodding and tried his level best not to let his agitation show.

"Hello Mister Rooley, how are you feeling?" She asked as she walked over.

Rose, who to Martin's recollection had never said a cross word in her life snapped at the young girl. "How do you think he's doing hooked up to this thing?"

"Rose!" Martin scolded.

"Sorry." She said, instantly regretting her words, she gazed down at the floor ashamed and miserable.

"That's ok." The young nurse said, she smiled to show there were no hard feelings but Rose's eyes were cast down and didn't notice. "How are you finding the oxygen mask?"

"Well, I don't like that I need it, but I guess it's better than not being able to breathe. That's the scariest thing I think, the lack of breath."

"I bet, whenever you feel uncomfortable have a little puff on the mask, but try not to use it too much we don't want you to become dependant on it ok."

"Ok." Martin replied, knowing he already felt dependant on it, terrified in fact of the thought of not having it as a kind of old mans security blanket.

"Can you guess what I'm here for?"

"Oh I don't know, blood pressure and pulse by and chance?"

"You're a fast learner." She said with a smile.

Martin relaxed a little, he liked the girl, she had a good bedside manner and it was eating through the barrier of bitterness he had built about himself. He was glad, these were alien feelings to him, he had always been a happy-go-lucky kind of guy and didn't like to feel miserable or morose, no matter how justifiable his reasons.

The nurse wheeled her trolley over, took the blood pressure cuff and wrapped it tightly around Martin's right arm. The cuff inflated and then the valve of the cuff opened slightly allowing the pressure to slowly fall. She placed the clip on his index finger to get an accurate reading of his pulse and after a couple of moments made some notes on his chart.

"All fine." She said with another smile, then placed his chart back at the end of his bed and undid the blood pressure cuff. She wheeled the trolley back into the corner of the room then returned to the bedside.

"Have you chosen something for lunch?"

"I'm not hungry." He replied.

"You need to eat, it's important to keep your strength up, I'll bring the menu back, there's a chicken Korma today, it's nice." Then she turned and strolled to the door.

When she had left Rose finally lifted her gaze from the floor.

"I didn't mean to snap." She said meekly.

"I know you didn't dear, it's a hard time."

She nodded slowly. "You just don't expect it you know, this is the type of thing that happens to other people, not to us, not to my lovely husband."

Her eyes were filling with tears and her bottom lip trembling. Martin placed the oxygen mask down on the bed spread and cupped his wife's hand in his.

"What will be will be, we have to stay strong."

"I know." She replied as the tears started rolling down her cheeks.

He patted her on the hand and then relaxed back into his pillow, staring up at the ceiling and wondering just how the hell he had let this happen.

Then the door was opening again and this time it was Purefoy who was entering the room. He wore a tailored suit and his parting was particularly neat this afternoon, as though he had been grooming in one of the waiting rooms. Martin wouldn't put it past him; he had always found the man to be arrogant and vain.

"Well, here we are again." He said as he crossed the room. This flippant remark did nothing to endear him to Martin, who stared over the top of his oxygen mask as the surgeon grabbed the chart from the bottom of the bed and flicked through the notes.

Rose tutted, she too had come to dislike the well groomed man but she needn't have bothered, negative remarks and gestures bounced off David Purefoy like raindrops from the top of an umbrella.

"So how are we feeling?" He asked as he continued to scan the chart.

Martin, who was growing tired of answering half baked questions about his well being sighed into the mouth piece of the oxygen mask, it made a deep guttural sound not unlike that old asthmatic arch villain Darth Vader and made him smile in spite of himself.

"I'm fine."

"You look it." Purefoy replied. Martin thought it was a funny thing to say under the circumstances, he felt anything but fine and was pretty damn sure he looked just as he felt.

"Do you have any news for us?" Rose asked, that hopeful but naïve look back on her face.

"No." Came the rather blunt response.

"That's reassuring." Martin muttered under his breath.

Purefoy nodded his head a couple of times and then placed the chart back on its clip at the foot of the bed. "Everything looks very good here." He said, seeming satisfied with what he had read.

"Everything looks good." Rose said with her eyebrows raised.

"What I mean is your husband looks good and stable at the moment, he looks strong."

Martin hated to contradict but he had never felt as weak in his life, he placed the oxygen mask back down on the bed. "I don't feel strong."

"Well sure, you're not going to feel exactly as you did, but trust me your vitals are very positive, I don't see any reason you can't go home."

"Go home!" Rose cried, standing from her seat. "Doctor look at him!"

"I am looking at him." Purefoy replied indignantly. "He looks as fit as a butchers dog."

Suddenly Martin felt very scared, something was wrong here, he didn't know what it was but he knew a brush off when he heard it, were they washing their hands of him?

"Mister Purefoy please, I don't feel strong enough to go home yet."

A look passed over Purefoy's face, but the intelligent man was quick to mask his true feelings, not quick enough though for the businessman to recognise it for what it was, the surgeon was agitated. Now his face was widening into his most persuasive smile, as though the fleeting reaction were nothing more than a figment of Martin's over active imagination.

"Martin, you're worried, I can understand that, but really you have nothing to fear, we're always a phone call away and I'm sure you'd be more comfortable in your own home. In these situations it's best to be wherever you are at your most comfortable and I think one's home ticks that box quite nicely."

"But I'm struggling to breathe." Martin almost pleaded, his eyes wide with alarm. "I need the oxygen mask; I don't think I can cope without it."

"Not a problem, we can get you one to take home with you, and a nurse to come along every day to change the tank and make sure everything's alright, how does that sound?"

"Well..." Martin said, starting to back down. Luckily for him his beloved wife was having nothing of the sort.

"I don't care how well you think he's doing, I don't even care how much you need this hospital bed. My husband pays for the best medical help and that is what we expect. If he says he isn't well enough to return home then you should honour that, and stop standing there with that smug look on your face! This is Martin's life, this is both of our lives, and we won't be part of a game involving bed count and success rates."

Her tirade over Rose fell silent, her chest rising and falling rapidly and a vein pulsing away in the centre of her head.

Martin looked up at her fondly, feeling immensely proud at that moment.

Purefoy looked down at the floor for a couple of moments, trying to gather his thoughts; the woman's reaction had clearly taken him aback. When he spoke again his voice was quiet and calming.

"Mrs Rooley could I have a word with you in private please?"

"Anything you have to say you can say in front of my husband." She said defiantly.

"Please." Came his gentle response, and there was something in his eyes that broke through her icy exterior and made her agree to his request.

"This won't take a minute." She said to Martin. He watched on, fearful once more as Purefoy turned and walked to the door, his loving wife following close behind. The door closed behind them and he suddenly felt very alone in the room. He could hear the soft beeping of the heart monitor and the sound of nurses talking in the station at the end of the hall, but otherwise it was silent. It felt creepy, something wasn't right here, why did Purefoy want him out of the hospital? It was clear he wasn't well enough to be heading home just yet. The creeping feeling that they were washing their hands of him returned and he suddenly felt very small and child like. He wanted someone to wrap their arms around him and tell him everything was going to be alright, just as his mother had done when he was a boy and he had fallen and scraped his knee. It would take one hell of a plaster to cover up this mess.

How long had they been gone now? Three minutes, four, five? He couldn't know for sure, but every minute felt like an hour. Martin couldn't remember ever being quite so terrified in his life.

Finally the door re-opened and Rose re-entered, Purefoy followed close behind, his eyes cast away from the man in the hospital bed. When Rose stepped up to his bedside it was clear to Martin that something had changed, but he couldn't put his finger on it. One thing was for certain though, his wife's entire demeanour was different to when she had followed the surgeon out of the room, she was calm for a start, and confident. Martin didn't know whether to feel reassured or all the more terrified.

She slowly crept up to the bed and took his hand in hers; Martin felt a sinking in his stomach.

"I'm being sent home to die aren't I?" He whispered, his eyes watering.

"No, nothing of the sort." Rose tried her most reassuring smile but Martin was feeling un-reassurable.

"What's going on Rose? Talk to me please."

"Everything's ok, there's nothing to worry about, but we have to trust Mr Purefoy now."

"I don't trust him!" Martin spat fiercely and the surgeon once more averted his gaze.

"You need to. He's doing all he can for you, I trust him and I believe him and you have to too."

"I'm scared Rose."

"I'm going to be there with you, all the way."

"But why? Do they need the bed or something?"

Rose cast her eyes to one side, struggling for an answer; Purefoy was quick to step in.

"It's nothing like that Martin, God knows you pay enough to keep your hospital bed, but statistics have proven that a comfortable environment is paramount to a healthy recovery."

"I'm comfortable here."

"What with nurses interrupting you every five minutes to do unnecessary blood pressure readings, come on, the only place you can get a decent rest is at home, we both know that, and rest is essential right now."

Martin sighed. He looked up at Rose with pleading eyes, but she was unusually strong to them.

"We have to go dear, I trust David enough to know that what he's saying is true."

"David, what so you're on first name terms now? What did he say to you out there?"

"I merely reassured your wife that I have your best interests at heart." Purefoy stepped in.

"I wasn't talking to you." Martin replied uncharacteristically cold.

Purefoy sighed and stepped to one side.

"It's true Martin, he simply explained the facts to me and the biggest of those is that more heart attack patients enjoy a full recovery in the comfort of their own home. We just want what's best for you, that's all."

Martin sighed again; he was losing his will to fight.

"I can see this is a fight I aren't going to win." He said resignedly.

"Don't think of it like that." Rose whispered.

"Your wife is right." Purefoy chipped in. "Don't think of this as a war between us, we all want the same thing, what's best for you, it's just that our opinions on what that is differ slightly. I know it's hard right now Martin, but please trust me, I know what I'm doing."

Martin cast his gaze down to the oxygen mask at his side.

"Ok, I'll trust you." He said weakly.

Rose let out a huge sigh of relief which Martin found strange given she was so vehemently fighting his corner not five minutes ago. He remained silent however; whatever had happened outside this room he knew that his loving and devoted wife would only ever have his best interests at heart; he had to somehow keep the faith in that.

"I'm going to need one of these." He said, gesturing to the oxygen tank.

"I'll arrange it myself." Purefoy said with a smile.

"When?" Martin asked.

"When are you to leave?" Purefoy checked his understanding. "There's no time like the present."

"Ok." Martin said with a slow nod. "Then I will ask if you could give us some privacy please Mister Purefoy, while I sort myself out."

"Of course." Purefoy nodded, then turned and left the room, closing the door behind him.

When they were alone Rose took her husbands hand in hers once more.

"Are you sure about this?" Martin asked, the fear still etched on his face.

"I'm not sure about anything anymore my love." She whispered. "But what choice do we have?"

Martin nodded reluctantly.

"Ok, I'll trust him. If I really have no choice I will trust that man. Will you help me gather my things?"

"Of course." She replied with a soft smile.

Twenty minutes later Martin was dressed in the clothes that Rose had packed for him earlier that morning, preparing as she always did for any eventuality. Purefoy had hurriedly discharged Martin himself and signed out the oxygen tank that he would be taking home with him. Again Martin found this strange; when had a surgeon ever bothered with the details? There was always somebody else to organise this type of thing. Martin made himself believe the surgeon simply wanted to provide an end to end service and put the thoughts out of his head.

With the short stay bag packed and slung over Rose's shoulder they made their way to the door, Martin was panting over this short distance and had to stop in the corridor and rest with his back to the wall.

"Wait here, I'll find that nice porter and ask if he'll wheel you out to the car park." Rose said, heading off down the ward.

Martin pressed his head back into the yellow paintwork, closing his eyes and waiting for his respiration to get under control. There were raised voices coming from the nurse's station down the hall. Martin turned his head in that direction and saw it was Purefoy and the young nurse who had attended him earlier. His curiosity pricked he prized himself away from the wall and slowly crept within earshot. They were stood part way into the little nook, facing each other angrily and had not noticed they were not alone.

"But why I don't understand why?" The nurse was saying, her hands on her hips.

"Yours is not to question why, yours is to do as you are told." Purefoy responded in his most patronising tone.

"But I've been taking down his vitals all morning; he isn't in any fit state to be discharged."

Martin drew in a quick intake of breath, they were talking about him!

"I appreciate your concern, but he's my patient, and I won't have you questioning my decisions."

"But..."

"No but's, you either shut your mouth and carry on with whatever duties fill your day or you'll be looking for a placement at another hospital, do I make myself clear?"

The nurse looked up at the surgeon with pure dismay. Martin could see her from his place by the wall but she hadn't seen him.

"Perfectly." She said eventually, though it clearly pained her.

Martin swallowed hard, completely dumbstruck with what he had heard.

"Good, now if you'll excuse me." Purefoy turned and walked down the ward in the opposite direction to where Martin was stood, the nurse turned and stepped back into the station where she resumed her paper work with a clear air of anger, humiliation and frustration.

The businessman swallowed hard, he was about to walk over to the nurses station when a voice directly behind him startled him from his thoughts.

"Mister Rooley." It was the Nigerian porter, he was stood behind a wheelchair and behind him was Martin's wife. "If you are ready."

"Of course." Martin said with a strained smile, and sat down on the soft cushioned seat of the wheelchair.

As he was wheeled down the ward with the oxygen tank in his lap and his wife at his side Martin felt a deep and troubling foreboding in his bones. Something was very wrong here, he just didn't know yet what it was.

14

With the oxygen tank always within hands reach Martin pulled his last will and testament from the folder in the bedroom safe. He opened it and scanned the details, sighing as he read the content; it was grossly out of date, written at a time when Sapient was just achieving blue chip status, but not yet the colossal empire it was today. Bill Brookes was Martin's solicitor and handled all such affairs; he would need to make an urgent appointment with him, as things stood without Martin's intervention in the event of his death the board could float the company on the stock market, milking what they could and burying a company with proud traditions, not least of which was the security of its staff, who would be left in jeopardy with such a move.

Martin shook his head and placed the folder back in the safe; how could he have been so foolish? Simple to answer really; it was easy to be blasé about death when you believed it was a thing that happened to other people, it was only when faced with the truth of your own mortality that it became necessary to get your affairs in order. He made a mental note to call Bill before bed that night and closed the safe.

He had been so full of doubts and fears when he returned from St. Cuthbert's that he hardly slept a wink that night, tossing and turning, reaching for the oxygen mask, staring at the ceiling and worrying about what little future he had left. He could be dead in days, and yet he felt like he had hardly lived. It wasn't true of course, not when you heard of children with leukemia and babies born with life threatening spine curvature, but it felt true to him as he was sure it did for everybody who had been given such earth shattering news. He had tried being positive and it had gotten him so far, but it all just felt so real now, and it was hard to be an optimist when the days were growing shorter and shorter.

Feeling tired and a little disoriented he had risen to a kind of numb acceptance of his fate; he had loose ends that he needed to tie, and he went about his business efficiently enough, taking his mind off his problems by calling what relatives he had left, making small talk, letting them know he still thought of them from time to time but avoiding the subject of his own waning health. Although he knew it was likely to be a shock when he eventually did pass he wanted to avoid difficult conversations where he had to relay the message again and again. He knew this was the coward's way, leaving it to Rose to break the news after his death, but he didn't want to spend what little time he had left nursing others through their grief.

He sighed and sat down on the bed, Rose was out on the common, clearing her thoughts so he had the house to himself. He really didn't want to waste away his day but he just felt so tired. Before he knew it he had taken off his shoes and lain down. No sooner had he closed his eyes there was a noise from downstairs. He ignored it and rolled over onto his side.

His eyes wanted to close so he let them, the heaviness of his eyelids too much a force to resist. His head sunk into the pillow and his breathing became deeper and slower, succumbing to the intense sleepiness. But that damn noise was still coming from downstairs, was it the phone? Whoever it was they could literally buzz off. He pulled the pillow around his head and held it there. He had that lovely orange glow behind his eyelids that you only get in the day time and a sort of fuzziness in his head that wasn't at all unpleasant; maybe forty winks wouldn't be so bad after all.

It couldn't be the phone the dial tone was completely wrong.

Martin opened his eyes and pulled the pillow away from his ear. He lay quietly on the bed listening to the strange noise from downstairs. It was a succession of beeps and a deep underlying vibration that occurred every five of six seconds. What's more it wasn't stopping. What could it be? It was completely relentless. It wasn't loud enough to be the smoke or carbon monoxide alarms and he was sure it wasn't the timer on Rose's huge Rangemaster oven.

Slowly he sat up on the bed, feeling nervous but not knowing why. What was it? He had never heard it before of that much he was sure. Could it be Rose's fitness app from her Apple iPhone, gone off unexpectedly downstairs? He doubted it, she was never far from her phone, how would she possibly live with herself if she missed the latest gossip because she had been foolhardy enough to leave her mobile behind?

His curiosity rightly pricked Martin stood up from the bed, took a long puff of air from the oxygen tank and then slowly head onto the landing. The noise was louder out here, and he was pretty sure he could pinpoint its location; it was coming from the living room. He was halfway down the stairs when a thought struck him; he stopped for a second, his hand on the rail, his breath caught in his throat.

It couldn't be, could it?

Feeling all the more nervous following this unlikely revelation Martin crept slowly down the stairs. He made it down into the hallway and stopped outside the living room door. Still the buzzing and beeping persisted. Martin stood in front of the partially open door feeling almost too afraid to enter.

Yesterday when he had returned from the hospital he had taken his oxygen tank up to his room and lain on the bed, taking the occasional puff and thinking about all that had happened. But before he had done that he had done something else. In the living room he had taken his wallet and his keys and dropped them on the coffee table in the middle of the room, and he had dropped something else with them as well.

Swallowing back his trepidation and fear Martin stretched out his hand and pushed open the living room door. He stepped inside and looked towards the coffee table and sure enough there it was, the source of the noise. The three rising tones continued and the beeper slowly turned about on the polished surface of the coffee table as the vibrating mechanism continued to connect. He had discarded it along with his wallet, no longer optimistic of his chances of it alerting him before it was too late; now here he was, stood in his living room watching as the green light flickered and the beeper continued its dance along the surface of the table. He realised he was shaking as he stepped further into the room, leaned down and picked up the tiny device. There was an off switch on the side and he flicked it now, following the instructions he had been given by Purefoy all those months ago. Then with his whole body going into shock and worried tears in his eyes, he left the living room by the door to the rear and came out into the huge perfectly kept kitchen. He passed the island with the decorative pots and pans hanging from their hooks above and grabbed the phone from the nook. Purefoy's number was written on the chalk board in huge white letters, it had been circled several times and underlined in Rose's neat hand, always the optimist that it would be needed some day. Martin hadn't shared her enthusiasm, and couldn't believe he was punching in the numbers now. He was so nervous that on his first attempt he keyed the digits in wrong and got a recorded announcement saying the number had not been recognised. He calmed himself down and followed the robots advice to please try again. This time he was more successful and the phone was ringing in his ear.

It rang twice before he was greeted by a female voice:

"Hello St. Cuthbert's how can I help you?"

"Oh hello my beeper has just gone off; I'm on a waiting list for a new heart."

"Your name and date of birth please."

Martin gave the information and waited for the receptionist to find his details on her system.

"I'll put you through now." She said, then there was unscrupulously annoying hold music chiming in his ear, luckily it didn't last long before Purefoy was on the other end of the phone, sounding harried yet excited.

"Martin thank God!"

"What is it?" Martin asked, desperately trying to calm himself from getting his hopes up, feeling out of breath both from his condition and anticipation.

"Fantastic news, we've got you a heart!"

Martin could barely breathe, he had heard the words come pouring through the telephone earpiece but he didn't dare to believe them. All of the colour had drained from his skin and he suddenly felt nauseous and weak.

"Did you hear what I said?" Purefoy continued when Martin didn't respond. "I've said I found you a heart, we're in business!"

"I – I heard you." Martin muttered. "I just c-c-couldn't quite believe it."

"Believe it, things are looking up Martin, how quickly can you get here?"

"Rose is out but she should be back soon, we can head straight down then, maybe an hour, ninety minutes?"

"Perfect, get here as soon as you can, we have a small window of opportunity here but we're going to take it. See you soon."

The line closed and Martin was left staring into space with the receiver giving a monotonous tone in his ear. Eventually he placed it back in its cradle, he drew in breath for the first time in what felt like an age and turned on his heels. He tried to take a step but his legs had turned to jelly and he collapsed against the marble worktop of the island unit, breathing deeply, his eyes wide and watering.

Purefoy's words kept playing around and around in his head; they had found him a new heart, he may just yet be saved. He leant on the hard surface, waiting for his heart to calm down, the last thing he needed right now was to get overly excited, and thought to himself how his world had just turned on its axis once more, but this time bringing something new; hope.

PART TWO: UNDER THE KNIFE

1

When Martin and Rose pulled once more into the car park at St. Cuthbert's the sun had disappeared behind a thick wall of cloud. The sky had turned a murky grey and it looked like rain. Martin, who had never been superstitious in his life, took it as a bad omen. He looked up at the sky with worried eyes, feeling trepidation in the pit of his stomach.

"Come on." Rose said with a smile. "This is good news, stop looking so worried."

They left the car and crossed the grey car park to the hospital.

Rose had arrived home when Martin had still been catching his breath at the kitchen counter. At first she had feared the onset of another attack, but there was something in his eyes, something she hadn't seen in some time, something that at first she couldn't quite put her finger on. When she had realised that it was hope, her own heart had given an involuntary lurch. He had explained to her about hearing the buzzing and beeping from downstairs, about the phone call to Purefoy, about the news that finally, when all had looked so lost, a new heart had been found. This was the news they had been waiting for, and it felt surreal to be finally receiving it.

Her bag had slipped from her fingers, making a soft thlump noise on the tiled floor, then her face had crumpled like tissue and her bottom lip had trembled uncontrollably. The tears were streaking down her face without any shame or regret and she scampered towards him with her arms open wide. Martin met her half way across the kitchen, catching her before she went careering into the island on unsteady legs, and held her in his arms, the two of them shaking and crying in the otherwise quiet room. It was a tender moment, the type which truly only comes about every once in a while and both were lost in its magic.

Twenty minutes later they were in the car heading into London, another forty minutes after that and here they were, walking into the huge reception area and taking the door on the right to the outpatients department.

Purefoy was already in the waiting area when they arrived and he personally ushered them through to his office, a warm smile on his face which Martin found strangely alien. He closed the door behind them and offered them a seat. Martin knew he should feel happy, ecstatic even, he had quite literally been delivered a lifeline, but he couldn't shake the deep guttural feeling of foreboding.

"So," he said when everyone was comfortable, "we finally have some good news."

"I can't believe it, we can't believe it can we Martin." Rose enthused.

"I must admit I'm finding it all a little hard to believe." Martin answered honestly.

"Well believe it, I got the call around ten this morning, just like the lottery your number has literally come up, I guess it was just your time."

"I'd given up hope." Martin said, his voice breaking slightly with the emotion.

"You should never give up hope Martin, never. But this is a very fortunate situation, and timely too considering the circumstances, we should be very grateful for the turn of events that have brought us here."

"Oh we are!" Rose exclaimed.

"So what happens next?" Martin asked.

"The ETA for the heart is ten o'clock tonight, it's being flown in by chopper from Newcastle, we'll be prepped and ready for its arrival, ready for surgery at midnight at the latest."

"What so soon?" Martin asked, panic stretched across his face.

"Yes so soon, I'm sorry I thought you realised, with a major organ transplant there is no time to wait, we have to get on and perform the procedure as timely as possible to have the highest chance of success."

"Oh, ok." Martin looked down at the floor, his face ashen; he had thought himself scared before, now he was utterly terrified. It was obvious really, how could he have been so naïve? There really was no time to wait.

"Don't worry, you're in safe hands." Purefoy reassured.

Martin looked up at the surgeon from across the desk. "And what err, what are my chances, level with me doc."

Purefoy thought for a second, he considered lying to his patient, Martin could tell by the complex changes in his features, but decided in the end that honesty was the best policy.

"It's an invasive operation on one of the most vital organs in the body, I'm not going to lie to you and say there are no risks."

'Yeah but you considered it.' Martin thought but didn't say.

"The truth is there are always risks involved, but I am certain you will pull through this procedure and go on to live a normal, happy life."

"Oh my God I can't believe this, that is so wonderful to hear." Rose said with a huge beaming smile.

"What about afterwards, what is the long term prognosis?" Martin continued to question.

"Considering the nature of the operation the prognosis is very good, around eighty-eight per cent of people survive to their one year anniversary with seventy-five per cent surviving for three years. After that you'd be pretty much in the clear."

"Only seventy-five per cent." Rose said, the smile fading from her face.

"Mrs Rooley that's a fantastic success rate for a truly invasive procedure, especially if you were to consider the statistics for walking out on the street and getting hit by a bus."

"Of course." She replied quietly, though the smile had not returned.

"So what happens now?" Martin asked. "Do I stay here? Get checked in. Or can I go home and pack some things?"

"Actually I wanted to discuss something with you with regards to that." Purefoy said, leaning forward slightly in his chair, and there was something in his demeanour that frightened Martin, he didn't know what it was and was sure the circumstances were just making him a little jumpy, but he felt it all the same. "With this type of procedure it's imperative that the patient in this case you are comfortable in their surroundings; the more comfortable the patient, the higher the chance of success. With that in mind I would like to propose that the operation be conducted in the comfort of your own home."

Martin was literally speechless; he sat across from the surgeon with his mouth hanging agape, wondering if he had actually heard what he thought he had. It was Rose who broke the silence.

"You want the operation to take place in our home?" She said, her face shocked and puzzled, much like Martin's.

"That's correct." Purefoy continued slowly. Martin could tell he was choosing his words carefully and once again wondered why this would be. "Hospital's can be pretty daunting places, after all when you visit a hospital it's usually because there's something wrong. The comfort of your own home is a safe haven, a place where you feel at your most relaxed. When considering an operation of this nature its important to take every detail into account, one of those details is the comfort of the patient; after all it is the heart we are talking about here, the organ most affected by the comfort or in fact discomfort of the patient. We need to ensure that your heart is as stable and healthy as can be before we perform the procedure, this means keeping you as comfortable as is possible under such difficult circumstances."

Martin considered this for a few moments, allowing the surgeons words to fully register before giving a response. When he was certain he had understood what had been said he continued.

"I appreciate that how the patient feels is of importance to the success of the procedure, so let me assure you that I would be at my most comfortable in the hospital."

"If you're worried about your house there really is no need, we would take great care to ensure the area was sterilised before the procedure and in pristine condition afterwards." Purefoy said, exasperation clear in his voice, he was not used to being challenged.

"All the same I'd feel more comfortable in the hospital, thank you for your concern."

Purefoy collapsed back into his seat, a look of hopelessness on his face that Martin found quite odd, after all why did the surgeon care where the operation took place? He thought for a couple of seconds, chewing his bottom lip, then he turned to Rose, an unexpected move.

"Mrs Rooley, somebody has to be the voice of reason here, your husband is clearly emotional which is understandable..."

"I'm not emotional!" Martin countered angrily.

"But somebody has to take a vested interest in the patient's wellbeing and as his next of kin that baton is handed to you." Purefoy continued as though Martin had not spoken. "Please would you talk to your husband?"

Rose squirmed uncomfortably in her seat. "If Martin would prefer the hospital maybe..."

"My wife doesn't need to answer on behalf of me I'm more than capable of answering for myself." Martin cut in.

Again Purefoy ignored the businessman and focused his attention on his wife instead.

"Rose," He said looking deep into her eyes. "The success of this procedure is vested in it taking place outside the hospital." He fixed her with a firm stare and something passed between them, Martin wasn't sure what it was, but suddenly his wife's entire demeanour changed.

Suddenly she turned and faced her husband, her eyes alive with understanding; it filled Martin with a curious dread.

"Martin I think he's right, I think we need to have the procedure at home."

"What is this?" Martin said, a look of puzzled concern on his face. "You two are in cahoots, why?"

"Oh will you stop it." She said with a rueful shake of the head. "You sound like a damn conspiracy theorist. Mister Purefoy wants what's best for you that's all." She smiled and suddenly she was Rose again, his wife of all these years, and Martin felt foolish for the creeping doubt that had been wrenching at his gut.

"I'm sorry." He said a little red faced. "I guess I'm just a little spooked is all."

"You're bound to be." She said, taking hold of his hand. "But all we want is what's best for you; I know you're scared, but that fear is clouding your judgment. If a surgeon at one of the best hospitals in London is telling you it would be better for you to be at home why are you doubting it?"

"I don't know." He said a little sheepishly. "It just seems a little strange that's all."

"I assure you its quite normal." Purefoy interjected.

"You don't have enough experience of this type of thing to possibly say what is and isn't right Martin, so trust Mister Purefoy, please."

Martin sighed and nodded his head reluctantly. "Ok, I'll trust you, I trust you both. If you say it's better for my wellbeing to be at home for the operation then I'll take your word for it. God knows it's hardly the important thing anyway, I've got a new heart, that should be the focus here."

"Amen." Rose said with a reassuring smile.

Martin sighed and turned back to the surgeon. "So, where do we go from here?"

"Well you're free to leave, but I'd ask you to stay home, no going out. The small team I'll be bringing to perform the operation will be with you by seven. I'll arrive with them, we'll prep. The heart will arrive around ten and like I say we should be good to go around twelve. Is there a bedroom, somewhere quite spacious?"

"We could use the gym." Rose replied quickly.

"Would this involve moving heavy equipment?" Purefoy asked.

"No, mostly just my yoga mats and a few lightweight pieces, nothing much really, I could move it all quite comfortably while Martin rests."

"That sounds perfect." Purefoy agreed.

"I guess that's that then." Martin said. "D-day."

"Someone will call you later this afternoon to finalise a few arrangements, but otherwise I think we're ready. Relax, this time tomorrow you'll be at the start of your recovery, with a whole new life ahead of you."

"New life." Martin muttered. "I thought I was already dead."

2

At a quarter after ten that night Martin sat looking out of his bedroom window at the car that had pulled into his driveway. He had expected the heart which he had been reassured had been flown in by helicopter to be delivered by ambulance, blue lights flashing, but it was a simple Vauxhall Zafira that made the delivery. Purefoy took receipt of it himself, nodding to the driver as he made his way back out of the private estate.

Purefoy carried the white case, about the size of a home filing kit back towards the house and disappeared from view, though Martin could hear him pottering about downstairs.

He had come to the bedroom to dress in his procedure gown, a blue thin piece of cotton that attached at the back with threads. Later, during the operation this would be removed, and only his underwear would remain.

They had arrived as promised a little after seven and started setting up the gym that had been emptied of contents earlier by Rose, for the operation. The room had been sterilised and blue plastic drapes attached to the walls and the floor so that no semblance to the room where Rose performed her exercises for the elder lady remained. It had taken them a good hour to fill the room with all the equipment necessary for the operation, including specialist lighting and a portable theatre bed, and another hour to prep their stations.

Martin had been surprised to discover only a handful of people would be present at the operation; the surgeon and two colleagues who he had yet to meet, a man and a lady. It didn't seem enough, but again he had to trust the surgeon's judgment. He looked at the clock on the bedside table now; ten-thirty, it wouldn't be long now.

He had to admit as he looked at himself in the huge wall length mirror, taking in the pale reflection that stared back at him, he was absolutely petrified. He was under no illusion as to the seriousness of the situation, and new heart or not this truly invasive procedure which he now faced was fraught with risks, and he may not live to see another day. His stomach fluttered with butterflies and his heart, that cause of so much anxiety these last six months beat rhythmically in his chest, causing the pulse in his temple to throb in time.

"Penny for them." The soft voice spoke at the door.

Martin didn't need to turn to know its source, that same soft voice had whispered words of love to him for decades, but he turned all the same, and smiled at her to show he was alright.

Rose stood at the bedroom door, her hands clasped before her, she too was all too pale and he knew instinctively that she was wracked with nerves.

"Come here." He said quietly, and she obeyed. They met on the soft carpet next to the bed and embraced, offering one another the comfort they so desperately craved. After a few moments Rose pulled apart from her husband and looked up into his tired face.

"How are you?"

"Oh, ok I guess." Martin looked down at his slippered feet, scrunching his toes inside their soft lining.

"You don't have to lie to me." She replied, as always he couldn't hide anything from his Rose.

"I'm scared, I won't deny it, I'm scared."

"So am I, but I keep telling myself how necessary this is, this heart is a good thing, it's a chance at a new future, without it there wouldn't be a future."

"Oh I know that." Martin spoke softly." "I'm just scared I won't be able to...won't be able to..."

"What is it darling?"

"I'm scared I won't see you again." Martin had to fight back the tears.

"Listen to me." Rose said, gesturing for Martin to sit on the bed, he did and she sat down beside him. "You're going to pull through this, the statistics are very much on your side, and when you do, when you wake to a bright new future, I'll be waiting right here for you, I'll be the first thing you see when you open your eyes."

"You promise?"

"I wouldn't have it any other way."

Martin smiled and placed his head on his wife's chest. He could feel the soft rhythm of her breathing and it comforted him. He must have been tired, awful tired from all the anxiety and fear, for he fell into a silent slumber, sat upright on the bed. The next thing he was aware of was his wife gently squeezing his hand, bringing him back into the here and now.

A little foggy and unsure he raised his head from her chest and noticed that the door was open; the surgeon, Purefoy was standing in the doorway, when he saw that his patient was awake he turned and head back in the direction of the gym.

"It's time." Rose said softly.

"What, already?" Martin replied, not realising the passage of time while he dozed on the bed, but when he looked at the bedside clock he saw that it was indeed time, a little after half past midnight in fact.

Martin drew in a deep breath and then stood from the bed, feeling a little light headed he grabbed for the oxygen tank, took a puff of air and waited for the wooziness to subside. Rose waited patiently for him to set his nerve, when she was sure that he had she took him by the hand and led him out of the bedroom and down the hall to the makeshift theatre.

Inside the room the medical staff waited for his arrival, dressed in their full procedure gowns and hats, their hands covered with surgical gloves. Rose paused at the door and turned to her husband.

"I can't be in the room with you, but I'll be right downstairs, I won't be sleeping til I know you're alright, and you are going to be alright."

Martin nodded solemnly. Rose leaned up and kissed him firmly on the lips.

"I'll see you soon my darling." She whispered.

"Goodbye Rose." He whispered back, hoping that his words were not an omen.

She stepped away with notable reluctance and crept down the hall, never taking her eyes from her husband, when she was finally out of sight Martin could hear her softly padding down the stairs and he desperately wished she would come back. Slowly, and with a deep feeling of foreboding he calmed his nerve and stepped into the room.

Purefoy was quick to greet him. "Hello Martin, please don't look so worried, you're in safe hands."

Martin took a look about the room; he really didn't recognise it to how it had been just that afternoon. The operating table was in the centre of the room, a soft white sheet pulled back ready for him, the portable lighting to the right and overhead. There were drapes covering the window and walls and also the floor, not a patch of magnolia could be seen. A work station to the left of the bed housed swabs, scalpels, bottles of antiseptic and various other tools that Martin had seen on those American hospital dramas Rose was always watching. A defibrillator that he regarded with some concern had been pushed into the right hand corner, ready for emergency use; Martin hoped it would remain in the corner for the rest of the night. Finally there it was, sat in its open case, the machinery keeping it pumping, the object of his salvation; his new heart. He stared at it with wonder, trying to figure out how something so small and fragile could hold the key to his very survival, then decided this was not a worthy train of thought to pursue, the last thing he needed right now was to dwell on the fragility of his situation. He turned back to the surgeon instead and smiled as warmly as the circumstances would allow.

"Let me introduce you to the team that will be supporting me tonight." Purefoy said. He gestured to the stocky man to his side, a slightly Mediterranean look to his features. "This is Ricardo Panettiere, he's your anaesthetist, supporting me with the operation we have Nurse Lucille Lily."

Martin nodded at the young woman who nodded back kindly, again he tried to block from his mind the operating theatres he had seen in those aforementioned dramas, where the room had been filled with people checking monitors and assisting the Chief Surgeon, he had to keep reminding himself that this was the reality, that was television, everything was over hyped on television, and really, what did he expect with all the cut backs these days.

The Mediterranean anaesthetist stepped forward and when he spoke Martin was surprised to hear a thick cockney accent.

"If you could step over here Mister Rooley I'll get you prepped."

Martin followed him to the side of the bed where the anaesthetist unfastened the tassels at the back of Martins gown and gestured for him to climb onto the operating table. There was a foot stool to the side which Martin used to gain height and when he lay down on the mattress the anaesthetist pulled his gown down to his waist and tucked the bed sheet into the waistband of his underpants. Martin felt exposed with the young girl in the room but tried to quell his feelings for the sake of the procedure.

"I'm going to put a needle into the vein in your hand, this is for the anaesthetic, you'll feel a slight prick as it goes in but it will only last a second."

"Ok." Martin said agreeably. He watched as the anaesthetist wheeled over a labelled bag of general anaesthetic and a tray of sterilised equipment. He quickly found the vein in Martin's hand and inserted the needle, as he had been warned it stung for a second then quickly faded. Ricardo taped the needle flat to Martin's hand and inserted the tube that led to the anaesthetic.

The businessman could feel his heart pumping away and wished he had his oxygen mask close to hand.

Purefoy stepped forward to address him.

"In a moment Mister Panettiere is going to apply the general anaesthetic, you'll be in a deep sleep within moments and won't feel a thing before you wake following the operation. Try to relax now, the hard part, the waiting is done. When you wake you're going to be a new man."

Martin nodded, trying his best to be brave though he could feel tears starting to prick at the corners of his eyes. He felt embarrassed, reduced at this moment to a small boy that has scraped his knee and desperately wants to be shown love.

The nurse, recognising the signs, stepped forward and took Martin's hand in hers, smiling warmly. Martin was grateful.

Purefoy placed his mask over his mouth and nose and started prepping his tools.

"Ok." Ricardo said, stepping forward once more and releasing a switch to the side of the bag. "I'm going to ask you to count backwards slowly from ten, can you do that for me."

But Martin wasn't listening, suddenly he was filled with a deep and foreboding panic, something was wrong here, this was wrong, he shouldn't be here he should be in hospital. The tears spilled from the corners of his eyes and coursed down the sides of his cheeks.

"Please." He said, looking up pleadingly into the face of the young nurse, Lucille she had been called. "Please I don't want to die."

She smiled down at him but didn't say a word and that was when Martin was sure, this was a plot, he had been fooled into this, they were going to kill him, probably after his money, and he had fallen for it, it was too late.

"Please, no pleeeaaaa....." His eyelids slid closed as the anaesthetic took effect.

"Is he under?" Purefoy asked, stepping forward with an antiseptic coated swab.

"He's asleep." Panettiere confirmed.

"Ok." Purefoy said. "Let's begin."

3

The darkness felt thick and comforting, like a warm blanket on a cool night; he drifted into it and was soothed by its colossal vastness. If you slipped into a lake of warm honey, the sensation would be similar to this. The man was mildly aware of a near and present danger, but for now he had neither the inclination nor desire to dwell on it, preferring instead to bathe in the honey, his head resting on its sticky warmth, his nostrils filled with its sweet aroma.

He didn't breathe, for there was no need for oxygen here, his body being naturally nourished by the opulence of its surroundings. He floated in the ether, his fingers tingling and his toes occasionally twitching as he slipped deeper and deeper into the abyss. There was a deep peacefulness that seeped into his pores and sucked at his conscious mind, drawing him into the security of the netherworld.

As he lay there in the darkness, the waves of warmth lapping over his still, motionless body, he became aware of a noise. It was a quiet sound, little more than the background twittering of his subconscious, but it was there all the same. It was a high pitched screeching, not unlike the sound of an electric drill or carving knife, but to Martin it was the sound of a small bird, chirping somewhere in the darkness. He sat up from the warmth of the ether, looking into the darkness, trying to determine the source of the sound.

There was a light in the distance, small but bright, and Martin floated towards it now, his feet not moving but his body being propelled forward on an invisible tide. At first the light was little more than a dot in the distance, but it grew and grew, becoming a circle of light the size of a plate, then growing to be greater than the darkness, until finally he was within the light with the darkness disappearing behind him.

Martin closed his eyes, for the light was at its brightest now, but slowly that too began to fade until he was stood comfortably within its core. His eyes blinked open and he took a look around. He was stood with his feet hovering a couple of inches off the floor in a room of brilliant white. Everything in here had been painted the same contrast less colour; the walls were a brilliant white, the ceiling and the floor, there was a brilliant white table with a brilliant white vase which held brilliant white flowers and the stems that stretched up to the petals were a brilliant white too. Martin felt in awe of the unquestionable blandness that surrounded him.

'Am I dead?' He thought. 'Is this what death is like?'

Suddenly, in contrast to its bleak surroundings, the bird whose song had mimicked some kind of sawing implement appeared in the far corner. It was a beautiful blue, the colour of a tropical spring and its feathers were plumed to perfection. There was a tiny red Mohawk atop of its head and a small yellow ring around its beak, but it was the dizzying blue that really caught the eye. Martin took a step further into the room, though his feet still drifted inches above the clear white floor. He looked up at the bird with real fascination, having never seen anything quite as beautiful in his life.

The bird seemed to notice him for the first time, fixing its eyes upon him; it blinked a couple of times then craned to look around the room.

'Hey there little bird.' Martin felt he had spoken aloud but his mouth never opened, the words were coming from direct inside his head.

The bird flicked its head from left to right, looking beyond Martin to the darkness that was in the distance behind him, then it looked back to Martin.

The businessman drifted closer still, wanting to be as close as he could in this sterile room to the object of beauty before him.

'Hey birdy, hey hey hey.' His whispered thoughts drifted across the stark white space.

Then something completely unexpected occurred, the bird took a look at him, blinked a couple more times, then in a voice he recognised but couldn't quite place said:

"Forceps, scalpel."

Martin drifted back a couple of steps, his eyes wide. Had the bird just spoken to him? Certainly its beak had opened and words had been heard, but a bird speaking? Surely not. But then, did it actually seem that strange? Really? For some reason Martin didn't think so, right here, in these surroundings it seemed like the most natural thing in the world. He allowed his nerves to settle and drifted back into the centre of the room.

The bird continued to regard him with only mild curiosity; it still perched up in the very top corner of the room, its tiny talons indented slightly in the brilliant white wall. Martin held out his hand, hoping the beautiful bird with the startling ability would leave its perch high up on the wall and fly down to him, but it just continued to stare.

Wanting to hear more from the bird Martin drifted up so he was directly beneath it, but when he stretched up his hand the bird flapped its wings and flew across the room to the adjacent corner. Frustrated Martin swivelled around; maybe it was a mocking bird? It was certainly mocking him now.

He was about to drift back closer to the bird when the room was suddenly ripped apart, it shattered around him in shards of brilliant white and he was thrust back into the darkness once more, only this time the darkness wasn't comforting, there was an aura about it, an angry red aura that was foreboding and pulsed within his subconscious. Trying not to panic Martin looked about himself, trying to find his way back to the room and the beautiful blue bird, but the room was gone, and the bird was no more. The red tinged darkness drank him in like golden liquor, surrounding him and creeping into his senses, making him terrified, his body shaking from the fear that ground into him.

'HELP ME!' He screamed inside his petrified mind.

The reply that came from the swirling red mist only served to further compound his fear.

"WE'RE LOSING HIM! THE DEFIBRILLATOR, QUICK!"

Martin's whole body shook with the tension, this darkness was threatening to consume him, he could already feel his mind slipping and his will waning at its constant pull. Was it possible for something to be darker than black? Before this he would have argued not, but now, being lost inside this amorphous black hole, only the red aura to provide any kind of contrast to the all encompassing darkness, he would most certainly argue the affirmative.

"COUNT IT! ONE, TWO, CHARGE!" The voice lost inside the ether demanded. "AGAIN, ONE, TWO, CHARGE!"

Every time the voice screamed 'charge' the darkness was filled with a brilliant white light, but it faded along with the voice.

"ANOTHER, ONE, TWO, CHARGE!"

Martin was blinded again by the amazing burst of light, this time it lingered a little longer and he stretched out his fingers, hoping desperately to grasp it in his hand, to pull it close, to drag himself back into its comfort, but it was just out of his reach.

The darkness took control again and this time Martin noticed something that made his fear grow like a tumour in his mind; the red mist was swirling around his feet. Martin swallowed hard, he knew that he was its desire; it wanted to consume him whole, to pull him into its vile red jaws where he would be lost in the darkness for eternity.

'No, no please, no, I want to live.' He mumbled in the terrified confines of his mind.

The light flickered again and Martin felt it flash before his eyes.

"ARE YOU GOING TO CALL IT?" The voice from inside the ether asked.

'Call what?' Martin thought, watching with terror as the red mist started to creep its way up his legs.

"NO DAMN YOU NO!" The voice continued, the ether glowing with the words.

'No, no please, let me live!' The voice within Martin pleaded, and again the light flashed within the darkness, making him shield his eyes from its glare. It faded again and though the ether had abated with the arrival of the light it continued its ascent up his legs now, but not before Martin became aware of something; the light had come when he had expressed his desire to survive, was this related? He wasn't going to take any chances.

'Let me live, I want to live.' He spoke again, and once again the brilliant light lit up the all encompassing darkness, it started to fade again but now Martin was sure, it was as though he had to convince the light that he belonged to it, not this vast black void.

"I want to live, you hear me, I want to live!" Martin opened his mouth and spoke the words and this time as the light flashed once more the red mist fully recoiled, drifting backwards into the darkness away from his floating body.

"I want to live, I want to see my wife, I want to hold her hand, I want to eat steak and ride motorbikes and look at the ocean, you hear me? I WANT TO LIVE!"

Suddenly his limp body was propelled forwards into the light, leaving the darkness behind him once more. He covered his eyes from the glare and allowed himself to be sucked into its brilliant acceptance.

Again the light started to fade; as it did he lowered his hand and found himself back in the room, the sterile (waiting?) room with the bland furnishings. He looked around for the bird but the bird had gone. He felt the comfort of the room as it drifted like blood through his veins. Then a soft voice spoke from behind him:

'Martin.'

The businessman turned slowly, fearful that red ether had returned to claim him, knowing that it would not fail this time. But it was not the ether, it was Rose. Rose as she had been all those years ago at the ice rink back in Bolton; the Rose with the mischievous eyes and the wavy auburn hair, the Rose who had reduced him to a quivering mess and caused his heart to flutter like butterflies on a soft breeze.

'Rose.' He said through the silence of the room, his lips never parting.

'It's time to come home dear one.' The Rose from long ago whispered in his mind.

Martin continued to stare, drinking her in with his eyes, remembering the look of her, the smell of her, the feelings that had flickered like pages from a book whenever she was around.

'Is it really you Rose?'

'It's time Martin.' She replied, her eyes fixed upon his. 'It's time to come home.'

'I want to come home.' Martin replied, almost pleadingly.

'Come home Martin.'

He drifted forwards and she held out her hand.

'Rose.'

He lifted his hand and their fingers met in the middle, a soft tingle running the length of his arm.

'Come home Martin, it's time.'

Their hands clasped and he allowed himself to be drawn to her, wanting to be drawn to her, needing to be drawn to her.

'Martin.'

He felt a flush as the room brightened once more.

'Martin.'

He was drawn into the brilliance of his surroundings and suddenly he was aware of nothing but the voice, the voice that drifted just out of reach.

'Martin.'

4

"Martin."

The voice spoke again and the businessman blinked his eyes a couple of times, but the light was too bright despite the curtains being drawn and he quickly closed them again, trying to protect his vision from the unexpected glare.

"Martin, wake up dear." The voice spoke again.

Feeling tired and weak Martin was reluctant to comply with the request, but the owner was not in the mood to let him rest and persisted with their infernal badgering.

"Martin, it's time to wake up now, wake up dear."

Slowly he blinked his eyes open again, managing to focus a little more on the room now; he focused for three seconds then drifted back, opened again for five seconds and drifted back, then was able to open his eyes for eleven seconds without the deep exhaustion dragging him back into its peaceful slumber.

"He's starting to come round." A new deeper voice spoke. "Nurse you can complete proceedings."

"Yes Mister Purefoy." Spoke a third voice.

Martin blinked again and then slowly opened his eyes, properly this time, his vision which had been blurry and devoid of colour coming into focus so he could see the woman who was sat at his side, smiling down at him. It was Rose, not as she had been all those years ago but as she was now, wrinkles around her eyes, hair grey and curled on top, the sensual curves of long ago lost under a baggy sweater, but equally as beautiful to the beholders eye.

A small gasp of air escaped his pursed lips as he looked up into her face, there were tears in her eyes but her smile was warm and inviting.

"Martin, you're here." She said, clutching his hand in hers and lifting it gently to her bosom.

"Where am I?" He asked, his voice a croak, his mouth and throat as dry as sand paper left discarded on the plains of a desert.

"Do you not remember?"

Martin tried to shake his head but his muscles were too tired.

"No." He said instead, a horrible coppery taste in his mouth. His eyes drifted closed again as his wife spoke but he squeezed onto her hand to show that he was still listening.

"You've had an operation, a serious operation, but it was a success, you're going to be ok."

"Operation." He repeated, trying to figure out what had happened in his muddled brain.

"That's right." Rose continued. "You had a heart transplant. Do you remember? It was a success; you're going to be ok."

"Success." He whispered, not really understanding the words but slowly starting to come around from the deep void of the anaesthetic. He opened his eyes again and looked around the room; he could see a woman in a surgical gown hastily packing up equipment and a man taking down drapes. Beneath were walls that he recognised, for they were his own, they were the walls of the makeshift gymnasium in his house.

"Thirsty." He said, his voice still hoarse.

"Can he have a drink?" Rose asked the lady that was packing away the equipment.

"A little water, but take it slow, small sips." The woman replied.

"Let me get you a glass of water." His wife said and rose from the bed. "It's so good to have you back Martin."

He tried to smile at her but even this seemed too much effort. There was a pain in his chest, a sore feeling and he looked down to where a deep pack covered the left hand side of his bare chest. He stretched out his fingers and touched it gently. But there was something else as well, despite the soreness in his chest and the vague befuddled feeling in his head, he actually felt better. He could breathe deeper and his heart actually felt stronger.

It was starting to slip into place now; the operation, he had been waiting for a new heart and it had come, right at the last second, the man taking down the drapes was the anaesthetist with the unusual name, the lady packing the crates a nurse. The surgeon who had treated him, who had saved his life by all accounts was called David something, David what? Prudence? Partridge? He knew it started with a P. Purefoy, that was it, David Purfoy!

"A success." He said out loud, liking the way it sounded. He had been so afraid, but the operation had been a success! He had a new heart and hope for the future, when all had been lost he had been pulled back again, back from the brink.

"Oh thank you thank you thank you." He whispered as a single tear trickled down from the corner of his eye.

Rose returned with the water, stepping to one side to allow the nurse to walk past with one of the crates. She stepped up to the bed and hunkered down next to her husband.

"It worked Rose, it worked." He said, his bottom lip trembled as he failed to contain his emotions.

"Try not to talk; I don't want you exhausting yourself." Rose replied. "Here, take a sip of this." She had placed a straw in the glass and she touched it to his lips. He opened his mouth and drank greedily, coughing as the cold liquid filled his mouth and slipped down his parched throat.

"Woah, slow down, you'll get me in trouble." She scolded jovially.

"Ah, thank you." He said, lifting his tired arm and mopping at his mouth with the back of his hand.

The anaesthetist had removed all the drapes now and the room looked almost normal again, sunlight was pouring through the gap in the curtains, it was morning.

"How long was I out?" He asked.

"A little over six hours, there were a few complications, but Mister Purefoy is a wonderful man, he's performed a miracle here tonight Martin."

"You must be exhausted."

"Oh like I could sleep, and anyway it was nothing compared to how exhausted you must feel."

As the nurse wheeled the defibrillator out onto the landing the surgeon stepped back into the room.

"Good morning Martin, good to have you back with us, how do you feel?"

"A little drowsy, a little sore."

"That's natural enough under the circumstances, I'm going to prescribe you something for the pain and there's a few medicines that you're going to have to take for a while but with a couple of weeks good bed rest there's no reason you shouldn't be back on your feet soon. Rose," He said turning to Martin's wife, "I'm going to need you both to look for signs of rejection, the new heart is to all effects a foreign body, shortness of breath, prolonged fatigue, fever, weight gain, inability to urinate, you call me ok?"

"I understand." Rose replied.

"We're going to move you to your bedroom now where you can get some much needed rest Martin, follow my advice and you'll be back on that golf course before you know it."

"Mister Purefoy, thank you." Martin said, his eyes leaking again. "Thank you for everything."

"It's my job." Came the reply. "But you're welcome. Ricardo, help me wheel Mister Rooley through to his room."

The anaesthetist nodded and together they wheeled the operating table out onto the landing and down the narrow stretch of hall to the master bedroom. Once there they carefully manoeuvred Martin onto the bed and the nurse straightened out the covers. The businessman lay panting on the bed, shocked at how such a small thing could cause such devastation to his body. The surgeon noticed the look.

"You've just had major surgery Martin, be patient, give it a couple of weeks and I think you'll be surprised at just how different you feel."

"Of course." Martin said, nodding his head slowly, feeling reassured.

The medical team left the room and carried on with their duties, packing up their equipment and turning the operating theatre back into a crude home gymnasium again. Rose stood in the door, a little puffy around the eyes, looking at her husband with real fondness.

"I can't believe we're actually here." She said gently.

Martin lay in the bed looking at his wife, something troubled him, something his wife had said coupled with a dream that was recurring to him now, a dream from when he was under the spell of the anaesthetic.

"Rose, you said there had been a few complications." He let the question hang.

"That's nothing for you to worry about now." She said, casting her eyes away from his.

"All the same, I'd like to know, what happened?"

Rose stepped into the room and sat down beside him on the bed; she stretched out her hand and cupped his right cheek gently in her palm.

"There was a horrible moment where it all almost went wrong, but it didn't happen, you're here and you're fine, that's all that matters."

"The red mist." He whispered, feeling the small hairs on the back of his neck stand to attention.

"What?" Rose asked, confused.

"Nothing." Martin replied quickly. "Just a bad dream. Rose, did I nearly die?"

She was silent for a while, wondering whether to burden him with such things so soon after surgery. In the end she relented.

"Yes, you nearly died. They had to use the thingy-me-bob, with the paddles."

"The defibrillator?"

"Yes that's it, the defibrillator."

"My God." Martin whispered in awe.

"Like I say that isn't the important thing, the important thing is that you pulled through, you must have really wanted to live."

"I did." Martin replied, thinking again of the dream. "I did want to live."

"Good." Rose said and leant forward to kiss him on his all too pale forehead. "Because I don't know what I'd do without you."

They were silent for a while, happy in each others company as the small medical team wandered up and down the stairs, packing crates of equipment in the back of their cars. It wasn't long before exhaustion overcame Martin and he drifted into a silent slumber. Rose listened for a while to the hypnotic rhythm of his breathing, feeling her own eyelids growing heavy. She slipped off her shoes and lay down next to him on the bed; she was just drifting off herself when a voice at the bedroom door roused her.

"Rose." It was the surgeon, David Purefoy.

Rose stood from the bed and met him at the bedroom door.

"Is he sleeping?" The surgeon asked.

"He's asleep." She replied.

"You're sure?"

"He's asleep." She repeated.

"Ok." Purefoy replied, breathing a small sigh of relief. "Well we're all just about done here, we'll be heading off in just a moment, I think we can count last night a huge success don't you?"

"We can, thank you Mister Purefoy."

"I'll be in touch, I'll want to see the patient every few days to see how he's progressing, this will be here, not the hospital. Remember what I said, any signs of rejection and you call me immediately ok?"

"I understand."

"The personal number I gave you, that's the number you call, under no circumstances do you contact St. Cuthbert's or any other hospital, do you understand?"

"I do." She said gravely.

"Good, I don't think I need to explain again to you what we've done here this evening."

Rose swallowed back her trepidation.

"I know the implications."

"Good." He replied. "I'll be getting along then, I'll see you soon."

"I'll see you out." Rose said, and watched as the tall man made his way down the stairs.

Rose turned and pulled the bedroom door closed behind her, catching a glimpse of her sleeping husband as she did so. He was worth it; she thought as she made her way down the stairs, her husband was worth it, whatever the cost.

5

It was two weeks after the operation and the pompous surgeon had been good to his word; Martin did feel like a new man, though it had taken the full two weeks to reach this stage. When he had woken from that first morning snooze following the operation he had felt as though he had been hit by a dumper truck, and then maybe reversed back over for good measure. Literally everything hurt; the pain in his chest was immeasurable, his arms and legs felt as though lead weights had been surgically implanted within them as he slept and his head throbbed with a deep, pulsing migraine, the like of which he had never suffered before.

In a panic he had called out for Rose, terrified that the heart was rejecting and he was going to die in his bed, only hours after his very salvation. Despite his protestations to contact Purefoy immediately his wife had remained perfectly calm, the surgeon had described in detail what to expect and although it was hard to see the man she loved in so much pain she knew it not to be unusual. Ignoring his pleas for medical help she had instead fed him two of the pills he had been prescribed and within a few minutes the pain started to ease, as did his fear. He slipped again into a deep sleep and woke some time around twilight, the evening bird chorus in full flow outside the bedroom window. Although still in discomfort the pain was not as agonising as before and this time he was able to deal with the situation.

The days went by as the days always did; some days were good and some days were bad. Some days Martin would wake and feel as fresh as a daisy, so full of life and energy and he would feel that this was the start of his new beginning, only to crash and burn again the next day, his stitches sore, his muscles aching, his mind muddled and confused. In this time Purefoy visited twice, once in the first week and again in the second. During his visits he would check Martin's blood pressure and pulse, ask him questions about his experiences so far and take a look at how the scarring on his chest, the stitches of which were dissolvable was healing.

Martin would describe the pains in his chest and the aches in his back and legs, the general fatigue that he felt most days and the surgeon would nod his head patiently before reassuring him that everything looked to be in good order. The pains were a natural part of the recovery process and the aching and tiredness were to be expected, he was after all well into his sixties now, not some twenty-one year old kid with fire in his belly and enough spunk to sink the Bismarck.

The surgeons visits would be a comfort to Martin, who often wondered if he had made the right choice in having had such an invasive procedure, in his pain and discomfort looking at his time breathing through an oxygen mask and counting down his final days through rose tinted glasses.

At the end of the first week he had left the house for the first time, it was mid July now and after a spell of bad thunder storms – apparently there had been flooding again in the West Country – the days once again were muggy and warm. Dissatisfied now with the breeze flicking softly across his face from the open window in the living room, and feeling more and more like some aging hermit, locked away like a prisoner in his own home, Martin decided to take a walk. It was too soon, the businessman made it across the courtyard and up to the small pedestrian gate that stood next to the huge electrified security gate and doubled up in agony. He was gutted to find himself racked with pains in his chest and lightheaded once more. Utterly exhausted he made his way slowly back to the house where he crashed down on the sofa, fell into a deep slumber and didn't wake until Rose returned from her bridge game four hours later.

This setback had been the catalyst for Martin's negative thoughts about his operation, it was lucky for him that he had pragmatic and realistic people in his life, the surgeon for one and his loving wife Rose to steer his thoughts back onto a positive path.

A happier day came at the start of the second week, when he received an unexpected visit from Peter Werth-Duncan, the man Martin had left in charge of Sapient during his spell of incarceration. It was good to see his friend, and Peter despite Martin's protests had been delighted in the progress he was seeing in his employer and friend. He had brought with him a huge bunch of chrysanthemums, stating he had had no idea what to bring as a gift for a man who had just undergone major heart surgery. Martin had laughed and joked anything but a huge bunch of flowers. Peter stayed a while, answering Martin's questions about the state of the company and how everybody was back at the office, talking about the latest signings for their prospective football teams; Chelsea and Bolton Wanderer's and chatting about the latest news stories, the on-going crisis' in Syria and Ukraine, the politician that had been caught literally with his trousers down in the House of Commons, the state of the pound against the yen, the euro and the dollar.

When the thin man left a couple of hours after his arrival Martin had been renewed with positivity, and he was sure he had this to thank for the optimistic nature that made his second week of recovery far more successful.

On the Wednesday of this week Martin had attempted to walk out once more, with Rose this time, and had made it as far as half way across the common before the tiredness took hold, he saw this as a huge improvement and was thrilled with the progress he had started to make. After a week of mostly liquid food; soups, blended dinners, risotto's, Martin was now starting to take on solids again, and this too helped to improve his mood and his outlook.

Now here he was, sat in his favourite chair in the living room, looking out at the courtyard and the sun that shone upon it and feeling for the first time like a new and changed man. He sucked in a huge lungful of fresh morning air that had drifted through the open window, felt a slight twinge from the area of his scar, but otherwise delighted at the capacity of his lungs. Now he could really focus on his time with the oxygen mask, gasping for air and feeling frightened of what was becoming of him. He really was a new man, the operation had been a success and he once more had the excitement and anticipation of a life left to live.

Rose, who had only left the house at times when Martin had absolutely insisted upon it, was out now at her dance class, and Martin was enjoying the peace about the house. The improvements that had been made over the last week were nothing short of remarkable and it was true that he felt twenty years younger than his actual sixty-eight.

He felt stronger, fitter, more determined, full of vigour and life, and all this in just two weeks, imagine how he could potentially feel in a month. Outside a bird was chirping away in the garden, in his life before the operation he would have dismissed the sound as just more background noise, but now he enjoyed the restless reminder of life. Little things that he would take for granted he now regarded with a reverie previously reserved for only truly remarkable occurrences; a sunset over the Bahamas, a trip to Silverstone for his birthday, his wedding day with Rose. Now the same elation could be found in the sun rising over his back lawn, the taste of strawberry jam on uncut bread, the sound of a lawnmower buzzing away in the distance. This new found zest for life would undoubtedly not last forever, but for the time being as he was lost within its beauty, he would treasure every experience.

Right now he was savouring the comfort of his favourite chair, he didn't think he had ever experienced comfort like it, or maybe he had and he had just taken it for granted. When Rose came home he was going to take her for a walk on the common if she was up for it, maybe even make a full circuit this time? Then dare he think it, would there be enough energy left for anything else? It had certainly been a long time, Rose would have the shock of her life when he suggested it, this was another area in which he felt different, and he couldn't wait to try out his new found libido. With a smile on his face Martin stood from the comfiest chair in the world and head to the kitchen, where he would think sweet thoughts while making a cup of the finest tea to be drunk from the most wonderful of mugs.

6

Later that evening Martin lay in bed, cuddled up to his wife, wearing only a pair of black cotton socks and a smile. Rose lay with her back to him, her hair tousled and her heart thumping away in her chest.

"What are you thinking?" Martin asked, kissing her in the delicate place just behind her ear.

"Two things." She replied a little breathlessly. "One that that was probably not advisable so soon after a major operation, and two that I need to buy David Purefoy a huge bottle of Scotch."

Martin chuckled and placed his arm around the top half of Rose's body, enjoying lying next to her skin on skin. God when was the last time that had happened? Five, six years ago? He was more used to seeing her in a pair of thick Donna Karen pyjamas than he was in the nude.

"I honestly can't believe that just happened," Rose continued, "I mean, I didn't think we'd ever do that again! And you've learnt some new moves."

Martin grinned behind Rose's back. "Not new moves, they've always been there, I just didn't have the energy to try them."

"Well I'm glad you found the energy now." She whispered with a sigh.

They were quiet for a while, just lying together between the sheets as the sun slowly disappeared over the horizon. Martin felt completely at ease, despite the slight twinge from beneath the gauze pack on his chest he was fully lost in the moment, so much so that in the quiet of the room he started to slowly drift off to sleep. It was only when he felt the slight tremble from his wife's shoulder that he was snapped back into the moment. He pushed himself up onto his elbow to get a better view and sure enough there were tears coursing down her cheeks.

"Rose, what's wrong? What's the matter darling?" He asked with real concern.

At first she couldn't speak, she turned slightly in the bed so she could look up at him, her bottom lip trembling.

"N-nothing." She managed eventually.

"I don't understand, why are you crying then?"

It took her another couple of moments to gain some composure, and when she had she was able to continue.

"I'm just so happy, I can't believe it, I can't believe any of it. My God Martin we came so close, I was so close...so close to losing you." The flood gates opened at this and she wept uncontrollably in his arms.

"Hey, hey now." He said, holding her tight, her ample bosom pressed up against his arm. "You didn't lose me though did you, I'm right here."

"Y-you're right here. D-don't leave me Martin, please don't ever leave me, I don't think I could stand it."

Martin used his free hand to wipe the tears from her eyes; they left a mascara smudge that trailed the length of her cheeks. "I'm going nowhere honey pie, you'd better get used to having me around again."

Roses face twisted into an almost ghoulish mask of her own features, she pulled him closer still and together they lay in the silence of the master bedroom, feeling the rhythm of each others heartbeats thumping away in their chests.

7

Martin pulled the gauze padding away from his chest and dropped it into the bin at the side of the sink. He looked at his reflection in the mirror, focusing on the long pink scar that ran slightly indented down the left hand side of his chest. The stitches had completely dissolved now and the soreness that he had felt from the healing scar tissue had seemingly gone with it.

A month had passed since the operation and though he had suffered a couple of minor setbacks his recovery had continued in a positive motion. He felt stronger and healthier day by day; his stamina was increasing and his appetite had returned after a lengthy hiatus. As the days progressed he started to wonder more and more about just how close he had come to the edge, and about what would have happened if his miracle new organ had not appeared, just at the right moment. He could be lying in a casket now, or burnt to ashes at a crematorium. The funny thing was despite him coming so close he had never actually decided on what he would want to happen to his remains. Now these thoughts seemed morbid and distant, he had a new lease of life and was still surrounded by the same positive aura he had felt a couple of weeks into his recovery.

Tracing his finger down the line of the scar he felt the soft tingle of his own delicate touch, but nothing more, no pain, no reaction from this strange foreign body inside his chest wall, no irregular hiccups in the pattern of his breathing. It was almost impossible to comprehend that a little over four weeks ago the paddles of a defibrillator had been pressed to his chest, and an electric shock given to stop the heart and suppress the ventricular fibrillation that had caused it to beat too fast and too erratically, nearly ending his new life before it had even begun.

Now here he was, happy and healthy, and though at a cross roads in his life, unable to forget the darkness of the past but thankful for the promise of the future, he felt confident that the worst of his recovery was behind him.

Martin smiled at himself in the mirror and grabbed for his shaving foam. He put a good squirt into his hand that foamed up in the shape of a whippy ice cream and lathered it over the bottom half of his face. As he grabbed his razor from the shelf and started to scratch away at the day old growth he started to think about David Purefoy. Such a strange man, a vain and pompous man but a man who had come through royally for him all the same. One thing struck him as odd about his recovery, and that was his contact with the surgeon. He had to say the after care he had received so far was not what he would have expected either before the operation or of the level of private care for which he had paid. In fact apart from those two short visits by the surgeon in the first two weeks of his recovery he had no further contact with the hospital.

Surely he should be visiting the hospital as an outpatient? But he had received no letters inviting him to consultation and very little word form the surgeon himself, checking up on his progress as he had been promised. Maybe he was being overly sensitive but he honestly felt that now the operation was over he had been discarded like a plastic bag, blowing in the breeze.

It would of course have been more of an issue if there had been any sign of the heart rejecting, but as he felt positive and healthy he let it go, though it continued to niggle at him from time to time.

Martin shaved until his face was smooth of stubble, then washed the remaining foam and fuzz away with cold water from the tap. As he was drying his face Rose walked in looking for her hair dryer, she stood for a second staring at Martin, then stepped forward and placed a hand on his bare midriff.

"You're starting to put on weight again." She said, not unkindly.

"I won't go back the way things were, trust me." He said defensively.

"I didn't say it was a bad thing, you needed to put on a bit of weight, you were too scrawny after the operation, I like to have something I can cuddle up to."

"Get a hot water bottle." Martin said with a grin.

Rose smiled and patted him on the arm before turning in pursuit of her missing hairdryer once more. She found it on the corner of the bath tub and head back out of the room.

Martin grabbed his shirt from the hook on the back of the door and after a spray of deodorant dressed in front of the mirror, watching as the scar disappeared behind the buttons of his top.

Maybe he should call Purefoy? Just call him up and say is this right? Am I supposed to be left to just get on with things? It felt unusual but maybe he was being paranoid again. He had hoped that these feelings would pass with the success of the operation but so far it had not been the case. Those niggling doubts just kept on a niggling.

And what was with the personal contact details? He knew the surgeon had a vested interest in his wellbeing but asking him to only contact on his personal number seemed unusual under the circumstances.

Then there was the operation itself, done in the comfort of his own home, rather than in a proper operating theatre in a hospital equipped to deal with any turn of events. He had accepted the unusual conditions at the time so desperate he had been to get a new heart, but now that the operation was a thing of the past it was troubling him again, he had just never heard of a serious procedure such as this being performed outside a hospital other than in the case of an emergency.

Oh what did he know anyway? Martin scolded himself for allowing paranoia to creep across his otherwise good feeling; he should be out enjoying himself now, taking a stroll in the park, maybe trying his hand at a few swings of the golf club or popping over to Knightsbridge for a celebratory meal, not worrying about the what's the why's and the how's.

But still, that small voice of doubt continued to whisper in his mind, and it was getting harder and harder to ignore.

Martin looked at the deep lines of worry on his forehead in the reflection of the bathroom mirror.

"Oh bog off!" He scolded, then stormed out of the room with his pants still unbuckled at the waist.

8

Two days later while Rose was downstairs watching the latest developments unfold in Albert Square, Martin sat on the bed that he shared with his wife, the laptop open before him. He looked down at the soft glow of the screen and sighed discontentedly.

He had decided that all this worry was no good for his health, and to embrace the new life he had been granted and stop dwelling on things that were out of his control. He had a new heart, a new lease of life and frankly what did it matter if things had been a little unorthodox to get him here? The fact was he was wasting the opportunity he had been given on things that frankly didn't matter, and now he intended to make up for lost time. And that was exactly what he did.

He had called up his old golfing buddies and arranged to meet them at the club, and though he hadn't been yet ready for more than a couple of practice swings he had enjoyed just walking the course with them, getting a little exercise and chewing the fat. Last night he had been good to his word and booked a table at Claridge's, surprising Rose with a gourmet meal at one of London's top restaurants, paying a little extra to secure the table and celebrating his rebirth in style.

It had been a fantastic meal, with enough wine to make him feel a little light headed but not out of control and enough chat and good humour to make the celebration feel special.

They had returned home, made love – four times since the operation now, more than the accumulation of the whole five years leading up to the operation, and gone to sleep. Or at least Rose had. Martin lay awake, staring at the ceiling and listening to the soft snores of his wife at his side, her arm still strewn about his naked waist.

The doubt had started to creep back in as he had pulled away from her, and now as he lay with the ever growing questions niggling at his brain sleep felt impossible. He had tossed and turned in bed, worrying about the level of after care he was receiving, about the circumstances surrounding the operation, about the strange behaviour of his surgeon before and after the operation and the more thought he gave it all the stranger it seemed. Three o'clock had passed, and then four, and as he lay there in bed, his troubled mind refusing to let him sleep, he had come to the conclusion that he was just going to have to confront the surgeon about it all.

Finally, his mind comforted at the thought of a pursuit for answers, he slipped into a deep and peaceful sleep and hadn't awoken until nearly ten that morning, the sunshine flooding into the room as his eyes flickered with confusion. Rose had already been downstairs, in front of the television in an ill fitting leotard, doing what looked like the Kiwi Haka in response to some young strumpet's motivational DVD. She made some curt remark about his new lethargic attitude and Martin thought if she only knew the half of it, before heading to the kitchen and fixing himself a huge mug of coffee and some bran flakes.

Now here he sat, the laptop open before him, searching the internet for clues on the type of care you would likely expect following a serious operation. He had already looked at several sites and had obtained some interesting data, but it wasn't sufficient. So he opened up Google and prepared to search again, this time he typed 'what after care can you expect after a heart transplant' into the search engine and watched as the first 24 results of over 100,000 possible links were loaded onto the page. Knowing that the first three or four results would be where he would find the closest answer to his query, he started here.

The first link he clicked on was the website for the NIH, a heart, lung and blood institute based in the states. The very first paragraph on the page made him feel cold all over, despite the warmth of the late summer morning. It read:

The amount of time a heart transplant recipient spends in the hospital varies. Recovery often involves 1 to 2 weeks in the hospital and 3 months of monitoring by the transplant team at the heart transplant center.

"Two weeks in the hospital." Martin muttered as he continued to read.

Monitoring may include frequent blood tests, lung function tests, EKGs (electrocardiograms), echocardiograms, and biopsies of the heart tissue. A heart biopsy is a standard test that can show whether your body is rejecting the new heart. This test is often done in the weeks after a transplant. During a heart biopsy, a tiny grabbing device is inserted into a vein in the neck or groin (upper thigh). The device is threaded through the vein to the right atrium of the new heart to take a small tissue sample. The tissue sample is checked for signs of rejection. While in the hospital, your health care team may suggest that you start a cardiac rehabilitation (rehab) program. Cardiac rehab is a medically supervised program that helps improve the health and well-being of people who have heart problems. Cardiac rehab includes counseling, education, and exercise training to help you recover. Rehab may start with a member of the rehab team helping you sit up in a chair or take a few steps. Over time, you'll increase your activity level.

"My God." Martin whispered, his eyes starting to water. He looked again at the words on the screen; heart biopsy, cardiac rehabilitation, counselling, he hadn't been offered any of this, why? Is it because it was an American website? Surely the level of after care in the UK couldn't be that different?

Starting to feel decidedly uncomfortable he clicked the back arrow on the menu bar and waited for the screen to return him to the Google results page. When it did he returned to the search engine and included the words 'in the UK' in his search topic, so that the whole question now read 'what after care can you expect in the UK after a heart transplant.'

After a couple of seconds the page loaded with a fresh list of sites to try. The second link down was for the British heart foundation, which seemed a pretty good place to find answers. He clicked the link and waited for the page to load.

The page gave general info on what to expect when going through the process of a heart transplant. He scrolled down past the sections 'who might need a heart transplant', 'How do I know if I'm eligible for a heart transplant?' And 'How long is the wait for a heart transplant', pausing to have a quick read of the 'what happens during a heart transplant operation' section and noting that nowhere did it mention that you may be asked to have the procedure performed in the comfort of your own home. Biting on his lip he scrolled down again and finally reached the information he was looking for, it was under the sub-heading 'what happens after the transplant' and read as follows:

Most people leave hospital within about four weeks after the operation, but depending on your condition, you may need to stay in hospital for longer.
In the first few months after your surgery you will need to spend a lot of time visiting the hospital – you might even need to stay near the transplant center. Your transplant team will talk to you about practical arrangements for after your surgery.

So that confirmed it, the level of after care you could expect in the UK was every bit as stringent as in the states, so why had he been left to fend for himself? Martin swallowed hard, not knowing what to do next. He was grateful to Purefoy for finding him a new heart and performing the procedure that had saved his life, but the way he had been left to his own devices in the time following the operation was nothing short of negligent.

A couple of brief visits the surgeon had made; checking his blood pressure and noting his pulse count, but that was it, and he'd not seen or heard from the man since.

Feeling deeply troubled Martin grabbed the laptop from the bed and made his way slowly down the stairs. Her exercises completed for the day Rose was bending over removing the disc from the player. The white haired man walked into the living room and sat down in front of his wife on the couch.

"I hope you've been looking for a holiday, Mauritius would be nice." She said with a smile.

"Look at this." He said, and turned the laptop on his knees so she could read what was on the screen.

"What about it?" Rose asked, with her own typical brand of indifference.

"Look what it says, look at the care I'm supposed to have received, counselling, regular appointments; I haven't had any of that."

"You feel ok don't you?"

"Yeah I feel ok, but that's not the point."

"Well what is the point?"

"What if I hadn't felt ok? Who would have known?"

"You'd have contacted David."

"Oh so it's David now is it."

"Oh stop it you're being silly."

"I'm just saying, wouldn't it be normal to invite me to a surgery? To have a discussion? For proper checks to be made? To check the heart isn't rejecting, that type of thing? It even says so right here."

"Well if it bothers you that much give him a call."

Martin nodded his head slowly. "Yeah, yeah I'll give him a call."

"There you go then." Rose said as he stood from the couch. "I'm sure you'll feel much better after you've had chance to talk to him."

Martin walked through to the kitchen, placing the laptop down on the island unit as he made his way across to the phone. There was a list of useful numbers on a small cork board to the side of the phone; he scanned it now, screwing up his eyes to read the small print. He huffed and puffed as he read down.

"What's the matter now?" Rose asked from the living room, mild annoyance in her tone.

"I can't read the blasted numbers without my glasses."

"Well where are your glasses?"

"I don't know, where did I leave them?"

Rose sighed and slowly shook her head from side to side. "David's number is right at the top, there's a star next to it."

"Oh." Martin muttered, quickly scanning back to the top of the page. He found what he was looking for and squinted out the digits, slowly punching them into the handset as he went along. Finally the phone started ringing, it rang just a couple of times, then the voice of the surgeon was on the line, telling him he wasn't available at this time and to leave a message.

Martin closed the call without doing as he was bid. He had been in business a long time, made a lot of calls to people he knew would not be happy to hear from him and knew all the tells. If the call went straight to voicemail it meant the handset was either switched off or out of coverage. If it rang several times and then went to voicemail it usually meant the call had been genuinely missed. But if a call went to voicemail after just a couple of rings Martin knew from experience the likely reason was that the receiver of the call had retrieved the phone from their jacket or trouser pocket, seen who was calling displayed on the screen and decided to send the call to voicemail.

Martin sighed and placed the handset back in its cradle. He walked back out of the kitchen towards the living room, pausing to fold the laptop closed on his way. Rose was just starting an episode of Holby City she had recorded on the couple's Sky Plus unit the night before. The businessman plonked down next to her on the couch.

"Did you get through?" She asked, her eyes never leaving the screen.

"Voicemail." He replied.

"Did you leave a message?"

"No."

"Well, he was probably busy."

Martin grunted and settled down to watch the TV show with his wife. She was probably right, he had probably sent the call to voicemail because he was busy right now, he was a surgeon after all, he could have been with a patient or studying some charts or attending a seminar with lots of men in tuxedos, patting each other on the back at the latest advancements in cardio-vascular medicine.

He could have been doing any of those things; it really was easy enough to believe, so why did he feel so uneasy? Why did he feel like the surgeon had avoided his call on purpose? Why did he feel like tiny ants were crawling their way along the base of his spine?

Martin swallowed back his anxiety and tried to concentrate on the programme; it was a good one today, an old man had just had a heart attack.

9

Having already left two unanswered voicemails on Purefoy's personal phone Martin was left with no choice than to try and contact the surgeon at the hospital, but again he met a brick wall, the receptionist tried to call through to his office and discovered that he had taken a leave of absence, expected to return at the end of August.

"He's avoiding me." Martin grumbled when he had hung up the phone.

"What because he's taken a holiday?" Rose replied, one eyebrow slightly raised.

"So he goes on holiday and my after care goes out of the window? That's not how it works, there should be a plan in place, someone to pick up my treatment, appointments, drop-in's, regular check-up's, I've just been left to rot!"

"Martin let it go, you're like a dog with a bone with this."

The businessman sighed. "I wish I could."

"Then do. Look the important things as far as I can see it is that the operation was a success and so far so good everything looks ok, you're feeling well, you are feeling well aren't you?"

"I feel great." Martin conceded grumpily, sitting down at the stool next to his wife in the kitchen.

"There you are you see, you feel great, so why are you beating yourself up over this?"

"I don't know." He admitted, starting to mellow. "You're right, I should focus on the positives, there are plenty of those."

"That's my boy." She smiled.

"And I am feeling much better. Talking of which there was something I wanted to run by you."

"Oh?"

Martin paused for a second, gathering his thoughts. "I'm thinking of going back to work."

"Back to work? So soon?"

"At the end of the month, it will have been over six weeks by then and I know that's still early but I am feeling good. Also, I need something to occupy my mind. All this conspiracy theory stuff, it's not me. I think I'm niggling at things because I'm bored."

"You always were a workaholic." She said with a sigh.

Martin tried to read her thoughts, he knew he would need his wife's approval if he was to return to Sapient, but at the moment she was a closed book.

"Well?" He said eventually, needing to prompt her.

"Well what?" She responded.

"Well what do you think?"

"Does it matter what I think?"

"Of course it matters." Martin mused on the fact that he thought the decision to be solely Rose's and she clearly saw it very differently.

"Martin I've never been able to keep you out of that office, God knows I've tried. If you think it would be beneficial for you to go back to work in a couple of weeks then go back to work, I could do with getting you out from under my feet anyway."

Martin smiled.

"But I insist that you take it easy." She continued quickly. "No takeover bids, no stakeholder meetings, no negotiations. You sit in the background."

"I was thinking of taking more of a back seat from now on to be honest anyway." Martin agreed. "I can leave the fraught end of the business to Peter; God knows he'd do a better job of it than me anyway. No it's the buzz I miss, the people; I miss the view from my office window."

"Well that's fine then; go to work if you must, anything to stop you moping around here."

"You're an angel." He said with a smile. "Two more weeks, then I'll be out from under your feet."

"You'll always be under my feet, and thank God for that little miracle." She said with a smile. Martin smiled too, and leaned forward to kiss her on the forehead before standing and walking out of the kitchen.

Rose watched him go, feeling relieved that the prospect of returning to Sapient had given him something else to think about other than his lack of after care at the hospital. It was important to her that he had something to focus on; he had started asking a lot of questions about his recovery, too many questions. Questions often led to answers, and there were some things that needed to stay in the dark.

10

Knowing that he would be returning to work soon Martin made sure the last two weeks of his time at home were spent in holiday mode. Day trips to the coast with Rose, eating ice-creams and snoozing on the beach in a pin striped deck-chair; following his buddies round on the golf course, chewing the cud and taking the occasional swing of a club, going out for dinner at the Hampton's or Luigi's on the high street and long walks on the common on an evening, watching as the sun sank slowly out of sight over the horizon.

The days had been stiflingly warm, and at night it had been so close that all the windows on the upstairs of the Rooley household had been left wide open, though little breeze had been felt despite this. It was a pleasant end to a long hot summer but as the August Bank Holiday weekend rolled around there was a sudden dip in the temperature, a cold front coming in from the Arctic and suddenly long trousers and jackets were once more on display when shorts and vests had been the strict dress code just days earlier.

Martin returned to Sapient on the Tuesday following the Bank Holiday, and as he pulled into his private parking space next to Peter's BMW, he felt pangs of nervous apprehension tingle away in his stomach. He hadn't told anybody of his imminent return and now regretted his decision, at least if they'd been prepared for his arrival he may not have had quite so many questions to answer. Adjusting his Saville Row tie in the rear view mirror he took a deep breath and stepped out of the vehicle. Martin had to bite back his anxiety as he marched up to the huge glass door and stepped inside. Deciding to arrive early enough to avoid the hustle and bustle of rush hour the foyer was only marginally busy, he was able to make it to the lift without anything more than a few cursory nods of the head and perfunctory good mornings. So far so good.

He took the lift up to his floor and walked across the gantry to the reception area, where Sheila was sat at her desk, typing away at her console. She looked up as he walked through towards his office and a look of shock passed her face, thankfully it soon turned to the beaming smile he often felt wasn't seen often enough on her pretty middle aged face.

"Martin, we weren't expecting you." She said, standing up.

"Oh God don't rise to attention, I'm not a school master, or the Queen."

She sat back down, red in the cheeks but the smile still on her face.

"Welcome back! It's great to see you again; the place hasn't been the same."

"Oh thank, thank you, you're too kind. Actually keep going it's nice to hear pleasant things." He said with a short laugh.

Sheila laughed too. "I'll contact Peter, is he expecting you?"

"No, nobody, I thought I'd surprise you all, see if you were throwing wild orgies behind my back, and if so I wanted to ask why I wasn't invited."

Sheila laughed again as he stepped up to his office and opened the door. "Could I not have any calls for the next hour or so?" He asked as he stepped one foot inside.

"Oh should I not contact Peter?"

"Peter's fine, I could do with a catch-up anyway, just not anybody else please, just an hour."

"Not a problem."

He thanked her and stepped through into his office, closing the door behind him. Martin took a look around, taking a sharp intake of breath; he had never expected to see this room again, and suddenly he was overcome with emotion. He leant back against the office door and waited as a wave of dizziness passed over him. He looked from the coat stand to his filing cabinet to his huge mahogany desk to his leather backed chair and finally to the huge picture window with the view of Canary Wharf.

With the feeling settling he peeled himself away from the door and walked further into the room, he placed his briefcase down on the desk top and plonked down into the soft cushion of his chair, turning slightly so he could look at London out the window. Hive minutes passed and he was still sat staring at the stunning view when there was a light tap at his door and Peter walked in.

The tall man walked into the room, a bemused smile on his face, shaking his head slightly. "You didn't think to call?" Was his opening gambit.

Martin let out a quiet chuckle and swivelled around in his chair. "What and give you prior warning? No, I wanted to catch you with your hand in the cookie jar."

"Oh? And what scurrilous activity does your twisted little mind think has been going on around here?"

"Fraud, embezzlement, monopolisation, trade secrets, loss leading, who knows what underhand practices go on when I'm not around."

Peter chuckled as he stepped forward, his hand held out. "You old bastard, how the hell are you?"

Martin ignored the hand and stepped up, giving the tall thin man a brief but firm embrace, when he spoke he was smiling from ear to ear.

"I'm great, I feel fantastic, the operation is looking like a huge success, I feel fighting fit, ready to take on the world."

"And you're sure this isn't all a bit too soon?" Peter said, pulling the chair to the front of the desk round next to Martin's and plonking down.

"I was going round the bend at home, besides summer's ending now, I figured it was time to do a bit of work for a change."

"I was starting to think we were going to have to scrape you away from the golf course with spatulas."

"No, no, truth be told I missed the place, it's good to be back."

"Well I've got to tell you it's good to have you back, everything's under control of course, it's just I don't think I do the fun side of business quite as well as you, the mood's been like a crematorium around here with you gone."

Martin laughed. "Yeah you never were known for your funny side around here."

"Hey, I'm misunderstood."

"Of course you are. So were there questions, you know, with me being gone so long?"

"Questions, rumours, you name it, my favourite was that you'd gone to Switzerland to have a sex change."

"You're kidding me?"

"I'm not, though I think it was started by John Swift in marketing as a wind-up to the cafeteria girls, but still I liked that one."

"Ha I'll bet you did."

"The biggest rumour was that you weren't well, pretty easy conclusion to draw after what happened at the Christmas party, not much I could do to quash that one."

"No I guess not." Martin replied solemnly.

"And then there's Sheila."

"Sheila?"

"Come on Martin she was like a dog with a bone, she wouldn't let it go, you know how much she cares for you, I had to tell her the truth."

Martin sighed. "Yeah I guess."

"She wanted to do a whip round for you but I told her you wanted to keep it under your hat for now, she didn't like it, wanted to contact you and let you know she was thinking about you, but she agreed to wait til you got back."

"Well that's very sweet of her, I'll make a point of going out at some point today and letting her know I'm ok. So how are things around here anyway? You run the place into the red yet?"

"You shouldn't joke, losing the pipeline contract cost us dear, we were looking at a dip in the market for the first time this year at the start of August but we managed to pull it back with some shrewdly timed press releases."

"You mean *you* managed to pull it back."

Peter shrugged. "It was a team effort."

"You're too modest, this place would buckle without you and you know it, it will be remembered."

The thin man smiled. "Well thank you, it's very good of you to say. So what's the order of the day anyway, you actually going to do some work or just sit staring at your view for a few more hours?"

"I thought I'd stare a little more, besides, why have a dog and bark yourself?"

"Don't I know it." Peter replied with a wry smile. "I should get the view instead of that damn awful window over looking the tube."

"Yeah well when I finally drop off this earth it's yours, unfortunately this little beauty means that will hopefully be quite a few years yet." Martin said, patting his chest.

"Yeah a new heart won't help if your morning coffee is spiked with arsenic."

Martin chuckled. "Haven't you got anything better to do than sit here threatening an old man? What am I paying you for anyway?"

"Oh you know, just the running of your business." The thin man said, standing up from his chair. "You're right though I do need to go, some of us have board meetings and trade discussions to hold, we can't all sit and stare at London."

"You'd better get on with it then, go make me some more money will you." Martin said as his friend strolled towards the door.

"I'll call back on you later; see how you're getting on. Oh by the way, fantastic start to the season by Bolton, two losses on the bounce, ouch, that's got to hurt."

"Whatever we achieve this season, whether it be mid-table mediocrity or otherwise, will have been achieved the hard way. You enjoy whatever trophies your billionaire owner has bought for you this season; I bet you feel really proud."

"Pride doesn't come into it, I just feel like a winner." Peter said with a sly smirk, then he was gone.

Martin swivelled back round in his seat to face the view, he always felt better after even a short catch-up with Peter, and he was starting to feel at home again. In a little while he would load up the reporting index and check out how they were faring on the stock exchange, then maybe take a walk down to HR and get an update on any people issues, but for now he was happy with his view, he could afford an easy day, it was his first day back after all.

Outside the window people dotted about the walkways to the side of the Thames like ants, their jackets fastened up against the late summer chill. There were dark clouds in the sky and it looked like it might rain, it made the view from Martin's picture window look foreboding and dramatic. It was with difficulty some ten minutes later that he prized himself away from the view and swivelled himself round to face his desk. He fired up the computer and waited for it to load. He was watching the bytes load up on the screen when impulsively he stretched out his hand and grabbed the phone. He fished his mobile from his pocket, checked the number he wished to dial and punched it into the landline, old habits die hard for an old timer like me, he thought as he slipped the mobile back in his pocket.

The phone was ringing in his ear, then after a couple of seconds it was answered by the now familiar voice of St. Cuthbert's daytime receptionist. She greeted him pleasantly and Martin had time to hope he wasn't becoming a nuisance before responding.

"Oh hello, this is Martin Rooley, I'm an outpatient of the hospital, I wonder if I could speak with Mister David Purefoy please."

"I'll just try cardio-vascular reception, if you could give me a moment."

"No problem."

Some awful pre-programmed hold music insulted his ears for about thirty seconds, and then a new voice came on the line."

"Good morning St. Cuthbert's."

"Oh hello this is Martin Rooley, I'm a former patient of yours, please could I be put through to Mister David Purefoy. It's really important I speak with him."

"Hold the line a second he's just walking past." The voice said.

Martin could hardly breathe, he hadn't expected he would get to speak to the surgeon and now he was about to he wasn't prepared for what he wanted to say. He could hear voices in the background, then the phone was being picked up again.

"Hello Mister Rooley."

"Yes."

"I'm afraid it was my mistake, it wasn't Mister Purefoy at all, he isn't actually in the hospital today, but I'll leave a message for him to call you."

"Thank you, if you could." Martin replied, feeling the bile start to rise in his stomach. He placed the phone back in its cradle and sat looking at it for a long time. That had definitely been the surgeon muttering away in the background, and he had asked the lady who had answered the phone to lie for him and say he wasn't there. The surgeon was avoiding him, of this he was now certain, but why?

Martin slumped back in his chair, feeling deeply troubled again. Outside the window London grew gloomier by the second.

11

The first day back at Sapient had gone better than he could have hoped. After much gazing at the wealth and opulence of Canary Wharf and the troubling phone call to St. Cuthbert's he had ventured out into the small reception area and eased Sheila's concerns over his condition. He was happy to do this; he knew he could trust her, she had always had his best interests at heart and was someone he considered a friend as well as a colleague.

Afterwards, with Sheila much happier hearing of his progress he strolled down to HR, where he spoke to Kim Gordon, the firm but fair head of HR about any people issues they were dealing with at present. Apart from a higher than normal absence percentage in sales everything was ticking along nicely, and this could probably be attributed to leave in the school holidays, and would likely even itself out when the new term started in the coming week. Martin asked Kim for a departmental breakdown on how leave was distributed in the school holidays and left happy that there weren't any major people issues at present.

Heading back to his office he had eaten an egg salad sandwich which Rose had packed for him that morning whilst looking at the latest financial index. Peter had been right, despite some major setbacks with their Eastern European prospects the share index had stabilised quite nicely, and the company was continuing to turn a healthy profit in a time when small independent businesses and major corporations alike were struggling to stay afloat.

A meeting of the department heads, led as always by Peter was scheduled for three that afternoon, and Martin attended for a short while, mainly to show his face and let everybody know that he was A) alive and well and B) still very much a man, contrary to the Sapient rumour mill.

It was nearly six o'clock when he had fully caught up on his email and had read up on the latest industry news and when he switched off his monitor he was happy with his first day back in the office. He was under no doubt that the following day would need to be more productive and he was looking forward to whatever challenges may lie ahead, most notably thrashing out with Peter how they were going to reaffirm the company's stakes in Russia and Eastern Europe.

He left the office via the main reception, waving goodbye to the friends and colleagues he passed on the stairs, and pulled his keys from his jacket pocket as he crossed the front of the building. He was about to press the lock release button on the side of the key when his phone started vibrating in his pocket. That was right, he had put it on vibrate when he had joined Peter's meeting of the department heads, he pulled it from his pocket and looked at the screen, instantly feeling the small hairs prick up on the back of his neck, but not fully understanding why. It was Purefoy, calling from his personal phone.

Swallowing back his unjustified anxiety Martin leant back against the door frame of his car and answered the call.

"Mister Purefoy, it's been a while." He opened unashamedly.

"How are you Martin? How are things?"

The question was put plainly enough but Martin could detect the agitation just beneath the surface, why was that?

"Good, good, I returned to work today."

"That's good, that's a big step. You must be feeling a lot better."

"Oh I feel wonderful, a new man, still a few twinges here and there where my ribcage is knitting back together and not quite ready yet to swing a golf club as I've found out to my peril, but otherwise fine."

"I'm glad to hear it, another couple of weeks and you'll be like new."

"That's the hope."

There was a pause on the line, when Purefoy continued he was speaking cautiously.

"Listen Martin, you've been trying to call me at the hospital, I thought we agreed if you needed me you'd contact me directly on my personal phone."

Martin could feel his anger starting to rise, he fought to control it.

"Well I called you several times on your mobile and left several messages, but I never heard back from you, it seemed natural to try and catch you at the hospital, why is there a problem with that?"

"No, no, no problem." The surgeon answered hurriedly. "It's just that I want to handle your after care personally, have that human interaction with my patient, to make sure you get the best possible care."

"Well like I say I tried to contact you on your personal number several times."

"I apologise, I must have missed your calls, what is it I can do for you?"

Missed his calls, what and the messages he'd left too? A likely story. Martin was cooling to this man again, in whose presence he had never been fully comfortable, there was just something about him that didn't fit with Martin's ideals, something sly, fox like and cunning, he didn't like it one bit. Again he kept his emotions in check by reminding himself the surgeon had saved his life, he deserved some respect for that, even if he was an unbearable toad.

"It's actually after care that I wanted to talk to you about; shouldn't I be booked into a surgery or something? I don't know, appointments, check-up's to make sure everything's going ok? Make sure the heart isn't rejecting that sort of thing."

"But Martin, we have met up, I came to your house."

"I know, and I appreciate that, but it was several weeks ago now and I just, I don't know…"

"What, you're feeling neglected?"

Martin bit down on his lip so hard that it started to bleed; the surgeon was backing him into a corner, making him feel foolish when he knew he had strong grounds to feel aggrieved.

"I've been reading on these websites…"

"Let me guess, NHS direct, British Heart Foundation right? Scare mongering sites, they convey the worst case scenarios with everything to cover their backs, otherwise there'd be a constant tide of legal action, then where would we be? No surgeons performing in hospitals because they're all in court rooms up and down the country."

Martin sighed. "I just…"

"Look," the surgeon interrupted again, "you read some things on a site you thought why aren't I getting that, you contacted me, I get it, and if you still feel like it's necessary to follow a set recovery plan despite being fit enough to return to work then we can do it, no problem, is that what you want?"

"I don't know, I guess so." Martin rubbed at his temple; he could feel a headache coming on.

"That's fine then, give me a few days, I'll set something up. Are you happy with that outcome?"

"I am, thank you David, I appreciate it, I do, and I appreciate everything you've done for me, sorry if I came across as ungrateful, that was not my intention."

"Its fine, we will get you whatever after care you feel you need, I promise, you are a valued patient of ours after all. I'll be in touch shortly, and if you need me again use the personal number, I can get back to you faster that way."

"Of course." The businessman replied reluctantly.

"Take care Martin." The surgeon said, then closed the call.

Martin sighed again and placed the phone back in his pocket; he climbed in his car, sat behind the wheel and regarded the deep worry lines on his forehead in the rear-view mirror. He had worked all day at Sapient and felt fine, two minutes on the phone with Purefoy and he was utterly exhausted.

12

Promises it seemed, at least in the case of David Purefoy, were made to be broken; the surgeon never called, never set up a meeting and never committed to the after care which Martin felt he deserved.

The businessman was aggrieved for some time, complaining to his wife at the gall of the man and remonstrating angrily each time he got the answer machine, leaving his messages that were calm at first, then angry, then finally just perplexed. By mid September he had given up all hope of any kind of after care and as October rolled around, with what leaves still remained in the trees turned all different shades of brown, Martin finally put it to bed. It was the right thing to do, it had been several months now since the operation, he was feeling just fine, fantastic actually and it was high time he moved on and started enjoying his life.

That had been his promise to Rose at the start of the month and he was true to his word; he put the whole sorry affair behind him, choosing to focus on the positives; he was alive, happy and healthy, what did it matter that he hadn't been hooked up to an ECG every now and then or wasted his time at countless appointments and check-up's? It just gave him more time for the things that actually mattered in life. Purefoy's lack of after care was actually a positive thing if you chose to see it that way, and if any complications occurred he would just contact the hospital directly, cut out the middle man.

Rose, relieved at this new outlook, had made the most of her husband's bright new demeanour and turned it to her advantage, persuading him to spend real quality time with her away from the office, just as they had before the operation, and her husband had rightly agreed. He had even agreed to the two week holiday to Maui she had booked for that coming April, having completely missed the hints she had left lying around the house like the open holiday brochures and the new one piece swimming costume she had picked up in Harrod's. She had her weekend's away with the girls and her activities and hobbies that kept her from boredom but she had married a man, not a business, and it was her desire to spend a little time with that man before a recurrence of the problems that had marred the first six months of the year.

To Martin's credit he had been more than happy to spend the time with his wife, who he had always loved unconditionally, and was now starting to see his own friends a little more too, especially now that he was finally capable of swinging a golf club again. The time away had done nothing for his handicap but he was sure with the new skip in his step he would soon be picking up the pace and maybe even putting up a bit of a challenge to his old chums in the occasional round.

Work still had its place, and Martin ensured he wasn't caving in to the growing desire to leave all the tough stuff to Peter, and was pulling his weight at Sapient just as he was pulling his weight at home, but he had a deeper love for his personal life now, no longer driven solely by the growth of Sapient; what's more he was actually enjoying the time that he spent away from the office, something he had been completely incapable of in his younger days.

Now here he was, a Saturday in early October, actually walking the length of Oxford Street with his wife while she shopped for presents for family and friends, her ruthless efficiency once more on display, though what was truly unimaginable was that he had joined her in the first place; Martin hated shopping! Actually detested it, he hated everything about it; from the queues to the patronising sales assistant's to the seemingly endless aisles of brightly displayed confusion. And yet here he was, Saturday afternoon on one of the busiest shopping streets in the world, perusing the displays with his wife, and only half grudgingly – the weather was cold and murky outside, not pleasant for swinging a club at all.

They had just entered Selfridge's and gifts for others temporarily forgotten Rose made a bee-line to the large selection of purses over by the escalator. Martin sighed; he had found the talent for making money around about the time his wife had discovered her own superior talent for spending it.

He shuffled over next to her, wondering why at sixty-eight years of age he still felt embarrassed and foolish when surrounded by ladies purses, shoes, jewellery and hosiery, and as for lingerie? He may as well open his mouth and call himself a post box, because nothing had the potential to redden his skin quite like a selection of frilly white bras and briefs.

Elegant gold streamers hung from the ceiling alongside giant baubles that sparkled and shimmered under the fluorescent lights; a huge Christmas tree adorned the centre aisle, its silver branches also sparkling.

"Is it Christmas already?" He asked, his eyebrows raised. "I thought it was only October."

"Honey on Oxford Street Christmas starts about the same time they pack away the string lined bikini's."

"But we haven't even had Halloween yet."

"If you like I can buy you a pumpkin outfit from the gift store, with a big round outfit on you'd look a bit like the old you."

"Ha ha." He said sarcastically.

"Maybe if you did a little Christmas shopping every once in a while you'd notice Christmas doesn't start on the twenty-fourth of December. What? You think I don't know you get your secretary to buy my Christmas presents, I've known for years."

Martin looked hurt. "She doesn't buy all of them!"

"Relax, Sheila has exceptional taste."

Martin continued to shuffle unhappily, trying to think of a really good present that he had bought for his wife off his own back; he had to admit that he was struggling.

"Look at this one, it's beautiful." Rose said, holding up a black purse covered in multi coloured dots. Personally he felt the dots made it look slightly ill, but he kept this thought to himself, thinking the sooner she decided on one she wanted to buy the sooner they could get out of here.

"Lovely." He muttered noncommittally, that was until he saw the price tag. "Four hundred pounds for a purse?"

"It's Chloe." She replied, as if this explained everything.

"Maybe you should let her have it back then." He said.

Rose smirked and patted him on the arm with her current purse, only two months old itself, then wandered deeper into the store still holding the new purse.

Martin sighed and followed her, wondering how companies could get away with charging so much for so little. A car he could understand, because the more you paid the better the quality, but a purse? Surely a purse was still a purse if you bought it in a posh London department store or if you purchased it down Kensington market.

A group of middle aged ladies were blocking the aisle, chatting loudly about their upcoming girly weekend to Brighton, another shopping peeve of Martin's, and he ducked around them, trying to catch up to his wife, who had now set her sights on the shoe aisle. Not wanting to hear the words 'wow', 'beautiful' and 'Prada' in a sentence, Martin made his excuses.

"I'm just going to take a look over here." He called out, gesturing to a gift display off to his right, Rose saw where he was pointing and smiled as she nodded, then she was gone, heading towards the shoes with the air of one about to give her platinum card another beating.

Martin wandered over to the display, looking at the gift boxes of toiletries and tins of sugared candy-cains, all at vastly exaggerated prices, well what was Christmas if not an excuse for a not so subtle blend of extreme commercialism and daylight robbery. He picked up a tester pot of a new aftershave called Dark River and gave it a sniff, recoiling slightly at the pungent odour. As he did he became aware of a man perusing the displays just a couple of feet away from him. He was a tall man, and stocky too, with thick black hair, greying slightly at the sides. He had a European look about his features and Martin recognised him straight away, though he couldn't place form where.

He had picked up a thick glass jar of sugared almonds and was inspecting the contents; blissfully unaware of the scrutiny he was receiving just yards away. Martin, who had placed the bottle of Dark River (it smelled more like stagnant pond water to Martin) back on the shelf, stared at the middle aged man, his brow furrowed as he desperately tried to place him. Maybe he was off the television, that happened sometimes, especially in London; you saw somebody you thought you recognised and bade them a greeting, only to discover you didn't actually know them at all, had in fact just seen them on a soap opera or one of those ghastly reality TV shows. Determined not to make a fool of himself today Martin shrunk back away from the man while he tried to remember his name.

It would be easy just to say hello, wait and see if the man recognised him, that would certainly help to fill in the blanks, but if he didn't recognise him then he could be within the category of TV celeb you mistakenly think you know; worse still if he did recognise him and started chatting away Martin would at some point have to admit that he didn't have a clue who he was.

Feeling the pressure of the situation weighing on him Martin turned his back to the man, and it was at that point that he remembered who he was.

The man with the thickset features and slightly Mediterranean look had been his anaesthetist, when he had gone under the knife in the makeshift operating theatre in his home; Ricardo something or other he was called. He had a name that sounded a bit like something you might find in a delicatessen or an espresso bar, and it was on the tip of Martin's tongue.

Palatin? Panarami? Pecaluto? None of them sounded right.

Oh what the hell, he had a first name, surely that would be enough? It would be nice to offer his heart felt thanks to the man for his part in saving his life, no pun intended.

Feeling the glow in his cheeks starting to rise Martin sidled up to the big man, and as he did his surname sprung to the front of his mind, as though it had been thrust there by some unseen force.

Panettiere! The big anaesthetist was called Ricardo Panettiere!

"Excuse me, Mister Panettiere." Martin spoke softly.

The anaesthetist turned around and looked at Martin, it took a couple of seconds for the recognition to register on his face, but when it did, he shrunk away from Martin with a look of horror.

Martin recoiled himself; shocked at the look he had received. Sure that the man must have mistaken him for someone else Martin quickly regained his composure.

"Mister Panettiere, Ricardo, I don't know if you remember me, my name is Martin Rooley, you were the anaesthetist at my heart operation back in the summer."

The bulky man took a quick look about himself. "I'm sorry pal I don't know you."

"It was an unusual operation, you came to my home, it was performed in the gym of my house."

"You must have me mistaken for somebody else." Panettiere replied gruffly, but Martin knew from the strong cockney accent that this man was exactly who he thought he was. So why did he look so agitated? Martin only wanted to say hello, to offer his thanks for giving him a second chance, yet he looked like he wanted to turn and run, looked in fact as though he had seen a ghost.

Maybe I did die that day, Martin thought suddenly, maybe that's why these people keep acting so weird around me, maybe I'm a ghost. He would have smiled if his own agitation wasn't starting to show.

"Well are you at least an anaesthetist?" He questioned.

"I have no idea what you're talking about." Panettiere hissed, taking another quick glance about himself, seemingly making sure nobody was eavesdropping.

"I don't understand, I just wanted to say hello and...."

"Look back off buddy." The big anaesthetist said, jabbing a finger at the flustered businessman. "I don't know you, I don't want to know you, I've never met you, so leave me alone."

Suddenly he shoved the jar of sugared almonds back on the shelf and made a hasty retreat to the exit.

"Wait!" Martin called out, feeling faint and a little nauseous.

"Don't you follow me!" The big man called back, making a few heads turn in the busy store, then he was gone, out into the murky grey of an October Saturday afternoon.

Martin stood by the display of over priced gifts, his new heart beating hard in his chest, looking towards the exit in confusion and fear. What had just happened? Why had he refused to acknowledge their connection? Why did he seem so angry and in such a hurry to get away?

Wiping a thin sheen of sweat from his forehead with the back of his hand Martin nodded his acknowledgment that everything was ok to the people still looking towards him with concern. Then with his cheeks flushed pillar box red, turned and went in pursuit of his wife.

13

"I wonder who it was." Martin said, disturbing Rose from the column she was reading in OK magazine; the would be King and his radiant wife had been on a month long tour of Australia and there was a full colour spread covering the highlights of the trip. Mrs Martin Rooley had always loved the royals and bought every copy of OK and Hello when they were blazoned on the cover. Her husband, who was more of a take them or leave them kind of guy when it came to Mrs Windsor and her many headline making relatives, had been sat in contemplative silence for the last ten minutes, had in fact been brooding ever since they got home from their shopping trip to the city. Rose had put it down to weariness, new heart or not he was sixty-eight years of age and a trip to the big smoke could be exhausting for a young man, but now she wasn't so sure. With some reluctance she placed the magazine down on the coffee table and looked across at him, sat at a sideways angle and peering out onto the forecourt, his face sullen and his eyes distant and vacant.

"Who what was?" She asked, knowing instantly that she would live to regret the question.

"Huh?" He said, turning and looking at her, as though he had not realised she was even in the room.

Rose looked down at her magazine longingly, not wanting to get into another conversation involving conspiracy theories relating to his heart operation; couldn't he just let it go already? It was true that over the last couple of months things had improved, but he was prone to lapse into old habits and frankly she was growing weary of the whole thing. He had been through a terrible ordeal, but he had survived, couldn't he just embrace his new life and forget about the past?

"You were wondering who someone was." She said, hating the sound of the words even as they fell from her mouth.

"Did I?" He asked, looking genuinely confused. "I didn't realise I'd spoken out loud."

"Ok, no harm done then." Rose replied, and stretched out her hand to her magazine.

"It's just I've been thinking," Martin continued, forcing his wife's hand to retreat back to her lap. "I wonder who they were?"

"Who *who* was?" Rose asked, feeling her anger rising but keeping it in check.

"The person you know, the heart." He said, gesturing to his chest.

"Does it matter?"

"I guess not, it's just, wouldn't you like to know, if it was you?"

"No Martin, I wouldn't. If it was me I'd want to let sleeping dogs lie."

"It's just that someone somewhere knows who saved me, I think I'd like to know a little bit more about the person who saved my life is all."

"They didn't save your life Martin; David Purefoy saved your life. They were just an unfortunate soul who was probably involved in an accident and was thoughtful enough to carry a donor card around in their wallet. Can't you just let this go?"

Martin sighed and sat back in his seat. "I just feel I need to show my appreciation or something."

"You can't show your appreciation to the dead Martin."

"Oh I know, but to their family, I mean I don't even know their name and somewhere there's probably a grieving family who misses them and may appreciate to know that their loss wasn't in vain. Maybe I could help them somehow, we're wealthy enough."

"I think the last thing a grieving family needs is some old rich guy from the city waving his wallet around and reminding them of their loss. Let this go Martin, trust me, no good can come of this."

Sighing for the second time Martin nodded his head slowly. "Maybe you're right."

Rose started to relax. It was short lived.

"But what if you're not."

"That's it." She said, getting to her feet. "I've had it with this; I can't take it any more."

Martin looked at her in stunned silence, shocked at her sudden outburst.

"You went through a terrible ordeal, I should know, I went through it with you, but you survived, you survived and you have a new life with a healthy heart. So what is it with this constant need to dwell on the past? You've been given a gift Martin, the greatest gift of all, the gift of life, yet you're wasting your time worrying about things that don't even need your concern."

"That's hardly fair." Martin protested.

"Isn't it? I thought things were getting better, you certainly seemed brighter. Now this, you may as well go back to square one."

"I only asked…"

"Oh I know what you asked Martin and I'm sure in your world it's ok to keep dragging up the ghosts of the past, but what about the people you could hurt along the way? What about the grieving family? What about me Martin? Huh? Did you ever consider how this could affect me?"

"I don't understand…"

"You wouldn't, that's because you live in your own little bubble, Martin Rooley land, where everything's a conspiracy and nothing can be left to chance. You have to know everything about everything, every last detail down to the who's and the what's and the how's and the why's. You can't just let things be, you can't just think hey I had a lucky escape there, gonna thank my lucky stars and go on with my life! You have to meddle, well you do that! But don't get me involved, you do what you like; you usually do anyway, but keep me out of it, cos I'm tired of this Martin ok? I'm tired of all the questioning and the conspiracies and frankly the lack of gratitude, and I'm not going to listen to it anymore, you hear me? I'm through! You go on if you like but keep me out of it."

Martin looked up at her absolutely dumbstruck, what had started as a simple enough conversation had left his wife red in the face and breathing heavily, her chest rising and falling under her thin blouse, and what's more it was the speed in which her demeanour had altered, it was as though he had flicked a switch inside of her that turned her from a placid loving housewife into a furious vengeful harpy.

"Rose…" He started, but cut himself short when he saw the look on her face, a look that could have curdled milk or melted butter. She stared at him for a couple more seconds, then turned and left the room, her magazine and the article on Will and Kate temporarily forgotten.

Martin stared after her, wondering what he had done to make her so unbelievably angry. He was a little shaken and quite upset, so he sat in his seat, listening to the padding as she made her way upstairs and the soft creak as she lay down on the bed. Martin went back to staring out at the forecourt, wasting his time and brooding on the past.

14

Rose hadn't wanted to be involved, but that didn't mean that he couldn't pursue his interest without involving her, especially if she didn't know there was in fact anything with which she could be involved. Despite Rose's anger and obvious disapproval Martin still believed it was important to learn a little more about the person whose heart was now pumping away in his chest, he would just have to be careful about how he went about his business. He rarely told his wife all of the details of his working day, so this would be just one more detail that remained unspoken.

Sat in his office looking out at his favourite view Martin mulled over his options; he couldn't contact Purefoy, he had done that before and it had gotten him nowhere, nor did he want to contact the hospital, the surgeon only ever called to reprimand him for contacting there. This left only one real option; he would have to do some digging himself. With the mornings papers scattered on the desk in front of him Martin leant forward and hit the button on his intercom.

"Yes Martin, how can I help?" Sheila asked, sounding alert and efficient as always.

"Can you track down Peter, ask him to come to my office at his earliest convenience?"

"He's in with marketing at the moment but the meetings due to end in twenty minutes; I can get him then, unless it's urgent of course."

"No, no, not urgent, twenty minutes is fine. Thank you Sheila."

"No problem."

The comms unit went quiet and Martin sat back in his seat, knowing that he really needed to focus on his work but finding more and more these days that distractions had an unhealthy habit of disrupting his day.

The twenty minutes passed quite quickly, by using the time to read the financial pages of the Guardian Martin was even able to convince himself he had been using the time productively, not including the five minutes he had enjoyed reading the cartoons in the Sun and the Mirror, well everybody deserved a break didn't they? At a quarter after twelve, as Martin's stomach started to grumble in preparation for lunch, there was a tap at his door and Peter Werth-Duncan strolled in. He was immaculately dressed in a dark grey Savile Row suit and what little hair he had left had been slicked down flat to his skull with Brylcreem. He smiled as he entered and nodded his greeting as he strolled across the carpet and plonked down in the soft cushioned chair opposite his employer.

"Summoned to the masters office, am I about to receive my first reprimand?" Martins friend asked with a twinkle in his eye.

"I don't think I'd dare." Martin replied, a small smile on his lips. "I'm just as scared of you as everybody else here."

Peter chuckled. "So what can I really do for you? It can't be advice on your golf swing; we both know you get plenty of practice at that."

"Actually I haven't been on the green all that much since the operation, but that's something I plan on rectifying, though you're right in thinking I didn't call you in here for work purposes."

"Oh, you taking me for lunch to Peppermint Tiger? Thanking me for the wonderful job I'm doing with a strip tease or two?"

Martin laughed, his head back against his head rest and his eyes squeezed shut tight; Peter always had this effect on him, sometimes he called him t o his office just to brighten his day.

"You wish, no this is a little different to that, I need your help."

"I'm listening."

"I want to meet the donor's family, but I don't know where to start in trying to find them."

Peter was silent for a while, he regarded Martin curiously. "Why would you want to do that?" He asked eventually.

"To pay my respects. I got to live at the expense of another human being. I feel I owe it to their family to show them that something positive came of their loss, to help them if I can, or if not just to have a chance to say thank you."

Peter sighed and rubbed at his eyes. "Are you sure that's really what you want? Do you think it's wise to dig up the past?"

"You sound just like Rose!" Martin said, feeling a little put out.

"Well maybe she's got a point."

"Maybe so, but I still intend to do this, so are you going to help me or not?"

"Ok." Peter replied with a sigh. "I'll make some calls."

"What about your friend, the private investigator?"

"Who Bill? Is that necessary? I was just going to call the hospital."

"It's not that simple. My surgeon, he's been avoiding me, and he gets antsy if I go behind his back."

"Ok, why has your surgeon been avoiding you?"

"I have no idea, but it's not my imagination, he has been avoiding me."

"You do know you sound like one of those crackpot conspiracy theorists right now don't you."

"And again he does an uncanny impression of Rose Rooley, get this man on Opportunity Knocks."

"You're behind the times old man, it's Britain's Got Talent these days."

"Oh, I thought you didn't watch television."

"I don't, but I make it my business to keep up with current affairs, I'm still holding out the slender hope that there may be a future Mrs Werth-Duncan somewhere out there."

"If there is you'd be apt to start your search at Battersea dogs home."

"Touché. Ok so the hospital's out of the question, maybe Bill could be of help, I'll give him a call, see if he can put the feelers out."

"Thanks, I'd appreciate it."

"No problem." Peter said, getting up from his seat. "Is that all you wanted me for? You don't want to know maybe how your business is performing? Anything like that."

"Why have a dog and bark yourself, besides, I really do have to work on that golf swing."

"You're right you do, well don't work too hard." Peter said as he head back to the door.

"Oh Peter." Martin said, stopping the man before he could leave. "I'd appreciate your discretion on this."

Peter nodded. "I'll be in touch when I have some information."

Martin nodded and watched as the door closed behind his friend.

He really did have to do some work now.

15

When Martin arrived home that night he was greeted by the wonderful aroma of roast beef and onions; Rose was in the kitchen, but when she heard him arrive she came to greet him at the door. She smiled warmly, took his briefcase and his jacket and led him to the living room.

"Hi." He said, wondering what was going on.

She sat him down in his favourite chair, then knelt down and slipped off his shoes without saying a word, then she fetched his slippers and slipped those on in return.

"Dinner will be ready in about ten minutes, roast beef, Yorkshire pudding, all the trimmings, in the meantime you can enjoy this, and this." She handed him the remote control for the huge wall mounted plasma screen, then poured him a large single malt whiskey.

"What's this?" He asked as he placed the whiskey down on the coaster at his side.

"An apology." She replied.

"What for?"

"For being a bitch." She replied, and instantly started to blush; Rose Rooley had been brought up to believe it was unladylike to use coarse language.

"I don't understand." He replied, though really he thought he did.

"I shouldn't have gone off on you like that on Saturday, it was wrong. Then I spent all yesterday brooding. It was very childish of me."

Martin leant forward in his chair and took his wife's hands in both of his. "I'm sorry too, all of this dwelling on the operation when I should be focusing on the future. I must have driven you quite barmy for you to blow off the way you did."

"You did yes." Rose said with a soft smile.

"Well I'm sorry, my promise to you is that I'll try harder, focus more on the positives instead of dwelling on the negatives. So what if David Purefoy's been a little negligent in his after care duties, he did save my life, and I really do feel fit as a fiddle. Things are going to change, I promise."

Rose smiled again. "Then I guess we're still friends."

"Always." He replied, returning the smile.

"I'll go finish up, come through in ten minutes."

"I'm looking forward to it." He said, and turned on the television.

16

Two days later Martin was sat in his office reading a report from HR on current absence percentages when Peter Werth-Duncan entered. He sidled up to Martin's desk with a smug smile on his face and placed a brown envelope down in front of his employer.

"What's this?" Martin asked, picking up the envelope.

"Open it." Peter replied, taking the seat opposite Martin.

Martin did as he was bid and thumbed open the envelope, he shook out the contents and what landed on his desk was a colour photograph. In it a young man, probably around his mid twenties smiled towards the camera, he was sat on a wall in front of a scenic coastline and was wearing a pair of khaki shorts and a T-shirt that read 'Boob inspector, first lesson free'. He was a handsome man with brown tousled hair and eyes that seemed to sparkle.

Martin looked at the young man and a lump formed in his throat. He didn't need to ask the question to know who it was he was looking at, but he asked it all the same.

"Who's this?"

"That is your donor, the man whose heart is now your heart."

"How did you get this?"

"I used Bill, he used his contacts. Easy."

Martin swallowed hard, his eyes not leaving the picture. He could feel tears pricking at the corners of his eyes and fought to keep them back. It was one thing sitting in your office as the king of the world, asking for information in a frivolous blasé way; but when faced with the harsh reality of those actions he was forced to acknowledge the real world and real lives that had been affected inside his own story. Here was a man, fresh, in the prime of life, so much ahead of him; marriage, possibly children, yet he was dead, and a much older man continued to live because of his untimely demise.

He felt like a leech, like blood sucking vermin that had preyed on someone far younger than him, someone far more vulnerable, somebody with their whole life ahead of them. It was wrong; it wasn't fair, and suddenly Martin was exposed to just how harsh a reality this really was, where a young man had died so that an old man could live.

The bile rose in his stomach, he was sure he was going to vomit, but somehow he kept it back.

"Are you ok?" Peter asked with real concern. "You've gone pale."

"Who was he?" Martin asked, ignoring the question to ask one of his own.

"His name was Edward Williams, Eddie to his friends, and he died in a motorcycle accident in Surrey, a little before you got the call from your surgeon friend, Purefob was it?"

"Purefoy, David Purefoy." Martin muttered, unable to take his eyes from the photo.

"Martin are you sure you're ok? You want me to call someone?"

"I'm fine I'm fine." Martin said, waving away the remark but rubbing at his forehead, his eyes screwed tight.

"You don't look fine."

"Really, I'm fine, go on."

Peter paused for a moment, making sure his friend really was fine, he wasn't convinced but he continued anyway, he and Martin may have been pally but the old guy also paid his wages after all.

"If you turn the photo over."

Again Martin did as he was bid and turned the photograph over onto its back, he was relieved, he didn't think he could continue looking into those still sparkling eyes without reeling from the nausea that was burning him inside; he didn't think he had ever felt so utterly guilty about anything in his life.

On the back of the photograph, written in black ink, was a ladies name, address and telephone number. The woman's name was Linda McGready, the number had the prefix 0207 and the address was just off Tottenham High Road.

"She's the mother of the deceased, that's her address and telephone number, in case you were still you know, wanting to go through with this."

"Why, do you think I shouldn't?" Martin asked, and he was aware what he was implying with the question, he actually hoped, was in fact pleading for his friend to talk him out of this. Now that this had become very real his desire to meet the family of his donor seemed whimsical and foolhardy, no wonder Rose had given him such a hard time.

But his friend did not commit to an answer. "I think that's a decision only you can make."

Martin nodded slowly.

"If you don't mind me saying," Peter said, the concern still very present, "you look terrible, should I have not done this?"

"No, no you did well, as always Peter you did well." Martin said, but he knew how drawn and pale he must look, for he felt it himself.

"Yeah well you look like you've seen a ghost."

"I don't suppose that's too far from the truth when you think about it." Martin conceded.

"No, I guess not, still I don't like how pale you've gone, let me call a doctor."

"I'm perfectly capable of calling a doctor for myself should I require one." Martin said, more testily than he intended. "Your concern is appreciated, but really, there's no need to wrap me in cotton wool, I'm fine. It's just, you know, seeing him, seeing the man, it was harder than I expected it would be."

"He didn't sacrifice himself for you Martin, it's important you remember that. He was just a poor unfortunate man who was involved in a terrible accident. It could so easily have been the other way around."

"Maybe it should have been."

"Nah, I don't think it would be fair to subject anyone to your dodgy old ticker."

Martin finally smiled. "No I guess not."

"You want my advice?"

"Always."

"If something feels uncomfortable it's usually for a reason, maybe this thing is better left alone."

"Maybe." Martin said, nodding his head slightly. "Maybe you're right."

Peter sighed. "Well don't let it keep you awake at night anyway, make your decision as soon as you can and stick by it, something like this, it's apt to drive you crazy if you think about it too long."

"That's good advice."

"I'd better go, I want to look at the revised eastern European proposals before I go home, you haven't forgotten I have my appointment this evening."

"I don't pay you good money to be forever taking leave." Martin said with a smirk.

"That's rich coming from the golf course kid."

"Take the time, heaven knows you've earned it, I may pop by before you go to run my eye over the report myself."

"You're considering actually working? Things are worse than I thought." Peter stood up and head to the door. Martin grabbed the photo from the desk, looking at the name and number on the back.

"Peter." He called out before his friend could leave.

The tall thin man stopped at the door.

"Thanks." Martin said earnestly.

"You're welcome." Peter replied, then slowly, he left.

Martin listened to the soft thud as the door closed behind his friend and chief confident. He looked down at the back of the photograph once more and the details that had been jotted there in Peter's investigator friend's neat hand. Then he turned the photo over and looked into those dazzling blue eyes.

"Eddie Williams." Martin muttered. His eyes were filling again with hot tears, so he quickly opened his desk drawer and slipped the photo inside, closing it so it was out of sight. His whole body was shaking and he felt nauseous and faint. He pushed his chair back, wanting to be as far from the offending photo as possible, and stood up. Slowly he walked over to the window, where he leant against the glass and looked out at the sprawling metropolis of London. He looked at the view but his thoughts were elsewhere, they were a jumble of untidy feelings, of motorbikes and hearts and grieving mothers, of old men that had been given a second chance and young men who had not.

Martin looked out of the window and wept, wondering if it would have been best if that first attack had finished the job.

17

The taxi pulled up to the kerb, Martin paid the driver and opened the door, stepping out into the brisk silence of a chilly October night. He pulled the collar of his coat tight to protect against the sudden drop in temperature and looked down at the scribbled address on the folded piece of paper. He looked around as the taxi pulled back away from the kerb and did a slow U-turn, ready to head back the way it had come. Martin pursed his lips, wanting to call it back, wanting to drive back to a nicer suburb of London and spend the evening next to a roaring open fire with his wife, watching television and eating Mr Kipling's baked fancies. He sighed, turned as the taxi disappeared out of sight and looked up at the dark row of terrace houses that lined the street, the bunch of flowers from the florist in the village tucked under his arm.

It had taken him several days to find the courage to dial the number on the back of the photo that Peter had given him; and then it had been several dialling attempts before he had plucked up the courage to actually talk to the person on the other end of the line. The first time he had found the courage the phone line had just rang and rang, the next time the line was answered by the soft voice of a woman, but the moment was gone and he ended the call without speaking, sending him back to square one. Finally, realising how ridiculous he was being, Martin called for a third time and spoke to Linda McGready, though he wasn't entirely honest regarding his intentions. Finding the situation all too emotional to address over the phone Martin had kept his intentions purposefully vague, asking the lady if he could talk to her regarding her late son. The woman had asked him what exactly it was that he wanted, but Martin had stood firm, asking for a little of the ladies time so he could fully explain. The woman had reluctantly agreed, and Martin had placed the phone back in its cradle with a hand that shook like a victim of Parkinson's disease.

Things had been better at home this last week after the initial storm, and rather than re-lighting the blue touch paper he had decided that dishonesty was the best solution. This however brought its own headaches, as in all their years of marriage Martin couldn't remember having ever purposefully lied to Rose, and it made him feel dirty and cheap. Still it was a necessary evil, and he had made the trip across London from the office, telling his wife he would be working late this evening. She had chastised him for working after hours, reminding him of his promise to take better care of himself, and Martin had taken the lecture on the chin, as his stomach softly turned at his deceit.

Now he stood on this quiet Tottenham street, looking up at the dark bricked building and feeling a little lost and very alone. He was just a stones throw from the lively main road that cut through the suburb, where youths hung outside fried chicken shops and late night hair stylists performed intricate weaves on girls who seemed to screech their every response. This was a part of town that Martin had little knowledge of, he was aware of the riots that had started here a few years earlier and had attended corporate events at the football ground once or twice but really Tottenham to Martin was as alien as Venus or Mars.

He sighed, looked down at his shoes, wishing he was wearing something a little less formal, then crept up to the path, divided by a pair of balding hedgerows, and slowly made his way up to the door. He checked the paperwork again, flat 2B, then stretched out his gloved finger and pressed the doorbell. There was a window to the left hand side of the door and a small pane of glass above, it was this that illuminated first as the light was turned on from within. Martin looked up, seeing the soft glow but not feeling its comfort, the first thing he had noticed was that there was no lamp shade, the bulb hung limply from its cord, straight from the ceiling.

What had he let himself in for? Why was he even here? Had he considered even for a second the implications of his actions? He was fighting the urge to scurry back down the path and disappear into the hustle and bustle of Tottenham High Road when a soft voice spoke from the other side of the door.

"Just a minute."

Martin's breath caught in his throat. He could hear a key turning in the lock, then the handle was dropping down and the door slowly opening.

The woman who opened the door to flat 2B looked tired and old, though Martin guessed her to be somewhere in her late forties. She had blonde hair that was coming through black at the roots and deep lines under her eyes. There was a small pink birth mark in the shape of a star, just below her hair line. She was skinny, she must have weighed no more than 130 pounds, and her jeans hung loosely about her hips. She was wearing a red blouse that was a good fit for her frame and when she poked her head around the door she looked anxious, on guard almost, Martin supposed that was natural enough in a neighbourhood like this.

"Yes." She said, using the word as a question.

"Oh hello, I'm Martin Rooley, we spoke on the phone."

"Oh of course." She said, putting a hand to her forehead in the age old gesture of forgetfulness. "Please come in."

She opened the door wide in its frame and Martin stepped into the narrow hallway. The flat was on two levels, with a staircase leading up to the floor above and the kitchen at the end of the hall. There was a small living area through a door to the right and it was here that Linda directed him. Martin walked through the door, noticing as he did the wallpaper that hung loose at the side. Dressed in one of his finest suits the gap between him and the middle aged woman was becoming increasingly evident.

He was led into the living room where he stood on the thin carpet in the centre of the room.

"Please, sit down." She said, gesturing to a battered leather couch that had seen better days.

"Thank you, oh…" Martin said, holding out the flowers.

"For me?" Linda enquired, looking genuinely surprised.

"Yes." Martin said, feeling flustered.

She took them from him and looked at the bouquet, allowing the aroma to fill her nostrils, she looked genuinely touched and this eased some of Martin's initial embarrassment.

"It's been a long time since anybody bought me flowers."

Martin smiled and sat down on the soft cushion of the sofa, feeling the air in the seat deflate beneath his weight. He took a look about the room, it was sparsely decorated, there was an old box television in one corner and aging floral paper on the walls, a wooden cuckoo clock was above the television, though it looked like it had stopped some time ago. No photographs or pictures adorned the walls, in fact for a woman who had recently lost a loved one there was no sign of a family here at all.

Linda sat down in the equally battered easy chair adjacent to the sofa and placed the bouquet down on the floor to the side. She clasped her hands in her lap and sat to the front of the chair, a gesture which told Martin that she was not yet comfortable in his presence.

"So, Mister…"

"Rooley, Martin Rooley."

"Right, right, Mister Rooley."

"Oh Martin please."

"Martin, right. And I'm Linda. What is this about Martin? I know on the phone you mentioned Eddie, I hope it's not more bad news."

"Oh no, no nothing like that." Martin said, feeling a connection with this woman who had suffered such a terrible tragedy in her life, or was it simply pity? He didn't know, but what he did know was that he wanted to help her in some way, if he could. She clearly didn't have two pennies to rub together, he wouldn't be able to offer charity, that would be insulting, but maybe there was some way he could help.

"What is it then?" She asked, still looking troubled.

"Mrs McGready, err Linda, sorry is it miss or Mrs?"

"It's Miss, but like I say, really it's just plain old Linda."

"Linda, is this your son?" Martin pulled the photo from his inside pocket and held it out to the middle aged woman, as she reached out to take receipt of it Martin noticed something that made his breath suddenly catch in his throat, but he battled hard not to let it show. On the inside of the ladies arm, needle marks dotted the area where the upper and forearm meet, the area looked purple and bruised, and there were specks of dried blood about the more prominent veins.

She took the photo and looked down at the young man in the 'Boob inspector, first lesson free' T-shirt, a small smile tracing the corners of her thin lips.

"That's my boy." She said softly. "That's my Eddie."

"The surname." Martin implied questioningly, finding his eyes drawn to that small star shaped birth mark in her hair line, it really was unusual.

"Eddie's father and I weren't married, he got his daddy's name, that's all he did get though, that bastard fled a couple of months after Eddie was born, haven't heard from him since."

"I'm sorry."

"What are you sorry for? It wasn't you who ran away."

They were quiet for a while; Linda looked at the photograph for a few moments then handed it back to Martin.

"Linda, I haven't been entirely honest with regards to my reason for calling on you today."

"Oh?" The woman said, looking ill at ease.

"Please, don't worry, I mean you no harm, quite the opposite actually. Were you aware that your son carried a donor card?"

"I was aware, some of his organs were donated after he died, at least something good came out of the whole mess."

"That's just the thing; I was one of the lucky beneficiaries of his tragic death."

"I don't understand."

"You see, at the back end of last year I was diagnosed with an incurable heart condition, I needed a donor or I was going to die."

"Oh my God." The thin woman said, her hands covering her mouth, finally understanding why this man had come into her life.

"Yes, yes, Eddie's heart saved my life. Because of your son, I'm still alive today."

"Oh wow." Linda said, sitting back in her seat for the first time, she had a look of shock on her face but Martin didn't think it was an entirely unpleasant one. After a while she sat forward again, looking now towards Martin's chest. "So you're telling me that in there…."

"Is Eddie's heart," Martin finished for her, "a part of your son still lives on inside of me."

"Wow." She was silent again for a moment. "This is just so much to take."

"I know, I'm sorry, and I'm sorry that I didn't make it clear on the phone why I wanted to see you, but I was afraid you'd refuse to meet me, and I so wanted to meet you."

"Why?" She said earnestly.

"To say thank you, to let you know what a wonderful, selfless person your son was, and to let you know that his terrible loss helped save the life of at least one other person. I guess I hoped that knowing that may somehow ease your suffering, even if only a little bit."

The words felt lame as they tumbled from Martin's mouth, how could it possibly ease her suffering to know that the tragic loss of a young man had helped preserve the life of the old fossil that was sat on her couch, sat there in his expensive suit and designer after shave while she clearly lived a very humble existence. But Linda surprised him, her mouth lifted into a smile again and it made her look younger, beautiful almost, and Martin could see in that smile the woman she could have been if life hadn't dealt her the hand it had.

"Thank you." She whispered, nodding her head slightly.

"No thank you, your son saved my life, I'm indebted to your family."

"Oh please, you owe nothing to me, I don't even carry a donor card myself, Eddie was a free spirit, I wish you could have met him but I guess that could never have worked."

"I guess not, only the circumstances as they are could have drawn us together."

"Hmm." Linda said, looking deep in thought but more at ease than she had before. Suddenly she snapped back into the here and now. "I'm so sorry, I'm forgetting my manners, would you like a drink of anything? Tea, coffee, something stronger?"

"Oh there's no need to trouble yourself."

"I'm having one."

"Ok then, a tea would be lovely, thank you."

Linda stood. "The kettle's upstairs, I use it for my hot water bottle, it gets so cold in these draughty old houses at this time of year, I'll go get it."

"Thank you." Martin said, watching as she left the room. He could hear the stairs creak as she climbed them and sat patiently on the couch; he looked across at the thin film of dust on top of the television and the curtains that barely fit the frame of the window. Then his eyes happened on the flowers lying on the carpet. He stood up form the couch and picked them up.

"I'll put these in some water." He called out, but there was no reply.

He padded from the living room down the hall to the kitchen. It was a relatively small room with old fashioned brown wooden units, it looked unlived in and cold. Where might she keep her vases? He surmised the wall mounted units might be the most obvious place and wandered across, but when he opened the first cupboard he was surprised to find it empty. He opened the second cupboard and then the third, these were empty too.

Martin's brow furrowed in confusion, he bent over and opened the base units, these were also empty. He had sensed the woman was short of money but to have no possessions at all, it just didn't make sense. With a slightly trembling hand he stretched out and pulled open the cutlery drawer; empty.

"What the Hell." He muttered, suddenly feeling afraid. What was going on?

"Is everything ok?"

The voice startled Martin and he spun around, feeling his new heart leap in his still healing chest. Linda was stood in the doorway, her own eyes wide with fear.

"I was err, I was, I just..." Martin stuttered.

"You were what?" Linda asked, crossing her arms across her almost non-existent chest.

"I was err, I was looking for a vase." He managed, though his heart was beating way too fast and he felt very hot under all his many layers.

"Oh I don't have one, I'll borrow one." She said with a strained smile.

"Yes ok, very good." Martin could feel the colour burning in his cheeks, he felt as though he had been caught doing something he shouldn't, why was that? Then he noticed that Linda's hands were empty, he used it as a way to change the subject. "You didn't find the kettle."

The skinny woman looked down at her hands, as if realising for the first time that she had gone upstairs to perform a task.

"Oh, it was in here all along." She gestured to a spot behind where Martin was standing, feeling foolish with the bunch of flowers. He turned around and sure enough there was the kettle, an old white plastic Morphy Richards on the kitchen worktop. It was the only thing that was there though; no microwave, no toaster, there wasn't even a bread bin.

"Oh, ok." He replied weakly.

"I'll err, I'll make that drink." Linda said, she walked past Martin towards the kettle still looking uncomfortable.

Suddenly, sitting in this house passing small talk with this woman and sipping tea in her sparse living room was the last thing that Martin wanted, in fact the very thought of being in this house a moment longer than was absolutely necessary made him feel light headed and weak.

"Oh that's ok, I really should be going."

"Already?" She replied, turning towards him from the kitchen unit, but what was that on her face, was that relief?

"Yes, yes it's been a long day, an emotional day, but it was lovely to have met you, I really just wanted to meet you, to pass on my heart felt condolences and to say how indebted I am to your family for the great gift your son has given me. I don't want to take up any more of your time." The words felt dirty and cheap coming out of Martin's mouth, why was he being this way? So she didn't have many possessions, was he really this judgmental?

That wasn't it though, something about this just didn't feel right, it didn't fit, and it was this that was making him feel like he was trespassing, that he shouldn't be here.

"Ok, I'll show you out." Linda was saying, but Martin didn't hear the words, he was too busy thinking about the empty kitchen units.

He padded down the hall and stopped at the front door, looking for a second up to the light bulb that hung loosely from its fitting in the ceiling. There was a small spider's web that clung to the wire casing; it stretched up to the corner of the hall.

"It really was lovely to meet you." Martin lied as he grabbed the handle.

"You too." Linda smiled, and for a moment Martin felt really foolish, as though he had made a poor judgment call from which it would be hard to recover. He paused for a moment, thinking what to say, but when no words came he stepped back out into the crisp night air and then turned slowly.

"Thank you again for the flowers." She said in that soft sweet voice of hers. "They really are lovely."

"You're welcome." Martin replied, feeling even more so that he had read too deep into the situation. Then the door was closing, and the moment was gone.

"Goodbye." Martin muttered, looking at the closed front door of the old terraced house. He turned and wandered back down the front path to the roadside. A gang of youths were heading his way from the far end of the street; Martin walked the opposite way and found himself back on Tottenham High Road. He noticed an off license and stood in the soft glow of its light while he gathered his thoughts. His heart was still beating, too fast and too hard and as he stood there in the cold Autumnal air he wondered how something so small could cause so much distress.

PART THREE:
PRIVATE INVESTIGATIONS

1

Like so many major European cities if you sat still for too long in London you got left behind. Bigger, taller, faster, smarter, you could visit year on year and still become lost in the ever expanding landscape. Buildings grew from the foundations up like hands stretching out of the ground, trying to wave on the clouds, transport links changed, updated, altered, upgraded until the route you had always taken becomes obsolete, you could walk into your local coffee house every day in a working week and be served each day by a different person, with a different accent from a different country to the last. It is a cosmopolitan city, a city that embraces change with the expectancy of a casual lover, a city that thrives on the diverse and the individual.

In London you can wear black eye make-up and ill matching clothes and nobody will bat an eyelid. In London you can prop up the bar of a different boozer every day of the calendar year without ever visiting the same watering hole twice. In London you can watch a Politician stand outside the House of Common's and give a speech about family values and morality in the afternoon and watch the same man slip into a private booth with an exotic dancer in Spearmint Rhino at night. In London you can be completely inconspicuous, or the centre of all attention. In London, anything goes.

This is the typical, big city ethos that attracts people of all walks of life to the capital; people looking for a break, people looking for a change, people wanting to find a new identity, people wanting to grow their opportunities, people wanting to escape.

Martin Rooley had come to London because it was the natural progression for his growing business to move to the business capital of the country. It had been hard for him to leave Bolton; Lancashire was his home, but he had understood that if he was serious about Sapient expanding then he couldn't rest on his laurels, relocating to the capital was the logical choice. It had been hard at first, the fast paced lifestyle just didn't suit his northern working class roots; but you could get used to anything in time, later still he had grown to love it; after all if you wanted to take in a show you had your pick of the bunch in the capital, same for if you wanted to visit a museum or dine at a world class restaurant. London had it all, and in time, though he still loved his birth town, London became his home.

Now, sat in his office, looking out once more at Canary Wharf, Martin felt a pang of homesickness the like of which he had not experienced in twenty years. Something wasn't right in his life, and he associated it with here, this city, this capital. For all the good that you could find in London it was easy too to seek out the bad, though it was harder for someone in a lofty position such as he, but that was because he didn't have a need to see the bad. London had provided him with a nine figure bank account, a huge house in the suburbs, a fleet of cars and no financial worries for the rest of his life. It had been good to him, and if he wanted he could turn a blind eye to the plight of the less fortunate. Martin felt he had done a pretty good job of this over the years, yes personally and also within business he made sizeable donations to both national and local charities, and Sapient also provided a community awareness project where staff could become involved in supporting local institutions and organisations such as soup kitchens and inner city housing projects. But these were simply great tools to help a man of his wealth sleep at night; he knew he could do more, and he knew that when he was spending four hundred pounds on a meal in Knightsbridge there were people in Peckham and Brixton and Tottenham that were surviving on less than a pound a day.

Visiting Linda had opened his eyes to the real world, he had seen how the other half lived and it had left him feeling uncomfortable and neglectful. He was a good man, he knew he was, but he also knew there was more he could do to help those that really needed his support, the lonely, the vulnerable, the sick, the poor, a company the size of Sapient had expectations to support its local community and it obliged willingly, but Martin had to wonder how much of this was to do with the greater good and how much was to do with meeting its corporate obligations.

He felt disappointed in himself and ashamed of his approach. How could he sit in his own living room with its picture window and plasma television and huge open fireplace when he had seen Linda's sparse home, with the wall paper hanging from the walls and the light bulbs that weren't even covered with a shade. Maybe he'd been in the big city too long; he certainly felt as though he'd forgotten his roots, and it was this that made him long for home, his real home where your neighbours had names and wherever you lived in the city you were still only ten minutes drive from the centre of town.

He had visited Linda to help in some way if he could, and he had left having done little more than dredge up the not so distant past and cause upset for both him and the poor unfortunate mother. What's more the way he had left had been inconsiderate at best, downright rude at worst. What had he been doing going through her kitchen cupboards anyway? It wasn't his place. So what if she had little possessions, did it make her a bad person?

But no possessions? Come on the cupboards were empty! The voice of disquiet argued again.

Martin shuffled uncomfortably in his seat.

And the vase Martin, what about that?

"What about it?" He muttered, staring out at Canary Wharf but not really seeing anything.

Come on, who doesn't own a vase?

That wasn't so strange was it? She clearly didn't have any money, why would it be strange that she didn't own a vase?

She said she had been a long time since anybody had bought her flowers.

"So what?"

Err hello, her son died; surely someone must have bought her flowers? A neighbour? A friend? A family member, a sister maybe or a distant cousin?

"Shut up." Martin whispered, not liking the sound of his own subconscious, not liking how much sense it spoke. He didn't want to think ill of the woman who had birthed his saviour, but it was true that something wasn't right; the pieces just weren't fitting together.

So what do you do now? He asked himself as he continued to stare with unseeing eyes. Go back? Harass the poor woman some more? Let it go? Forget the whole sorry affair and get on with your life? He knew that this was the sensible choice, continuing down the path he was currently on was bringing nothing but hardship, confusion and pain; the problem was he just wasn't sure that he could do that. He needed answers, and he needed to help, seeing the poor woman's humble home had cemented that into place if nothing else.

Martin sighed and leant over, placing his head down on the hard wood surface of his desk. Why couldn't he just let this go? Rose was right; he really was like a dog with a bone. He closed his eyes and nursed his wrinkled forehead with his hand; he could feel a headache coming on.

2

Two hours later and Martin's DB5, which he had fallen in love with all over again after seeing the latest Bond film, pulled up to the kerb outside the terraced house in a small back road in Tottenham. He killed the engine and sat for a while, trying to steady his nerve.

This time he hadn't called ahead, he had come here on impulse when leaving work and was a little hesitant with regards to the purpose of his visit and what should be his next move. He had many questions, but wasn't certain of the means to ask them. Feeling there was no alternative than to approach the situation head on and accept whatever may come Martin opened the car door and stepped out into the cold night air. Although the street was again deserted Martin was conscious of leaving such a valuable car in a rough neighbourhood and triggered the alarm and the locking mechanism before leaving.

He hadn't taken more than two steps before something struck him as odd; at the end of the path, where the hedgerows met the street, a 'To Let' sign was attached to the gatepost. So what? He told himself, these were flats, it could be any one of them that was up for rent, but a sinking feeling in his gut told him otherwise.

He stepped up to it and looked at the sign, 'Wright Brothers letting agency', and below it, attached to the sign, a smaller panel that displayed 'flat no. 2B'.

"What the hell?" He muttered, feeling vacant and confused. He stepped onto the short path that led up to the house and looked at the darkened windows where light had glowed on his last visit. Again he had that creeping sensation that something just wasn't right. Slowly he wandered up the garden path, wanting nothing more than to turn, get in his Aston Martin and get the hell out of Tottenham. But he held his nerve and walked up to the front door. He pressed the button for flat 2B, just as he had done two nights ago, and waited for any sign of life from inside. But none came, and after two minutes, several presses of the bell and nothing but silence and darkness from the other side of the door, Martin accepted that there was no-one home.

When he had been here before, the living room, which was to the right hand sider of the door had long draped curtains, worn with age and ill fitting for their surroundings hanging in the window; now he could see these were gone. Taking a look about him to make sure nobody was watching – the last thing he needed right now was to be branded a prowler by some nosey neighbour and spend the night in a cell – Martin decided to take a look inside. He placed his foot on the small jutted out wall to the side of the door and grabbed the window pane for support, then using his arms as leverage hoisted himself up so his face was level with the bottom of the glass.

Martin used one hand to steady himself and the other to shield his eyes from the glow of the street lamp, then leaning with his forehead pressed to the glass, he peered inside. He swallowed hard; it wasn't particularly easy to see very much of anything with the darkness of the room being matched by the darkness of the street outside, but by cupping his free hand around his eyes and using just enough glow from the lamp a couple of yards down the street he could make out enough. The room was empty. No big box television, no battered sofa or threadbare easy chair, the room had been sparse of furniture when he had visited on Tuesday, but it was completely empty now.

That uneasy feeling was rising again, starting in the pit of his stomach and working its way up his spinal cord, tingling every nerve end on its way to his brain, where it would undoubtedly cause another bastard of a headache. He stepped down from the wall and paused on the garden path to gather his thoughts.

What the hell had happened? Had she really moved out since he had visited just two nights ago? She certainly hadn't mentioned anything to him then, but then why would she? It's not as though she was obliged to let a complete stranger in on the various intricacies of her personal life. But it just seemed so odd; surely his visit hadn't prompted her swift departure? He didn't see why it would, but so much had seemed off since his procedure that nothing would surprise him any more.

Martin walked back down the path towards his car, but paused once more at the To Let sign. Beneath the company logo there was a contact number, Martin looked at the Rolex on his wrist; quarter past six, would they still be there? He doubted it, but grabbed his mobile from his pocket anyway. He dialled the number and waited as the line rung in his ear; he expected it to either kick in to an answer machine or for the line to simply ring and ring, and was surprised when after only two rings the call was answered by a woman with a hard cockney accent.

"Hello Wright Brothers property agents how can I help you?"

"Oh hello, I wasn't expecting anybody to be there."

"You were lucky, you just caught me, how can I help you sir?"

Martin paused, how could she help him? It wasn't like she would know why the tenant had suddenly vacated the premises, he carried on regardless.

"You have a property up for rent, flat 2B, Bill Nicholson way."

"Just give me a second while I bring up the details."

He could hear her tapping away at her computer, a few seconds later she was back on the line.

"Ah yes, two bedroom flat in Tottenham."

"That's the one."

"Yes this one's only been on the market a couple of weeks but we've already had a lot of interest, rentals always go quickly in this area, we have a couple who are wanting to sign this weekend but haven't confirmed yet so there's time to steal the property if you wish but you'll have to be quick."

Martin's breath was caught in his throat; surely she hadn't just said what he thought she had?

"Sorry did you just say...?"

"There's still time, but you'd need to come down to the office as soon as possible, I'm afraid I'm leaving now but..."

"No no no, not that, sorry, did you just say the flat has been to let for the last two weeks?"

"Give me a second. Yep, came available on the 9th, so just under two weeks actually."

Martin rubbed at his forehead with his free hand; he could definitely feel another migraine coming on. How could this be possible? How could the flat have been available to rent for the last two weeks when he had visited the current occupant there just two nights ago?

"Are you still there?" The lady asked on the other end of the line.

"Sorry yes." Martin replied, his eyes screwed tight. "I was just wondering, well I'm actually trying to get in touch with the previous occupant."

"The Polumbo's?"

"No, no not the Polumbo's, I don't know the Polumbo's."

"Then I'm afraid you've got your wires crossed, the Polumbo's rented the property from us via the landlord for the last three years, nice family, Italians, always paid on time."

"No, no!" Martin could feel himself becoming exasperated and tried to keep his cool, but it was hard when everything around him seemed so wrong and out of place. "Listen I don't know any Polumbo's, it was the woman I was looking for, Linda McGready."

"I'm sorry sir no-one of that name has rented this flat while I've worked here, and I've been with the company for four years now."

"But I visited her here just two nights ago!"

"I'm afraid you're mistaken, the flat has been empty for nearly two weeks. Are you sure you got the flat number right? I'm looking at flat 2B, Bill Nicholson way."

"Yes, yes, I'm stood outside right now!"

The line was quiet for a few seconds. When the lady returned she sounded cautious, sensing that Martin was losing his cool. "I'm sorry sir; I don't know what to tell you."

The businessman rubbed at his forehead, trying to think but not understanding anything. "That's ok." He said eventually. "I'm sorry to have troubled you."

"I'm sorry I couldn't be more help." The woman's tone softened now, mimicking Martin's behaviour.

"Thank you anyway." Martin replied, and closed the call, not wanting to continue the discussion any further. He placed the phone back in his pocket and looked back up the path to the darkened windows of the flat. Now he knew it for sure, it wasn't his imagination, something was very wrong here, and he had absolutely no idea where to turn next.

3

The following Saturday morning was cool and crisp, but dry with the occasional sunny spell, ideal conditions in fact for a visit to the golf course, at this time of year anyway. They were stood on the green of hole twelve; Bert Etherington the CEO of Tulip Farm cakes lining up his shot, while the rest of the guys continued to dig for the latest details in Sebastian's fling with the sexy inner city barmaid.

"I'm sure you're looking thinner." Davey said as he regarded his old friend, and Martin and Bill knew straight away where he was heading. "Must be all the sex."

Sebastian sighed and placed his nine iron back in his golf sack. "Won't you ever give it a rest?"

"Show me some topless photos and my lips are sealed forever."

"I never knew you cared." The handsome man shot back with a grin. "Look I'd love to take you up on any offer that kept that motorised gate you call a mouth closed Davey but sadly I must politely decline."

"Because you don't have any?" Davey asked.

"No, because the lady and I are no more."

All of the guys stared at their friend, Bert even paused mid swing, the silver haired man simply returned to rearranging his golf bag.

"You can't leave it at that!" Davey blurted out.

"What can I say? It ran its course. It was never a forever thing."

"Great, just great." Davey seemed more put out at the news than Sebastian.

"I'm sorry, I know you wanted all the details but now there really is nothing to tell. The truth is I need a little time back to myself, try to find out what it is I'm actually looking for."

"Great, so now we get to go back to talking about Bill's irregular bowel movements!" Davey cursed.

"Hey!" The big man whined, clearly hurt, Davey didn't seem to notice, he was busy wondering where he would fill the void in his own sexual fantasies now his lucky son-of-a-bitch of a friend had let him down.

Martin heard all of this but not directly; it was like background chatter, the kind of mutterings created by the extras in movies when the leading stars go to a restaurant or the park. He was in the moment but away from it at the same time; his thoughts batting back and forth like an over worked ball at a tennis match. Besides, his interest in Davey's constant badgering about Sebastian's love life had faded for him with the summer, and he was secretly pleased that they could move on now to something – *anything* else. Even Rose had lost interest, her bridge club buddies were currently fascinated by her friend Celia's new neighbour who came and went at unusual hours and always carried parcels wrapped in thick brown paper.

In truth these days it was hard for him to think about anything other than the circumstances surrounding his unorthodox heart operation. After a brief and enjoyable hiatus he had gone back to dwelling on the situation, though never in front of Rose, that would be a really quick and easy way to land him in hot water. But if he was sat at his desk, if he was taking a bath, if he was out buying supplies or even yes on the golf course with his friends, his mind kept wandering back to what had happened, cross examining the details and trying to make some sense out of it all.

The procedure itself had been strange enough; although not an expert in the practices of an operating theatre he had never heard of an operation performed in a patients home before, not unless it was an emergency situation and there was no time to get to the hospital. He supposed he should have questioned it more at the time, he had a little, but he had not satisfied his curiosity, he supposed he had just been relieved that he was getting a heart at all. Maybe he had questions that he needed answering now, but who was going to answer them? Not David Purefoy that was for sure, the surgeon wouldn't even take his calls. Why was that? And why had he received close to no after care at all when he had undergone major surgery? It just didn't make sense.

Now there was a new twist in the tale; Linda McGready. The mother of the deceased had been happy to meet him at her North London home; but the flat had shown no signs of a life she had led with the man whose heart had literally saved Martin's life. He was her son, even if their relationship had been strained it would be expected that there was at least one photograph of him, especially after the event of his death. But there had been nothing, in fact the flat had hardly looked lived in at all, especially when you considered the bare cupboards in the kitchen. Even the poorest of people from the humblest of backgrounds own some possessions, or so Martin believed anyway.

Then on his return, when he had needed to question her about all of the troubles on his mind he finds the flat empty, and what's more according to the letting agent the lease had never been in the name of Linda Mcgready, had in fact been assigned to the Polumbo family less than a fortnight preceding Martin's initial visit.

The last two nights he had lain awake, trying to find a reasonable explanation for all that had happened, but there was none. Something was badly amiss here, and he no longer knew who he could trust. He was even having his doubts about Peter, after all it was his private investigator that had provided him with the whereabouts of the family of the donor. He knew that this was ridiculous, but the situation was making him edgy and nervous.

If Linda Mcgready really was Eddie Williams' mother then why had she felt the need to create a false address? And if Linda McGready wasn't Eddie Williams mother then who was she? And what was her involvement in this strange and ever changing story? And there was something else as well. Purefoy had told him that his new heart was being flown in from Newcastle, yet when Peter had handed him the photo of Eddie Williams he had said the accident had occurred in Surrey; like everything else in this tale, to Martin it just didn't sit right.

The only appliance that Linda McGready had owned was a kettle, of course it was, she had needed this to offer him a drink, thus keeping up the appearance of a normal family existence, but he hadn't been expected to go into the kitchen, that was why the cupboards and drawers had been empty, because he wasn't supposed to see them. Then she had said she would fetch the kettle from upstairs, though it had been in the kitchen all the time, so why had she really gone upstairs? Simple, to make a call, whoever she was and whatever she was up to Martin was sure of one thing, she wasn't acting alone.

So the real question, the biggest humdinger of them all, was what the hell was he supposed to do now? Contact the police? And say what? He'd sound like a crackpot conspiracy theorist and be marched out of the station. Approach Purefoy? Possibly, though he was reluctant to make any kind of contact with the man at this stage, not without proof. Proof? Proof of what? He didn't even know what he was accusing the surgeon of! All of this was just a headache that he wished he could cure with ibuprofen or paracetamol. Maybe Rose was right, maybe he should just learn to let things go.

"Earth to Martin, come in Martin." It was Sebastian, and he was looking at Martin with amused bewilderment, they all were.

The businessman snapped from his thoughts and came quickly back into the here and now.

"Sorry." He said distractedly.

"It's your shot." Sebastian said, frowning slightly.

"Of course, sorry."

"You ok buddy? You were really gone there." Bill asked.

"I'm fine, I'm fine." Martin said, pulling his driver from his golf bag.

"Poor guy was probably wondering what he was going to masturbate about now we don't have your little filly in our lives." Davey said, this brought laughter which disguised Martin's embarrassment. Sebastian clapped him on the back as he lined up his swing. For now, thoughts of dead donors and mysterious middle aged women were temporarily withdrawn from his mind.

4

There were pasty crumbs all down his suit front, when Martin noticed them he brushed them down into the foot well of the Aston Martin, again he was reminded of the old adage – you could take the boy out of Bolton but you couldn't take the Bolton out of the boy. He tucked the Ginsters wrapper into the glove compartment and looked through the car windscreen at the row of shops that lined the short parade.

First in the row was a launderette, then a gold pawn shop, a hair salon that specialised in weaves, a café with the original name of 'Apocalypse Chow' and an Indian takeaway that had one window boarded up. Right in the centre of the row, between the hair salon and the café was Wright Brothers property agents. It had a green lettered sign with a white background and the display window housed several property cards. Martin switched off the engine and climbed out of the car, locking it behind him as he marched up to the front door.

Visiting such an establishment brought back all sorts of memories for Martin; sourcing his first flat at the tender age of nineteen back in Bolton, then three years later being able to walk into the same estate agents and place down a sizeable deposit on a two bedroomed semi detached, what would become his first family home with his new bride. The move to London and the agents who had come to them, showing brochures for properties for which his old chums back on the estate could only dream. The agents who had secured the first Sapient address in Chigwell and the agents who had signed the very lucrative deal some years back to bring them to Canary Wharf. Finally the agents who had secured the pay up front deal for the property he now shared with Rose; the one that had been home now for more than seventeen years.

He had come a long way since signing that first rental agreement; a boy with hardly any hairs on his chest, just starting out in the world with his wild ideas and ambitions, one eye always free for a slightly raised skirt or a full bosom. Who would have believed where life would have taken him? Certainly not he, and certainly not his working class parents, God rest their souls.

But all of this was just distractions; ways to fog up his thought process and throw him off track, a self defence mechanism that was kicking in to prevent him from continuing this foolish charade. If he walked through this door it was possible he would open other doors, metaphorical ones for which there was no return, was he really ready for that? He was sixty-eight for God's sake; who did he think he was? Jason Bourne? James Bond? He wasn't either, he was a silver haired man who should be already claiming his pension and enjoying his retirement; but like everything else in his life he persisted, pushing on when others would have given in a long time ago.

What's life without a little adventure? However misguided. He thought as he crossed the pavement and stepped up to the front of the letting agents.

He took a quick look in the window before he entered, nothing unusual here; the display cards all looked legitimate and the office inside looked reputable enough. If there was anything fishy going on within the confines of this particular address they kept it covered with a very respectable looking little business. Martin sucked in a deep breath and opened the door. There was a beep from the sensor as he entered and the lady behind the nearest desk looked up from the stack of letting slips she was perusing. There were two desks in the room, both occupied by women, the one with the lady directly facing Martin, and another to the left, just through a narrow alcove in the wall, this one at a ninety degree angle to the first, so its occupant spent her working day facing the first lady.

Both women were somewhere in their late thirties to early forties, both wore slightly dated business suits, both had sandy golden hair that hung down to their shoulders and both were slightly over weight. In fact the only discernible difference between the two was the one through the alcove was currently wearing glasses. Sisters? Possibly. But really what did it matter?

"Hello can I help you?" The first lady greeted with a smile.

"I wonder if you can." Martin said, stepping into the office and allowing the door to close behind him. "I called up the other night enquiring about the flat you have to let on Bill Nicholson Way in Tottenham."

"Two bedroom flat, listed under Harvey Butters." The lady through the alcove informed.

"I know the one." The first lady said, Collette she was called, Martin noticed from her name badge. Also, he couldn't mistake that strong cockney accent;

this was the lady he spoke to on the phone. "Were you interested in renting the flat?"

"Oh no, nothing like that."

"I didn't think so, not wearing a suit like that. Are you the gentleman I spoke to last Thursday evening?"

"Yes, yes that was me." He said, pointing to his chest with his fingers as though this would aid her somehow.

Suddenly the lines around the ladies mouth and eyes were tighter; she had clearly hoped she had heard the last of him.

"How can I help?" She asked again, managing to hide her frustration behind a slightly weary smile.

"May I?" Martin said, gesturing towards the chair to the front of the ladies desk.

"Of course." She replied, and sat back down herself.

Martin sank down into the soft cushioned chair and placed his car keys in the pocket of his suit jacket. "Thank you." He said when he was comfortable. Sensing that there was more to this conversation than the usual boring letting agreement the lady through the alcove with the striking resemblance to Collette watched on, ignoring the photocopies that just moments ago she had promised herself would absolutely be done by lunch.

"I know you mentioned on the phone that the flat hadn't been rented by anyone since the Italian family left two weeks ago."

"The Polumbo's, that's right."

"But I checked the address, I didn't make a mistake, I definitely visited a lady by the name of Linda McGready at that apartment last Tuesday evening; I just wondered if there was anything, anything at all that you could tell me."

"I can tell you that you watch too much American television, they're flats not apartments, but like I told you on the phone, that particular flat has not been occupied since the Polumbo's left."

"But that's what I don't understand, why was this lady there? If the house was rented by this Polumbo family, and hasn't been rented since, what was she doing there?"

"I don't know, squatting maybe?"

"No, no, this wasn't a squatter's house, it was furnished, she lived there."

"I'm sorry but as I told you on the phone, that isn't possible, we handle the letting of that property, have done since long before the Polumbo's moved in, if there was another occupant we would know."

Martin sighed, placing his hands down on the soft fabric of his tailored trousers. What had he expected? After all this was exactly what he had been informed on the phone, why should coming here in person make any difference?

"Ok, ok I'm sorry for wasting your time." He said reluctantly. It looked like whatever conspiracy theory had been clogging his mind for the last three months had finally hit a brick wall. Maybe it was time to let sleeping dog's lie.

Martin stood up to leave, as he did he noticed the lady through the alcove; she was no longer listening intently to their conversation but looked deep in thought. Martin paid this no heed and head to the door.

"Thank you for your time." He said as he pulled open the door, sounding the connection from the sensor once more.

"I'm sorry I couldn't be more help." Collette replied, and this time she actually looked genuine, though she was probably just relieved to be seeing the back of him. Let's face it, he was hardly a good advertisement for their business if he was walking around saying he had seen people living in a property they had to let.

He walked across the pavement to his car with a deep feeling of disappointment rooted in his bones. Playing Columbo was one thing, and yeah he supposed it had been kind of fun living with the intrigue while he still had a viable quest for answers, but now that those answers had run out he was left with the possibility that he would never know why the things that had happened did in fact happen, and that was a thought process that was likely to keep him awake at night for quite some time to come.

Sighing heavily he unlocked the Aston Martin; he was about to climb in and drive off when a voice behind him commanded his attention.

"Excuse me." It was a female voice, but softer than that of the lady he had just been speaking to. Martin turned around and saw that it was alcove girl. She was stood in the doorway of the property agents, shielding her eyes from the glare of the sun.

Martin locked the car again and walked over towards her; she let the door close behind her and met him about half way.

"I'm sorry I didn't catch your name."

"Martin, Martin Rooley."

"I'm Ronette Weaver; did you say that you visited the flat on Bill Nicholson Way last Tuesday?"

Ronette and Collette, Martin mused, they even had sound-alike names. "That's right yeah, Tuesday, does that mean anything to you?"

"A little, I'm not sure how much I can tell you."

"Please, anything you could tell me would be a great help." Martin could feel his hope starting to build and he tried to control it, this could be just another red herring.

"I got a call, must have been the Friday before the date you're referring to, from a man who wanted to rent the flat for just one day."

"Just one day?" Martin's eyebrow rose slightly as he comprehended the notion.

"That's right yes, just one day, it was very unusual."

"Did you get the name?"

"He didn't leave one."

Martin chewed on his lip, he could feel the skin crawling across his bones, this was truly unusual indeed.

"What did you tell him?"

"I told him we didn't do one day leases, that we couldn't help him."

"And what did he say?"

"Nothing, just asked me who the landlord was for the property."

"Did you tell him?"

"Not at first, it kind of goes against our confidentiality agreement you know, but he had a way, I don't know, he was smooth. I gave him a name, nothing else."

"Will you give the name to me?"

Ronette sighed. "I shouldn't, but I don't know, you seem harmless enough. You promise me you're not out to kill anybody?"

"I only want to talk to the lady; I don't have beef with anybody."

"I believe you." Ronette replied, but she still didn't look happy. "Ok, I'll tell you what I told him, after that you're on your own. The landlords name is Darren Fryers."

"Thank you." Martin replied earnestly.

"So what is this all about anyway, it kind of sounds intriguing?"

"I wish I knew." Martin said honestly. "It's probably nothing. But I need to find out, just in case it is something."

"Wow, keeping your cards pretty close to your chest there."

Martin smiled.

"Just be careful ok, whatever you're into…. I don't want to state the obvious here but you're no spring chicken."

"You think I'm old now, you should have seen me in June." Martin said with a smile, and unlocked the Aston Martin once more.

Ronette regarded him with intrigue, then she smiled, nodded and head back to the office.

For Martin, as he started the engine, he felt a renewed sense of hope; if he had known what was to come he would have perhaps not felt so positive.

5

The farm, which was situated in the middle of the Berkshire countryside, covered almost seventeen acres of land, the farmhouse itself was a grade two listed building and the grounds were well maintained by an abundance of hired hands. This was a cattle farm and cows grazed in the fields to either side of the track that led down to the house as Martin slowly brought the car down the lane. Today he was in the Range Rover, much more practical than the Aston Martin for a journey across the counties and nice and comfortable when he had been stuck in the traffic on the M25. He didn't do much driving anymore but when he did he always enjoyed it; it was a rare chance to just sit and gather his thoughts and he always listened to the talk shows on the radio, they were often full of amusing characters and seedy politicians trying to cement their manifestos. He had lost his respect for politicians after representatives of all of the major parties had touted Sapient for funding in the run up to the last two elections. He was well aware of the advantages a successful business could have with getting into bed with a party that was tipped to rule, but he preferred all of his business to be out in the open.

He brought the car to a stop in front of a huge barn, the tires crunching on the asphalt, and killed the engine. He looked up at the house, an impressive double fronted barn-dominium with huge bay windows that looked out onto the forecourt, and pulled the keys from the ignition.

Yesterday he had cancelled a couple of meetings that had been pencilled into his diary (he had still to get used to the electronic calendar on his PC that Sheila had painstakingly set up for him) and spent the morning with the phone book open in front of him, dialling all of the Darren Fryers on record and asking if they were the same Darren Fryers that owned Flat 2B of the house on Bill Nicholson Way. He was disappointed to find that none of the Darren Fryers in the Greater London area were indeed the one they were looking for.

At three o'clock he did what he should have done in the first place and asked Sheila for her help. She disappeared with the name scrawled on her notepad and no questions asked (something he absolutely loved about her) and returned twenty minutes later with a number.

'Will that be all?' She had asked with a proud smile and Martin had applauded once more her undentable efficiency.

So he had the number, and he had the name, the next step had been an uncomfortable five minute conversation with Darren's wife Sylvie who had wanted to know right there and then why someone was so interested in talking to her husband. Martin didn't know what problems in the Fryers' marriage had caused this mistrustful nature but he had felt for poor Darren all the same. Reluctantly she had agreed for Martin to visit them and provided the postcode that would locate them on the businessman's built in sat nav.

And now here he was; sat in the Range Rover in the driveway of what looked like a thriving farming business, ready for his meeting with Darren Fryers. It would be a sluggish two hour journey back to London in the rush hour traffic, there was no time like the present. Martin opened the door and stepped out into the yard. He took a look about himself; a huge oak tree dominated a small patch of grass to the far side of the farm house; to the side of the barn were two grain silo's and a small garage that housed a couple of Massey Ferguson tractors, the wheels caked in mud. There was a path that ran round the side of the barn, which was literally covered in muddy footprints and a gate in a fence that ran directly behind the tractor garage that led into the grazing fields. At the front of the house a large ginger cat snoozed in the small triangle of sun that shone through the houses single skylight onto the otherwise cool courtyard.

Martin was walking up to the front door when a voice from the barn startled him.

"Can I help you?" He hadn't seen the young man in the dirty coveralls as he had been working far back in the dark shadows of the barn, but now he crept out into the mid day sun. He was somewhere in his late teens to early twenties, with a classic young mans hair cut, all gelled spikes that looked lethal to the touch, and his cheeks were smeared in dirt and sweat.

"Oh yes, thank you." Martin said, stepping forward. "I'm here to see Darren Fryers."

"Give me a second." He said, and stepped up to a white cordless phone that was attached to the barn wall. He punched in a three digit number and waited to be connected through to the house.

"Yes." The curt voice on the other end of the line came through the speaker, and though it was such a small simple word Martin found it instantly recognisable; this was mister Fryers delightful wife Sylvie.

"Gentleman here to see Darren." The young man informed.

"He's out in the paddock."

"No problem." The young man was about to end the call when the voice came again.

"Wait; did they say what it was regarding?"

The young man covered the mouthpiece on the phone and looked to Martin. "What is it about?"

"I just need to speak to Mister Fryers about a property he owns in London."

The young man nodded and lifted the phone back to his ear.

"He wants to speak to him about a house in London."

"I'm coming down." The line went dead and the young man placed the phone back in its cradle.

Martin's heart sank.

"Lady of the house will be right with you."

"Thank you." Martin said through pursed lips, and watched as the young man went back about his business to the back of the barn.

A couple of minutes went by; Martin stood tapping his Gucci loafers on the dusty forecourt and enjoying the feel of the sun on his face on this cold October morning while light hammerings came from the barn where the young man was working on fixing a damaged fence post.

If in doubt, clout. Martin thought as the front door to the farm house opened and a middle aged woman stepped out. She was quite striking; not pretty, but attractive in a careless kind of way. She wore her dyed blonde hair tied back in a messy ponytail and was wearing riding jodhpurs, knee length boots and a padded gilet over a roll neck sweater, pretty much standard fare for a farmers wife, at least according to the magazines and TV shows Martin had seen.

"Mister Rooley?" She enquired as she cut the distance between them.

"That's me yes."

"We spoke on the phone, I'm Darren's wife."

Martin held out his hand and when he realised that she wasn't going to take it quickly placed it back down by his side.

"Please call me Martin." He said with a warm smile, trying to win her over, but it seemed she had already cast her judgment on his character, there was no going back now.

"Darren's out back, I'll take you to him." She turned and head to the path at the side of the barn, Martin followed wondering if the treatment was personal or if she was this joyful all of the time.

The mud was quite thick in places where it had fallen from the bottom of well worn work boots and Martin inwardly cursed not bringing more appropriate footwear; he had just assumed they would be meeting indoors.

She led him to the back of the house where a third grazing field, equally as large as the two to either side of the driveway could be found. To the back of the field were two storage sheds that looked to have had better days; a man in a long green wax jacket – more standard fare for the farming community – was rolling coils of barbed wire and storing them by the door of the first shed.

As they walked across the field with Martin being careful not to splash mud on his suit trousers, Sylvie questioned him..

"So what is this about?"

"Oh, just a general enquiry really." Martin replied, feeling uncomfortable, he didn't know what the situation was between the husband and wife but he didn't want to make it worse by disclosing any information that would land the master of the house in any trouble, instead he quickly changed the subject. "You have a lovely house here, really impressive."

"Hmm." She said non-committedly, her features drawn and tight. Luckily they had nearly reached the farmer and Martin couldn't have been more pleased. He turned when he heard them approach, panting at the exertion of his duties.

Darren Fryers was somewhere in his mid forties; with thinning ginger hair and deep lines about his eyes and his mouth; when his wife approached he frowned and his forehead creased so dramatically it reminded Martin of the seating compartment of a rubber dinghy.

"Darren, this is the man I was telling you about, the one that called about the Tottenham flat."

"Oh yes, I remember." The farmer said, and his face creased into a pleasant smile, easing some of Martin's concerns. He was wearing thick work gloves but he removed these now and stretched out his hand to the businessman. Martin took it in his and the farmer gave him a firm shake.

"You can head back if you like Sylvie." Darren said, and the middle aged woman tutted, then turned and head back across the field. When she was firmly out of earshot he spoke again. "You'll have to forgive my wife; she isn't going to win any personality awards."

"Oh she was fine." Martin lied with a small smile.

"If you consider Genghis Khan to be fine then I guess my wife can also be considered so. Not her fault, got myself into some bad gambling debts a few years ago and now she has problems with trust; trusting me mainly but she's always suspicious of strangers.

Martin was surprised at the mans frank nature; in a time when so many secrets clouded his judgment it was quite refreshing.

"So, how can I help you? I understand you have an enquiry regarding the Tottenham property, you don't want to buy it do you? Please God say you want to buy it."

"Sorry no, nothing like that."

"No I didn't think so, I'm not that lucky. You ever get into property?"

"No, I was tempted once or twice but never took the plunge."

"You did right not to, it's a fools game. I used to own seven different properties in the Greater London area, good place to buy as there's constant demand for cheap housing. All was good, back in the early noughties I was making a small fortune, then the bottom fell out of the property market and I'm left sat on a huge steaming pile of negative equity. I only have three properties now; one in Enfield, one in Redbridge and the Tottenham property. Biggest mistake I ever made; I hate travelling into the big smoke, that's why I always use an agency, saves me the journey. Anyway I'm babbling, sorry I didn't catch your name."

"It's Martin, Martin Rooley, I'm the CEO of Sapient Trans Global, we have offices in the city." The words had left his mouth before Martin could stop them, and he wondered why he had divulged so much information, most of which wasn't even relevant to the conversation. Maybe the younger mans unbridled frankness was rubbing off on him, but whatever the case if this ginger farmer before him was involved somehow in whatever conspiracy surrounded his operation then he had just given him his real name and a good way of being able to track him down. Oh well, it was too late now.

"How can I help you mister Rooley?"

"Oh Martin please."

"Ok, how can I help you Martin?"

"The property on Bill Nicholson way in Tottenham, it's currently up to let right?"

"Yeah." Darren said nodding. "Previous occupants moved out a couple of weeks ago, damn pain in the arse if you ask me."

"And the properties been empty ever since?" Martin prompted.

"What is this about?" Darren asked, suddenly becoming cautious.

"Mister Fryers..."

"Darren."

"Darren, are you aware that a lady was using the property, actually claiming to be a resident there while the property was up for lease?"

Darren sighed, the rubber dinghy marks back on his head. "I knew it, I knew this would come back to bite me in the arse, I just knew it."

"Knew what?" Martin asked, all of his senses pricking to life.

"They assured me that what they were doing wasn't illegal, from the look of you I don't think you're a cop, what's your interest in this?"

"I'm not a cop." Martin reassured, excited at the turn of events. "I assure you I am who I say I am, I'm just an old businessman from the city, and my interest in this is purely from a personal perspective; I just need to find the lady who was at that house, that's all."

Darren nodded slowly, it was lucky for Martin that he was a naturally trusting person.

"Why do you want to find her? What has she done?"

"She hasn't done anything, not to my knowledge anyway." Martin sighed, oh well, in for a penny, in for a pound. "I had an operation; heart transplant, at the beginning of this year, the lady is the donor's mother, I was hoping to find her and I don't know, thank her for her son's sacrifice."

"I see." Darren said, his face relaxing. "Congratulations on your successful operation, at least I assume it was successful, you want to thank the lady after all."

"Thank you." Martin didn't say anything more, he wanted to wait and let the farmer fill the silence. When it became too uncomfortable not to fill the void Darren continued.

"Look I don't know what I can tell you, if you're after the ladies whereabouts I'm afraid I can't help you; I didn't even get her name."

"McGready, it was Linda McGready. Anything you could tell me could be a help, please, anything at all. It's imperative that I track her down."

"Ok." Darren sighed again; he gazed out across the field with far off distant eyes. "A couple of weeks ago I get a call from a guy saying he wanted to rent the flat, I'm like great, just call the agency and they'll get you sorted, then he says no, he just wanted to rent it for one day."

"Did you get his name?" Martin asked, his eyebrows raised.

"Ken Smith."

Ken Smith; great, an assumed name if ever he'd heard one.

"What did he say he wanted the flat for?"

"He didn't say, just assured me it was all above board, and that if I agreed he'd give me two thousand pounds for one days rent."

"Two thousand pounds?"

"Yeah I know, ridiculous, I mean the place is falling down, it's not like a Chelsea penthouse."

Martin was quiet for a moment, allowing everything he had been told so far to absorb; if somebody had paid two thousand pounds for the privilege of renting a dingy North London flat for one day they were clearly desperate, but why? It didn't make sense, had they done this on his behalf, to convince him that this woman was really who she claimed to be? He didn't know, but a thick weight in his gut told him he didn't like it one bit.

"So what happened next?" He asked eventually.

"I had to meet the lady at the flat, she'd have the money. I wasn't too happy about it, it's a ninety minute journey, one way, but you know, two thousand pounds is two thousand pounds. Sure enough it wasn't a hoax, she was there, and she had the money."

"Was Ken Smith there?" Martin asked, not wanting to get his hopes up but hopeful all the same.

"No, just the woman."

Martin sighed. "Yeah, I thought you were going to say that. I'm assuming you never met this Ken Smith fellow."

"That's right; it was all done over the phone."

"Is there anything else you can tell me?"

"I don't think so, that's about all there was. Ken Smith said the flat would be left as they'd found it the following day and it was. I will tell you this though, when I let this woman in the house, Linda McGready you say she was called? I let her in but I wasn't happy about leaving her there I can tell you that."

"Why?" Martin asked earnestly, thinking back to the quiet, unassuming woman he had met at the flat.

Darren Fryers looked at Martin, his face a picture of disdain. "Because she was a junkie."

6

Outside the sky was grey and overcast, rain threatened in the heavy clouds and there was a chill wind to greet the start of November; but inside the Merry Berry Delicatessen it was like a summer's day in a tropical paradise, it always was in here, which was why Martin liked it so much. It was situated just on the corner of West India Avenue and Cabot Square, literally a stones throw from the front door of Sapient Trans-Global, and as such was the perfect spot to grab a quick bite to eat or a travelling coffee.

Inside it was all hanging vines and moisture sucking yucca's, with a long self service counter at the back, its glass display cabinet always crammed full of delectable pastries and cakes. In the old days, before his heart had waved its little white flag of surrender, such a delicacy would have been a daily occurrence; these days it was just an occasional treat. Not that it would ever steal the crown from Gregg's mind – sticky buns 59p – but to Martin the Merry Berry was a close run second.

He had been sat looking at the service charters that had been provided by their shipping contractors in the Netherlands when Peter had turned up unannounced and insisted he join him for coffee. Martin; who rarely needed an excuse to put his work on the back burner these days practically leapt at the chance. Now they were sat at a table by the window, looking out at the approaching storm; Martin with a hot chocolate with whipped cream and a vanilla slice and Peter with a cappuccino and a chocolate éclair.

"Id love to be able to eat one of these without getting cream on my chin." The younger of the two men said, taking a generous bite of his cake.

"I'd love to sit opposite a man capable of eating a cake without resembling a three year old boy." Martin replied, smiling to show his words were all in jest.

"I'd be careful what I wished for if I was you. Give it another couple of years and all your meals will be spoon fed to you by a fat woman in grey sweat pants. Meals on wheels my friend, it's just around the corner."

Martin laughed. "Touché."

Outside the first spatters of rain broke from the angry looking clouds and patted down onto the grey tarmac. In another five minutes it was likely that without an umbrella even the short trip back to Sapient would leave them resembling drowned rats.

"So what did you think of the new marketing proposals?" Peter asked, dabbing cream from the corner of his mouth with his napkin.

"They were fine, I mean it's not going to set the world on fire but we're not trying to rival a Hollywood blockbuster here; I think the mail drops and the trade one pager should be fine."

"Agreed, it's like I've been saying to the board, we're not currently in the market to acquire new business but in order to stay both commercial and competitive we need to get more from the customers that we already have, what are their shipping needs? How can we further connect their business? If we can sell the benefits to their own organisations there's no reason we can't capitalise on some pretty serious growth, especially if the Eastern European contracts come through, everything is resting on those."

Martin took a sip of his hot chocolate and nodded slowly. "So what is this really about?"

"I'm sorry?" Peter replied, faking puzzlement.

"Come on Peter, I love you, you know I do, but you're a workaholic, I'm always giving you grief for the hours you put in, God knows out of everybody that punches a metaphorical clock at Sapient you deserve a break the most, but it's been an awful long time since I've known you to take one. So why now? And don't say to discuss the marketing proposals because we both know this could have been picked up on email."

Peter sighed and looked out of the window, one hand supporting his chin. "Is it that obvious?"

"Peter you are without a doubt the owner of the finest business mind I have ever met, but you can't act for toffee, if you cut down your working hour's maybe you could join an amateur dramatic society."

"I'm glad to hear I'm so transparent, remind me not to represent the company in any more negotiations."

"Stop avoiding the subject, what's on your mind?"

Peter sighed. "Ok, I'm worried about you."

"You're worried about me?" Martin replied, genuinely confused.

"That's right I'm worried about you, so I thought I'd bring your here and top you up with sugar in the vain hope that the rush will send your jaw into over drive, that you might actually level with me for once."

"Peter what are you talking about?" Martin said, feeling anxious, though he didn't know why.

"We're friends as well as colleagues Martin, you'd agree with that wouldn't you?"

"Of course."

"Well as your friend I'm concerned about how distant you are at the moment; I'm not talking about work, no offence but you've been pretty distant from your responsibilities as CEO for some time now, no I'm talking distant in yourself. You're always staring off into space, you rarely talk these days and if you do it's usually brief and to the point and you generally keep yourself to yourself most of the time, you just sit up in your office and generally don't get involved."

Martin was a little taken aback; he had known he had been a little distant of late, there had just been so much on his mind, but he hadn't realised just how obvious it had been. This troubled him.

"Peter I'm sorry, if you feel I've been neglecting my responsibilities..."

Peter was shaking his head. "No, no that's not it, I'm not concerned about you pulling your weight, I actually encourage you to take a bit of a back seat now, especially with everything that happened earlier in the year. This is more about you as a person, you seem withdrawn. Not yourself, as though there's something on your mind. Your health is still ok isn't it?"

"its fine, I'm fitter and stronger than I have been in years."

"Good, I'm glad to hear it."

"Look Peter, I'm sorry if I've been worrying you, but I'm fine, really, like you say I've just been taking a bit of a back seat of late, maybe even concentrating on my potential retirement."

"Now I know there's something wrong, you'll still be at Sapient when they wheel your coffin out through the reception doors."

Martin smiled, Peter did not.

"As long as that's all it is, I was worried, I don't know, I thought maybe this could have something to do with that address I found you, the donor's mother."

Martin cringed but tried not to show it; he had hoped to avoid the topic of his current situation and now here it was, blatantly staring him in the face. What did he do now? Peter was his friend, but he was still having trouble with knowing who he could trust, and though it made him feel like a bit of a scab he didn't want to open up to his colleague, not yet at least.

"No, no nothing like that."

"Well how did that go?" Peter pressed. "You never said, did you call her?"

"I did more than that; I visited her at her home."

"Wow." Peter replied, one hand covering his mouth. "What was that like? I've got to admit if it was me I don't know if I'd have had the guts."

"It was fine, we chatted for a while, I brought her flowers, I don't think I'll be seeing her again."

Peter was nodding slowly. "That's good. So are you satisfied now, has it put this to bed for you?"

"I think so." Martin nodded, hoping he was a better liar than his friend.

"Well, you've done it now; I guess you can finally move on."

"Oh I intend to, and I intend to get more involved too, maybe not with the full in's and out's of the operation, but more on a personal level. I'm sorry I worried you."

"That's ok, it would just be good to have the old Martin back, personality wise, no-one wants to see fat Martin again."

The businessman laughed, though inside he was concerned, if his instincts were correct, and they usually were, then his problems were only just getting started, and keeping to his word might be harder than he could ever anticipate.

"Drink your coffee, it's getting cold." He said, and looked out of the coffee shop window at the oncoming storm.

7

Martin Rooley was a firm believer that in life, you pretty much got what you paid for; if you paid thirty five pounds for your fiancé's engagement ring you can pretty much count on the mock gold it is made from turning green on her finger within a couple of years, if you pay the silly money that he and his golfing buddies did for luxury cars that was what you were getting; luxury. Heated leather seats, walnut dashboard, built in satellite navigation, cruise control, even self parking on some models. You got what you paid for. That's why when looking for a private investigator to track down Linda McGready, Martin chose the most expensive in the book.

He could have used Bill and would have been confident of some positive results; but could he trust that his case wouldn't somehow make it back to Peter? Bill was Peter's friend after all. Not that he harboured any doubt around his friend; not any more at least, but he still didn't want people knowing what he was up to, not yet anyway.

Thomas Spence was a former MI6 code breaker who had retired with a sizeable pension at forty-five and set up his own private security firm in 2006. Although primarily they offered short term security options for visiting dignitaries, pop stars and politicians, they had a separate investigative division that focused on private case work for people willing to pay a little extra for the latest techniques and the utmost discretion. Martin was one of these people.

Trojan Horse Security had their small but very impressive headquarters in Reading; when Martin visited them on a Friday morning in early November the place was already buzzing with activity. He was meeting with the main man, mister Spence himself, as had been his desire when he had made the appointment, and a young smartly dressed lady who smelled exquisitely of expensive perfume ushered the businessman to his office on the third floor.

Everything was chrome with a soft green under lighting that made it look modern and sleek. Even the desk, where the big man with the shortly cropped hair was sat looking at a case file, was like a huge chrome tablet, its edges curved like a Lamborghini. He looked up from his work as Martin and the young secretary entered, a friendly smile on his face.

"Mister Rooley?" He enquired.

"Yes, but Martin please."

"Please take a seat Martin." He gestured to the chair on the other side of the desk as the secretary quietly left the room.

Martin sat down, thinking as his bottom planted firmly on the angular chair that they had negated the need for comfort in their vision for the offices.

"Can I get you a drink, tea, coffee?"

"No I'm fine thank you."

The big man nodded. "Did you find us ok?"

"It was fine, took a couple of wrong turns through the diversions but found my way back alright."

"Those damn road works, they're a nuisance. They've been fiddling with the pipework out there since the summer, half the time there isn't a damn person working on the site."

"I have to tackle the M25 every day, I feel your pain."

Spence let out an appreciative laugh, showing he understood Martin's pain. "So," he said, settling down to business, "how can we be of assistance?"

"I'd like you to find somebody for me."

"A missing person?"

"Not exactly."

"Ok, I'm intrigued, but before we begin, first a little insight into how we operate. We're a relatively small firm, twenty-two employees with around a dozen or so sub contractors. You probably noticed a lot of activity on your way in, we have a major security operation today for a high stake client, so we're just getting ready to begin proceedings. This type of job covers the bulk of our role, ninety per cent. The other ten per cent is private investigation work, but we pride ourselves in giving the same dedication and focus to the ten per cent that we give to the core of the business.

Our clients come from all walks of life, though we tend to deal with high end businessmen such as yourself and the more affluent members of society. This is because the service that we provide doesn't come cheap. I make no bones about this, we aren't in the business of trying to undercut our competitors in the market; what is important is that the service we provide and for which our client base is generally very satisfied is of good value; the product to meet the price tag.

We get results, and we get them fast. We have technology that surpasses the traditional methods still used by the majority of our competitors. What's more we guarantee absolute anonymity for our clients, all of which are provided a case worker, in your case me, who will deal solely with the client and that client alone until a satisfactory resolution to the assigned task. Nobody else will have access to your information; nobody else will know your name or the reason for your visit. All of this we guarantee with the assurance that if you aren't completely satisfied with the service we provide you will of course be entitled to a full refund; in ten years of business we have never had to exercise this right.

In return we ask only that you will be as discreet with our information as we are with yours. Recommend us by all means, we are a growing business after all, but any information you receive and any methods you are privy to as part of your investigation must remain of knowledge to you and you only. Is this clear?"

"Perfectly." Martin replied, wondering how many before him had sat in this office and listened to this well rehearsed speech.

"And are you comfortable with the terms of this agreement?"

"I am."

"Excellent." Spence said with a smile. He fished in his drawer and pulled out a sheet of A4 paper, complete with a yellow and pink carbon copy underneath. "This is our confidentiality agreement, if you would take a moment to please read and if you agree to the terms just sign and date at the bottom."

"Of course." Martin took the document from the burly former agent and carefully read the small printed terms and conditions of service; there was nothing in there that either surprised or concerned him so he signed and dated and handed the form back to the private investigator.

"Very good, very good." The big man said, scanning the signature. He then ripped off the two carbon copies and handed the yellow sheet back to Martin. "This is your copy, please store somewhere safe. Now, please tell me a little more about this missing person of yours."

"It's a woman, a lady, by the name of Linda McGready, though I suspect that may have been an assumed name." Martin began. "I met her a few weeks ago at a flat in Tottenham that later transpired not to be her address at all. It's a long story, but basically the lady has information I need and that's why I need to track her down."

"Your reasons for finding the lady are your business, and will stay that way as long as your reasons for finding her are legal and do not break any national or international laws. Our only objective thus far is to find her."

"That's good." Martin replied, feeling reassured. "I can assure you that my reasons for finding the lady are all above board, I just need to speak with her."

"You mentioned you'd met with her before."

"At her house that's right, it was Flat 2B, number 18 Bill Nicholson way in Tottenham. But it wasn't her house; you see I met her there, and then later when I went back to visit again, she was no longer there, in fact she had never actually been there. It's kind of hard to explain."

As Martin had been talking the investigator had been making notes on his electronic pad, now his right eyebrow raised inquisitively, but to his credit he kept to his word and did not press the businessman for the finer details, sticking instead to the facts that would support him with his case.

"Can you describe the woman to me?"

"Average height, slim, very slim, skinny you might say. Late forties I'd guess. She has blonde hair, dyed, and a small birthmark just in her hair line."

"What shape?"

"Pardon?"

"The birth mark, what shape was it?"

"Oh, it was kind of shaped like a star, quite unusual."

"Star shaped huh, this is good. What about eyes, what colour were they."

"I'm sorry I didn't notice, if I had to guess I'd say blue but I couldn't say it with any certainty."

"Ok, anything else you can remember about her, anything at all?"

Martin sighed. "She had needle marks on her arm."

The investigator looked up from his electronic pad. "She was diabetic?"

"I don't think so."

"I see." He said, and noted it down. "And what is your relationship with the woman?"

"Oh just a passing acquaintance really." Martin replied, he could imagine the investigator wondering if she was just a passing acquaintance why he was so desperate to speak to her and why he was willing to pay so much money to discover her whereabouts, but again he said nothing.

"Ok so let me go over the details as I have them recorded; you're looking for a lady by the name of Linda McGready though that could be an assumed name. She has a connection to flat 2B at number 18 Bill Nicholson way in Tottenham, North London, though not as her permanent residency. She's a passing acquaintance so has no familiar connection with you. Average height, skinny, dyed blonde hair and a small star shaped birth mark in her hair line. A history of possible recent substance abuse. Have I captured everything?"

"I think so yes."

"Ok." Spence looked up from his notepad and tapped his stylus against the surface of his polished chrome desk. "I'll be honest with you it isn't much to go on, but hopefully it's enough. Are you sure there isn't any further information that would support my investigation.

Martin paused; he was considering telling the investigator everything, from the unusual operation to the mystery third party, the person who had rented the flat on a one day lease from Darren Fryers, then at the last second changed his mind. Deciding his best policy, for now at least, was to play his cards as close to his chest as possible.

"That's everything."

"Ok." The investigator said nodding. "Well give it a couple of days, I should have something for you, it might not be everything, but I should have something. The next matter is one of a contract to be drawn up between us, of what your expectations are and what you feel is an acceptable fee to meet those expectations. This is handled by our finance department; they'll need to take your personal information. Usually we look for fifty per cent of the fee paid in advance with the further fifty per cent paid on the satisfactory conclusion to your case. Of course as I mentioned earlier the advance fee would be returned should you not be fully satisfied with the service."

"That sounds reasonable." Martin replied.

"Excellent, then let's get down to work. Shall we?" Spence said and gestured towards the door.

Martin nodded, and standing from the uncomfortable chair followed the ex MI6 man out to settle the bill.

8

If Martin had thought early October was Christmassy on Oxford Street then he had not anticipated the sheer Yuletide madness of early November. It was as though Santa Claus and the infant baby Jesus had vomited red and green glitter the length and breadth of the street, leaving no store window or shop front untouched. It was supposed to invoke yuletide cheer whilst reminding the happy shopper just how few shopping days there actually were left until the big day, but to Martin it was just a distraction. Tomorrow night was bonfire night; couldn't we as a nation please celebrate this before getting all over awed about an event that was still the best part of two months away? He guessed there just wasn't enough commercial value in ole Guy Fawkes.

Not that he was an old stick in the mud; Martin loved both events in equal measure – what wasn't to like? Pie and peas, bonfire toffee and parkin pigs could easily be matched by a full turkey dinner, Christmas pudding with lashings of brandy sauce and icing covered mince pies – but lately the only thing he could actually muster any enthusiasm for was finding Linda McGready.

Now he was back again, fulfilling a pastime that he hated, conscious in the knowledge that he had recently been more often than not neglecting his wife; this was his way of making it up to her. Surely there had to be a better way than this? He thought as he was practically shoulder barged out of the way by a woman outside Waterstone's busy yelling obscenities into her mobile phone.

There was a fellow in a flat cap selling horse chestnuts on the corner of Regent Street; Martin stopped and bought a bag to help him through the ordeal.

Rose somehow didn't see the same horror in a day's shopping as her husband and was laden with bags from various stores, a huge smile on her face as she made a bee line towards the huge Selfridge's department store. This alone filled Martin with untold dread; it would be all too easy for him to become lost amongst the numerous floors and aisles and departments and he feared if this happened he may never again be found; or if he was it would be by a security guard long after the store had closed, a gibbering wreck that would have to be confined to a nut house.

Swallowing back his deepening dread Martin pocketed his bag of nuts and followed Rose through the huge revolving doors. His eyes instantly wandered over to the place he had stood, almost exactly a month ago to the day, when he had bumped into the Mediterranean anaesthetist who had refused to acknowledge his existence. That had been the turning point; the moment when he had known that something was definitely not right about the circumstances involving his operation. A month on and what did he know now? Zilch. He was still in the dark. Martin wondered if he would ever have an answer to his questions, it was looking increasingly doubtful.

With the dotted Chloe purse she had purchased this time last month tucked under her arm Mrs Rooley happily wandered over to the designer handbags and took another good look, much to her husband's dismay.

"Seriously how many handbags can one person need?" Martin asked with notable frustration.

"Darling handbags are like shoes, you can never have too many."

"Yeah, tell that to Zola Budd."

"Honey if I was going to take shoe advice from anybody it certainly wouldn't be Zola Budd."

"No, it would probably be Imelda Marcos." He muttered in reply. He threw a horse chestnut into his mouth, wondering why he hadn't suggested the cinema or a nice meal out or the theatre or basically anything that wasn't this mind numbing soul sapping torture. But no, he had suggested a spot of shopping in the city, now he would just have to deal with it. The only pin prick of light at the end of a very long, very dark tunnel was that at some point they would have to factor in lunch, which for him at least was a much more pleasurable pastime.

His phone was ringing in his pocket; Martin fished it out and looked at the screen.

"I have to take this." He said to his wife, feeling his cheeks starting to redden.

"Ok but if it's the office remind them that you are the boss and today is your day off please."

"I will." He said, and wandered over to a quiet corner of the store. As it turned out it wasn't the office on the line at all; it was Trojan Horse Security.

"Mister Rooley?"

"Speaking."

"It's Thomas Spence from Trojan Horse Security."

"Hello Thomas, good to hear from you."

"Can you speak?"

Martin looked about himself, cautious that he wasn't being overheard. "It's safe."

"I have some news for you."

"Already, that was quick." Martin had only visited Spence at his office the day before.

"I was confident of getting some information fairly quickly, we have an extensive network that we use to track down missing persons and with all the CCTV in Britain nowadays it's hard to stay hidden for long. That said it was more traditional methods that led us to your lady."

"You've found her?"

"Not exactly, but we're closing in, what we do have is a name and a last known address."

"A name?"

"Your instincts were correct; Linda McGready was an assumed name; the woman's real name is Abigail Tardy."

"Wait a minute." Martin said and wandered over to a perfume counter where a young blonde girl was visibly watching the seconds go by on the huge round clock above the escalators. "Excuse me, do you have a pen please, and perhaps some paper?"

"I've got a pen." She said and handed over a black biro. "No paper."

"It's ok, these will do." Martin replied, and took a handful of tester strips from a small jar next to a huge display of something by Kim Kardashian. He wandered back over to the quiet corner and perched next to the wall. "Sorry Thomas carry on."

"From searches under medical records we were able to trace three women who would now be in their mid to late forties each with a star shaped birthmark in the Greater London area."

"You have access to medical records?"

"We have access to a lot of things. The key though wasn't the birthmark, it was the drug dependency. From the three ladies we'd narrowed it down to only Abigail had a history of drug abuse. She's been prescribed methadone no fewer than five times; the girl's a junkie alright. What's more she got careless, she'd used the name Linda McGready before, she was jailed for three months in 2009 for benefit fraud, she'd been claiming a pension under this name, a deceased neighbour of hers, for six months."

"This is unbelievable." Martin said, feeling his heart beating way too hard in his ribcage; he had also broken out into a sweat and his fingers were gently trembling where they were wrapped around the toughened plastic of his phone.

"With this information it was easy enough to track down her last known whereabouts, you got that pen?"

"Go on." Martin said, jotting the name Abigail Tardy on to one of the tester strips, he slipped this in his pocket and took out another.

"Seventeen Brighton Terrace, Brixton, though she may not be there any more as her parole officer last had contact with her there in 2014."

"I see." Martin said, noting down the address.

"This is just the information we have so far, but we're confident we can trace her from here, may just take another couple of days."

"No, no don't do that." Martin said, concerned that if guys as big as Spence started asking around, especially ones that were former MI6 agents, Abigail may go to ground and then he was right back at square one. No, he wanted to handle this himself. "I'll pick it up from here, you've done great, thank you."

"But the job's only half done, this is just a lead, we don't yet have a positive ID."

"Really, you've already surpassed my expectations; I will of course pay you in full."

"Are you sure?"

"I'm positive Thomas, really, you did great."

"Ok, well you know how this works; the remaining sum will be automatically debited from your account, though I have to say it's not usual for me to take a fee without completing a job."

"You have no cause for concern I am one hundred per cent happy with the service you provided, and I know where you are should I require your services again."

"Ok, you're the customer; I have to respect your wishes."

"Thank you." Martin said, starting to relax. They said their goodbyes and the businessman placed the mobile back in his pocket, absent-mindedly taking another horse chestnut from his pocket and popping it in his mouth while he settled his thoughts.

So the woman was not who she had claimed to be; where did this leave him? Somebody was trying to cover something up, but who? And why? Knowing that Peter had provided the details that led him to the woman cast further suspicions over his friend, and this made him feel uncomfortable and sad. Why had she lied? Why had she claimed to be the mother of his donor? None of it made any sense.

Martin sighed resignedly and looked over to where Rose had been stood a couple of minutes ago; she was no longer there but with a bit of a wander he found her once again perusing the Jimmy Choo's in the footwear section.

"Don't even say it." She said as he ambled over. "There's no need, it's written all over your face, our date's over isn't it."

"I'm so sorry." He said, and once again his cheeks reddened as he surmised the apology would be the only truthful thing he would say from here on in.

"What is it this time?"

"HR issue, corporate fraud, nothing major but they need a senior member on site and with this being a Saturday…"

"It has to be the CEO, surely you pay people so you don't have to deal with this type of thing."

"It's my business; it wouldn't be fair for me to call in any favours."

"What about me Martin, when are you going to devote a little time to me?"

He could see how upset she was and felt decidedly guilty about it, but not guilty enough to sway him. "I'll make it up to you I promise."

"You'd better." She said with a sullen look. "Go on, get out of here, you were under my heels anyway."

"Thank you." He said, and kissed her cheek. He left the store via the same revolving door he had entered by and quickly hailed a cab back to the offices, where they had left the car before making their way into the city.

On the journey his thoughts kept returning to Abigail Tardy, who had claimed the identity of a dead neighbour to steal her pension allowance.

9

When he had left that morning he had seen no reason not to drive him and his wife into the city in the Aston Martin; he had not anticipated the turn of events that would lead him to regret that decision just as he had not anticipated leaving his wife stranded in the middle of London, laden with shopping bags on a busy Saturday afternoon. Pulling up to the side of the kerb now though his mistake was clearly evident; you couldn't be inconspicuous in the heart of an area like this in an Aston Martin; it was the same mistake he had made in Tottenham, but to a greater degree. Here he stood out like a sore thumb; Brighton terrace in Brixton wasn't a side street like Bill Nicholson way had been, it was a busy thoroughfare, it was all high rise flats and discount stores, he couldn't have been less inconspicuous if he'd walked down the street naked with a traffic cone on his head singing 'the Chattanooga choo choo.'

There was one parking space left but it was for permit holders only; he would just have to take his chances, he was pretty sure he could cover the fine should he receive one. Martin pulled into the space and killed the engine.

He leaned forward and peered through the windscreen at the street about him; getting a fine was suddenly the least of his concerns. This was a less affluent borough of London to the ones he frequented, he didn't like to conform to stereotypes, not even in the darkest most secretive corners of his mind, but it was hard not to consider the possibility of being mugged or beaten or having his car stolen or vandalised when he was a rich man in a poor man's neighbourhood, a metaphorical fish out of water.

Martin drew in a deep breath and opened the car door. Somewhere above him loud music was playing, it must have been coming from one of the balconies of the high rise flats, but he couldn't trace its source. On the corner three black youths in huge puffer jackets were smoking and talking loudly in what Martin thought of as 'street talk', it was all 'homes' this and 'word' that and 'shizzle-ma-nizzle', a term for which the businessman could determine no decipherable meaning. It certainly wasn't the Queen's English and served no use he could muster than to further compound his fear that he was very much out on a limb here. He looked down at the tester strip with the address crudely written in biro; 17 Brighton Terrace. There were houses over the road from the high rise flats so he crossed the street to get a closer look.

"Hey geezer, what you doin' roun' here rich boi." One of the youths shouted.

"Nice wheels homes nice wheels." Another joined in.

Martin ignored them and quickened his pace; he was terrified that they might leave their place on the corner and follow him down the road, but they didn't, for now at least he was safe. There was laughter as he nearly tripped stepping back up the kerb but that was about as harmful as it got.

The building directly over the road was a betting shop, the sign stating it was number 23; next door at number 21 was one of the discount stores, then it was a derelict building and finally, at the property he deemed to be number seventeen a dry cleaners. Martin looked down once more at the address, wondering what had gone wrong. He took another look about himself, wondering if there was perhaps another number seventeen, or maybe he'd misheard the private detective. Either way he had been foolhardy to take on the responsibility himself.

Having no other option Martin slipped the address back in his pocket and entered the dry cleaners. The shop was empty apart from a small Chinese man working on the steam press to the back of the building. All about him clothing hung wrapped in cellophane bags, ready for collection. Martin stepped up to the counter.

"Excuse me; I wonder if you could help me."

The small man turned from what he was doing and regarded Martin with notable curiosity; he was clearly not the type of client for which the man was used.

"Yeah." He said, his accent strong.

"I was looking for number seventeen, Brighton Terrace."

"Yeah, this sev'teen." The man said, slapping his hand against his chest to further cement his point.

"I was led to believe that somebody lived here." Martin said, feeling exhausted by the constant brick walls that he was coming against.

"Not here, sev'teen B." The man replied.

"Sorry?" Martin said, feeling more confused than ever.

The man pointed up to the ceiling. "Sev'teen B."

"Seventeen B, there's a flat?"

"Yeah sev'teen B, flat."

"How do I get to the flat?"

The man pointed to the window and then gestured left. "Stair."

Stairs to a flat above the shop, Martin nodded his understanding. "Thank you." He said, then head to the door. He stepped outside and looked above the shop front and sure enough there was a single window that looked out onto Brighton Terrace. To the side of the shop was a slim alleyway between it and the discount shop at number fifteen; Martin walked into it and noticed a scuffed black door about halfway down the alley. It was already partially open, so Martin opened it further and poked his head around the door.

"Hello?"

No answer. A staircase ran up to the floor above the shop from directly behind the door, after a moment's hesitation the businessman stepped through and slowly climbed the stairs. The staircase was narrow and steep, with hard cheaply tiled steps underfoot and plaster crumbling from the walls. A single light bulb hung from a casing in the ceiling atop the stairs, but it wasn't switched on so the only light in the narrow corridor came from the gap in the open doorway below.

Martin reached the top of the stairs a little out of breath, he may have a new fully functioning heart but he was still sixty-eight, and those really were steep stairs. The door at the top of the stairs was closed, but he could hear soft murmurings from beyond it, which he guessed to be coming from the television. He waited a moment to catch his breath and then knocked.

At first there was no answer, so he rapped a little harder, there were voices, this time not from the television, and a shuffling of feet coming towards him, then the door was opened and a mans head peered around the frame.

He was of ethnic origin, short with drawn listless features and a shortly cropped afro hairstyle. He was wearing baggy sweat pants and a yellow vest and his thin arms poked out of the sides like match sticks. He regarded Martin, who was dressed in comfortable slacks and a sweater from Harvey Nicholls as a scientist may observe a brand new species.

"Oh hello, I wonder if you could help me..." Martin began.

"TINA!" The small man bellowed, turning from the door and leaving Martin confused and a little deaf in one ear.

The door swung back a little on its hinges, leaving Martin's view obscured, but he could still hear the voices from the other side.

"What?" A loud female voice enquired.

"Someone at the door."

"So?"

"So go answer it."

"You answer it."

"I just did."

"And?"

"It's some geezer."

"Well what does he want?"

"I don't know do I."

"Well tell him to fuck off."

"You tell him to fuck off."

"I is watchin' Hollyoaks in'I."

There was a pause long enough for Martin to consider turning and fleeing down the stairs, then the woman's voice cam again."

"Fuck's sake Raymond!" There was heavy footfall from beyond the door, alarmed at the noise Martin took a step back so that he was almost pressed up against the wall to the right hand side of the staircase, then a woman about the size of a double decker bus and a half swung open the door and stared out at him, the expression on her face making it very clear she was unhappy at being disturbed from her soap opera. She too was black and had wild hair that stuck out from her pudgy head at irregular angles. "What do you want?" She asked, and for a moment Martin was so taken aback that he couldn't for the life of him remember why he *had* come here.

Luckily, just before he felt sure this mammoth of a woman would either throw him head first down the staircase or pick him up and snap him like a twig over her huge gelatinous knee, he had a flash of recollection.

"Abigail Tardy!" He blurted, and air gushed from his throat, he had not been aware he had been holding his breath.

The woman's features scrunched like a balled up piece of paper, which did nothing to allay Martin's earlier fear.

"What about that bitch?"

"I need to find her, can you help me?"

"I don't know nothink about that bitch." She went to close the door and Martin was quick to step forward and place his foot in the way, a brave move, especially considering the woman's current mood.

"Please, I just need a little help."

"I don't know you, what is I gonna help you for anyway?"

"Please, I just need to find Abigail Tardy, I know she used to live here."

"Why do you want to find her?"

"That's my business."

"Is she in trouble?"

"Would it make a difference if she was?"

The woman was silent for a moment; Martin used the gap in the confrontation to quickly gather his thoughts.

"Yeah I know Abigail, but I ain't seen her in months. Who are you her dad or somethink?"

"No, no, not her father, I'm just, I don't know, an acquaintance."

"Is you her customer?"

"Her customer?" Martin asked, feeling more confused than ever. "No, no I'm just, err, I'm just a man who needs to speak to her that's all."

"You need to speak to Abigail you need to go to St. Pancras"

"St. Pancras. As in the station, you mean at Kings Cross?"

"Yeah, with all the other whores."

"Abigail's a prostitute?" Martin asked, his eyebrows arched.

"Like you didn't already know, pervert."

"You've been most helpful, thank you." The businessman said, and quickly made his way back down the stairs. Then the woman's voice bellowed out from behind him, making the skin on the small of his back crawl like it was covered by thousands of tiny ants.

"You see that bitch you tell her she still owes Loretta the fifty notes!" Then the door was slammed shut, and Loretta undoubtedly returned to her soaps.

Feeling his heart pounding in his chest Martin ducked out into the alleyway and quickly hurried back out onto the street. He was disheartened to see the youths who had acknowledged him earlier gathered around his car, peering in through the passenger window.

"Hey homes, what you packing under the hood?" One of them asked when they saw him approach.

"Sorry, I'm in an awful hurry." Martin said, finding some truth in the words, he wanted nothing more than to get away from this God awful place and as quickly as possible.

"Don't be like that granddad we is just making conversation."

Martin unlocked the car and climbed inside. "Sorry." He said, feeling flustered and afraid.

"I fink he's pee'd his pants!" One of the youths shouted, and all three laughed.

Martin hadn't, but he checked his crotch just the same, considering the circumstances he really wouldn't have been surprised if he had. He started the engine and the car pulled away from the kerb, leaving the three boys, who really were just kids clowning around, still laughing on the roadside. It wasn't until he was passing through Lambeth heading towards Westminster that he finally calmed down. But his mind was still muddled; he didn't understand any of this. What the hell was a drug addict prostitute doing pretending to be the mother of the donor of his heart?

The plot was thickening around him, but Martin Rooley no longer felt like Columbo or Poirot, in fact he didn't think he had ever been so out of his depth in his life.

10

There was a café on the corner of Granary Square that Martin had been to a number of times on various trips into the city. It was a quarter after ten at night and was bitterly cold, somewhere close to freezing, when Martin stepped through the front door and up to the counter he was happy for the momentary warmth. He ordered a coffee to go – removing the plastic lid and leaving it on the counter – and reluctantly made his way back outside.

He had already done three full circuits of St. Pancras station, walking in the shadows as much as was possible, and although he had seen several ladies of ill repute; none had been the one he was looking for.

Walking down Pancras road in the direction of the hospital he pulled his collar tight against the chill wind. Again he battled with his thoughts; what was he doing here? Why was he walking these inner city streets, pursuing this ridiculous fool's charade when he should have been tucked up in bed. He was sixty-eight years old, not some young buck out to make a name for himself, why couldn't he just let this drop and move on with his life. The answer was simple; pride. He had been lied to, and more than once, and he was damned if he was going to let it lie without at least finding out the reason why. Somebody was purposefully trying to fool him, but who? Peter? Purefoy? Both? He didn't know, but he had a feeling there was more to the story than he currently knew, and it may not all be above board, why else had someone gone to such great lengths to keep him from the truth? Knowing this it was impossible to let it go, so he tried to ignore the cold that was creeping into his bones and walked on past the hospital.

The breath formed in front of his face like a cloud every time he exhaled, turning onto Granary Street and heading towards the train tracks. Here the road passed directly beneath the lines; he didn't like this bit, it would be all too easy to be the victim of a mugging or a savage beating and over what? The few coins he currently had in his pocket? You read about this type of thing all the time in the papers, and if it happened to him it would be big news indeed; the millionaire businessman getting his pocket picked in one of London's notorious prostitution hotspots. The Sun and the Daily Star would have a field day; his good name and his reputation would be dragged through the mud, it was frankly not an option, he would have to tread carefully.

As it turned out he needn't have worried; no gangs of youths hung in the tunnel beneath the railway lines, no local hoodlums were currently scouring the area for ageing millionaire businessmen out on a late night stroll. There was however a middle aged woman stood by the tunnel wall, her fake fur coat covering a pudgy body in a black PVC Basque. Martin had seen her the other three times he had made this journey, business must have been slow, and he was aware of how it must look. He tipped his head low and made his way into the ill lit tunnel, trying to avoid eye contact, but the woman had clearly misinterpreted his intentions.

"Looking for a good time darling?" She said as he passed for the fourth time.

"No thank you." He said, and hurried his pace.

"Come on love you clearly want it, why else would ya keep coming round?" Her cockney accent quite grating.

"No really, I'm ok, thank you." He said, thankful for the darkness of the tunnel for his cheeks were burning red.

"Poof." She muttered as he hurried away from her; he really couldn't come round this way again, it was becoming embarrassing. He made it to the end of the tunnel and the formidable red brick structure that was St. Pancras station came back into view. It really was a hugely impressive building, to think it had become home to prostitution and drug abuse within its vicinity was a crime against architecture.

From here he could also see the clock tower of the Midland Grand Hotel, which formed a part of the station; nearly half past ten now, Rose would be tucked up in bed with a good book, he wished that he was there with her.

He carried on up Granary to the bridge that crossed the Regent's canal, watching as a couple of cyclists out for a late night ride took the Grand Union tow path and disappeared out of sight, then he was back onto Pancras Road and facing the front entrance to the station once more.

This was pointless; he was wasting his time. Really, what were the chances of actually finding her; this was one of the largest cities in Europe, he may as well have been searching for a strand of hay in a huge pile of needles.

Taking a sip of the coffee to keep warm he looked about himself; he was running out of options. There was little point in performing the same circuit again; if she hadn't been there before she was unlikely to be there now. He was reluctant to head home just yet, otherwise this whole night would have been pointless, but at the same time he didn't want to spend too much longer out in the cold on a ridiculous wild goose chase. He looked up at the looming façade of St. Pancras International, home of the famous Eurostar, then across St. Pancras road in the direction of Kings Cross. Deciding he was better off trying here than working the same circuit again Martin crossed the road.

Turning left towards York Way he made his way around the back of the huge station to where the train lines terminated for central London. Here a couple of ladies were plying their trade on one of the secluded corners, but neither were the particular lady he sought. As he watched a car pulled up, a window was wound down and after a couple of seconds both ladies climbed in the back. Somebody's in for a busy night; Martin thought as the car pulled away and head towards the A5200.

He followed its general direction around to the far side of the station, and walked past the long row of shops to the side of the busy main road. A couple of gentlemen were settling down for the night in the doorway of the Harry Potter shop; they pulled their battered sleeping bags up to their necks and attempted to shield the worst of the chill wind by bending an old TV box and using it as a shield. Martin's heart went out to them as he passed by; he may be cold, but at least he wouldn't be spending the night here. He wanted to give them the change in his pocket, to tell them to buy a hot drink to keep them warm, but he understood that he needed to stay inconspicuous so instead walked on by, the men didn't pay any notice, they were used to this.

His own coffee was lukewarm now, so he took one final swig and dropped the remainder into a bin on the corner of Euston road. He had made it to the huge front façade of Kings Cross station; still busy even at this time of night, and watched as the glass doors opened and closed as people made their way to and from the station.

Normally he could people watch for hours, especially if he had a comfortable chair, a sticky bun and a cup of hot chocolate, but now the frantic movement made him feel anxious. He wasn't getting anywhere fast stood here on this street corner looking at the constant human traffic; if he was going to get answers to any of the multitude of questions that were fogging up his already over crowded brain he was going to have to take more decisive action. With his hands in his pockets to ward away the chill that was trying to creep into his finger joints he marched towards the glass doors of the station; a couple of moments later he was inside and out of the worst of the chill.

The huge grand entranceway to Kings Cross station opened up before him; the high domed ceiling arching down to stone walls that encased all of the usual station outlets; Boots, WH Smith's, Journey's Friend, The Cornish Pie Company, Subway. Above these a huge wall mounted monitor displayed the up and coming arrivals and departures to the station; there weren't many left now; it wouldn't be long before this part of the station closed down for the night. To the rear were gangways and security gates that led to each of the eleven platforms. People were milling around, some using the shops that were starting their nightly close-downs, others looking up at the board, some just waiting around for their train or a loved one to arrive. Martin took it all in, looking about the place, trying to spot his prey amongst the thinning crowd.

Suddenly out of the corner of his eye he noticed something; a thin blonde haired woman was standing to the far side of the foyer; she was wearing what looked from a distance like a knee length fake fur cost, just like the woman in the railway tunnel, and Martin just bet that underneath there wouldn't be very much left to the imagination. It was her, he was sure of it; with his new heart pumping a little faster Martin made his way in her direction. He crossed the distance, his shoes squeaking on the polished floor, the fingers of his hands jiggling at his sides.

As he came closer she turned on her heels so that her back was turned to him; but it was the same slender frame and the right height and build, it just had to be her.

Martin quickly tried to gather his thoughts; he would be of little use to his quest if he found himself tongue tied and his mind a blank. He needed hard questions that would give him the answers he desired, and he needed to ask them fast, before she decided he was trouble and she didn't want to be seen with him. She was younger and probably fitter than him, if she decided she was going to scarper he felt pretty sure there was little he would be able to do about it.

Just fifteen feet now; she was shifting her weight from foot to foot, a clear sign of impatience; Martin still didn't have his thoughts in check but he had decided to simply shoot from the hip, it was far from perfect, but it would have to do.

He closed the distance between them, not giving her a chance to turn around, then reached out and grabbed her gently but firmly by the shoulder.

"We need to talk." He said as the shocked woman spun around. Then he was stumbling backwards, his face equally as shocked as the woman's; it wasn't her! They had a similar look, a similar build, similar hair, but this lady was most definitely not Abigail Tardy, and the coat he had mistaken for a cheap fur imitation was in actual fact a very nice wintery fleece, beneath which she wore an elegant black knee length dress.

"Who are you?" She asked, her eyes large and afraid.

"I-I'm sorry." Martin stuttered. "I thought you were…"

"You ok Liz?" A voice interrupted from directly behind the businessman, this time it was he who spun around, and was greeted by a concerned looking middle aged man with greying hair, at his side were two tired looking children, each carrying an identical Pizza Hut balloon.

"I...it was...it was a mistake, I'm so sorry." Martin spluttered, feeling his cheeks starting to burn, he could feel sweat on his forehead and was suddenly very hot beneath the lining of his jacket. He turned back to the woman who looked very relieved at the timely arrival of her husband. "I'm so sorry; I thought you were somebody else."

"Ok, you startled me." She managed, starting to relax.

"I'm so sorry, please, have a pleasant evening." He said flustered, and quickly made his way as far from the family as he could across the concourse. He could see the signs for the tube station and head towards them; this night was done, the sooner he was on a train and away from here the better.

His night a disaster Martin took the escalator down into the tube station and followed the signs to the Northern line.

11

Mid day.

He had sat watching the wall mounted office clock for the last twenty-five minutes, just as he suspected half of the customer service department did when it was creeping up to five o'clock. The seconds had passed slowly but he had watched their continual circular motion with numbed comprehension. He wasn't waiting for something to happen, just as his chums in the service team would wait for the magical hour of home time, but had rather fallen into a sort of steady trance. The gentle tick-tocking as the second hand continued its onward journey was hypnotic to his fragile mind, and he had watched it with the same awareness of his actions as a baby smiling at a doting parent as it passed wind.

Everything ached; literally everything, from his ankles to his lower back, from the muscles in his neck to the balls of his throbbing feet. He had to face facts; he wasn't a spring chicken anymore, and all this running around, searching for answers was starting to take its toll. What did he expect; he must have walked four miles last night, he was sixty-eight years old for Christ's sake. He may have the heart of a thirty year old but the rest of him was ready for the knacker's yard.

Martin sighed and rubbed at his head, wanting nothing more than to jump in his car and head for home, maybe hit the sack for an hour or six, but he knew he wouldn't; he's stick it out until six o'clock, just as he always did, CEO or not, there were some things that never changed.

The previous nights events kept playing on his mind; how was he supposed to find Abigail in such a huge area? I mean Kings Cross, it was massive! And even then he would have to be there at the same time she was; last night while he had been wandering the streets around St. Pancras station she could have been tucking up in bed with a customer in a cheap hotel or sat home watching the soaps, wherever home was. She may not even be a prostitute anymore, if she had been in the first place, it could have simply been a damning statement from a bitter ex housemate. There were just so many potential opportunities for failure that it made him feel tired and out of his depth.

So what now? Should he call up Spence at Trojan Horse, tell him what he had found out and get him to dig a little deeper? Should he continue his search of the area around the two huge railway stations, one with its connections to the north the other with the whole of Europe? Should he try and figure out a different way of tracking the woman down, or of continuing his quest for answers in a different vein all together? Or should he simply admit defeat and put this whole sorry affair behind him once and for all? He knew one thing for certain, the latter certainly sounded tempting.

Just think; he could finish up here tonight and make the journey back home, safe in the knowledge he had nothing more pressing to his time than watching television and eating dinner, he'd be just like the vast majority of the country, and it sounded absolutely fantastic.

Martin sighed and leaned back in his seat. Whatever he decided he couldn't keep neglecting the notes he needed to cross examine for the upcoming end of year report; it may be still over a month away but already the department heads were submitting their data for his approval and it wasn't going to be accepted or declined sat in his inbox. He opened up the first mail and started to read. It was from Bill Bent, the head of Consumer Enterprises and was a basic round-up of activity by quarter for the year. It was a well written piece, full of facts and figures and charts and graphs, you had to hand it to old Bill, he was a sucker for detail, but halfway through the second page of the report Martin found his mind wandering again. It was just impossible to concentrate on work when he had so much going on in his personal life. He clicked the little lower case E icon on his desktop and loaded up Internet Explorer. After a few seconds the company homepage appeared, so he clicked on the browser panel and typed in the URL for Google. In the search panel for Google he typed in 'prostitution hot spots London' and clicked on the magnifying glass. The first ten hits appeared on screen, without waiting to check what he was entering Martin clicked on the first link.

Just then his intercom sounded on his desk, he hit the receive button and heard the soft tones of his PA on the other end of the line.

"I've got those reports you asked for, the ones from marketing, I just need your signature and I can forward them on to HR."

"Bring them through." Martin said, and a couple of moments later his door opened and Sheila walked in. She was carrying a small stack of papers that she cradled carefully against her bird like chest.

Martin gestured her over and she came and stood at his side, placing the papers down before him.

"You look tired." She said as he quickly scanned the first paper.

"I'm fine, just not sleeping very well that's all."

"Any reason? I hope you're taking care of yourself."

"There's no need for concern I can assure you." He said as he finished reading and signed the first document.

Sheila didn't reply, but after a few moments as he was continuing to sign the duplicate copies she let out a small "oh" and when Martin looked up she was looking down to the floor. He ignored her and finished signing the forms, when he looked up she was still looking down, her cheeks a little red as though she were flustered. Strange.

"You ok?" Martin asked.

"Yes, fine thank you." She replied, then quickly gathered up the signed forms and hurried to the door. "I'll get these over to HR straight away." Then the door closed behind her.

Martin smiled his first genuine smile of the day. He liked Sheila a lot; she was quirky. Then he turned back to his PC and his jaw dropped loose as he saw what his secretary had:

On the screen a young girl wearing a revealing outfit that left little to the imagination was bent double, her bottom pointing at an irregular angle as she blew a kiss to whoever was watching, above her in giant red lettering was the words' XXX babes.com, dirty girls direct to your door!'

12

Martin sat in the window of what was quickly becoming his favourite coffee spot, warming his hands on the thick ceramic of the white porcelain mug. From here he had a perfect vantage point over the front vestibule of St. Pancras station and a pretty good view of Kings Cross in the distance. It was his third night in a row on stakeout duty and it had not gone unnoticed at home.

He hated lying to Rose; when you had been married as long as they had there were certain things which were just natural to veto; lying was one of them. But what choice did he have? He still remembered how she had blown up when he had hinted at digging deeper into the strange situation surrounding his operation; if she knew just how deep within that investigation he had become embroiled she would probably bury him under the patio, and he hadn't undergone invasive surgery to be dead a few months later at the hands of his own loving wife.

As he had left the house shortly after supper a deep weight had settled in his gut; he had lied, again. It was becoming all too frequent. Tonight was a continuation of a major HR problem involving work place fraud that had to be handled outside office hours. He knew she wouldn't suspect him of any foul play; he was way too old to be fooling around with anybody and as far as she was concerned didn't have a devious bone in his body, but this only made matters worse. He almost wished she did suspect something; she could challenge him about it and he would happily spill everything, from his meeting with a woman he believed to be Linda McGready to hiring the private dick. He would receive one hell of a tongue lashing, maybe even receive the silent treatment for a couple of days, but anything was better than this horrible double life.

Martin sighed and looked down at his coffee, three quarters gone now, black and strong, enough caffeine to keep him going for hopefully another hour or so, if only it could somehow medicate the deep aching in his back and in his legs as well.

He had worked out a new figure of eight route that led him around the back of St. Pancras and across the front of Kings Cross before circumnavigating this station and returning to the front of St. Pancras again, and had walked it three times already tonight. Last night he had done his original route a couple of times before discovering his new, more efficient route, the night before that had been the disastrous misunderstanding with the lady and her pizza loving kids.

Three nights, and no results. He couldn't keep this up much longer; even Rose would start to see through his thinly veiled lies if he did. On top of this it was starting to drain on his morale, it was like his lifelong support of Bolton Wanderers; there were only so many negative results you could stand. He drained his coffee and looked over to the counter; he was toying with the idea of getting another cup, this one to go, when something out of the corner of his eye suddenly caught his attention. It was a flash of red, so striking against the darkness of its surroundings that it would have been very hard to miss. He swivelled around on his chair and pressed his face up close to the glass.

The red had been the material of a figure hugging dress, too tight and too thin for the conditions tonight, but the perfect attire for somebody trying to gain the attention of a potential client. The thigh length boots were the same devilish colour, but were PVC to the dresses thin cotton. Even the lipstick, as scarlet as it was could be seen from this distance, but despite this vulgar contrast to the quiet unassuming woman he had met in a rented flat on Bill Nicholson Way, there was no mistaking he had finally found his prey.

Martin's heart felt as though it were literally lodged in his throat, he could barely breathe and definitely not blink as he watched the thin woman cross Pancras road in the direction of Kings Cross. Abigail Tardy, who had paraded as Linda McGready in an attempt to fool him into believing she was the mother of his donor, but to what gain? He wasn't going to find the answer sitting here with his jaw hanging loose like a Venus fly trap.

Quickly he pushed back his chair, the metal feet scraping on the worn tiles, and made a dash for the door. A blast of cold air hit him as he stepped outside, he lifted his collar up to protect his neck against the worst of it and hurried in the direction she had gone. He could just see her stepping up onto the pavement leading up to the station and quickly gave chase.

He was in luck; she stopped on the corner of Kings Cross to adjust her dress and this gave Martin the valuable seconds he needed to close the distance between them before she disappeared through the front doors of the station and out of sight. There were cars starting to appear through the changing traffic lights on Pancras road and Martin had to hurry across, feeling a stitch start to gather in the right side of his chest. He comforted it with the palm of his hand, knowing he had no time to stop and rest, and continued on his way.

Up ahead Abigail was on the move again, just a few paces from the station now, he wasn't going to catch her before she was inside.

Martin stopped at the kerb, panting and out of breath. "Abigail wait!" He called.

It worked. The middle aged prostitute stopped dead just as she was about to walk through the sliding door and into the station. She turned around, but when she saw Martin there her face stretched in surprise and horror. She paused for a couple of seconds, a rabbit in the headlights, and it was just enough time for Martin to be on the move again, inching towards her. He knew her intentions instantly; she was going to run, and he was damned if he was going to make it easy for her, he hadn't spent three nights staking out this dark and gloomy part of London just to lose her again now.

Though he was still struggling with the pain in his chest – all too reminiscent of the pains that had got him into this whole sorry mess – he had one thing in his favour, Abigail was struggling to run in the huge heels of her thigh length boots, Martin noticed and it was the impetus he needed. Spurred on by the change in fortune he clutched his pained chest tight and made a dash on his weary legs towards her. He caught hold of her arm just as she was passing through the sliding door and spun her around so they were standing face to face in the entrance to the busy station.

Recognising how it must look, a reasonably high profile businessman propositioning a prostitute in the doorway of one of the busiest rail stations in Europe, Martin pulled her into the shadows to the far side of the entrance.

"Leave me alone!" She said trying to struggle out of his grip, her make –up plastered face a mask of misery and concern.

"I need to speak to you." Martin replied unfazed.

"I don't know you leave me alone."

"Oh I think you do." Martin replied with determination.

"I've got nothing to say to you!" She spat angrily, still trying to struggle out of his grip.

"First you don't know me, then you don't have anything to say to me, which is it huh?" He asked. "Look, I'm going to let go of your arm, don't try to run, I mean you no harm, I just want to ask you a few questions."

"I've got nothing to say to you!"

"You've already said that, but I think you do, I think there's a lot you can tell me."

"Yeah." She said, looking straight at him in a challenging manner. "And why should I?"

"Because I've done nothing to hurt you, and I don't deserve what's happening to me, and because you owe it to me for lying to me about who you are."

Abigail let out a sharp mocking laugh.

Martin pursed his lips; he could see he was going to get nowhere trying to reason with her. "Ok, if that's not a good enough reason for you, how about if you don't tell me what I want to know I'll go to the police and tell them you've been using the name Linda McGready again, I'm sure they'd be interested to hear bout your latest parole violation."

The prostitute's shoulders slumped and she leaned back against the wall; Martin knew from her crestfallen expression that he had her on the ropes. Just then the huge glass sliding doors opened and a dozen or so commuters walked out into the cold night air. Martin gently manoeuvred the woman deeper into the shadows, afraid of being spotted and, God forbid, recognised. It wouldn't look too innocent to Rose if he had been photographed having a close quarters conversation with a lady of the night outside a busy city railway station.

"Look, I don't want to hurt you any more than I'm sure you wanted to hurt me, but I need to know why you lied to me, why you pretended to be the mother of my donor, there had to be a reason for that and I need to know what it is. Please."

Abigail shook her head in exasperation, still looking beyond Martin for any possible means of escape, but for the time being she was resigned to being stuck here in this difficult situation. "I knew I should have never got involved in this." She said with real regret.

"Involved in what?" Martin coaxed.

"Whatever this shit is!" She spat angrily.

"Just tell me what you know."

"Some guy, he stops me in the street, says he'll pay me five hundred pounds if I go to a house with him, I figure just another day in paradise, but he said it wasn't like that. He wanted me to pretend to be somebody, told me some rich guy was gonna come asking a lot of questions and I had to play a role. I told him I play plenty of roles in the bedroom but I ain't no actress. He says I'll be fine and goes through what I need to say and what I need to wear. I tell him to fuck off, so he up's the ante, a grand now. I'm not rich like you I ain't in no position to turn down a thousand quid."

"So you agreed to play the role."

"Yeah I agreed to it, so would you if you were in my position. He says to me we need to come up with a character name; I suggested Linda McGready, he seemed to like it. I don't know who he was, I don't know why he wanted me to do it and frankly mister I don't care, what I care about is getting paid, and he was good to his word on that so as far as I'm concerned the matters closed."

"And at no point did you feel you were doing something wrong? That you were being deceitful?"

The prostitute slowly shook her head, the mocking smile back on her lips. "It must be fucking fantastic to be up there in your ivory tower. It was business; I was doing a job, unless you hadn't noticed my day to day job isn't exactly kosher either."

"When we were at the house, you went upstairs to get the kettle, but it was already in the kitchen, I know because I saw it, you must have known that too. What were you really doing while you were upstairs? You were calling him weren't you? Your contact."

"So what if I was?"

"Can you give me the number?"

"I don't have it anymore, he took my phone, said I could buy a new one with my earnings."

"Well can you describe him to me?"

"I don't know, I only met him a couple of times."

"Please try, it's important."

Abigail sighed. "Tall, broad shoulders, thick wavy hair, real stick up his arse, acted like he was better than me, Eton type, well educated but no manners."

"Purefoy." Martin whispered, having his worst fears realised.

"He never gave a name."

Martin could feel a chill in his bones and it wasn't from the cold November air. His eyes were watering and his brain felt cluttered with a multitude of disturbing thoughts. When he didn't speak for a while the middle aged woman took her opportunity.

"Look, I've told you what you want to know, now let me go."

"Fine, fine." Martin said, nodding his head slightly, but his eyes were glazed and distant, deep in thought.

Abigail started slowly edging away from the wealthy businessman, sliding along the wall in the direction of the glass entranceway to the station. Before she could get there though she stopped, looking hard at the man she had so callously fooled.

"Piece of advice, whatever this thing is, let it go."

"I can't." He said, looking up at her. "I'm in too deep."

"That guy paid me to mess with you for a reason, if he wants to cover something up it's because he doesn't want you to know. He must be half your age, what are you anyway? Seventy? Seventy-five?"

"I'm sixty-eight!"

"Doesn't matter, that fact is you're in over your head, let it go."

"Thanks for the advice." Martin said, his shoulders sagging now he had found what he had come for.

"So err, you gonna dob me in or what?"

"No, our business is done."

Abigail Tardy nodded a couple of times, then slipped away from the businessman and disappeared through the glass front doors of the station. Martin watched her go, feeling more and more helpless with every passing second. Maybe she was right, maybe he was in over his head. Purefoy had paid a complete stranger to act in a conspiracy, to cover up something he was desperate to keep from Martin, something that related to his heart transplant, he had a few ideas and none of them filled him with anything other than anxiety and fear. After a couple of moments staring into space, trying to gather his muddled thoughts he followed the prostitute through the sliding doors of Kings Cross station.

Had she really told him everything that she knew of the conspiracy? He would perhaps never know for sure, but he felt that she had. So what now? Confront Purefoy? It seemed like the only viable solution. If the surgeon felt he could con Martin and get away with it he had another thing coming. He decided as he walked through the station in the direction of the Northern line that he would sleep on it for tonight, no good could come of him challenging the surgeon now, he needed a clear head and a good line of questioning readily prepared.

Martin scanned his Oyster card and took the elevator down to the station floor, where he would take the tube to London Bridge and change on to the Jubilee line towards Canary Wharf. His heart was thumping away in his chest; he paid it no notice.

13

Back in his office Martin was pacing the thick carpet in his bare feet, travelling the length of the picture window back and forth like a stalking predator. Once again his working day had been less productive than that of the most basic of introductory staff on his wage bill; he had done nothing, literally nothing. Not unless you could count trying to decide whether to confront Purefoy about what he had discovered as meaningful work, somehow he felt the shareholders who had heavily invested in his good name and his business would not.

He was in too deep to just let this go, but he couldn't just go steaming in all the same. What exactly was he accusing the surgeon of anyway? Whatever it was it can't have been legal; nobody would have gone to such lengths to cover their tracks if the business they were conducting was legitimate. And why? No money had changed hands, so if something illegal was going on here who were the beneficiaries? He was one for sure, he had received a new vital organ that had literally saved his life; but as far as he could see he was the only winner here. If Purefoy had acted unethically in a bid to save his life what had been in it for him? Martin had met the man, he could be sure that this was no act of charity; in fact he doubted if the man could even understand the word.

Then there was the Devil in him, the small voice that kept telling him to let it go, that whatever the circumstances the man had saved his life, to be thankful and leave it at that. But he couldn't shake the feeling that there was something truly appalling behind all this that would make any kindness he had received pale against the weight of its knowledge.

The one thing for which he was finally certain was that the operation that had been performed on the upper floor of his ample home had not been done with the knowledge of either his private healthcare contractors or the NHS.

He had known at the time that something wasn't right; it was ludicrous when you thought about it, the idea of having such a serious operation performed in a non emergency scenario within the confines of your own home. But he had wanted to believe; oh yes he had wanted to believe, had wanted it with every ounce of his swiftly decaying heart. So he had ignored that curious inner voice and allowed it to happen. Not wanting to think about the what if's, not wanting to think about the why's or the how's, just wanting to be well again, just wanting to not leave his wife a widow, his business in need of a new CEO. He had ignored his better judgment in the pursuit of his own survival, but to what cost? To what cost? Martin had some ideas, but he was scared to even acknowledge them, scared that it made him at least in part complicit to something potentially truly horrible.

He had to know. Whatever the outcome, whatever the consequences, however it made him feel about himself once the truth was finally out, he needed to know what had happened, if only to quieten those small soft voices that were talking all the more frequently now in his mind, he needed to finally put this business to rest.

Martin crossed the carpet and plonked down in his soft leather chair, he scrunched his toes on the carpet as he picked up the phone and dialled the number that he knew now by memory. After a couple of rings it was answered by the soft voice of the on-duty desk nurse.

"St. Cuthbert's Hospital, cardiovascular, how may I help you?"

"Oh I wonder if you could, I was hoping to speak with Mister David Purefoy please."

"Please hold the line while I try to connect you sir."

"Thank you."

The line clicked and then some awful twenty year old hold tone was ringing out its tuneless travesty in his ear. Martin pulled the receiver away from his tortured ear and waited to be patched through to the surgeon, his heart beating fast in his chest. He wasn't exactly sure what he was going to say, but if he dwelled on it any longer it was likely to drive him crazy. Then the voice of the desk nurse returned and he placed the handset back to the side of his face.

"I'm sorry sir Mister Purefoy isn't in the building at the moment, in fact he hasn't been seen for a couple of days, is there anything I can help with?"

Martin sighed with frustration, as per usual when he needed to speak with the surgeon he was nowhere to be found.

"Not really no, I need to speak to the Doctor. Could you tell me how I can get in touch with him please?"

"I'm sorry I'm not able to divulge that type of personal information…"

"I already have his personal number, but you can bet he won't be answering on that, it's his address I need."

"I'm sorry sir, I wouldn't be able to provide that type of information."

Martin screwed his eyes shut tight and gently tapped the handset receiver against his forehead, his frustration oozing from every pore.

"Sir, are you still there?"

"Sorry yes I'm still here, could you pass me through to the anaesthetist's please?"

"Hold the line."

The awful toneless chimes sounded in his ear again and Martin crumpled back in his seat, waiting for the call to be acknowledged. Finally, after what felt like an entire concert by the toneless deafening squawk band the call was picked up by a woman with a deep Surrey accent.

"St. Cuthbert's how can I help you?"

"Oh I wonder if you can." Martin said, leaning forward. "I was hoping to have a word with one of your anaesthetists."

"Are you a relative or a friend?"

"No, no, nothing like that, more a grateful patient that wants to thank him for looking after me."

"This line needs to be kept open sir in case of emergencies; any thank you's can be delivered in person or by letter."

"Oh this won't take long, I promise not to block your line up for too long."

The lady sighed. "Ok, who was the anaesthetist you wanted to thank?"

"Ricardo Panettiere."

There was a pause on the other end of the line, when the lady came back on the call there was caution in her voice.

"Is this some kind of joke?"

"No joke, why?" Martin asked, his curiosity pricked.

"When is Mister Panettiere supposed to have performed as your anaesthetist?"

"In the summer, why?"

"There must be some mistake."

"No mistake, it was definitely him, why does that surprise you?" Martin could feel a cold chill working its way through his bones, he could hardly breathe.

"You're mistaken. Either that or you're trying to be funny, either way I'd like to free up this line now please."

"Please, I don't understand." Was all Martin could say to prevent her from dropping the call, but it worked. When the lady spoke again it was in a hushed tone.

"Ok I don't know your real reasons for wanting to speak to that son of a bitch and frankly I don't care, but I am certain of one thing, that man did not perform as your anaesthetist this summer, not in this hospital or any other. Off the record to get you off my case, Ricardo Panettiere dosed the anaesthetic wrong for a four year old child who proceeded to be awake through major bowel surgery; he was struck off nearly three years ago."

Martin's breath caught in his throat, he had not expected this.

"So you see," the lady continued, "he can't be your man, now if you'll excuse me I have work to do."

"Ok," Martin mumbled, feeling flabbergasted once more, "I'm sorry for the confusion."

"Good day sir." Came the curt response, then the line went dead.

Martin placed the handset back in its cradle and slumped back in his chair. The deeper he swam into this pool of deceit and lies the more he became entwined in its mystery. Panettiere struck off for the most horrendous case of professional negligence that Martin had ever had the misfortune to consider. A four year old boy awake throughout major bowel surgery; the implications were both terrible and terrifying. Staring up at the ceiling Martin puffed out his cheeks and rasped a huge exhale of breath towards the air conditioning unit.

His intercom buzzed on his desk.

"Yes." He said, pressing the receive button and nursing his temple with his free hand, he could feel a headache coming on. Hell this whole sorry mess was nothing short of one long troublesome headache.

"Rose is here to see you." His PA's voice came through the speaker on the side of the intercom unit.

Martin sighed, just what he didn't need right now, he pressed to talk again: "Send her in."

A couple of moments later the door opened and his wife walked in, a huge smile on her face. Martin tried to return it but it was strained, he hoped it wasn't too obvious.

"Hey." He said as she walked across the plush carpet and sat down in the chair opposite him.

"I missed you this morning." She said, the smile never faltering.

"Sorry, another early one, there's just so much going on here at the moment, you know how it is."

"Early mornings, late nights, you seem to be forever at the office these days, what happened to cutting back."

"It's temporary; things will get back to normal pretty soon, I just have a few things I need to tie up that's all. So what brings you here?"

The business like tone to her husband's voice finally made the smile falter, though Rose tried hard to regain it, though a worthy effort it would prove to be in vain.

"I just thought it would be nice to pop by, say hello, it's been a while since I did that. Is that little café still around the corner, the one with the pretty cake counter?"

Martin couldn't believe this, all he wanted to do was sit and give some serious thought to his next move in the mystery that was rapidly unravelling about him and here she was talking to him about cake.

"Yeah, yeah it's still there."

"Well," she said, looking hopeful but starting to feel a little crestfallen, "I thought maybe we could go for a spot of lunch, maybe you could get a slice of that nice coffee cake you like."

"It's a lovely idea." Martin replied, trying hard to smile. "But I've just got so much on, some other time, definitely."

"Oh, ok." Rose replied, her eyes looking sad, Martin noticed and it made him feel bad, but he really didn't have time for this, not if he was going to get to the bottom of whatever was happening in his double life.

"What time do you think you'll be home?" She asked, forcing a thin tired looking smile.

"I think I'm going to be late again." He said, thinking what he really wanted to do was spend some time going over his options and knowing he wouldn't get that opportunity at home, where Rose would want him to sit down and watch Downton Abbey on the Sky planner.

"Tonight?" She asked, the mask finally dropped, now she looked utterly horrified and Martin didn't know why, in fact it was starting to bug him, could she not see he was busy?

"I'm afraid so, like I say we just have so much on at the moment, and I know I promised I'd start cutting things back at work and I will it's just that tonight really isn't a good night to be heading off early, it would give out the wrong message when so many others are going to have to be staying back too, you understand don't you?"

"Yes, yes." She said, nodding slowly, a strained smile on her face.

"Thank you, I promise things will get back to normal soon, it's just been one of those weeks you know, Hell one of those months!"

"No problem." She said, and slowly got up to leave."

Martin felt a little guilty. "I'm sorry you came all the way down here, if you'd called first..."

"Really, it's fine." She replied, but her tone was clipped and Martin knew it was likely he would be in the dog house for his behaviour later; what's more he was pretty sure that he'd deserve it. All the same he allowed her to go, walking her to his office door, but when he placed a kiss on her cheek before she left she did not return it, did in fact flinch slightly at his touch.

Oh well, he thought as she said her goodbyes and closed the office door behind her, he may feel the heat for this later on but at least for now he had the much needed peace he so desired. Martin slumped back down in his chair and swivelled slightly so he could look out once more onto his favourite view.

He breathed a deep sigh and tried to regain the thought process he had started moments before Rose's unexpected interruption.

Then there was a knock at the door and his sigh this time was one of exasperation; what did he have to do to get some peace around here?

It was Sheila; what's more she looked concerned.

"You got a minute?" She asked.

"Of course." He replied, gesturing for her to come in, already knowing he was being more pleasant to her than he had been to his own wife; the regret of the earlier conversation was starting to weigh on him, maybe he should call her on her mobile, arrange to meet her for lunch after all.

Sheila crossed the office and stood in front of him on the other side of his huge mahogany desk.

"I don't mean to pry, but is everything ok?"

"It's fine yes, I have a few things on my mind but otherwise I'm tickety-boo, why?"

"It's just Rose, well, she seemed upset as she was leaving."

"She wanted me to go for lunch, I didn't have time that's all, and I told her I'd be working late, I think she was hoping I'd be home at a reasonable hour but I've got a few things to do."

"Today?" Sheila asked, her eyes looking troubled.

"Yes today!" Martin felt completely exasperated, and he was struggling to stop it from showing, what was so special about today?

"You've forgotten haven't you?" Sheila stated, looking troubled on behalf of her employer.

"Forgotten what?" He almost bellowed, starting to feel really agitated now.

"It's Rose's birthday, I added it to your calendar and put early reminders in for last month and the beginning of the week." The PA had gone red at the cheeks but this was clearly not her fault. Martin slumped back in his seat; of course, Rose's birthday! And Sheila had put the reminders in, he had seen them but they had not registered, he had been too preoccupied with his own selfish needs.

"Oh God." He said, feeling utterly horrified at his terrible error, no wonder she had looked so hurt, no wonder she had been so stiff when he had leaned in to kiss her!

"Do you want me to try and catch her?" Sheila asked, gesturing back towards the door.

"No, I'll call her on her phone, my God Sheila you could literally be a life saver!"

The PA nodded and started to turn to the door. "If you need anything, let me know."

"Could you order a bunch of flowers quick? A big bunch. A really big bunch!"

"I'm on it." She said with a smile and head from the room.

Martin leant over and picked up his desk phone, as he dialled another number he actually knew from memory he reflected on how he could have been so stupid. He had never missed Rose's birthday, did in fact enjoy her special day more than his own, he had always preferred giving presents to receiving them, but somehow he had been so preoccupied that the day had almost slipped by without him even noticing.

I need to spend more time at home, I'm neglecting the one I love on the trail of a pointless venture, he thought, and made a decision there and then to let the whole sorry affair go. Life had to go on, he couldn't waste any more time on something so vastly out of his control.

In his ear the dial tone finally kicked in.

14

Salvaging Rose's birthday wasn't easy, but he pulled it off; just. At first she had absolutely no intention of letting him off the hook; she was mad at him and frankly he didn't blame her, what's more she intended to make him suffer. At a table in the window of the Merry Berry Delicatessen Rose sat in brooding silence while her husband grovelled for her forgiveness. He had been an ass, she deserved better, he hadn't meant to treat her with disrespect, of course her birthday was important to him, he was going to make it up to her; his mouth was saying all the right words but the frosty exterior wasn't showing any signs of an early thaw.

Then salvation arrived in the form of four men in pin striped suits, spotted dickie-bow's about their necks, straw boaters atop their heads; a barbershop quartet, there to perform Mrs Rooley's favourite song – 'Don't sit under the apple tree' by the Andrew's Sisters. It was a stroke of genius, and it melted away all of the ice and tension in four voice a cappella harmony.

When the song had come to an end and the gentlemen had wished the now sixty-four year old a wonderful day the birthday girl had leant over the table and smacked a huge grateful kiss on the left cheek of her equally grateful husband, who in turn had made a mental note to display his gratitude to his PA who was no doubt responsible for this latest stroke of genius.

Now that he was back in an upward keel he had absolutely no intention of letting it slip again. While Rose was in the toilet Martin called through to the office. After thanking Sheila for saving him from a bit of a hole he set his PA off on another couple more extra curricular activities; well, he was the boss, if he couldn't bend the rules a little when it was he who footed the wage bill then who could?

They finished a light lunch of toasted bagels and coffee cake, all washed down with a cappuccino for Rose and an English breakfast tea for Martin, and made their way outside, where the businessman informed his wife he had taken the rest of the day off, and they were heading onto Oxford Street to finish the shopping trip he had cut short previously.

This time he'd served an ace for sure; Martin knew his wife and of all her many and varied hobbies shopping ranked the highest, and by a considerable margin. What's more knowing how much her husband hated the pastime, and the fact that he had left what she believed to be another busy day at the office to share the time with her, cemented his place firmly in Rose Rooley's good books.

He didn't moan, he didn't grumble, he didn't slouch behind or complain of sore feet; in fact Martin was the perfect shopping companion that afternoon, suggesting items that may be of interest to Rose and complimenting her when she proceeded to try them on. It was when they broke for coffee and a rest in the Costa near Selfridges that the text he had been waiting for came through. Once more Sheila had come up trumps, and Rose's forgotten birthday was not only salvaged but propelled to new heights.

"So what have we got planned for tonight?" He asked as she took a sip of her skinny latte.

"I haven't got anything planned." She replied.

"That's where you're wrong." He said with a smile. "We have an early table at Hibiscus followed by the evening performance of your favourite West End musical 'Phantom of the Opera'."

Rose was speechless, a Michelin starred restaurant and tickets to her favourite show, it really was turning out to be a wonderful birthday, and if she had known the strings that Sheila had needed to pull in order to mastermind such a last minute coup she would have been doubly impressed.

The couple continued their shopping spree, buying outfits more suitable to the evening's proceedings, and had their bags and day clothes picked up by one of Sapient's three limo drivers and transported back to the office. After a quick refresher where Rose reapplied her make-up in the toilets of Harvey Nichols the couple were ready, and they made their way to Mayfair for their early dinner. It was an exquisite meal, each course an explosion of flavour on the taste buds, and when they left a little after seven-fifteen they were both in culinary heaven, as well as being a little tipsy from the two bottles of champagne the businessman ordered to accompany the meal.

They hailed a taxi from the restaurant that took them to Her Majesty's Theatre where they arrived just in time for the evening performance. Sheila had secured them a box that adjoined the grand circle that was the perfect spot for when the huge chandelier came crashing to the stage, and though Rose had seen the show at least half a dozen times she still gasped at this particular moment, cried during her favourite of the love songs and applauded the operatic performance of the lady playing Carlotta Giudicelli, a vibrato that seemed to reach out and touch the very eaves of the old West End theatre.

When the performance came to a close some time after ten both Rooley's were on their feet applauding the show. As the performers took their bows Martin reflected that he had seen the show at least a couple of times since moving to the capital, but this was the first time he had really enjoyed it.

In fact, as they made their way across London in a black cab hailed from the theatre the businessman had time to reflect on the entire day. He had enjoyed the show as he had enjoyed the meal, he had enjoyed the look on his wife's face as he had been able to unveil his surprises; Hell he had even enjoyed mooching round the shops earlier that afternoon. When he really considered how the day had panned out if he excluded the horrendous faux pas of actually forgetting it was his wife's birthday, then the only part of the day that he hadn't enjoyed was in pursuing the mysterious surroundings relating to his heart operation.

Rose sat happily, looking out of the window of the cab as the heart of London disappeared behind them, the miles slowly ticking down on their journey home. Martin looked at her, so happy, so content, and wondered just what he was doing with his life. He had really enjoyed himself today, couldn't in fact remember the last time he had felt so happy, so fulfilled, and realised he had been spending too much time focusing on the negative aspects of his life. H e was healthy, he had a wonderful wife and good friends, he had absolutely no financial concerns, the business was doing well much in contrast to the general economy, and yet he was spending his days wallowing in a world which brought him nothing but confusion and misery.

Why?

When he really gave it some serious thought what benefit was there in continuing this foolish charade? So what if Purefoy had acted a little off the books? He had done it to save his life! He ought to be grateful, not spending his days on some 16th Century witch hunt. He had a life to live, he had learned the hard way that life was short, had almost in fact found himself at an abrupt and terrifying climax to his life; he needed now to learn how to enjoy his days ahead, to live his life in a way that reflected the amazing gift he had received.

The couple arrived home and exhausted made their way to bed; it had been a long day. As Martin relaxed back into his pillow he realised he was feeling something strange, a feeling he had not had for a very long time; it was a feeling of contentment. He slipped quickly into a deep and nourishing sleep, a small smile still pressing at the corners of his mouth.

15

The sun had no clear definition in the sky, and the temperature, whatever it may be was irrelevant to Martin as he stepped through the open doorway of Sapient Trans Global and outside. If it was unusually warm for the time of year it was lost on Martin; his mind wasn't settled on anything in particular, in fact it was fair to say that at this present time he had no thoughts at all, but this did not support him in having any awareness of anything that was happening around him, what's more, at this particular time, Martin also did not notice that he was being superficially numb to his senses.

There were three things of which he was aware; he had been at the office and now he was leaving, he was heading out of the office on his way to a certain destination; he was yet to discover what that destination was.

None of this concerned Martin; in fact concern was an emotion that at this present time would have been alien to him, he was surrounded by an aura of contentment that negated the need for any other senses or feelings.

That was however all about to change.

He reached the kerb and paused for thought, not having an understanding of where he was currently headed this seemed a logical step, but it made what was about to happen all the easier for his abductors.

The white van, rust down the entire right panel, screeched around the corner of Cannon Drive from the direction of Hertsmere Road and came to an abrupt stop directly in front of the shocked man. The side door slid open and two masked figures leant out, grabbed Martin by the upper arms, and dragged him into the van, badly knocking his shin on the lip of the storage compartment. He felt no pain, was too shocked to feel any pain, but all at once his senses were alive and kicking, blood pumping through his veins, a million different thoughts firing into the Broca's area of his brain.

He was thrown roughly to the uncovered floor of the van; he hit his back hard against the corrugated metal and rolled onto his side, a wave of panic filling his body and clouding his judgment. Instinctively covering his face in case of attack Martin looked up at his captors, there were two of them in the van and through the opening to the front of the compartment he could see another masked assailant driving. He was thrown against the side of the van as the vehicle quickly turned a corner, then was able to prop himself up on his elbows, breathing way too fast. That was the first time that he properly noticed the masks. The largest of his captors wore a plastic mask that covered the majority of his face; the hood of a sweatshirt had been pulled up to cover the back portion of the head. When the features of the mask became apparent it made the gorge rise in Martin's throat; the plastic had been moulded into the shape of his wife's face, he was looking at his captor, and the dead plastic rudimentary features of his wife were staring back.

The smaller of the two in the back of the van wore an identical hoodie, it too covered the back portion of their head, but their own mask was moulded to resemble somebody completely different; Peter Werth-Duncan.

Martin gasped, wondering with growing dread who these people were and what exactly they wanted with him.

"Everything ok back there?" The driver called through the open window in the back of the cab, and Martin couldn't be sure, but he thought he recognised the voice.

"Everything's fine." The larger of the two assailants in the back of the truck replied.

"Good, hold on back there." The driver called back, turning round slightly as he manoeuvred through the streets of the financial capital of England, and when he did Martin caught a slight glimpse of the mask he wore. He couldn't be certain, but he was pretty sure this one had been moulded to resemble his golfing buddy Bert Etherington. Martin didn't find this strange; for the time being he was too preoccupied with the simple and startling fact that he had been snatched from the street outside his office in broad daylight , thrown into the back of a transit van anddriven at high speed to God knew where.

I'm a wealthy man, is this a kidnapping? Am I going to be ransomed for money? Martin wondered as he tried to gather his thoughts. One thing was for sure he wasn't going to get any answers sitting mutely on the floor of this van.

"Who are you?" He asked, looking up at the two masked assailants who regarded him with all the caution of a snake handler attempting to charm a particularly spirited cobra.

"Shut up!" The bigger of the two spat, pointing a meaty finger at the businessman.

"What do you want with me?"

"I said shut up!"

"Ricky…" The other assailant started; Martin was startled to hear a female voice beneath the mask that bore the resemblance of his friend and colleague.

"No names you stupid bitch!" The man wheeled angrily on his partner.

"It ain't gonna matter, he's not going to be able to tell any of this."

"That's not the point, now the pair of you just shut your holes." He leaned back against the wall of the van and folded his arms huffily across his ample chest.

The woman's words were not lost on Martin, who sat staring back at them in abject terror; why would he not be able to tell any of this? What were they going to do to him? One thing was for certain, this was surely not a case of kidnap and ransom, which tended to work best when the captive was still alive to be ransomed!

He desperately tried to gather his thoughts, trying to think of anything that may help him out of a situation that was quickly spiralling out of control, but in his panic his mind had reverted to that of a baby in the womb; all pink spots and dreamlike lapses.

The van hurried on, its destination as yet unclear, but every time it sped round a corner the three in the back were rocketed back and forth, the two who were standing using hand rails to keep themselves on their feet.

Martin's eyes scanned the floor of the van for something, anything he could use as a weapon, but apart from a thin film of dust and the three of them gathered in the back the compartment was empty.

Think, you have to think! He scolded himself, feeling completely incapable of finding a solution to his problem. Wherever they were heading they were heading there fast, probably breaking the speed limit, surely his biggest hope couldn't be that they would be pulled over by a traffic policeman?

"You're making a big mistake here." He tried to reason. "Just let me go and we can forget about all this. I won't even go to the police, you have my word."

"I told you to shut up." The bigger of the two masked assailants responded.

"I'm a very powerful man; there will be people looking for me you'd do a lot of time for this."

"You think I'm scared of doing a little time?"

"All I'm asking is you see reason, I have money, I can make you rich beyond your wildest dreams, just let me go and we can work something out."

At this the smaller of the two, the woman stepped forward.

"We don't want your money ok, talk can't save you now, so do as my friend here says and shut up, or I'll take him off his leash."

"What's going on back there?" The driver called through the hatch.

"Nothing, it's under control." The beefy one replied.

They didn't want his money. Ok so what the hell did they want? Whatever it was it couldn't be good, if these people were not financially motivated then his chances of getting out of this alive had just drastically reduced.

Martin slumped back against the floor of the dirty van, feeling the vibrations from the exhaust pipe beneath him, he was still breathing way too fast, he needed to calm down, the last thing he needed was to bring on another cardiac arrest! What's more it was impossible to have any coherent thought with all this blood pumping through his veins. He closed his eyes and tried to steady his breathing, to make it regular and slow the pumping of his over worked heart. He tried to think of things that would soothe him; like the face of his wife or the 9th hole of his favourite golf course or the sun drenched beaches in Bali, but it was as though he were seeing all these images through a dark veil.

Using the face of his wife as reassurance, that was a joke as well, right now the face of his wife had been adorned by an aggressive thug who had snatched him from the street and intended to do God knew what with him once they reached their destination.

The van careered around another corner and the businessman was thrown hard against the right hand wall, he hit his arm and a bolt of pain exploded up its length, but as quickly as it came it faded. For whatever reason, any pain he was feeling was short lived, though he didn't acknowledge this at the time.

They intend to kill me, Martin was thinking as he settled again on the floor of the van, they intend to kill me, but why? What is in it for them? Publicity? Fame? Infamy? He didn't know, but he needed to find out, it could be the key to getting him out of here. He was about to open up a new line of questioning when the van suddenly screeched to a halt.

His efforts to steady his racing heart had been in vain, it was beating ferociously once more now, he looked from one masked face to the other in ever increasing panic.

The engine died and a couple of seconds later the drivers door was opening, he could hear footsteps on a gravelled surface and the thump as the door closed again, then the compartment door was sliding open. He had been right; the mask was of his old golfing buddy Bert Etherington. He didn't have chance to register how strange this was, suddenly he was being pulled to his feet by the two in the back and forced back out into the early afternoon sunshine.

His eyes blinked at the light as he was surrounded by his three captors, and when his vision came back into focus he took a quick look at his surroundings. They had brought him down an alleyway between two buildings; it was a dead end at a concrete wall straight ahead and the ramshackle remains of what appeared to be a derelict factory was to either side. There was a trade door with a corrugated shield to secure it, but it wasn't locked and the man with the Rose Rooley mask pulled on the chain to wind it up into its fitting while the businessman was frogmarched by the other two to the now visible wooden doors. The woman opened the doors and together they walked inside.

It was dark inside the old factory, but unlike a lot of derelict buildings it had managed to retain all of its windows, and though some were covered with dusty sheets of acetate, some light did manage to creep through; it was enough for Martin to consider his surroundings. The factory floor was huge, about the size of an average football pitch, with stone pillars painted navy at the bottom and sky blue above to support the roof which was bowed in places. The dark hulks of machinery, possibly textile were dotted about the floor and a staircase to the left led up to the unseen floor above. There were doorways at regular intervals leading to rooms beyond the main factory floor and it was to one of these that the captors led him now.

"Look, who are you people? What do you want with me? You can't get away with this!" Martin tried to assume control, but his voice cracked and let him down, revealing his true feelings.

"I thought I told you to shut up!" The big man in the Rose Rooley mask replied sternly, and shoved him hard in the back.

"That's ok, not much longer now." The other man, the one with Bert Etherington's face disguising his own reassured his friend.

Martin knew that voice, had heard it before, it was a posh voice, the voice of a man with a private education, but he wasn't given time to place it; they reached the third door down the left hand wall of the factory, about twenty feet before the staircase that led to the upper floor, and the woman with the Peter Werth-Duncan mask opened it and gestured inside.

Martin stepped into the darkness behind the door, feeling his heart rate suddenly skip into overdrive. He could feel them crowding behind him but for now was unaware of what terrors awaited him in this room.

Suddenly the arc sodium light overhead flickered into life, revealing to him in the dim glow exactly what was in store. He looked about the tiny room, with its ancient tiled walls and poorly built suspended ceiling, and tried to fight back a scream that was threatening to escape him. An operating table had been made up in the centre of the room, and to the sides were an ECG machine and a table with various surgical instruments prepped and ready for use. He turned in fear to his captors and drew in a quick breath when he saw who they were.

Martin's captors had removed their masks and were holding them at their sides; he had known he had recognised the voice of the driver, and he wasn't surprised now he looked upon him in the flesh; it was David Purefoy. The big man, the one who had looked so out of place with the mask of his loving wife to disguise his features, was the anaesthetist; Ricardo Panettiere, and the woman was the nurse who had supported the operation, though he couldn't place her name right now.

"You!" Martin said, his bottom lip starting to tremble. "What the hell do you think you're doing bringing me here?"

"You could have just got on with your life Martin, enjoyed the gift you'd been given, but no, you had to go snooping around." The surgeon said. "Now you've left us in a bit of a position."

"I don't know what you're talking about." Martin defended, taking a step back towards the operating table.

"You know exactly what I'm talking about."

"Well, what if I do? Just what in the hell is this all about anyway? Dodgy operations in people's houses, prostitute's pretending to be the donor's mother. Just what kind of a scam needs a cover up like this anyway?"

"I guess now you'll never know." Purefoy replied.

"What do you mean?" Martin asked. The three captors who had performed the likely illegal operation in his home took a step forward, and Martin backed up until the backs of his legs just under his posterior were pressed against the plastic coated fabric of the table bed.

"What we mean is that you've left us no choice, we could have all lived happily ever after, but you had to put your poisoned beak where it doesn't belong and now we're all left to suffer, well we have our side all neatly tied up, but you're the loose string, and we can't go having any loose strings now Martin can we? You can understand that."

"What are you going to do?"

"Why, we're going to take it back." Purefoy said with a sly smile.

"Take what back?" Martin asked, though he feared he had already guessed.

"Your heart of course."

Martin's eyes widened in horror, the man was clearly a lunatic, he needed to escape! He looked at the gap between the surgeon and the nurse whose name he couldn't quite remember and thought about making a break for the door. Before he could even take a step towards freedom the strong hands of the anaesthetist had clutched him roughly about the upper arms and were pressing him back so he was sliding backwards onto the table.

"No!" He shrieked in shock. He struggled against the big Mediterranean looking mans grip but it was no use, he was just too strong. Now the nurse was here too, circling about him and grabbing him by the shoulders, trying to force him down.

"For God's sake restrain him!" Purefoy ordered as the businessman was forced flat on his back on the operating table.

"Please, David no! You don't have to do this! For God's sake David please! I promise I'll stop snooping! I won't go to the police; I won't tell anyone about this, you don't have to do this!"

"I'm afraid it's too late for that." Suddenly the surgeon was out of his casual clothes and was dressed from head to foot in a surgical gown and mask. As he was forced into the leather straps that bound his arms tight to the table Martin noticed the anaesthetist and the nurse were too in full medical robes. He didn't find this strange just as he had not the masks they had worn in the street, he was too terrified for such emotions.

"Shall I prep the anaesthetic?" Panettiere asked as Martin wriggled within the restraints that trapped him like a fly on a spider's web.

"There's no time for that." Purefoy replied, pulling on a pair of procedural gloves. "Open his shirt."

The tiny nurse leant over him and ripped open his shirt, buttons flying off the side of the table, revealing the curly white hair of his chest and the long thin scar from the original operation.

"No, please God David no!" Martin pleaded.

"Scalpel." Purefoy said from behind his mask.

The nurse handed him the knife and Martin looked with petrified eyes towards the blade that glinted in the reflection from the arc sodium lights.

"Oh God, oh no!" He squeezed his eyes shut tight, unable to bear it any longer.

"Making the first incision." Purefoy said, and suddenly, with excruciating pain, the scalpel was cutting through his skin as though it was made of butter.

Martin screamed into the darkness behind his closed eyelids, and then his eyelids were not closed anymore, they were open, and the darkness was the result of the closed curtains in the safety of his own bedroom.

At his side Rose stirred but did not wake, in reality he had only let out a small terrified yelp, the real scream had occurred solely in the dream. He sat up in bed, breathing too fast and too hard, feeling at his chest beneath his pyjamas to make sure he was still in one piece. He looked about the room, afraid that this was the dream and the horror inside the abandoned factory the reality, afraid that Purefoy and his goons were hidden somewhere in the shadows of the room, ready to attack him once more. Of course they weren't, the room was silent, the only sound that of the central heating that Rose insisted on using throughout the night in the cold months.

It was ridiculous that a dream could leave him so unbelievably petrified, but petrified he was, and as he settled back into the comfort of his pillow, pulling the duvet back up to his chin, he couldn't shake the horrible feeling of disquiet. It would be a long time before sleep would comfort him again, and until then he was left with his thoughts. Yes it had only been a dream, but a dream based on too much reality. Was he really in a position to let this go? What would be the consequences if he did? Then he thought back to the sensation of the scalpel cutting through his un-anaesthetised chest wall. What would be the consequences if he didn't?

16

Martin had visited quite a few places in his quest for answers, but Campden Grove in Kensington was the first time he had felt within his comfort zone. This was the type of area he was used to frequenting in London, not Tottenham, not Brixton, not Kings Cross. He felt an utter snob for even having these thoughts and in deep shame of completely betraying his roots, something he swore he would never do, but when he pulled the Aston Martin up outside the tall white fronted town house he was pleased for once that he wouldn't be worrying he was going to return to his vehicle to find it either up on bricks or gone.

The dream had been enough to convince that putting the mystery surrounding his unorthodox operation behind him was simply not an option. In hindsight he didn't know what he had been thinking, never finding out the answers to his multitude of questions would have driven him halfway to the loony bin and back. He needed to understand why he had been lied to, deceived and avoided as much as he needed air to breathe or water to hydrate.

It had been a restless night in bed, tossing and turning, the questions spinning around and around in his mind, the dream still fresh, with an element of fear still coursing through his veins. Eventually he had got up, gone downstairs, made himself a hot milk with a shot of single malt Scotch and sat looking out on the forecourt, trying to get his thoughts straight. He had showered, dressed and headed out to the office before Rose had even woken and spent the journey into London in contemplative silence.

The first thing he had done on reaching his office was to plonk down in his chair, drop his briefcase under his desk and dial the hospital on his landline. Again there had been no sign of the surgeon at the hospital, it was thought he could be ill or taking a leave of absence. Martin wasn't convinced; he tried Purefoy on his personal number and when he had no more luck there he decided to take matters into his own hands; it was easy for the surgeon to avoid him when he was dialling over the phone but how would he fare when the businessman confronted him face to face? He hoped that this was one question he would be able to answer now.

He had reached this point by calling on his contact at Trojan Horse Security; Thomas Spence. For a nominal fee he had asked the investigator to obtain for him the home address of one Mister David Purefoy, and the investigator had not disappointed; in fact it had taken him only fifteen minutes to acquire the information and in the time it had taken Martin to read through the mornings emails he had been back on the phone with news of a positive outcome.

And now here he was, sat in the Aston Martin looking up at the four storey town house and wondering if the surgeon was home. One thing was for sure he wasn't going to find out sitting here. Martin opened the car door and stepped out onto the quiet Kensington street.

The house with its imposing white washed walls and duel bay windows was in by no means the largest on the street, some a little further down the road were nearly twice the size, but Martin guessed there to be at least four bedrooms and probably a couple of bathrooms here, and in this part of London you were looking at a seven figure mortgage. Martin wondered if he had come by such a property by reputable means; a heart surgeons salary was not to be scoffed at, but this was a six million pound house.

Gathering his thoughts, trying to piece together a line of questioning that would get him the answers he desired Martin slowly ambled up to the small gate that protected a narrow paved walkway leading to the royal blue front door. It was quite a dull morning but no lights illuminated the Purefoy residence. There was a lamp in the bay window to the right hand side of the door, but this too was currently not in use.

All this anticipation and it looked as though the surgeon wasn't even home. Swallowing back his disappointment Martin lifted his hand and knocked hard on the solid wood of the door, but when his hand connected the door clicked off the latch upon which it had barely set and slowly opened with a small creak, it had not been properly closed.

Martin drew in a quick breath, surprised to see the door creep open; he was looking now down a fairly decent length hallway, with doors to the left, the right and the rear and well carpeted stairs leading up to the floor above. Unsure how to proceed Martin took a furtive glance about himself, feeling like he was the one who had done something wrong. He knew that Purefoy didn't have a family; there was certainly no wife, children or live-in lovers on the records recovered by Spence, but that certainly didn't mean the house would currently be unoccupied.

"Hello." He called into the silent hallway, there was no reply. He leaned a little further through the door and tried again. "Hello." Still nothing.

Feeling suddenly on edge Martin took another look about himself, mindful of being observed, then, comfortable that he was not he stepped into the cool hallway and pushed the door closed behind him. Great, he was a trespasser now, that was something new to add to his CV.

"Mister Purefoy, are you home?" He called out; peering up the stairs for any sign of movement, there was nothing. It was so quiet in here Martin could hear his heart thumping away in his chest; he swallowed hard, wondering what his next move should be. He acted on instinct, stepping deeper into the hallway, his footfall sounding very loud on the blue, black and white tiles beneath his feet. There was a sitting room through a door to the right but this was empty and silent, so he moved on to a door on the left, that led to a comfortable looking living room, with a thick Persian rug surrounded by soft fabric sofas and a huge chestnut bureau in one corner that no doubt housed the television.

Martin exhaled and noticed the vapour of his breath before his face; winter was creeping up quickly now, but it looked as though the central heating hadn't been used in some time. Had the surgeon fled? If so then why? He stepped away from the door and considered his options; he was at the foot of the stairs now, should he carry on his search of the house or get out before the surgeon came home and found him trespassing? More so if the surgeon had been acting in an underhand way what would be his reaction if he did come home and find him snooping here? Was he in danger right now?

Feeling he needed to break the awful silence Martin peered up towards the hallway at the top of the stairs and called out again:

"Mister Purefoy, its Martin Rooley, are you home?" The only response was the soft whistle of the wind through the eaves; if the surgeon was home then he was choosing to ignore his former patient, nothing new there then. He was about to take the first step upstairs when he noticed something coming from the room at the end of the hall, a smell, a pungent unpleasant odour that made him want to block his nose.

Now his heart kicked into overdrive, fearing the worst he stepped past the bottom of the stairs and slowly made his way down the hallway towards what he suspected was the kitchen. The door stood only slightly ajar, revealing nothing of what lay beyond, Martin reached the end of the hallway and held out a slightly shaking hand, slowly he pulled the door open by its wooden side and peeked into the room beyond.

He had been right; this was the kitchen, a dining kitchen to be precise with a large teak dining table and matching chairs to the centre and the kitchen units and appliances about the sides. There was a picture window that looked out onto a small courtyard garden to the rear and brass pans and utensils hung from hooks in the low ceiling. This room was warmer than the others as it was currently being heated by a huge Arga oven, permanently ticking over; Martin surmised though nice in the winter it would be a real bugger when the warm weather came round.

The smell was stronger in here, though Martin couldn't currently find its source; maybe the oven? He took a step into the room and took a proper look around. That was when he noticed the partially opened cellar door. He had missed it at first as it was directly to the left of the door he had been peeking through, but now he noticed it standing slightly ajar and took a tentative step towards it.

As soon as he pulled the door open two things struck him; it was icy cold in the area below the house, as a cold draught billowed up as soon as the door creaked open, and down here was definitely the source of the disgusting smell.

"Jesus." Martin whispered, looking towards the relative safety of the front door with watering eyes. No, if he wanted answers, somehow he instinctively knew that they began this way. Suck it up buttercup, he thought, then turned his head from the door and took a huge lungful of slightly cleaner air before taking that first terrified step down.

He had known what he would find in the cellar of the old townhouse in Kensington before he had even set down, but seeing was believing, and only with the confirmation of his own eyesight would he truly believe the inevitable truth.

It grew colder and darker the deeper he descended into the depths below the house, though he was able to remedy at least one of these problems before he was fully immersed in the cellar; there was a light switch on the wall that he had missed as he first started down, but as he looked behind him to the daylight creeping through the kitchen window above he noticed it and quickly tracked back to switch it on.

There was only one dim bulb, hanging by its cord from the ceiling of the cellar directly below the kitchen, but it was enough to give decent visibility, and Martin made his way cautiously back down the stairs. The smell was overpowering now, the businessman had to block his nose with his thumb and index finger to stop it from violating his senses. At the bottom of the stairs he turned into the gloomy cellar and was confronted by what he had already gathered as his worst fear.

The room was divided into three sections; the main chamber that was the core of the cellar, then two smaller compartment rooms to the rear. The first was a former coal cellar that had been converted into a downstairs toilet sometime in the last century; it certainly looked as though it had not been used in a long, long time. The other housed an ancient boiler, which looked bulky and inefficient towards today's standards but Martin bet it had stood the test of time, without the need of a regular British Gas check-up or service protection contract.

Dusty bottles lined the walls in different shades, shapes and sizes, undoubtedly part of some long abandoned collection, though a rack in the corner housed the new wine collection with bottles of red from around the globe, some of the labels looking particularly expensive; this was the collection of quite a connoisseur.

There were bin liners of old clothes thrust into the far corner and a few rusting tools dotted about the floor, but it was what was bunched right in the centre of the room, beneath the cobweb infested single bulb that had caught Martin's attention.

It was a man, propped up with one arm and one knee bent at an impossible angle, he wore comfortable house clothes and his face was out of sight, pressed into the floor, but Martin would recognise that slightly curly, slightly greying hair anywhere; the man on the floor was David Purefoy.

Then, in the shadows cast by the dim bulb Martin noticed with horror that the body was face down in a sticky looking maroon coloured puddle; this was how the mans decaying blood appeared in the darkness of the cellar.

The man wasn't moving, the man wasn't breathing, the man was dead. Martin felt the gorge rise in his throat, his gag reflex was working and the next thing he knew he was vomiting fresh DNA all over the cellar floor. He bent double in the cold room, his chest rising and falling, mopping the sweat from his forehead with the back of his hand. Then he turned his head and looked down at the cadaver once more; he needed to be certain. Slowly he stepped forward, not wanting to get any closer to the stinking foul mess on the floor but knowing he had little choice. He bent down close to the side of the body, fearing that at any second a hand would lash out and grab him around the ankle. It was foolish of course; David Purefoy's days of movement were gone. He took in the pallid, waxy looking skin and the shocked, pained look in the dead mans eyes; then he noticed the wound that had surely killed the surgeon and his gorge was rising once more.

This time he managed to control it, but it was close. On more detailed inspection he could not miss the jagged gaping wound in the surgeon's neck, and the congealed, clotted blood that was caked about both the throat and the floor beneath; somebody had slit David Purefoy's throat.

Martin stumbled backwards against the side of the cellar steps; he was feeling light headed and faint. He had to get out of here. In a panic he looked across at the pool of vomit on the cellar floor and was suddenly terrified of the implications. Oh my God what have I done? He thought in terrified wonder; his finger prints were all over the house!

Suddenly torn between the need to retrace his steps and try and conceal the fact that he was ever here and the desire to flee this house of the dead as quickly as he possibly could Martin found himself in a terrified stupor. What was he thinking? He was no master criminal, even if he tried to clean away the evidence he was bound to miss something, he had to get out of here and now!

Still light headed but starting to think a little straighter Martin stood upright, took one last pained look at the surgeon, lying face down in a pool of his own mess, and quickly fled up the flight of steep stone stairs. He flicked the light off at the top using the cuff of his shirt, knowing this was an extreme case of closing the stable door after the horse had already bolted but unable to help himself, and crashed through the door into the kitchen, which seemed much brighter after the dimness of the cellar.

"Oh God, oh God, oh sweet baby Jesus!" Martin whimpered, his arm pressed against his trembling lips. He looked about himself, feeling completely incapable of coherent thought, then he looked down the hallway towards the closed front door and knew that he simply had to leave, and now.

He was just passing through the kitchen, about to enter the hall when something caught his eye. To the left of the door from where he was now standing, the opposite side to the open cellar door, a modern telephone was hung on the wall in a cradle. To the left of the phone was a pad, also hung to the wall for jotting down notes whilst on the phone. He didn't know how he had noticed it, something must have pricked in his subconscious as he tried to exit the room, but notice it he had, and now he stared at the pad with wide unblinking eyes.

Amongst various names and numbers that had been scribbled over a period of time and calls, was the letters MR. MR – Martin Rooley. To the right of the initials was a crude drawing of a love heart, and directly beneath this, written in the same shade of blue so almost definitely in relation to the letters and drawing above, was a phone number.

Martin stepped forward and with a trembling hand ripped the front sheet from the notepad. Even in his panic he noticed that where Purefoy had pressed down on the front sheet the letters had been engrained into the next five or six pages beneath. He ripped these free too, not wanting to leave anything for anybody else to go on but him. Then he was racing down the hallway to the door, where he exited as calmly as he possibly could, stepping out into the cold November air like a man who had made a mid morning visit to an old friend and was now heading for home. If anybody saw him now he hoped he would not be memorable. He looked about himself but the street was still quiet, for this at least he was thankful.

Feeling very vulnerable and suddenly very, very old, Martin climbed into the driving seat of the Aston Martin, gunned the engine and drove as patiently and carefully as he could away from the scene of the grizzly crime.

17

When Martin had been a boy growing up in Bolton his friends had dared him to crawl through the drainage pipe that led from the storm drains that backed onto their estate to the farmer's field beyond the recreational ground.

The pipe itself was about two and a half foot high and approximately 500 metres in length, in fact although the pipeline was perfectly straight it was not possible to see daylight coming through from the opposite end, only bleak darkness greeted a curious observer. It was made of concrete and its entire length ran beneath the recreational ground and the waste lend that separated the estate from the farmland.

Long had it been rumoured, amongst the group of adolescent boys at least, that the Devil himself lived somewhere in the tunnel, earning the pipe the nickname 'Satan's hideout'. Though all the boys knew this to be nothing but harmless ribbing amongst friends, none of them could shake the feeling that something could be watching them from its place in the darkness when they had dared to crawl a couple of feet inside.

It had been during their summer break from school, a time to be treasured amongst all adventure seeking children that they had taken a break from playing boy soldiers to once more peer into the void beyond the entrance of the pipe line. A constant trickle of water escaped from the end of the pipe, disappearing down the grated storm drain and soaking their feet as they bent to once more goad one another into seeking out the Devil himself.

On the morning of the fateful dare Martin had been the proud recipient of a smile from Yvonne Macgruder, the first girl at St. Thomas Chequerbent infant school to start developing breasts, and it had been this innocent exchange that had caused a jealous Jerry Brown to goad his friend into finally plucking up the courage to make it all the way to the farmers field at the far end of the pipe.

Martin, who had been in an exuberant and dreamy mood ever since receiving the said smile was currently of the inflated opinion that he could take on the world and all its armies and still return the victor, and so it was on that warm August morning so long ago that when he had been challenged for the umpteenth time to meet the Devil in his hideout, he had readily accepted.

Standing ankle deep in the cold flowing water he had enjoyed the fanfare of his childhood chums, he had received a smile from a reasonably pretty girl (but a reasonably pretty girl with the beginnings of real womanly breasts!) and now he was to prove his bravery in a show of bravado he was sure would become legendary amongst his friends.

It wasn't until he was a third of the way into the tunnel, with the excited cheering of his friends long behind him now and the darkness starting to fully take hold that Martin had realised how foolish he had been. On all fours, his legs and wrists soaked from the constant flow of water, only an inch between the top of the pipe and the arch if his back, he was suddenly very afraid. In the darkness of the tunnel it was all too easy to imagine the horned fury of Beelzebub bearing down on him, but it wasn't this he was most afraid of, it was becoming trapped in the tunnel and not making it out to the other side. What had he been thinking? If the roof were to cave in or if he suffered some as yet unknown injury no parent or adult would be able to crawl in here and rescue him. He was entirely at the mercy of his own pre-orchestrated fate and only he could get him safely to the other side.

It would be closer and easier to crawl backwards to his friends, but would he ever outlive the humiliation? So with over two thirds of the dark wet tunnel remaining his only option he felt was to continue, but he was becoming weary, his back and his legs were aching and he didn't know if he had the strength to make it to the other side.

In the cold wet darkness of the tunnel Martin Rooley started to panic.

He could feel his heart hammering against his rib cage and there were beads of sweat standing out on his forehead, he was breathing way too fast and he was shaking from sore head to sodden toe. He had crawled on through the panic, but now he was just about halfway through the tunnel and unable to move any more. Martin collapsed forward onto his front, having to spit out the water as it tried to fill his mouth and nostrils with its putrid minerals. This was it; he was going to die in here, cold and alone in the all encompassing darkness of the tunnel. He had never been more certain of anything in his life. With tears stinging his eyes and thoughts of his mother and the pot pie he should be eating for his supper, Martin started preparing for the end. He had never felt as utterly helpless in all his young life.

It goes without saying that Martin did make it to the end of the tunnel, our tale would be a short one had he not, but it had taken determination the likes of which he had previously felt incapable to get him back on all fours and crawling towards the exit. It had felt like it would never come, but eventually the tunnel had started to slowly get lighter; he almost dare not look forward in case it was a mirage, but after a while he could taste the freshness of the air outside and when he dared a quick glance upright he had seen he was only twenty feet or so from the end of the tunnel and freedom.

He had emerged from the tunnel cold, wet, filthy, but utterly fulfilled with the joy of life. Weeping joyous tears he had escaped quickly over the barbed wire fence that was the boundary to the farm and made it back across common ground towards his friends.

Now, sat at home with the television news on in the background, Martin felt as though he was back in that tunnel from so long ago, or a metaphorical tunnel at least, for he had been plunged once more into darkness, and like that small boy of so long ago felt utterly helpless.

The TV news anchor was currently discussing the escalating problems erupting once more in the Gaza strip, where a school of Palestinian primary school children and their teachers had been gunned down in a mortar attack in the middle of the day, but not five minutes ago the news had been focused on the prominent British heart surgeon who had been found stabbed to death in his Kensington home.

It was the twenty-eighth of November, two days since his own discovery of the bloody corpse, and the body had been finally discovered by the authorities after a neighbour had tipped them off after a strange smell had started coming from next door.

The TV report had talked of a dedicated heart surgeon, a hero in the cardiovascular circle with over five hundred successful transplants under his care, a passionate lover of the arts and a kindly gentle man, none of which were terms that Martin found described the man he knew. It advised of the body's discovery and how the death could only be attributed to suspicious circumstances, but the part that connected with Martin the most was when the reporter announced that Scotland Yard at present had no leads.

No leads. This was good. So, they had undoubtedly discovered the orgy of evidence he had left behind; the finger prints, the vomit at the foot of the body, but of course with him having no prior convictions as yet there was nothing to tie the evidence to him.

This was his predicament. Every ounce of his body now found itself so out of its depth that he was desperate to hand over everything he had learnt about his mysterious operation to the police, but if he did that how long would it take for the finger prints and DNA to be tied back to him? What then? A media frenzy as he became the chief suspect in a murder investigation?

He really had no choice, for now at least he was back in the tunnel, completely on his own and totally out of his depth.

The fear that the evidence in the cellar could lead back to him was magnified by a thought that had been troubling him since discovering the body; he had made a nuisance of himself at the hospital, calling on a regular basis in a desperate attempt to speak with the surgeon. Would Purefoy's colleagues and friends put two and two together and consider him a suspect? And if so would they inform the police? Martin didn't know, but the uncertainty weighed heavy in his stomach like a meal eaten after midnight.

So Purefoy was dead, that much was for certain, but who had killed him, and why? Was it in relation to his own on-going concerns? It was impossible to know for sure, but Martin had relied on his instincts many times in life, good instincts had led him to where he was today, and his instincts were telling him this was all connected somehow.

The last two days had passed like individual weeks; with Martin sure that the doorbell would ring at any minute and there would be a detective with a couple of uniformed policemen for support, wanting to take him in for questioning. It hadn't happened yet, but now that the body had been discovered officially surely it was just a matter of time?

Rose was out; the bridge club girls were meeting at Claridge's for an early dinner, so he had the house to himself.

Martin pulled the crumpled note paper from his pocket and looked at the scrawled script for what felt like the hundredth time. MR was the initials, with a crudely penned love heart and a number beneath. MR, it could mean anything, but with the drawing at its side the businessman felt sure it stood for Martin Rooley heart. Then there was this number, an 0207 Borough of London number, but not his number, so whose number was it? If it was in relation to his heart then it could be a clue to help him unravel this whole sorry mess. Of course it could also be nothing.

He had been considering calling the number for two days now, but simple fear had prevented him from taking the necessary action. He needed to get a grip; if he didn't get to the bottom of what was going on here he could be accused of the murder of a prominent British surgeon, there was already enough evidence to tie him to the scene, he was going to have to man up and stop putting the inevitable on hold.

Martin drew in a deep breath and then blew out his cheeks. With sweaty palms he reached out and picked up the phone from the bedside table. With foresight he dialled 141 before dialling the number on the notepad, so that whoever answered the phone would not have access to his number. Then the dial tone was ringing in his ear, it rang a couple of times and he suddenly realised he had absolutely no idea what he was going to say.

Quickly he slammed the phone down hard in its cradle and sat on the bed panting, sweat breaking out on his forehead, he suddenly felt very hot and very clammy.

"Come on come on get a grip!" He challenged himself, and stood up so he could pace the bedroom carpet. He caught sight of himself in the full length bedroom mirror and looked into his sleep weary eyes. "You're going to go to prison!"

This was all the motivation he needed. Withholding his number once more he perched on the edge of the bed and dialled the number scrawled on the pad. After a couple of rings it was answered.

"Hello." The voice on the end of the line not so much greeted as stated.

"Hello, may I ask who I've dialled please?" Martin asked, his hand clutched tight around the firm plastic of the receiver.

"No you can't, fuck off!" Came the gruff response.

"No wait please!" Martin said in a panic. "I just need to ask you a few questions."

"This ain't fucking Google Mate, now fuck off and don't call this number again."

The line clicked off and Martin was left sat on the bed listening to the dialling tone, his heart once more racing away in his chest.

Who the hell had that been on the other end of the line? What connection could they possibly have with a prominent British heart surgeon? Putting Purefoy with the gruff man on the other end of the line seemed as alien as connecting Prince William with Albert Steptoe.

Martin placed the handset back in its cradle and sat on the bed with his head in his hands. Things were starting to quickly spiral out of control now; if he didn't act as quickly himself he might yet find himself accused of the murder of the surgeon, or worse, far far worse.

He had become embroiled in something that was far darker than the innocent seeming mystery he had set out to investigate, and as he was dragged down into a dark underworld of crime and violence, he found himself wishing he had remained ignorant after all.

18

On a dark and bitterly cold evening at the start of December Martin found himself stood in a deserted alleyway between a row of shops. He had his winter jacket fastened up to the neck, a scarf and a pair of leather driving gloves but they were doing little to withstand the icy gusts of wind that were blowing down the alley. Martin pulled the collar of his jacket up to protect the bottom of his face from the worst of the chill and stepped into the shadows to the side of the alley.

He had left Rose at home, listening to her Perry Como Christmas album and putting up decorations, this time with the excuse that he was meeting the boys for an early Christmas drink. She had seemed to fall for it and was happy enough it seemed battling with the tree and the tinsel and the baubles; Rose always decorated on the first of December, she liked to make the absolute most of all the Christmas sparkle, she said it was the only time of year you could get away with showing off your gaudy side.

Another call to Thomas Spence at Trojan Horse had led him here, to this seedy part of London where betting shops and strip joints were two a penny and high rise blocks of flats littered the skyline. This was Peckham, and it was home to Eze-link cars, a private hire taxi firm operating out of its small Goldsmith road base station. Although Spence was able to trace the number to the station this wasn't the number that the rental firm advertised to its taxi needing clients; this was a private number, and it wasn't to be found in any phone directory or website. It had taken specialist technology perfected by the CIA out of Langley Virginia to trace the number. When Spence had first tasked his technology guru Adam Seeley to locate the line it had bounced him round from Taos, New Mexico to Redon, Ille-et-Vilaine, Brittany, from Imperatiz, Brazil to Aberystwyth in Wales. This was a sophisticated worm that took time and patience to hack, it hadn't been easy, and it hadn't been cheap, but the team at Trojan had traced the line to this small private hire firm in Peckham and now Martin was here to take a closer look.

"When you ask for a name and address of a prostitute and drug addict it arouses no suspicions, and I'm happy to help you with your enquiries." Spence had said on the phone when returning with the news. "But when you're asking us to track down a sophisticated telephony system for people who clearly don't want to be found it concerns me, it concerns me a great deal. Are you sure you're not biting off more than you can chew here Mister Rooley?"

"You don't need to worry about me." Martin had replied calmly. "Just keep cashing the cheques and helping me out when I call, everybody's happy then."

But it had all been bravado, when he had learned of the trouble Trojan Horse had had in trying to locate the line it had made him wonder exactly what he was up against. This was no longer a conspiracy that involved a surgeon, an anaesthetist and a young female nurse; now the said surgeon was dead and he was dealing with matters that were spiralling rapidly out of his control.

It was good to know that he had Spence to fall back on, but he was under no illusions, he was in this on his own, and the way things kept falling apart this truly was a terrifying thought. Martin stood shivering in the cold alleyway between the betting shop and the Clove and Anchor pub, looking across the street to the small ramshackle building that housed Eze-link cars.

A battered and graffiti scrawled green door stood closed next to a dirty window that was lit from within by a single bulb. The building itself was small and lopsided with a hand painted sign above the door. Even from this distance Martin could see that the paint was peeling from the window frames; the whole place was in need of a decent make-over. It was hard to believe that this was the home of the sophisticated telephony system that had given Trojan Horse so much trouble to detect; maybe there had been a mistake?

Occasionally shadows would move in front of the window, but from this distance it was impossible to make them out; it was no good, he would have to get closer.

Martin stepped out of the shadows and crossed the busy street in the direction of the private hire firm. Two girls not dressed for the weather passed him by, giggling and holding each other about the waist, clearly they had been enjoying the revelries of the local drinking establishments. Martin felt a momentary pang of envy towards them; oh to be so young and carefree. Knowing that if he gave it much thought he would lose his nerve, Martin drew in a quick breath and pulled the handle down on the graffiti troubled door.

Inside the small building was pretty much the same as the outside; in need of repair. There was a small cubby hole office with a barred open window to talk to the on duty controller, a small waiting room to the left and a closed door to the back of the room. In the waiting area was a battered old leather couch that looked as though if you sat on it you could either get a nasty cut from a protruding spring or catch plague from the plethora of undetectable stains. The filthy carpet tiles were coming away from the floor and patches of dusty concrete could be seen beneath, the walls were covered in age old signs and posters, some peeling at the corners and the whole place smelled of tobacco smoke and sweat. The building did however have one thing in its favour, it was at least warm, and with the weather like it was outside this was a pretty big pro in a sea full of cons.

Sat in a battered old plastic coated chair patched up with gaffer tape was an enormous Asian man with a thick black beard and glasses that he'd fixed with sellotape. He was in the base captain's office and was wearing a cream polo shirt with huge sweat stains under the arms; his huge belly was currently propped on the desk in front of him. A communications radio and maps were on the desk before him and a TV raised up on the wall was showing the football highlights from Match of the Day.

"Yeah." The man said without looking up from the slice of pizza he was currently shovelling into his mouth.

"Oh a taxi please." Martin said, thinking on his feet, he had every intention of finding out if this was a genuine private hire company.

"Where you heading?" The fat man asked between chews, looking up at the businessman for the first time.

Now here was a predicament; Martin didn't want to give either his home or his office address as he didn't want it on the records of the firm should anything come of it later.

"Her Majesty's Theatre, the west end." He said after a moment's hesitation. He could always catch the tube back to the office from here where his car would be waiting for him.

"Be about five minutes." The dispirited man replied, and nodded with his head towards the waiting room. Then he was on his radio, signalling for the nearest car to return to base. So this is a genuine taxi firm then, Martin thought as he ambled into the waiting room and with some reluctance sat down on the sticky couch.

In the background Gary Lineker was talking to Alan Shearer and Robbie Savage about the controversial incident in the game between Chelsea and West Ham, though Martin heard the words they were not registering, he was entirely focused on his surroundings. So, he had ordered a taxi and one was on its way; maybe the private hire company was a front for something else, but they still ran a genuine taxi firm from the same location. But if this was a front then what exactly were they fronting for? Nothing seemed out of place in here, this was a regular looking taxi base right down to the greasy wallpaper and the cobwebs in the corners of the ceiling.

Martin couldn't help but feel frustrated; if it was answers he seeked it was unlikely he would find them here.

Suddenly a phone was ringing in the little cubby hole office; Martin's ears pricked to attention, every nerve in his body tingled with anticipation, was this the number that Spence and his Trojan Horse cohorts had had so much trouble locating? The line was picked up by the fat base controller.

"Eze-link cars.......yeah..........yeah...........where are you going?...............What name is it?.............. Be about ten minutes................ No problem, be with you soon."

Martin settled back into the couch, feeling disappointed and a little agitated, unless it had been some pretty well constructed code the call had been a genuine customer wanting a genuine ride in a genuine private hire vehicle; whatever he had been looking for when he came here he was pretty sure he wasn't going to find it tonight.

Listening as the base controller used his radio to dispatch another car Martin considered his options; should he continue to wait for the taxi to determine if this was definitely a legitimate private hire firm, or should he cancel his request and try and think of another way to discover whatever secrets were being hidden here in this smelly little room?

The more thought he gave it the more he became convinced that Spence's colleague Adam Seeley had made a mistake; what connection could there possibly be between this Peckham based taxi firm and David Purefoy, the recently deceased surgeon who had performed an unorthodox heart transplant? It was ludicrous; there couldn't be anything to connect them, Seeley had made a mistake, the worm had bounced them all around the globe whilst trying to locate its source, it had simply done its job again and bounced them here, an innocent little business in the South East of London. He had made up his mind; he would change the destination of his cab to his actual home address and give Spence a call in the morning, let him know there had been an error.

He was about to stand up and let the base controller know of his wishes when the door to the back of the waiting area opened and a tall, thin man stepped into the room. Like the fat man in the cubby hole office he was of Asian descent, with long gangly arms and short cropped hair that spiked down his forehead like spiders legs. He was dressed in jeans and a black Fenchurch hooded top and he was carrying a stack of papers that he held close to his scrawny chest.

The thin man was quick to close the door behind him as he stepped into the waiting room, which aroused suspicions in Martin about what lay beyond.

With his senses alerted he tried to remain impassive as he watched the thin man walk up to the counter.

"Zee, process these." He said, handing the forms through the gap in the barred cubby hole.

"Safe." The fat man replied, accepting the forms.

Then the thin man was turning and heading back to his private room. He gave a cursory look at Martin as he passed, who looked down at his shoes, not wanting to make eye contact. Even with his head bowed, Martin could still see the thin man make eye contact with the fat man, and nod backwards in his direction.

"Taxi to the west end." The man known as Zee said quietly.

Thin man nodded slowly, then turned back to the closed door. Trying to remain as inconspicuous as he possibly could, Martin watched from the corner of his eye as the thin man opened the door wide enough to step inside the room beyond the waiting area; he didn't see much, but it was enough to offer further intrigue. There was another small office beyond the closed door, with a small desk which housed a telephone and a computer. It could of course simply be the office for the private hire firm, where taxes were paid and wages cleared, but it could also be so much more. Whatever it was Martin had decided that he hadn't fully given up on Eze-link cars just yet.

The door closed and Martin was once more alone in the waiting room; desperately trying to think of his next move, but before he even had time to consider his options the fat man in the base controllers chair was summoning him from his place in the cubby hole office.

"Taxi's outside." Was all he said.

Martin drew in a breath, wanting desperately to have more time to investigate further, but alas his time was up. Slowly he got to his feet, feeling his knees pop as he rose from the disgusting sofa; he took a sly look at the door to the back of the room, then head for the exit, nodding to the man in the office as he left.

The car was indeed waiting outside, and it was a genuine private hire vehicle, that on his instruction and at a cost of twenty pounds took him into the centre of London in the direction of Her Majesty's Theatre. But what else was Eze-link cars, and what was in the room behind the closed door?

19

Above the betting shop that faced onto Eze-link cars was a flat. When Martin had called unannounced and told the young Nigerian family currently occupying the residence of his plans, they had politely asked him to leave. Martin had then handed over ten thousand pounds in crisp fifty pound notes and unsurprisingly the situation quickly changed. The flat was now Martin's, on a one week lease arrangement, and the young Nigerian family were back visiting family in Ibadan.

He had played the CEO card quite well, calling Sheila to say he would be taking some time out to hit a few balls and do a little Christmas shopping. Nobody had complained, after all, wasn't that the general opinion on the shop floor of what most CEO's do? Sadly he hadn't played the husband card half as well. How could you explain to your wife that you would be working late again when he had already been so frequently absent from home? He was neglecting her he knew, and neglecting his responsibilities as a husband, but if he didn't get to the bottom of whatever was going on here somebody else could die, and he couldn't have that on his conscience.

After securing the flat Martin had visited Cameraworld in Fitzrovia, where he had laid out £1,799.00 on a Nikon D610 camera with a Tamron 28-300mm lens, capable of zooming in up to fifty times the current view. Martin had dabbled with a bit of photography as a hobby back in the seventies, and had felt well within his comfort zone when making the purchase. So, armed with the camera, a note pad, his laptop and enough supplies to feed a small army, he had started his first stakeout.

The small but functional living room of the flat had a window that looked out onto the road and more importantly the taxi rank across the street. There was a yellowing net curtain that reminded Martin of the paper doyley's his mother used to put out when they had guests over for tea, and it was perfect for looking out onto the street with little chance of being spotted in return. A two-seater couch that had seen better days and a rickety old wooden chair were the only furniture in a room that smelled of tobacco and spices, Martin had chosen the couch and wheeled it, more difficult than it sounds with two broken casters, over to the window.

And so he had sat, for three days and the best part of three nights, staring at the rundown building over the road and making notes in both his notepad and on the laptop. Martin would sit there for hours, watching the various comings and goings at the small business and making his notes. At around seven-thirty he would head for home, arriving back a little before nine. He would eat a decent meal, have a shower, and after spending a little time with his wife his thoughts would start drifting back to the flat once more.

The three hours or so he spent at home were a welcome relief from the monotony of the stakeout, but he was also terrified of missing something important, so he would wait for Rose to be soundly asleep, then sneak out of the house again, making his way across London to Peckham and Eze-link cars. Here he would spend the night drifting in and out of sleep on the battered old sofa, a kaftan rug pulled up to his neck to keep out the cold, and when he was able to stay awake watching the glow cast from the lights of the taxi rank across the street.

It wasn't an easy task performing a stakeout, it certainly wasn't as glamorous as it appeared on the cop shows that he liked on T.V., where they could skip through large time periods in order to keep the viewer hooked with the more glamorous elements of the mission; but there was little to consider glamorous here. On the whole the majority of what occurred at the premises was no different to the average goings on at every other private hire firm in the greater London area; people came, they ordered taxis, vehicles would pull up outside and a few seconds later the customers would be climbing in, ready to head off to wherever their destinations may lie. The business seemed to operate on a 12 hour rotational shift pattern, which switched over to the new shift at six pm each day, meaning the drivers and base controllers were either working a six am to six pm shift, or vice-versa. The drivers were kind of hard to keep track of, though Martin was trying his best, taking photos from his perch in the flat as they appeared and then scanning them onto his laptop where he stored them in their own zipped file. A little easier were the base captains, as there were only two, one for the night shift and one for the day. The one Martin had met the other night, the one with the huge yellowing sweat stains in the armpits of his shirts, was the night captain, the day captain was a small

Asian man with a bald head, probably somewhere in his early fifties. Both were heavy smokers and Martin had managed to capture several decent shots of them as they worked on their habit on the doorstep of the taxi rank.

All of this was fine, but it was not these people for whom Martin was most interested; it was the thin man, the one with the spider leg hair, the one who had enquired about Martin when he had been sat on the sticky couch, and the one who had disappeared through the door to the back of the waiting area. He didn't know how he knew, intuition he guessed, but this man appeared to be in charge. *In charge of what?* Well that was another question, what could you be in charge of in the back room of a small London private hire firm other than the daily running of a small London private hire firm? But it was something about the door, and the room beyond it, and the fact that the thin man had made absolutely certain Martin did not see into the room as he came and went about his business.

The thin man had of course appeared, and Martin had managed to take a couple of pretty decent pictures of him as he left the building, walking down the street in the direction of Peckham police station and the retail park, though the businessman felt pretty certain the police station was most definitely not his destination. On the few times this had occurred Martin had craned his head as far into the corner of the window frame as he could, trying to get as much of an idea of the man and his destination before he disappeared out of view. It was no good; he was still none the wiser. A couple of times he had considered following the man, but he was young and fit, probably somewhere in his mid to late twenties, and there was no way that Martin would be able to keep to his pace. Instead he had loaded his photos into the thin mans own personal file, and continued with his stakeout.

Eze-link cars advertised itself as a 24 hour private hire firm, but this wasn't strictly true; there was a thirty minute window each morning at around four am where the base was left completely unmanned. This was a quiet period at the rank, where the nights hectic rush was finally over and most of their customers were settled down in bed, this was also the time that the fat night controller left the premises temporarily unmanned. The first morning that this had occurred Martin had watched the fat man lock the door and wander down the road out of sight. He had sat confused, wondering what was going on, until thirty minutes had passed and the man who had been referred to as Zee returned. On the second morning, when the fat man had appeared at the door again, Martin had quickly grabbed for his coat and run for the stairs, making it out onto the street where Zee was just disappearing around the corner. Martin had followed him the five minutes down the road to the 24 hour McDonald's, where from a distance he watched the base captain devouring a couple of Big Mac's, large fries and a thick shake, the breakfast of champions. Wondering if the mans employers were aware that their captain left the rank unmanned each morning in order to fill his belly, Martin returned to the flat.

Most of his time in the rented room above the betting shop was spent like this; watching the everyday comings and goings of a small business in the South East of London, but on the evening of the third day, when Martin was just about to pack up and head for home, something of note did finally happen.

He had been packing his camera into its padded carry case, tucking the zoom lens into its separate pouch when a car had pulled up outside the rank. Now this was nothing unusual, after all it was the nature of the business for cars to be arriving and departing from the base at regular intervals, but it was the type of car that caught Martins eye; it was a silver Rolls-Royce Phantom, the windows blacked out to conceal the interior of the car and it's occupants from view. Martin, who had always been a bit of a motor hound, had owned a Phantom himself in the early nineties, and recognised it as soon as it pulled up to the kerb, this was certainly no private hire vehicle.

His curiosity pricked Martin quickly reopened the case and pulled out his camera, attaching the zoom lens as the driver emerged from the vehicle. He wore a suit with tie and a cloth hat, a chauffer if Martin had ever seen one, and walked around the side of the vehicle to open the back passenger door.

Martin was just in time; he powered up the camera and quickly adjusted the aperture in time to snap a couple of quick shots of the man getting out of the vehicle. He was a tall man with thick brown hair and tinted glasses; he wore an impeccable suit, tailored to perfection and carried a briefcase in one hand. With him was another man, less well dressed but smart all the same, thin with a balding head, an assistant for sure. Martin got his best opportunity when the man took an anxious look over his shoulder, affording the man watching from over the road the best angle of his face, quickly Martin took the opportunity, firing off another couple of shots.

Stood in the shadows behind the net curtain that reminded him of his mothers' doyley's back in Bolton, Martin watched with wonder as the sharp dressed man and his assistant walked through the door of Eze-link cars. A couple of minutes later the Phantom pulled away from the kerb and disappeared around the corner of Marmont Row.

Taking his coat off and placing it back on the arm of the sofa, Martin settled back into his observational routine; he couldn't leave now, not when things had just become interesting. What the hell was such a powerful looking man doing entering a small Peckham taxi firm? It certainly wasn't to get a ride; he already had his own driver.

For the next thirty minutes Martin watched the front door of the small building with frustration, nothing much was happening. A couple of customers came and went and the night captain came out for yet another cigarette, but on the whole all was quiet at Eze-link. Martin passed the time uploading the photos he had taken of the mysterious man in the expensive automobile. Once loaded into the file Martin clicked a couple of times to enlarge the image, wanting to get a closer look at the man. Zoomed in another couple of times the photo became quite grainy, he had focused too quickly with his zoom lens and it had not been allowed enough time to adjust to the shot, but even in these conditions Martin knew that he recognised the man, though for the time being at least couldn't place from where.

The thirty minutes passed slowly; Martin's stomach grumbled and he thought about what Rose would be cooking up at home, then the Phantom appeared once more at the kerbside and Martin quickly lost all thought of food. He raised the camera, waiting in anticipation from his place behind the net curtain, and was rewarded for his patience when after a couple of minutes the door to the private hire firm opened and the two men stepped back out onto the street. Both looked anxiously about themselves before the driver opened the door and they disappeared back into the safety of the vehicle. Martin, who had already taken numerous pictures of the driver and his two well presented passengers, now focused his lens on the license plate of the vehicle, firing off a couple of shots just in time before the car manoeuvred back down the road and out of sight.

Martin sat back in his seat trying to think, but he was tired and oh so hungry, so again he packed up his things and head for home, feeling confused and unsure for about the millionth time since this whole sorry mess had begun.

20

With the electric gate closing behind him under the soft whir of its motor Martin pulled the Aston Martin up to the side of the house and wearily climbed out. He was exhausted, three whole days and two whole nights on the couch in the pokey flat, with barely enough nourishing sleep on which to function was starting to take its toll. His eyes were heavy and sore and his body ached from being scrunched up on the couch for long periods of time, his shoulders felt very heavy as he trudged across the forecourt to the front door. Maybe he would take a night off from the stakeout, try and get his mind off the case for a while and spend a little time with his wife; maybe get six or seven hours sleep in the bargain.

Right now the thought of just putting his feet up on his own couch, watching a bit of television, taking a hot shower and eating a home cooked meal sounded like the top prize in a gala auction. Unbeknownst to him none of this would materialise, for as he slipped his key in the lock he was blissfully unaware of how events were about to rapidly descend to new depths of misery.

The door opened and he stepped through into the hallway, sighing as he unfastened his coat. He closed the door behind him and was about to walk through to the kitchen when he noticed his wife stood at the bottom of the stairs.

"You made me jump." He said with a huge beaming smile, after the day he had spent behind the net curtain in the small flat in Peckham she really was a sight for sore eyes.

Rose didn't reply, just stared at him, a frosty demeanour was his only greeting.

Feeling suddenly very cautious and a little on edge Martin's smile faded as quickly as it had appeared.

"Is everything ok?" He asked, knowing from the look on her face that it most certainly was not.

"I don't know Martin, is it? Is anything ok?"

"I don't understand."

"Where were you last night Martin?" She asked, the hurt in her eyes betraying the anger on her face. So he had been found out, but how much really did she know? The businessman sighed once more, and took a moment to hang his coat up on the hook next to the door; it did little to buy enough time to come up with a convincing excuse.

"I was here."

"No you weren't, don't lie to me Martin, you weren't. I woke in the night, I got up to use the bathroom and you weren't there, your side of the bed was cold, the covers weren't even turned back, you hadn't been there all night."

"Last night….. oh God yeah last night." Martin said, trying desperately to think on his feet, but his brain was tired and not up to the challenge of trying to dig him out of a hole, his cheeks turned scarlet red as he dug himself in a little bit deeper. "I got a call from the office, we've got auditors coming in this week and some departments didn't have their affairs in order. Bit of a bloody nightmare to be honest, the whole HR department was in, trying to straighten out our affairs."

"And you've been there all week?" Rose asked, her eyebrow slightly raised.

"Yeah, yeah like I say it's been a nightmare, getting back on track now though." Martin could feel his stomach clenching in knots, he hated lying to Rose, but really, what choice did he have?

"No you haven't." She replied matter-of-factly. "No you haven't Martin. You haven't been there all week. I know you haven't, you haven't been there at all this week, and do you know how I know? Because I called up to talk to you and your PA informed me you'd taken the week as leave, taken time in fact to spend with me. Do you know how humiliating that was?"

Martin felt his legs suddenly turn to jelly.

"I'm going to ask you one more time Martin, and I want the truth, where have you been tonight?"

"Rose…" He said, taking a step forward, his hands outstretched, palms up to show he came in peace, but his wife's cold tone and bitter stare stopped him in his tracks.

"Don't you *Rose* me. Where were you Martin?"

The businessman sighed for the third time, feeling like a rabbit in the headlights, he put his head to his hands and considered telling her the truth, telling her the whole sorry story from his mistrust of the operation to the death of David Purefoy and the link to Eze-link cars, but before he could speak she said something that bounced the thought right out of his head again.

"Be honest with me Martin, are you having an affair?" Tears were welling in the corners of her eyes now, but the businessman was so flabbergasted that he let out a short barking laugh, he couldn't help it, the idea was so completely leftfield to him that it had completely taken him off guard.

"What? That's absurd." Was all he could manage.

"Don't laugh at me Martin, this isn't a laughing matter, I want to know where you've been this week, and why you felt the need to lie to your wife."

The smile which had formed on his lips at the absurdity of the accusation quickly fell away, and he was left in the tricky dilemma of telling his wife the truth, and accepting the many consequences that would come with that decision, or thinking of a way out of this sorry mess.

As it turned out he didn't need to worry, not just yet anyway, he had paused too long, and Rose wasn't in the mood to be deceived any more than she already had been.

"Fine." She spat through thin white lips. "You keep your secrets, but you keep them away from me, you can sleep on the sofa tonight."

And with that she turned her back on him and quickly climbed the stairs to their bedroom, where she closed the door behind her.

Martin stood in the hallway, feeling hollow and utterly drained. He slipped off his shoes and padded into the living room, where he sat down in the darkness on his favourite chair, and wept like a child.

21

Define irony; the desire to return to your own warm bed following two uncomfortable nights on the sofa , only to be confined to a sofa again when you got there. Was that irony? Martin wasn't sure, but it was damn inconvenient, and it was damn uncomfortable, and he felt damn inconvenienced being in that situation. Not that he blamed Rose, how could he, she hadn't done anything wrong. He was in the dog house and deservedly so, he had lied to her repeatedly about where he was going and what he was doing. It had also been easy to lie to himself; to say he had been protecting her from the escalating strangeness of the situation, but it simply wasn't the truth. The truth was that it was more convenient to keep her in the dark, to not have to answer her myriad of questions, to not have to justify his actions, to not have to listen as she tore him to pieces once more for not appreciating the wonderful gift he had been given.

This wasn't the case; of course he appreciated the fact that he was still alive, and he knew he owed a lot to David Purefoy and his team for ensuring that was the outcome, but if something underhand, something potentially illegal had occurred to make this happen, then that was something he simply couldn't ignore, even if he was the lucky benefactor.

Rose had every right to be angry with him, and he certainly didn't hold it against her for banishing him to the sofa, but as he lay under the thin blanket, his back aching, uncomfortable with his legs poking over the end of the arm, he wished he had been able to think of something, anything that would have spared him this indignity.

Maybe it was for the best; if he had come clean about what was really going on he could be sure that she would use every means at her disposal, from sexual exploitation to hurt indignity, to try and deter him from his current course of action, and he couldn't do that, not now, he was in too deep; in fact he was up to his neck and without a buoyancy aid. He could be thankful for one small mercy; his wife was not a great lover of the news, deciding decades ago that if all they had to broadcast was the negative side of life then it could stay the business of those that were involved. This blasé attitude to current affairs had meant that the violent death of David Purefoy had completely passed his wife by; he hoped that this would remain the case, for at least as long as it took to get to the bottom of the whole sorry saga.

Martin looked at the clock on his mobile phone, quarter past two, he sighed and placed it back on the floor next to the couch, after a couple of seconds the soft glow from the display faded to black and the living room was cast in darkness once more. Earlier he had heard Rose weeping from upstairs; it had filled him with sadness and pity and made him want to rush up the stairs and take her in his arms, but he knew his wife, and now was not the time to start rebuilding broken bridges. Eventually, thankfully, the weeping had stopped, and all had been quiet from the upper level of the house now for over two hours.

It wasn't going to be easy to clear the air with Rose, and that was why it was doubly important to get to the bottom of this mystery as soon as he could, he felt sure that if Rose could see he had been acting for the greater good she would be able to find it in her heart to forgive him. In the meantime it looked as though there may be a few cold shoulders to come until he could.

Martin sighed and rolled onto his side, pulling the thin blanket up over his shoulder. There was so much to consider, not least of which how to make amends with Rose. He hated falling out with her, and though it seemed ludicrous to him the very notion that he could be having an affair, no matter how alien, the thought had indeed entered his wife's mind, and it was the darkness he had created in her heart that had led her to this conclusion. By trying to be a good man he had become a bad husband, lying, neglecting, forgetting her birthday, just what type of man was this whole sorry mess turning him into? Not the type he had ever been, and not the type he had ever wished to become, but he couldn't avoid the facts, it's the type of man he was now, and he was only really left with two choices:

1) He take what was increasingly becoming the sensible option and put the whole saga behind him, focusing on patching things up with the love of his life.

2) He take the road less travelled, and continue pursuing answers in a situation that had already long since spiralled out of his control, putting his marriage and maybe even his life in danger.

It was an impossible choice, either way he couldn't win, whatever his decision there would be consequences that could have long term ramifications for him, his wife and possibly countless others. Feeling sick to his stomach and weighed down with the sheer weight of his problems, Martin placed his head in his hands and tried to block out all thought. It was of course impossible; his head was spinning with a thousand different questions, and he felt sure he would still be mulling them over when the sun finally appeared over the horizon, but sometime a little after three his exhausted mind finally weaved a little white flag of surrender and he slipped into a troubled sleep.

He awoke to the sound of the telephone ringing in the kitchen, feeling disoriented and confused. Then he pieced together in his mind the events of the previous evening and received a painful weight in his stomach for his trouble. He checked his watch, quarter past eight; this was the latest he had slept in in years. Sighing he sat up on the couch, feeling pins and needles in his feet and a dull ache in his back from sleeping on the soft cushions of the sofa. After a few rings the telephone gave up its monotonous drone; Martin wasn't concerned, it was probably only a cold caller anyway, but it did make him wonder why his wife hadn't answered the phone at the side of the bed.

He stood from the sofa and walked to the bottom of the stairs.

"Rose?"

No answer. Slowly he climbed the stairs, already knowing what he would find when he got there. He wasn't surprised to find he was right, but this didn't stop a dull ache working its way through his body to his heart, sitting heavily in his stomach and making his head feel even wearier, his eyes twice as tired.

Rose was gone. The bed was made but her overnight bag was missing from the wardrobe, she hadn't left a note.

Ok, well you're in this now, may as well see it to a conclusion, Martin thought as he looked with sorrow at the empty bed.

His decision made Martin showered, shaved, dressed and packed his own bag with changes of clothing and essentials. This done he went downstairs and forced down three Shredded Wheat with half a pint of milk, not feeling hungry at all but knowing he would soon need the energy. He rinsed the bowl and sat down at the kitchen counter with a pen from the drawer and Rose's notebook open before him. It wasn't easy, but with some regret he forced himself to write the most difficult letter he had penned in his life. It was only short, but it took him the best part of twenty minutes to jot down everything he wanted to say, pausing only to rest his aching wrist. Done, he placed the pen back in the drawer and read through his words.

My darling Rose,

You are hurting and you are angry right now. I don't blame you for this, you have every right to be, but know that all my actions, everything I've done, I've done to stay true to the man you somehow fell in love with all those years ago.

I've hurt you, I know I have. I haven't been a particularly good husband of late, but know it's not because of you. I have some things going on right now that I have to get straight. I can't explain what they are but I promise you dear one when this is over I will sit down with you and explain everything.

I'm going away for a while. You won't be able to contact me, but know that my leaving is to protect the life we have built together, not to damage it more than I already have.

I know all of this will seem a little nuts to you right now, but please believe me when I say I really don't have any other choice.

I will return soon, and when I do, we'll have that chat, and I promise to start to try to make it up to you. God knows I hope to get the chance.

I love you.

Marty

P.S. How could you think there was someone else? It's always been you xx

Martin closed his eyes and tried desperately to block out the tiny voice of doubt, the one that was calling him a fool on a fool's errand, the one persistently filling his thoughts with uncertainty. Then he placed the note down on the kitchen counter, picked up his bag and head for the door.

22

The door to the taxi rank opened and the fat man known as Zee emerged; he locked the door, lit a cigarette then slowly ambled down the road in the direction of McDonald's. Martin, who had been watching with anticipation, waiting for this moment to arrive, watched him turn the corner at the end of the street and then quickly made his way to the door.

He had spent the day back at the flat, watching the general coming's and goings, taking his photograph's and documenting the images in his files, updating his timeline with any unusual activity, for which today there had been none. Since the Rolls Royce Phantom had dropped its distinguished passenger at the firm a couple of evenings ago everything at Eze-link cars had been business as usual. Customers came and left as passengers, shifts rotated on time as usual and cars pulled up to the kerb outside the office, but they weren't super cars, they were reliable affordable vehicles chosen by men on average wages who made their living on the road; Volkswagen's, Vauxhall's, Nissan's.

The argument with Rose and the fact that until this situation was resolved he was for all intents and purposes homeless had weighed heavy on his mind. At around five pm the previous evening his mobile had started to ring; Rose. She had returned home from wherever she had spent the day mulling over her own version of events and found his note, now she wanted to talk. He had been desperate to answer, to hear her voice, to tell her that everything was and would be ok, but he had not. In the end he had understood that if he had taken the call from his loving wife the chances were he would never get to the bottom of this terrible mess, for she would have wanted him home, and he would have undoubtedly relented. With a heavy heart he ignored her first, second and third calls, and when she left a message for him following the third attempt he deleted it without listening, though tears had stung the corners of his eyes as he did.

That was it then; his decision was definitely made, for better or worse he was in this now until the bitter end. Martin had settled back on the couch and the evening had progressed as it had before, quietly watching life continue on the street below. At around nine pm a ferocious argument had broken out between a man and a woman somewhere outside the door of the flat, Martin had listened on nervously as the pair tore strips off each other, swearing, screaming, cursing and berating. Finally, after what felt like an eternity, and several protestations from other flats within the complex, all was quiet again.

At nine o'clock Martin had used the greasy remote to turn on the television in the corner. He had watched the TV news, wanting info on the David Purefoy murder investigation, but there had been nothing. It was hard to determine if this news, or indeed lack of it, was good to him or bad.

Feeling exhausted from the night he had spent on the sofa at home Martin had allowed himself to drift off to sleep on the battered old couch pushed up to the window, but not before setting the alarm on his mobile for three in the morning. When it had finally sounded some four and a half hours later he had risen reluctantly, taken a bleary eyed look out at the street below, then dipped into his bag and produced the clothes he had packed especially for this particular excursion; black cotton slacks, a stretch black polo shirt and a baseball cap a friend had brought him back from the States, which until this evening had remained unworn.

The adrenaline that had pumped through his veins at the thought of what was to come was enough to shake any notion of sleep from his deeply deprived body and mind, he felt alert and sharp, ready for whatever was to come, and at four am, just as with the mornings he had spent in the flat before, his moment arrived.

As Zee was strolling his way down Marmont Row, the only care in his world right now the choice he was going to make from the delectable range of cuisines on offer beneath the golden arches, Martin was crossing the silent road in the direction of the closed private hire firm.

With his heart beating hard in his chest Martin ignored the front door and walked two buildings down to an alley that he assumed ran to the back of the small row of shops. He wasn't disappointed, though he was faced with a bit of a climb to scale the wall that separated the flats that backed on to the buildings with the small courtyards to the back of the shops. He grabbed a plastic crate that had been discarded along with some old tyres and several bin liners full of rubbish in the corner of the lot. Martin placed it portrait against the wall and propelled himself up onto the lip of the brickwork, swinging his leg over into the empty space beyond the wall. Not giving himself too much time to think Martin swung his trailing leg over the wall as well, and as the crate toppled and dropped to the floor with a small thud, he did too, the impact sending shock waves through his tired ageing knees. He rubbed the pain away and then straightened up, taking a look at his surroundings. Martin stood in a small yard area than ran around the back of the three shops in the row; overflowing bins lined the wall and the drains were overflowing where they were blocked with leaves, the water soaking the cracked paving in the yard. Knowing that the taxi rank was the last in the row Martin moved to the door to the far side of the yard. He had feared it would be a security door, or worse still that there would not be a rear entrance to the building at all, but the door here was little more than a standard wooden panel in a timber frame, an old brass handle with a standard keyhole the only notable security; at last he had finally caught a break.

Martin pulled the crowbar he had retrieved from his own garage when he had left home the previous morning from the waistband of his pants, and looked at the door. He was pretty sure the building wasn't alarmed, as on no occasion of observing the fat man taking his morning stroll had he ever seen him do anything other than lock the door, but that didn't mean he couldn't be overheard breaking into the building just the same. It was a risk he was going to have to take, he was only going to get one chance at this; after today with this method of entry they would know that somebody had been into the office, and security would undoubtedly be tightened.

Placing the flat, sharp end of the crowbar into the tiny crack between the door and the frame Martin pressed against the metal with his hands, using as much force as he could to jar the lock. He only succeeded in taking a big chunk of wood out of the frame that bounced off his belly and landed on the wet floor next to his feet.

"Damn." He whispered and placed the flat side of the crowbar into the gap once more. This time he nestled the crowbar under his arm and used the weight of his upper body to lean against the bar, causing the door to bend against the frame and the gap between the two to increase. There was a terrible creaking sound that was only equalled by the sound of Martin's exertion, then all of a sudden the latch popped free and the door swung open with a sharp crack.

Martin looked first at the door where a large split had appeared in the frame and then into the darkness of the small room beyond. This was when he produced the second item he had brought along especially for this excursion, a small battery powered torch. Martin flicked the button on the chrome handle and pointed it into the darkness, he took a look about himself, making sure he wasn't being observed, then entered the building.

With his heart beating fast and hard Martin closed the door behind him and stepped a little further into the room. It was a fairly small square area with a desk in the middle and filing cabinets lining the wall. There were two doors in the room, the one Martin knew of that led out into the waiting area of the private hire firm and another to the left. He made his way here first, using the soft glow from the torches beam to light his way. He pulled the door open and checked inside; nothing but a small toilet cubicle; Martin closed the door again and stepped back into the main room. He shone the torch at the desk; there was a computer and scattered papers that had not yet been filed away, the desk phone looked interesting so he took a closer look. It was an ordinary landline unit, but in the XM24 port on the back a connection cable led to a small black angular box covered in dials, Martin was no expert but he could be sure this was the scrambler unit that had caused Trojan Horse so many problems.

Pulling the soft cushioned chair free from the leg well Martin sat down, placing the torch on the desk top so it gave off light as he scanned the documents on the desk. The thin man may have been suspicious of Martin as he sat waiting for his ride, but he had a lot to learn about personal security; he clearly felt that with the scrambler unit whatever business he was conducting in this office was safe, for on the desk was a plethora of damning information. Was it evidence? That remained to be seen, but it was information for sure, and Martin was positive it could help him in his quest for answers.

Amongst the first of the papers he perused was a short dossier on the man from the Rolls Royce Phantom. There was a photograph attached to the upper right hand corner by a paper clip and Martin took in his features, knowing he had seen the man before. Then he read the information printed on the page and everything sank into place. The name at the top of the page was Chris Forbes, and though the occupation field had been left blank Martin knew enough from the name to be able to fill in the blanks. Chris Forbes was the chief executive officer of Brave New World Media, a publishing firm that produced a number of successful online subscription only magazines and newspapers, and that was why Martin had recognised him, a couple of years ago Forbes had attended a conference held by Sun Village to promote their new range of luxury apartments in the Indian ocean region. Neither had purchased anything that day but they had chatted briefly over canapés; though Martin had found the man quite pompous and arrogant and made his excuses to leave.

Continuing to scan the dossier Martin could not find any connection to the multi-millionaire news mogul and this small South East London taxi firm. Then he turned the page, and was faced with a private medical report from North Haringey Hospital; Forbes had lung cancer.

Martin sat back in the seat, this couldn't be a coincidence; Forbes was in need of a major organ just as Martin had been.

With his curiosity well and truly kindled Martin placed the dossier back down on the desk top and picked up the torch. There were drawers under the desk; Martin focused the beam here as he tried them. They weren't locked, security really was lax here. The first thing he noticed as he shone the light inside the top drawer caused a surge of panic to flow through his already heightened senses; it also confirmed to him that whatever was going on in this back room within this South East London private hire company was less than legal. Within the thin top desk drawer was only one item, but it had clearly been left there for easy access, and that thought filled Martin with dread. It was a handgun, a large black handgun. Martin, who had never held a gun in his life, not even a paintball gun on an office away day, couldn't have guessed at the make and model, but he didn't need to know the specifications to know that it was big enough and ugly enough to blow a football sized hole in a man from fifty paces.

Beads of sweat had formed on Martin's forehead and his mouth suddenly felt very dry, parched even, he slid the drawer closed and was about to go for the larger compartment underneath when he thought he heard something from outside the room. With his breath caught in his throat Martin pushed the chair back and quietly stepped up to the door that led back into the waiting room. He could see the soft glow of the single bulb creeping under the door and stepped up to it with growing trepidation. There was a deadbolt on the door, as quietly as he could he reached out and slid it back, then with his heart hammering away in his chest he pulled the door open just a crack and peered out into the waiting area. All was quiet, the room was empty, he had either heard a noise from outside or it had been his over active imagination, playing tricks on his high wired system.

Exhaling a huge sigh of relief as the sweat coursed the length of his cheeks Martin made his way back to the desk and plonked himself back down in the soft cushioned chair. How long had he been here now? Ten minutes? Fifteen? He couldn't know for sure having left his watch and his phone back at the flat, but he needed to speed up whatever the time, if these people carried guns as a way of life he didn't want to get caught rifling through their private affairs.

Sliding the larger of the two drawers open Martin peered inside, shining the torches beam down so he could see what he was doing. Inside were a couple of bound ledgers and an official looking book with a red and black binding. He pulled this book out first and flicked through the ear marked pages. Inside were lists of foreign sounding names written in English, with a calendar of dates and times in chronological order. Martin, who had been in haulage and dealt with shipping his entire adult life, knew this for what it was straight away, the port authority timetable for the Shandong province of China, but what business did the thin man with the spider leg hair have with it?

Martin placed the timetable back in the drawer and pulled out the two bound ledgers, flipping the cover of the first over. Each page had been divided into crudely drawn out sections to highlight different collections of data. In what Martin assumed to be the almost illegible handwriting of the thin man, were columns separated for name, age, weight, organ, amount paid and amount pending. He scanned down the list, reading names and perusing their data.

Harold Fincher...54...180 pounds...left kidney.....£54,000.00...N/A

Elizabeth Bentley...48...152 pounds...retinas...£15,000.00...N/A

Malcolm Avery...57...222 pounds...heart...£65,000.00...N/A

The list went on and on, Martin turned page after page, reading through name after name; the people in this list it would appear had all paid large amounts of money for organs; so it was true, the thin man was in the business of illegal organs.

"Christ." Martin whispered, looking down at the journal with watering eyes. He continued to read, unable to stop though he had found what he was looking for, amongst the pages were at least two names he recognised; one a leading director in the pharmaceutical industry and the other a Conservative politician, to Martin's knowledge the current acting MP for East Finchley. Martin flicked to the back of the book and wasn't surprised to see the last name in the register was that of Chris Forbes. Then he had another thought, and started flicking backwards through the pages from Forbes, it only took a couple of pages, but when he saw what he was looking for a sickly feeling washed through his body and settled in his gut like concrete. He looked down at the words on the page with eyes that were clouded in disbelief.

Martin Rooley...67...approx. 190 pounds....heart....£65,000.00...N/A

Martin stared at the page for some time, he stared until his eyes felt strained and his head started to hurt, then, unable to stare any more, he slammed the cover of the book closed and slipped it back into the drawer with slightly trembling fingers.

So he finally had an answer as to why the operation had been performed in the unusual surroundings of his own home; it couldn't be performed in a hospital as it was an illegal operation, his heart was illegal, an organ supplied by an underground trader. Martin clutched at his chest feeling vulnerable, exhausted and racked with guilt. But why damn it? Why had Purefoy done this? According to the ledger the heart had cost sixty-five thousand pounds, but who had paid for this? Surely not Purefoy, he had been no knight in shining armour.

Feeling deeply troubled Martin grabbed the second ledger and flicked over the neatly bound cover. Like the first it had been divided into crudely mapped out sections, with column headers written in almost illegible script. This time however the payments that were displayed on the pages were outgoings as oppose to the incoming payments listed previously.

This time the columns had been divided into 'name', 'role', 'amount' and 'paid by'. The names in this particular journal were irrelevant, but the roles could not have been more important, they outlined as much as anything just how deep this operation went.

Xang Pyo...border guard...£500.00...Yang Lu

Anthony Thomas...border guard...£750.00...HM

Lee Young Chang...chief of police...£3500.00...Yang Lu

These were clearly bribes, money paid for people to either turn a blind eye or help out with the illegal trade of human organs, and from the looks of some of the roles on display in the ledger it wasn't just border guards and ferrymen who were complicit, it was police officials, politicians, airport security personnel. This was a large operation, he was in deeper than he ever could have imagined.

Martin couldn't believe how lax the thin man had been with his security; there was evidence enough here to open a criminal investigation that could lead to his incarceration for a very long time.

Flicking through the pages something else became apparent; there were two names that appeared regularly in the 'paid by' column; Yang Lu and someone with the initials HM. Putting two and two together Martin figured HM to be the initials of the thin man, and Yang Lu no doubt his opposite number on the Chinese side of the operation. With a sudden flash of inspiration Martin shone the torch about the room, looking for a waste bin, he saw it in the corner and quickly made his way over. Bending down he started to rummage through, amongst the sweet wrappers, empty coke bottles and polystyrene trays he found what he was looking for, crumpled up junk mail. Martin smoothed his hands over the paper, straightening it out as best as he could, it was from a credit card company offering their latest fantastic deal, but this wasn't the important part, he looked up to the very first line; 'Dear Mister Malik,'.

"Malik." Martin whispered, placing the paper back in the bin. He found more of the evidence that he was looking for right at the bottom of the waste bin, an envelope, addressed to the Eze-link cars address, and for the attention of one Mister Haroon Malik.

"Haroon Malik." Martin mouthed the words, letting the name roll off his tongue, he was congratulating himself on his superior detective skills when a noise suddenly startled him from his revelry; a key was turning in the locked front door.

On the floor of the small office to the rear of the taxi rank Martin Rooley's heart seemed to suddenly drive up and wedge in his throat; his petrified eyes looked to the closed door that separated him from the main floor of the office and his hand clutched the envelope in a balled fist, the fingers white at the knuckles.

The front door to the private hire firm opened and then closed again, then a man was coughing somewhere nearby, but obstructed from sight by the thin wall of this secondary office. In a panic Martin dropped the envelope back into the bin and looked about the room; the ledgers were still on the desk along with the paperwork he had been scanning earlier. He could hear the man, probably the fat base captain Zee moving about in the cubby hole office to the side of the waiting area and as quietly as he could crept over to the desk where he grabbed the ledgers and placed them back in the drawer. His violently shaking hand was just pushing the drawer closed when a new terror almost froze him to the spot in a temporary paralysis. Another key was turning, this time to the office in which he stood.

Martin had just enough time to reflect on how stupid he had been before the door was swinging open, letting in an arc of light from the room outside the door. Why had he returned to clear the desk? They would know there had been intruders as soon as they saw the splintered back door, so why had he tried to cover his tracks? It was ludicrous; he should have made for the door as soon as he heard the fat base captain return.

It was too late now; the petrified businessman stood like a badly carved statue, waiting to be discovered and whatever terrible punishment the fat man would inflict.

Martin was not a religious man, he didn't believe in fate and he had never held true to the old adage that everything happens for a reason; but what happened that night in the back office of the private hire firm in South East London could only be described as a modern day miracle.

The door to the office opened, and Martin stood, a paralysed fear etched on his face, as the fat man walked in, and was somehow completely oblivious to the presence in the room. Knowing where he was heading and how he was getting there he didn't switch on the light, which kept Martin at least partially hidden in the shadows, but also, like so many young people these days, the man was completely engrossed in his phone, and walked through the room and into the tiny toilet cubicle without once lifting his eyes from the screen.

Too shocked to breathe the panic stricken man quickly evaluated his options; there were really only two, stay or run. If he stayed he risked being caught when the man finished in the bathroom, if he ran he risked being heard leaving, and though the man was overweight he was Martin's junior by at least thirty years, and could still catch him as he tried to make his escape.

Martin crouched down at the side of the desk, breathing hard, listening to the heavy flow of Zee's urine as it splashed into the bowl, there was a change in the flow as the fat man missed his target and peed all over the toilet floor, then the last few drips were hitting the bowl and the familiar sound of a fly being zipped. Martin held his breath.

Zee lumbered out of the toilet, still looking at the screen of his mobile, Martin watched as he stepped back out into the light of the waiting area and pulled the door closed behind him, the latch clicking into place.

The businessman slumped onto his behind on the floor of the tiny office, letting out a huge exhale of breath. He needed to get out of here, and fast. In the other room the television came to life, tuned to a late night roulette game; this would be good cover for his exit. Quickly he positioned himself first onto his knees, then up to his feet, feeling a twinge in his back as he did so. He moved as quickly as he could over to the door. With sweat literally pouring from his face Martin opened the back door and stepped into the cool early morning air. He closed the door behind him and turned to face the wall.

Suddenly a fresh fear crept into his bones, on the other side of the wall he had used the crate for purchase, on this side he had nothing. Fearing he would not be able to make it over Martin picked up the crowbar from the side of the splintered door frame and stepped up to the wall. It was at least a foot taller than him, and there was very little he could use to propel himself up the rugged surface.

In a dizzying panic Martin looked around, how could he have been so foolish, he should have brought the crate over with him. It was too late now, he had to make his escape or be caught here trying. Reaching up and grabbing the top of the wall Martin placed his foot in one of the gaps in the pointing, he pulled with his upper arms and managed to get so his head was up above the rise, but his foot slipped and he landed back down on the uneven concrete at the back of the office.

Panic flooded Martin in a wave, he was going to die here, they were going to find him and they were going to kill him. These were hardened criminals who carried guns as a way of life and he was a sixty-eight year old soft in the middle businessman who had never so much as touched a firearm.

Calm, stay calm, you have to stay calm and focus, he chided, summoning all of his energy, all of his will. Taking a couple of deep breaths Martin opened his eyes and sized up the wall once more, he stepped forward, placed his hands on the top, found his grip once more with his foot, and when he felt back in some form of control, pulled with his arms whilst pistoning his foot out to propel him back up the wall. It worked. This time Martin made it up to his chest past the lip of the wall, and as he started to slip back down once more he kicked out his feet, connecting with the brickwork and using what was left of the ageing muscles in his legs to thrust him up and onto the top.

He sat there, panting, his muscles screaming with the exertion, but thrilled to be out of the dirty old yard. He looked down at the floor below him, then dropped down into the alleyway behind the shops, a spasm jolting through his knees as they impacted against the old cobblestones.

Not wasting any time to nurse his shattered legs Martin darted out through the alley and back onto the main road, avoiding the light that was glowing from the window of the taxi rank. He walked a little further up the street and then crossed over, making his way back to the relative safety of the flat, his heart still pounding away and his head muddled with a thousand new thoughts.

23

Harvey Mullins considered the empty bottle of port in his lap with the air of a man disgraced that the world would allow such a tragedy to occur. He lifted the bottle, placed the neck to his lips, and with a long lizard like tongue cleared the rim of any remaining drops. Then the said bottle was discarded amongst the rest of the debris at his feet and the old man was up and away, walking with style and panache despite the alcohol that was coursing his system. He danced across Romilly street in the direction of the off license, which was situated right next door to one of his old haunts from before nature had been so cruel as to rob him of his income, the Coach and Horses. He looked in the window eagerly at the suits and tourists who were enjoying a quiet lunchtime drink in this busy Leicester Square pub, then made his way next door, feeling in his threadbare pocket for his change.

He entered the shop, pirouetted and then bowed to the owner who shook his head in dismay, then stepped up to the wall of alcoholic treats with a look that could only be described as desire on his tired old face.

"Not you again, I bloody told you earlier, you give my customers a bad name."

"Gupta my good man, a bottle of your finest port, and may God and his angels surround you in the comfort of their majesty."

"Not bloody Gupta, my name's Suhail." The man in the turban grumbled, but he moved his castered ladder over beneath the port just the same. He climbed up and brought the port down from the second highest shelf, then placed it down on the counter. Harvey eyed it greedily, already relishing the fiery burn of that first euphoric swallow.

"Eighteen pounds." Suhail said without taking his hand from the bottle.
Harvey looked down at the change in his hand.

"We seem to have an ever so slight miscalculation of the funds," he slurred, "would you accept seven?"

Suhail took the bottle and placed it back on the shelf, much to the old mans dismay.

"Gupta my good man you are being a terrible hound. Ok ok I will consider my tipple if I must, tell me my valiant young servant of the masses what delights will my seven English pounds provide on this fine December day?"

The Asian man leant under the counter and produced from the refrigerated unit a four pack of Tennents that he placed next to the till matter-of-factly.

Harvey eyes the beers with a look of abject horror sketched across his once handsome features. "My good man," he said indignantly, "one may have found oneself on hard times but one is not yet at such a level of undignified desperation."

Suhail placed the beers back into the fridge with a grunt of disapproval, though the skinny man was indeed one of his best customers the smell that emanated from him was enough to make the most hardened of drunks consider his life choices.

"Nothing else, you leave now." Suhail said, waving his hand towards the door.

Harvey eyed the bottles in the display desperately. "What about the vodka?" He blurted, losing his feigned dignity in his fear of leaving empty handed. He pointed to the shelf where a small bottle of unbranded Polish vodka rested beneath a hand written label on fluorescent green card stating £8.50.

Suhail sighed and grabbed the bottle from the shelf. "Seven pounds." He said reluctantly, holding out his hand for the coins.

"Gupta my man you are a scholar and a gentleman." Harvey blurted, handing over the change and grabbing the bottle from the counter. "As I have said to her Majesty the Queen on many of her frequent visits to the square, when sampling the delights of rural London why not pay my good friend Gupta a visit, his cheery disposition and good old fashioned standards will make your visit a delight of which to treasure."

"Please just go." Suhail sighed, putting the change into the till and shaking his head with dismay.

"My good man, I bid you adieu." The old man bent and gave an almost perfect bow, before exiting the shop with his prized possession tucked into the waistband of his trousers for safety.

Harvey scurried down Romilly street, licking his lips, already anticipating that first fiery rush. The St. Anne's churchyard gardens were his destination, though his altar of worship was the bench beneath the trees to the bottom of the gardens, and his deity of choice the God of hard liqueur. Harvey liked to joke that he came to the church yard to trade the Holy Spirit for plain old spirits, a sleight at a God who had had the audacity to cut short the career of the greatest living thespian in the history of the capital.

Opening the gate with a rusty creak the old man skipped past the side of the church and out back into the small patch of tree lined gravestones that had been his binging spot of choice for the last five years. He rubbed his hands together, not warming them from the cold, but needing to keep them busy; they desperately wanted to fish the bottle from the waistband of his trousers and unscrew the bothersome lid, but he would not, he could not, he was a slave to his desires and his desire right now was to enjoy the drink from the comfort of his favourite bench.

As he drew near to his place of worship he glanced up towards his destination and what he saw repulsed him enough to make the skip in his step momentarily falter; someone was sitting on his bench! In the five years that he had made the rusty old bench in the church gardens his home from home he had only twice before had the misfortune of other people; once had been an old lady who had stopped for a rest, the other a young mother with a pram, both had had the good sense to depart on his approach. Let's hope today's intruder had the same good manners, or they could find themselves on the sorry side of a vicious tongue lashing.

Feeling certain that the unexpected visitor would be only a temporary problem Harvey marched up to the bench with his head held high.

The man was sat to one side of the bench, leaving the other side unoccupied. These days it was generally considered courtesy that if a person was sat on a bench the portion of the bench that was unoccupied would remain so, a kind of unwritten etiquette amongst modern day bench users, but this wasn't to be the case today. Fixing his eyes firmly on the man with the soft white hair Harvey took his seat, and made sure he was a couple of inches closer to the man than was reasonably acceptable. To his resounding horror his invasion of the intruders space did not have the desired effect; in fact when he sat down and gave a cursory glance at the old fart to his right he was mortified to find the stranger smiling back at him.

Of all the undignified, disrespectful, inharmonious acts that Harvey Mullins had had the misfortune of being privy to in his seventy-three years on this planet; this had to be the daddy of them all!

Ok, so his mere presence on the bench and his crafty invasion of space hadn't been enough, surely the vile oath would depart once the retired actor began to partake in his favourite pastime. Keeping his eyes firmly fixed on the intruder; Harvey unscrewed the cap from the vodka bottle and without taking his eyes from the white haired gentleman, took a heroic swig.

The liquid burnt his throat and left a warm tingling sensation in his chest as it made it's way down his gullet, it was sheer bliss; Harvey closed his eyes, savouring the moment, but when he opened them again moments later he was horrified to find that the intruder was not horrified at all, in fact he was smiling at Harvey as though they were old friends.

This was frankly monstrous! What was he to do now, drop his trousers and wave little Harvey in the vile intruders face? It was an idea, though if that too didn't work he would be left standing in the cold church yard with his trousers down and his flaccid penis in his wrinkly old hand as the stranger potentially continued to watch on, unscathed.

"Good morning." The white haired stranger spoke, still smiling.

Great, now he wants to converse, Harvey thought with dismay, maybe if I blank him he'll get the message and finally toddle on.

But the stranger was completely unfazed; he just continued to smile that soft sweet smile, never taking his eyes from the old drunk.

"I see you're a vodka man." He continued, nodding to the small bottle of Polish spirit in Harvey's hand. "Never was a fan myself, me, I prefer a drop of this." The stranger slipped his hand inside his expensive looking jacket and produced a bottle of Taylor's 1985 vintage port, and not a small bottle either, a full size bottle, the cork removed but still full to the brim.

Harvey was so stunned that he almost dropped the vodka, this was one of the best ports on the market, and though a connoisseur of the tipple he had never been fortunate enough to try the 1985. His tongue darted out of his mouth and wetted his lips, he couldn't help it, he had never been so close to such a delicacy in all his years, and now here it was, within a foot of where he sat in this lonely old church yard. Maybe God had finally ended his campaign of hate towards the old thespian and finally produced one of his true miracles as a way of saying sorry for forsaking him for so long? Whatever the reason, it didn't matter, what mattered was that the vintage was within his grasp, he just needed to work out how he got his worthy little hands on it.

As he watched on, water filling his eyes and his throat suddenly as parched as the Sahara, the white haired gent pulled a small plastic cup from his pocket and poured in a measure. He glanced away from Harvey towards the church and swallowed the liquid in one go.

"Ah, that hits the spot." He said, pouring himself another measure.

Harvey was leaning in close, unable to take his eyes from the bottle and the beautiful blood red liquid in the bottom of the see through cup. He knew that he must resemble a dog, salivating at the sight of a juicy steak, but what the hell; he had played worse roles than a hound in his time, and with lesser reward.

The intruder lifted the cup to his mouth and was about to empty it of its contents once more, when he suddenly paused, as though noticing the old drunk's desperate advances for the first time.

"I'm sorry old boy, can I shout you a drop?" The intruder asked, suddenly redeeming his earlier misdemeanours in Harvey's eyes.

"Well sure, sure, I mean if you fancy a little company, I don't mind sitting with you a while, I think it's terribly important to be sociable to one another in these darkened days wouldn't you say so old pal?"

"I totally agree." The white haired gent nodded with a smile, and produced a second cup from his jacket pocket. He poured out a measure, a generous one at that, and handed it to Harvey with a knowing wink.

The bedraggled former thespian grabbed it from the other man's hand with the speed and agility of a honed athlete, and held it to the left side of his breast, protecting it in case the man changed his mind and tried to take it back.

He did not, just sat there with that soft sweet smile on his face, looking towards the church to allow his companion to truly savour the moment.

Harvey, a little more relaxed lifted the plastic cup up to his chin, allowing the rich aroma of the port to drift up his nostrils, heightening his senses, then, with that same athletic agility, he knocked back the cup and allowed the liquid to fill his mouth. Oh sweet nectar! Sweet nectar of the Gods! There were chestnuts and wood bark and spices and grapes, luscious, luscious grapes, and they danced on his taste buds like tiny angels, fluttering their wings and singing in harmonic chorus on his tongue. Then the liquid was coursing his throat, coating his trachea in its bitter sweet exuberance and providing a fire in his gullet the likes of which he hadn't enjoyed in years. He looked down at the cup in his hand with awe.

"Oh sweet angels of heaven!" He breathed as the fire started to abate.

"Another?" The white haired man asked with a smile, and Harvey could have smothered him in kisses, and would have done had he not feared it would scare his new companion away. Instead he nodded eagerly, then watched with huge bulging eyes as the old gent filled his cup once more, this time to the brim.

"Allow me to introduce myself, my name is Martin Rooley, it's a pleasure to make your acquaintance."

"I assure you, the pleasure is all mine." Mullins replied, his entire countenance changed towards the stranger now he was the lucky benefactor of the vintage port, the vodka bottle lay forgotten on the bench at his side, he would no doubt renew his interest in it once this white haired stranger went on his way, but for now there were finer delicacies to enjoy.

"Harvey Mullins, why do I recognise that name?" Martin asked, tapping his head thoughtfully as the old man considered the drink in his hand, wanting to savour the experience this time around. "Wait, you didn't once play King Lear at the Royal Lyceum Theatre did you, would have been around the late eighties if I remember rightly?"

"Lear, Hamlet, Macbeth, even Monsieur Thenardier, my boy I've played them all."

"I can't speak of the others but I'll never forget that production of King Lear," Martin replied, doing a little acting himself, "your portrayal was so haunting, so commanding, I have to tell you, I cried, I actually cried."

"Well that's the art you see my boy," Harvey beamed, his ego generously massaged, "being able to captivate, being able to draw in one's audience, the ability to transport them to another when and where, that's the gift."

"A tremendous gift, it was an unbelievable performance, an unbelievable night, tell me, what are you doing now?"

Harvey recoiled slightly, as though slapped, but the old thespian hadn't trod the boards at some of the West End's premier theatres to lose his composure in a church yard in Central London, and to the untrained eye his momentary lapse would have been little more than a flicker of emotion. The beaming smile that followed was as genuine as the hardened plastic grin of a carnival mask, but the actor was willing to play another role if the rewards continued to be plentiful, if and when they dried up he could drop the act once more.

"I'm retired." Came the short out of character reply.

"Retired? No way, what a waste."

"Oh age catches up on all of us my man, even you."

"Oh come now, there must be plenty of roles for men of a certain age, surely yours is a vocation of which you only retire by choice."

"Quite." Mullins replied with a strained smile. "And indeed that is what I did, retired by choice."

Martin, who knew otherwise, wasn't about to let the moment slide, he had engaged the old actor in what he knew to be his favourite subject, now he intended to exploit the situation.

"But you must still get the call of the stage? That desire to be back in front of an adoring public?"

Harvey, who had thought of little else since being struck off the actors guild of Great Britain after exposing himself on stage while drunk in a debacle performance of 'The taming of the shrew' in 1991, only nodded. Feeling sullen and hoodwinked into delving into archives he had long since stored in his mental attic, the old thespian knocked back his drink, hardly tasting the flavours this time, but needing the rush.

"To be honest I don't really think about it." He lied, looking away from Martin and staring off into space, his empty cup in his hand which was resting in his lap.

"You should," Martin leant in close and refilled the cup with the dark red liquid, "you're too good to go to waste."

Whether the compliment had struck a chord with the old actor or having his cup refilled with the delectable port, Mullins spirits were temporarily lifted, and he raised his drink in salute to his new friend, who raised his own in return.

Martin watched as Harvey lifted his cup, tilted his head slightly and allowed the crimson liquid to slip between his lips, his eyes closed tight in ecstasy. The alcohol must be really coursing through his veins now, even for an old hand like Harvey; now seemed as good a time as any to make his proposal.

"I was thinking," Martin said as he poured himself another measure, he didn't want the drink, didn't in fact even like it, but he needed their meeting to seem genuine, "us meeting today like this, it must be fate."

"Fate? I'm not sure about fate old boy but it is jolly good fortune, it's not often you meet fellow connoisseurs in these parts, just leery football fans and weekend tourists."

"Oh fate can grow from the most unexpected of encounters." Martin continued. "I mean, what are the chances I would get talking to an actor, one I know of to be damn good at his trade, just at a time when I require the services of a professional actor myself." The businessman could only hope that there was enough alcohol inside the old drunk now for him to not consider exactly how fortunate the situation appeared.

"You need an actor?" Harvey enquired, his three years at RADA on display with his theatrically raised eyebrow. "You putting on a production?"

"Not quite," Martin replied, "more like a one man show."

Harvey considered this for a moment; the alcohol and the ambiguity of the situation were numbing his senses, had he just been offered a job?

"I'm not sure I follow your meaning old bean."

"I need an actor, I have one here with me now, I would very much like to acquire the services of said actor for a little project I have in mind."

"Oh, and what's in it for me?"

Martin smiled. "Money, of course, and all the Taylor's vintage you can handle."

Harvey smiled a thin lipped smile, then held out his dirty hand for Martin to shake. "I hope you've got a large wine cellar."

24

It was of course no coincidence Martin and Harvey meeting on that cold December morning; it had been pre-ordained by the businessman after carefully selecting the old drunk for his purposes. Trojan Horse had again been the providers of a full background history of the man after Martin had requested details of a down on his luck actor habiting in the London area; it had transpired there were quite a few from which to choose, and Harvey Mullins had been top of Martin's shortlist.

Martin had never seen King Lear in his life; but he had used it as a way to break the ice between him and his target after studying the details of Harvey's former career.

It had seemed he had been quite the thespian in his day, performing leads in some of the biggest productions in the West End, but a thriving party scene and easy access to alcohol had taken their toll and by the mid eighties Mullins was a certified alcoholic. He had stumbled through his productions for a few more years, acquiring roles from the good name he had earned in the seventies and early eighties but by the early nineties producers had stopped returning his calls, he had found himself slipping further and further down the casting sheet and had used alcohol to numb the nagging uncertainty that had started to cloud his better judgment. It all came to a head in that fateful performance of 'The Taming of the Shrew', Trojan providing press clippings that had covered the whole sorry incident, recording the moment that would conclude Harvey's time on the London theatre circuit for good.

It had been a difficult few days leading up to this moment; first of all there had been the constant calls from Rose, desperate for information on his whereabouts and what he was doing; the poor soul was worried half to death about him and after ignoring the first, second and third barrage of calls and texts he had responded with a simple message – PLEASE TRUST ME, I LOVE YOU, I WILL BE HOME SOON. It hadn't been the end of her messages but they had abated at least a little from this point on. He had been racked with a terrible guilt, it was Christmastime after all and this was the second time his dodgy old ticker had caused a disruption to the festive proceedings.

This hadn't been his only concern; both Peter and Sheila had called regularly too, Rose no doubt having contacted them fearing the worst for her absent husband. He had lied to both, telling them not to worry and that he just needed time out to manage his personal affairs. Peter had been willing to hold the fort in Martin's absence, just as he had done following the operation, but it was clear that his friend was not happy, too much was being withheld from him and he had made his feelings well known.

What could Martin do? He wanted nothing more than to confide in his friend, to get some support in dealing with the dark underworld for which he had become a part, but there was still that nagging doubt, could he trust his friend?

On top of all this there had been a disturbing break in the David Purefoy murder investigation; a witness had come forward claiming they had observed an elderly gentleman fleeing the scene around the time the murder was suspected to have taken place, he had been spotted after all. The only thing that was continuing to work in his favour was the photo fit the television news had displayed looked absolutely nothing like him.

Still, it was a new clue, and with the DNA and finger prints he had left in the house how long did he really think it would be before Scotland Yard came knocking at his door? With this in mind Martin had made a sizeable withdrawal from his current account and was now moving hotels every two days and paying for his rooms with cash, trying as best as he could to stay one step ahead of the police.

Now he stood in a rented room above a shop in Islington, running the retired actor through the details of his role. Mullins was to act as the instigator of a conversation between Martin and Haroon Malik, the adviser to a multi-millionaire corporate banker in need of a new heart, having watched countless detective shows in his time Martin knew that when going under cover it was always best to keep the details as close to the truth as possible without actually giving away any of the facts, this way you were less likely to stumble on your answers when questioned.

He had spent the morning on Savile Row, fitting Mullins out with a new suit before heading into Knightsbridge where the man was treated to a hair cut, wash and blow dry, close razor shave and a manicure. Now that he looked the part it was Martin's responsibility to ensure he was aware of what he was up against and determine that he was comfortable being placed in that kind of danger. The businessman had been surprised; fully expecting the flouncy old actor to run for the hills when he heard the detail behind his latest assignment, the last thing he had expected was Harvey to positively relish the idea of walking into the danger zone. Scared that it was the booze that was doing the talking Martin had pressed the idea home, but Mullins was determined, he wanted this job.

Martin's biggest fear was the booze; could he keep Harvey clean long enough to appear at the offices sober, the old actor assured that he could, but Martin wasn't so sure. If Harvey turned up for his meeting with Malik half cut the game was over, what's more Harvey himself could be in terrible danger.

In the room above the shop Harvey looked down at the details; bullet points for the meeting that Martin had drafted, reading them like a script. Earlier they had made a difficult call through to Malik, requesting a meeting. The hardened criminal had been naturally suspicious, drilling Mullins on how he had obtained the number and cautiously refusing to enter into any conversation over the phone about a potential deal, claiming that he didn't know of any reason the adviser would want to meet with him and stressing that he was simply the owner of a South East London private hire firm, but despite this he had agreed to a meeting; and Harvey was set to join him at the office that very afternoon.

"Are you sure about this?" Martin asked for what felt like the hundredth time.

"Quite sure old boy quite sure." Harvey nodded, still reading the dossier.

"Less of the old boy, you can't talk like that in the meeting, it won't work."

The actor looked up from the paper, genuine distaste in his stare. "My boy I am frankly astounded you would say such a thing, I am a professional, I would not proffer to advise you upon your line of business, for it is an area for which I have no expertise, please allow me the same courtesy."

"Ok ok." Martin said, holding up his hands to show he was sorry. "Point taken. This isn't a game Harvey, these are real life criminals, gangsters no doubt, if things go bad….."

"If things go bad you call the police, they may arrive in time they may not, that I believe is the risk I have to take."

"You don't have to do anything."

"Correct, I do not, but if I may rephrase, that is the risk I am willing to take."

"Why?"

Harvey, whose eyes had dropped back to the crib sheet, now looked up seriously for what felt like the first time. "Why?" He repeated, as though he had not understood the question.

"Yes, why, why would you want to do this? I don't believe it's for the money, I don't believe it's for the booze either." Martin was looking at the ageing actor with real tenderness; it was perhaps this that made Harvey open up so honestly. He sighed and placed the paper down at his side.

"To feel alive again." He said softly. "To prove to oneself that one still can. To prove that there is still more to Harvey Mullins than the liquor that courses his veins, even if only to oneself"

The actor finished talking and picked up the paper again, making sure he was fully prepared before entering into what could potentially be his final character.

"Are you ready?" Martin asked gently.

"I could use another glass of Taylor's, just to settle the nerves."

"Not now, you have to stay clean, just until after the meet, then you can have all the booze you can drink."

"Thought you might say that." Mullins said with a sigh. "Ok ok you're the boss. In that case I will commit to being as ready as I'll ever be."

"Good." Martin said with a brisk nod. "Then it's time."

25

The Nigerian family that lived in the flat over the road from Eze-link cars welcomed Martin with open arms when he called unannounced again that afternoon, why wouldn't they? This was a very lucrative relationship for them, and proved so again when the man with the white hair offered them a thousand pounds in cash for the use of their flat for a couple of hours and no questions asked. So Martin once more had sole use of the flat and the family were heading to central London to do a little impromptu Christmas shopping.

Once more the battered old sofa was pushed up to the net curtained window; once more Martin sat with his camera in his lap and his notebook at his side. The television was on in the corner, some programme showing people trying to get the best deals for salvaged junk, Martin wasn't paying it any attention. In fact it wasn't until the adverts that he even noticed it was on. It was one of the major department stores, the ones that seemed to have limitless advertising budgets at this time of year that managed to draw his attention from the window. It was the usual gushy affair; children, big smiles, woolly hats, proud parents, full of sentiment and intended to give you a warm glow inside and to then associate that glow with the store, the type of thing that Martin usually scorned for the truth of what it was, just another marketing department trying to wrangle a few more pounds out of an already cash strapped Britain; but this time was different. This time when the advert came to an end Martin found sentimental tears pricking at the corners of his eyes. And why? Because he missed home of course. Because he missed his wife. Because it was Christmas, and rather than spending it with loved ones, celebrating at parties and gatherings and countless functions, he was here, in this smelly flat, finding himself dragged deeper and deeper into a world for which he had no business in becoming embroiled.

Letting out a deep sigh Martin picked the remote up from the arm of the couch and silenced the television. He didn't have time for sentiment; sentiment was for people who had the luxury of ignorance. He had been one of these people for sixty-seven happy years, but now, in his sixty-eighth year, this luxury had been cruelly snatched away. The scales had fallen from his eyes, and he was seeing the world as it actually was; cruel, hard and unforgiving.

Feeling a little more in check after taking control of his emotions Martin turned back to the window and peered outside; it was nearly three o'clock, Harvey should be arriving soon. No sooner had this thought entered his mind did a black London taxi turn the corner and pull up outside the private hire office.

After a couple of moments the back passenger door opened and out stepped Harvey Mullins, AKA Reginald Porter, personal assistant to corporate banker Martin Lachance, both names that the businessman was quite proud of and which fitted his beliefs for how a character name should sound. He had kept the first name for his character the same as his own to prevent him from tripping up during conversation, a trick he had learned from watching the BBC secret agent series 'Spooks'.

Resplendent in his thousand pound suit Harvey straightened out his lapels and watched the cab pull away from the kerb, then with his back straight and his shoulders level he stepped up to the front door of the office and walked on in.

This was it; game on. Martin started the programme on his laptop that Thomas Spence had uploaded for him just the other day, it would be his eyes and ears in the meeting, unfortunately the technology didn't stretch to Martin being able to communicate with the actor, but fingers crossed that was an interaction that would not be necessary.

On the skin of Harvey's left hand was an almost invisible patch containing a tiny, microscopic camera and microphone, to the casual observer it would look like no more than a couple of freckles, Martin desperately hoped that Malik would fall into this category. The state of the art equipment had not come cheap, but it was imperative, for Harvey's safety as much as Martin having full access to what goes on in that small room at the back of the waiting area. There were a couple of anxious moments where the screen remained blank as the image buffered, then after what felt like an anxiety racked eternity the picture appeared.

Could he trust the old actor to pull this off? Martin wasn't sure, maybe it hadn't been a good idea to choose somebody with an alcohol dependency, maybe this whole thing was one big bad idea. Oh well, it was too late now.

With his foot anxiously tapping away on the threadbare living room carpet Martin turned his attention away from the window and focused fully on the screen of his laptop. At present Harvey's hands were by his side, so it was difficult for Martin to tell exactly what was going on, the only thing for which he was certain was that he was stood in the waiting area, for he could see the sideways on projection of the battered leather couch he had sat on himself about a week ago.

Why was there no sound? Was there something wrong with the programme? Had he set something up wrong? Martin was no technological genius, a long way from it, and panic started to set in. There was absolutely nothing coming from the speakers of the laptop. Should he call Spence? He knew he shouldn't have trusted technology, or at least trusted himself to use it!

Looking back towards the window and the business front across the street Martin could only wonder what conversations were already taking place. His heart was racing and there was sweat standing out on his forehead; his communication with Harvey had been cut solely to the visuals, and this meant he had no way of determining how the meeting was progressing and if the old thespian had landed in any trouble.

How could he have been so stupid? This was a foolhardy quest from an old man who had watched too much television and thought of himself as more savvy and detective minded than he actually was. Unsure of how to proceed and feeling desperately afraid as on camera Harvey was moving towards the back office, the small bald day captain leading the way, Martin was about to grab his phone to call Mullins, when he suddenly had a flash of inspiration. Using his tired arthritic fingers to move the cursor Martin hovered over the audio icon in the bottom right hand side of the screen. A sound bar appeared along with a small red cross and the word 'mute'. Martin unclicked this box and suddenly the speakers were filled with deep luxurious sound.

Martin collapsed back into the sofa, feeling utterly exhausted, he really wasn't cut out for this. He allowed himself a couple of moments to breathe, compose himself and relax, then he sat up straight again and turned his attention back to the screen of the laptop.

"Of course." Harvey agreed, answering some question asked by the bald man that Martin had not heard.

The bald man nodded his head then Martin was looking at the back of his head as he turned to the door. He knocked three times, then after a moments hesitation the door opened and there was Malik, just as Martin had remembered him, the well oiled spider's leg hair, the dark clothes, the steely, focused stare. A strong gust of wind would probably have toppled the thin man, but there was something about him, something commanding that made you take him very seriously, and Martin leant back away from the screen at his presence, feeling his heart trip into an even faster beat.

"Mister Porter?" Malik enquired, his voice sounding very loud through the laptops speakers.

"That is I." Harvey replied, and then Malik must have gestured for him to step into the room as the camera attached to Harvey's hand showed him moving forward into the small office space beyond the waiting room.

"If you don't mind Mister Porter, I'm sure you can understand my precautions?" The thin mans voice crackled through the speakers, but Martin didn't know to what he was referring, his current view with Harvey's hand at his side was a sideways on angle of the near side wall and the door from which they had just entered.

"Of course." Martin heard Harvey reply.

Then there was a rustling and patting sound and all became clear, Malik had gestured for his base captain to search the old actor for any weapons or wires. Martin's breath caught in his throat and he waited anxiously for either the meeting to continue or the swift demise of Harvey Mullins.

"If you could just open your shirt." Malik's voice persisted.

"Am I to sing a sad ballad too?" The old actor replied, and Martin was pleased, he believed anybody would be curt in response to these circumstances.

"Please accept my apologies Mister Porter, but you must understand that my business requires the upmost discretion, I can't afford to be taking any chances."

"I understand." Harvey replied, then the camera was momentarily lifted as Harvey unbuttoned his shirt, revealing his scrawny chest to the equally thin man before him. Satisfied that he was not wearing a wire Malik nodded, and Harvey was once again fastening his button, the motion from the camera on his hand causing Martin to feel a little queasy as he watched the image bounce and jostle.

"Pockets are empty, all clean." The base captain remarked, satisfied after thoroughly patting Harvey down.

"Good." Malik replied. "If I could just have your ring please Mister Porter."

Martin swallowed back the golf ball sized lump that had formed in his throat.

"My ring?"

"That's correct, your ring, I will of course give you it back once our business concludes."

Harvey removed his ring, a worthless trinket Martin had purchased to complete the PA's image, and handed it to Malik, who dropped it into a glass of water on his desk; he really was more cautious than Martin had expected, especially considering the lack of security when the businessman had broken into his office the other night, or perhaps it was because of this. Remembering the gun that was in easy reach in the top drawer of Malik's desk Martin hoped with all his transplanted heart that he had not made a gross error of judgment here.

"A little dramatic don't you think?" Harvey said, Malik just shrugged.

"Please Mister Porter, take a seat. You can leave us now." The illegal organ trader said to the short bald base captain, who Martin heard but didn't see padding away and closing the door behind him.

Harvey stepped forward and pulled the seat out at the opposing side of the desk to Malik, Martin looked away as he did this as it was all a little erratic to him on camera, then there was the familiar scrunching sound of weight being applied to a leather cushion, and the view steadied once more. He had sat as Martin had instructed, with his left leg crossed over his right knee, his hands clasped about his left knee, giving Martin the optimum view of Malik and the room.

The intimidating man had taken the seat at his side of the desk and was regarding his new potential customer with a notable mix of caution and greed.

"So mister Porter, you mentioned on the phone that you may have a potential client that requires my services, but I don't understand why you would need to see me in person, we are a traditional private hire company, we are happy to conduct our business either over the phone or through the base captains."

"Let's not be coy mister Malik, we didn't come here to discuss taxis, your potential client has no need for them, having a fleet of limousine's at his disposal, besides, do you give all your taxi customers a thorough search before they embark on a journey?"

Martin had to smile, he was impressed, Mullins was playing the part perfectly. In his experience PA's to wealthy businessmen did tend to be straight to the point no nonsense people, it was the only way they could handle their clients needs.

Malik surprised Martin by smiling thinly. "Ok, then let me talk equally as frank in return, where did you get my number?"

"From the late David Purefoy, my client's consultant surgeon before he sadly passed."

Martin had known that this strategy was a risk, any mention of the surgeon, who was the subject of a current murder investigation, could make the trader clam up and refuse to continue with the meeting, but what choice did they have? It was the only connection they had to the business that was really practiced behind closed doors here in central Peckham, without Purefoy they couldn't justify even knowing of Malik's very existence.

"Purefoy." Malik muttered looking down at his hands. He was silent for a few seconds, long enough to make Martin anxious again, then he slowly shook his head and looked back towards Harvey and the tiny camera on his hand. "I guess some people don't fully understand the need for discretion."

"Oh, I would have thought someone like Purefoy would be a dream for somebody in your business, a surgeon with an on-going list of potential wealthy clients."

"Only if he could hold his water, besides, what business is this you're referring to? As I've already said, we're a private hire firm."

Martin grimaced; Malik was the dictionary definition of caution, there was no way he was going to get involved in any discussion of any illegal matters today.

"Ok, if that's the way you want to play it." Harvey replied. "Then let me talk in a manner for which you will be comfortable. My client has a need for your services, whatever you say those services are. My client would very much like to meet with you to discuss becoming a potential customer of yours. My client has a desperate need for those services. My client has the disposable income to match whatever your fee would be, and my client fully understands the need for the utmost discretion."

Malik nodded slowly. "Ok, what guarantees do I have that your client is good for the money? You sitting here in a fine suit talking on his behalf is hardly the collateral I require to make my business happen.

"My client assures me that should you agree to meet with him, he would be more than happy to pay half of the cost of the service up front, with the other half being secured once your dealings with him are complete."

At this turn of events Malik's eyes positively sparkled, it was even visible on the poor quality of the laptop feed, and Martin chewed on his lip anxiously; they had him.

"Ok." Malik replied, his greed outweighing his caution for the first time. He leant over and pulled something out of his drawer, Martin had a momentary panic when he thought he might be reaching for the gun, then he produced a notepad and pen and slid them across the desk towards the PA. "Why don't you write down your clients specific needs and I'll consider whether it's something my company are able to support with."

"Ok." Harvey replied, and pulled the pad and pen towards him on the desk. Martin didn't see what it was the old actor had written, for his view on the laptop as Mullins wrote on the pad with his other hand was of the suspended ceiling of the office, Mullins' left hand being flat on the desk top as he worked. Then he was sliding the pad and pen back across the desk and Martin's view of the proceedings was restored.

Malik nodded slowly. "Ok, I don't understand how we can be of service to you, your requests don't seem to be something a small private hire firm could support with, but maybe if I met with your client he could help me to understand a little clearer."

"That would be most agreeable." Harvey replied, and Martin was finally able to relax a little, the old actors work here was done.

"Ok, then let us arrange a time and we'll take it from there."

"With my clients specific needs time is of course of the essence, he has asked me to assure you that any time would be fine, the sooner the better."

"I understand, shall we say this evening then? Perhaps seven-thirty?"

"That sounds perfect."

"Ok, then I look forward to meeting your client this evening mister Porter, please assure them we will do all in our power to fulfil their needs."

"Excellent." Harvey replied, then the image became unstable again as the actor got to his feet. Martin mopped at the sweat that had formed on his head and snapped the laptop closed, he needed to get downstairs to meet with the driver he had organised from Sapient.

Harvey stepped out of the office and crossed the waiting room to the door, nodding to the bald base captain as he exited the building. Outside the black cab which Trojan Horse had assisted Martin in acquiring for the afternoon turned the corner. The thin man opened the door and climbed in the back, surprised to find Martin already there waiting for him.

The businessman smiled and held out his hand as the black cab turned around the corner away from Eze-link cars. The actor relaxed at the gesture and shook his employer's hand, smiling himself now.

"So how was that for you old boy?"

"Perfect." Martin replied. "Seriously Harvey you were a revelation, I hoped you'd be good but that performance far exceeded my expectations. It was like you actually were Reginald Porter, PA to Martin Lachance, Corporate Banker, seriously inspired."

"One does try." Harvey gushed, theatrically adjusting his tie.

"You did more than try, you succeeded." Martin continued. "You got me an in, and that's all I could hope for, I just hope Malik opens up a little more in his meeting with me."

"He was certainly a closed book." Harvey agreed.

"Anyway, I thought a little celebration was in order, a little drop of the red stuff?"

Martin pulled a bottle of Taylor's vintage port from inside his winter jacket and a plastic tumbler to accompany it. Harvey's eyes sparkled at the sight, his tongue darting out and wetting his lips in that lizard like fashion. Martin found it repulsive, but poured a good sized measure of port into the cup and handed it to the old thespian.

"Oh glorious nectar, how I've craved you so." He said, holding up the cup so he could worship its contents, then greedily he tipped the tumbler to his mouth and emptied the contents down his gullet, flinching slightly at the burning of his throat, relaxing as it abated, heating up his insides pleasantly like smouldering embers.

"Good?" Martin asked.

"Good? Good is not a word to describe this feeling, good my dear boy does not even come close."

"I'm glad." Martin said, looking at the thin man who had rested his head on the back seat rest of the taxi and closed his eyes in sweet ecstasy. "Because it's your last."

Suddenly the eyes were open, regarding Martin with suspicion, concern and contempt.

"What do you mean?" He asked, and Martin could physically see his chest rising and falling where his heart was suddenly pounding away, driven into overdrive by the fear of what he had just heard.

"Exactly what I say." Martin replied coolly. "You're too talented a man to waste that talent on the booze, and I've checked, there's plenty of work for a man of your years on the stage, you've just got to get dried out to be able to pursue it. I've checked you into the Priory, where you'll be given all the support you need to conquer your Demons."

"You can't, you can't!" Harvey spat, furious at what he was hearing.

Martin continued as though the actor had not even spoken. "When you're sober you will be given the contact details for Barry McGuire, a theatrical agent currently looking for a lead in a Samuel Beckett production due to open its doors in the West End in the spring. This man owes me a big favour, you're the payback."

"I'm not listening to this, stop this taxi, stop this taxi right now!"

The driver from Sapient turned his head, concerned, but Martin gestured for him to carry on.

"You can't do this! You promised me money, you promised me drink!"

"I'm not going to be responsible for you drinking yourself into an early grave. I lied about the booze, and for that I'm sorry, the money you will earn doing what you love, it will just take a lot of patience and a lot of will to get there, have you got that Harvey? Or are you too much of a coward to take control of your own destiny?"

Harvey stared at Martin, confused and unsure; the businessman took the opportunity to make his escape before the argument could get out of hand.

"Stop the car." He commanded the driver. The cab pulled over to the side of the road where Martin opened his door and stepped out onto the road. "Carry on straight to the Priory, make sure Mister Mullins is treated with dignity and care."

The driver nodded, as Martin closed the door Mullins lashed out, but only managed to strike his fist on the frame of the door.

"You're a thief, a fucking thief!" He screamed indignantly. Martin ignored him and pushed the door closed, stepping around the back of the car onto the pavement. Harvey was still screaming indignities and hammering on the back window of the cab as it pulled away from the kerb and head in the direction of the Priory. Martin felt no remorse, he knew that the old actor would thank him later, if he lived long enough to be thanked that was. He had a meeting to prepare for, and time was of the essence.

26

At seven-thirty the same privately hired black London cab that had escorted Harvey Mullins kicking and screaming all the way to the Priory turned the corner of Goldsmith road and came to a stop outside Eze-link cars. Martin, dressed in his finest suit, freshly showered and shaved, asked his driver to keep driving around the block until he received his call, at which point he was to return to the drop off immediately in order to make his collection.

Satisfied that the man understood the importance of keeping close at hand, Martin stepped out onto the pavement and closed the door behind him. The taxi pulled away from the kerb and Martin watched it go, feeling an uneasy desire to hail it back and climb back inside, asking the driver to take him as far away from this building and this situation as was humanly possible. But he didn't, and when the black cab disappeared around the corner the white haired man swallowed back the outright fear that was threatening to fully take control of his senses and walked up to the splintered wooden door of the taxi rank.

It was the fat base controller Zee, who had almost caught Martin snooping in the office to the back of the waiting area who was on duty when the businessman stepped in from the cold. When Martin stepped up to the cut through he looked up from the girly magazine he had been flicking through and regarded him with about the same energy as a drunken sloth, MacDonald's every day for breakfast would do that to you.

"Yeah?" He said in his deep Barry White'esque voice.

"I have an appointment with Haroon Malik." Martin said crisply and coolly, just before having to fight back a sudden wave of panic when it occurred to him he may not be supposed to know the organ traders name. Luckily the fat man didn't seem to notice, and as he nodded absently and pulled his hefty frame from his poor hard working chair Martin allowed himself a small sigh of relief.

Zee exited the cubby hole office from the far side and stopped outside the back office door, he knocked and waited, a couple of moments later the door was opening and Malik was there, peering out into the waiting area with his usual hostile gait.

"Your seven-thirty's here."

"Good, send him in and do the search." The thin man said.

Martin, who had been stood to the back of the waiting area and trying to steady his overly fraught nerve, looked at the man and felt a natural wave of abject terror course through his entire system. What was he doing here? This was absolute madness! He needed to escape; he needed to escape and now! Before it was too late!

"Come on through." Zee said from his place at the door, and though Martin's mind screamed at him to run for the exit his feet disobeyed and his jelly-like legs started shuffling forwards towards the small office at the back of the building and its terrifying custodian.

He closed in on the office and suddenly it was too late to leave; he was in this now, and had to see his part through or he really could be in trouble.

"Mister Lachance." Malik said, offering his hand. "Welcome."

"Thank you." Martin replied, he shook the young mans hand and felt a moment of revulsion that he hoped he had hidden well. They walked into the office and the fat man Zee followed close behind.

"I hope you don't mind, but my associate here is going to perform a bit of a body check on you, you never can be too careful in my line of work."

"Of course." Martin replied with a strained smile, after Harvey's visit earlier today he had been expecting this. Standing to the back of the office with his arms raised Martin allowed the fat base controller to pat him down. He checked in his pockets, ran his hands up his legs, checked inside his shirt and even took a look in his ears, a thorough examination if ever there was one. Having seen Harvey's ring end up in a glass of water on Malik's desk Martin had entrusted his wedding ring to his driver, he wasn't about to risk such a sentimental item as collateral damage in his investigation.

"Is this really necessary?" Martin asked as Zee patted down his chest, checking for wires, though Martin was the CEO of a blue chip organisation in the FTSE top 100, he wasn't like a lot of his compatriots, and had to feign the arrogance that would be expected of him in a situation like this.

"I'm afraid so." Malik replied, sitting down at his desk. "I can't afford to be taking any risks, I hope you understand."

"Fine." Martin huffed, hoping his act was as good as Harvey's had been.

"He's clean." Zee said when he had finished patting down.

"Good, you can leave, make sure we have plenty of cars on tonight it's that festival in Brixton." Malik said to Zee, who nodded in his usual lethargic way, and then left the office, closing the door behind him. "Please, take a seat mister Lachance."

Martin stepped forward to the chair positioned across the desk from Malik, the same one that Harvey had occupied that very afternoon, and when he did he noticed for the first time the newly fitted reinforced steel door that led out into the dirty yard out back. Martin wondered what panic Malik had felt when the discovery had been made, and just what kind of trouble the fat base captain had endured for not preventing the intrusion. Sitting down in the soft leather seat he couldn't help a momentary gush of pride; he hoped the thin man had been scared, in fact he hoped he'd been petrified. It was of course naïve to have any positive thoughts so early in the meeting, and Malik's opening words were enough to wipe them instantly from his thoughts.

Malik had been gazing at him from across the desk, his fingers laced together as he contemplated whatever was on his mind, and when he finally spoke it sent an icy chill into Martin's chest.

"Do I know you?" The words were innocent enough but they were weighted with so many potential hidden connotations that Martin momentarily froze, completely losing his composure and crumbling like a small boy asked to talk in front of his class.

"I don't believe so." Martin finally answered, trying to keep his voice as steady as possible.

"I've definitely seen you somewhere before." Malik continued unfazed. "Are you sure we haven't met?"

Then it struck Martin, how could he have been so stupid? Malik had seen him when he had hired a taxi from the Eze-link office the previous week. Quickly he tried to think of a way out of this difficult opening gambit.

"I'm a corporate banker, I gave a few interviews to the national press during the global economic crisis."

"No, no that's not it." Malik was shaking his head slowly, Martin could practically see the cogs turning in his brain as he mulled it over, his calculating eyes piercing into the businessman's. "I don't watch the news, not my thing."

Martin swallowed hard; his throat was suddenly very dry. He was going to have to come clean about how Malik recognised him, and just hope that his answer was sufficient to satisfy the man. "I got a taxi from here last week; I think you were in the office at the time, that's probably it."

Malik nodded slowly. "Use a lot of private hire firms do you Mister Lachance? I thought a man like you would have his own driver."

Martin felt like a bluebottle, caught in a spider's web, his eight legged menace slowly closing in on him, this wasn't going at all as he had hoped and he suddenly felt completely out of his depth. He needed to stay calm, needed to stay in character, he had to have learned something from Harvey, and he needed to be able to produce a similar amount of believability as his predecessor now, that is if he wanted to stay alive long enough to see it to new year.

"Ok, you've got me." He said slowly, sitting as comfortably as he could in the seat to try and show that he was relaxed. "I don't take a lot of taxi's, you're right, and yes I do have my own driver. He drives me round in a Bentley if you must know the details, quite a snazzy little number. I took the cab because I wanted to get a closer look at your operation, I was satisfied with what I saw, which is why I'm sitting here today. Now are we going to talk business or do you have any other pressing concerns?"

Malik smiled thinly. "Of course." He replied, and then pressed a couple of buttons on the keyboard in front of him, taking a look at the monitor for a couple of seconds before turning back to Martin. "I'm a cautious man Mister Lachance, I'm sure you can understand that. With this in mind as I'm sure your associate informed you I don't talk openly about my business dealings, but from the requirements I've been provided I believe I can be of service to you."

"That's good to hear, I understand your need for caution, but I have to be frank mister Malik, at some point we are going to have to speak openly and honestly, despite all your best protestations, it's simply necessary in progressing through any kind of negotiation."

"I agree, and there is a time and a place for such conversations, but they don't happen here. Today is about getting to know one another, an opportunity if you like for us to determine if us working together is the best course of action for everybody involved."

"I'm afraid that's not good enough." Martin replied in his best Corporate Banker guise. "As I'm sure you can appreciate time is very much of the essence, I need to know when I leave here this evening that you are going to be pursuing my interests in the swiftest timeframe possible."

Malik smiled that thin smile again that made Martin want to rip out his own thin white hair by the fistful. "Speed is not something for which you need to be concerned mister Lachance; I assure you none of my competitors have a success rate with a turnaround quite as fast as mine. I pride myself in what I do, but I also pride myself in self preservation, I need to know that my clients understand the need for discretion and that by working in a certain systematic way my operation will still be thriving in years to come, I'm sure *you* can understand that."

Martin nodded slowly. "Ok, I accept your terms, though I have my reservations."

"It's natural to have some reservations, most of my customers do, you're paying for a service, you want that service to be fast, efficient and deliver an expected result, I can guarantee you all of that."

"That's excellent in words mister Malik, but success isn't built on words alone, I have a large capital investment as well as my own personal wellbeing invested in this exchange, I need more information."

"All of which will be made available to you at the necessary time, as I said mister Lachance I do not discuss the finer details of my business arrangements here at this time, however I can assure you that all of your needs and requirements will be met."

"Not good enough, I need to know for starters where the organ that I'm paying for is being sourced from."

Malik had been tapping away at the computer again which was making Martin nervous, but he stopped now and glared across the desk at the businessman.

"I have absolutely no idea what you're talking about, this is a private hire company, we hire out taxis for commercial and private use, and if you insist on continuing to inject wild fantasy into our proceedings I will have no option than to ask you to leave, and our business here will be done."

Martin swallowed hard; Haroon Malik was not one to suffer fools gladly, even rich fools who provided large financial rewards, he would have to tread carefully from here. Frustrated that he was getting nowhere fast he nevertheless nodded his head slowly, maintaining eye contact with the criminal despite the overwhelming urge to look away.

"Now that we have an understanding, let me search our archives to ensure our service can fully meet your needs and requirements."

The thin smile flashed out again and Martin could have screamed; here he was putting himself right in the midst of major danger and potential harm and yet it appeared that the risk wasn't even going to pay off with any serious leads. It was all too easy to think of the handgun that he knew to be in reaching distance next to Malik in the top drawer of the desk, so he battled to block it from his mind, it would do him no favours to have a meltdown of nerves now.

The thin Asian man was still peering at his screen, he finished typing, paused for a few seconds, then a smile lit up the corners of his thin lipped mouth. This smile was unlike the other smiles he had falsely used today, this one looked cunning, devious, and it made Martin feel suddenly very exposed and afraid, akin to a rabbit caught in the headlights of an oncoming truck.

"Bingo." He said, practically salivating at whatever he was looking at.

"Is everything ok?" Martin asked, sensing that for him at least, things were far from ok.

"Oh yes, they're ok, in fact they're more than ok." Malik replied, turning finally from the screen, the mischievous smile still on his face; he resembled a small boy that was using a magnifying glass to project the rays of the sun onto a trapped ladybird. It made Martin feel sick with fear.

"Can we get back to the matter at hand? Time as I've mentioned is short." Martin said, though he was aware that he had broken out into a sweat and that his cheeks and forehead had turned scarlet red, destroying any believable cover he had fashioned in the process.

"I don't think so." Malik replied coolly. "In fact I believe our business here is done."

Martin, whose mouth felt as dry as the sands of the Sahara desert in the summertime, clasped his hands tightly together in an effort to stop them shaking. "Oh, and why is that?"

"Because you're not who you say you are." Malik let the statement hang in the air, the smile never faltering, to Martin it felt as heavy as a medicine ball bearing down on his chest; everything suddenly felt very surreal, could this really be happening? Could he really have just been found out by a potentially dangerous criminal? Every nerve end in his body was jangling as though tiny alarms had been set off; still he tried to keep his composure.

"This is absurd." He replied when he was certain his voice wouldn't betray him and crack like a twelve year old boy going through puberty. "I don't have to sit here and listen to this."

Martin pushed back in his chair and was about to stand when Malik's smile suddenly turned to a vicious scowl, he pointed at Martin and suddenly there was no chance of escape, his legs had turned from jelly to a substance that vaguely resembled custard.

"Stay there!" The thin man demanded, his icy stare cutting right to the core of Martin's fear, and he was trapped in the chair in this quiet back room, the sweat that had started on his forehead now soaking his back, turning his Savile Row shirt from sky blue to navy in the process.

Malik turned the screen so it was facing the businessman; on it was an article from the Financial Times, dated 24th December 2015. 'Sapient CEO suffers cardiac arrest' the headline exclaimed, below it was Martin's mug shot, taken from his current security ID card. He had a momentary lapse of wondering how the newspaper had come to obtain the picture, then his mind was dragged quickly back into the here and now, and the more pressing matters at hand.

He knows who I am. He knows who I am! How the hell am I going to get myself out of this one?

"Martin Rooley, Chief Executive Officer of Sapient Trans Global, a multi national haulage contractor, we could have used your knowledge when we were trying to negotiate the shipping of our goods from Chinese to international waters. Sadly doesn't say anything here about the banking industry, which tells me you've been telling porky pies."

Martin squirmed in his seat, there was no response he could give to the man and so he did what he felt best under the circumstances and stayed quiet.

"You honestly think I wouldn't do a background check? You honestly think I'm that thick? You think you can run an operation like this without taking some precautions? Oh don't worry I know I can talk freely now, you ain't wearing no wire. In fact alarm bells were ringing when my man was giving you the search, you made a fatal error mister Rooley, not that I wasn't suspicious already."

"Oh yeah, what was that?" Martin found his voice, trying desperately to stall for time while he considered his limited options.

"Your scar."

Martin closed his eyes in frustration, he understood what the man was saying, the scar from his operation, he had insinuated that he needed Malik's services in sourcing a replacement heart and yet here he stood right in front of the black market organ trader with a scar on show that suggested otherwise. Of course he could have claimed it to be a previous transplant that was now coming to the end of its usefulness, but what was the point? Malik knew exactly who he was, and he had him over a barrel.

"I believe you've already benefitted from my experience mister Rooley, using David Purefoy as your contact was another mistake, after all it was Purefoy who made the initial contact for your own heart transplant, now the surgeons dead, which leads me to my own conclusions. Did you kill him?

"You mean you didn't?" Martin blurted. In hindsight it was probably not very self preserving to ask such a leading question but he had been so surprised to discover that the criminal was not responsible for Purefoy's death that he had been unable to stop it.

"Not me my friend." Malik replied with a sneer. "But let me assure you, I have no issues with doing what is necessary to protect my own survival."

The Asian let the threat hang in the air; Martin, who had already seen the gun in Malik's top drawer didn't need reminding of this fact.

"I'm sure you will."

Malik leant forward, his elbows resting on the desk and his hands clasped together.

"What do you want?" He asked, sizing Martin up like an anaconda stalking its prey.

"I don't follow."

"Of course you do. You've come here under an assumed name, probing for information about my affairs. It isn't because you need an organ yourself, cos you've already had one, so I ask myself, what is it that this little white haired fool wants?"

Martin felt trapped in the thin man's stare; if it was possible to have sunk any deeper into the sticky office chair he would have become part of the plastic.

"Nothing, I don't want anything."

"Hmm, a likely story. Mister Rooley if I may be frank, you do not cross a man like me lightly, not if you have any good sense anyway, so let's start again, what do you want?" Malik was losing his patience now, Martin could see the veins in his arms throbbing where he had placed his hands flat on the surface of the desk, the small vein in the side of his temple was throbbing too, he was running out of time.

"I wanted information." He admitted, trying to gauge just how much information of his own he should concede. "I wanted to know whereabouts my heart was sourced, for personal reasons, I wanted to thank the family of the donor, and I didn't think if I came right out and asked that you'd be free with the information."

Malik regarded him for a while as one might examine the contents of a particularly colourful specimen jar. When he spoke there was enough of an undercurrent of malice in his tone to frighten Martin very badly.

"You're lying, you're lying to me again and I don't have time to waste on pointless little boys' adventure stories. Shall I tell you what I think? I think you're a white knight. A do-gooder. A busy body. I think you're on a one man crusade to get the girl and kill the baddies, a silver haired James Bond, license to shit his pants at the first sign of trouble. I also think you're the ageing fool who broke into my office the other night and went through my personal and business affairs, well tell me white knight was all the trouble worth it? Does it feel like you're about to dismantle the bomb with one second to go? Or does it feel like you're out of your depth? Does it feel like you're a couple of shit answers away from winding up in a shallow grave somewhere in Epping forest? How does it feel big man? How does it feel?"

As the Asian gangster known as Haroon Malik had been talking Martin had stared back, wide-eyed, his brow sweating profusely, his hands clutched to the arms of his chair with fingers that had turned white from the pressure. He was a dead man; he had come here as Malik had suggested on a one man crusade and was now close to swimming with a pair of concrete shoes in the Thames, just like some blabber-mouthed Johnny-come-lately in a bad 1940's gangster movie. He tried to speak, but all that escaped his throat was a dry wheezy croak.

Malik heard the sound and a vicious cackle erupted across the room.

"James Bond!" He shrieked with real glee. "You're so pathetic I could almost let you go, give you a pat on the back and send you home to your mummy. But we both know I can't do that." Then the Asian man did something that really did almost empty Martin's bladder right there in the middle of the office; he bent down and pulled the gun from the top drawer of the desk. He held it loosely in his hand, pointed in Martin's general direction, it looked very heavy and cumbersome being held from such a thin wrist, but Martin had no doubt the man knew how to use it, had no doubt in fact that he had used it several times before.

"Any last words?" Malik asked, almost casually.

"Yeah. Martin managed to somehow reply though his throat now felt like the epicentre of an inferno. "Aubergine."

"What?" Malik said, a bemused look on his face. "Aubergine? What the fuck are you talking about aubergine? You've lost it mate, fucking lost it. Now tell me old man, what the fuck am I supposed to do with you huh?"

Martin just sat in the chair, all sweaty and wracked with nerves, he had decided from here on in that silence was the best policy.

"Not in the talking mood huh? Let's see if you still feel that way when I've rammed the barrel of this gun down your throat. My guess is you'll be all talk then, my guess is you'll be begging me for your sad pathetic life."

Martin felt sick, the Asian man was actually enjoying this now, he could tell from the sly look in the thin mans eyes and the moistness of his lips as he talked; as though he was actually salivating at the possibility of putting a bullet into the old man.

"What do we do?" Malik muttered, leaning back in his chair, then, slowly, he began to rise.

In his sodden chair Martin crunched his teeth together tight, ignoring the advice of his orthodontist who had remoulded the pearly whites in his ageing gums five years ago.

The thin man was making his way slowly around the desk, toying with his prey, ready to make that fateful strike when all of a sudden there was a huge commotion from the next room. He turned around, startled at the sound, and quickly stuffed the gun into the waistband at the back of his trousers.

It sounded as though the Sunday parade at the Rio carnival had just come singing and dancing into the tiny waiting area at the front of the office. Looking now like a small boy who had seen his ice cream cornet pulled from his sticky grasp by a much bigger, stronger boy Malik made his way tentatively to the door.

Martin, who had been both expecting and hoping on this disturbance, readied himself.

When the thin man opened the door he looked out into the waiting area with a look of shocked disbelief sketched across his angular features; under different circumstances it could have been quite amusing.

In the tiny waiting area were at least a dozen party revellers, all wearing bright clothing, some in colourful wigs, some pulling party poppers, some blowing on horns, all were dancing around the tiny area as though it was the main stage of the Glastonbury festival while the fat base controller known as

Zee desperately tried to calm the pandemonium. It was utter chaos, and so bewilderingly unexpected that it had completely caught the black market organ trader off guard.

Martin did not waste the opportunity; he had crept up behind Malik as he had stared out at the revelry beyond, and now, sensing his utter bewilderment took a deep breath and then slipped past him through the door and out into the melee beyond.

The businessman immersed himself into the crowd, looking back at the thin man as he was surrounded by party revellers, watching the criminals face change from shocked disbelief to quiet understanding as the people in their brightly coloured outfits ushered him in a whirlwind of noise and emotion towards the door.

Malik was nodding his head now, a sly smile on his face as he watched Martin make his escape; he had underestimated the businessman, but it wouldn't happen again.

Martin made it to the door and was about to slip out into the cool December chill when Malik's voice cut across the room.

"I'll be seeing you Rooley." He said, his eyes cold and calculating. "I'll be seeing you real soon."

Knowing this to be true Martin nodded slowly, he had won the battle, the war was yet to be decided. He slipped out onto the well lit street and was bustled by the crowd towards the waiting black cab. The back door was opened and he slid onto the back seat as the last of the revellers stepped out of the office. As Martin watched a white van screeched to a stop outside the taxi rank and the side panel door opened; all of the party goers piled inside in a blur of fantastic colour, then, like the taxi it was pulling away from the kerb.

Turning in his seat so he could get a good look out of the rear window Martin stared back at the office, terrified that Malik and his fat companion would be giving chase. They were not, but he saw them at the window, staring out on their captives escape and wondering how the old man had gotten the better of them.

As the car turned the corner Martin slumped back against the seat, feeling absolutely exhausted. He had started a war, now he needed to win it.

27

The lift seemed to be taking an age to climb to the fourteenth floor, but then in Martin's heightened state of panic everything was taking too long. The black cab journey back to the hotel had taken too long, his trek across the lobby had taken too long and he could be damn certain packing up his belongings would be a task he would find time consuming and stressful as well.

Finally there was an audible ping and the doors slowly slid open. Martin turned left out of the elevator and crossed the short corridor where he pushed through a fire door, turned right and came to a stop outside room 1421. He used his key card to gain entry and stepped into the room. As soon as the door closed behind him and the latch was safely secured, Martin felt a wave of dizziness wash over him and he stumbled over to the bed. He knew he didn't have time to rest, but if he didn't lie down and close his eyes for five minutes he was likely to faint, and that would not suit his present situation at all. He had no doubt now just how dangerous a man Haroon Malik was, and he was under no illusion that the man didn't have the means at his disposal to track him down fairly quickly, and if that was the case then he could be here at this hotel at any time, or worse still, at his home; with Rose.

Martin allowed his head to sink into the soft pillow on the luxuriously large bed; he wanted nothing more than to slip off his shoes, climb under the covers and allow the exhaustion of a truly terrifying day send him into a deep and peaceful slumber. But there was no time for that; it would be reckless and foolhardy. Instead he waited for the worst of the dizziness to fade, then slowly forced himself into an upright position.

Sitting on the bed with his Gucci shoed feet pressed into the thick hotel carpet Martin reflected on how close he had come to actually slipping off this mortal coil for good. If it hadn't been for the safe word he had set up with Thomas Spence and the Trojan employees who had caused the scene that had masked his escape he may not still be breathing right now, and that thought scared him, it scared him badly. Martin had settled on the safe word of aubergine, wanting to make sure it was something he would definitely not use as part of a normal conversation; if he had been getting somewhere with Malik the last thing he would have wanted was a bunch of fake party revellers turning up and spoiling things because he had inadvertently triggered his safe word as part of a normal conversation. It had been a comfort knowing that Spence and his colleagues could hear everything that happened in the room through the tiny listening device that had been implanted deep in his ear, but it had also brought about its own problems; he had been given no choice other than to level with the private security boss about his intentions, and the agent had not been happy. It had taken Martin a long time to persuade him that it was his intention to go about his mission with or without his help, and it was this bullish persistence that finally paid off. Spence had agreed to support him on his quest, but had insisted on the safe word so he could get his people to spring him out of the confrontation at the first sign of danger.

Now Martin knew that relationship was over; from here on in he was on his own. Slowly, reluctantly he forced himself to his feet, then stepped into the bathroom, the lights being triggered from the sensor above the door. He pulled a pair of tweezers from the complimentary toiletry bag on the bathroom counter and looked into the wall sized mirror, not liking the dark ringed eyes that stared back at him.

Who am I? Who have I become? He thought, feeling like a stranger in his own skin. He turned his head slightly so he could look from the corner of his eye at his right ear as he worked, then he placed the parallel prongs of the tweezers into his ear, and fished around for the listening device. It was tiny, no more than the size of a pencil eraser, and he managed to snare it on the second attempt. Carefully he pulled the flesh coloured device from his ear canal, and with it wedged between the prongs of the tweezers, filled a glass with water from the sink, then proceeded to drop it in. There was a tiny plop as it entered the water, then it sank to the bottom of the glass and came to a rest on the bottom. Martin watched it's descent with mounting fear, knowing what this symbolised for his journey from here. Thomas Spence and his Trojan Horse employees had been his security blanket to this point; knowing that from here on in he was on his own was deeply unsettling, but he had no choice. Thomas had made his feelings quite clear; he was unhappy with the way Martin's personal vendetta was proceeding and wanted it to end, the businessman was pretty sure that he would have pulled his support anyway, for fear of getting the old man killed, or not preventing it from happening at least. Martin, who didn't have any choice but to see this through, took one last look at the listening device, then stepped back into the bedroom.

His next port of call was an essential one, and it was going to be far from easy. Martin sat on the corner of the bed next to the nightstand and picked up the phone from its cradle, he dialled one of only a couple of numbers he ever remembered by heart and waited for the call to connect. It rang six times in total before a tired, weary voice answered on the other end.

"Hello."

Martin hesitated, his breath caught in his throat, just hearing her voice again in a time of turmoil made him weak at the knees, longing to see her, to rest his head on her bosom and be comforted, to have her stroke her long fingers through the thin patch of white hair on the top of his troubled head.

"Martin?" Rose enquired gently. She had known it was him, even in his silence she had known it was him; if at all possible this made him pine for her all the more.

"Yes." He said weakly, squeezing his eyes shut tight and collapsing backwards onto the bed with the phone pressed tightly to his ear. What a joy it was to hear her voice, what sweet comfort.

"Oh my God Martin, thank God! I've been so worried, are you ok? Where are you? You haven't been answering my calls, come home, please God Martin come home, I'm not angry anymore, I just want to see you, I need to see you, please Martin please!"

He listened to her plea with a heart that ached not only from his own personal longing but from the guilt of the burden he had enforced on her; she was fraught with worry and close to tears, he had done this. He wanted nothing more than to tell her everything was alright, that he was coming home, that he would be with her soon, but he knew that to do this would be to confine her to her doom, to confine both of them. He needed to stay strong; now more than ever he needed his backbone, he had to fight every urge in his body and see this thing through; the consequences if he didn't were unthinkable.

Steeling himself Martin blocked out all sense of sentiment.

"Rose, I need you to listen to me, and I need you to hear me well. I'm ok, I'm safe and I *will* be home soon, God willing we'll be together soon. But I have a situation that I'm trying to address, it's a matter that won't go away and I need to see it through. Now the important bit; I need you to leave the house Rose, right now. Don't pack a bag, don't even bother to lock the door, just grab the keys from the counter, get in the Range Rover and drive up to your sisters in Bolton. I want you to stay there until you hear from me again."

"Martin what are you talking about?" Rose asked in an unsteady voice.

"I don't have time to explain, but you're in danger, I need you to leave the house right away."

"You're scaring me Martin!"

"Good, it will pay you well to be a little scared right now, but if you listen to me and you do as I say there will be absolutely nothing to be afraid of. I don't have time to explain but I promise I'll explain everything soon. Please, do as I say Rose, leave now."

"No! No I won't!" She cried. "Why should I? You're not giving me any reason! Why should I leave?"

"Because some very bad men are going to be looking for me, and my home will be the first place they'll try! They could be there any minute Rose and you don't want to be there when they arrive!"

The line was silent for a few seconds, when Rose spoke again her voice was shaky and afraid.

"My God Martin what have you gotten yourself into?"

"I promise I'll explain everything soon, but now you need to leave."

There was a pause again, this time when Rose broke the silence her voice was filled with a tired reluctance.

"Fine, but you have a lot of explaining to do."

"I know I do." He agreed, his eyes still closed, his arm covering them as though he wanted to completely block out the light.

"I guess I'll go then." She said with a weary sigh.

"Drive carefully."

"You be careful too Martin, I don't know what you're up to, but you're scaring me very badly."

"I know, and I'm sorry."

She paused again, as though waiting for some other word of comfort; Martin wanted nothing more than to give it to her, but this was neither the time nor the place.

"Fine, goodbye then."

"Goodbye Rose." He said with an ache in his heart worse than any pain he had felt before his operation. The line clicked dead and he slowly stretched out his hand and fumbled the handset back into its cradle on the bedside table. He lay like that for some time, feeling terribly weary, his arm still covering his eyes. What had he done? His wife was in danger in their own home, just what the hell had he done?

Letting out a pained sigh he slowly sat up straight on the bed, every muscle ached and he felt all of his sixty-eight years. Malik had been right; he had seen himself as a crusader, the white knight sworn to protect the innocent, but it was a fairy-tale, a fallacy, the real world was nothing like the adventure tales of Zorro and the Lone Ranger that he had enjoyed as a boy, the real world was a snake, it was cruel and calculating and if you weren't careful you were likely to get bitten. The real world could swallow you whole and there wasn't a damn thing you or anybody else could do about it.

Martin flicked open his mobile and scrolled through to his contacts list; Sheila had set this up for him and it was her that he called now. His PA's personal mobile answered after a couple of rings.

"Martin?"

"It's me, I'm sorry to call on you after office hours, I never would normally but I'm in a bit of a tight spot and I could use your help."

"Of course, I'm just glad you're ok. We've been worried about you, have you spoken to Rose? She's been calling daily, asking for news of you; I didn't know what to say."

"You didn't need to say anything, and yes I'm fine thank you, so don't worry about me."

"Ok, if you insist, though I see it as part of my job to worry, just so you know. How can I help?"

Ten minutes later Martin's travelling belongings were packed back in his holdall and he had checked out of the hotel. He took the car from the underground garage and was speeding across London towards home. He knew it was a risk to be heading there at all with Malik on his tail, but there were items that he absolutely needed that made the risk necessary.

The journey passed in a blur, his mind was a muddle of thoughts and confusion and before he knew it he was turning into the forecourt of his lavish home, the electric gates creeping open before him. He pulled the Aston Martin to a halt right outside the front door, wanting to keep a fast escape a possibility, and exited the vehicle.

Martin looked about himself nervously; it was close to ten o'clock now and the sky was dark and littered with stars. All was quiet; if he was being watched the would be stalker was not as yet making themselves known. Swallowing back his fear Martin stepped up to the door and tried the handle, it was locked; luckily this was the only advice that Rose hadn't taken, he unlocked the door and stepped inside.

All was quiet in the dark hallway; it was all too easy to imagine Malik or one of his goons lurking somewhere in the shadows, watching and waiting. Without flicking on the lights the businessman quickly strode up the stairs, needing to keep moving, scared that his fear could render him useless, he would be done then for sure.

He crossed the landing to the bedroom; he could still smell Rose's sweet perfume lingering in the air and it made him crave for her. How long had it been since he had seen her gentle face? Since he had held her in his arms? He honestly couldn't remember; too long. The small silver Christmas tree stood in the corner of the room; there were three trees in the house; one in the living room, one in the kitchen, and the small one in here. Martin had never understood the need for more than one, but looking at it now made him feel lonely and close to tears. He wished he had been here to help her with the decorations. He had always been too busy, one way or the other, usually work commitments, and he regretted now not taking the time to help her trim up the house, for the first time in his life it seemed something that would be a pleasure rather than a chore.

Sighing he walked around the side of the bed and opened his wardrobe door; in the alcove below the lowest shelf was a tin file holder where Rose stored all the important documents. The key was left not so securely on the top of the tin. Martin removed the tin and placed it on the soft carpet in front of him. He took the key and clicked open the locking mechanism, pulling the lid back ninety degrees on its hinge so he could peer inside.

There were five separated compartments in the tin; house, car, bills, bank and miscellaneous, all written in Rose's careful script. He ducked into the miscellaneous compartment and quickly found what he was looking for. Martin looked at the picture at the back of his passport and the many stamps that filled the pages before it. Then he slipped it into the pocket of his suit trousers and closed the lid on the file holder. He placed this back in the wardrobe and then pulled the large suitcase from the top shelf. He opened it on the bed and began quickly filling it with clothes, underwear and toiletries from the en suite bathroom.

Rose had always packed the bags for whatever venture they were escaping on; she was meticulous, using every last ounce of space, Martin was a little more haphazard, everything would no doubt be creased beyond recognition when he reached his destination. Oh well, he didn't have time to worry about anything as trivial as a pair of creased slacks or an un-pressed shirt.

Finally he grabbed the chair from affront the vanity table and placed it directly in front of the far left hand wardrobe door. He stood on top of it and pulled a glass jar from behind a couple of folded up duvets. Inside was over two thousand pounds in unused fifty pound notes; emergency money that had been stored up high for countless years; well if this wasn't an emergency he didn't know what was. Martin unscrewed the lid, pocketed the money and threw the jar back on top of one of the duvets. Then, without placing the chair back in front of the vanity table he zipped up the case, grabbed the handle and head for the stairs. He took them two at a time to the bottom, where he stood panting for a second, the case next to him on the floor.

While he caught his breath Martin took a look about the darkened hall; he could see through into the living room with the huge Christmas tree in the corner and the sparkling Angel decorations bought on a shopping spree to Tiffany's in New York a couple of years ago. He could see the couch where he had spent many an evening with the remote control on his lap and the television tuned to some cop show or other. If he turned his head slightly he was facing down to the huge dining kitchen with the island in the middle and the pots hanging overhead, to where Rose had prepared many a sumptuous meal, meals fit for a king. These were small things; things that in his former life he had taken fro granted, but how he craved them now, how special they felt to this man standing on the edge of the abyss.

There was a lump in Martin's throat, he swallowed it back with some difficulty, then he picked up his case, walked to the door and stepped outside. The cold air hit him like a slap in the face. Martin locked the door, taking a nervous look around as he did so, then he climbed back into the Aston Martin, gunned the engine and drove out of the huge double electrified gates towards his destiny.

PART FOUR: THE CHINESE CONNECTION

1

    With the landing gear released the Boeing 747 touched down smoothly on the tarmac at Qingdao Liuting International Airport. Flying China Southern from Heathrow it had been an arduous eighteen hour journey, stopping once to change planes at Seoul Incheon International in South Korea, but finally the weary traveller had reached his destination. He stepped off the plane into the humid mid afternoon heat and walked down the stairs with his carry on bag over his shoulder.

    The airport wasn't huge, not when compared to Heathrow where he had started his journey, but to Martin it may as well have been, to Martin it could have been the size of a small planet. On the plane it had been easy, half of the passengers had been English as had half of the crew, but here he was receiving the earliest indications of how far out of his comfort zone he had just travelled, he was a stranger in a strange land, and it was already starting to show.

He followed his route through to baggage claim by following either the crowds or the recognisable symbols on the signposts, there was no point trying to read them as not only were they written in Mandarin, there weren't even any decipherable letters, Chinese symbols guiding the way.

Luckily the flight information was written in English as well as Mandarin and Martin found his carousel easily enough, and with his suitcase collected wheeled out through customs into the arrivals hall.

In hindsight it would probably have been a good idea to get Sheila to book him a transfer as well as the flight and hotel, but as he hadn't he would just have to muddle his way through.

Even in the shade of the canopy at the front of the airport it was stiflingly hot, and Martin had to remind himself that it was almost Christmas. He queued in line for a taxi and when his time came he climbed in the back of the yellow cab, thankful that it was a recognisable colour and closed the door behind him. Instantly he was clawing at the collar of his shirt, the car was not air conditioned and it was like an oven inside. The driver had his window wound right down but this made little difference with the outside temperature at the hottest point of the day being so high. Welcome to China, he thought as he scrambled the hand written note from the pocket of his trousers. He could barely read his own writing, pulling the car over to the side of the road when Sheila had called him back with news of the bookings two nights ago he had quickly jotted down the details, now he read them back, hoping he had not made an error in his haste.

"Please could you take me to the Qingdao Sailing hotel?"

The driver, a thin man with even thinner hair, just stared at him.

Great, Martin thought, and so it begins.

"Qingdao Sailing hotel." Martin repeated.

The man replied in very fast, very high pitched Mandarin, and Martin's heart sank. Great, his fears had been confirmed, the man didn't speak a word of English.

The man continued to talk, pointing at something to Martin's right. He looked at it, feeling jet lagged and stressed. It was a small grey plastic box with a display window and keys, on each key was both a symbol in Mandarin and its closest corresponding English letter. With Mandarin not having an alphabet and literally thousands of different symbols for prospective students to learn this was never going to be an exact science, but the man seemed insistent that Martin use the equipment.

"I don't understand, I don't know how to use this." He said in a panic, wishing not for the first time that either Sheila or Peter were here to guide him. He had known the language barrier was going to be an issue, he just hadn't known it would happen so soon.

Martin slid over to the other side of the seat where the plastic box was attached to the back of the front passenger chair, he looked down at it with growing dread, technology always having been something he felt was for younger men than he. There was a fairly obvious start button in green to the left hand side so he pressed this and the display came to life.

"Err, ok." He muttered, sweat forming on his brow, he could honestly say he felt as stressed now as he had when he had been staring down the barrel of Malik's gun, ridiculous but true.

On the screen several national flags had appeared, none of them were the St. George's cross, there was a down arrow so he pressed on it and felt a moment of pride when more flags appeared, there was still no English flag, but there was a Union flag, so he tapped on this and an egg timer appeared.

"Come on come on." He muttered, feeling the pressure with the other taxis in the queue waiting in line.

Finally a message appeared on screen:

Please enter the name of your destination

Thank God, English. Martin looked down at the scrap piece of paper, hoping he had spelt the name of the hotel correctly when taking the details from Sheila, then with his usual one finger typing style, he tapped in the name of the hotel.

Nothing happened.

Martin looked down at the screen frustrated, then back at the driver. He was no help, just stared back at Martin with a look as confused as the businessman felt must be etched on his own.

Then he had a sudden moment of inspiration, and remembering the Windows media course he had been forced to take several years ago when it became apparent his business practices were becoming antiquated, he hit the enter key at the side of the letters.

A new message appeared on screen:

One moment please, we are working on your request

Then the screen went blank and at the front of the taxi the radio suddenly burst into life. A voice spoke in Mandarin and then the driver picked up the CB and gave his response. A moment later the car was pulling away from the kerb; Martin didn't know exactly what had just happened but he hoped to God the message had been relayed correctly or this could be just the start of his difficulties. He relaxed back against the uncomfortably hot fabric of the seat and looked out of the window at the unfamiliar landscape unfolding before his eyes.

The area surrounding the airport was very much like that surrounding airports the world over, all tall fences, industrial estates and cheap looking hotels, but as soon as they pulled onto the freeway the landscape changed and Martin was reminded again that he was far from home.

There were hills in the distance, but they were unlike any hills Martin had ever seen, they certainly didn't resemble anything in the Yorkshire Dales. When they passed through small townships the shops looked poky and unkempt, the displays and signs above the doors in the same foreign symbols that had baffled him at the airport. Even the people, with their vastly different appearance both facially and in the way they dressed, made Martin long for the comfort of the land he knew so well. He had never been to this part of the world before, and on first impressions didn't think he would be returning any time soon.

Luckily, as they crossed a bridge separating the land from the crystal blue sea and approached the centre of Qingdao, the landscape changed again, tall skyscrapers and office blocks littering the horizon before breaking to the rugged landscape in the distance. With the blue waters of the East China Sea stretching out to touch the base of the glass adorned skyscrapers it was not unlike Miami where Martin had holidayed a couple of times back in the early nineties and this went some way towards easing his trepidation.

Through the centre of the city the stiflingly hot taxi weaved in and out of the traffic, down Xianggang Middle Road, turning right onto Xinpu road and down towards Donghai Road West. Finally it turned through a mass throng of people milling around a quiet residential street and through onto the Binhai Walk Road. The imposing four star Qingdao Sailing Hotel was right next to the Olympic Sailing Centre and the taxi pulled up right outside.

Martin looked up at the building, suitably impressed. When he had spoken to Sheila on the phone she had been flustered at the cheap cost of the rooms in this industrial Chinese city, with most going for as little as fifteen pounds a night. At thirty one pounds the Sailing Hotel was one of the best she could find on short notice, all the five star hotels being fully booked, but she needn't have worried, it looked perfect for his needs. Besides, Martin had never been one for the Dorchester or the Four Seasons anyway, his PA just assumed being the CEO of a major corporate empire this would be the norm, but truth be told he had always been happy in a Premier Inn.

Unsure how much to tip Martin handed over 500 Chinese Yuan Renmimbi that he had converted back at Heathrow and the driver smiled gratefully. The journey had actually only cost a quarter of this but Martin wasn't to know, he was just glad to finally be at the hotel. He grabbed his bags and walked up to the door where a young good looking man in a red uniform and hat, which

Martin guessed would be quite uncomfortable in this heat, greeted him with a bow. Martin returned the greeting and the doorman gestured him inside.

His bags were taken by a bellman who also smiled politely and then Martin was at the front desk of the ultra modern reception area. The young attractive girl on reception beamed an enigmatic smile at his approach and with barely a trace of accent spoke to him in his mother tongue.

"Good day sir, welcome to the Qingdao Sailing Hotel, how may I help you today?"

Martin felt his shoulders relax; he was so relieved to hear somebody speak to him in English that he was sure his face was currently distorted with the goofiest of grins.

Five minutes later he was fully checked in and rising to the eighteenth floor in an elevator as fast if not faster than any he had ever travelled in back home. The doors opened onto a plush corridor with soft lighting due to the huge picture window that looked out onto the sun drenched street below. In this hotel all of the signs and numbers were duplicated in English as well as Mandarin and he had no problem locating room 1808, where he inserted his key card and watched the tiny light on the handle locking mechanism turn green.

The businessman stepped into the room and took a look around. Another wave of relaxation washed over him as the tension of the last forty-eight hours was momentarily put to one side. The room was nothing short of beautiful, with a huge picture window looking out to sea and sleek modern furniture, a huge plasma TV on the wall. The bathroom was sparklingly clean with a large walk in shower as well as Jacuzzi bath; all modern amenities had been covered. It was the bed though that really caught Martin's attention, so warm and inviting in the air conditioned room.

He didn't waste any time, slipping off his shirt, trousers and shoes martin climbed between the sheets, the exhaustion of his journey here and all that had happened before weighing on him like a poisonous cloud. He relaxed into the pillow; the sheet pulled up to his bare shoulder, and was asleep within seconds.

2

Martin's eyes blinked open and he looked about the room with momentary confusion. He felt disoriented and it took him a few seconds to find his bearings and realise where he was. Then he remembered all that had gone before and he let out a weary sigh. His head dropped back to the pillow and he closed his eyes again, allowing himself a few extra minutes in bed. His hands traced over his body as he lay, he was clammy with sweat despite the coolness of the air conditioning, his mouth was dry too but he had nothing at hand with which to quench his thirst.

Groaning he rubbed at his face with his palm and then blinked his eyes open again, this time staring at the brilliant white ceiling of the hotel room. What time was it? He couldn't tell from the light creeping in through the open curtained window so he rolled over onto his side and picked his Rolex up from the bedside table. Ten thirty am, how could that be? He had arrived here in the afternoon, how could it now be morning? Then he checked the date and lo and behold it had progressed to the twentieth of December; he had been asleep for over sixteen hours.

Martin groaned again and forced himself into a sitting position. How could he have let this happen? It was easy of course; he was exhausted, had been managing on hardly any sleep for weeks now, his shattered brain had needed to rest and had seen its opportunity and taken it. The businessman shuffled to the end of the bed and drooped his legs over the side, yawning and rubbing at his sleepy eyes.

He plodded across to the bathroom, dropped his underwear, urinated for what felt like ten minutes, then climbed into the shower and washed the sweat and grime from his skin. Twenty minutes after this he was dressed in a pair of thin cotton pants and a short sleeved pale yellow shirt, clothes he had bought for evening meals in the Maldives with Rose, and heading out to explore this fascinating new land.

The elevator doors pinged open and he stepped out into the huge reception area. He was too late for breakfast and his stomach growled discontentedly, his raging thirst had also not abated for he had not dared drink the water from the tap for fear of it unsettling his guts.

Walking out of the hotel, bowing once more to the porters who guided his way, Martin stepped out into a much cooler day than before. This part of China, due to its position on the coast, could see lower temperatures than other major Chinese cities, and Martin instantly regretted not bringing along his jacket. He looked back at the hotel, considered making the journey back to the eighteenth floor and decided he could live without it. Despite the morning chill it was a pleasant day, with a brilliant blue sky and a sun that crept behind the tall buildings and brightened the street about you as you moved.

Taking the roadway past the Olympic Sailing Centre Martin crossed a small bridge over the estuary and followed a busy looking road towards a lively looking thoroughfare. Here designer shops and boutiques lined a short pedestrianized zone that was overlooked by the huge skyscrapers above. With his white hair and westernised features Martin attracted quite a lot of attention as he strolled through the thoroughfare, it made him a little uncomfortable as groups of giggling teenage girls snapped photos of him on their iPhones and middle aged men passing in the street made no disguise of their intent to gawp at him like some exotic breed of fish in a tank. It made him feel quite ridiculous and he hurried as fast as he could to the end of the lane.

Through the alleyway to the back of the pedestrianized zone a walkway at the side of the water led past a confused mix of German, Oriental and typically modern buildings, the German occupation of 1898 owing to the cities diverse and varied landscape. Martin walked along feeling a little more comfortable amongst recognisable architecture. There was a small grocery store in the shade of St. Michael's cathedral, the seat of the Bishop of the Roman Catholic Diocese of Qingdao, and Martin entered it under the arc of its undecipherable sign.

It was warm and sticky inside, with a smell of cooking meats coming from a curtained off area to the back of the tiny store. The man sat on the small wooden seat amongst a litter of exotic sellable items looked to Martin to be a hundred at least; his skin was stretched and paper thin and what teeth he had left were little more than brown stubs protruding from his ageing gums.

Martin looked at the over-stacked shelves with mounting dismay. There was absolutely nothing that he recognised, and all of the packets were covered in

Chinese symbols and strange designs. He scooted down, looking at things that resembled dog chews but had cartoon pictures of children devouring them on the packets, strange spice smelling balls in net bags, a dark liquorice looking substance in sticks that smelled of cat food and bags of shells that looked a little like fortune cookies, but which had a picture of a smiling fish on the label, its friendly demeanour seeming to identify that it was happy to be caught in a trawler boats net and chopped up to be put inside the shell of a fortune cookie.

At the end of the short aisle, down on the floor beneath a stack of sickly looking sweets, Martin found what he was looking for. He didn't need to speak Mandarin to recognise bottled water, and he grabbed a litre sized bottle from the floor, a picture of a mountain on its unreadable label. Martin took it to the counter and handed it over to the old man, who regarded him like a new species of life form that had just landed in the middle of Shandong Province. Still having absolutely no concept of the currency Martin handed over a note to the old man, who shook his head and waved it away. Martin could feel his stress levels starting to rise again, was every interaction in this country going to be this difficult? He didn't even know if the note had been too much or too little but seem as how it had been the same note he had used to pay for his journey form the airport yesterday he figured too much. Well what could he do? He didn't have any other money and he doubted if they took Visa.

"Keep the change." Martin said, placing the note back down on the counter, then he left the store before the old man could complain.

Back outside Martin hurried away from the tiny store, feeling way too stressed over such a simple transaction. He screwed the cap off the bottle as he walked and put the spout to his lips. The water was warm and not particularly pleasant, but it put out the fire in his throat and settled his growing dehydration. He downed half the bottle, then screwed on the cap, letting out an almighty belch as he did so. He looked around embarrassed but nobody had heard.

He followed the road down past the church; he was at the top of a hill now and had a magnificent view of the ocean on the left hand side. Down past a row of traditionally oriental buildings he could see what looked like a street market in full flow to the right, so he head this way, curious as to see the ware's on display and to how they may differ from the markets he had attended back home. Taking another mouthful of warm water Martin strolled down the road past the traditional houses and came to an intersection in the quiet street, where he crossed over to the market.

Nanshang market was unlike any market Martin had ever attended before; it was in fact a real eye opener as to just how far from home he had travelled. This was a bird and pet market, and the commotion coming from the various cages and stalls made a din quite unlike anything the businessman had heard before. Martin walked through the cluttered walkways staring at the countless displays with wide eyes and a slack jaw. He had always been naïve as to the ways and cultures of other countries, and had only been keen to learn more on the rare occasions that a business venture had hinged on his learning a little about an associate in another country. Martin's holidays with Rose were generally to places where English food, English customs and the English language were second nature; Shandong Province wasn't one of those places.

On his right cats in cages pawed at the bars that kept them prisoner while on the left stack upon stack of tiny wooden cages housed equally tiny exotically coloured birds, all chirping and tweeting in unison. Further down there were tanks of squid and lobsters and water filled trays of terrapins, all bunched together and climbing over one another for space; it reminded Martin of the photographs he had seen of the holocaust victims at Auschwitz who had clambered naked as the day they were born over one another for air as the gas had been dropped into the chamber. Martin had never really been much of an animal lover but the sight of these poor creatures filled him with a deep sadness and he couldn't help wondering what PETA would make of all this.

He made his way out beyond the raucous animal section and was pleased to enter a more serene part of the market selling fake designer handbags and shoes and row after row of carefully preened bonsai trees. Seeing the shoes and bags made him think of Rose, and this made him long once more for home; he quickly cast his feelings aside and continued on his way.

Suddenly a delicious aroma filled his nostrils and he was reminded that he hadn't eaten in nearly twenty hours. His stomach grumbled on cue and he looked around for the source of the smell. In the far right hand corner of the market smoke was rising from a quarter that was cordoned off with blue and white border material. Thinking the smoke could be from a barbecue or grill Martin started in its direction. He was thinking of Borough market back in London, where he stopped whenever he could to sample the delicious gourmet food on offer; minted lamb burgers in focaccia baps, gourmet sausages, full hog roasts that tickled the nostrils and tantalised the taste buds and cheeses and meats from some of the finest producers in the world.

Of course this wasn't Borough, wasn't even London for that matter, but if the food in the market was half as good as that in the Imperial Palace restaurant in Kensington he was in for a treat, and he couldn't help but salivate at the thought.

Martin walked over to the entrance to the segregated food court and turned in expectantly, his stomach omitting a growl of anticipation. On first glance it was actually quite a lot like Borough market back home; with stall after stall of steaming pots and skewered meats. There were people milling about and some sat over bowls of rice and noodles at trestle tables in the centre of the court.

Every stall was manned by a couple of eager owners, vying their trade and gesturing for customers to come take a closer look. In his current state of hunger this seemed like a very good idea indeed, and Martin strolled into the cordoned off arena with his stomach rumbling.

At first all seemed fairly normal, the smells were not unlike those that you could enjoy if you took a stroll through China town in London's busy west end, but it was on closer inspection that it transpired that things were not as they had at first seemed.

Some of the stalls were serving standard fare, pots of steaming noodles and prawns or oysters served in a type of broth. Others displayed roasting meats that were basted in a deep red sauce that looked genuinely very appetising. There were thin pancakes filled with duck and bean shoots and dishes of rice and sizzling beef in a warm sticky looking sauce. All of it looked delicious, and would have been the perfect antidote to the raging hunger that was starting to make Martin feel dizzy and faint, but these weren't the only stalls. There were others that displayed such outlandishly unusual goods that the businessman suddenly and unexpectedly lost his appetite.

Giant deep fried spiders were on offer at the stall to Martin's left, to his right whole ducks heads, which had been boiled with vegetables and stock. Seriously, Martin thought as he looked at the tiny woman gesturing for him to come closer, how much meat could there be on a ducks head?

Further down the row two men in dirty looking jackets were selling whole Qingdao Bay crabs, deep fried in oil and then battered. With the coating on the outside it was clear that the shell of the crab was supposedly part of the dish. Martin could only wonder at the hours it would take to pick this out of your teeth.

All of this was bad enough, but it was when he meandered past the last stall at the end of the row that he really lost his appetite, and nearly threw up onto his shoes in the bargain. As well as more traditional delicacies such as skewered pork meat and bowls of tasty looking dumplings, the stall was also selling scorpions skewered on a stick, and as he watched an old man with more wrinkles than teeth bit into what could only have been a baby chicken, deep fried and impaled on a stick. He bit its head clean off and chewed with his gums, fat dripping down his chin. It was this that almost caused Martin to lose what little sustenance was left in his stomach, and he hurried back out of the food court with his stomach lurching and bile filling his throat.

He hurried back along the displays of fake designer bags and shoes and again through the worryingly ill treated animals and appeared back at the entrance to the market, where he hurried out onto the street as far from the smell of the cooking as he could, he came to a stop next to a crudely balanced lamp post.

Breathing deeply, sucking in air and bending over so he was facing the pavement, Martin unscrewed the cap from the top of the bottle and splashed the lukewarm water in his face. It did little to ease the griping in his stomach, but he rubbed it into his cheeks, his eyes and his forehead, trying desperately to settle the fire in his belly.

He stayed like that for some time, panting heavily, his stomach slowly turning. Passers by who had regarded this stranger in a strange land with curiosity earlier were now positively fascinated by him. One old lady even took a photo of him as he stood bent double at the side of the road. Martin ignored them all, wanting nothing more than to be as far from the market as possible. As soon as his stomach no longer felt as though it was going to eject its meagre contents, he stood up straight, took a couple more deep breaths, and with his head feeling light and dizzy continued down the road.

It was cool in the shade and he was glad; the heat of the sun was not something he wanted to feel right now, his body felt hot and clammy as it was. He couldn't believe how quickly he could have lost his appetite having been so hungry before, but then he thought of the old man biting down on the neck of the tiny fried bird with his gums and it was all very clear.

Swallowing the last of the water from the plastic bottle Martin dropped his litter into a bin and unsure of where he was heading took a look around. If he turned left he would make it back to the coast, where he could follow the shoreline back to the Olympic Sailing Centre and his hotel, turning right would lead him deeper into the city, and whatever lay within. He needed a plan, simply walking around hoping for inspiration was getting him nowhere, and he didn't want to be here in this strange city so far from home any longer than was absolutely necessary. He should return back to the hotel, take a lie down on the bed and try and formulate his next move.

It made perfect sense, was of course the sensible thing to do, but something, instinct maybe made him turn the other way and cross the road in the direction of the city centre.

He was walking blindly, no knowledge of where he was heading or what he intended to do when he got there, but he had always trusted his instincts, they were the reason for his success in business, and he was going to trust them now.

Martin crossed over at a quiet intersection in the road and travelled in the direction of an area populated by blocks of flats about five storeys high. There was an alley between the separate buildings and he could see the high rise buildings of Qingdao's busy financial district in the distance. Although he had only been walking for close to twenty minutes it was clear that he had wandered now into a poorer part of town. Compared to the neat little oriental houses he had wandered past a few moments ago and the splendour of his hotel and the affluence of the waterfront, this was like a whole new world.

Washing hung from lines between the buildings and a maze of poorly fitted wiring criss-crossed spider web fashion from posts and junction boxes high up on the walls. Like all overly populated areas if you were quiet enough you could hear the general hubbub of life in the cheap housing, some of it just general chitter chatter, others the more heated debate brought on by tough living. There was graffiti marking the walls and litter in the street and the whole area evoked an air of depravation and poverty.

Feeling a little uneasy in this deprived part of town, just as he had done in Brixton and Peckham and Tottenham, Martin looked over his shoulder to the shoreline in the distance and the high rise hotels and business centres that were dotted there. It would be so easy to turn around, to simply head back the way he had come, but something was telling him he was supposed to be here, that there was something here that he needed to see, and it was a voice he had learned not to ignore.

"Remember your roots God damn you Martin." He whispered to himself for reassurance. "You weren't born with a silver spoon in your mouth so just remember your roots and try to stay calm."

He pushed on towards the gap in the apartment buildings, wondering what it would be like to be so poor and to gaze out each day upon the wealth and opportunities just a stones throw away. It wasn't fair, the world wasn't fair, there was no balance and no justification for it and it made a man in his position feel very humble. Why had he been so lucky? For that's all it had been, a combination of hard work and luck. But why had his hard work landed with opportunity when for so many others it brought nothing but poverty, a hand by mouth existence. It was sickening, and Martin could have cried with misery and guilt.

Instead he swallowed back the lump that had formed in his throat and walked into the alley, looking up towards the noises coming from the individual apartments as he walked. A small boy, no more than five, with no shirt on and slipperless feet sat on an ancient looking tricycle to the far side of the alley. As Martin approached he gave a giant grin that revealed two missing teeth right at the front of his mouth, then pedalled with all the ferocity of an Olympian into the small yard to the back of the nearest building. Martin watched him go, feeling warmed by the encounter. He shouldn't be scared here; these were just people, flesh and blood like him, having little money did not instantly make you a bad person, it would serve him well to remember that.

At the end of the alley the narrow pathway reached a kind of pedestrian crossroads, where you could turn left or right along the backs of the first two apartment blocks or carry on forward to the next pair. Still not knowing his reason for being here, but feeling sure he was on the right track just the same,

Martin chose to carry on, walking into a new alleyway that separated a block of flats once more to either side.

Towards the end of the narrow lane a large beige coloured wall separated the roadside from the tiny yard space at the back of the latest block of flats. Dozens of sheets of paper were attached to the wall, some flapping in the gentle breeze where the stickiness had gone on the tape that held them in place.

As Martin drew near a middle aged woman walked up to the wall with a sheet of A4 paper in her hand, she looked towards Martin as he approached and the look on her face and in her hollow, sunken eyes was so haunted that for a moment Martin was paralysed with shock.

The lady, her shoulders sagging as though a huge weight bore down on them, found a place on the wall and added her own poster, sticking it in place with adhesive tape that she had brought along especially.

Martin wanted to talk to her, to ask if she was alright, but a combination of the shock of her appearance and fear of the language barrier kept him in his place. Instead he watched as she finished hanging the poster and waited for her to walk away. She did, but not before regarding him with those lost, empty pupils again. Martin shivered; it was like looking into the tiny Chinese woman's very soul. He waited for her to disappear back around the corner from which she appeared and then ambled up to the wall, his mouth feeling very dry.

Hand written Chinese symbols adorned the poster, Martin of course could not understand a single one, but he didn't need to speak the language to understand what this was, he knew that from the picture alone. A black and white photograph in the centre of the page showed a young boy, no more than eight years old, he was sat on a wall wearing shorts and a short sleeved T-shirt, he was smiling at the camera, his eyes happy and bright.

This was a 'missing' poster, just as you might see at the back of the Big Issue back home. The child had gone missing, the woman was undoubtedly his mother.

Martin took a step back and took in a wider view of the wall.

"Oh sweet God." He muttered in horror, as dozens of different faces on dozens of different posters stared back at him.

3

The restaurant in the Qingdao Sailing Hotel served excellent dishes, many of which were fresh catches from the days haul. Although Martin's appetite had been temporarily dampened following the incidents both in the alleyway and the decidedly un-British food market, it had returned with a vengeance some hours later, his stomach protesting that upsetting imagery or not, twenty-four hours was quite long enough to have to wait for a meal.

He had ordered the scallops to start and the sea bream for main and although it was cooked in unusual herbs and spices it was nevertheless delicious and quite filling, which was a blessing as he didn't recognise anything on the dessert menu.

From time to time as he tucked into his fulfilling meal the image of the old man biting the head from the baby chick would return and his stomach would give an unpleasant lurch. At these times he screwed his eyes shut tight, waited for the image to pass and then took a mouthful of cold water. Eventually with his meal complete he sat at the table looking out onto the crystal blue waters of the ocean, feeling a little better with his stomach finally full. Earlier that day he had returned to the hotel in turmoil, feeling as lost and alone as he had at any point since this nightmare started to unfold. He had picked up the phone in his room and been close to dialling the number he had stored for Rose's sister back in Bolton. He had needed to talk to her, to hear her sweet voice on the other end of the line, but in the end he had placed the handset back down, hanging his head in dismay. Speaking with Rose would be counter productive; it would just make him long for home all the more. Instead he had laid back on the bed and screwed his eyes shut tight, trying to blank out the images that had caused him to flee back to the waterfront in horror.

With his plate pushed to one side Martin reached into the pocket of his trousers and produced a folded up sheet of A4 paper. He opened it now and looked down at the image on display. This was one of the missing posters from the alley, but not that of the child; he didn't think he could cope with looking for too long at that one. This was one of the older posters, one that looked as though it had been on the alley wall for some time. The writing was illegible to a man who had never uttered a word of Mandarin in his life, but the image was of a man, probably somewhere in his early to mid forties, his hair swept over to one side to cover over a pretty substantial bald patch, his narrow eyes focused on the camera. He wasn't smiling in the photograph, but Martin could still detect an element of warmth, this was a good man, he didn't know how he knew but he knew it all the same. What's more this man was somebody's son for sure, and potentially a husband and father too, he could have siblings who were missing him and friends who were concerned about his whereabouts. He was an average Joe, just another missing person in a city that seemed rife with them, and was certainly nothing special; but to Martin he symbolised his very reason for being here, and though the mysterious disappearances could have nothing at all to do with his own reason for travelling to the far reaches of the earth, it gave him something with which to focus his attention, and a place to make a start.

Charging his meal to his room Martin grabbed his jacket and head back out of the hotel, walking this time with a purpose, after grabbing a map and some basic directions to his destination from the young man on the concierge desk. He was heading back in the direction of the financial district and the tall buildings that battled for attention on the skyline. To get there he cut through a busy shopping arcade and through more German colonial buildings that looked so out of place in this far flung corner of the planet. It was nearly four o'clock now and the streets were still full of people going about their business, still his western looks attracted attention, he could certainly not go about his own business quietly here.

He turned into a busy square, checking his location on the map that had been scribbled on by the pleasant young concierge, and found his bearings from the McDonald's in the far corner. He crossed over in that direction, wondering if there was anywhere on earth where Ronald McDonald and his happy bunch of cohorts hadn't laid their roots, and turned down a much quieter street lined with impressive looking buildings. The one he was looking for was right at the end of the row, then Union flag hanging from the gantry at the top of the building. This wasn't the British embassy; the closest was in Guangzhou, but a small consulate office that handles local issues involving British citizens travelling in the Shandong Province area. Happy to finally have some small semblance of a purpose Martin checked his pockets for the missing person poster and then trotted down the street in the direction of the building; he arrived and skipped up the stairs two at a time to the heavy oak door.

The room beyond the door was small yet lavish; with a tiled floor, oak panelled walls and red velvet drapes half covering the windows. There was a giant portrait of Winston Churchill on the left hand wall and Queen Elizabeth the second on the right. Two desks at the front of the room were housed by busy looking clerks, one completing some paperwork and stacking her completed files in a neat pile on her desk, the other a young man who was supporting a harried looking woman with a passport situation. At the back of the room a long counter housed three more positions, though two were currently unoccupied. A small western looking man with only a few thin strands of hair remaining on his head and dark horn-rimmed glasses sat in the occupied position, staring at his computer screen as though it displayed the weeks winning lottery numbers.

Martin stepped forward, the missing poster in his hand, the young female clerk looked up from her paperwork and gestured for him to come forward.

"Hello, how can I help you?" She said with a pleasant smile. Her accent sounded familiar, not Bolton, but definitely Lancashire, maybe Preston or Blackpool, it was reassuring in this unfamiliar landscape to know he wasn't the only Brit in the whole of Shandong Province.

"I wonder if you could."

She smiled and gestured to the seat at the desk in front of her and Martin accepted the gesture and sat down. For the first time he noticed the armed guard, dressed in British army coveralls and carrying an SA80 assault rifle, the standard firearm of the British military, standing at the bottom of a flight of stairs that led up to the floor above and scanning the room patiently. Martin didn't know if his presence reassured him or made him nervous, he tried to ignore him as he spoke to the young girl but it was unpleasant knowing he was probably under scrutiny right now. He slid the piece of paper across to the girl who looked down at it with a puzzled expression on her face.

"I'm fairly new to Qingdao, in fact I only flew in yesterday, but I have concerns about the number of missing people there seem to be in the city."

"Ok." The woman replied, looking more puzzled than ever. "What was it you were wanting us to help you with?"

"I don't really know." Martin admitted. "I was maybe hoping you could give me some pointers as to where I could raise my concerns; I was kind of hoping this would be a good place to start."

The lady sighed and looked down again at the sheet of paper.

"I'm not sure what I can tell you, this is the British consulate for Shandong; we deal with diplomatic situations and minor events involving British citizens travelling abroad; are any of the people you're looking for at least of British heritage?"

"No." Martin replied dejectedly. "At least not to my knowledge."

The woman sighed again. "I don't know what I can tell you; maybe you need to try the police? They would handle all the missing people's enquiries in the city."

"Yeah I guess." Martin said, though he was thinking of the ledger in Malik's office with detail of all of the bribes in reputable positions in Qingdao's police force, his disappointment showed and the lady took pity on him.

"Give me a second." She said, and stood up from her seat, she left the poster on the desk and Martin took the opportunity to fold it back to a quarter its original size and deposit it into the pocket of his jacket. He watched as she approached the counter to the back of the room and spoke to the middle aged man with the ridiculously thin hair. They spoke for a couple of minutes, then he looked at the monitor again on his computer while he tapped away at the keyboard. Martin looked over his shoulder straight into the eyes of the British guard, who just happened at that moment to be looking back at him; the businessman quickly turned back around and refocused his attention on the consulate staff. After a couple more moments tapping away the man scribbled something on a piece of paper and handed it to the girl, she turned and head back towards Martin, thanking her colleague as she went.

"Ok." She said as she sat back down. "It's not much, but it's a start, that is if you are serious about your concerns."

"I am." Martin replied. "Really."

"I can see you are." She said with a warm smile. "This is the address of a local charity, it translates as 'Lost and Found' in English, they specialise in tracking down missing people. If you have concerns related to missing people, they would be a pretty good place to start."

"Oh thank you." Martin replied, genuinely relieved to have traversed the brick wall he had come up against.

"Don't thank me yet, they may not be able to speak English, let alone help you, but between them and the Qingdao City Police Force it gives you a pretty good place to start."

"Thank you, I really do appreciate it."

"Well you have the phone number and the address there; I would assume they're open standard business hours. You mind if I ask you a question?"

"Sure." Martin replied, feeling suddenly cautious.

"Why the concern? This is a big city, all big cities have an abundance of missing people, Qingdao is no different, so why here?"

"I don't know, I guess the pictures just touched me."

The lady nodded her head slowly. "Ok, well good luck."

"Thank you." He replied, gesturing with the note paper. "And good day."

Passing the guard at the foot of the stairs Martin left the British consulate, a new destination to investigate, though checking his watch he had probably missed them for the day. Not to worry, he would head to the hotel and try and get some rest, in the morning his search could continue.

4

That evening as he was once more battling the jetlag that left him exhausted in the day and full of energy at night, the phone in his hotel bedroom roused him from his thoughts. He had been thinking of Rose, thinking about what she must be thinking, laying low at her sisters while her husband for all intents and purposes disappeared off the face of the planet. The sudden noise in the otherwise silent room had startled him quite badly, but when he regained his composure and stretched out his hand to the telephone he had felt quite sure that it would be her; that she had tracked him down and was about to beg him to come home. As it turned out he was only half wrong; he had indeed been tracked to this hotel room in distant Shandong Province; China, but not by his doting wife.

"Hello." He said, his voice croaking slightly; this was the first time he had spoken in nearly four hours.

"Martin?" The voice on the other end of the phone spoke his name as a question.

"Peter." Martin replied, his shoulders slumping back into the bed sheets; Rose demanding he come home he could handle; his second in command was a wholly different adversary.

"Thank God." Peter replied with notable relief. "Martin what in God's name are you doing in China?"

"How did you know I was here?"

"It doesn't matter how I knew, what matters is I know, and I need to know what in the Hell you're doing disappearing off to the other side of the world without giving any indication you were leaving?"

"Peter you have to believe me when I say I had no choice." Martin, resigned to having to defend his actions as best he possibly could, closed his eyes and placed his naked arm over his face, so his closed eyelids resided behind the puffy skin in the joint in the middle.

"Why though? What the hell are you doing there?"

"I wish I could tell you, really I do, but you wouldn't believe me if I tried."

"Why don't you try me?"

Martin sighed. "I can't really I can't, trust me I wish I could my friend, but I have to figure this out for myself."

"Are you in some kind of trouble?"

"No, no, nothing like that." The businessman lied. "Consider it...business."

"You can't be trusted with business, that's why all the big decisions come to me. Seriously though Martin what's going on? Is it something to do with your heart?"

"What makes you say that?" Martin asked startled, removing his arm from his now open eyes and sitting up slightly in the bed.

"Come on Martin you've been obsessed with the operation ever since it happened, all that need to speak to the family of the donor, morbid if you ask me. Look do I need to be worried? I guess that's all I want to know."

"No Peter, you don't need to worry, but I thank you for checking in on me."

"When are you coming home?"

"I don't know yet, not long, a couple of days maybe." He replied, relaxing back against the mattress once more.

"Two days, that's what I'm going to give you, if I don't hear back from you by then I'll be on a plane myself."

"No Peter, please, don't do that."

"So stay in touch, two days Martin, contact me in two days."

"I will, I promise."

There was silence on the line, Martin knew that his second was reluctant to accept the vague details he had been given. Eventually he sighed, resigned to the fact his employer was not going to give anything away lightly. "Ok. Martin, are you sure you're ok?"

There was something in his voice, something so gentle and caring that Martin almost caved in, almost broke down and unloaded everything, but that inner steel reasserted itself just in time, and against his strongest desires he lied once more.

"I'm fine, I really have to go now, I don't know what time it is in London, but it's two o'clock in the morning over here."

"Oh, yeah, sorry." Peter replied.

"Thank you for calling Peter." Martin said earnestly.

"Why do I feel like I'm turning my back on you in your hour of need?" Peter said unhappily.

"Goodnight Peter." Was martin's only reply.

The balding man on the telephone line thousands of miles to the north west let out another deep, guttural sigh. "Goodnight Martin." He said, then the open line was ringing in Martin's ear.

The businessman placed the handset back in the cradle and rolled onto his back, staring up at the ceiling. In the quiet of the room he was thankful for his friends call, somebody had been worried about him, this was strangely reassuring. Ten minutes later, soothed by the tone of his friends' voice, he was sound asleep.

5

In the end he had gone to the police, for all the good it had done him. His long peaceful rest on his first night in China had been a fluke brought on by a combination of extreme exhaustion and jet-lag. But now the seven hour time difference between Shandong Province and home was starting to take effect, and if it hadn't been for the unexpected call from Peter he was in no doubt that he would have laid staring at the ceiling for many more hours.

He had awoken a little after nine, feeling confused and disoriented, and slowly forced himself out of bed. He could easily have given in to the temptation and buried his head back in the soft pillow but there was work to be done, and it wasn't going to happen from here.

Thankfully he hadn't missed breakfast, for his stomach was growling again, though he wasn't expecting the virtual slap in the face he received from another dip into China's strange culinary practices. Whole fish, with the heads still intact may be the order of the day in this part of the world, but to Martin it was enough to make him queasy yet again. There were also bowls of rice and noodles and curry dishes and seasoned tiger prawns; it was like there was no distinction between breakfast and the rest of the day. Thankfully there was also a small table of pastries and fruit and he indulged in this hungrily, watching with some amusement the expressions of other western tourists who discovered their breakfast fate for the first time too.

Following another visit to his new concierge friend he was armed and ready for his day ahead. It was another cold day, with temperatures probably little higher than they would have been back home. Martin, who had wrongly assumed that every part of China was hot and humid all year round hadn't been prepared for this eventuality and his thin summer jacket did little to keep out the creeping cold.

While he had laid awake, tossing and turning and wondering if he was ever going to find sleep, he had come to the conclusion that his next port of call really ought to be the local police station, after all if they weren't aware of the problem on their very doorstep then it needed pointing out to them. His intention was to stir up a bit of a hornets nest, see if anything emerged from his actions. Unfortunately as with most good intentions, it didn't transpire that way.

The station had been crowded and rowdy, with uniformed officers going about their business while members of the public and apprehended criminals sat at desks waiting for processing. There was a desk sergeant on duty for people who walked in off the street but the queue to speak to him was the length of the building and he didn't appear to be in any hurry to speed it along.

With little other choice Martin stood in line, but after ninety minutes of waiting he had still only been halfway down the queue. Feeling agitated he had left the queue and attempted to speak to an on duty officer, who was stood at the water cooler reading a message on his personal phone, but it had of course been fruitless; the man didn't speak a word of English, and after staring at Martin as though he were some form of creature beamed down from Mars, he turned and walked away beyond the cordoned off area restricted to members of the force.

The queue was now twice the length it had been when he had arrived, it would take several hours from here if he were to join it again. Wondering if any of the many locals in the queue were here regarding missing relatives Martin cut his losses and head back out into the bright December sunshine.

It was mid-day; the police station was located in the middle of a bustling square; Martin strolled down the steps and looked to his next option; the Lost and Found charity. The problem was that it was not located in the centre of town, it was on the far side of the map in a place called Huiquan; too far to walk yet he didn't fancy another difficult taxi experience. Looking about the square he noticed his next best option. He had never ridden in a rickshaw before, but there was a first time for everything.

The man attending the nearest cart looked to be about a hundred, and skinnier than a supermodel before the Milan fashion expose, but when Martin showed him his destination on the map he nodded enthusiastically and the businessman climbed on board.

It wasn't long though before guilt started weighing on Martin's conscience; here was this man, clearly much older than he, pulling his and the carts weight along on a journey that had seemed too far for him to walk. What had he been thinking? This was a mistake, and with the pittance the man had charged for the journey it felt like extortion. Half way to his destination Martin had made his excuses and departed the rickshaw, giving the confused old man a sizeable tip before walking away. He didn't think he would ever get used to the strange customs in this land; he was just too long in the tooth. He journeyed the rest of the way to Huiquan on foot, and by the time he reached the tiny industrial street that housed the small charity building, he was tired, his feet hurt and he badly needed to relieve his aching bladder.

Still, he was here, he could rest later, for now it was finally down to business, he'd just have to somehow cross his legs and hope for the other to pass.

Lost and Found was located through a plain looking door beneath a sign adorned with Chinese symbols; there would have been no way for a person who didn't speak Mandarin to recognise they had reached their destination if not for the locations telephone number, which was displayed in the window and matched the one on the piece of paper Martin had received from the British consulate. Tall factory buildings surrounded the tiny office and at the far end of the street you could just make out a strip of blue where the ocean swept into Huiquan bay.

Desperately hoping to find someone inside that both had a basic grasp of English and could help guide him on the right path, Martin opened the door of the charity and stepped inside.

The office consisted of one large room in which Martin now stood, and two smaller office rooms to the rear of the building. From what Martin could see these housed a small admin room with a photocopier and fax machines and the other was home to a decently equipped meeting area. To the back of this room was what appeared to be a staff toilet; Martin looked at it longingly, finding it increasingly difficult to ignore the urgent call of nature. Instead he looked about himself at the room in which he was standing, the main hub of the Lost and Found foundation. Three desks in the room were occupied by three Lost and Found employees, two ladies and one gentleman. The man and one of the ladies were currently dealing with members of the public who had come in to discuss their own situations; the remaining lady was free and now gestured for Martin, who was the only other person in the office at that time, to come forward.

As he did he finished his brief scan of the office; it was a pleasant and well kept room with all the usual amenities, water cooler, notice board, fire extinguisher, but it was impossible for your eye not to be drawn to the far left hand wall, where dozens and dozens of black and white photographs hung on the wall, each with it's own detailed description, again in Mandarin so impossible for Martin to read, each with its own timeline and case handler. This was clearly the display of current cases that the foundation were working to resolve; missing persons who the charity had committed to trying to locate.

Finding it hard to take his eye from the wall Martin stepped forward and sat down in the plastic seat opposite the young woman. Even sat down Martin could tell that she was tiny, no more than four foot five, and she was very slight to boot, she probably weighed no more than 90 pounds, and would be blown from her feet if a stiff breeze came in from the East China Sea. Still, her smile was warm and genuine and a pleasant invitation was a good place to start.

"Hi, I'm wondering if you can help me…" He began, then he noticed the look on her face and he knew that the good start had come to an abrupt end; she didn't understand a word that he was saying.

The young woman replied in Mandarin and Martin could only shake his head in dismay.

"I'm sorry, I don't understand, I don't speak Chinese." He said, very slowly and very carefully, like it would make a difference.

The young woman continued to talk in her native tongue and Martin slumped back in the chair, feeling already that his journey both to the charity building and to China as a whole had been a complete waste of time.

Then the lady at the next table, a pretty girl with long dark hair was talking to the woman at Martin's desk. They exchanged dialogue for a few seconds then the first woman nodded in understanding. The two stood up and exchanged places, with the new woman explaining to her customer what was happening.

Martin watched all this with renewed hope, then the woman was describing to her colleague where she had got to with the case she had just been working and that was that, Martin had a new person with whom to try and break the language barrier. She sat down in the previous woman's chair, smiled at him and opened her mouth to speak.

"Hi, I'm Su Lin, how can I help you?"

"Oh thank God!" Martin said with a huge exhale of relief.

The woman laughed. "I take it this isn't the first time you've struggled to be understood."

"Not even the fifth." Martin replied with a relieved chuckle.

"Well, make the most of it, I can't promise you'll be understood on your journey from here."

"Travelling here has made me realise just how ignorant I am to the ways of the world." Martin said wearily.

"Not at all, our culture is very different to yours; it can take some getting used to. You should travel out to the country at some point; it will blow your mind."

"I'm sure it would, but for now I think I'm pretty much on all the sensory overload I can handle. May I say your English is impeccable."

"Thank you, I will accept the compliment, now, how can I help you?"

Martin sighed, knowing after a pleasant and all too brief exchange that it was now down to business.

"Well, I wonder if you could. You see, I'm not trying to track down a missing person, more, I'm trying to find out why it is they're going missing in the first place."

At this the man at the far table, the only male employee currently on duty at Lost and Found paused mid conversation and looked over towards Martin. The businessman noticed but didn't think anything of it.

"Ok." Su Lin replied after a moments thought. "I'm not sure I follow you."

"It's difficult to explain, but I've noticed there seems to be a bit of a missing person problem in Qingdao, I was wondering if there was a reason for that?"

"There is a missing person problem in all the cities of the world, Qingdao is no different, but it is true that there are more missing people in Qingdao than we would certainly like."

"Yeah I keep hearing that. Is there a reason for the disappearances? Is there anything at all you can tell me?"

Again the man at the far table looked in Martin's direction, seemingly curious as to his line of questioning. He was middle aged, probably in his early forties, with jet black hair that was swept into a side parting. He was wearing a lemon coloured shirt and had a tired and weary expression that Martin had witnessed before. After a few seconds he went back to his conversation, but Martin couldn't help but wonder what it was that was pricking his curiosity.

"I don't think there is any one specific reason." Su Lin continued. "There are many different reasons. Sadly abduction is a possibility, certainly in the very young, these cases are generally police matters, we just help out where we can. Domestic and financial situations can force people to move from their homes; they don't always tell people where they are moving on to and this can leave a void in people's lives. Homelessness is a big factor; sadly this is something like most major cities that we do have a problem with, and when people become homeless it can be difficult to track them down. That's where we come in, we provide comfort and support for those who have lost someone and act as an intermediary so those that are missing have a way of being found. Unfortunately not everybody does want to be found."

"I see." Martin said, nodding his head slightly. "Is that all of the reasons?"

"There could be many different reasons, it's impossible to list them all. I'm sorry I still don't understand your interest in this mister..."

"Rooley, Martin Rooley. I apologise for my manners, or lack of them. Just generally curious I guess, I saw a few posters about town and I was wondering if there was anything I could do perhaps to help?"

"Well we're always in need of more volunteers; with Lost and Found being a charity organisation we rely on the support of local volunteers to cover our obligations. We like to outreach to the community, spread the word of what it is we do and how we can help and volunteers are essential for this."

"That sounds very worthy." Martin enthused. "But alas I don't think I'll be in town long enough to be able to lend a hand. So just to reiterate, to your knowledge, there isn't anything say, underhand to explain the missing person problem in Qingdao?"

This time the man at the far table made no attempt to disguise his curiosity; he stopped mid conversation and turned to stare at Martin, a look of concern on his face. It made the businessman decidedly uncomfortable. Then the person at his table was demanding his attention again and reluctantly he turned his eyes back to his customer.

"As I mentioned, abduction is always a possibility, but this would be a police matter rather than something we would have any direct involvement in, but if you are asking if this is more of a problem here than anywhere else then no. Qingdao is a good city, with good people and a strong community spirit. People go missing from time to time, it isn't unusual."

"Ok, thank you." Martin said, nodding slightly.

"I'm sorry I couldn't be more help to you."

"No not at all, you've been most helpful. Thank you for your time Su Lin."

"You are most welcome. If you find you are going to be around longer than you expected and you change your mind about our outreach programme you know where we are."

"I'll keep that in mind." Martin said, pushing back his chair and getting to his feet. "Thank you again."

Su Lin nodded and Martin head to the door, as he pulled at the handle he noticed in the reflection from the glass that the man from the far table, the one with the weary looking eyes, was staring at him again. Martin thought he would have known even if he hadn't seen the reflection; he could feel the weight of the mans stare on his back. He opened the door and stepped outside, feeling agitated and frustrated to boot. His latest line of investigation had brought up no new information, if anything he was even further away from the answers he required than he had been before, for now he had nowhere left to turn.

Martin sighed and looked about the street, trying to gage his next move. Then a more pressing problem took his mind from his frustrations and he was relieved to have something else on which to focus his thoughts; for his need to relieve his bladder had returned with a vengeance, and if he didn't rectify this little problem soon it could make for a rather embarrassing situation.

6

In a small square halfway between Huiquan and the centre of Qingdao he had managed to relieve his aching bladder. The public toilets were like nothing he had ever seen before; each individual cubicle looked like something that would fit in well in a science fiction movie like Star Wars or Alien and all of the facilities were motion sensored and hands free. A robotic voice guided you through the unusual process, thankfully in Mandarin as Martin would have struggled to go at all; no matter how desperate had he received a running commentary to the proceedings.

He had returned back to the hotel sullen and moody and had lain on the bed for a while wondering just what the hell he was doing here. Like really, what had he been thinking? Flying half way round the world on some ludicrous crusade; a man of sixty-eight years, arthritis in his wrists and in his knees, what was he doing?

Depressed and lonely, with only days to go before Christmas, Martin picked up the phone and dialled his wife at her sisters. Ken had answered; Martin's brother in law, he was pleased, Ken was a man of few words, if it had been Moira he would no doubt have received quite an ear full. After a few seconds his wife who he missed so badly was on the line.

They talked for a while; Rose begging Martin for information, for what he was doing, for where he was, for when he was going to come home, for why she had needed to flee to her sisters. How could he answer? What could he really tell her? He had reassured her as best as he could and promised to at least try to be home in time for Christmas. She was lonely, and she was scared, this was the second Christmas in a row ruined for no fault of her own and it made

Martin feel incredibly guilty, and when he hung up the phone after twenty minutes he felt even worse than he had before.

Sitting on the bed with his shoulders slumped and his arms dangling between his legs he glanced across at the mirror on the hotel bedroom vanity unit; he didn't like the reflection that stared back at him. He seemed to have aged an awful lot in the last thirty or so days. The lines under his eyes looked deeper, the ridges on his forehead like the grooves at the bottom of a rubber dinghy, his skin a pallid grey that made him look ill. He was low on sleep and pushing his luck for a man of his years, and he knew it. But he was trapped by his own actions; he couldn't return to London with Malik on his tail, and in China he was a small fish in what was transpiring to be a very large pond. He needed answers, and he was getting nowhere fast.

Martin rubbed at his eyes, feeling the beginnings of a headache pulsing away in the far off vortices of his brain. This was no good; he didn't have a clue how to proceed with his investigation, but he sure as hell wasn't going to be home in time for Christmas sitting around this hotel room feeling sorry for himself.

Outside night had fallen as the sun had disappeared below the horizon; Martin grabbed his jacket and the missing poster he had taken from the alley wall and stopping to force out a quick pee; he didn't want the turmoil of his ageing bladder catching him out again, he washed his hands and head for the door.

The friendly doorman bowed to him as he gestured him outside and Martin did the same, wondering if he was managing the local customs correctly or making as he feared a complete arse of himself. The night was cold, almost bitterly so, and the thin jacket he wore over his thin shirt did little to keep out the chill. Again he was reminded of his ignorance and naivety, having just expected it to be hot here all the year round. It would serve him in future to maybe do a little research before taking a trip; but his position had made him lazy, he had a PA who handled all that, only now did he realise how pampered he had been.

He walked through the quiet streets, tall skyscrapers on his right hand side, German colonial buildings on his left, with no idea of where he might be heading. He was walking blind, hoping that inspiration would strike him as he travelled, but at present his mind was blank.

A cold wind blew in from the sea through the gap in the buildings to his left and he pulled the collar of his jacket shut tight, wishing he had some gloves to cover his exposed fingers; this would do nothing good for his already worsening arthritis. Grimacing as the throbbing ache started in his knuckles and slowly made its way down the length of his fingers to the connection of his hands Martin bit back the pain and walked on.

When travelling in a foreign city it is easy to follow the routes you have taken before, fear of getting lost and not being able to find your way back the key driver to this; so Martin found himself walking past the tiny shop, closed now for the night where he had purchased the warm bottle of spring water. At the top of the hill he passed the oddly named for these parts St. Michael's cathedral, lit up with halogen lamps that made it look quite striking on its stoop high up above the city. Martin paused for a while, enjoying a moment of tranquillity and peace, then he was moving again, back down the road towards Nanshang market, also closed now, bordered up to prevent access, the stalls that could be seen beyond the periphery empty of contents, stark and bare where yesterday they had been alive with activity.

A couple of people passed him in the street; this time not regarding him as an odd specimen from outer space but rather completely ignoring his existence, this was fine, he didn't want to feel trapped inside a goldfish bowl anyway.

On reaching the intersection at the end of the road it became clear to him what his intentions had been when he set out on this particular journey, and although his feet had guided him here absentmindedly he now knew that his subconscious had known his destination all along. Just as he had trusted his instincts the day before, he did again now, and allowed them to lead him back towards the slums on the outskirts of town.

His feet felt sore in his inappropriate loafers and his knees were throbbing as he ambled towards the dark looking tower blocks that loomed on the skyline like a vortex that sucked the light from the moonlit sky.

Passing through the alleyway in which he had ventured the day before a deep feeling of unease crept into his body. This place could be pretty intimidating in the daytime, but at night, when the shadows were at their darkest and the walls seemed somehow taller and thicker, the gaps between them smaller, it was all too easy to feel vulnerable and afraid.

Noises from the apartment buildings could be heard from every angle; TV sets turned to game shows and documentaries, arguments between husbands and wives, the crying of children, the barking of dogs, it all added to the uncomfortable atmosphere and made the housing estate seem somehow menacing, though it was only the dwelling for people, human beings just like him. He tried to focus on this as he made his way down the alley, looking over his shoulder every few seconds to make sure he wasn't being followed.

What was he doing here? Did he even know? He had hoped to perhaps bump into the woman from the day before; the one with the haunted eyes who had displayed the poster of the missing child. But even if he had found her it was highly unlikely that he would have been able to break the language barrier, so just what in the hell had he been thinking coming to such a place once the light had crept out of the day?

He was standing in the open area at the centre of the four huge apartment buildings; the place where the posters that were taped to the alley wall flapped in the breeze and the age old fences separated the thoroughfare from the tiny yards to the back of the apartments. His mouth felt very dry and his heart was beating away quickly in his chest. Looking about the place seemed deserted; everybody in their apartments doing whatever people do on an evening in this part of the world, with all the various noises that accompany it. This had been a bad idea.

Then he noticed a young boy, possibly the same young boy he had seen the day before, pedalling his tricycle down the alley at the back of the two apartment blocks to the left. The wheels made a deep scraping sound as they rotated along the cracked paving of the alley and it echoed down to where Martin was standing. So many missing people, children amongst them and some parents still allowed their children to play out alone after dark; it made Martin frustrated and angry. Feeling it was his duty to ask the child to go back inside he started down the alley to his left, unaware as he did that he was being watched.

It wasn't until he was about halfway down the narrow lane that he became aware that there were more than just he and the child in the alleyway.

Martin stopped still in his tracks; he watched as the child came to a stop at the end of the alley, turned and gave him an almost toothless smile, so it was the same child as the day before after all. Then he pedalled left out of sight; the plastic wheels continuing their unearthly din as they continued on their journey.

Martin stood incredibly still; the small hairs on the back of his neck standing tall like sentries to a royal palace. Then, slowly he turned his head ninety degrees and arched his hips so he could look back over his shoulder; when he saw the man that was slowly making his way towards him he almost lost control of his bladder, almost. He was young; no more than eighteen, with spiked black hair and a huge padded puffer coat that made him look twice his actual size. But it was what glinted in his hand from the reflection of the moon that almost brought about the embarrassing accident; the youth was carrying a knife.

Terrified with the young man bearing down on him Martin turned back around, ready to flee forward in the direction the little boy had disappeared; but it was futile, the alleyway ahead was blocked by two more oncoming youths, one wearing a baseball cap turned slightly to the side and the other with a hooded top, the hood pulled up to slightly obscure his face. Both carried weapons; a baseball bat for the one with the cap of the same sport, though Martin doubted very much that he was a fan of the Red Sox or Dodgers, and a thick chain wrapped around the fist of the other.

"Oh God!" Martin whimpered in abject fear as the youths closed the distance between them. With his eyes wild and terrified the businessman looked to the tall fences that enclosed the alleyway and wondered if he could make his escape that way; but of course it was futile, these young men were less than a third his age, if he tried to escape that way they would be on him in an instant. He had no choice than to try and talk them down; but with the language barrier that separated them this could be like hoping for the sky to rain fifty pound notes. He stood his ground; the breath in his throat coming rapidly, his chest rising and falling beneath his thin summer jacket and hoped that their first instinct would not be to hit him or stab him or worse.

The youths reached their intended target and surrounded him, cutting off any hope of escape. Their eyes burned with hatred and they brandished their individual weapons to show the stranger that they meant business. The one in the baseball cap, the one who had clearly never struck a ball with his bat in his life, padded the thick end against his open palm; it made a dull thwacking sound in the confines of the alley. Knife man; he of the oversized jacket that made him look a little bit ridiculous, held his weapon up next to his face, snarling viciously at his prey. Then the same man was talking at him, seemingly questioning him from his tone, but in a language that Martin could not even hope to understand, and any dream of being able to talk his way out of this vanished like a teardrop in the rain. Why were they talking at him in Mandarin? Surely they could see that he was a westerner!

"I – I don't understand!" Martin replied, his hands held up in surrender.

In response he was shoved from behind and stumbled forward past he of the over sized jacket. Though he was ahead of the pack now there was no chance of escape, as he felt rough hands grab him from behind, the long fingers digging into the blades of his shoulders with excruciating pain. With his eyes squeezed shut tight, in too much blistering agony to currently feel any fear, Martin was frogmarched back down the alley in the direction he had come. He was shoved hard into the space between the buildings and though he landed hard on his arthritic knees he was thankful at least that those vicious fingers were no longer digging into his skin.

"Wait, please, you don't understand..." He pleaded as the three youths circled him. The one with the chain came forward and swung his weapon about his head. Martin could hear it whirring in the air and he thought this is it, this is the moment I finally meet my maker. But instead of striking him with it the young man with the hood of his top pulled high allowed it to sail a few inches high of his head, close enough for the thin hair on the top of Martin's head to get caught in its slip stream.

The businessman stumbled backwards onto his behind, letting out a groan of terror as the hooded assailant allowed the chain to drop back to his side as he stepped backwards. There was no let-up though; now the youth with the knife was stepping forward again. He was talking either at or to the terrified man in an aggressive tone, but Martin couldn't understand a word. This didn't stop him from gesticulating with the knife in a manner that led Martin to believe he had absolutely no fear in using it on him.

"Please, please God I don't understand!" Martin said with his hands outstretched in surrender. It was to prove a costly mistake. As quick as a flash the youth struck out with the knife and sliced his palm open in a two inch long wound.

Martin yelped in pain and clutched his wounded hand close to his chest. Hot blood was flowing from the open wound and he looked down at it in dawning horror. This was no game; these young men intended to either hurt him very badly or kill him on the spot. But why? He could understand if they were after money, this was after all a poor part of the town; but so far not one of them had checked him for a wallet or cash, not one of them had seemed interested in the expensive Rolex quite clearly on display.

With his hand screaming for attention Martin shuffled backwards on his bottom towards the wall with the posters that flapped gently in the breeze. It was useless; he was entirely at their mercy, he knew it and they did as well. They had anticipated some futile attempt at escape and now the youth with the baseball bat circled back behind the old man and hampered his escape with a swift shove of his booted foot into the trapped mans back.

"Ah!" Martin cried out in surprise and pain. "Oh no, oh please no! Please don't hurt me!" He pleaded, but the youths looked completely disinterested in mercy.

Now baseball cap boy was talking at him from behind; Martin raised his hands, both the wounded one and the one that was desperately trying to steady the loss of blood, up to cover his head. He was terrified that the young man intended to bring the heavy end of his bat crashing down onto the back of his head; at his age a blow like that would be the end of him for sure.

"I don't understand God damn you!" Martin shouted, hoping that somebody in one of the many nearby apartments would hear him and call for help. "Can't you see? I don't speak your language!"

His outburst did little to dissuade the young men, in fact if anything it only served to spur them on, now all three came at him at once. Baseball cap had dropped his bat to his side and was kneeling now behind the injured man; pinning the old mans arms behind his back so that the blood from his wounded hand dripped down the back of the waistband of his trousers, soaking the top of his underwear. As he did this the other two came forward and crouched before him; the hooded man using his free hand to grip Martin by the chin and force his head back while he of the over sized coat dropped down to one knee and raised his blade so it was only an inch from Martins left cheek. He was completely trapped; whatever they were going to do was about to come to a head, and he felt sure this interaction would not have a pleasant outcome. But before the young man could use the knife to cut at his skin again a new voice could be heard from directly behind the two youths at the front. They turned in its direction and on seeing who it belonged to both got back to their feet; though the third continued to hold the businessman in position with his behind firmly planted on the cold and poorly paved floor.

There was a brief exchange in their native tongue which meant nothing to Martin; for all he knew they were discussing the weeks lottery numbers, but any exchange was a way of separating him from the blade of the young mans knife, and was welcome as a result.

More words were spoken, the new man seeming to assert his position when the younger voices argued their point. Then the two young men at the front separated, and though Martin was still pinned to the ground by the youth in the baseball cap he could see clearly for the first time the stranger who had halted the horrifying act of violence for which he was unjustifiably suffering. Martin looked up at him; thinking at first that he must know the man from television, or a Jackie Chan film maybe, as he recognised him straight away, a strange occurrence in this far flung corner of the globe. Then he understood this for what it was; a ridiculous notion brought on by a state of extreme panic, and the identity of the new man became clear:

It was the man from the charity organisation; Lost and Found, the one who had paid him so much interest in the office earlier that day, the one who had stared at him as he was talking to the young girl, Su Lin. Now he was here; clearly working alongside these youths, and as he stepped forward between the two young men and stared down quizzically at the man trapped on the floor of the dirty alley, the businessman felt his eyelids begin to flutter.

No, God please no, not now! He thought in panic as the world about him went grey, but it was no use, a combination of blood loss and abject fear had taken its toll, and as Martin slipped into unconsciousness, he was thankful at least that he wouldn't feel whatever was to come.

7

With a groan that seemed to come right from the insides of his gut Martin's eyes blinked open and he looked up at the ceiling fan that rotated slowly above his head. He felt fuzzy and weak all over and his mouth was very dry. His tongue flickered out and snapped at the white crust that had formed in the corners of his mouth. He was aware that there was a dull ache throbbing away in the corner of his temple and that he was heavy with a deep feeling of lethargy, as though he had run a marathon the day before and was waking to the after effects of too much exercise.

Blinking against the force of eyelids that felt very heavy and threatened to close Martin struggled to remain conscious and to determine where he was and what he was doing here. He was laid on a hard wooden futon in a small room with minimal furnishing. There was a television in one corner; the old fashioned box kind with wooden panelling straight out of the eighties. A couple of pictures on the wall but he was too far away and his eyes not yet focused enough to determine who or what they were of. A plate and a saucer had been placed on a small plastic table about three feet away and a pair of chopsticks clung to the side like stick men dangling from the edge of a cliff.

This triggered something in his brain; chopsticks – Chinese food – Chinese people – China!

China, he was in China; he had flown here a couple of days ago, fleeing his troubles in England and trying to discover the secret to his unorthodox heart transplant. He was staying at a large hotel next to the sea, something to do with yachting, it had a restaurant in which he had eaten fish and looked out at the boats along the harbour. So what was he doing here? In this strange room, laid on this strange furniture while above him a white plastic ceiling fan continued its constant rotation.

Martin sighed and tried to sit up; but a wave of nausea washed over him and he flopped his head back onto the hard pillow, waiting for the dizziness to pass. He closed his eyes, waiting patiently for his pulse to settle, for his energy to rise; while he waited he tried to gather his thoughts. He had been at the hotel, he had spoken to Rose, to sweet sweet Rose who he missed so dearly, and it had made him feel guilty about leaving her alone once more at Christmas. It was Christmas! This too struck him as odd; there was so little sign of the season here. Later he had taken a walk; he had seen the animal market, all closed for the evening and the catholic cathedral that looked so out of place in a land of strange symbols and colourful lanterns, a land of strange people who he had assumed would be Buddhists or Taoists rather than Christians. He had assumed so much that had turned out to be untrue; like China was bathed in constant humid sunshine and that every other person was well versed in the Queen's English. He had been naïve; a stupid old man and his assumptions that had served little to answer any of his plethora of questions.

With the dizziness finally settling Martin took a couple of deep breaths and then slowly lifted himself into a sitting position. As soon as he saw the blood stains on his jacket which was draped over a chair in the corner and on his trousers he remembered the situation that had caused such a horrific blood loss and a fresh wave of panic erupted in his brain.

He had been attacked by the three youths; they had cut him with a blade and threatened him with a chain and a bat. Martin lifted his hand, remembering the feeling as the blade sliced at his palm. It had been wrapped in a bandage that was held in place with adhesive tape; small dots of blood had soaked through on one side. Now that he was focusing on his bandaged hand he could feel the cut throbbing beneath the dressing. No wonder he felt so weak; he had suffered quite a blood loss and the fear of worse to come was enough to make anyone a little trembly at the knees, and a sixty-eight year old man against three youths should feel no shame at this.

Martin placed his shoeless feet on the floor and tried to stand up; as he did the door opened and the man from the alley, the same man that had been staring at him at Lost and Found, walked in. A fresh wave of dizziness washed over him as he tried to put weight on his feet and he dropped back to the seat with an undignified plop, feeling exposed and vulnerable to possible attack with his head spinning as it was.

But surely that was ludicrous? If the man had wanted to hurt him he would have had the perfect opportunity with him unconscious in the alleyway. Instead he had brought him here, dressed his wound and laid him on the futon, but why?

"Don't try to stand, you are not in any state for this right now, you sit."

The man's English wasn't to the level of Su Lin's earlier that day, but it was good, Martin was relieved that he would not at least have to try and break another language barrier. But with his head throbbing and his stomach churning it was hard to find any positives in his current situation. He placed his head in his hands and waited for the world to stop spinning around him. While he sat like this the man stepped further into the room and sat at the chair on which his blood stained jacket was draped. Eventually the dizziness settled and Martin was able to focus at last on the oriental man before him.

Still dressed in the clothes Martin had seen him in at the charity organisation earlier that day, (or was it the day before now? It was hard to tell how long he had been unconscious with no clocks in the room and it still being dark outside the apartment windows) the man was just as he remembered; early forties with jet black hair pulled into a side parting, a stern face but not unkind, eyes that looked to have seen too much.

"Who are you?" Martin asked when his racing heart had finally started to settle.

"I will ask the questions." The man replied, putting Martin, who had just started to relax, firmly back in his place. "The question is, who are you?"

Martin thought about this for a moment; should he come clean and tell this stranger why he was here, not just in China but in this poor district of Qingdao? Or should he lie? Make up some tall tale to try and worm his way out of this difficult situation? It didn't take long to come to the conclusion that honesty was the best policy; he may be groping in the dark but he couldn't help getting the impression that this man may be the first step in getting back on track with his investigation since boarding the plane back in London.

"May I have some water?" He asked, partly because his throat was parched and partly because he wanted a little more time to consider his options. How much should he tell? He was trusting his instincts again, putting his life on the line in the unjustified belief that there was good in this stranger, based on his actions so far. This could yet prove to be a costly mistake; he had after all had at least some form of contact with the three youths who had attacked him at the back of the apartment block.

"Ok." The man nodded, he got to his feet and slowly padded out of the room. Martin could hear the tap running in the kitchen that must have been just beyond the near wall, and as he tried to gather his thoughts he also wondered if it was safe for a westerner to drink the local water? You've been slashed on the palm with a knife Martin, threatened with a baseball bat and a chain and brought to a place against your will whilst unconscious and you're worrying about getting an upset tummy? Might be time to grow a pair and get a grip of them.

The man returned with a tall glass of water which he held out to Martin. He took it gratefully and took a large mouthful. He could taste the minerals within that made it ever so slightly different to the Thames valley water that he drew from his taps every day; but it was essentially still just water, and it tasted cold and crisp and soothed his parched throat, taking with it the thick layer of fuzz that had been forming on his tongue. He finished drinking and placed the empty glass down on the floor by his feet, breathing a little quicker as is always the case when you take a drink a little too fast. When Martin looked up again the man had returned to his seat and was waiting patiently for this silver haired stranger to stop wasting his time and tell him what he wanted to know. After careful consideration Martin decided that he would be telling the truth after all, but he was going to dish out his reason for being here one morsel at a time; hoping to promote a healthy dialogue of conversation in return that would perhaps answer a few burning questions of his own.

"My name is Martin Rooley; I'm the CEO of a major corporation back in my homeland of Great Britain."

"See he oh?" The man said, his thin black eyebrows raised.

"CEO, it means the man in charge, the boss if you like."

"Oh." The man nodded, understanding the meaning now but not why he was being told, he clearly wanted to cut the crap and get down to the nitty-gritty. Martin however after being attacked in an alleyway and brought to this stranger's home whilst unable to defend himself was in no mood to oblige too willingly. He would get to the conclusion in whatever way he saw fit, and starting at the beginning for him was it. Then, as quickly as he had decided to trust the man, he was overcome with caution, and was suddenly very wary about just what information he was willing to release."

"Something happened in my homeland that led me to travel here to Qingdao, something that I believe is related to the problem you are having here."

"And what problem is that?"

"People are going missing aren't they?" Martin was looking directly at the man when he spoke and the tiny flinch at the corner of the stranger's narrow eyes was not lost on the businessman.

"This is not unusual; all large cities have problems with people going missing, we are no different, I believe we have already made this clear to you, when you came to the charity today. So why here, tell me why you come here, why you asking all sorts of questions about missing people?"

"Not yet." Martin replied firmly; he was still nervous, but was also still trusting in his instincts, and right now they were telling him that this man was not a threat to him, and somehow he was important in his quest for answers.

"Oh?" The man replied, his eyebrows stretching up on his forehead again.

"That's right, not yet, there's something I want to know from you first."

"And what is that?"

"Your name."

The man smiled thinly, it was not a smile derived from warmth.

"I do not believe you in any position to start asking questions of me."
Martin nodded slowly, not taking his eyes from the strangers.

"Maybe." He said after a short pause. "But maybe also it's you who are wrong, and I am exactly where I need to be right now to ask a few questions of my own."

"And how have you come to this collusion?"

"Conclusion." Martin corrected, and watched as the mans eyes narrowed to even thinner sockets, surprised at his growing confidence. "I'll tell you how. Because I have information that you want, perhaps need, and you need me to give it to you. Because you're desperate for this information, as I believe rightly or wrongly that you have a large investment at stake in the answers. Because I believe you realise that I am not a threat to you, and I strongly believe that you are no threat to me. And because I believe we are both striving for the same goal, looking for the same answers, and I believe if we put our heads together we can get there a lot sooner than we can on our own."

The man looked at Martin with a look on his face that was hard to read; was it confusion? Astonishment? Or as Martin suspected, hope.

"My name is Young Pyo-Chang; and you are right, you are not a threat to me." He said eventually, and Martin was left to muse the fact the man had not yet committed to not being a threat in return, there were some strong barriers at display here that may take a little persuasion to overcome. That was ok, he needed an ally right now and he was prepared to devote the necessary time, getting the man's name was a promising start.

"Do I call you Young?"

"You can call me Chang, everybody does. And you are Martin."

"That's right." The businessman replied, nodding slowly. "Ok, another question, the youths in the alley, who were they?"

"Yooves?"

"Youths, young men, the ones who attacked me and did this." Martin held up his hand to highlight the meanly wrapped bandage, the dots of blood a little larger now. "Who were they?"

"It is not what you think."

"Oh even I don't know what I think yet, but I do know that being set upon – attacked, by three young men who had age and vitality on their side is not how I would expect innocent parties to behave.

"That was regretful."

"You're damn right it was regretful." Martin replied, feeling his confidence grow by the second. He was angry too; he had been attacked by three youths, completely unprovoked, they had slashed his hand and threatened his life, and this man appeared to be involved somehow. "They could have killed me, what if I'd had a heart attack?"

"I apologise, the boys, they are very how you say...headstrong, but they are good boys."

"Where I come from good boys don't outnumber three to one people four times their age then attack them with deadly weapons."

"Where you come from the children probably don't need to guard and protect their own homes."

This time it was Martin whose eyebrows rose in wonder.

Chang sighed; he looked down at his clasped together hands for a few seconds, seemingly at battle with his own thoughts. His decision made he looked up at the white haired man before him; doubt etched across his features, he had however made up his mind and he was going to run with it, whatever the cost.

"Do you feel capable of taking a little walk?" He asked finally.

Martin nodded slowly, and though he knew this was progress he couldn't help the burden of doubt that bubbled away just below the surface.

8

They had to walk down three flights of stairs to get to the exit that led out onto the street and Martin couldn't help but wonder if the man had carried him unconscious up those same stairs earlier that night alone or if he had been helped by the three youths. Surely it had to be the latter? This again made him wonder about the three young men and what it was that had caused them to attack.

The night was cool and crisp, you could smell the salt blowing in on the breeze from the ocean and the ozone in the air; they were smells that Martin had always enjoyed, but tonight it was hard to find any enjoyment with his mind full of questions and the palm of his hand throbbing like a bastard.

"This way, follow me." Chang said, and walked back through the alleyway that separated the apartment buildings. They came to the place where he had been attacked by the youths and Martin couldn't help but look over his shoulder; making sure he wasn't being stalked once more. Under the soft glow of a light from one of the apartment buildings he could see drops of crimson red blood that had dried on the cement floor in the place where he had been slashed by the knife. It made him feel queasy and he wondered what would happen if he just turned and ran. Would the Chinese man allow him to escape? Or would he give chase, maybe bringing his three young friends along to help with the pursuit?

Then he was passing the wall with the countless posters of people, lost from their families and friends and as he looked one flapped slightly in the breeze; when it settled the face of a young girl, no more than seven stared back, a happy smile on her face, her narrow eyes so full of innocence and wonder. He couldn't run; he was as involved in whatever was happening here as he could ever be, he needed to see this through to the end, and if that meant following this man through to whatever it was he wanted Martin to see then so be it, that was just how it had to be.

Through the alley and out beyond the apartment buildings you could once again see the tips of the skyscrapers that littered the skyline in the more affluent part of town, but before you got there you had to navigate through a maze of factory buildings that were undoubtedly the source of employment for many of those who lived in squalid conditions on the estate from which they had just come.

The Chinese man didn't say a word as he led Martin along on this cold dark night, with the businessman wondering again what time it must now be; his Rolex was no longer on his wrist, but he felt sure it had not been stolen, rather the man had removed it when applying the bandage that was temporarily supporting the wound in his injured hand. Whatever the reason he would need to get the watch back, it had been a gift from Rose two Christmases ago, and he was not going home without it.

Rose, he thought as they marched on down the darkened streets, how he missed her. How long had it been now since he had last seen her? He couldn't even remember. Now he came to think of it he had also lost all track of the days, how long was it now until Christmas day? Surely only a matter of days. It was easy to forget it was the festive season at all in this part of the world. He was sure that some parts of Qingdao must be decorated for the season, but if they were he was yet to lay eyes on them.

"I need to be home for Christmas." He muttered as he walked along.

Chang turned his head as he walked. "What did you say?"

"Nothing." Martin replied, he hadn't been aware he had spoken out loud. "How long was I unconscious?" He asked, to break the silence as much as anything.

"Not long, two hours maybe." The Chinese man replied. "We are here."

A few more paces down the road he came to a stop at the reinforced door of a darkened factory building. Two hours, Martin thought as Chang took a key from his pocket and slid it into the lock, which must make it almost midnight now. The dark haired man placed the key back in his pocket and pushed the heavy old door open wide.

"Come on in." He said, then stepped into the darkness beyond the door.

Martin looked at the opening, too much like the gaping mouth of a giant with that all encompassing darkness beyond, and swallowed back his growing anxiety. Why had the man brought him here? Why had he entrusted his life to this stranger? He could feel his heart thudding away in his chest and remembered a time when his biggest fear was that it was soon not going to beat at all. Those days seemed so long ago now, in a different life. How had things changed so dramatically?

Sucking in a quick breath Martin found his courage and stepped through the door into the factory and whatever lay beyond.

"I used to work here." He heard the man say from somewhere in the darkness. "This was my factory. I tried to sell many times but the Chinese government will not allow the sale until the rot has been removed, I cannot afford to do this."

There was a click from somewhere behind Martin, close to the door, he drew in another breath, of fear this time that something was creeping up on him in the dark, then the overhead light was flickering and after a couple of seconds the room was bathed in light.

Martin blinked a couple of times as his eyes adjusted to the new brightness, he turned and saw Chang stood by the door, where he had just flicked the switch, then watched as the dark haired man closed the door behind them and slid the bolt across. Swallowing hard Martin tried to control his fear, then took a look about the room.

It was only a small space, probably about eighteen by twenty feet, and was occupied only by a small desk in one corner that was stacked high with papers and a giant wall mounted board to one side. It was this board that commanded Martin's attention. It ran the length of the room from the doorway in which they had entered to a further door to whatever lay beyond at the far end of the room, but it was what was displayed on the board that made Martin's eyes widen in wonder and fear. Similar to the wall display at the charity Lost and Found, Chang had displayed his own investigation into the disappearances in Qingdao. There were photographs of missing persons, highlighted maps of areas of disappearances, timelines and copies of police records and statements, and although everything on display was accompanied by unreadable Chinese symbols one thing to Martin was clear; this was more than just a personal investigation, this was one mans obsession.

"This used to be my office, the factory was through there." Chang said, pointing to the door at the far end of the room.

"What is all this?" Martin asked, nodding towards the wall board.

The Chinese man was quiet for some time; when he finally spoke his voice was solemn and drained.

"This is how I have spent my time for the last four years."

Martin stepped up to the board, looking at the countless images that stared back at him. Men, women, children, some older people but not many, most of the images were of people below the age of forty, and this left an unpleasant taste on the tip of Martin's tongue. Chang stepped up behind Martin and regarded the wall display gravely.

"The boys who attacked you saw you as a threat, it was lucky I came along when I did, it may not have been so fortunate otherwise."

Martin glanced down at his bandaged, throbbing hand, he didn't feel fortunate, but he understood what the dark haired man with the haunted eyes was implying.

"Why did they see me as a threat?"

"Recently some residents, including those boys, have taken to patrolling the streets about our neighbourhood. There is no trust towards strangers now. That is why you were attacked; they saw you as a stranger and a threat."

"There have been a lot of people going missing from your housing estate haven't there?"

Chang nodded slowly.

"It started a few years ago now, but the problem seems to be..." He closed his eyes for a second, struggling to find the right word.

"Escalating?" Martin suggested.

"Yes, yes, escalating." Chang said with notable relief.

"What are the police doing about this?"

Chang smirked; it was an altogether unpleasant look on his chiselled face.

"The ones who are not involved themselves do not see it as a serious problem."

Martin was quiet for some time while he gathered his thoughts; he looked back at the board and considered all that had happened on this long and strikingly unusual evening. The man had brought him here; to what was clearly a very private domain, and opened up to him about the dangers that surrounded his way of life, it was only fair that Martin gave a little back in return.

"Ok, I'm going to tell you what I know; it isn't much, and it may not even be relevant, but I always trust my gut, and my gut tells me it is."

Chang's narrow eyes had widened at Martin's words; he was desperate to understand what this strange man knew and if anything he could tell him would support his own on-going quest for answers; Martin hoped he would not disappoint him.

"Almost a year ago to the day I suffered quite a serious heart attack. When I was examined at the hospital it was determined that my heart was quickly dying. I needed a heart transplant, and if a suitable heart wasn't found pretty soon I wasn't going to live."

Chang was listening intently, his arms folded over his chest, trying to piece together Martin's words with his own situation in Qingdao, and what had brought the old man to travel here at all.

"Things looked pretty bleak for a while," Martin continued, "but then suddenly a suitable heart became available. I didn't think much of it at the time; I was just so relieved to finally have a suitable donor. But the operation itself, the heart transplant, though I must say a highly professional job, always seemed incredibly strange to me. It was performed within my own home rather than a hospital, and there was no after care as you might expect with an operation like this. Oh I know what you're probably thinking, I was incredibly naïve to go along with this in the first place, but we met with the surgeon at the hospital and he was so insistent this was the norm, and well, when you're so desperate for any kind of good news at all, you're willing to believe anything."

Martin sighed and rubbed at his head, he suddenly felt very tired.

"Would you like a seat?" Chang asked, pointing to the plastic chair that was pushed beneath his cluttered desk.

"I'm ok." Martin replied weakly. "I just have to get through this."

Chang nodded slowly, keen to hear more. After a moment's pause Martin continued.

"Anyway life went on; I recovered from the operation and was back in good health again. But I started getting suspicious you know, some things just didn't seem right, didn't add up. Anyway to cut a long story short I was able to trace my own operation back to a rather nasty black market operation performing out of London, England. I broke into their premises one night and found some information that linked me with an operation that they have running from here in China."

"What sort of operation?" Chang asked.

Martin sucked in a quick breath. "The black market trade of major organs."

He had feared that the Oriental man would recoil in shock at this, but he simply nodded, as though he had been expecting it all along. Martin wondered not for the first time just how much he already knew.

"Anyway." Martin said, picking back up the thread. "I found myself in a little trouble back in England with some rather unsavoury characters; I needed to lay low for a little while but I couldn't afford to let my own private investigation go cold, so I followed the one lead I already had and came here. That's it, or most of it anyway, barring a few details, that's my story."

As he had been talking he had watched as Chang had followed along, noticing the little winces in his eyes when he struggled either with Martin's dialect or the slang terms he had used but basically following along quite well. When he finished the Chinese man stood in contemplation for a few moments, when he spoke it became clear he was having a little more trouble with the story than Martin had at first realised.

"So, you have a new heart, you receive illegal organ yes?"

Martin was cautious, unsure where Chang was heading. "Yes, but I didn't know it was illegal when I received it."

"You didn't know?" The Oriental man replied doubtfully, a small sarcastic smile on his face that Martin didn't much care for.

"That's right I didn't know."

"You are rich businessman."

"Yes but..."

"You paid for illegal heart."

"No! That's not what happened!" Martin replied indignantly. "I didn't know it was illegal when they performed the transplant, I only found out much later on."

"So somebody else paid for the heart." Chang had crossed his arms in front of his chest, unsure right now what to believe.

"So it would seem."

"Why?"

"I don't know why!" Martin barked, feeling flustered and angry at being challenged, he was after all trying to help this man, a man who it could be argued had taken him hostage; he didn't yet know if he was out of that particular sinking ship, couldn't he just accept what he was telling him. "I've been trying to find that out for myself, do you think I'd fly all the way to China and spend my time looking up missing person cases if there wasn't any truth in what I was saying?"

"Calm down, I am not saying I don't believe you, but it is quite a story you are telling me."

"Yeah well you haven't heard the half of it. I'm right though aren't I, all these people," he said, gesturing backwards at Chang's display, "you believe they're involved somehow don't you."

The dark haired man rubbed at his chin and looked beyond Martin to the evidence on display. "Not all of them." He replied eventually "But some yes."

"Tell me what you know." Martin requested, feeling his nerves start to settle again after a fraught moment. His hand was still throbbing and he wondered if he may need proper medical attention at some point.

"Qingdao is very wealthy city, some events of the Olympic Games were held here, but there are many poor neighbourhoods. It is the same in all big cities."

Martin nodded, thinking of some of the places back in London that his own investigation had taken him.

"But in Qingdao our problem with people missing is much bigger than err, than average."

"How do you know that?"

"At charity we have outreach programme to other parts of China; based on population size we are twenty-five per cent higher than the next highest city; Shanghai. There is a problem in Qingdao, and I believe a large reason for the missing people can be tied together."

"What is it that makes you think that?" Martin asked, wanting to press Chang as much as was possible for the answers he needed.

"Many people go missing in all cities. People move away without telling anybody where they are going, this happens. Mental illness can force people to disappear; some people lose homes and jobs and need to move on. Then there are children, some become lost, some become how you say, abducted. It happens. What I am saying is that not all cases of missing person in Qingdao is suspicious, but when twenty-five per cent more than Shanghai…" Chang shrugged as if to say 'what do you think?'

Martin nodded; he turned so he was fully facing the board.

"So the people on here…" He began.

"Divided by category. On left are cases under suspicion, in middle I am not sure, to right hand side natural cases."

Martin looked over at the photographs and print outs of people on the far side of the board; they were mostly older people.

"Why have you discounted these?"

"If you pay lot money for new heart you want it from old person?"

"So you believe me then?" Martin said, turning back to face the dark haired man. "You believe some of these missing people are missing because they're being harvested for organs."

"It doesn't matter what I believe, I have no proof."

Martin bit down on his lip and turned back to the board; he moved now to the left hand side, to the pictures, print out's and photographs of the people Chang suspected to have been abducted. Here was a young man; somewhere in his early thirties, next a young girl, pig-tailed hair sticking out at right angles from the sides of her pretty head, then a woman, probably late twenties, attractive, long dark hair, even longer legs, and then the same young girl he had seen on the wall in the alley to the back of the housing estate. Martin sighed gravely, hoping this would all turn out to be some kind of horrendous misunderstanding.

"What makes you think all of these people are missing due to suspicious circumstances?" He asked when he finally managed to block the image of the two small children from his mind.

"I don't know for sure, how could I? But all these people come from poor background, government flats, shanty towns on outside of Qingdao. None of these people have reason to leave, all leave behind people grieving, grieving parent, grieving husband or wife. Some had good jobs, good life. Not rich, but happy."

"And you say you haven't told the police?"

Again Chang let out that small humourless laugh. "There is no help from the police here."

Martin thought of the ledger he had seen in Malik's office, the one with the payments to police officers and border agents and government officials, and wondered just how deep the corruption in this city ran.

Martin turned again and cast his eyes at the board; something was definitely amiss here, in this large and provincial city, but how was Chang involved, he wanted to know more about the man, and what was driving him to pursue such a soul destroying venture.

"So this was your factory." He said as a way into the conversation.

Chang had wandered over to his desk and taken a seat on the plastic chair.

"Still is, just doesn't produce anything anymore."

"What did you used to produce?"

"Textiles; at one time twenty machines operated beyond that door, twenty four hour day. I employed two hundred workers, all are gone now."

Martin gazed over to the door, thinking of his own empire back home.

"What happened?"

Chang gazed off into the distance, his eyes vacant and weary. "I lost interest."

Suddenly it all became clear to Martin, as though a veil had been lifted from his eyes. He stepped forward to Chang's desk and picked up a framed photograph that could be just seen poking up from behind the huge stack of papers. It was a family photograph; a rather stiff looking one, with a stiff looking Chang next to a stiff looking but pretty woman with short bobbed hair, the only thing that was not stiff in the photograph was the little girl, who grinned at the camera with her pigtails sticking out from the sides of her head.

"Oh God." Martin whispered, feeling the grey hairs on his arms stand up like sentries. He turned and looked towards the board where on the left hand side the same girl grinned back from a black and white print attached with colourful pins. "Your daughter."

Chang didn't say a word, just stared off into the distance, that same haunted look on his face. No wonder the man had devoted the last four years of his life to this quest, no wonder it had become his obsession. Finally he turned and looked at Martin, and when he did the businessman felt that he could see deep into the Chinese mans very soul. Swallowing back the terrible lump that was restricting his windpipe Martin spoke once more:

"And your wife?"

"Alive, not missing, living with banker in financial district." Chang said after a moment's contemplation. "When Chao-Xing disappear, my marriage not survive, too many problems, too many memory. I try to keep things together but my heart wasn't in it. Soon after Chao-Xing go missing the factory closed, lots of people lost jobs, it wasn't good. Meifeng left around same time, that was when I moved to the flat."

"You lost everything." Martin said, placing the picture frame back on the desk, feeling like he shouldn't be touching such a sacred artefact.

"Not everything, I have my photograph, and I have my memory." Chang replied.

"Chao-Xing." Martin said, testing the name on his foreign tongue. "What a beautiful name."

"It mean morning star." Chang replied with a smile.

Martin felt sick to his stomach; he ached for the loss this poor man had suffered and it made him angry, in fact it made him furious; how could this be happening? How could it be happening and nobody seemed to care? Well somebody would care, he didn't know how but he was determined; this evil had to be stopped.

"This is why you work for the charity."

"It is a good source of information, plus pers….pers…"

"Perspective?"

"Yes, perspective! Charity helps find people, not all are related to this terrible evil. People are found and families are happy, this is helpful to me."

"You're a good man Chang."

"You don't know me." He replied.

"I know enough."

Martin thought about how long Chang's quest for answers had gone on and related it to his own; four years, he couldn't imagine the mental torture of such a long investigation. He was about to ask something else when the man with the dark haired side parting raised his hand, stopping him before he could speak.

"There are lots of questions, and lots to discuss, but now the hour is late, you must rest, and so must I. May I also suggest getting your hand properly seen, I am no doctor."

Martin nodded; the man was right, there was so much more to discuss, but the hour indeed was late, he needed to rest if he was going to be of any use at all in the morning.

"We will meet back here tomorrow, around mid-day, that should give you time to go to the hospital, you think you can find your way back here?"

"I think so." Martin replied with a nod. "So I'm free to leave then?"

Chang smiled. "You are free to leave, the question I ask is will you return."

Martin smiled, then he took one last long look at Chang's board, and the little girl with the big smile and the dark pig tails, and with a shiver that ran the length of his spine and shuddered within his shoulders he head to the door.

9

Despite his own private health care Martin was a huge advocate of the NHS; it was his reason for voting Labour after the last Tory government had enforced the need for privatisation; but the service he received at the Qingdao Municipal Hospital International Clinic was second to none, what's more it was conveniently located right next to the Olympic sailing centre, just a stones throw from his hotel. Within an hour he was stitched and re-bandaged, professionally this time, but with a bit of a dint in his finances, not that it was particularly noticeable when those said finances stretched to eight healthy figures. He left the hospital with a goodie bag of pills and antiseptic creams and head back to the hotel for a quick bite to eat in the only local restaurant he trusted. Afterwards he dropped off his things before heading out to meet with Young Pyo-Chang.

The day was much warmer than it had been the last couple of days and as Martin walked the streets in the direction of the old factory he was able to take off his jacket and drape it over his arm, enjoying the feel of the warmth of the sun on the back of his neck. He was pleased to have met the Chinese man the night before, it gave him a new direction and a feeling of purpose in his ongoing quest for answers, but he was saddened by the mans heart breaking tale of woe, a story that made his own misadventures seem very small and inadequate in comparison.

Martin and Rose had never been blessed with children, but he knew that if they had they would have treasured their child with all of their hearts; to lose a child was the most awful thing he could comprehend for a parent, and to have the fear of how that child may have died and to have to live with that pain was a horror he didn't even want to comprehend.

The sun gleamed on the surface of the ocean to his left; he looked out at it, wishing he was viewing it under different circumstances, circumstances that would perhaps allow him to enjoy the twinkle of the suns rays on the gentle waves as they lapped against the line of the shore. Instead he felt pensive and nervous, unsure of what the day would have in store, and if he would still be breathing at the end of it. It wasn't the type of feeling that made gazing at the sea a pleasurable activity.

His thoughts turned to the three youths who had attacked him in the alley the previous evening. He had thought they were just thugs, out to mug or murder; but they had been vigilante's, trying to protect their homes from a much larger threat. It didn't excuse their behaviour, didn't even come close, but after seeing Chang's wall with the countless photographs of missing persons it was at least understandable. Strangers had taken people they had perhaps loved and cared for, and strangers were threats. It was an ugly world in which the three young men lived, and despite the pain in his hand Martin couldn't help but feel sorry for them.

Before leaving the hotel Martin had turned on the cable in his room to check the date on CNN; 22nd December, give or take the time difference between the USA and China, that meant he had to have this wrapped up in the next two days if he was to return home to Rose in time for Christmas. It didn't seem likely; an old man and a poor ex factory owner against an underground crime syndicate that stretched across at least two continents and had roots in local government and a somewhat corrupt police force. Also, what did they really know? So they suspected that at least some of the missing persons on Chang's list had been abducted to harvest their organs, how could they prove it? Where did they even go about starting to investigate such a claim? The police were certainly no help, and it wasn't as though either man was blessed with the investigative skills of a Hercule Poirot or a Lieutenant Columbo. No, right now sitting down to a turkey dinner with the love of his life seemed about as far away as the moon.

What must she be thinking? Hidden away at her sister's house back in Bolton. What questions must they be asking? Then he thought of Sapient; what was Peter thinking about his careless abandon of his role? What about Sheila? Or Perry Nuttall in HR? And how long would that abandonment continue? If he didn't manage to somehow get to the bottom of this, clear his name in relation to Purefoy's murder and bring down a ruthless criminal organisation in both England and China he could pretty much rule out a return to British soil for the foreseeable future. When he thought of it like that it made his stomach churn angrily and his respiration became tight and restricted, so he blocked it from his mind as best as he could and continued on his way.

One step at a time, that was the only way he could think of this, it was the only way he could associate his bizarre life with some kind of normality. The first step; find the factory. When they had walked these streets the previous evening he had been following Chang, and although he felt he had retraced his footsteps pretty well, he still found himself completely lost. All of the buildings looked the same. All were of the same red brick, all had tall walls and dusted windows, all had dark black reinforced doors and chimneys that seemed to stretch up to the clouds.

Martin came to a stop on one street, sure he had already wandered down this road, was he walking in circles? Flustered and agitated he was about to start walking again when a voice from his rear startled him.

"It seems you are lost."

Martin turned and there was Chang, standing in the doorway of the factory building to his left. He breathed a sigh of relief; he had been on the right track after all.

"Come on in." Chang gestured, then ducked back inside his old office. Martin followed, though regretful that the warmth of the sun was cut short the second he stepped through the door. He closed the door behind him and stepped again into the cool and gloomy office space, letting his eyes drift from the desk with the huge pile of papers stacked high and the old family photograph, to the huge wall board with its countless photographs and maps and statements, to the man who stood in the centre of the room, a plain white shirt tucked into his pants, his arms folded across his chest.

"I wasn't sure you would come." He said when Martin stepped forward.

"Believe me, I have little choice."

"I have something for you." Chang said, then fished in his pocket. He pulled something free and held it out to Martin, who took it gratefully; it was his watch. Normally he would wear it on his left wrist, but with this one bandaged he carefully fastened it to his right, where it felt alien on his arm, but at least he knew that it was safe.

"Thank you." He said, when he had finished struggling with the clasp.

"I see you took my advice." Chang said, gesturing to Martin's professionally bandaged hand.

"All handled with that fabled Chinese efficiency I might add, very impressive." Chang smiled. "Come on, we have much to discuss."

"Have we?" Martin enquired genuinely. "I feared there was little more to say."

This time the smile on Chang's face was wry. "What do you think I have spent four years doing? Twiddling thumbs?"

It was Martin's turn to smile; he was delighted to learn there was more to the current story yet to unfold. "Tell me what you've learnt."

"Come." Chang said, and gestured to his desk where he had positioned a second chair. The two men sat down and the one with the jet black hair pulled a thick ledger from his drawer. He opened it and Martin was witness to page after page of photographs, clippings, maps and schedules, all noted in the Chinese mans careful script, that damn symbology that Martin couldn't hope to read if he went to night school lessons for a decade.

"What is all this?" He asked, fascinated.

"This is my investigation."

"Did you take these?" He asked, pointing to the photographs.

"The one thing I managed to keep from my breakup with Meifeng, aside from this factory was my camera. Photography used to be hobby, now important part of investigation."

"They're very good." Martin complimented. "Explain to me what I'm looking at."

"So, when Chao-Xing disappear we were assigned special task force officer, Lieutenant Riu-Jian. He try to find Chao-Xing but not get anywhere. I started to get f- err...frus..."

"Frustrated."

"Yes, frustrated with his actions. It was as though he didn't care. I make complaint but they keep me assigned to Riu-Jian. One day we are at home when there was a knock at the door. It was another policeman, a detective Kong Lee, who said he wanted to help us but not in an err, official, err..."

"Official capacity."

"That's right, official capacity. He told us he believed Chao-Xing had been taken by mistake. Chao-Xing disappeared while playing with a friend in a poorer part of town than where we lived when we were a family. Because of this Detective Lee believed she had been taken thinking she was a resident of the government flats. He said lots of people go missing in poor parts of city and poor parts of cities close to Qingdao. Detective Lee didn't trust his fellow officers; he believed some of them were involved somehow in what was going on. This made me very worried, if we couldn't trust the police who could we trust? Lee had his suspicions of what was happening but he didn't tell me straight, he was afraid I would panic. Instead he took me here."

Chang pointed to a photograph in the ledger of a huge red bricked factory, not unlike the one he was in now, with a huge smoking chimney and dark mesh covered windows. It had been taken from behind a perimeter fence and a dirt track circled the factory, cutting it off from its neighbouring buildings.

"What is this place?" Martin asked, feeling a chill starting in the base of his spine.

"This is where they bring the people they abduct." Chang said with a cold look on his face. "See here." He pointed to another picture, one that had been taken with a telephoto lens. In it an armed guard in civilian clothing was patrolling the exterior of the building, his machine gun held in both hands as he walked.

Martin swallowed hard. "Go on."

"I try to dig for more information from Detective Lee, but he is either reluctant to tell or he don't know. We watched from a distance a few times, trying to see what was going on, and I started to lose faith in his beliefs, I was going to go back to Lieutenant Riu-Jian and beg him to help me find my little girl. Then something happened that changed everything."

Chang looked down at the photographs on the cluttered page, gathering his thoughts, Martin waited patiently for him to continue, though his trepidation was growing with every moment that passed.

"Lee was a heavy drinker; he liked Japanese Saki and American whisky, and he drink both in equal measure. When he drink Lee's jaw got loose, and he talk a lot, too much. One night he told me he had fight with station commander when drunk, accuse him of covering up what was really happening in Qingdao. Lee tell me he was thinking about handing in his badge and his gun, couldn't take the corruption anymore. He was very drunk and very upset. Then he stopped calling. Just like that. I wait a couple of days but still no show. This was not like him. So I go to station and ask after him and they tell me he moved away, just like that."

"You don't believe them?"

Chang shook his head. "Detective Lee care, he the only one who did. He not leave without saying to us."

"They killed him." Martin replied, feeling the chill start to work its way upwards towards the back of his neck.

This time Chang nodded, and there were tears prickling at the corners of his eyes.

"My God." Martin whispered; although there was no proof, he knew it to be true, those trusty old instincts again. "Then what happened?"

Chang sighed. "Now I knew what Lee tell me is true. Somehow Chao-Xing disappearance is related to much bigger picture. My only lead was the factory; so I start to do stakeout, watching as people come and go."

"If they'd have caught you they'd have killed you." Martin said, thinking of his own stakeout of Eze-link cars.

Chang nodded again. "Time went by; I start to lose connection with Meifeng, and with my job as factory owner. Things start to slip apart."

The Chinese man fell quiet and Martin had time to reflect how his own marriage and work life had been affected by his own quest for answers. Would they see out these problems? His business was certainly safe in Peter's capable hands, but his marriage? He wasn't so sure. Poor Rose had suffered just as much as he during this last six months, and who knew how much longer it would actually be before both he and Rose could return home and start over?

The thought terrified him, he was too old to start over, and he couldn't imagine his life without his love, as Chang had spent the last three and a half years without Meifeng. With a lump in his throat and tears close by he tried in vain to push the thought aside and waited patiently for Chang to continue. When he did he seemed morose, as though the memories of his breakup and his failed business on top of the disappearance of his daughter had taken their toll on his morale. Who could blame him?

"Anyway, Meifeng leave and I move to government flat. I didn't have my job, my daughter or my marriage but, I had something new, something to replace them."

"Your investigation." Martin whispered, feeling all too cold in the old factory.

Chang nodded. "My investigation, my obsession. For four years I gather notes, take photographs, find clippings and statement. Waiting for something to happen, waiting for sign, then you come."

"Me? A sign?"

"I needed something, someone. Someone to help me, to give me courage."

"And you think I am that person?"

"You are going to have to be." Chang replied matter-of-factly.

Martin tried to swallow through the painful lump in his throat. "Tell me what else you learned."

"When I sell my car I buy scooter, small bike, it help me get from government flats to factory. I hide the bike in bushes and spend my day watching with binocliars."

Martin didn't correct Chang but he did afford himself a small smile, hearing the mispronunciation from a grown man in the same vain of a small child was wryly amusing despite the circumstances. Then he reminded himself that a small mispronunciation in a second language was a damn sight better than his ability in reverse, and all at once the little slip up didn't seem quite so amusing. Chang, who hadn't even noticed Martin's amusement, carried on regardless.

"You see here." He said pointing to a photograph of a woman with long dark hair being led towards the factory door. "Man has hand on arm, this woman is being led."

"Why is she not fighting? If she's being led against her will I mean?"

"My guess, they are drugged."

Martin nodded slowly.

"Lots of examples of this." Chang flicked through the pages, showing various photos of varying quality, all of people being led towards the door, some looked positively docile as they were marched towards the old factory.

"This is damning evidence." Martin said excitedly. "If any of these people can be identified as any of the missing persons currently on record then the police force here have to take notice."

"Maybe," Chang agreed, "but are you going to be the one to raise it? After what happened to Detective Lee?"

Martin pursed his lips. There must be plenty of officers that could be trusted within the Qingdao Municipal Police, but Chang was right, how were you to know those you could trust from those that were corrupt? It was a dangerous play, they needed another option.

"Ok, for now no police, but we're going to need someone on our side."

Chang nodded. "I keep watch, sometimes in day, sometimes in night. Most activity at night. Deliveries come deliveries go. But I notice some deliveries handle with more care than other. Also, people being led into the factory, but people never coming back out, and all the time, the chimney is blowing out smoke."

"This is where you became suspicious of what was going on inside the factory?"

"Not at first, at first I couldn't understand what was going on. But one night when one of the special deliveries was being made, I watched them load a plastic compartment into a van and I decide to follow."

"My God I have no idea how you're still breathing."

"It is only by God's will that I still am. So, I follow the van on my scooter, keeping a distance behind, this wasn't hard, it was difficult to keep up! The van pulled into an old airfield; this was strange because this was an old military airfield that hasn't been used since the nineteen-eighties. I left my bike at the side of the road and took a closer look.

There were guards at the airfield but only a few, none in uniform so not official runway. The package was transported onto a small plane and after a few minutes it left, flew away with the container. Here look."

Chang flipped the pages again and this time pointed to a photo taken between the loops of a chain link fence of a small bi-plane; directly in front of it was a man in civilian clothing holding a machine gun. The photograph was quite grainy but again this was damning evidence that something was seriously amiss in Qingdao.

"After this I start to observe the airfield, watching from a distance; taking photographs and keeping notes. Only activity happen when delivery being made. Airplane turn up, twenty to thirty minute later van arrive and parcel loaded on board. Twenty minute after plane leave airfield quiet again. When delivery being made three to four guards patrol airstrip, but any other time, only one guard. So, I wait until after airplane leave, knowing this would be optimum time to take a look around, and I climb over the fence into the airfield.

I waited until the guard was patrolling the far side of the strip and made my way to the small tower next to the runway. I found these."

Chang pointed to photographs he had taken of log books and maps found in the tower.

"See this," he said, pointing to one of the photographs that showed a detailed flight plan, "the plane take the package to Xiagong island, just off coast of Qingdao, from there larger plane take package to distribution point in Tainan City; Taiwan."

"Then to England?" Martin asked, thinking of Malik's operation back in London.

Chang smiled, but there was no humour in it. "England, Germany, Switzerland, United States of America, Russia; all over the world."

"My God." Martin whispered in horror, feeling the enormity of his situation weighing on him again. He looked down at all of the information Chang had managed to gather in his four year tenure as sole investigator of the hideous crimes in this wretched city. He didn't know whether to be impressed or horrified; maybe a steady mixture of the two was the right way to feel. "All of this was just left out, with only one guard on duty? It all seems a little reckless."

"You can afford to be reckless when protected by police." Chang replied, and Martin guessed he was right.

Martin sighed, looking down at the information gathered on the table, trying to work out exactly what two men with a combined age of nearly one hundred and ten could possibly do to bring down a vast criminal empire, an empire that was protected by those that were sworn to protect, and it made him feel weak, he was very glad to be sat down right now because if he had not been he felt sure he would have fainted.

Chang, recognising the look on Martin's face, placed a reassuring hand on his new friends shoulder.

"So what do we do now?" The older of the two asked, genuinely at a loss for how to proceed.

"Now, I take you to the factory." Chang replied, and Martin felt his stomach shift uncomfortably. He wanted to run and hide, to call Malik and tell him he was sorry and that he wouldn't keep prying into his affairs, but he was trapped, trapped in a world for which he desperately wished he could be ignorant , just as he had been before. With his heart beating away in his chest Martin reluctantly nodded, secretly wishing the Chinese man had remained a stranger.

10

Chang's tiny scooter was no way for two grown men to travel the ten miles out of the city to their destination. With that in mind they shared a taxi out of town, with Martin feeling guilty when the Oriental man insisted on covering half the fare.

At Chang's instruction the taxi pulled to a halt at the side of a dirt track, a mile shy of their destination. They needed to remain inconspicuous and pulling up in a taxi outside the factory gates would not be the best way to go about this.

They had packed Chang's trusty camera, his binoculars, a small amount of food and water to keep them going and the wire cutters from the middle aged man's toolbox. Not wanting to arouse any suspicion Chang had chatted to the taxi driver in Mandarin about taking a visiting friend bird watching on the salt plains outside town. The driver had nodded along agreeably enough but not asked any real questions, finding the topic of conversation a little dull, which was perfectly ok with the instigator of the conversation. Confident the driver had bought his story Chang paid for the journey with the accumulation of his and Martin's money and the two men climbed out.

It was really quite warm now with the mid day sun beating down and Martin worried about his skin burning as the two men watched the taxi disappear back down the beaten old lane.

"Well, we have a bit of a walk." The dark haired man said, picking up the bag of food and water and gesturing to an overgrown track that led up the hill adjacent to the road.

"Lead the way." Martin replied, and followed the other man onto the crumbly track.

The ground underfoot was not hazardous, but it was far from ideal in Martin's Gucci loafers. Every time he stood on a rock about the size of a golf ball it punctured into the underside of his foot and caused a sharp pain, and his six hundred pound shoes were dirty and worn within minutes of strolling up the hill. Ignoring the pain he kept up the pace behind Chang, who was walking with purpose along the winding path, which was gradually rising uphill and leaving the road running parallel below them. There was a slope of yellow grass that ran down to the roadside, about two hundred feet now; Martin looked down wondering at the lack of traffic on the road. It really was quiet out here, with only the occasional caw of an overhead bird and the steady droning of the crickets to keep them company.

They walked in silence, each lost in their own thoughts as they made their way along the path. About half a mile from where they had left the taxi they came to a mesh fence; it ran down the slope to the roadside and continued ahead along the side of the path.

"This fence surround factory." Chang said matter-of-factly. He continued forward along the path without so much as looking up. Martin, who hadn't spent the best part of the last four years staking out the factory, stopped for a moment to take a look. If the perimeter fence was anything to go by then the factory was undoubtedly huge. Where the road met the fence a locked gate obstructed entry to the site. To the side of the gate was a sentry post, from this distance it was hard to make out but Martin was fairly certain it was manned. He looked for a few more seconds, trying to see where the road continued into the factory grounds, then carried on, quickening his pace slightly in order to catch his Chinese friend.

They walked along, with the fence towering above them on their immediate right; with Chang leading the way, walking with his eyes cast to the floor, and Martin following obediently along behind. He could see how the road wound along its route below them along a desolate looking area of wasteland. Old tires and scraps of waste metal littered the ground, amongst muddy puddles and mounds of weed covered earth. As they drew closer to their destination the road split in two, with one lane continuing along forward, while the other forked to the right, taking the traveller to what Martin suspected would be the rear side of the factory.

Another slight rise had to be traversed to get to Chang's chosen destination, and on reaching the brow of the hill the old factory came into view for the first time. Martin couldn't help but pause at the boundary fence and stare, his jaw slightly agape. The giant red bricked monster looked to be more fitting to Victorian London than the Shandong Province of China, but it was here, and it was as real as the skyscrapers in downtown Qingdao. Its tall looming walls were occupied by mesh covered windows that made it impossible to see inside. The red brickwork arched over the window panes was detailed in intricate fashion around the buttresses, but the effect wasn't pleasing on the eye, on the contrary the whole building looked daunting and foreboding, like a dark blot on the landscape or an optical illusion that caused your stomach to gripe if you stared at it for too long. On top of the building was a giant redbrick chimney, smoke billowing from its spout; the very sight of it caused Martin's skin to crawl, looking at it was all too like the images he had seen of Birkenau and Belzec, and he couldn't help but wonder how close those similarities ran.

Chang had come to a stop at a point on the brow of the hill where a double trunked tree ran up the side of the perimeter fence. There was a divot in the earth that Martin guessed had been made by four years of the Asian man sat observing the factory. It was a good spot, you were safely obscured from view by the cover of the tree but between the twin trunks had an excellent view of everything that was going on below. Martin hunkered down next to Chang who had sat in his favourite stakeout spot and was taking his binoculars out of their faux leather case.

"What do you think?" He asked, genuinely intrigued as to Martin's initial reaction.

"It's vile." Martin replied, then when he realised the man hadn't understood he clarified his point. "It's dark, and it's dirty, and if I was a more superstitious man I'd say it reeked of pure evil."

Chang only nodded, that same solemn look on his tired face.

"Here, look closer." He said, handing over the binoculars.

Martin took them from him, not wanting to see the building any closer than was absolutely necessary, but not wanting to show this to his new friend. He raised them up to his eyes and looked down through the gap in the tree trunks. Through the holes in the wire mesh fence he could see the path that ran around the side of the factory. Again this was littered with old debris and puddles, as though no care was taken in the upkeep of the building. There were a couple of garages to the left hand side of his vision and a couple of patrol jeeps were parked outside. He scanned a little further to the right; he could just make out from here the spot where the road split in two, and if he adjusted the focus on the lenses he could see the top of the sentry booth that sat next to the gate, but not the gate itself as this was obscured by a couple of sorry looking trees, their branches long since robbed of any foliage by the constant plume of smoke from the enormous chimney.

"Look." Chang said, pointing to a spot near to the right hand corner of the factory; he had opened the bag of food and was tucking into a home made spring role, a couple of bean sprouts protruding from his mouth as he munched. Martin followed his gaze with the binoculars and drew in a quick nervous breath; just coming into view from the far side of the factory was an armed guard, all dressed in black with his machine gun held in both hands. Martin didn't know what type of gun it was, though he had seen a lot of action movies in his time and would like to hazard a guess at an AK-47, but really what did it matter? It was the type that would tear a huge hole in your side should the man take a fancy to firing it at you.

"You want?" Chang asked, holding the bag of food open for Martin to see.

"No thank you." He replied; he had felt quite hungry when walking up here but he had suddenly lost his appetite. Instead he lifted the binoculars back to his eyes and watched the guard slowly make his way along the perimeter of the building, when he disappeared back around the far left hand corner he lowered them and addressed Chang again. "So what do we do now?"

Chang swallowed the food he had been slowly chewing in his mouth and regarded Martin with a strained smile. "Now we go in there."

"What?" Martin blurted, unable to disguise the shock on his face.

"Why else do you think I brought you out here?"

"I don't know, to observe, to make notes." Martin bleated in absolute panic.

"The time for making notes is done; the time for action has arrived."

"This is crazy, we can't just stroll on in there, there are armed guards down there."

"We have to know what is happening inside that building."

Martin bit down hard on his lip and when he tasted the coppery taste of blood on his tongue he knew that he had bit down hard. "Shouldn't we at least wait until night?"

"No, at night time guard doubles. More movement at night. Trucks coming and going, we need to go in day."

For this Martin had no answer; he drew in a deep breath and waited patiently for his heart to slow to a steadier pace, when it didn't he accepted he had little choice than to try and use the adrenaline coursing through his veins to his advantage.

"Ok," he said with a trembling bloodied lip, "but for the record, I think this is insane. Do we even have a weapon?"

"No." Chang admitted. "Even if we did we wouldn't be able to fight them off. The key is to not get caught."

"Not get caught, great, that's good advice, I'll try and remember that."

"Come on, we can leave our bags and equipment here."

"Where are we going?"

"To the corner of perimeter fence, best cover from there."

Martin looked up the hill slightly to where the perimeter fence came to an abrupt stop at its corner post. Then he followed the line of the hill down to where it met with the back of the garages he had spied earlier. Chang was right; if they were going to enter the facility – and he still couldn't believe he was actually contemplating this with a reasonably sane mind – then the area behind the garages would provide the best cover.

"Ok." He said reluctantly, and watched as Chang took the camera strap from round his neck and laid it next to his bag and binoculars next to the split roots of the tree. When he stood Martin remained seated for a while; he was willing his legs to work but they felt weak and jellylike. He was also breathing too fast, he wanted to calm his nerves but right now it felt impossible.

"Are you coming?" Chang asked, genuine concern on his face.

"Just give me a minute ok." Martin replied, squeezing his eyes shut tight; he didn't think he had been this terrified when Malik had pointed the gun at his head.

This is insane, you're going to get yourself killed, get out of here, leave now! He was taunted by the terror that was creeping through his pores, and was concerned it was going to get the better of him, that in a moment he actually would be fleeing back down the path with the Asian man staring after him. Then a new image came into his head, an image of a small girl with narrow eyes and pigtails on the sides of her head, a girl that was smiling at a camera on a happier day, long ago. He tried to block the image, to force it away, he didn't want to think of that, he had been happy in his ignorance, but the image persisted, forcing its way into the forefront of his mind where it pulled at his conscience and toyed with his good nature.

"Oh screw you!" He spat angrily, his eyes still squeezed shut tight, causing Chang to take an involuntary step backwards.

"Are you ok?"

"Fine!" Martin replied angrily, opening his eyes and finding the strength to move first into a kneeling position then up onto his feet. "At least I know now why you brought the wire clippers."

Chang only nodded, then he turned and made his way up the hill to the corner of the perimeter fence, keeping low so as not to be seen from below. Martin followed, keeping the image of Chang's daughter as his motivation against his escalating fear. When they reached the corner the two men crouched down low while the Asian man removed the wire clippers from his trouser pocket.

"Do we at least have a plan?" Martin asked as his friend started snipping a hole in the mesh fence.

"We can't enter by main entrance, but there is side door to left of building, we take that and look for evidence."

"Surely we need the camera, if we're going to prove there's something going on here?"

"It's too bulky, any photos I can take on my phone, that will have to do."

"I hope you know what you're doing." Martin sighed, unable to fully believe this wasn't some warped dream, that he wouldn't wake up in a moment in the soft linen of the Qingdao Sailing hotel and breathe a huge sigh of relief, or better still, at home in bed with Rose, and the whole thing had been one sorry nightmare.

"Not really." Chang conceded. "But we will get nowhere doing nothing."

Martin had to admire his honesty, no matter how foolhardy.

Chang clipped the individual prongs of the fence in an upwards line about a foot high; then with sweat pouring from his face he snipped away at the wire diamonds to the left and right of the bottom of the fence, so he could when finished draw them apart like curtains. He did this and made a gap that both men could squeeze through if they laid on their bellies.

"After you." Martin said, looking at the gap in the perimeter fence with real trepidation.

Chang nodded, then lay down so his belly was flat to the yellow grass of the plain. He poked his head through the hole then shuffled his shoulders through, using his elbows to pull him along. Once his shoulders were through the rest of him was easy, a lot like giving birth, Martin thought with a terrified smile as he watched the Chinese man slither through.

"Ok, now you." Chang said, crouched low at the business side of the fence.

Martin drew in a quick breath, had another fleeting notion of simply running away back down the hill in the direction they had come, then got himself into a laying position so his head was inches from the opening. He pulled himself forward, shimmying so his shoulders would fit through the gap and thinking as he did there was no way he would have fit through this hole before his operation. As he was pulling himself through his back caught on one of the jagged spikes left by the wire cutters, tearing his shirt and his skin. He grunted in pain as he pulled himself free, then dragged his legs through the hole.

"Let me look." Chang said, manoeuvring to the back of Martin so he could catch a glimpse of the damage. "Just a scratch, you'll be ok."

Martin soothed the scratch with his fingers through the small rip in his clothing, when he pulled his fingers back there was scarlet ion the tips, but Chang was right, it couldn't have been a deep wound or the fingers would have been covered. Still, it hurt.

There was a small grove of trees about half way between the back of the garages and the perimeter fence; keeping low Chang descended towards it. Martin had one last stroke of the scratch on his back, then followed the Oriental man down the hill.

They made it to the cover of the trees and knelt down behind one of the thicker trunks.

"Look." Chang said, pointing down the hill. The sentry who had been making his rounds a few minutes ago was back, just turning the far side corner of the factory, walking slowly along the back wall with his machine gun held across his midriff.

"When he gone, we go." Chang said. Martin nodded, feeling a lead like weight in his stomach. They watched as the sentry travelled on, his eyes darting left to right, probably desperate for some action, a couple of idiotic ageing men perhaps who thought they could change the world but were little more than deluded pulps of flesh waiting to be cut apart by machine gun fire. The thought did little to ease Martin's growing trepidation, but he swallowed his fear and watched as the guard disappeared out of sight.

"Ok, come on." Chang said, confident that the coast was clear with the guard heading back round the far side of the building. He took a look around, and when he was happy that nobody was watching from beyond the darkened windows of the factory he shuffled down the remainder of the hill on his behind, coming to a stop behind the corrugated exterior of the rear garage wall.

Martin, sick now with anticipation, waited until Chang was safely holed up at the back of the garage and then followed his lead, keeping low but not shuffling on his bottom as his friend had done for fear he would not get up again afterwards. He made it to the safety of the garage and hunkered down next to Chang, breathing hard.

"You ok? The dark haired man asked; Martin nodded, though he felt anything but.

"Where's this door?"

"Down the left hand side of the building." Chang replied, then nodded in the general direction with his head.

"Ok." Martin said, his breath coming rapidly. "And what do we do if we get there and the doors locked? Or if it's open and there are a hundred armed guards on the other side?"

"If there are a hundred armed guards on the other side of the door Martin I think it safe to say we die." Chang said with a soft smile. It was intended as a joke, a way to lighten a too fraught mood, but it did little to raise Martin's spirits. "Come on, I will lead the way, before the guard comes back."

There was a gap between the two garages, just wide enough to fit a man; Chang slipped into it and edged his way down to the end. Martin followed. It was cool between the two pre-fabricated buildings, a pleasant feeling with the sweat that was pouring down Martin's back. He waited for Chang to reach the end and then slowly started his sideways shuffle down to the front end of the garages. The Chinese man turned and watched him come, when Martin was about halfway down he nodded some reassurance to him, not wanting to speak out loud now they were nearing the factory, and slipped back out into the sunshine.

Martin made it to the end of the gap in time to see Chang duck back out into the sunlight and cross the twelve feet between the garages and the corner wall of the old red brick factory. He was about to follow him when a startled and angry cry froze him to the spot and turned his insides to jelly. Paralysed with fear the businessman looked out from his place between the garages as Chang spun in the direction of the sound, alarm etched across his own face. His startled eyes were wide as he noticed for the first time the two guards who had been taking a cigarette break in the shadow of the garages. He raised his hands in surrender as they rushed towards him, machine guns raised.

With his stomach feeling like t was trying to squeeze its way out of his body via his windpipe Martin watched on in horror as the first man reached a terrified Chang and thrust the barrel of his machine gun into the side of the startled mans face. He was barking something in his native tongue and though Martin didn't speak a word of the language he could imagine what was being said. Who was he? What was he doing here? Was he alone? Panic encircled him, he wanted to cry out, to give his friend a chance of escape but he was rigid with absolute terror.

Suddenly the second guard came into view and as with the first started barking questions at Chang, stood with his back to the gap in the garages, his own weapon aimed at the intruder.

Martin could hardly breathe, the Chinese guard was stood no more than a foot in front of him; the slightest noise would alert him to his presence. The man was about half a foot shorter than Martin, which gave him the advantage of being able to see over his shoulder to what was happening at the corner of the factory. It wasn't pleasant viewing; Chang's eyes were squeezed shut tight, the barrel of the machine gun still poking into his cheek, the guard was still bombarding him with questions and occasionally the terrified Shandong Province man gave a startled and terrified response.

Then Martin noticed something else, and it made his breath catch in his throat. The guard that was stood directly in front of him, the one who had foolishly turned his back to a second intruder, had a handgun clipped to his belt. It was about three inches from Martin's own hand; he could stretch out his hand, grab the gun and help his friend. Martin contemplated this as the guard that was interrogating Chang suddenly struck out with the butt of his gun and sent it crashing into the side of the mans face.

Martin watched with startled eyes as his friend was sent crashing back against the wall of the factory, banging his head hard on the brickwork in the process. His hands that had been raised above his head instantly dropped to both his cheek and his head trying to comfort the pain. Martin looked down again at the handgun as the first guard dropped his machine gun to the floor and produced from a sheaf attached to his belt a long, curved blade. Martin had seen these in movies, usually in films like Scarface and Casino, films with gangsters and molls and people with names like Tony Collucci and Baby Face Pauly, but never in real life. The sight of the blade sent a fear coursing through him the likes of which he had never felt before, not even in the offices of Eze-link cars. He was frozen to the spot in terror as the guard pushed Chang back against the wall and pressed the tip of the blade into his cheek, just below the eye. Even from this distance Martin could see the drop of blood that formed instantly from the wound, and as the drop slowly traced its way down the curve of the Chinese mans cheek Martin could easily have vomited. His eyes dropped down to the gun in the guard's belt holster, the one that was only inches from his own hand.

Come on! You know what you have to do! You know you have to do this! He commanded, but it was as though he was under some deep paralysis, as though he had been bitten by a poisonous spider or snake and that its venom had caused a comatose state. But that wasn't it; what was freezing him at this moment that commanded action, was fear; fear for his own sorry life.

Tears pricked at the corners of his eyes as he looked up again at the angry guard that was still berating Chang with questions, still pressing the blade into the terrified mans cheek. To Chang's credit he had clearly not given Martin up, for he still stood here unobserved, in the relative safety between the garages, if only he could muster the same courage.

His hand twitched as he tried to will it into some kind of response, but it was no good, what he had known all along had just been confirmed; he was a coward, a stupid old man with no place in this world of terror.

Just as this thought was entering his brain, as his hand was flopping back uselessly to his side, as the front of his pants was filling with warm urine and the first tears starting to course his cheeks, the guard decided the time for talking was through. As Martin watched on in horror he lifted the blade, pressed his free hand across Chang's chest, and slit his throat with the knife. Blood gushed from the open wound and soaked the Chinese mans shirt in an instant. Then in little over a second, his eyes were flickering and a wheezing gasp was passing through his lips. He dropped to the floor in a lifeless heap as the guard looked down on him with a sadistic smile on his face.

Martin could barely breathe, his eyes steadfastly refused to blink; he looked out on the moment his new found friend was brutally murdered, murdered by the same people who had undoubtedly murdered his daughter, and nearly passed out at being witness to such an inhuman act of violence. Then the guard that had been in front of him was stepping forward, wanting to get a closer look at the twitching body as the guard who had dealt the killer blow leaned over to wipe his blade on the dead mans clothing. Martin could not take any more, he didn't care if it was the wrong time to make a move or not; he had to get out of here, had to get out of here right now. He slid back down the narrow gap, manoeuvring his body so his shoulders were pressed one in front of the other, giving him enough space to slide backwards to the rear of the garage. He made it and slipped out, pressing his back to the corrugated wall. He was absolutely drenched in sweat and shaking from head to toe, but he was going to head back up the hill and to hell with the consequences.

   With legs that wanted to collapse under him he quickly ascended the hill, not even bothering in his haste to keep low, and when he made it to the top and out through the gap in the fence without getting caught he didn't feel an ounce of gratitude; right now he didn't feel a thing.

   With a dark fog enveloping his body and his mind the shuddering mess that was Martin Rooley stumbled down the hill along the line of the perimeter fence and made his escape.

11

In the Qingdao offices of the Shanghai Daily News a man sat on a plastic seat in the waiting area with his head in his hands. He was sixty-eight years old but looked at this moment in time closer to ninety. His shirt was torn at the back and was dotted with blood about the tear. He had a bandage on one hand which was smeared with dirt and his skin was coated in a thick sheen of sweat. His hair, which had been washed clean at the start of the day was now matted and clumped together with a mix of sweat and grime and his skin had the frazzled aroma of burnt pork.

Martin was aware of his condition, was aware that the young couple who shared the waiting area with him had moved to be as far from him as possible, was aware that the clerical staff and journalists who passed through the offices were regarding him oddly and possibly discussing him when they returned to their work stations. He was aware of all of this, but he was also aware that there was little he could do about it, and more importantly he didn't care. There was enough of a burden on his troubled mind already without worrying about what people thought of him. Let them look down their noses at him, let them comment on his appearance and his smell, let them point and jeer, what did he care? He couldn't understand them anyway and even if he could they were insignificant. He wondered if they would be so judgmental if they could see the contents of his bank accounts. Maybe if they could they would consider him an eccentric millionaire; blessed with finances but bereft of any sense.

A low sigh passed his lips as he gazed down at the paper cone of water held in his trembling hand. He took a sip; it cooled the burning in his throat, it was bitter sweet. The cooling of his parched throat was a pleasant feeling, but he didn't deserve to feel pleasure, he didn't deserve to feel anything but remorse. He could have saved Chang, the gun had been just inches from his stinking cowardly hand, he could have saved him and he had failed to even try. Now the man was dead, his throat slit like a gutted pig, his life cruelly snatched away as had been his beautiful little daughters before him. Martin considered all this in his mind and wished he could cry. If he could cry he would be consumed by grief, and grief was a feeling he could accept, instead the tears refused to budge, confining him in a cell built solely out of guilt. It was good that he couldn't cry, it was what he deserved.

For years he had watched heroes such as John Wayne and Clint Eastwood, Steve McQueen and Charles Bronson; tough guys who had not hesitated in the face of adversity, who had found the courage to stand tall against all odds, to face up to their fears and when push came to shove use their strength and their valour to defeat whatever evil stood in their way. Martin had watched their movies and their shows, had revelled as the good guys had taken on the bad and come out on top, had enjoyed the triumph of good over evil and had told himself, foolishly it seemed now, that when the chips were down he too could be the hero.

Some hero he had turned out to be today. Wherever Chang was now; he sure wasn't looking down on Martin Rooley and thanking him for his bravery. It was the Chinese man who had been brave; even under such terrifying circumstances, with a machete and a machine gun pointed at his face, he had not given Martin away. Chang was the hero, and Martin was little more than a coward who had been too scared to save him.

Martin ran his fingers through his greasy hair, crushing the paper cone in the palm of his bandaged hand, what was left of the water splashing out and landing on the tiled floor with a dull plop. His stomach churned angrily, as it had done that day in the market place, a day which seemed so long ago now.

For what felt like the twelve-thousandth time since starting this miserable charade Martin wondered just what the hell he thought he was doing? He had watched his movies, seen something wrong and fool-heartedly felt that he could fix it. Well he'd done a real swell job of that; his wife was miles from home, hiding away in fear and confusion, he had angered an underground crime syndicate with roots in some very high places and had lost the only other person with whom he could truly share his ordeal. All in all he made a pretty crummy hero.

"Misser Woowey." A high pitched voice spoke from somewhere on his left. Martin looked up to see a hauntingly thin girl with wire rimmed glasses attempting to converse with him from the relative safety of the busy office annex. She really was skeletal, probably no more than seven stone when soaked to the bone, though for now at least this was far from Martin's concern.

"Yes."

"Misser Lau will see you now."

Martin got to his feet, every muscle in his body screaming out in protest, and followed the young girl through into the main office complex of the news room. She led him past a complex grid of active desks where junior reporters sat typing at their desktops or talking loudly on the phone, talking to be heard over all the commotion, and through to a quieter row of small offices on the left. She paused at the door of the third office down, rapped on the door and then opened it. She briefly spoke something to the man inside in her native tongue, then gestured for Martin to enter. He did as he was bid and waited for the door to close behind him.

"Please sit down." The man at the desk pointed to the seat opposite his desk, though with a look on his face that suggested he was going to disinfect that same chair the moment Martin left.

The businessman did as he was bid and with an audible creak from his tired old knees sat down. The man opposite him leant forward, placing his elbows on the desk in front of him. He was wearing a crisp white shirt, loose at the neck with his tie slightly askew. He was somewhere in his mid forties, with hair not unlike Chang's, but slightly more balding on the top. His face was lined and aged, a heavy smoker Martin guessed, and he had eyes that suggested he had seen it all; Martin, who had seen a fair amount himself in recent weeks, begged to disagree.

"My name is Bao-Zi Lau, I am a reporter for the Shanghai Daily, I unnerstan you have a story I may be interressid in."

"That's correct." Martin replied. "Not just a story Mister Lau, I've got you the scoop of the century."

Lau sat back in his chair, regarding this curious Westerner with intrigue.

Martin had stumbled back up the road that led from the factory in a daze; shivering from head to toe though the day was warm and the skies clear of rain. He hadn't been able to fully comprehend what he had just witnessed. Although he had seen the grisly remains of James Purefoy in the basement of his Kensington home he hadn't actually watched on as the life had escaped his body. Seeing Chang die had been Martin's first witness of a murder, and it had shaken him badly. With emotions bordering somewhere between heartbreak and acute remorse he had wandered the ten miles back into the centre of Qingdao. His pores filled with sweat, his hair matted and lank, blisters causing agony he truly felt he deserved on his heels and between his toes, Martin had walked on like a man in a dream.

Cars that passed by either slowed to get a closer look at him or sped on past, afraid if they slowed that the strange looking man now walking along the side of the busy highway would somehow access their vehicles if they did not. He was lucky not to have been picked up by the police as he travelled along, but it was the only way he felt that luck had indeed blessed him this day.

It was as he was breaching the outskirts of the city, with the Qingdao skyline in his peripheral vision that he became aware of what he needed to do. It really was his only option now; he had to go to the press and tell them everything. It had been easy enough to find them; there were three newspaper buildings in Qingdao, but this was by far the largest, a national press, that was exactly what he needed. And so here he was, filthy, smelly, battered and bruised, but determined to bring what had happened to his friend and so many before him to the public eye.

Martin sat in the poky office, his head throbbing with the onset of a migraine, and thought about where he should start. Lau waited as patiently as a man as busy as he could, hoping that the strange looking man before him wasn't yet another time waster in a day that had already served him three.

"What I'm about to tell you, I can't afford for you to take lightly." Martin started. "I mean that quite literally. My name is Martin Rooley, I am the Chief Executive Officer of Sapient Trans Global, a major corporation and FTSE one hundred company."

Lau's eyes widened at this; the man before him clearly didn't look as though he had two pennies to rub together let alone a vast business empire.

"Oh I know what you're thinking." Martin continued, recognising instantly the look on the Chinese mans face. "But I assure you its true, and you can verify that information yourself with a couple of clicks of your mouse. But for now, you have to hear me out. I had an operation, about seven months ago now, a heart transplant. Everything was alright at first, but after a while I started to become suspicious of the details surrounding the operation."

As Lau listened on, a look of mild interest and little more on his lined face, Martin told the story of how he had come to arrive in Qingdao. He told of the agonising wait for a new heart, and how one had suddenly and miraculously become available; he told of the operation itself, how it had been performed in his home rather than in a hospital, and how after the operation it had seemed almost impossible to get any kind of after care. Then he told of his own investigations into what had occurred; he spoke of Linda McGready who had transpired to be Abigail Tardy, of Trojan Horse Security and Darren Fryers, who had rented his house on a one day lease. He mentioned travelling the length and breadth of London, talking to people, searching for clues and how eventually he had come to discover the body of David Purefoy, the surgeon who had performed his transplant, in the basement of his multi-million pound home.

At this point Martin expected Lau to look shocked; surprised at the very least, but he just continued to sit with his arms on the desk in front of him, that same look of mild curiosity on his face. Unperturbed Martin continued, telling of how he had followed the trail to Eze-link cars and it's proprietor Haroon Malik; of breaking into Malik's office and piecing together the evidence that linked the Asian man with an underground operation right here in Qingdao, China.

Again there was nothing from Lau, he just continued to listen patiently, as though hearing about a black market organ trading syndicate sourced from his hometown was something he contended with every day.

Battling hard to hide his growing frustration Martin carried on, telling of how he had flown out to China to avoid the threat back in London and coming upon the posters of the missing persons in the alleyway between the government flats. He told of Lost and Found, and about meeting up with Chang who had for all intents and purposes saved him from the youths who had mistaken him for one of the abductors.

At this point Martin had to pause; thinking of Chang had brought him close to tears, he had a lump in his throat the size of a golf ball and it was hard to speak around it.

"Excuse me." He said, attempting to take a sip from the now empty paper cone, when he realised his parched throat was not to be whetted he crushed it in his hand, all the while thinking about the blade that had cut the mans life from his body.

Slowly, with care, Martin told of how Chang had taken him to his former place of employment, the abandoned factory that was now his base of operations, and how the man had admitted to losing his own family through abduction; first his beautiful little girl, then his wife, collateral damage in his escalating obsession. He told of how Chang had discovered the whereabouts of a factory on the outskirts of town where he believed the missing were taken, of the countless hours he had spent staking it out, taking his pictures and documenting it all in his journal. He told of the airbase and how Chang believed the organs were flown from here to a small island off the coast, and then on to their destinations in various cities around the world. Finally he spoke of today, of the reason he appeared now before this man in tattered, filthy clothing, blood drying on his back and starting to seep again through the bandage on his hand. He told of cutting the wire fence and attempting to break into the old building, of how Chang had been captured and how the man had died. He told it all, or most of it anyway, to his eternal shame he was unable to tell of how he had been in a position to save the man, but had been too much of a coward to try. His story done, Martin let out a huge sigh of relief and relaxed back into the plastic chair.

Looking up at the clock that had been ticking away behind Lau's desk he noticed that twenty minutes had gone by; it had felt like only moments. Then he looked at the journalist, at how he still sat patiently, his hands stretched out on the desk before him, that same look of bemusement on his face. Martin could have screamed. How could he be so obtuse? Was he being deliberately ignorant? Or did he simply not believe him? He could agree it was definitely quite a story, but surely any journalist worth his salt would want to at least make further enquiries.

Then a new thought crept into Martin's mind, an unpleasant thought, a very unpleasant thought indeed. What if the journalist was also involved somehow? Was that why he still sat there, that small smile on his face? Was he waiting for Martin to spill everything he knew while he decided exactly what he should do with him?

The disquiet was growing in his bones like a cancer when the man finally broke the silence:

"It is quite a story you tell."

"Not a story." Martin said, shaking his head. "No, not a story no. A story would suggest that it had been made up, and I can assure you none of this was, all of it happened."

"I'm not saying I don't believe you." Lau replied patiently, so patiently in fact it made Martin want to lean across the desk and smash his face into the monitor of his Apple Mac. "You think we don't know what goes on here?"

Martin was shocked, whatever he had expected from this conversation he had not expected this. "You know?"

"Of course we know some fings, we are not ignowant Misser Woohey."

"I'm not suggesting for a second that you are, but if you know of what is going on here why do you do nothing about it?"

"Same weason as evwybody. No evidence. This thing, very corrup, government, police. To take this on, you need evidence. You have Misser Woohey?"

Martin pursed his lips. "No, not exactly, but I can take you to the factory, you can get all the evidence you need."

"No, no, no Misser Woohey. You need evidence."

"I can't believe this." Martin said, gripping his head in frustration. "A man has died, a man has been murdered, in fact dozens if not hundreds of people have been murdered, and you're not willing to do anything about it?"

"Not not wiwing, need evidence."

Martin sighed, he had hoped the story alone would be enough to at least prick the journalists curiosity, and though he felt he had done that, there was no way he was going to put it to print in his name without some hard solid facts with which to back it up. Then, just as he was feeling completely helpless once more, Martin thought of the plethora of evidence at his disposal, Chang had documented four years worth of evidence in his journals; photographs, journals, flight plans, he had it all.

"I can get you the evidence."

"You can?" Lau enquired, thin black eyebrows slightly raised.

"I think so." Martin replied. "If I can get you the evidence, if I can bring it here and land it on your desk, do you promise me you'll take this story to press?"

"Take story…"

"Write the story, do you promise me you'll write the story?"

"If you can get me hard evidence, I wite storwy."

"Ok, I'll get you the evidence." Martin stood up from the seat, feeling determined. But before he could march out the door Lau grabbed him by the arm. Martin turned to face him.

"Misser Woohey, journawist look into missing person before, journawist become missing person. I need evidence, pwoof, I not wite storwy without."

"I understand." Martin said, nodding his head slightly. "You'll have your evidence." Then he turned and walked back out into the busy news room, adrenaline pumping through his ageing veins.

12

With his feet sore and blistered and his arthritic knees giving him hell the last thing Martin wanted was another trek across town; but after his taxi experience on his first day in China he was reluctant to travel this way again, so he gritted his teeth and started his journey on foot. He could see the basic path he needed to take to reach his destination but finding his way there through the maze-like city streets was not going to be easy, especially as he didn't have Chang to guide him this time.

Chang, who had suffered so much loss at the hands of these evil bastards, his sacrifice would not be in vain, if it was the last thing Martin did he would serve the man the justice he so rightly deserved, he owed him that much at least.

He was still shaken from the horrific events earlier that day, but with the fire in his belly Martin had the impetus to journey on, to find his closure.

This time last year he was still two days away from the cardiac arrest that would turn his entire world upside down. Now, three hundred and sixty-five days later that world that he had known was little other than a distant memory. The man that had sat in the big chair in the big office with the views over London meant little to him now. Everything seemed little; from world haulage in which he had made his fortune, to marriage and family. None of it mattered and all of it mattered; or at least none of it would mean anything if he couldn't draw a line under this new and unnervingly hideous side of his life. He wanted to go home, he wanted to return to his beloved wife, to hold her in his arms and to wish her a merry Christmas, but all of that would remain out of reach as long as the trade remained in operation.

"So it doesn't remain in operation." Martin muttered, drawing a curious look from a passing Chinese couple as he weaved through the streets, his whole body throbbing with a mixture of exhaustion and adrenaline. He tried as best as he could to keep the high rise government flats in view, for he knew that Chang's old factory was somewhere between the mans home and where he was now. It wasn't easy, they would regularly be blocked from view by equally tall buildings, but by keeping his wits about him and trusting both his bearings and his instincts he slowly plodded along until eventually he came to the dark and gloomy streets that housed Qingdao's blue collar district. From high rise office blocks to traditional Chinese homes, intricate in design, to unusual in their context German colonial buildings and finally to here; the red brick walls that loomed up on either side of the near silent streets. It was late afternoon and the workers would be soon leaving for home, some of them anyway, and the streets would be busy once more, but for now the only sounds Martin could hear was the tweeting of the birds and the distant thrum of machinery.

Street after street after street he traversed, feeling completely disoriented, just like he had this very morning when the middle aged man with the sad eyes had found him wandering with no clue as to his whereabouts. Chang wasn't here to help him now; Chang wouldn't ever help anyone with anything again. The thought sent a painful wrench deep into his gut and Martin had to force himself to carry on walking. What he really wanted, what he wanted more than anything, was to sit his weary body down on the cracked pavement, bury his head in his hands and cry. Cry for his own miserable situation, cry for the ache he felt over missing his beloved Rose, cry for all the missing, and the truth behind their absence from life, and cry for Chang, a man who had wanted to do good, and had become a victim all over again.

What was the use anyway? Even if he found the factory the door was undoubtedly locked.

"Then I'll kick it down." Martin said through gritted teeth. He didn't have time to feel sorry for himself, he needed to deliver Chang's evidence to Lau, or he could be stuck here permanently. With renewed vigour he marched on, ignoring the charley horse that was kneading into the muscles of his right thigh.

He turned a sharp corner and came face to face with the block of flats he had walked from just last night with Chang, he was definitely on the right track, so he traced his steps back on the route he had taken twice already and after another couple of turns was pretty sure he had reached his destination.

Although all the streets about this part of town looked unquestionably the same the white iron grill covering the windows on the building to the far end of the street was definitely familiar. If he was right, and he was sure he was, Chang's old factory should be coming up on the left.

As Martin drew close an uncomfortable feeling started stretching its claws out into the pit of his belly; something wasn't right here. One of his biggest concerns had been that the door would undoubtedly be locked and he would have to break into the old factory building, but as he approached he realised that the opposite of this problem could be far more troublesome to his plans.

The black reinforced door was standing ajar, a slither of darkness running the length of the frame. Martin couldn't have been certain that Chang had locked it when they left earlier that day but he was damn sure he had at least closed the door. Something was very wrong here.

His nerve ends were jangling again, a state for which he was becoming all too familiar, as he closed the distance between the slightly open door and himself. Someone has been here, that small voice of disquiet spoke in his mind, and perhaps they are still here now. He steeled himself, preparing for whatever may lie beyond the door, preparing to scream or to run or God damn it to fight if need be, and when he reached the door he paused for a moment to gather his nerve, but not too long; waiting too long under these circumstances would see his nerve dissipate all together.

Ok, you can do this. Martin closed his eyes, drew in a deep breath, then pulled the heavy door open.

At first he didn't see anything; looking into the relative gloom of Chang's murky old office after being out in the dazzling sunshine caused white spots to dance before his eyes, but as his retinas became accustomed to the change in light the room before him became clear, and the truth of what he was seeing hit him like a slug to the guts.

Beyond the door in this industrial part of town no thugs or hoodlums waited with guns or knives or machete's or baseball bats, no grisly remains had been laid out on display, waiting for the animals to come and dine, no corrupt police officials lurked in silence, waiting to question with methods best served in rooms such as this anyone who happened to come along.

Beyond the door in this industrial part of town was very little indeed, and it was this that caused the businessman from Bolton, England to almost drop to his knees in desperation.

Somehow, with his heart as heavy as it had ever been, Martin stumbled into the coolness beyond the door, and looked about the room with a mix of resignation and futile hopelessness.

At some point between them leaving the factory early that afternoon and Martin arriving back here now, somebody had come and cleared out the factory. Not a patch of evidence remained in the room, it was as silent and empty as an age old tomb. With his throat clicking from the drought on his tongue Martin looked at the huge wall board, filled now with nothing but pins and dust. Here and there tiny scraps of paper still clung to some of the pins, where their contents had been removed in a hurry. Then he looked over to the desk, where piles of paper and ledgers had been stacked earlier that day, now only Chang's framed family photo stood silent sentinel on the desk, nothing about it to distract from its own air of tragedy.

Martin swallowed hard, feeling a pain like the onset of laryngitis as his dry throat forced through the motion. He literally couldn't believe his eyes. Whoever had murdered Chang had either discovered who he was no doubt through their contacts in the police department, or had simply known all along. The thought was truly terrifying, and it left Martin completely without an avenue with which to follow. He could head to Chang's house, see if there was any evidence there, but he could bet if they had discovered the evidence in the factory then it would be the same in the flat.

Sick to his stomach, his head swimming with misery and despair, Martin turned and head out into the early evening sunshine. He took a deep breath, then slowly made his way back in the direction he had come. He was not going to call back on Lau, he wouldn't waste his time. The man had made it clear he would do nothing without some solid evidence, and now Martin had nothing.

It was over; his time in China had finally drawn to a close; there was nothing more he could do. His foolhardy attempt to be a beacon of light in a sea of darkness had transpired to be what he had always feared; as futile as trying to swim through molasses. It was time to go home.

13

It was after seven at night when a concerned looking bellman opened the door to this haggard and exhausted man. Martin nodded to him as pleasantly as he could, and then stepped into the air conditioned foyer with his head hung low. He hadn't eaten since breakfast, but he felt no hunger as he trudged slowly across the tiled floor to the elevator.

He had reached a decision on leaving Chang's old place of work; it was time to accept defeat, it was time to go home. He would get the first available flight out of China, even if it meant having to wait in Paris or Lisbon or Hamburg or Bonn. He would slowly but surely make his way home, where he would contact his wife and have her brought to his side. He would go to the police, tell them his story, his full unedited story, including the parts in which he had broken the law himself, and demand protection. He would swear to testify in court to the things for which he was accusing and he would admit his own misgivings, including finding the body of David Purefoy and not alerting the necessary authorities. He would do all of this and to hell with the consequences, it was after all what he should have done in the first place. If he had to serve a little time himself for breaking and entering or perverting the course of justice then so be it, frankly at this moment in time he was too emotionally exhausted to care. All he wanted now was to be home in time to wish his beloved Rose a merry Christmas. If he could throw a hot shower into the mix he guessed he could be satisfied.

Lifting an arm that felt weighed down with lead he poked the button to summon the lift and waited with his head hung low, eyes blinking against the tiredness that was trying to pull him under. He could sense the eyes of the other guests and the previously pleasant reception staff bearing into him but he didn't care; he'd like to see how they looked if they had suffered as he had today.

There was a soft ping as the lift arrived and then the doors were opening. A middle aged Chinese couple stepped past him out into the foyer, both glancing back at him as they passed and whispering not very subtly under their breath. Martin chose to ignore them as he had chosen to ignore the others before them, and stepped into the yellow glow of the lift with his eyes still cast to the gleaming tiles. He pressed the button for his floor and as the doors closed softly he closed his eyes, too exhausted to hold it back any longer. He was pretty sure that if the journey had been just a minute or so longer he would have fallen asleep right there, stood up with his behind pressed against the handrail. That same soft ping again alerted though and he lifted his head in time to see the doors slowly sliding open.

Martin stepped out into the well carpeted corridor and followed it down in the direction of his room. In a semi daze he stumbled along, his feet working on muscle memory to lead him in the direction of the comfort of his room, his shower, his bed, his bag with his change of clothes and the telephone from which he could make his reservations.

So exhausted and numb to the brain was he that when he arrived at his destination he had actually lifted his card key up to the card slot before he noticed that the door was standing slightly ajar. What's more the light was on inside the room. Now it was a small possibility no matter how unlikely that either he had forgotten to close the door behind him when he had left that morning or the maid had when doing her rounds. However, neither he nor the maid would have switched the light on in the room, for the sun rose over the sea line horizon beyond his bedroom window and bathed the room in glorious natural light from six am; neither he nor the maid had any reason to ever use the lights in the room during the day.

Within seconds of him noticing these unusual occurrences the tiredness that had threatened to engulf him in the elevator was gone. In its place was a hot and fiery burst of Adrenaline that shot through his veins like cocaine, heightening all of his senses and snapping him from his stupor. He was totally awake and totally alert, a pharmaceutical company that could successfully bottle this sensation could reap the rewards of that success for a lifetime.

With his eyes wide and bug like, Martin stretched out his fingers, too soon after noticing what was wrong for fear to take hold, and pushed on the door. It crept gently open, revealing the destruction inside the room an inch at a time.

Somebody had been here all right, and from the mess inside the room he was pretty sure it wasn't the maid, if it was she could forget about a tip. His clothes lay strewn about the floor, his bag wide open on the bed, the covers of which were in disarray. The drawers in the vanity table hung open as did the ones in the cabinets at the side of the bed. His belongings such as his toiletries and mobile were strewn about the floor and a chair had been smashed to pieces where somebody had either been searching it for anything that may be hidden there or taking their aggression out on it when they discovered there was nothing.

Swallowing against the painful lump in his throat Martin took a step into the room, allowing the mindless destruction to slowly sink in. This was a targeted attack, somebody had discovered who he was and where he was staying and had come here either to find the man himself or learn more about his intentions. But who? The likely answer was the same people who had murdered Chang, and if they knew who he was then he was in even greater danger than he had originally thought.

Martin stepped up to the dresser to get a better look at the damage in the room, thinking he could be in hot water with the hotel management if they saw the room like this. As he did a noise from the bathroom startled him back into the moment; the toilet was flushing, whoever had caused this mess was still in the room!

Freezing to the spot Martin stared at the closed bathroom door, all thoughts of showers and beds and airport telephone calls ripped from his fragile mind. He could hear somebody moving about inside, they padded across the floor and turned on the faucet over the sink. In outright panic he looked towards the door, but he had come too far into the room, they could be back in the bedroom before he was able to escape, and that could be very bad indeed. Thinking quickly Martin looked towards his only other option; the narrow linen closet next to the flat screen television. Without further thought he stepped backwards towards it and as quietly as possible pulled open the door. The space inside was a little tight between the ironing board and the spare bed sheets and towels, but he slid in and pulled the door closed behind him just as the bathroom door opened and the intruder re-entered the room.

The closet was the old fashioned kind; with horizontal slats that offered Martin a decent if slightly obscured view of the room beyond the door, and when the fat man entered, scratching his arse and yawning, the businessman knew instantly who he was.

The last time he had seen the Eze-link cars base controller he had been looking harried in his cubby-hole office as several Trojan Horse staff pretended to be party revellers in order to aid Martin with his escape; now Zee was here, in China, in Qingdao, and most disturbingly of all in his hotel bedroom.

How had they tracked him down? There was no way they could have traced his path to here, but somehow they had, and it only served to further display the resources that these gangsters must have at their disposal.

The fat man pulled a stick of gum from his pocket and peeled off the wrapper; this was dropped to join the rest of the clutter on the carpet. As he popped it in his mouth he turned his back on the closet door, and Martin saw with mounting horror the handle of the gun that was sticking out of the waistband of his sweat pants.

Barely able to breathe, Martin hid in the closet, watching as the fat bearded man plodded about the room, kicking at items of clothing on the floor and chewing his gum. There was nothing here to see, so providing the man had not been tasked to camp out here until Martin returned the businessman was fairly confident that he would leave soon, he just needed to wait it out until he did.

Zee blew a huge bubble, quite impressive under other circumstances, that burst and left gum residue in the whiskers of his beard, then fished in the pocket of his sweats for his mobile. He found it and settled down on the edge of the bed, scrolling down whatever it was he was reading on the screen.

Cramped up in the tiny cupboard, barely room to breathe let alone move, Martin sighed in frustration. He didn't know how long he could stay in this position, with his back pressed up against the shelf that housed the iron and the Chinese equivalent of the Corby trouser press. He shuffled uncomfortably in the narrow space, quietly moving his right buttock so it wasn't pressed into the side of the ironing board. The movement disturbed a thin layer of dust that had gathered on the underside of the shelf, it puffed out into the space around where Martin was standing, tiny speckles floating in the air like stardust. He knew what was going to happen before the dust had even affected his sinuses; he had been prone to sneezing fits his whole life, why should now be any different? This knowledge was possibly what saved Martin from almost certain death that evening, for he was able to reach up his hand and pinch his nostrils tight before the sneeze took effect. If he had sneezed out loud the fat man reading messages on his bed would have known it for what it was straight away, and caught or killed him where he stood. By pinching his nostrils shut tight Martin was able to stifle the sneeze, making a dull sound that alerted Zee to a potential problem but now what it was.

The fat man turned his head sharply at the soft sound, eyeing the cupboard suspiciously. He moved his bulky frame into a position where he could reach around and grab the silver jewelled handgun from his waistband. Martin sucked in a terrified breath, his eyes still misty from the sneeze, as the large man pushed himself up from the bed and slowly started to edge towards the closet.

Martin stretched his hand around his back, tracing his fingers along the shelf without taking his eyes from the approaching man. The tips stroked along the side of something plastic and he knew he had found what he was searching blindly for. His arm screamed with pins and needles as he stretched out further and wrapped his fingers tightly about the plastic handle.

With eyes as huge as space hoppers Zee reached the closed closet door, the gun raised in his hand. He reached out his free hand, found the handle and pulled. The door swung open and when it did Martin struck the iron out with all the force he could muster in the enclosed space and sent it crashing into the fat mans face. The result could not have been any better; Zee didn't even yelp in either surprise or pain, the shot was perfect, it had rendered the big man instantly unconscious. He collapsed to the floor like a dress shop mannequin, his back and his head perched against the side of the bed. A small trickle of blood dripped down from one nostril, the Asian man was alive, though his eyes were shut he was visibly breathing from his mouth and his chest was rising and falling in regular motion.

Martin, racked with terrible shakes from adrenaline and fear, stepped from his place in the closet, unable to take his eyes from the unconscious man. He kept expecting him to move, to maybe fling out his free hand and grab him by the ankle, but the man would not be moving for some time. Slowly Martin started to relax. Somehow he had done it, the unexpected victory was the catalyst that he so desperately needed. Quickly he dropped down to the mans side and prized the bling covered gun from his grasp. It felt too heavy in his hand, like a death weight, but he held on to it all the same. He had to move fast, who knew how long he had before Zee either came round or one of his equally abhor able colleagues came looking for him.

Unable to take his eyes from the man lying on the floor of his hotel bedroom Martin backed up towards the bathroom door. He crept back into the room and flicked on the light, ignoring the smell that met him, at least he knew now what the big man had been doing in here; all those McDonald's needed to come back out somehow.

Martin stripped off his shirt, taking a quick look at the thin cut and the clotted blood that had formed a small scar on his back, then he ran water from the cold faucet and rinsed his body, his hair and his face. He stripped down to his underpants and splashed cold water onto his legs, cooling them down and washing away some of the sweat.

When he stepped back into the room he expected to see the man rising from his stupor, so he left with the gun raised in both hands; but Zee was still unconscious. Martin placed the gun down on the bed and grabbed some fresh clothes from the pile on the floor. He quickly dressed into the darkest clothes he could find; some black suit pants and a dark grey polo necked sweater, then turned and grabbed the gun from the bed. He tucked it into the waistband of his trousers, hoping he wouldn't accidentally blow off one of his testicles, and head for the door. He took one last look at the stagnant man, thinking I did that, then left, closing the door behind him.

Heading down the corridor at pace he made his way towards the employee stairway, wanting to avoid the lift in case it was being watched. He couldn't go home now, they could be waiting for him at the airport; there was really only one thing he could do, and the thought of going back there made the small hairs on the back of his neck stand out like silent sentinels.

14

By the time he reached the tree with the split roots that wound up the side of the perimeter fence Martin, despite his growing anxiety, was consumed by a ravenous hunger. The bag of food was right there, next to Chang's trusty camera, right where they had left it. Martin grabbed for it and fished inside. Seeing the camera had brought memories of that afternoon crashing back into his exhausted mind, but he needed to control the sentiment; Chang was gone, if he didn't have something to eat soon he was apt to join him imminently. He produced a couple of spring rolls from the bag and munched them down in two large bites. Then he ducked back inside, brought out something that may or may not have been some kind of chicken wrap, and devoured this too. Whatever it was it was absolutely delicious, and his grumbling stomach thanked him for it. Satisfied he had eaten enough to increase his waning energy levels Martin dropped the bag back to the floor, picked up the camera and continued on his way.

He came to the corner where they had cut their way into the compound and was surprised to see that the hole was still there. The intruder's way of entry into the facility had as yet to be discovered, though Martin was sure it would not remain this way for long. Not wasting a moment he hunkered down and slid through the gap, being careful not to catch his back again on the jutting wire of the fence.

Halfway through the hole a terrible thought occurred to him; what if they had discovered the hole in the fence and had left it on purpose? What if they were watching him now from afar, waiting to see if anybody else would be foolish enough to try and gain access to the old factory?

Martin gritted his teeth and continued to shimmy through the gap; if that was the case then so be it, for he was fresh out of ideas, this, as far as he could see, was his only option.

He made it to the other side and lay on the yellow grass with his back pressed against the floor, waiting for his heartbeat to steady. He felt reasonably safe under cover of moonlight, with his dark clothing blending him into his surroundings quite nicely. He lifted the camera and switched it on, looking through the view finder to the path below that ran around the side of the building. He could see the spot where his friend had been brutally murdered earlier that day and it made the food he had just eaten churn uncomfortably in his belly. Chang had been right; the facility was better guarded on an evening, with twice as many sentries as he had witnessed earlier. Perhaps they had lain on more guards following the intrusion earlier that day. It didn't matter, what mattered was how he was going to get past them. The one thing he was hoping they would not anticipate was for someone to try the same plan twice. This was his hope anyway. He intended to slide down the slope on his backside, make it to the back of the garages, shimmy through the gap between the walls and head to the doorway Chang had made him aware of on the Western side of the building.

Foolish old man, he thought, and had to suppress a terrified laugh; he was glad that it did not make it past his lips, in these circumstances it would sound all too like the joviality of a madman.

He closed his eyes and counted to ten, hoping when he opened them again that he would have been steeled from a new found inner resolve, but all that waited for him was the same deep pooled anxiety that had prevented him from saving his friend. Oh well, he couldn't lay here all night waiting to be captured; if he was going to get caught he wanted it to at least be while attempting to do some good, not lying on the soft grass, too terrified to move. He manoeuvred into a sitting position, and keeping an eye on the pathway below slowly made his way down the hill. He could feel the straw-like grass under the material of his polo shirt as his legs pistoned him down the slope, his hands pushing against the ground to give him extra purchase. He made it to the bottom and climbed with an audible pop of his tired old knees into a standing position behind the garages.

"Come on come on." He muttered under his breath, trying to find the nerve to slide back between the garages; a place that had encapsulated so much horror for him earlier that day. The only motivation he had was the thought of finding the evidence he needed to be able to escape this Hell hole, and he wasn't going to be able to do that standing here. It wasn't much, but apparently it was enough, because a couple of seconds after having the thought he was pivoting his shoulders to be able to slide between the gap in the two garages. His polo-neck scraped along the garage wall as he made his way down, making a soft shushing sound that he hoped could not ne heard from the other side. His hand held on to the camera, the strap safely around his neck, and when he neared the end he raised it to his eye and looked through the view finder, zooming in to see if there were any guards in his limited vision. There were not but that didn't mean they weren't just beyond the garage wall, just as they had been that afternoon. Martin reached the front of the garage and waited a moment, gathering his nerve. He drew in a deep breath and then poked his head slightly around the corner.

The coast was clear; no guards sat smoking on the old tires to the front of the garages, no patrol guards were currently circumnavigating the building, he could see a torch beam bobbing up and down in the distance but it looked to be moving the other way. This was it, this was his chance, he could stand here all night in the safety between the garages or he could try and do some good. The former seemed all too tempting, so he forced himself to look to the corner of the building, where Chang's throat had been slit and his lifeless body had slumped to the dirty floor. Anger crept into his veins, it was a good feeling, a powerful feeling, it spurred him on, recklessly maybe, but if Marie Curie hadn't been reckless with her own health radiation therapy may have remained undiscovered.

"You're no Marie Curie." Martin whispered in the silence between the garages. "You're a foolish old man with a death wish."

Despite this Martin counted to three, his chest rising and falling very quickly now, then stepped out into the space to the front of the garages. Discarded cigarette butts littered the ground in front of the abandoned tires; there was an arc sodium light that illuminated the corner of the building but apart from a couple of dirty puddles the area was deserted. He turned to his right and looked down the side of the old factory building, he was just in time to see the torchlight disappear around the corner, and as it did another appeared, heading in his direction, another guard was doing the rounds in the opposite direction, and was heading Martin's way!

The businessman drew in a sharp breath then disappeared around the side of the building. A large rock wall was separated from the factory by the pathway; it provided ample shadow despite the light that was penetrating from above. As he made his way down the western side of the building he had time to hope his friend had been right, for if there was no door between here and the far corner of the building he didn't think he would have enough time to make it back into the relative safety of the garages.

He slid down the wall, his eyes huge orbs that desperately searched out their quarry, feeling more and more desperate the deeper down the alley he travelled. Then he saw it; jutting out slightly from the straight factory wall, it was undoubtedly a doorway. He breathed a sigh of relief and then wondered why; literally anything could be beyond the door, from a guard dog to an armed patrol unit, but if he didn't allow himself one minor victory at a time he may not make it through this sorry nightmare.

Taking a look over his shoulder to make sure the guard wasn't turning the corner behind him – he wasn't – Martin made it to the doorway. It was a steel reinforced door, the kind you would see in a bank or jewellery store, when Martin tried the handle he wasn't surprised to see it was locked. He bit his lip in frustration, what had he really expected? Before he had time for the disappointment to truly register he became aware of a change in the light to the corner of the factory; it was the torch beam, the guard was coming!

With no time to either make it back to the safety of the garages or to the next corner of the building Martin ducked into the shadows by the wall, pressing himself as far back against the natural rock as he could. It wasn't ideal, but with his dark clothes to blend into the surroundings it was his best shot. Glancing down to the end of the factory wall he could see the circular motion of the torches beam, cutting through the darkness and bobbing from left to right, up and down, corner to corner. The light brightened, then the guard was there, turning the ninety degree angle at the end of the factory wall and strolling down in Martin's direction. He was holding the torch in his hand, but even from this distance it was all too easy to see what was in his other, Martin recognised it from many an eighties action movie; it was an Uzi 9mm.

It was impossible to take his eyes from the weapon as the guard made his way slowly in Martin's direction. One squeeze of that deadly trigger would tear the businessman to shreds. He could hardly breathe; he was barely concealed here in the shadows next to the wall, the guard was apt to see him for sure. Then another break in the light occurred to Martin's left and he turned in time to see another patrol guard, torch in hand, turn the corner at the opposite end of the alley.

Martin's breath caught in his throat; now there was twice the chance of him being seen, twice the chance of him being caught, twice the chance of him being mown down in a hail of deadly fire.

The two men walked toward one another, lowering their torch beams so as not to dazzle the other; what do you know, even brutal killers could be courteous, and as they approached it was the arrival of the second guard that transpired to save Martin from almost certain detection. Had the original guard continued his observation of the perimeter wall he would have undoubtedly seen Martin cowering in the shadows next to the rocks, but having his colleague here was a distraction, and as the men approached one another they remained completely oblivious to the terrified Englishman cowering just yards from where they stood. Martin could hardly breathe; he clamped his lips shut tight, refusing himself the slightest chance of alerting them to his presence.

The men spoke in their mother tongue, their voices sounding high pitched and rasping to Martin, who would have despised their sound if they had spoken like Greta Garbo. One switched off his torch and attached it to his belt, then fished in his pocket and pulled out a pack of smokes, some brand Martin had never seen before, clearly Chinese. He offered one to the other guard who took it gladly, lighting it from the tip of the first guard's cigarette.

Martin watched the soft orange glow as the man took a drag of his smoke, secretly hoping that it gave the man cancer, and that he died a slow painful death with nobody to offer him comfort. It wasn't a particularly nice thought, but considering what men like these had done to Chang Martin felt it was justified.

The men exchanged what Martin assumed to be pleasantries, not understanding a single word they were saying, and then the first took a deep drag of his cigarette, dropped the butt to the floor, and stamped it out under his foot. They exchanged a few more words, then the first guard was continuing on his way, grabbing his torch back from his belt loop and switching it on as he continued in the direction of the far corner of the factory. The second guard stood for a second; his back pressed against the factory door, and took another long drag of his own smoke.

From his position right next to the door he was practically looking straight at Martin, but somehow whatever Gods existed both in Europe and far east Asia were smiling down on him this evening, for the guard seemed to look straight through him. He finished his smoke and dropped it to the floor, then, just as Martin felt he could hold his breath no more, he turned to the door and pulled a loop of keys from his belt. He found the right one and slid it into the lock, then turned it and listened as the bolt was drawn back.

Martin watched as the man opened the door on what looked to be a dimly lit corridor beyond and stepped inside. Then he pulled the door closed behind him and Martin was alone once more in the alley. He let out a huge exhale of breath, then sucked clean air into his pained and oxygen deprived lungs, panting as an old man will when dabbling in the realms of the clinically insane. Had the guard locked the door again behind him? There was only one way to know for sure. Creeping from his place in the shadows Martin stepped back onto the dirty path and up to the door; he reached out his hand, grabbed the handle and turned. To his utter amazement the door opened inwards and he could see himself into the corridor beyond. He didn't have much time; the guard had probably just taken a quick loo break and would be back at any moment, he had to act fast.

He stepped into a cool shadow filled corridor with floor tiles that lay askew of their positions and walls that were crumbling from within. There was a dank smell in the air and the fluorescent lights that lined the ceiling flickered in time with the sound of dripping which could be heard coming from a room nearby.

With wide eyes and a heart that was drumming out a calypso beat he slowly made his way forward. Any of the doors that led off from the corridor could lead to the toilet, if that was indeed where the guard was currently ensconced, Martin was very aware that one false move here could lead to his capture and most likely his demise, he had to tread very carefully. Without a clue as to where he was going or what he was indeed on the hunt for he randomly chose a door, it was one of the ones on the left of the corridor, and stepped up to it. He placed an ear to the door, listening for any sound from inside. When there was none he steadied his nerve, took a look over his shoulder to determine that he wasn't being watched and carefully pulled on the handle. The door crept open and he looked down into another ill lit corridor. He opened the door wider, stepped on through and then pulled the door closed behind him.

Now there were two doors separating him from the relative safety of the exterior of the building; he was actually doing this then, he could scarcely believe it himself. Swallowing through a dry, parched throat he made his way slowly along. There were no doors down here, but the corridor branched to the right at the end. The smell of dampness was stronger down here, as though a tonne of bed linen had been dipped in a stagnant pond and left to fester in a corner somewhere. Mildew clung to the walls and empty cigarette packets were discarded here and there amongst the litter of ancient butts.

Martin made it to the end of the corridor and paused before turning the corner; he poked his head round instead, ensuring that the coast was clear before turning. It was, so he battled against his desire to turn and flee this hellish place and crept along the side of the wall. He came to a small rectangular room, boxes were piled high against the wall and a couple of ancient tarpaulin's had been draped over a hospital gurney with a broken wheel. In one corner a huge spiders web was doing en excellent trade in mummified creepy crawlies, it was not the type of thing Martin wanted to be looking at when in such a foreboding location.

Only one door led from this room and it was on the wall opposite where Martin now stood, Martin sidled up to it, not wanting to reach out his hand to its cold handle but willing himself on all the same. He drew in a quick breath and then pulled the door gently open. He was in luck, the short corridor beyond was also empty and silent, there was a single door that was closed at the end, Martin fumbled his hand across Chang's camera for comfort, an aid to remind himself just why he was here, and then slowly walked towards it. Again he stood and listened, making sure all was quiet from beyond, when he was happy that it was he battled with his emotions for the final time that day and then slowly opened the door.

It opened up into a fairly large square room completely filled with filthy stainless steel kitchen units. There was a filthy stainless steel double basined sink with a filthy stainless steel shower head attached, filthy stainless steel work units that covered filthy stainless steel storage compartments and a filthy stainless steel rack with filthy stainless steel utensils hanging from it. Amongst the many filthy stainless steel artefacts on display here the ones that most caught Martin's eye was the two huge and equally filthy stainless steel meat cleavers.

The white haired man swallowed against that sickening lump that was forming in his throat; just what kind of operation was carried out in a room like this? And what exactly was the purpose of those grisly looking cleavers?

He stepped a little further into the room, all of his senses heightened, and in such a state it came as little surprise that he jumped in shock when the door clicked shut behind him. He stood staring at it for several moments, breathing all too fast, his heart beating way too hard. Finally his eyes narrowed from the football shaped protrusions that threatened to pop right out of his skull and he was able to unlock his petrified limbs and move again.

"Get a grip." He whispered, blinking at the moisture in his eyes. "You hear me now, get a grip."

He walked over to the huge double basined sink and peered inside. It was empty bar a thick wall of lime-scale and a neat coating of grime. The tiles above the sink were filthy and covered in grease, it made Martin's stomach turn to look at them, and the smell, like nothing he could describe, but if he was forced to try he would say it was week's old pork that had been left out in the sun. As he was about to turn from the sink something in the plughole caught his eye. A thin red rim circled the drain, and caught in the mesh of the plug dish was a tiny clump of flesh. Martin tried to swallow and found he was incapable; surely no meat would be prepared in this disgustingly filthy room, which left only one conclusion.

Martin lifted Chang's camera, activated the flash, and took a photo of the incriminating sink hole, hating every second that he had to look at the offending clump of doughy flesh. The flash was very bright in the gloomy room, the click of the camera very loud, it seemed to echo from the walls, though he knew that was a ridiculous notion.

Lowering the camera again Martin stepped back away from the sink, feeling his gorge starting to rise. Was this where they dismembered the bodies, ready to be burned in the incinerator? It was a terrifying and sickening thought and Martin battled to keep the meagre rations he had eaten down.

Suddenly a noise from out in the corridor alerted his senses. His head turned with the agility of a hawk, staring at the closed work room door. There were footsteps heading his way, and voices, he heard a door open and then they were closer still.

At first he did nothing, he was rooted to the spot in panic, then thankfully, he managed to pull himself back to his senses and used the adrenaline that had fired into his system to propel him into action. The footsteps and voices were growing louder still, just yards away from the closed door of the room in which he stood now as he took a survival instinct look about the room. In his terror he could have missed it, but luckily for him he did not. One of the stainless steel units had a sliding door that stood slightly ajar, from where Martin stood it looked empty; there was only one way to know for sure. He dropped to his knees, ignoring the flare of pain that rocketed up his thighs from his arthritis. He slid the door fully back and peered into the unit; completely empty. The voices were right outside the door as he clambered into the space, pulling the sliding panel almost completely shut as the door opened and three men entered. They were wheeling a hospital gurney with a crudely wrapped shade on top. They closed the door behind them and wheeled the gurney into the centre of the room.

Martin, who had left a slither of light in the door panel peered out, barely able to breathe as the three Chinese men relaxed back, two against the units at the opposing side of the room and one right next to where Martin lay, in fact if he pressed his head right up against the top steel panel of the unit and squinted down he could just make out the mans right leg.

They spoke loudly in Mandarin; Martin couldn't understand a word and he didn't care, he just hoped that their discussion would cover up the sound of his own laboured breathing. He glanced across at the Chinese man to the right side of the gurney, who had pulled a cigarette from behind his ear and was lighting it with a pink, plastic disposable lighter. He lit the tip and took a deep drag of his cigarette, blowing smoke out into the already murky air. As they continued their discussion one of them produced something from his breast pocket, Martin watched on from his place beneath the filthy worktop, petrified that they would turn at any instant and find him skulking down below their line of sight. As he watched on he realised what it was the young man had produced and his heart sank. The man who had lit the cigarette pushed the gurney to one side of the room then helped his friend as he produced a crude table made of old boxes and a trio of rough chairs. The man who had reached into his pocket now opened the cigarette pack sized box and started dealing the cards; he was here for the long haul.

Already uncomfortable, his arm and shoulders aching from laying on the cold, hard surface, Martin closed his eyes and tried to block out the world.

15

Martin blinked a couple of times then let out a huge pained gasp as pins and needles sawed into the joints of his knees and down his entire right side. He tried to move his head and bumped it instead against something hard and metallic. Confusion swept through him and for one awful second he thought that he was dead, or had been buried alive inside an ill fitting coffin. He drew in fast, deep breaths, and pressed himself up on one elbow. He banged his other arm against the roof of the coffin and it let out a dull thud in the otherwise silent room. Then he noticed the slither of light coming from the gap in the door and he manoeuvred to look outside.

Suddenly it all came flooding back; this was no coffin, it was a stainless steel unit in a wash down room inside the cursed factory. He must have fallen asleep while the men sat playing cards, and he had awoken to the silence of the room, still hidden in his place inside the storage unit. He was lucky that the room was empty now, for the noise he had made when he had awoken would have been enough to alert the deaf to his presence. The thought gave him a chill that ran the length of his spine; this was no place to be complacent with your surroundings.

Feeling suddenly claustrophobic and more than a little bit stiff inside the metallic tomb he stretched out his hand and pulled back the sliding door panel. He poked his head out, taking a quick look around to make sure he really was alone, and then crawled out of his hiding space with every muscle in his body jangling. As he stood he marvelled on the fact that he had fallen asleep; with his life literally hanging in the balance he had somehow found his way to the land of nod, a truly remarkable feat under the circumstances. The exhaustion of a terribly trying day had overcome him, as had the steady drone of the card game going on outside his place of sanctum. He had lain for a while, listening to the soft voices of the men speaking in some language that he would never understand, calling out their cards or asking for new ones from the bank, some time later his eyes had grown heavy, that was the last that he could remember.

Now he stood up straight and groaned as his muscles started popping back to life. He was racked with aches and pains from his night in the uncomfortable cell, but feeling the blood rush back into his system, waking up his limbs and tingling in his digits was pleasant enough. He looked down at his watch; it was a quarter after six in the morning on the twenty-third of December, just two days now before Christmas. Again his tired and bullied mind tried to return to his wife; again he refused to let it, this was no time for sentiment.

The gurney was still pushed up to the near wall with the indistinguishable form beneath the protective drape. It was obvious what he would find if he stretched out his hand and removed the cover, but Martin was helpless to stop himself. He steeled his nerve, not wanting to see the body that undoubtedly lay beneath, but knowing that he had to, if he could get a photo it may serve as the evidence he needed. Taking in a quick breath Martin whipped back the cover, only to be faced with more rolled up drapes; there was no body here. Exhaling breath in a bizarre mixture of disappointment and relief Martin took a step away from the gurney and rubbed his eyes in frustration. Then he took another look about the room; there were two doors, the one from which he had entered the room and the one directly opposite that led beyond the room. The way he saw it each door represented a choice; he could cut his losses and make his way back the way he had come, giving in to his desperate will to survive, or he could delve deeper into the factory, continue his quest for answers with a blatant disregard for his own safety. As strong as the pull was to head back through the first door Martin knew that this was only a temporary solution; Malik's goons were still hot on his trail, if he didn't find the evidence he needed how long could he actually survive on the run? At his age he didn't think it was very long.

For a long time he stared at the door, wanting with an almost profound desperation to be back outside the perimeter fence and heading down the path that led far from this God forsaken factory, then he squeezed his eyes shut tight, shook his head from side to side miserably and head towards the second door. He grabbed the handle and gently pulled the it an inch or two open, just enough for him to peek through and ensure the coast beyond was clear. A single light bulb hung from its dusty cord, flickering incessantly, it gave an almost strobe-like effect to the murky corridor beyond the door that made Martin feel a little nauseous. He lowered his gaze, pulled open the door and hurried down past the offending bulb. He made it to the end of the corridor and turned the corner at the end. An orange glow was coming from a large open space at the end, so he made his way towards it, when he reached the end of the corridor he discovered that the soft orange light was actually the natural glow of the sun as it crept above the horizon and shone through the large slanted windows that littered this side of the factory wall.

Martin guessed that he had worked his way to the front of the factory, and he gazed now into a huge open space that would have once housed whatever machinery for which the factory had found its purpose. Now it was silent and empty, the floor layered with a thick coating of dust, disturbed only by the foot tracks of the guards who passed this way on whatever errand they currently served. Martin waited a few moments to ensure he was alone in the enormous chamber, then slowly made his way along the left hand wall, heading towards a steel double door crested with ornate brickwork in the far corner of the room.

How much further into this hellish factory did he have to travel before he found something of what he was looking for? So far he had almost scared himself to death and for what reward? A photograph of a red ringed drain and a small clump of flesh that on camera could have been literally anything.

He was about halfway down the chamber when a noise froze him to the spot in fear; the door to the right of the empty space was opening. Quickly he ducked behind a crumbling pillar, and watched with wide eyes as a dark haired Chinese man casually walked through the room. His footsteps were very loud and echoed from the high ceiling as he made his way along. Luckily for Martin he did not see him lurking in his hiding space to the back of the room, but carried on towards the same double doors for which Martin was heading. As he got beyond the spot where Martin crouched in fear the businessman noticed the pistol grip of the handgun that protruded from his pants at the back, and it served to remind him just how out of his depth he really was.

The door opened and the Oriental man disappeared through, there was a soft swooshing sound as it closed behind him and then all was quiet in the huge empty space once more. Martin let out a pained gasp, he hadn't even been aware that he had stopped breathing until now, and stepped out from behind the battered pillar.

He was reluctant to follow the man through the doors, there was after all at least one man that way that could potentially end his life, but the only other option was the door in the opposing corner, and who was to say that the man hadn't just left a dozen armed guards through that way.

"In for a penny, in for a pound." Martin muttered, and followed the direction the man had taken, just as he had intended to do. He crossed the enormous room to the double doors and stood to one side, listening for any movement on the other side, when he didn't hear anything he drew in another deep breath then opened the right hand door a couple of inches. All was quiet beyond; sunlight was streaming through a large window that took up most of one wall in what was a relatively small room. The walls were white washed and lockers lined one wall. There were benches around the edges of the room and a filthy looking toilet and shower cubicle in one corner. Shirts and jackets were hung on pegs attached to the walls above the benches and shoes were stuffed out of the way on the floor. This was clearly a changing room, where the guards could come and change into their standard black attire, Martin found it wryly amusing, was there a clocking in machine as well? It seemed ludicrous, but to the criminally insane he guessed this was still a job.

Listening for a few more moments, just to be sure, Martin plucked up his courage and stepped into the factory changing room. The door slid closed behind him with that same soft swooshing sound and left him fully immersed in the room. He took another look around, considering looking for some other attire to change into, something that would help him blend into the background, just like Roger Moore in an old seventies Bond movie. It was a pointless thought on a number of levels; one it was highly unlikely he would find anything that fit him, two he was already dressed in black and grey, just like the armed guards who patrolled this facility, and three it made little sense in trying to blend in anyway, he could make his clothes look like those of the enemy but his face and his hair were a dead giveaway, he couldn't have looked less like a member of a Chinese criminal organisation if he had painted his face orange and wore a party hat and frilly cravat.

Martin sighed and stepped up to the window; from here he could see out onto the dusty forecourt to the front of the building. As he watched a guard stepped out into the sunshine, yawned and kicked up dust with his scuffed old boots. Martin slid back slightly against the wall in order to stay out of sight, though he remained in view of the forecourt. He was about to continue through to the other side of the changing room when he noticed a car drift into his line of sight from the direction of the road. It was a black limousine, the type of car that businesses used to ferry clients to their destinations, he had several himself at Sapient. As he watched the car made a huge arc, sending up a cloud of orange dust in its wake and came to a stop about ten feel from where Martin was standing.

The driver's door opened and out came the chauffer, dressed much as you would expect a chauffeur to dress; grey suit pants, pressed jacket and shirt, dark tie, grey cap and thick black shades. He stepped down to the back passenger door and with his leather gloved hand opened it wide, gesturing politely for his passenger to vacate the vehicle.

When the leg poked out from the back of the car Martin was surprised to see it was clad in tracksuit bottoms, a sneakered foot finding purchase on the gravel surface. But as the man stepped out Martin understood; this man truly was a big player in this particular game, but not one to dress in the manner of formal business. Haroon Khan, tall, skinny, his bony features surrounded tired looking eyes, the hair atop still overly gelled and combed into those wiry spiders legs.

Martin swallowed hard, his eyes huge and unblinking; he could feel his heart thumping away and his hands were gripped together, the knuckles as white as snow. He watched as Malik was ushered along towards the front entrance which appeared to be a little to the left of where Martin now stood, looking more than a little irritated to be up and attending to business at this ungodly hour. They were met at the door by a heavyset man in a suit, but Martin could not make out his features without pressing his face right up to the glass, and he didn't want to give up his position of relative safety unless he was absolutely forced. That said he needed to know what Malik was doing here, if he could get some photographic evidence of the meeting it may be enough to persuade Lau to go to press with the story. It was a slim chance but it was one he knew he had to take, and if that wasn't enough to spur him on he thought he could hear whistling coming from the huge chamber from which he had just come, quickly he made his way around the corner of the shower to where another door led out towards the factories main entrance.

He could hear voices from the other side, but he could also hear the whistler getting closer to the changing room, in a blind panic he ducked into the shower cubicle and pulled the mildew stinking curtain closed. As the door to the changing room opened he quickly turned the tap on the shower and pointed the head away from him, firing the water straight down towards the brown stained drain.

Through a tiny gap in the side of the curtain he saw the whistler, a middle aged man with a receding hairline enter the room and walk up to one of the lockers. Martin could barely breathe, if he decided to talk to his colleague in the shower Martin would be discovered for sure. Luckily the man was just coming off his shift and had nothing on his mind than getting home to bed. He continued to whistle as he changed from his industrial work boots and slid on a pair of battered old sneakers. Then he grabbed a jacket from his locker and a pair of Ray Ban sunglasses and head for the door, not stopping to close his locker door, in the world of major crime Martin guessed petty theft wasn't an issue.

The room fell silent again apart from the relentless thrum of the water spouting from the shower head; Martin switched it off at the tap and allowed himself a deep, luxurious breath. Slightly damp from the back spray of the shower he stepped from the cubicle and took a look about the room; satisfied he was alone he crept back around to the back of the shower cubicle and up to the door. All was quiet outside now, he assumed the voices he had heard moments earlier to have been Malik and the man he had flown all the way from London to meet; he hoped he hadn't missed his chance. Opening the door a crack he peered out into the corridor. From his place in the changing room he could see the huge double door entrance to the factory, the doors stood open and the early morning sunlight lit up what would have otherwise been a gloomy entrance foyer with numerous doors and corridors leading from its sides and rear. Two men stood guarding the door, each holding a machine gun of some kind and smoking cigarettes, Martin thought that if he had a pound for every time these guys lit up a smoke he could most likely give up the haulage business for good.

To the opposite side of the foyer a glass panel separated what would have once been the factory offices, back in a time when the factory served more of a purpose than pain and misery, Martin figured this would be where the mystery man had taken Haroon Malik. He opened the door another couple of inches and looked out at the two guards, they were talking contentedly with their backs to Martin, if he was going to move he needed to do it now before more people arrived and before he lost his chance with Malik.

For a minute he was too afraid to move, if the men turned and saw him as he passed he would likely be killed on the spot, just like Chang. Quickly he ducked back into the changing room and took a look around. There was a navy blue New York Yankees cap hanging from one of the pegs, it wasn't much of a disguise but anything was better than his silver hair and wrinkled face. He adjusted the strap at the back and pulled it on his head, pulling the peak down low, then he stepped back up to the door and steeled his nerve. If he was going to do this he couldn't be sneaking about in the shadows, he needed to walk out there with confidence, like he belonged here. It was a great thought in theory, but stepping casually out twenty feet away from where two trained killers carried machine guns and orders to kill on sight was no mean feat.

Nevertheless it had to be done; Martin closed his eyes, drew in several sharp breaths and then as quietly as possible pulled open the door. He stepped out into the foyer and walked as quickly and casually as he could across to the corridor to the side of the glass partition. He walked with his head down and from the corner of his eye he was sure that he saw one of the guards turn mid conversation and stare straight at him. He didn't slow his pace, just kept on walking towards the sanctum of the corridor and the guard continued his conversation, turning back to his friend and speaking in that same foreign tongue that had been Martin's enemy since the moment he had landed in China.

He reached the corridor and let out a huge rasping sigh of relief, putting a hand to his chest in a bid to steady a heart which was beating uncontrollably beneath his sweat soaked polo shirt. He could still hear the steady conversation of the guards and this steadied his nerve, as long as they didn't sound alarmed, as long as their voices were not drawing closer, he felt he had gotten away with his brazen show of courage, maybe God was on his side after all. When he felt that he had his nerve back under control Martin turned and looked down the corridor. The darkened passage led parallel to the glass partitioned offices, no lights illuminated the way, in fact Martin thought he could see a shattered bulb hanging from the cord of one of the fittings. The glass was frosted so it was impossible to see inside, but if Martin listened carefully and blocked out the noise of the guards he thought he could just make out a couple of voices coming from down the corridor.

With his camera tucked under his arm Martin made his way down the corridor, comfortable that he blended in with the shadows. He passed three dusty wooden doors, each leading into its own glass partitioned office space before he came to the door from which the voices emanated. Unable to make out exactly what they were saying he traced his steps back to the next closest door and ducked into the office. Office was a strong word for the devastation that awaited him; the suspended ceiling had caved in and panels and plaster dust littered the floor, the ceiling gaped like a yawning mouth and the rotting wood of long abandoned desks was smashed into pieces in the corner of the room. Rat faeces were everywhere, making Martin pinch his nostrils closed in disgust and green mould crept up the two plastered walls in the room. The frosted glass separated the room from the office to either side, and when Martin looked to his left he could see the shape of the two men sat in the room to that side. The businessman ducked low and hunkered down in the shadows next to the partition, listening in to the conversation as best as he could.

"………journey Mister Malik."

"If you could hold up your end of the bargain I wouldn't have had to make the journey in the first place." This was Malik, and now Martin could determine the difference in the depths and tones of the voices he could follow the conversation a little easier.

"You can point finger all you want, but you lose Rooley in London, you caused this, it could have all been stopped by you."

Martin swallowed hard, they were talking about him!

"Don't fucking start with me Wang, I've been up all night flying to this fucking shit-hole, I'm tired and I'm irritable. One of my men is in the fucking hospital because of that prick and I want to know what you're doing about it?"

"Relax, we have a saying in China, 'coming events cast their shadows before them', your man will be found."

"You fucking chinks, all about your fucking proverbs, well we have a saying where I come from too; 'time is money', and this little fucker has cost me a lot of both."

"You need to calm down, find perspective, meditate. Your man is wandering blind in a land he doesn't know or understand. The police will not help him, the government will not help him, now his only friend out here is dead too. It won't be long before he tries to flee the country and when he does we will be waiting for him."

"I'm glad you're so sure, at least one of us has confidence."

"He has nowhere to go, he was stupid to come here, he knows this, it is only a matter of time before he reveals himself to us."

There was a sigh from the adjoining room; Martin guessed that it was Malik. "Ok."

The man who Malik had referred to as Wang laughed. "You see, was there really a reason to be up at this time, I like to stay in my bed until lunch."

"Well my flight landed at five and I wasn't in the mood to go to a hotel."

"You are too pent up my friend, later I take you to excellent massage parlour, see if we can't rub away some of your frustration, for now, as you are here, how about a little tour of our facility."

"I suppose that would make sense."

"Mister Malik, you are an important client, you will be well looked after in your time in China, let me show you around the place, let you see how your money is spent, later we can enjoy delicious Chinese food, I don't want you to worry, your friend will be found, and when he is we will serve him swift Chinese justice."

Sat on the floor of the dilapidated office, only inches from where the two men were talking, Martin gripped his hands tightly together, trying to control the trembling that was running through his fingers.

"Fine." Malik replied in his usual matter-of-fact tone.

"Come." Wang said, and Martin watched as his shadow rose from his chair. "I think you are going to be impressed."

The shadows beyond the glass partition moved and twisted as the first man gestured towards the door and the two men moved out of the room. Martin could hear them leaving the office next door and steeled himself in case the man known as Wang decided to start his tour in the dilapidated office next door. He heard voices and the shuffling of feet outside the room, then they had passed and their commotion grew more distant. The businessman let out a breath, feeling thankful for his healthy heart, there was no way his old one could have coped with this relentless stress.

So Wang was clearly the facilitator of the operation here in China; but what good did that do Martin? He was frustrated at having missed his opportunity for photographs, and with both men partaking in an incriminating conversation he had found himself wanting for any kind of recording device; he was sure in hindsight that he could have done it on his phone somehow, but he was sixty-eight, not eighteen, technology would always be a mystery to him.

With a groan as his muscles protested Martin stood up from the cluttered floor, brushing plaster dust from his dark pants. He held Chang's camera in one hand, the strap about his neck, then quietly made his way back to the door. As he peered outside a couple of men were walking from the back of the foyer to the exit. Martin quickly ducked back inside and waited for them to pass. When he was sure the coast was clear he opened the door again and peered back outside, all was quiet so he tip-toed out of the office and made his way back towards the foyer. At the end of the darkened corridor he looked out into the sun drenched space, trying to decide on his next move. To the rear of the foyer the room opened up into a wide looking corridor that branched to the left, as there was no sign of Wang and Malik he decided this would be his next port of call.

The guards at the sun dazzled entrance were still engrossed in their conversation, their backs turned to the inside of the building, with his head low and the cap still there to disguise as much of his face as possible Martin adopted a proven philosophy and marched out into the foyer as though he had every right to be there. Again the plan worked, and he crossed the space unnoticed. The corridor beyond with the aged yellowing plaster branched in two directions, Martin took the path to the left for he could hear distant voices on his right, he made it to a wooden door and paused to gather his thoughts.

He had been incredibly lucky so far, he had literally been here for hours now and had so far managed to avoid any contact with the dozens of armed guards and morally redundant workers who had made this their profession, surely if he continued in this manner his luck was bound to run out soon? It was a risk he had to take, without evidence Lau wouldn't take the story to press, without the story going to press he was stuck in this nightmare forever, however short that may be with hardened thugs on his trail.

Martin grabbed the handle of the wooden door and pulled; it opened onto a room bright with morning sunshine. It was a large space, one that would undoubtedly have housed more machinery in a time when the factory was part of a less menacing industry; now it was empty, with only rusting bolts and brackets protruding from the whitewashed floor to provide any clue as to what had happened before. The floor split into two levels, with a slope to the left leading down to a second floor space that ran parallel to the first room, about eight feet lower down. A dusty white rail separated the two, preventing any unfortunate accidents in the days when the room would have been alive with activity. There was an unpleasant odour in this room, different to the stale and musky smells that had accompanied his journey so far; this wasn't a smell of damp and decay, but something far less pleasant.

Due to a wall on the right that housed a small abandoned office space the far right hand corner of the room was obscured from view; it wasn't until Martin ambled down to the end that it opened up to him and he pressed back to the wall in panic. There was a guard in the room, stood with his back to a reinforced steel door, about a hundred yards from where Martin was standing.

His chest was rising and falling as he remained fixed to the wall, wondering what he should do. He could double back the way he had come, try the corridor to the right, but there had been voices that way too, besides, what was beyond the reinforced door? Why was there somebody left to guard it? If he was looking for answers, those finely tuned instincts were telling him they lay in here.

"Come on come on come on!" He whispered, trying to find the courage to peel himself away from the wall. It was easier said than done, a hail of machine gun fire could turn him into so much ragu in a matter of seconds. Knowing that he was blocked from view by the office wall he slid back towards the door he had entered by and edged over to the other side. Using the theory that if he couldn't see the guard the guard more than likely couldn't see him, he crouched down low and shuffled forwards towards the ramp that separated the room onto the two split levels. It was about five feet forward that the right leg of the guard came back into view. Ok, he would have to get even lower, time to think like a snake, it was literally as low as he could go. As quietly as he could Martin swung the camera strap around so the camera was pressed against his back and hunkered down to the floor, placing his flattened legs and chest flush to the dirty concrete. With his mouth just an inch from the ground he used his hands and knees to slowly slither forward, keeping as low as he could as he moved so the guard in the far corner would not see him. It was hard going, and incredibly painful on his elbows and knees, but he persevered, he was pretty sure that a hail of bullets slamming into his head would hurt more.

Inch by inch he crept forward, until his head was below the level of the upper floor on the downward slope. If he could get far enough down the ramp so that his entire body was below the upper floor level he could raise up a little from a laying position. He used this as his motivation as he scraped his knuckles and his knee caps on the unforgiving concrete, pulling himself further and further forward. It was exhausting, and he was terrified that his laboured breathing as he edged on and on would eventually become audible to the guard.

Then another thought struck him, one that was even more terrifying than the thought of being heard; what if somebody came into the room now? Entered the room by the same door that he had, and saw him laid down on the floor making his way down the slope. It would almost be comical if the connotations were not so grave. He just had to keep the faith that they would not; somebody had been looking out for him so far, he had to believe that it would continue to be this way. In a similar vein what if there was close circuit television in the room? Somebody could be sat in a control room watching him right now. He had to believe that there wasn't, the crime syndicate could afford to be blasé with the police in their pocket, besides, he had not seen a camera so far, hopefully it would stay that way.

Eventually he was far enough down the slope to be several feet below the level of the upper floor, feeling protected from view by the ascending wall to the side of the ramp, increasing inch by inch as the slope descended lower, he pushed up into a press-up position, then with his knee at a right angle, gently rose so he was crouched down at the side of the wall. From this position he could peer over the lip of the rise, there was about a ten inch gap before the white painted metal rail started. He could see the guard, stood looking bored at the reinforced door. He was a stocky man with close cropped black hair. His gun was held across his chest at a seventy-five degree angle, again Martin was unsure of the make or design, but he knew a machine gun when he saw one and he had watched enough Sylvester Stallone movies to know the damage it could do to him if he was caught. He noticed something else as he crouched staring at the guard; his fear of being heard panting as he made his way down the slope had been unfounded, the man was wearing iPod earphones.

Ok, so maybe he could fire off a couple of shots from Chang's camera without the man hearing the sound of the shutter. This would be good evidence indeed, not enough for Lau to go to press but a talking point for sure. Keeping low he lifted the camera, switched it on and aimed the lens at the guard. As he did something else caught his attention, he was zooming in on the guard, trying to get the best possible shot when he noticed the deadbolt on the door. It was the kind you slid across from the outside, the kind that you used when you weren't trying to prevent people from getting in, but to stop something getting out.

He clicked the button on the top right of the camera a couple of times, feeling conscious of the sound it made as he took his photos despite the earplugs of the guard. With his head back below the rise he took a look at his shots, they were pretty good, showing a clear image of the guard, his machine gun and the door behind him. It wasn't enough though, and he knew it, the shots didn't prove anything, he needed to see what was beyond that door.

Martin poked the top half of his head up above the floor of the upper level, looking across at the guard and the mysterious door; he was considering doing something to try and attract the guard's attention, knowing that this was both rash and dangerous, when a bleeping sound brought him back to a reasonable level of sanity. The noise made him duck back out of sight, but a moment later he realised what it was. It was the radio unit that was attached to the guard's lapel; somebody was trying to contact him.

As the businessman listened to him answer the call, speaking words that would always sound like gibberish to him, a terrifying thought entered his mind; there was a camera after all, hidden somewhere in the room, and the guard was being alerted to his presence, in a matter of seconds his time on this earth could be up. He glanced down the slope in a panic, looking for an escape route, a door or a shutter back to the outside, but there was nothing, the door he had entered the room by was the only door in the room.

Then foot steps crippled any hope of escape, for he was paralysed with fear, unable to move a single limb, as though rigor mortis had set in and turned his muscles to cardboard.

He waited in anticipation and fear, knowing that any second now the guard was going to turn the corner at the top of the rise, he would bark something undecipherable in his native tongue and Martin's sixty-eight years on this earth would come to an abrupt end in a hail of fire and bullets. He screwed his eyes shut tight, drew in his breath, and waited for the inevitable end.

The next sound he heard was the door creaking on its ancient hinges; at first he couldn't understand it, then when he recognised it for what it was he felt it could only be more guards coming to join in on the action. He waited with his eyes clamped shut for the real terror to begin, and waited, and waited.

All was silent in the room.

Martin forced his eyes to slowly open, and starting to feel light-headed allowed himself a small intake of breath. It was still silent. How could this be? Afraid to turn his head he stared straight forward at the white washed wall, listening out for any sound. He was scared that if he turned his head the guard would be there, directly behind him on the upper level of the room, taunting him like a cat to a mouse.

This is insane, force yourself to look Martin force yourself to look!

With muscles that seemed to creak he slowly turned his head, feeling sure he would be crying out in fear in just a moment, but there was nothing. Nobody stood behind him on the upper level; nobody stood watching him at the top of the rise. Breathing properly now he gently moved into a sitting position, all his joints feeling as though they needed a good oil. Nothing, the room was silent and empty.

Martin pushed himself up to his feet and looked about the room, it really was empty, the sound of the door had been the sound of the guard leaving, but for how long? This terrible mistake had got to end, he had to get out of here and now!

The door!

It was like a scream in his brain; Martin ambled to the top of the rise, torn between his desire to run and his need to look in the room.

Leave now and it was all in vain.

Yeah but I'll survive.

For how long exactly?

With a throat that felt as dry as burnt leaves he looked across at the reinforced door, the dead bolt slid shut to keep something firmly inside, this was why he had come, he felt it in his bones, it was in every ounce of his being, he simply couldn't afford to pass this opportunity by.

"Thank you Lord, thank you for watching over me." He whispered in the quiet of the room, and made the sign of the cross over his chest. Then he was hurrying over to the far corner of the room, to the storage container and the reinforced door.

The smell, the nasty one that had curled his nostrils when he had entered the room was stronger from here; he tried to ignore it, needing to remain focused on the task at hand. He took a look over his shoulder; he was still alone in the room. He paused at the door, gathering his nerve. His hand was trembling as he lifted it to the bolt; there was a loud clang in the otherwise silent room as it slid back, metal on metal. Beyond the door something stirred, a low murmur started and Martin withdrew in fear.

Needing to remind himself why he was here, needing to picture Chang as he slid lifeless to the floor, needing to picture Rose as she hurried up the motorway to hide out at her sisters in Bolton, needing to visualise the picture of the cute little girl with the pigtails, the one that had smiled from the picture on Chang's wall, Martin called on every ounce of courage he had left. Then he stepped back to the door, and with a heart that wanted to burst out of his ribcage pulled on the handle, the heavy door slowly swinging open to reveal what lay beyond.

It was the smell that hit him first; the businessman recoiled from the enclosed space in repulsion, covering his nose and his mouth with his arm, his eyes watering. It was like every bad smell he could muster in his fragile mind all rolled into one; blood and piss and shit and vomit, but mainly shit. It made his stomach lurch and for a second he feared he was going to add to the stench by throwing up himself. Somehow he controlled the urge and with the bile rising in his throat stepped back up to the door. What he saw made every hair on his ageing body stand to attention, made every nerve end jangle as though he was being probed with an electric current.

Inside the darkened room, cowering back from the entrance, covering their eyes from the sunlight that now lit up their prison home, a dozen Chinese captives cowered in fear. Amongst them were men, women and children, all were naked, all were filthy and severely malnourished, all pressed back as far as they could from the man at the door, terrified that they would be the next to leave the room, never to return. There was filth all over the floor, a horrible swill that was clearly a mix of faeces and urine; it was on their skin and in their hair. A terrible cacophony had started as he had opened the reinforced door, a sound loud enough to cover any other sound that may have occurred in the well lit room outside this terrible cell. With his mind in turmoil, with the horrifying wailing from inside the foul smelling cell, Martin did not hear the man who had entered the room.

Staring into the space that was occupied by these poor pitiful souls in an ever increasing mix of panic and terror Martin could not muster a single positive thought; he was completely overcome with emotion and fear. Then the hand locked onto his shoulder, and any hope of leaving this place alive was gone.

16

It was of course the guard; returned to his post from whatever task had been called of him, now in the possession of a high profile target, one that his unit had been briefed upon when they started their shift. Now he was his, and he looked forward to being the one to deliver him to his superiors. With the barrel of the machine gun pressed into Martins back he had closed the heavy metal door and slid the bolt back into place. The assets once more secure the Chinese man shoved hard into Martins back with his weapon, and the businessman, panting in terror stumbled forward.

He was led back the way he had come, out through the door, down the narrow corridor towards the foyer of the factory. His legs were weak, almost jelly-like, and more than once he nearly stumbled. It was as though every muscle in his devastatingly tired body had finally waved the white flag of surrender, and now he was utterly exhausted, only his heart, that cursed muscle that had caused all of this pain and misery, was still active, and it thumped away angrily in his chest, reminding him with every beat that he was a part of this awful shame.

The man barked orders as they moved, but Martin didn't understand a single word, he didn't need to to recognise the trouble he was in; he was never going to leave this factory, the best he could hope for now was a quick death. They entered the sun drenched foyer, the guards at the door turning and staring at the old man in the baseball cap, being subjected to an almost constant barrage of abuse from the man behind him with the gun. The commotion also alerted the two men in the office, the ones who had returned from a brief tour of the facility, and they appeared at the open office door looking more than a little bemused.

The one referred to as Wang simply stared open mouthed, but it was when Haroon Malik, gazing over his shoulder laid eyes on the terrified businessman that all Hell truly broke loose.

"You!" He snarled, pushing past his Oriental counterpart and marching down the narrow corridor to the foyer. Martin was pushed forward by the guard, adrenaline rushing now he was delivering his prize, and the old man collapsed to his knees in the middle of the open space.

Malik, who had always been an act first think later kind of a guy walked straight up to the bedraggled man and kicked him with all his force in the side of the head. The white haired man hit the floor hard, his head smacking off the cracked tile floor of the foyer and bouncing back again. At first he was so dazed that he didn't even feel any pain. For a second the room went white, as his brain struggled to remain conscious, a high pitched whine started in his ears, then, finally came the explosion of pain, it was as though his left ear and all of the left hand side of his face had been doused in petrol and set on fire, he would have screamed from the all encompassing agony if his breath had not caught in his throat.

The British-Asian crime lord, bent over the flailing man with a look of absolute fury on his features was screaming out words but to Martin, with his ears ringing as they were he may as well have been speaking in Mandarin as well. All he could hear was a muffled blur, and he was thankful for that at least.

It wasn't to last, gradually the hearing in his hurt, throbbing ear returned, noises and sounds at first, then words, and finally full sentences.

".....wh....hu.....chee.....I don......forget.....you think.....fucking kill you.....And if you thin......or going to get out.......ive you've got another thing com.....'"

"Calm down calm down my friend, let us see what we have here." It was the one who had been referred to as Wang; he had stepped up to the scene before him and placed a hand on his counterparts chest. Now, as Malik turned away in disgust, the Oriental man took another step forward and peered down at Martin, who lay on the floor feeling dazed and confused, clutching at his burning ear as if it might actually fall off.

The man was somewhere in his late forties, possibly early fifties, with a perfectly round face and thick black hair not unlike Chang's. He wore brown rimmed spectacles with amber vision lenses and had a thin moustache that reminded Martin of the old comic book character Fu-Manchu. He regarded Martin closely for a few seconds, the way you may regard a particularly unusual specimen in the rare fish tank of an aquarium, then he leaned back with his hands planted firmly on his hips and let out a huge belly laugh. Under other circumstances it may have been quite a jolly sound, but to Martin, lying on the dirty factory floor, fearing for his very existence, it was a terrible sound; full of angst and menace.

"This is the one? This is who caused all of the problem?"

"Don't misjudge that one Wang!" Malik stepped forward again, a look of blind hate on his face. "That little fucker's caused me a whole world of problems."

"He is just old man!" Wang said, the smile on his face never faltering.

"Old men have had plenty of time to learn their tricks, and this one's as wily as they come."

The Chinese man, no longer smiling, looked up at the guard who had marched Martin into the room and spoke to him in his own language, it sounded very brisk and business-like, not like the tone he had used before at all.

Still brimming with pride at his successful coup the guard allowed his gun to swing from its strap on his shoulder and leaned down to lift Martin to his feet. At the door the two sentries still watched on, enjoying the unexpected show that was helping pass their morning shift.

With his hand still pressed firmly over the searing pain in the side of his head Martin tried to stand up straight, but a combination of fear, exhaustion and unbelievable pain made him sag, and he slouched before the Chinese man with his knees trembling and a deep ache forming in the base of his spine.

"So, you are the cause for my friend here flying all the way from England."

Martin didn't reply, he couldn't even bring himself to look at the man, just stared down at the floor resigned to his inevitable fate.

"Are you alone?"

Martin nodded slowly. The Chinese man seemed satisfied, nodding himself.

"You can't take his word for it." Malik said, staring at Martin with a look that could have curdled milk. "He's a tricky old fucker, and he's had people working with him before."

"Maybe so, but he is a long way from home now, I think he is working alone." The Chinese man walked slowly around Martin, regarding him with fascination, the old man that was single-handedly trying to save the world.

"Martin Rooley." He said, as if testing how the name sounded out loud. "You are interesting character. Important man, head of major corporation, and yet here you are."

"You won't be needing this." Malik said stepping forward, and swiped the camera from around Martin's neck. The businessman watched it go with regret, his worst feelings confirmed, any hope of this ending rightly were gone.

"Did you find anything of interest?" Wang asked with a mocking smile. Martin just stared back at him, the pain in his face which had been flaring and urgent at first slowly turning to a dull throb.

"Guess it doesn't matter anymore." Said Malik, who proceeded to throw the camera hard at the tiled floor. It bounced about a foot high, breaking into three separate pieces, then he brought his sneakered foot down hard on the body of the camera and smashed it into roughly a thousand more. Martin swallowed and looked down at the floor. Resigned to the fact that he was unlikely ever to feel the breeze on his face again he battled to find the courage to voice his true opinion of the two men before him. When he eventually spoke it was in a dry cracked voice, but he soon found his composure, after all, he had nothing left to lose.

"Y-you may have won the battle….but you won't win the war."

"What you say?" Wang asked incredulously.

"You heard me, kill me if it does you, but know that I won't be the last, and next time, the person who comes for you may be younger and smarter than me, then you'll have nowhere to hide."

Wang threw his head back and laughed heartily again. Malik stared at Martin like something that had just crawled off the bottom of his shoe.

"You are very brave, I like that, but you are the first to challenge us and you will be the last. There is no happy ending here, not for you, not for your friends in the dungeon."

"How can you sleep at night?" Martin asked, looking at the Chinese man with real disdain.

"With over one hundred million Yuan in my account, I sleep very soundly my friend." The hateful man said with a smile and gave Martin a friendly pat on the arm.

"We're wasting time here, get rid of this son of a bitch and have done." Malik said, stepping forward and expressing his opinion with vigour.

"Patience my friend." Wang replied, placing a hand on his compatriot's chest to restrain him. "Mister Rooley will be taken care of, but first, I must have my curiosity satisfied."

Malik stepped back with a huff, looking towards the door in agitation, he had no jurisdiction here, had this been in London Martin had no doubt that he would have been lying in a pool of blood already, the life draining from his body.

"I hear about you, my friend here tells me your story." Wang said, turning and addressing Martin once more, who tried to stand as tall as he could under the other mans stare, not wanting to cower in his final moments on this earth. "You needed new heart, we provided that heart, without it you surely die, so tell me my friend, why this crusade? Surely you owe us your life do you not?"

"I was grateful for my heart." Martin said through dry, cracked lips. "For sure, more grateful than I'd ever been, but I didn't know where it had come from; I would have never chosen this, what you people do disgusts me."

"We do what we do so rich cunts like you can live!" Malik spat angrily, striding forward and pointing at Martin, again Wang had to restrain him. The guard shuffled nervously, clutching the pistol grip of his gun; at the door the two sentries grinned in excitement.

Biting his lip to control his ever escalating temper the British-Asian man turned on his heels and faced the door once more.

"You will have to forgive my friend; he doesn't see you like I do." Wang continued when he was comfortable Haroon wasn't going to lash out again. "I admire you Mister Rooley, so full of your British pride and principles, but really, where has it got you? You may have done very well in business, but in the real world, you are nothing but a tiny woodland mouse."

"Rather a woodland mouse than a sewer rat." Martin replied.

This time Wang did not laugh, nor did he smile, just regarded the white haired man before him coolly as he considered his options. "You are very quick to judge, but I am in the business of saving lives."

"You are in the business of kidnap and murder." Martin replied unfazed. "Try as you wish, you can never justify your actions, you are an evil man, and when your time comes, you're going to burn in Hell, you all are."

Wang's patience, like his furious colleagues before him, had finally reached its limit. He looked beyond Martin to the guard and spoke to him in his native language.

"And now it is with regret that your time is up my friend." Wang returned his attention to Martin. "You are going to be tortured to find out everything you know, then you are going to die."

Martin swallowed back his fear, desperately not wanting it to show to this pitiful man, but it was hard, he had not anticipated the possibility of torture, and the mere mention of the word had brought with it an urgent need to pee.

"About time too." Malik said, turning to face the businessman again.

"Would you like to stay and watch the proceedings?" Wang asked, as though he had asked if the other man fancied a couple of tickets to that night's game.

"You think I want to stay here any longer than I have to? I'm on the first flight back to London; I can sleep on the plane." Malik replied indignantly. "Make sure that son of a bitch is in the incinerator by noon."

"As you wish." Wang replied with a small smile. Then he addressed the guard in Mandarin once more, and suddenly the machine gun was prodding Martin in the back again. The guard barked undecipherable orders, and Martin turned in the direction he was being shoved.

As he was forced from the room Martin took one last longing look at the sunshine outside the doors, fearing it may be the last time he ever saw it again.

17

It had been Christmastime, just as it was now, only it felt Christmassy, unlike here. The decorations were all up and hanging from the trees and the lamp posts in the town centre and the shop windows, adorned in reds and greens, displayed their wares to the busy shoppers who rushed for last minute gifts and delicious goods to eat. It was Christmastime in Bolton in the late nineteen-sixties and all was well with the world.

The Christmas tree outside the Albert halls had been planted on a slight angle this year, causing tutts and hmmphs from disapproving passers by, but the young couple hardly seemed to notice. They were in love and the lights and ornaments that hung at an obscure angle could not cut through that innocent adulation that only the young seem to find in one another. As they crossed the road by the Octagon theatre three men wearing leather jackets, their hair slicked back with Brylcreem, walked out of the front door of the Balmoral. Two were smoking cigarettes with no filters and the third still held his half finished pint glass in one hand. Revellers, enjoying the Christmas spirit, or perhaps 'spirits' was more apt.

The young couple paid them no heed as they hardly did anyone these days as they walked up the road towards the bus station, but as they passed the one with the pint glass purposefully pushed the young woman's bag from her shoulder.

"Hey! She protested, turning to face her aggressor.

The men, who had passed by now, turned and laughed, one of them grabbing at his crotch and giving it a good squeeze to show just how sorry he was.

The young woman's partner, flushed with love for his blushing damsel and in need of showing he was man enough to stand up for her when the chips were down, was not going to miss a display of bravado that could cement him even deeper in the girls affections.

"I think you should apologise." He said, stepping forward and puffing out his chest like a peacock. His mistake was apparent at once. There were three of them; there was only one of him. What had he been thinking? He should have just put his arm around her shoulder, told her to ignore them and continued on their way. What's more she would have probably respected him for it; but this was the nineteen-sixties, still a few decades away from the age of new men, and one simply didn't cower away from defending his woman's honour.

"What you say?" The one with the beer glass snarled. His two friends stepped forward and stood by his side, their cigarettes billowing smoke from their nostrils and the corners of their mouths.

Swallowing back his sudden pang of fear, knowing he could only continue with his foolish show of guts now that he had started, if he was to turn away now he could be branded a coward forever, and he loved the young woman way too much to ever allow that, the young man stepped forward himself.

"No don't!" The young woman protested, speaking the only words of sense in the whole sorry charade.

"I said I think you should apologise." The young man repeated, hoping the waver in his voice would not betray him.

"Is that so?" Beer glass exclaimed, and stepped up so he was only inches from the young mans face, his friends joined him and surrounded their prey like hyenas hunting in a pack. The young man, petrified now but still determined not to show it, tried to lift his hands to push the man away, but before he could his friends had grabbed him by the arms.

"Hey!" The young woman screeched, her eyes huge with terror, and as she watched on the thug who had pulled her bag from her shoulder lifted his pint glass and smashed it hard into the young mans face, covering him in a thick foam of beer suds before his lip was split in three places and blood gushed from the wound. The young man dropped to the floor as a Chelsea boot came crashing into the side of his head, making him see stars.

It could have all ended very badly indeed if the cavalry hadn't arrived in the form of the landlord of the Balmoral, coming out to grab a lungful of fresh air from the smoky fog inside the pub. The young woman rushed to him for help and heavyset northerner that he was he had chased the men away down the street, claiming when the young man had come round that the boys had been spoiling for a fight all evening.

All was well in the world again, and although badly shaken, the young couple had made it home safely, enjoyed a wonderful Christmas together and gone on to live happy and fulfilling lives.

It had been for many years the single most terrifying experience of Martin Rooley's life, but that was in a time when he had not yet learned that his heart was slowly dying, when he had not been threatened with a gun, when he had not entered a secure guarded facility and discovered the naked captives of a terrible underground crime ring.

Now, sat on a wooden chair in a filthy room in the old factory, he had a brand new entry in his ever growing chart of terror; and it had entered straight in at number one.

The fat man laughed as he looked down at the ever growing pool on the floor and the dark stain that was forming on the front of Martin's trousers. He bellowed something that Martin couldn't understand, but if he had spoken Mandarin he was pretty sure that the fat man was mocking him for having just pissed his pants in outright fear.

He had been brought to this room by the guard that had caught him snooping in the filthy cell, the barrel of his machine gun pressed into his spine the whole way. They had wou0nd through the seemingly endless corridors with Martin staring down at his feet, resigned to his fate. Eventually they had arrived here, in a white tiled room with a huge patch of green mould on the ceiling. There were no windows; a single flickering bulb hung from its cord, making Martins eyes blink every few seconds, it seemed cruelly unfair that this was to be the last light he would ever see. The guard had brought the rickety wooden chair from a store room to the right and had made his captive sit while he radioed the true master of ceremonies for what was to come.

The beefy man had arrived some ten minutes later, practically salivating at the prospect of a little early morning torture. What struck Martin as ludicrous though, as he sat and waited for the fun to begin, was the realisation that the man didn't speak a word of English. What was the use of torturing him for information if he didn't understand a single word that was being said?

Wearing a sweat stained shirt and jeans, his hair tied in a ponytail at the back, the fat man had commanded the guard to watch over Martin while he taped his hands together at the back of the chair, then, satisfied the old man wasn't going to cause him any trouble, the guard was dismissed. He left the room reluctantly, clearly wanting to stay and watch the show, but fat man liked to work alone.

It had been fairly simple at first, a little bit of mocking from the greasy heavy-set man followed by a couple of swift punches to the gut. Those first initial slugs had the same impact as a sledgehammer to the stomach, and Martin doubled over in shock and pain, his head lolling down to his legs as he battled to regain his breath.

Could this really be happening? He was the CEO of Sapient Trans Global, a FTSE 100 company. He had enjoyed a hugely successful business life but prided himself in being an even greater success in marriage. He was a happy man, had lived a happy life, a comfortable life, just what in the hell was he doing here, sat in this seat, being tortured by this horrible man, waiting to die? It was surreal, and though the hope remained that he would at some point wake to find this was all a terrible dream, it was fruitless to give it any serious thought. He was going to die here, alone in a foreign country, in a world that he didn't understand, and there wasn't a damn thing he could do about it.

Then, as the man continued to laugh and to jeer, another thought crept into Martin's horrified mind, and the implications made him shudder. How had Malik known that he was here? He had made it clear that he had flown to China personally to ensure of Martin's capture, and was heading for the first flight back to London now that it was done. But how had he known? It troubled the businessman as he stared at the floor, desperately trying to fill his aching lungs with oxygen.

Somehow, to this point, Martin had managed to hold his water, but the urge to pee was becoming as excruciating as the torture, he could feel the piss right at the tip of his penis, and his balls ached in desperation.

Suddenly a hand lashed out and struck him across the face. Martin's head rocked back and bounced around for a couple of seconds as the impact started to register. The pain was incredible, like a red hot poker had been pressed into the side of his face, it flared from his jawline to his temple, and he felt lucky that his cheekbone had not been shattered by the blow. The feeling was short lived; the other hand struck out and connected with Martin's left eye, connected hard. His head rocked to the right and a low gasp escaped his throat. Blood exploded from a wound in his eye socket and dripped down, clinging to the corners of his eyes before streaking down his cheek and collecting at his chin. For a couple of seconds he saw stars, they danced before his eyes impairing his vision. When he had read of this in books he had always thought it to be a myth, but what do you know, it was actually the truth, if you took a big enough whack to the head you really did see stars. When his vision slowly returned he noticed for the first time that he was alone in the room. He tried to lift his head up straight; it was the only positive move towards escape that he managed before the man returned. In his hands he held a red box covered in dials, about the size of a small record player. Two cords protruded from the box with bulldog clips at the end, a final shorter cord held some kind of hand trigger. Martin, who had seen enough Bond films and crime dramas to feel pretty savvy on torture techniques knew it for what it was straight away, and that was when his bladder finally released.

Martin pissed, boy did he piss, it was like a camel piss, and it soaked his trousers and formed a huge pool of stinking liquid on the floor. Great, now he had to die in piss wet trousers, could life be any crueller? It seemed it could, for the fat man, surprised at first at the sight of the white haired man pissing his pants, now threw back his head and roared triumphant laughter. Martin wanted to cry, to throw back his head and cry as he had done as a child when he had fallen and scraped his knee, but that was one pleasure that he would not allow this disgusting man. Instead he squeezed his eyes shut tight and tried to block out the world. It was hopeless; there was no happy place, not when you were consigned to death in a stinking hell hole on the far side of the world.

He could feel heavy, rough skinned hands lifting up his polo shirt, it gathered in a roll beneath his armpits, tight enough to not slide back down. Then an index finger was tracing the length of his scar, and Martin thought that he might scream. He didn't, somehow he managed to keep his emotions in check, but it was far from easy. Then the electrodes were attached to his chest, they stuck to his skin around his wiry white chest hair, just above each nipple.

Slowly Martin opened his eyes, just tiny slits at first, then the full eyes. He didn't want to see what was about to happen, but he needed to know when the shock would come, needed to brace himself at the right time. The fat man had his back to him, fiddling at the dials on the old red box, Martin pulled at the tape that bound his hands; it was no use, there was no give there, and even if there was, what could he do? The man outweighed him by at least a hundred and twenty pounds; he'd squish the old man like a grape.

Satisfied that he had set the machine up at the right level the fat Chinese man turned back to where Martin sat, the box emitting a low hum that the businessman found decidedly unpleasant, nothing good could make a noise such as that.

The Oriental man, a huge grin on his fat jowelled face, asked Martin something in his native tongue, exasperated the white haired man shook his head from side to side.

"I don't understand you! Don't you see?"

Unperturbed Wang's chief torturer continued to grin his goofy grin, then waved the hand paddle in front of Martin's face.

"You don't need to do this." Martin said, knowing it was useless but needing to try, even if he did understand it wouldn't make the slightest bit of difference, still he persisted. "I have money, a lot of money, you could be rich, just get me out of here, please get me out of here." In his desperation his emotions almost betrayed him, but he fought back the tears just before they slipped from his eyes.

The fat man was still taunting him with the hand paddle, tapping it with his free hand and waving it before his captives bruised and bloodied nose and all the while the horrible red box gave off its sickening drone.

"Do it then, just do it." Martin said resignedly, his head lolling as the pain in his face throbbed like a living thing.

The torturer uttered something in Mandarin, then with his narrow eyes widened in excitement pulled the prongs together on the hand paddle and a jolt of absolute misery exploded in Martin's chest. He yelped in shock and pain, he had known that it was going to be bad but this was so far beyond anything he had expected. The thin white strands of his hair stood to attention on top of his head and his chest felt as though it were burning, like the short white hairs had actually caught fire, Breathing rapidly as the pain subsided Martin looked down to make sure this was not the case. It wasn't, it just felt as though it was.

Now the tears did spill from his eyes, he couldn't help it, if anyone could contain their emotions through a situation like this they were a stronger man than Martin. He no longer cared; he just wanted this misery to be over.

"Please, please I'll tell you anything you want." He pleaded between pained breaths. "I'll tell you anything you want but please no more."

The fat man just laughed, then he crossed back to the red humming machine a couple of feet away and turned the wattage dial a little higher.

"Oh no, oh no please no." Martin begged, his eyes wide with alarm. Again the fat man waved the paddle before him, wanting to savour the terrified look on the old mans face.

The pain had been unimaginable with the dial turned low, now the man had notched it up another couple of degrees Martin wasn't sure if his body could handle it, nice young heart or not. His breath came in rapid bursts, behind his back his fingers laced together and squeezed until the knuckles turned white, he steeled himself, waiting for the inevitable pain.

As the Chinese man pressed on the hand paddle once more Martin drew in a sharp breath and squeezed his eyes shut tight, fearing they would pop right out of their sockets if he didn't. This time the shock that blasted through his chest lifted him a couple of inches off his seat, his arms spasmed, quivering against the impact and his teeth rattled in his skull. It was an almost unimaginable level of pain, and a tiny yelping sound escaped his mouth as more piss puddled on the floor. Martin crashed back down into his seat, sweating from head to toe and shaking violently as the evil torturer bellowed laughter again. His pants were sodden with urine and the pool on the floor had grown bigger still, Martin was glad his instruments were still in order, he felt that second shock would have fried his balls for sure.

Then the man was turning back to the machine; Martin watched him go with dazed, confused eyes. Surely not, surely no more? He watched as the man turned the dial further still and a string of slaver dripped from his lip, landing in a small pool beneath the electrode that rested above his left nipple.

Surely a higher voltage would kill him? Maybe this was a good thing; he was going to die anyway, may as well get it over with.

"Rooooose." He muttered as the man turned back with the hand paddle. Although slumped in the chair, resigned to his fate, martin became aware that his hands were now a little looser in the duct tape behind his back, that second shock must have jerked him loose of his restraints.

Was there hope? It was foolish to think so, but it was human nature, the mind wanted to believe even when the odds were stacked so heavily out of favour.

Then the man was turning to him again, and was Martin imagining this or had he just licked his lips in anticipation? If the last shock had made him piss his pants, surely a higher voltage would have him soiling his trousers too? He may be resigned to his fate here but dying in shitty underwear was not a prospect that he relished.

His chest was rising and falling rapidly as he looked up into the narrow eyes of his torturer, hoping to find any level of humanity there; it was hopeless, the man was actually enjoying this. Martin didn't understand how anybody could get off on hurting another human being, but this man clearly was, there was no chance of appealing to his better nature for he didn't have one.

Suddenly the man pressed on the paddle again and a shock with all the force of a lightning bolt jolted into Martin's chest, sending him a foot into the air and ripping his left hand out of the duct tape in the process. His heart stopped beating for what felt like an eternity, though in reality it was only a matter of seconds, and when his flailing body came crashing back down onto the wooden chair the pain that coursed his body jangled every nerve. He drew in a sharp breath as his heart kicked back into operation and collapsed back in the chair, his head lolling backwards, his tongue hanging from his mouth like a hot Doberman. He was shaking from head to toe, his whole body filmed with a fine sheen of sweat, and he felt nauseous and weak, his head throbbing as though he was in the throes of a severe migraine.

"No more…… please…….. no more." He muttered, knowing it was futile but not able to prevent himself.

When he was a young man, still years away from the life changing events that would map out the course of his life, he had worked one summer in a textile mill; one hot July afternoon he had lost his concentration while loading cotton into a bottom feeder. He had slipped and caught his hand between the pressers, an excruciating pain that had him screaming and crying in agony. It had taken three burly men to prize the press apart, and when they did Martin's hand was crushed like a burst balloon. That was his summer of labour over, and he had spent three months in the Royal Bolton Hospital with his shattered fingers wrapped in a heavy cast. He had not suffered pain like it for the next fifty years; today that pain had been doubled.

He was still panting heavily when he realised that his hands were free of the restraints that had held him prisoner, they were hanging freely behind his back. So what? He couldn't overpower this man, he was huge.

Maybe he didn't have to.

The man was back at the machine again, his gut pressing into the table and turning it into an ugly looking sideways V, with one half of the letter on top of the table and one half beneath. He reached out to the dials, turned it up a little, thought better of it then hitched it up to full power. The hum from the red box became unbearable, like the sound of a plane taxying on a runway, there was smoke starting to billow from the fan on top as well; the fat man was pushing his luck and he knew it, but the temptation to cause the ultimate pain was too much for him to possibly resist.

Martin watched all this with mounting horror, knowing that his ageing body really couldn't take any more, then an idea occurred to him and he realised that the evil mans persistence could also be his downfall. It was a slim chance, a one in a thousand long shot, but a slim chance was better than no chance at all. Martin lifted his feet off the floor and propped them up onto the bar at the bottom of the chair, as the man turned around to face him again he readied his tired arms, tensing and un-tensing them behind his back to get his circulation flowing.

The man stepped forward, the same slack jawed expression on his round features, until he was only a foot or so away from Martin, he wanted to be up close and personal to the action when this one went off. The businessman readied himself, knowing this was the difference between success and almost certain death. In the background the machine continued its deafening hum.

Martin knew he had to time this just right, if he was too quick the fat torturer would anticipate his move and prevent it, if he was too slow he would be fried in the chair like a rasher of streaky bacon. He watched the mans eyes twitching from left to right, looking for the tell tale signs. The man waved the paddle before his face, that was the first sign and Martin brought his arm as far around his side as he dared. Then the tongue flickered out and licked at his sweaty lip; that was sign two, Martin drew in a quick breath. The hand holding the paddle paused before the fat mans chest, Martin watched the vain in the Oriental's right arm pull and the muscle tense, this was the third sign and the most important of all, it was now or never. With his breath caught in his throat and his feet safely raised form the dampness on the floor Martin shot his hand round the front, grabbing the wire to the electrodes attached to his chest, pulling then releasing his hand as the fat men pressed on the paddle. There was just enough time for his expression to turn from triumph to shock to outrage, all in the space of less than a second, as the electrodes were dropped into the pool of piss that surrounded Martins wooden chair.

There was a huge bang as the electric charge exploded into the puddle of urine which acted as a conductor and sent a deadly charge of electricity through the fat mans hand which held the paddle and on through his body, sending shock waves through his nervous system that would in turn fry his brain.

The fat man squealed, a terrible sound, much like the mewling of a dying pig, to the side of the room the machine exploded in a hail of sparks, crackles and bangs, smoke billowed up from the top of the torturers head and his eyes rolled up to reveal only the whites. He staggered for a few seconds, a steaming corpse on legs, then collapsed to the floor landing in a heap in the puddle of piss that had been his demise. To the side of the room the machine gave out a couple of hissing pops, and then like its owner, met its untimely end.

Martin sat in the chair, his eyes huge and wild, looking at the man on the floor with the smoke escaping his loosened jaw. He couldn't believe that it had worked; he couldn't believe that he was free. Afraid to place his foot in the pool that surrounded the fat man, fearful there may be still some charge left lurking there, he stretched out to the left and found a dry part of the floor, then with his muscles aching and his body shaking he pushed himself up from the chair and took a step to the left. His legs buckled beneath him and he collapsed to the floor, panting, his body convulsing in spasms. He waited a few moments, wanting to close his eyes and block out the deadly pain that racked every joint in his body, but he was afraid he would slip into unconsciousness, and then all of his troubles would be for nothing. Instead he rolled onto his back and waited for the worst of the shakes to calm, when they did he dragged himself to the edge of the room and sat with his back to the wall, looking down at his chest where two black scorch marks blotted his skin, the white hairs above his nipples singed away.

He had to move, had to get away from here, he had been granted another chance and he had to take it, grab it with both fists. Letting out a pained gasp he managed to pull himself into a half standing position, with his body bent over his trembling knees. He side stepped around the still steaming man and edged towards the door. He didn't know what lay in the corridor beyond, for all he knew there were a dozen armed guards just waiting for him to make his move, but he didn't care, he hadn't died at the hands of the evil torturer, and he didn't intend to let the victory go to waste.

With his breath still coming in short, sharp gasps, and his tortured body and puffed up face shrouding him in untold pain, Martin opened the door of the filthy torture chamber and stepped outside.

18

Escape, get out of here, find the exit and run, as fast and as far as he could. This had been his prime motive when he had left the room, an impulse that had been almost impossible to overcome. There had not been an army of armed guards standing sentry in the corridor, there had not even been one; this was how little a threat they saw him. Martin hoped that he could use this to his advantage, initially in his plans to escape, and then, as both his guilt and his better judgment took hold, in his quest to free the fateful prisoners. He simply couldn't leave them here, even if he hadn't needed them to make his own end his conscience could never be clear knowing he had left them to die in that stinking room; he would rather die himself, and with the odds stacked so heavily against him probably would.

The maze of corridors that extended from the torture chamber were exactly that to Martin; a maze. He didn't recognise a single turn, when he had been led along them by the guard who had captured him looking into the prison cell he had been in a desperate and terrified frame of mind, positive that he was walking to his death. He hadn't noticed a single thing, and now, still desperate, still terrified, but with a renewed sense of purpose, he found himself lost in the endless myriad of rooms and passageways that filled the enormous derelict factory.

A couple of times as he made his way slowly through the factory he heard voices ahead; on both occasions he froze paralysed with fear, luckily for him on both occasions the voices drifted into the distance and he was free to continue his search.

He passed through a dingy corridor with a spider's web that covered three quarters of the ceiling and came to a small grey room with a staircase leading up to the next floor. He hadn't even considered what may be on the upper floors of the factory; what if there were more rooms with more prisoners, trapped in a den of their own filth, awaiting execution on the surgeons table? Martin couldn't allow himself to think of that, he had more on his plate than he could handle considering how he could free the prisoners that he was already aware of. Besides, in the slim possibility that he would actually succeed in his mission he would hopefully bring the curtain down on this whole sorry institution, and anyone that was trapped on the upper floors of the factory would too be free.

Keep telling yourself that, the sly voice that taunted inside his mind whispered, keep pretending you're gonna get out of this, if that's what makes you feel better. You have no chance of escaping the building with your head still attached to your shoulders, and you think you're going to do that and free the prisoners into the bargain? Well good luck to you champ, you're gonna need it!

"Shut up!" Martin snarled under his breath as he edged down another corridor with his heart thudding away like the huge bass drum of an orchestra.

As he reached the door at the end of the hall he wondered if the fat man had been found yet, he thought not, or there would be sirens blaring and guards searching the building, or so he assumed. Still, it paid to keep his wits about him. He opened the door at the end of the corridor and stood looking at the floor space before him. It was a largish area with two doors leading off to the left, a door directly ahead and two swing doors to the right that were currently standing open, hooked to the walls at the bottom. There was noise coming from this room, a kind of grinding mechanical sound, like a generator or a large industrial fan, and the sound of someone whistling as they went about their business. There was a smell too, a deeply unpleasant smell, different to the smell of the faeces caked cell but just as pungent, it was how Martin would imagine an abattoir to smell when the animals were brought in for slaughter.

With his nostrils furling Martin looked back the way he had come. He really didn't want to head into the space before him, not with the smell attacking his senses and the imminent threat of the person or persons beyond those doors. On the other hand if he was to turn back now he was heading back in the direction of the dead torturer, and it wouldn't be long now before he was discovered. When that happened Martin wanted as much distance between him and it as possible. Biting his lip, with his stomach turning in knots at both the smell and the ever increasing fear, the businessman slid beyond the door and allowed it to close behind him. He stood there for a few moments, taking in deep lungful's of foul stinking air and trying to keep his gorge down, then when he knew he simply had no other choice, he crept slowly towards the room with his hands clenching and unclenching at his sides.

Again he reflected on how dramatically his life had changed; from the mild mannered gentleman of business, growing fat and lazy in his ageing years, to a maverick rebel with a vendetta against a global crime ring. It really did defy belief, and it was not lost on him as he crept up to the open doors and slid to a position where he could peer into the room without giving himself away.

The whistling was louder now, some tune that Martin recognised but couldn't place, and it was filled with the jovial spirit of those content in their role. Martin didn't know how anybody could feel job satisfaction plying their trade in a place such as this, but if he understood the nature of pure evil perhaps he wouldn't be the man he was, and he was thankful for the ignorance.

The room that opened up beyond the double doors was fairly large, probably around the size of the interior of a small bank or meeting hall. The walls were coated black with soot and there was a thick veil of black on the floor, decorated here and there with foot prints. Tables and gurneys lined the edges of the room, stacked high with various tools and implements and a line of hooks on the left hand wall housed several thick industrial aprons. At the centre of the room, the real focal point of attention, a huge furnace stood with its doors wide open, the flames licking away within and sending tendrils of smoke billowing up the dark cylinder of its chimney. Martin thought of the huge red brick chimney that stood tall on the roof of the factory and realised he was now looking at its base. He discovered the source of the happy whistling stood directly in front of the incinerator. He was a smallish man with closely cropped black hair, and as Martin watched he was grabbing objects from the gurney at his side and tossing them into the fire. Luckily for Martin he had his back turned, and with the noise coming from the huge industrial furnace would not likely hear Martin as he sneaked on by. The businessman was about to do so when he noticed something else, it was resting on one of the tables just a couple of feet from the open swing door; it was the mans gun, still in its holster, the strap hanging down the side of the table. If Martin could grab this without the man noticing it would certainly increase his chances of success. With his mouth dry of spit and his eyes refusing to blink, Martin gave himself no time to consider his options; if he did this he would back out for sure, so instead he stepped into the room.

The man continued to whistle away, Martin did not take his eyes from him as he edged into the room and up to the table, every nerve end on edge. As he approached the table two things happened; he realised what it was the man was tossing half heartedly into the incinerator, and he remembered the tune that the man was happily whistling.

As Martin watched, the man, blissfully unaware of the stranger just a matter of feet behind him, grabbed a severed arm from the gurney and threw it into the furnace, just as he moved on to the chorus of Mungo Jerry's 'In the summertime' in that same high pitched warble.

Martin didn't know if it was the shock of seeing the body parts lying on the table, and the blasé way in which the man was going about his business, or the fact that he had the audacity to do it while whistling a happy summer tune, but something inside Martin snapped. Grabbing the gun from the table and pulling it from its leather holster he marched up behind the working man, ready in his fury to shove him as hard as he could in the back, sending him tumbling into the flames that were eradicating the evidence of this Hell holes sad victims.

At the last minute, as the man grabbed from the gurney a leg cut off at the thigh, bone sinew protruding from the lacerated end, Martin's conscience thankfully took charge, preventing him from an appalling act from which he would likely never recover. Instead of pushing the man into the flames as he had intended, Martin gripped him by the back of the neck and thrust hard forward, cracking the mans skull hard against the burning hot lip of the giant oven. He collapsed beneath Martin's fingers like a sack of limp clothing, and dropped unconscious, blissfully unaware of what had just happened to him.

Martin looked down at the body at his feet, breathing in short sharp gasps, thankful that he had not just become a murderer himself but enraptured to have sought out at least some minor vengeance for the victims of so many awful crimes. Then he looked down at the gurney, topped heavy with dismembered body parts and his stomach shifted uncomfortably. Adding a further touch of macabre to the already grisly proceedings, as Martin looked upon the bloody remains of the latest batch of victims he noticed the top half of a human head, cut off from halfway through the nose, staring back at him. It was the final straw, the final sorry insult, with the gun in his hand pointed toward the floor the sickened man stumbled from the room, just in time to keep his guts on the inside and his sanity frailly intact.

19

The sickness passed fairly quickly and was replaced unsurprisingly by the crippling and debilitating fear. He was racked by an anxiety so intense he could have quite easily curled into a ball in the dark recesses of the factory and waited until he was discovered. Only the equally pressing desire to be free of this unholy nightmare kept his feet pressing forward, though he didn't know how long he could go on with this as his only motivation. Luckily, if inspiration was what he required he found it shortly after leaving the grisly furnace room.

He was following another corridor, with doors on either side and a dusty old fluorescent light on the mouldering ceiling, when he came to a place that he actually thought he recognised. Not wanting to build up a hope that could later be dashed Martin kept his emotions in check, but when he opened the door at the end of the corridor he knew for certain he had been right. He was back in the huge former work space floor, with the pillars and the sun drenched windows; he was pretty sure he could find his way back to the prisoners from here, it would involve him making his way past the guards in the foyer again but it was a risk he would have to take.

Peering through the door, checking that the coast was clear, he ducked inside and slid behind the first pillar. He stood there panting; listening for any sign of life, but the room was empty. Martin stood, listening to the sound of his heart as it thudded its rhythmic beat, then quickly pressed on, keeping low, the gun still in his sweaty hand and feeling like an alien artefact, weaving between the pillars and heading towards the door that he knew to house the changing rooms. He made it there and checked over his shoulder before pressing on, remembering the guard who had walked this way little over an hour ago, in a time before he had become a torture victim. The coast was clear, so he pressed his ear to the door, listening for any sign of life beyond. All was silent; Martin pursed his lips and gently pushed on the door. It crept open and he peaked inside; the changing rooms were empty. Slowly he entered the room, closing the door gently behind him. His chest was rising and falling and he was panting quietly as though he had run a great distance, his eyes darted about the room, failing to believe he could be actually still alive in this place. Satisfied that he really was alone in the room, nobody lurking in the filthy showers or hiding behind an open locker door, ready to pounce, he quietly crossed the small room, manoeuvred the shower cubicles and stepped up to the next door. This one would require far more courage, for he knew for sure at least two guards would be standing sentry at the doorway to the factory. Martin jostled from foot to foot, his trousers still wet from where he had pissed them a little while ago and uncomfortable when he moved, but the nerves were making him restless, there was only one thing for it, he would just have to keep on moving.

Opening the door a crack he peered out into the ramshackle old foyer. It was just as he had left it an hour or so ago; the dusty floor, the bowed ceiling, the filthy windows of the abandoned office rooms, only now all was silent, no violent criminals remonstrated in this sterile area, only the ghosts of the conflict remained where the floor was clear of dust in the place he had been forced into submission. He took a look right, from this angle, with the wall blocking his view, he could make out only one of the guards. He stood with his back to the old man, looking straight ahead to where the dirt track led back out to the exit. Slowly Martin crept forward, allowing the door to close softly behind him, it clicked shut and he tip- toed out and to the left, heading in the direction he had taken after eavesdropping Malik and Wang's conversation. He could see the other guard now, luckily for him also stood with his back to the foyer, and slipped backwards towards his escape.

Martin found the door he had been looking for and slipped beyond it, he didn't realise that he had been holding his breath until it all came rushing out in one long exhale. He stood with his back to the door, trying to regain a little composure, he was going to need it from here, he was nearing the makeshift cell, and that meant more confrontation.

He looked down at the gun in his hand, he didn't even know how to switch off the safety, he would just have to hope that if he could conjure up enough bluster the guard would buy the charade, it was the only hope he had.

Slowly he edged down the dank smelling corridor; the only sound that of his own heart beating away faster than was surely good for him. In fact it had been beating away like the rhythm section of a steel band for the last twenty-four hours or so, if he wasn't careful he was going to wear out another heart, then where would he be?

Taking the left turn at the end of the corridor he paused to catch his breath, a thick mop of sweat had plastered his thin white hair to his forehead, he brushed it away distractedly and stood looking at the door before him. Beyond this was the large room that housed the foul smelling prison cell, he was going to need every ounce of courage if he was going to pull this off. Actually he needed more than that, he needed every ounce of courage, a whole barrel full of luck, and whoever or whatever is watching over this mortal coil to cut him a bit of slack.

"God be with me." He whispered with his eyes closed. The palm of his hand felt very sweaty on the handle of the gun. What would happen if he went marching into the room and dropped the gun because he couldn't keep his grip? He brushed the thought away, he couldn't afford any negativity.

Ok, this is it; don't give in to your fear. Martin drew in a deep breath, closed his eyes, steeled his nerve and grabbed for the door handle.

The man who entered that room was not the mild mannered Lancashire boy who had shunned the traditional image of corporate businessmen and made his fortune through honesty, integrity and an ethos to put his customers and his companions at the heart of everything he did; the man who entered that room was nothing short of the Devil.

The guard on duty was not the same guard who had caught Martin peering into the cell; this one was taller, with a closely cropped haircut and a dopey expression on his slack jawed face. As the door came crashing open and the frantic looking man in the grey polo shirt and black trousers burst into the room, a look of pure fury on his face and a black desert eagle pistol held out at arms length, the gangly man very nearly peed his pants. He had taken this job because it was easy money, stand around all day feeling important, flexible hours, easy work and you got to hold a gun, he never thought for a second he may one day have to use it. This was the luck that Martin had been hoping for; he doubted if the mans predecessor would have been caught so unprepared, and he wasn't going to let the momentum slip.

"Get down, right now, down on the floor!" He snarled, rushing across the room, closing the space fast in an attempt to give the man no time to reach for his weapon. He didn't know if the man understood his words, but the gesture was clear enough, dipping the barrel of the gun quickly every two seconds to emphasise a downwards motion. The man did not reach for his gun, just let the automatic weapon hang from the strap at his side, and lifted his hands in surrender, a terrified look on his young face.

"Get down you hear me, right down now, down on the floor!" Martin was just a couple of metres away now and closing ground fast, but the man clearly didn't understand, oh well, plan B. With the adrenaline bursting through him like wildfire he reached the trembling young man and spun him around with his free hand, so he was facing the reinforced steel door of the cell.

"Sorry." Martin muttered through pursed lips, then brought the pistol grip of his gun down hard on the back of the mans head. This wasn't the movies, in the films Martin watched when you got struck on the back of the head with a gun you dropped to the floor unconscious. Instead the man let out a horrified scream as his skull split in two at the back. Martin winced at both the sight and the sound, horrified at his own actions as the man gingerly touched his fingers to his blood stained cranium. Then he remembered the poor souls trapped beyond this door, and all sentiment went out the window. Quickly and efficiently he brought the gun down another two times, staining his hand in sticky red blood as the man finally did slip into unconsciousness. He slumped to the floor with blood dripping down his neck and pooling beneath him.

Martin looked down at him with sick fascination, feeling elated and horrified in equal measure. Then the ever pressing finger of time was on him again and he quickly stepped back into action, any second now that door that he just arrived through could burst open, and when it did his luck would run out for sure.

It was only adrenaline keeping him on his feet now, his injuries from the savage beating in the foyer, his subsequent torture at the hands of the fat man and the fatigue from days of over exertion and stress were desperately trying to take hold, luckily fear was a strong motivator and he was able to find the energy to move on.

With the gun transferred to his left hand he stretched out his trembling right and slid back the inch thick deadbolt, listening to the creaking clunk and the final slam of metal on metal as it connected with its housing. He pulled on the door, his arm feeling as heavy as the thick steel it was trying to shift, and slowly it crept open.

When he had looked into this terrible room before he had not been prepared for the horrors that would be plagued upon his eyes, this time he was, and although he steeled himself to take in the gruesome vision it did nothing to soften the blow. It was a full sensory overload, from the sight of the poor souls, naked, filthy, huddled together in fear, to the smell of the room, the sweat, the piss, the shit, the stink of death, to the sound as they groaned in abject terror, sure that one of their number was about to be taken from them again, hoping in vain that it would not be them.

There were close to twenty bedraggled Chinese prisoners in the room, men, women and children, their hair matted in sweaty clumps, their faces streaked from dirty tears, and when the door opened once more they raised their naked arms to block the sunlight that dazzled their increasingly nocturnal vision.

Martin stared at them, his jaw loose, unable to comprehend how man could be so inhumanely cruel to fellow man, and for a moment had absolutely no idea of what to do. His eyes felt weary at the horror, his lip trembled as though he was close to tears, but really what he felt was anger, a blinding anger against those that had caused this scene. And guilt, he couldn't deny it, the guilt of knowing that the heart that beat inside his own chest and kept him from his own early burial had come from a soul such as this, locked in a room, miles from home, from friends and family, terrified and confused. No he hadn't known that this was the source of his salvation, but he had been wise enough to smell a rat from the outset, and his own desperate urge for survival had made him ignorant to the truth, and it was an ignorance that he had bore by choice.

Yes, well, all that is in the past, and you can't repent your sins without action! The voice in his head was right, he had to act, and act fast.

"My name is Martin Rooley, I'm here to help." He said, his voice wavering slightly.

A low moan came from within the cell, they hadn't understood him, they cowered towards the back of the cell amongst the filth and the shadows, pressing as far back into the steel wall as they possibly could.

"Please come." He called urgently, desperately trying to make them understand. "I don't want to hurt you, I'm here to help! I want to get you back to your families."

The commotion rose again, Martin sagged at the futility of the situation, then, slowly, a small woman crept from the back of the group. She was a tiny thing, probably in her early forties, covered in shit and filth of every description, her hair lank with grease. She stared at Martin in a look that could have only been hope, and suddenly the businessman felt it too.

"Help?" She said, her face a torture of desperation and disbelief.

"Yes! Help! I'm here to help you, you have to come quick!"

With a speed that defied her malnourished frame the skinny woman turned to the huddled throng and spoke to them in wild, urgent Mandarin. The same look of disbelief filled the faces of the terrified prisoners, but something glinted in all of their eyes, it was a beautiful glint that nearly brought tears to the corners of Martin's, they had lost all hope some time ago, now it had presented itself again, Martin only hoped he wouldn't let them down. It was one thing to lead these people to believe he was their salvation, it was a completely different other to actually pull such a wild feat off.

Slowly they crept forwards, still bent over, still covering their modesty, still covering their eyes from the glare of the sun. Martin gestured for them to come, checking over his shoulder, watching for the door to come crashing in. At his feet the guard gave a small shuffle, his head lifted then dropped again as though the strain was too much, his cheek plopping down into the blood that had soaked the floor. Martin watched with concern, fearful he may have to administer another blow, one that could potentially kill the man in his current state, luckily it was not needed, he fell silent again, his body only moving with his own laboured breathing.

The prisoners had reached the opening in the door, the women with their arms around the shoulders of the children, who pressed their faces into the stranger's naked sides, terrified that this was some kind of cruel joke, that they would all now find themselves in whatever place it was their brethren had disappeared.

"Come on come on." Martin gestured frantically. Finally the filthy captives emerged from the foul smelling cell, their eyes which were slowly becoming accustomed to the light darting about the huge open space beyond the confines of what they had come to think of as their home.

The businessman found the tiny woman, the one who had seemed to understand him earlier.

"You speak English?"

"A little." She replied, though the word was pronounced 'liwel'.

"Ok, tell everybody not to be afraid, tell them to trust me, tell them I'm here to help, but tell them that we need to move quickly and we need to be extremely careful and extremely quiet."

The scrawny woman turned and for what felt like an age addressed the Chinese in their native tongue. There were nods of agreement and some mild response, but Martin thought the interaction to appear reasonably positive. Good, he hadn't known how he was going to get out of this place with only his self to worry about, now he had twenty naked newly freed captives in tow, the odds against him hadn't just increased, they had just closed the book on his chances of ever getting out of here alive.

Oh well, better to die with a clean conscience than to live in the knowledge he had left them in this place of misery.

"Come on, we have to move, now." Martin waited for the woman to translate and then turned and head for the door.

It was strange, under any other circumstances the businessman would have been horrified to find he was in the company of over a dozen naked human beings, with bits dangling from top halves and bottoms, needing to avert his eyes but drawn back to such private places like a magnet. But this was different, the extremity of the situation vastly outweighed any embarrassment, and the fact that they were naked and matted in their own filth was the least of his concerns; getting them out of this place alive however was.

They reached the door and Martin peeked outside; the coast was clear. It would be oh so easy to head back the way he had come, to make it to the foyer and smell freedom from the open double doors of the factory, but that way was covered by at least two guards, and Martin thought he had stretched his luck to the absolute limit where they were concerned. There was only one thing for it, he was going to have to travel back through the maze of corridors in the hope of finding his way back to the side exit, where he had entered the building the previous evening. Reluctantly he looked towards the door that led out towards the foyer, then turned in the opposite direction and led the prisoners deeper into the ground floor of the factory.

There was some murmuring and chatting amongst the group as Martin led them along, after a while he turned to the skinny woman and reaffirmed the need for absolute quiet. She relayed the message and the group fell quiet, just a small girl, no more than six weeping into the side of one of the Oriental women remained; Martin allowed her this, she had earned it.

Slowly but surely the ragtag mob made their way through the vast network of corridors that formed the majority of the ground floor of the facility, with Martin in the lead, hoping he looked like he had at least a thimble of a clue what he was doing. At one point voices could be heard ahead, Martin gestured in panic for the group to be silent and this time even the little girl managed to hold back her sobbing. He waited, the gun raised up next to his face, for the men to appear, but again the voices faded into the distance. Martin let out an exhausted sigh; whoever was watching over him on this ludicrous quest apparently still had his back.

They journeyed on, at times Martin thought he recognised the path he had taken, only to find himself either at a dead end or not in the place he thought that he had been at all. Other times he resigned to being as lost as he had ever been in this mausoleum of horrors. The group followed close behind him as he negotiated the dank mouldy corridors, walking through rooms and cross junctions that looked like all the rooms and cross junctions they had journeyed through before. Finally they had a breakthrough. With his resolve sagging Martin reached a door and listened for voices beyond; there were none, all was quiet. He slowly opened the door and found himself in what he believed to be the room he had fallen asleep in the night before.

He drew in a quick breath, he could see the sink with the filthy faucets and the rows of aluminium containers, he looked to the one in which he had managed to find some peace and saw the door was still standing ajar. Could this be it? Had he finally stumbled upon a way out of here? If so he was pretty sure he could find his way back to the exit. There was only one way to be sure. Martin walked up to the double basined sink with his group of followers huddled in the doorway behind him and looked in. It was still there, the tiny clump of flesh that had so turned his stomach some nine or ten hours ago. If he had known the horrors that would follow from that point perhaps the tiny chunk of flesh would not have had quite the same effect.

"Ok," Martin said, finding the English speaking woman amongst the assembled throng, "I know where I'm going, come on."

He walked to the door at the opposite side of the room and again listened for signs of life beyond. Comfortable that all was clear he pressed on, with the naked Chinese following close behind. It occurred to him as he slipped quietly into the next corridor that he had only considered as far as their escape into the open, he had not given any thought to how he was going to get twenty naked men, women and children beyond the perimeter fence and back to the relative safety of Qingdao. Oh well, he would just have to cross that bridge when he came to it, at this moment in time he couldn't allow himself, even in his wildest dreams, to believe that it would ever be a problem he wouldn't need at some point to address.

They shuffled along the corridor, Martin following his nose back in the direction he believed he had come, some murmuring and the sound of many shoeless padding feet behind him. He still held the gun out in front of him, still unsure of whether the safety was actually switched off, still feeling a million miles from Clint Eastwood in the Dirty Harry movies he so loved, but determined to do everything he could to get these people to freedom.

There were a couple more corridors to negotiate and then they were back in the side atrium, a small area with several doors leading from the main thoroughfare, and directly in front; the door to freedom. Martin drew in a quick breath, utterly mystified that he had actually managed to lead them all this far, maybe he would have to address the small problem of the perimeter fence after all!

"Ok." He said, more as reassurance to himself than to address the crowd. "Keep close to me now."

He only managed one step towards the exit door and freedom, and then the voice to the back of the atrium froze him to the spot.

"Bravo Mister Rooley, bravo."

The small hairs on the back of Martin's neck abruptly stood to attention, water pricked the corners of his eyes, his mouth suddenly felt very arid. Martin turned slowly, the group about him following his stare.

There stood Wang, a small smile on his face, his hands clapping together mockingly. To his side one of the guards, and in his hands, aimed at the petrified group, an Uzi submachine gun.

20

Wang and his companion stood at the foot of the atrium, looking at the pitiful band of escapees before them with real contempt. The crime lord stood with his hands on his hips, that same mocking smile stretched across his thin lips. The guard stood with the small cylindrical barrel of his gun pointing into the centre of the group, his finger on the trigger, itching to pull.

Martin, though holding a deadly weapon himself, stood slump shouldered, with the gun hanging in his hand at his side. He had known it was all too good to be true, his luck had to run out at some point and it seemed that time was now. He looked dejectedly at the two men before him, hoping now only for a swift end.

"I must say you impress me Mister Rooley."

"Oh please, we're about as deep as we're ever going to swim, call me Martin."

Wang's smile grew wider. "Ok, Martin, I am very impressed with your ingenuity, with your tenacity, with your will to survive."

"Am I supposed to be pleased with the compliment?"

"You are supposed to be dead, and yet here you are, and with some things that belong to me."

"They're not things, they're people, and they aren't yours to own."

Wang's smile faltered, but only for a second, and when it returned it was wider than ever before. "It is a shame that you do not see the possibilities before you Martin, a man with your particular skills, I could use him in my organisation."

"I'd never work for you."

"I know you wouldn't, and that is why sadly you must die, but before you do, I'm going to remove that heart that you have grown so attached to, I think you owe me its value for all the trouble you've caused me today."

"Do as you please," Martin replied with a shrug of his shoulders, "I apologise for my crudity, but frankly right now I don't give a shit."

Wang chuckled, at his side the guard's eyes darted from person to person, with little or no grasp of the English language he didn't know where this conversation was heading and his finger on the trigger of the Uzi was becoming itchier still.

"Ok, this has gone far enough, I have important work to attend to and as exciting as this mornings events have been it is time to draw them to a close."

Martin drew in a deep breath, letting it out in a slow exhale. "Do what you must, but let the children go, I beg of you please, let the children go."

The smile reappeared on the crime lord's face. "Very commendable Mister Rooley, sorry, Martin, but alas I cannot help you there. You see the children are my most valuable commodity, if you think the heart or lungs or eyes of an adult goes for a good price, you should see what people will pay to save their children!"

Martin's lips drew together in a pained grimace, his hand tightened on the pistol grip of the Desert Eagle. He wanted nothing more than to raise the weapon and shoot the vile man between the eyes, but he knew that his hand wouldn't get above waist height before he was cut to ribbons by the fire of the semi automatic.

"You disgust me." He said instead, enjoying the momentary pinched, slapped look that came across the Chinese mans face. Then he composed himself, and after a few seconds the smile also started to creep back into his features. It sickened Martin, but before he had chance to register his disgust a shrill scream rose up from the centre of the crowd.

Everybody in the room froze apart from the person who had let out the unearthly scream, in the end it was this that saved Martin's life. The screamer was a naked Chinese man with a slight pot belly; he rushed from the centre of the crowd with his hands raised high above his head. Martin watched him charge the two men at the foot of the room with his jaw slightly agape. He wasn't alone, Wang's smile had been replaced by a look of shock and confusion, and an almost identical look was etched onto the features of the guard at his side.

The rushing man cut the gap in seconds, but he wasn't quite fast enough. His moment of immobility brought on by the bizarre turn of events passed, the guard recognised the danger to him and his employer and pulled on the trigger of the Uzi. Fire rained from the barrel of the snub nosed gun, deafening in the small room, and turned the screaming mans guts into a mess of blood and torn apart organs. The quality of the scream changed from one of rage and triumph to one of pain and absolute misery. The mans eyes screwed shut tight as the bullets tore his insides to shreds and sent the life quickly slipping from his body. He stumbled on, his feet still carrying his lifeless body until he collided with the guard, slumping naked into his arms, trapping the mans weapon beneath his warm corpse.

Martin stared at this horror with wide open eyes, and as he did, a voice of panic screamed inside his mind: This is it! Now! This is your chance! Do something! Now!

Wang's mouth hung agape as he watched his enforcer struggle beneath the dead weight of the prisoner, he knew he needed to act and act fast before the situation slipped out of his control but he was completely without motion. Martin noticed this and finally snapped out of his paralysis. While the guard struggled with the bloodied cadaver he raised the Desert Eagle, blanking out the voice that screamed in his head: Not that! You're not a killer! Anything but that!

He ignored it, he had no choice, he had to ignore it! Martin pointed the gun, still feeling alien in his hand, at the head of the guard, then with his eyes narrowing into slits pulled the trigger.

The guard's eyes may have been narrow, but in that moment they were as wide as golf balls, when the white haired man pulled on the trigger, he sucked in a quick, terrified breath, and let it out again a moment later when nothing happened.

Martin's fear had become a reality; the safety mechanism was activated on the weapon.

Recognising that the play had just momentarily swung back in their favour, Wang screamed a panic stricken order at the guard, reverting in his distress back to his native tongue.

As the businessman turned the gun over in his hand, looking for the switch to activate the weapons deadly firepower the Chinese guard finally struggled free from beneath the dead prisoner. The bloody body slumped to the floor, landing at the guard's feet with a sickening plop.

The crowd screamed, raising their hands before their faces, the children burying their heads into the sides of the adults as Martin found the catch and switched it on. He was in a race against time now, it was him or the guard, he knew if he took the time to aim he would be beaten, instead he raised the gun only to waist height and pulled quickly on the trigger, sucking in a deep breath and holding it in his tightened mouth as the gun exploded in his hand, bucketing his arm backwards with the report.

The bullet missed its target by a good two feet, taking a chunk out of the plaster to the left of the guards head, but it was enough to throw the man off guard, who ducked in fear at the deafening roar of the gun. Martin wasn't going to waste his chance again, as the guard looked back at the hole in the wall that could have been a hole in his face; Martin raised the gun again, tensed his arms to counter the kick back of the weapon, and fired twice. Screams rose up from the crowd, some of the women covering their ears from the din as the guards chest exploded in a sea of blood. He collapsed back against the atrium wall, banging his head hard against the plaster, and dropped lifeless to the floor right next to the naked body of his own victim.

Wang stared in horror at his dead security blanket, equalled by the look of horror from Martin, who was staring at the smoking gun in disbelief, unable to comprehend that he had actually just taken a human life.

One of the children was crying now, long distraught wails that brought the white haired man back to his senses just in time to see the crime lord ducking down to retrieve the sub-machine gun from the hands of the dead guard.

"D-don't you move!" He screeched, not liking the sound of his own voice, it sounded way too like the voice of a mad man.

Wang instantly jumped up straight, his hands raised in the air, wearing the expression of a man who was clearly not used to staring down the barrel of a gun.

"Mr. Rooley, come on, we can work this out. I have money, lots of money, I can get you money. I can get you out of here, is that what you want? I can get you all safely out of here. A helicopter, I have a helicopter, I can get a helicopter!"

"Shut up!" Martin screamed back, his hands shaking around the handle of the gun. His head was spinning from the crazy events and he needed time to think. As he was desperately trying to get a coherent thought into his stress addled brain the tiny woman who had understood him in the darkness of the prison cell stepped forward and appeared at his side.

"Is this man who took us prisoner?" She asked in her broken English.

"Yes." Martin replied without even thinking.

Before he knew what was happening the woman had turned and addressed her fellow naked, filthy escapees. She was barking something quickly and shrilly in Mandarin that hurt Martin's ears. He didn't need this right now, whatever this was; he needed to be at home, in bed, sleeping off this whole nightmare.

Whatever was being said in a language that Martin would never understand, it made all of the blood wash out of the crime lord's face. Wang stood with his head slowly shaking from side to side, a terrified look of helplessness in his Chinese eyes.

Suddenly, before Martin could even comprehend what was happening, several of the ragtag mob broke from the crowd and rushed the petrified man. Amongst them were several men and a couple of women, including her of the broken English. As Martin watched on in horror, the gun sagging in his tired arms, the screaming mob pulled the sharp suited man down to the floor. He was pleading something in Mandarin as he was sent crashing to the dirty floor, but the prisoners, who had suffered the most humiliating and terrifying of ordeals, were in no mood for mercy.

A writhing mass of bodies descended upon him, kicking, punching, biting. The mans head was lifted from the cold tiled floor and sent smacking back down, not once but several times. Blood erupted from a huge split in the back of his skull and as Martin watched on his eyes rolled up to the whites and mercifully for him he slipped into unconsciousness. This didn't stop them, their fists rained down on his face, on his torso, on his legs, his hands and his feet. Naked knees came crashing into his skull, shoeless feet stamped down on his chest, breaking his ribs like twigs.

The crowd that had held back recoiled in horror, some of the adults covering the eyes of the children; Martin watched on in sick fascination, feeling any hope of salvation for his poor tortured soul waning with every second.

Finally, one by one, and with shocked looks in their eyes as though they couldn't understand what had just happened, the attackers stepped back from the bruised and bloodied corpse of the man that had held them prisoner in this most awful of places. They walked backwards in a zombielike state, a vacant quality to their stares as they looked down at the bloody work of their own hands, until eventually only one naked Chinese man remained, his flaccid penis hanging limp amidst a mass of thick black pubic hair as he squealed uncontrollably and continued to rain punches down on the corpse of the crime lord.

Slowly, as his own awful wailing died to a low warble, the man recognised that his fellow killers had pulled away from their barbaric act, and he rolled away from the dead man on the dirty floor of the atrium.

The corpse was now there for all to see, and Martin struggled to hold whatever was still left in his stomach within.

Wang's suit hung from his lifeless body in tattered shreds, what flesh remained could no longer be used to identify him, it was a bloodied mess. About his head several teeth lay in pools of crimson blood and one eye hung loosely from its socket, dangling next to a bulbous, fractured cheek.

There was crying and moaning in the room but Martin hardly noticed, he just continued to stare at the cadaver with a growing separation from reality. It was only when the skinny woman, blood matted to the palms of her hands, gently grabbed him by the material of his grey sweatshirt and looked up into his shock induced eyes that he finally broke his stare.

"We go now." She said simply. The businessman nodded his head slowly, no longer feeling in charge of any situation. Slowly he turned to face the terrified group, knowing that he had to find the courage to somehow go on, then stepped forwards towards the exterior door.

He made it to the door on feet that seemed to somehow glide several feet above the floor, listening to the sound of the soft footfalls behind him as his group of damaged souls followed on, then he grabbed the handle, turned and then pulled.

21

Sunlight hit his face and caused his eyes to squint momentarily. It was lucky that this happened, for a guard was just turning away from them around the corner of the building; if Martin had seen him he may have ducked back inside, and what then? More fruitless journeying through the seemingly endless corridors of the factory.

Instead his eyes became accustomed to the change in light and when they did the guard was already gone. Feeling a little more under control following the harrowing incident in the atrium he stepped outside and looked about himself. The coast was clear; he knew that if he ventured left he could lead the prisoners back to the garages and up the slope to the hole in the perimeter fence where he had twice made his entry into the compound. Right would take him back in the direction of the main entrance to the building, which was heavily guarded and from what he had seen bereft of any real cover.

Opening the door a little wider the businessman slid out, taking in huge lungful's of clean air, filling them up and letting them out in greedy gulps. If this was what it was like for him after only one night in the frightful place how sweet must the air taste for the group that followed, whose stifled air had reeked of sweat and shit and piss for all their time in captivity.

Martin turned and placed a finger to his lips, giving the internationally recognised motion for silence, then he crept along the path to the side of the factory wall, heading towards the corner of the facility as his naked companions followed close by, their faces still etched in terror, covering their eyes from the glare of the sun.

Reaching the corner he gestured for the group to stop, sympathising with them having bare feet on this new rough ground. He pressed himself flat against the factory wall and took a peek around the corner. A guard was walking slowly down the gangway to the back of the huge building, but fortune was continuing to shine on Martin, for he was walking away from the group with his back turned. Without waiting for him to disappear around the corner – who knew how much time they had before another guard appeared walking in the opposite direction – Martin turned the corner and stepped into the middle of the path between the garages and the factory wall. He didn't notice the open garage door, was in fact too engrossed in ensuring the group of naked Chinese followed him around the ninety degree angle in the wall as quietly as was humanly possible. If he had have noticed he may have seen the man who was climbing into the drivers seat of a large delivery truck. It wasn't until the engine roared into life that Martin became aware of the presence, and he froze to the spot in panic.

The front end of the truck appeared from within the garage and started to turn onto the rough track to the rear of the factory; it wasn't until the driver had manoeuvred the vehicle onto the straight that he became aware of the bizarre event in his direct line of vision. His eyes set upon the group of filthy, naked men, women and children and the white haired westerner dressed all in black and grey and his mouth dropped open with a plop of his lips. He pressed down on the brakes and the truck stopped just inches from where the first of the newly freed prisoners stood.

Acting only on impulse Martin raised the hand holding the gun once more and aimed it at the man in the driver's seat.

"Out, get out now!" He commanded, gesturing in quick motions with the gun in case the man didn't understand the words. The man opened the door and jumped from the vehicle, his hands raised in surrender to the sides of his head, his mouth still wearing that small O of surprise.

"Quick, get everybody into the back of the truck!" Martin commanded the skinny woman, who nodded her head in frightened understanding.

Suddenly there were shouts from somewhere to the far end of the factory wall; the guard who had been patrolling this area and walking away from the group had turned around amidst the commotion and discovered the botched up escape attempt. He was screeching something in Mandarin and was running back along the length of the building, his AK-47 raised in his hands.

"Quick, move!" Martin yelped, but too late, shots rang out along the narrow track and one of the prisoners, standing only inches from Martin, suddenly jerked backwards, slamming into the front of the truck, his chest exploding in several jets of crimson red blood. He dropped to the floor lifeless to the side of the truck, Martin watched him fall in outrage and horror. Without even thinking he gritted his teeth together and raised the Desert Eagle, firing it three times at the guard, all three shots missed their target and sent puffs of dust and exploding brick flying from the factory wall. Although the shots had missed it did cause the guard to duck into cover, giving the group valuable seconds to board the back of the vehicle. They scrambled aboard, screaming and crying, pulling each other up into the relative safety of the truck, dragging the children on board, finding solace amongst the boxes and crates in the back of the storage compartment.

The driver of the truck was gone, disappearing up the side of the hill and covering his head with his hands as though this would protect him from a rain of bullets from an automatic weapon. Martin watched him go, still feeling like he was being driven by some unseen force, then climbed up into the drivers side of the truck as more guards appeared around the far corner of the factory. They instantly dropped into combat positions, aiming their assault rifles as the businessman released the brake and pressed down hard on the accelerator.

"Come on you bastard!" Martin cursed through pursed lips as the truck slowly ambled forward, directly before him the guards were firing their weapons, the shots very loud in this quiet valley. Martin ducked down so his head was directly below the wheel but kept the vehicle pointing straight forward as he attempted their escape from the facility.

Suddenly the glass of the windscreen spider-webbed in a thousand different shards, it would have been impossible to see, but then more bullets hit the glass and shattered it inwards, missing Martin's head by inches and coming to rest in the panel to the back of his head. Glass shattered down into his lap, cutting his arms and his face in several places. He let out a small gasp of pain but gritted his teeth and pressed down harder on the accelerator.

The guard who had first fired upon the fleeing prisoners ducked out of his hiding place at the worst time and was crushed beneath the wheels of the oncoming truck, Martin felt the bumps as he was crushed first between the wheels at the front of the truck and then the ones at the back and squeezed his eyes shut tight at this new horror. But he kept the truck guided forwards and was now bearing down on the guards to the end of the track. They were still firing; trying to hit the tyres, trying to stop the truck from making its escape, but now became aware of their imminent danger and dived into cover around the corner of the factory.

The truck screeched out into the open roadway that led back up the hill to meet the main road under a hail of bullets from the guards gathered by the factory wall. They hit the side panels, the passenger door and the fuel tank, leaving a trail of diesel in the trucks wake as it roared away from the factory and towards the ramp up to the exterior gate.

Martin's tensed arms were shaking visibly as he gripped onto the wheel; his face wore the expression of a madman as the truck struggled up the hill with the weight of the terrified passengers in the hold. The wind blew through the glassless window and ruffled the thin hair atop the businessman's head as the gate appeared before them. Two guards who had likely heard the commotion from below them were quickly sliding the mesh gate back into place, trying to block the oncoming vehicle's escape. Martin, who had seen plenty of car chases on plenty of cop shows over the years was not perturbed, did in fact feel a surge of adrenaline kick in as he dropped the truck down a gear, pressed down hard on the accelerator and lowered his head below the wheel once more in anticipation of the impact.

The front bumper and grill of the truck collided with the mesh and metal gate as the guards leapt to safety, there was a huge clatter as it was torn from its fixings and a couple of wild screams from those gathered in the hold, then the truck was through, out onto the dusty road dragging half the gate behind them.

Martin screamed in triumph and punched the ceiling of the cab, not quite able to comprehend that he had actually just successfully escaped the compound, and with the majority of the captives released and heading to freedom with him. He was breathing heavily, each breath a huge lungful of clean Oriental air followed by an exhale that blew out his cheeks like a puffer fish. He couldn't stop now, he had to get to town, and fast. Again he worked his way through the gears, listening to the roar of the engine as the truck raced on.

Sweat poured from his hairline and traced down his cheeks in dirty rivulets, for the first time since being trapped in the room with the sadistic torturer he could feel his wounds, from the cuts and bruising about his cheeks and eyes to the burning in his chest, and he winced at the pain. On top of this every inch of his body throbbed with exhaustion, his eyelids felt incredibly heavy and needing to squint against the morning sun made it all the more difficult to combat the desire to simply close his eyes and allow the sleep to overcome him.

No! These people were depending on him, his own survival was depending on him, he had been through so much, he wasn't going to give it all up now, not when he was so close!

Martin bit down on his lip hard enough to draw blood, and when he felt it trickle down his chin and could taste its coppery flavour in his mouth he was once again within the moment, ready to finish this in whatever way he could.

That was when he noticed the fuel meter, he couldn't be certain but he was sure when he climbed into the truck it had been somewhere close to the halfway mark, now it was only a little over the quarter tank level. How could that be? He had only gone a couple of miles. Then he remembered the hail of bullets and how some of them had made contact with the escaping truck, they must have hit the fuel tank! Martin squeezed his lips together in frustration; oh well, it would have to do.

In the distance he could see the silhouettes that would soon take shape to become the skyscrapers on the horizon of Qingdao, he reckoned somewhere in the region of seven miles away, if he kept a steady pace maybe, just maybe the truck would make the distance.

He briefly wondered how everybody was doing in the back, had they in fact all made it on board the truck before he had driven away from the factory? He could only hope for now that this was the case; in his minds eye he kept seeing the innocent man who had lost his life in the alley at the back of the factory, just like Chang before him. No time for sentimentality now; he had to get these people to safety.

The truck continued to groan as it cut down the miles, soon they would be back onto the freeway that led into the centre of town, they would then start to see more signs of life, he didn't know given the circumstances if this was a good thing or a bad thing. It was at this time that Martin happened to look into the wing mirror to the driver's side of the cab, and noticed for the first time the two motorcycles that were bearing down on them fast from the rear.

The old mans breath caught in his throat, his eyes stared at the oncoming cycles with mounting horror; would this nightmare never end? There was nothing he could do, he was already driving at maximum speed, and the motorcycles were closing the distance fast.

"Son of a bitch!" Martin whispered, unable to take his eyes from the approaching bikes, he could just make out the dark uniforms of the guards who rode them and the automatic weapons that were dangling from their straps at their sides.

It was probably still a couple of miles to the freeway, at this rate he would be there in less than seven minutes, he had to get rid of them somehow before then, he was conspicuous enough driving a bullet riddled truck with no windshield without a couple of heavily armed bikers on his tail.

The first bike was closing fast; tearing up the dusty road with the driver bent low over the handle bars. He reached the truck and veered slightly right so that he could speed along the side of the truck. Suddenly he was at the side of the cab, waving frantically for Martin to pull over.

"Fuck you!" The businessman screamed, he wasn't normally one for profanity but this was far from a normal situation.

The biker didn't speak a word or English, but he could tell by the driver's aggressive tone that he was in no mood to comply. Keeping one hand to balance the bike he grabbed for the handle of the machine gun and raised his weapon so it was pointing directly into the cab of the truck.

Martin didn't have time to think; if he paused for thought the dark haired man could unload the clip into his face and that would be the end of everything. Acting on instinct and instinct only he quickly pulled hard right on the steering wheel and sent three and a half tonnes of heavy duty vehicle crashing into the side of the flimsy bike. Martin just had time to see the look of abject panic on the young mans face as the truck collided with him. There was a sickening crunch as the bike and its rider disappeared beneath the wheels, a thud and a dragging from beneath, then the escaping vehicle was free, though the tires left a trail of blood that streaked along the dusty road in crimson tracks.

Refusing to look in his mirrors, not wanting to see the latest fatality caused by the ever thickening blood on his hands, Martin brought the truck back straight and pressed down harder on the accelerator.

Suddenly shots rang out from behind and Martin was forced to address the problem, glaring into the wing mirror to the side of his head. The second rider, seeing his quickly dying friend clutching a string of intestines that were hanging from his gut at the side of the road, had apparently taken umbrage to this and was now taking matters into his own hands. Screams pierced out from the hold as the bullets panged from the back of the truck, sending sparks flying in all directions. The rider lowered his weapon and allowed it to swing loose from his shoulder, grabbing the handles with both hands and leaning forward as he quickly increased his speed.

Watching all this with mounting tension Martin knew that he only had one chance; the truck was travelling at approximately fifty miles an hour, the bike coming up behind must be doing seventy at least to break the distance so fast, timing was going to be key.

The start of the freeway could now be seen about five hundred yards up ahead, it was now or never. Keeping his hands pointing the vehicle straight forward and his eyes firmly pierced to the wing mirror Martin wobbled his leg on the accelerator, making sure he had life in his calf, that it had not become subjected to pins and needles, cramp or fatigue. He waited until the bike was just a couple of metres from the back of the truck, then, taking a deep breath he slammed down with all his weight on the break and the clutch. The tyres screeched as the truck came to an unexpected halt, sending a cloud of orange dust up from the dirty back road. The move was all the more unexpected on the rider of the oncoming vehicle, who saw what had happened too late, and went smashing into the back of the truck at seventy-five miles per hour.

There was a terrible smacking sound as metal collided with metal and a wall of petrified screams
rose from the rear of the truck, but not from the owner of the destroyed motorcycle, the only sound that escaped his lips was a muffled gasp as he was propelled from the seat of the bike and sent crashing face first into the lower roof hang at the back of the truck. With no helmet to protect his head he didn't stand a chance, his face crumpled on impact like a fist into a freshly

baked pie, sending blood, bone and muscles exploding in a grisly shower down the back of the hold.

Martin, who could see none of this from his place in the cab, waited anxiously to find out if his plan had worked. Smoke was drifting up from the tyres and dust was filling the air around him, but there was still no sign from behind other than the whimpering and moaning of his travelling companions. When after almost a minute nothing had happened he restarted the stalled engine with a badly shaking hand and slowly pressed down on the accelerator. There was a gut wrenching screech of metal from the rear as the battered bike was dragged along for the first hundred yards, then it broke free and clattered to a stop on the quiet road. Martin didn't know what had become of the rider, and he didn't want to know, it was enough to know that for now at least they were reasonably safe.

Increasing his speed as he reached the end of the dirt road Martin breathed deeply, trying to slow the beating of his wildly erratic heart, and signalled for the truck to enter the slip road that led onto the freeway.

The skyscrapers looked closer now, with the city only a little over five miles away, and suddenly a busy Chinese morning erupted around him, as he left the quiet, scarcely used road and entered the bustling freeway with its speeding cars, bikes and lorries.

It was a three lane strip of tarmac that led directly to the ring road that circled Qingdao; Martin entered on the slow lane and though the speed limit on the freeway was a steady seventy-five miles per hour it seemed that few were paying heed to the restriction. Cars buzzed by at close to a hundred miles per hour, going about their business in brisk fashion as the battered truck struggled to make fifty as it ambled along in the far right hand lane. A couple of cars slowed as they drew alongside the truck, their drivers gawping at the white haired man that was driving this death trap down one of the busiest freeway's in Shandong Province with no notable windscreen and diesel flowing from the badly damaged tank in a dark spray. Martin ignored them, he had problems enough of his own without worrying about how he may look. He took a cursory look at the fuel gage, just under quarter of a tank left; he thought he might actually make it.

Then suddenly, as was becoming the norm in this newfound crazy existence, everything went to Hell in a handbag again, and Martin slumped over the wheel in utter disbelief. They had been on the freeway for less than two miles, and apparently that was all it took for the businessman to find trouble once more. He looked in the wing mirror as the wind lifted his hair from his brow and chewed on his lip with escalating concern. In the distance, but closing fast, were the flashing lights of not one but three speeding police cars. Martin had no doubt they were here for him, just as he had no doubt they had not been called because of the un-roadworthy state of his vehicle. These were corrupt cops, called to track down and capture the man in the stolen delivery truck by the very men he was fleeing. This was a whole new nightmare; it was one thing to be responsible for the death of a couple of hired thugs and a major crime lord, but killing a policeman, in broad daylight on a busy Chinese freeway, was a step into the land of the ridiculous. There could be no hope for him if that was to happen; even if he was to survive, the odds of which had just suddenly and cruelly been slashed again; he would spend the rest of his days rotting in some Oriental prison somewhere, seeing out what was left of his days in a dingy cell.

"God damn it!" He cursed in frustration, unable to take his eyes from the mirror, watching as the other vehicles occupying the road veered out of the way to make room for the oncoming authority.

Trying to pre-empt their next move Martin cut across the lanes of traffic into the fast lane, where the road was at its busiest, hoping in some lame way that they would somehow miss him amongst the traffic.

The police cars were speeding down the freeway in direct formation, one after the other, their lights flashing, their sirens blaring in the morning bustle. They were only a couple of hundred yards back now, and any hope Martin was harbouring that perhaps they weren't here for him after all, that perhaps they would catch up to him and then speed past on their way to their true destination, were savagely dashed as they cut into his lane, the first vehicle flashing its front headlights repeatedly in an attempt to catch his attention.

Maybe they were here to help? Maybe somebody, Lau perhaps, had got wind of his predicament and sent them to guide him safely back into the city.

Yeah right, maybe his beloved Bolton Wanderers would win the Champions league.

His poor old heart, that organ of seemingly endless misery, was thumping so hard in his chest that it actually felt as though a small man had become trapped within his ribcage and was now attempting to punch his way free. Sweat stood out on his brow, shimmering in the morning sun, before sliding down his filthy, blood streaked cheeks and coming to a rest in the thickening stubble about his chin. The hands that clutched the wheel did so in a vice like grip, his knuckles white from the pressure he was unconsciously applying.

Suddenly two of the cars broke from the pack, leaving the one car behind him in the fast lane, still flashing its lights with a passion close to obsession. He knew exactly what they were doing as they dropped gear and sped up alongside him, had seen the manoeuvre performed on 'Police, camera, action' at least a dozen times, but knowing what was happening was of little use, he was helpless to prevent it, they were simply far faster than he could ever hope to travel in the beat up delivery truck. As he watched on helplessly the lead vehicle sped up alongside him, then overtook him, so the back left corner of the police car was at a diagonal to the front right corner of the truck. As this was happening the second car sped up alongside him and kept pace with Martin, so the two vehicles were travelling at parallel to one another on the busy freeway. The final piece of the jigsaw occurred when the lead car increased its speed again, and when it was about ten feet in front of the truck swerved hard left and into his lane. The action was complete, he was completely boxed in, all that remained was for the lead car to start applying its breaks and the whole sorry affair would come to a dramatic close.

Martin, resigned to his fate but sick to his stomach at coming so close to both his and the captives freedom, looked right at the driver of the patrol car that ran parallel to him on the busy road. The driver was holding the wheel with one gloved hand, dark shades covering his narrow eyes, as he leaned against the frame of his open window and gestured with his free hand for the foreigner to pull over. Martin ignored him, he may have been resigned to his fate but he would be damned if he wasn't going down without a fight.

Suddenly red lights were filling his vision as the car in front applied its breaks, Martin, who had been anticipating the move, tensed his hands on the wheel and braced himself for impact. The driver of the squad car upfront had expected Martin to notice his move and brake in time, this would continue until the speed of the cars were slow enough for the driver of the entrapped vehicle to find no alternative but to pull onto the side of the road. The surrounded fugitive would then do one of three things; they would give themselves up quietly, flee the scene or stand and fight. What the driver of the squad car up front had not anticipated was the frazzled and dangerously close to the edge mind of the man driving the truck. Martin had absolutely no intention of allowing the manoeuvre to succeed, and at the moment the brake lights flared in his vision he dropped the gear and slammed down hard on the accelerator.

There was an almighty crunch as the trucks metal grill collided with the hard moulded plastic at the back of the police car. Martin took some element of satisfaction in the surprised, hurt look that flashed across the face of the driver as he was shunted forward a couple of metres, almost losing control of his wheel. He regained his composure just in time and brought the car back onto a steady path, but he was clearly shaken, and when he next looked miserably into his rear view mirror Martin was glaring back at him with the eyes of an escaped lunatic. The driver up front, who had been given the description of the man he was to bring to swift justice, had been excited at the prospect of an easy takedown, now he lowered his gaze, looking like a frightened rabbit, caught between the headlights of an oncoming truck on a starlit country road.

"Take that you bastard!" Martin shouted, then stared hard right at the driver of the car running parallel to him, letting him know in no uncertain terms exactly who they were dealing with.

This was all good and well, but Martin was well aware that it was all just stalling tactics. They were going to find a way to bring the vehicle to a halt, even if it meant they tailed him until his rapidly diminishing fuel supply ran out and the truck came chugging to a halt at the side of the road. If that was to happen it would all be over; he would stand no chance against this much resistance, he had been lucky until now, but that luck could only last for so long. He needed another plan, and fast.

Then he saw it, a possible way out of this latest nightmare, approximately five hundred yards up the road. He had one chance to make this work, and that was the only chance he was going to get; there was no room for error, one slight mistake, a misjudgement of timing or a badly executed manoeuvre and the chance would be gone. This had to be perfect.

In the distance the slip road that led to a small suburb on the outskirts of Qingdao grew closer. He had to pick the perfect moment; too soon and the men in the squad vehicles would anticipate his move, too late and he would blow his chance.

Martin sucked in deep breaths, only daring to look at the exit from the busy freeway from the corner of his eye in case either the driver up front or the driver to his side got wind of his intentions.

"Come on come on come on!" He muttered, not daring to blink in case he missed his chance despite the wind that continued to billow through the empty windshield.

Three hundred yards now, two hundred and fifty, two hundred and twenty five. Martin's fingers flexed and un-flexed around the sweat soaked steering wheel, his hair was stood on end giving him the appearance of a deranged psychopath and despite the ever rushing wind his clothes stuck to his body in a stinking coating of greasy day old sweat.

One hundred and fifty yards, this was it, this was his chance, miss it now and all was undoubtedly lost. Martin wasn't going to make that mistake. Quickly drawing in a huge lungful of dirty freeway air he pulled hard right on the steering wheel, catching the back bumper of the squad car up front again and sending it shunting forward once more before slamming hard into the drivers side door of the car to his right, the driver wearing a mask of petrified confusion as he was forced spinning out of his lane and into the inside lane where he almost hit an elderly woman in a battered green Toyota. A gap as wide as the adjacent two lanes appeared and the truck entered it fast, reaching the exit lane just in time to cut across the narrowing slipway to make his escape, but leaving no time for the cars that tailed him to understand what had just happened.

As the truck disappeared down the exit ramp Martin looked up and to his left, watching as the police cars continued past the exit along the freeway, their drivers still too stunned to be able to react in time to the sorry situation.

Martin screeched in triumph, punching his fist against the roof of the truck hard enough to damage his hand, but he wouldn't feel that until much, much later, when he was back on a plane to England, unaware that he would soon be watching as someone he cared for dearly lay dying in a pool of their own blood.

22

There was a cough and a splutter as the engine, starved of petroleum kangaroo jumped a couple of times, then came to a stop at the side of the road with the engine stalled, the yellow fuel light the only thing still illuminated on the dash.

Martin sighed, tried the engine a couple of times, listened as it clicked over but found no ignition, then switched it off, leaving the key dangling in its place. That was it then, with all the fuel gone it was a foot race from here, and a race it would be, even if they were confronted by honest policemen or women, of which he had no doubt there were many, they would still be in hot water given their current predicament. No, he had to make it his target, it was their only hope.

It hadn't been easy, but Martin had led the band of terrified, naked Chinese through the narrow streets on the outskirts of Qingdao, able only to use his intuition and general sense of direction to lead them back into the city; all of the signposts were in Mandarin, so no help there. Slowly they had wound their way forward, with the white haired man craning his neck at regular intervals to try and catch a glimpse of the inner city skyline in the distance.

There had been no further sign of the officers who had tried to box him in on the fast lane of the outer freeway, though he had no doubt they wouldn't be far behind; it wouldn't have taken them long to double back to the exit and give chase through the quiet suburbs, maybe they would even know a short cut, could be lying in wait for them around any corner. For now however there was no sign, and for that at least Martin was thankful.

Now he sat at the side of the road, looking at the empty fuel gage and contemplating his next move. The safest thing would be to go on alone, make his way to his destination and return for the refugees once he knew the coast was clear, but if their pursuers were to travel this road the battered, empty wind-screened truck was not particularly conspicuous, and the prisoners would be in trouble once more. There was only one thing for it; they were going to have to all go together.

On the positive side he had managed to lead them right back into the centre of Qingdao, so their destination to his reckoning was no more than three or four streets away, on the negative side this was the heart of the city, where business men and women, shoppers and tourists lined the streets in droves, leading nineteen naked and filthy captives through these streets and remaining unnoticed was simply not on the agenda.

"Ok, let's do this." Martin said, aware that a white haired foreigner in a bullet ridden truck with no windshield was already drawing attention on this busy inner city street. Oh well, so they were going to get a few funny looks, compared to what they had all been through and the imminent danger still surrounding them that was the least of their concerns.

The bruised and bedraggled man opened the driver's door of the camouflage green truck with a grunt of exertion and jumped down onto the tarmac, feeling the impact in his tired, arthritic knees. He winced at the pain and hobbled around the side, feeling every bit of strain and effort his ageing body had been subjected to in the last twenty-four hours. Already a small crowd had gathered at the side of the street, camera phones were raised in hands, Martin wondered how many more would appear in just a few moments. He opened the hatch at the back of the truck and looked up into the faces of the terrified Chinese gathered in the back. At first he didn't see her, one sorrowful dirt streaked face blended into the next, then, thankfully she appeared, pushing to the front of the crowd, seemingly aware of the importance of her role as the only English speaking captive.

"Thank God." Martin muttered, then he addressed her directly. "We need to get out of here; the truck is out of fuel, so we need to go on foot."

"On foot?" The woman replied, her eyes confused and more than a little bit scared.

"Yes, on foot." Martin replied, then placed the palm of his left hand flat and used the index and middle finger of his right hand to imitate a pair of walking legs, it was an internationally recognised gesture and the woman nodded with understanding, though the fear had grown in her eyes. "Please can you tell your people?"

The woman turned and spoke to the assembled throng in her native tongue, who too went through the motions of both understanding and great fear at pretty much the same time. The little girl was weeping again, one of the women still comforted her, but now she looked as though she could use a little comfort herself.

It was funny, but the newly freed captives rather revealing state had become as normal to Martin now as the paintwork of a well seen wall, but he was still acutely aware that when they left this truck, with penises dangling and breasts on display, pubic hair all matted and filthy, pandemonium was likely to ensue.

Well, they were just going to have to deal with it.

"Ok, are you ready?" Martin asked the skinny woman. She nodded gravely, looking both terrified and determined at the same time, then the white haired foreigner was gesturing for them to climb down from the truck, and slowly but surely the people were shuffling forwards.

He hoped to God that his sense of direction in this far flung corner of the globe was as keen as he hoped, or this could be a very short trip.

The first of the assembled group reached the edge of the truck, it was a man, somewhere in his mid to late twenties, really it was hard to tell under all the grime, he poked his head out of the side of the truck and looked around nervously, seemed to think better of it and ducked back inside. Martin had feared this would happen, now they were back in the city, away from the understanding confines of the factory, they were becoming conscious once again of the fact they were as naked as the day they arrived kicking and screaming into this world.

"Come on," Martin said, gesturing with his hands for the man to jump down, "it's our only chance!"

The man didn't speak a single word of English, but he knew all too well what the white haired saviour was saying. Nodding his head slowly and reluctantly he crept forward once more, looked out again at the crowd gathered at the side of the road, then jumped down from the back of the truck to the roadside below, cupping his private parts in his hands to try and keep at least some small semblance of modesty.

A surprised chorus of gasps rose from the crowd, just as Martin had suspected, hands were suddenly darting into pockets, pulling out smartphones to capture the moment in all its glory.

Let them, Martin thought as he gestured for the next person to step forward, the more evidence of the existence of these people the better.

The next person dropped down, bending over in an attempt to protect her dignity, then the next and the next. One young man caught his foot on a sharp stone and hopped around holding his injured foot in his hand, his penis bouncing up and down much to the delight of the crowd, which cawed with laughter at the sight. The children were handed down, Martin grabbing them beneath the arms and lowering them to the floor, this was the point when the crowd, which had doubled by now and was spilling out onto the road, let out a drone of disapproval.

One by one the holding area at the back of the truck emptied, until all that was left was the one skinny woman who had come to Martin's rescue when he had needed an interpreter.

"That evywun." She said in her thick accent, and then, with one arm draped across her tiny breasts and her other covering her thatch of curly pubic hair she sat down on the open truck door and slid down to the ground.

Some of the crowd had moved in for a closer look, lifting their cameras before their awe struck faces and capturing the moment that a delivery truck in the centre of Qingdao just unloaded its contents of nineteen filthy, naked Chinese.

The crowd of naked refugees looked to their newfound leader for guidance, their eyes desperate and pleading as the bustling crowd drew closer.

"Come on." Martin said, and quickly marched down the street in the direction in which he hoped to find his destination. The crowd of onlookers, growing by the second, followed. As they passed shops and cafes and places of work people within became aware of something truly spectacular going on outside, and drew to their windows like moths attracted to a softly glowing light. Their expressions when they saw the mob that passed them by were always the same; the hands that covered the open jaws, the eyes so narrow the most of the time so wide at the sight of the melee.

If this were in Paris, or London, or midtown Manhattan, where protests and street theatre and flash mobs were a part of everyday life, the sight of so many naked bodies in one place would still have caused some kind of controversy; but this was none of those places, this was the land of dictatorship and strict enforced rulings, and what was going on right now on the streets of Qingdao was simply unthinkable.

Martin couldn't let this concern him; yes in Shandong Province, China it was likely that being naked in the street would lead to incarceration, maybe even punishable by death, but considering the alternative this was a risk he felt sure to be worth the effort.

They reached the corner and Martin looked about himself, trying to get his bearings, he could see the roof of the building he was trying to reach rising over the top of the smaller buildings in the near distance and looked for a way to navigate the streets towards it.

"This way." He said, and marched on, the soft padded footsteps of the shoeless souls behind him thrumming away on the tarmac. They passed another row of shops and a whole new group of surprised onlookers quickly grabbed in their pockets or purses for their mobiles, whatever else happened on this already manic day Martin felt sure that they would all be internet stars by the end of it. The old man had heard of YouTube but never used it himself, if he had been aware of the term 'going viral' and understood its meaning he would have bet every last penny he owned, quite a sizeable pile of brass, that his ragtag bunch of followers would be viral by seven that night, and he wouldn't have been wrong.

Past the row of shops he tried his luck down an alley and came to a dead end. Cursing his misfortune he led them back in the direction they had come, still covering their most private areas, the young girl still weeping uncontrollably, through the maddening crowd.

Martin was looking further up the street, trying to determine if there was a way through to the road beyond this way when he felt a sudden heavy clout on his arm. It didn't hurt, but it did shock him, and he turned in surprise to see an elderly Chinese lady preparing to take a second swing. The businessman was able to duck in time, but he couldn't avoid the torrent of abuse that poured from her outraged mouth, luckily for him he didn't understand a word of it, but even with the language barrier what it was he was quite able to detect her disgust at his vulgar display, and so close to Christmas as well! Behind them on the street the gathered crowd roared with laughter, this really was the last thing they had expected when they had left their homes that morning, Martin ignored them, and the old woman to boot, and carried on in the direction he hoped would lead them to safety.

The naked refugees followed close behind him as he rushed on down the road, turning at the end and crossing a small road to what he hoped would be the right spot. At the end of the road they reached a wider street, this looked familiar to Martin and he looked to the right; there it was, the Qingdao office of the Shanghai Daily News.

The sigh of relief that passed his lips was like a warm comforting blanket on a cold and bitter evening, they were just a few hundred yards from safety. Then a sound shrilled in his eardrum and turned the warmth to the coldness of an icy finger from a frozen lake. It was a police siren, and he had no doubt for whom it was intended. Even if these were genuinely good cops they would still be in a whole world of trouble if they were caught here on the street; they had to move, and fast.

"Come on!" Martin shouted, and ran down the street in the direction of the tall glass building as fast as his sixty-eight year old legs would allow. The panic stricken brigade followed suit, their bare feet slapping against the concrete as they pursued their saviour in the direction of the news building.

If the car turned the corner and saw them, making it to the building would not be good enough, they had to disappear inside the building before the police car arrived. The sirens were getting louder, and definitely heading in their general direction; Martin dare not turn round, just kept facing forwards, cutting the distance to the tall glass building as the breath wheezed from his chest.

Finally they reached the double fronted glass doors; Martin yanked on the handle and pulled the right hand side open. For the first time he tried to gage the distance of the police car, to determine if it had yet turned the corner at the end of the busy road, but he couldn't see past the naked jostling bodies, the smaller children being carried now, as they followed him to this place. They didn't know why they were here, they didn't know yet if they were safe, but the white haired foreigner had rescued them from their terrible ordeal, they would have each followed him anywhere.

Holding the door open wide Martin ushered his terrified followers inside, their naked, filthy bodies passing him one by one as he finally got to look down the street; the police sirens continued to blare but the cars were as yet nowhere in sight, this was good, he just hoped they wouldn't be alerted to their whereabouts by some camera wielding busy body. The last of the group slipped through the door and disappeared inside, Martin was quick to follow, pulling the door closed behind him, and even though it was completely transparent he felt much safer with it closed between him and the street. He was just in time to push his way to the front of the self conscious group, who continued to protect their modesty to the best of their ability, in time to see a fraught looking security guard rushing their way. He was wearing a blue suit and must have been Martin's age at least, probably even older. The businessman could see the busy news room beyond the waist high glass partition about fifty yards ahead, he wasn't about to let this jumped up pensioner stand between him and the end of this sorry mess.

As the guard neared Martin prepared himself; the man was shouting something in mandarin that made a couple of the group, ladies who had been through enough of a fright for one day, flinch back against their fellow escapees. The businessman, who despite his time surrounded by this colourful and exotic language had not picked up a single word, did not allow it to even register. He had been shot at and tortured by hardened thugs this morning; one old man wasn't going to cause him any trouble. Without waiting to discover how the man intended to control an unexpected mob of naked trespassers, Martin waited until the old man was just a couple of yards away, then struck out his right fist. It connected firmly with the mans jaw and sent him tumbling to the floor, no doubt seeing birds tweet about his head just like in the old warner brothers cartoons.

"Sorry." Martin said with genuine empathy, then stepped over the dazed man and headed in the direction of the news room. "Come on!" He said, ignoring the receptionist who was momentarily too stunned to act, and climbed the glass partition into the noisy open space.

The escapee's followed, climbing the flimsy barrier, having to reveal their naked forms as they used their hands to scale the partition, the men lifting the children into the area beyond.

The wave of awe that quickly swept the busy news room that morning began at the corner desk, the one closest to the barrier, but as this startled young man tapped the shoulder of the busy junior reporter to his left, it started a chain reaction that quietened the floor in seconds and left nearly a hundred office juniors and editorial assistants frozen to the spot in wonder. Their eyes, slanted by the nature of their origin, were wide now, and as they looked upon the scene before them they each understood with their finely tuned journalistic instincts that something big had just interrupted their busy day, and whatever it was the Shanghai Daily News had just landed the scoop.

Ignoring their gormless expressions Martin hurried down the side of the news room towards the small row of offices on the left, gesturing for the crowd that had gathered behind him to follow. He didn't have time to worry if Lau was even in his office, the thought flashed across his mind at about the same time that he pulled on the door handle and saw the man sat their at his desk.

The reporter, who had been mid call to his chief editor, looked up and saw the group of naked, bedraggled souls that filled the doorway to his office, leading them the strange Englishman who had stirred up his interest in the old missing person case again, and the phone dropped from his hand, clattering against the side of his desk where it hung limp from its cord. His jaw dropped loose and the gum he had been chewing rolled out of his mouth and landed with a dull plop amongst the clutter of his crowded desk. He stared in disbelief at the scene before him, completely incapable of speech for the first time in his life, as he did so the white haired man took a step deeper into the room and regarded him with a look of exhausted finality.

"You asked for proof," he said, spreading his hands to draw attention as if some were needed to the group of naked Chinese to his rear, "here it is."

PART FIVE:
A SHADOW OVER
CHRISTMAS

1

The privately chartered Lear jet touched down at Gatwick a little after noon on Christmas Eve. Martin, who had slept the entire thirteen hour journey through arose from his deep slumber as the wheels connected with the tarmac of the runway. The businessman groaned, feeling disoriented and stiff from lack of movement. His injuries, of which there were many, all sang as he returned to the land of the living, some dull and distant, others like the swelling about his eye socket and the singed area on his chest more immediate.

He took a look around; the passenger bay was empty apart from the single flight attendant who sat with her back to the rear of the cockpit, waiting for the captain to give the signal that she was safe to go about her duties.

The Chinese authorities, embarrassed by the sudden surge of media speculation surrounding one of their leading cities, had started proceedings to have Martin contained in the country until such time as to question him about his damning accusations. Knowing this could be a lengthy process indeed the businessman had used his new found media fame to postpone these arrangements until after the holidays, and with a call to Sheila back in England had chartered the first private jet out of the Orient, leaving on the promise of returning to Shandong to support the police with their enquiries in the new year.

Outside a cold and grey cloud hung over England's capital like a death bag, the ground was wet from an earlier downpour and the distant terminal building was lit up like the Christmas trees that adorned its hallways and waiting areas. Less than twelve hours from now presents would be left waiting under elaborately decorated trees, ready for eager and expectant children to rip at their paper coverings, excited at what Santa may have delivered, turkey's would be defrosting for the morning, when they would be stuffed and basted, ready for roasting, champagne would be on ice for young couples excited at their first Christmas in their new home and the foil of mince pies, the litter of badly chewed carrots and the empty remains of eagerly poured glasses of sherry would wait beneath chimney stacks for their benefactors to discover the first signs that he had been. All of this would be happening, in houses up and down the length of Britain and beyond, but Martin had never felt so distant from the spirit of Christmas in his life.

Sighing and rubbing at his eyes he reflected on the last year; a year that had seen him develop from a happy-go-lucky man of business to a breaker of multiple laws, most notably manslaughter, in some eyes maybe even murder. From the operation to his own investigation, from his near miss at Eze-link cars to his time in China, it had certainly been a rollercoaster, with more lows than highs. It had been a journey of intrigue and suspense, of mystery and absolution, and amazingly had come to a head a year to the day in which it had started.

Who was I back then? Martin thought, thinking of the pot bellied man who had stood to give the address at the annual office party. Who am I now?

A voice over the intercom interrupted his thoughts and brought him back into the room.

"This is your captain speaking, we've landed safely at Gatwick International airport, the local time is just coming up to twenty-five past twelve, the outside temperature is just below three degrees so a bit cooler than back in Qingdao, make sure to wrap up warmly before heading out. Your flight attendant

Suzanne will be with you shortly to see to your safe exit from this Lear jet 85.On behalf of Eastern Charter Direct I would just like to thank you for flying with us today and would like to be the first to wish you a safe onward journey, and a very Merry Christmas."

The intercom fell silent and a moment later the flight attendant was unbuckling her belt as the engine softly died. A car was making its way slowly across the strip in the direction of the landed jet; Martin had an idea the driver of the vehicle had been eagerly awaiting his arrival for some time.

"Did you have a nice flight mister Rooley?" The Oriental flight assistant with the distinctly British name asked with a warm smile.

"I had a nice sleep that's for sure."

"You will have needed it."

"You can say that again." The white haired man said, then stretched out his arms, feeling his joints loosen and spring back to life with a pleasant tingle.

"Make sure you grab any personal belongings before you leave Mister Rooley."

"I will." He replied with a pained smile, then watched as she went back to her duties cleaning the cabin, there wasn't very much for her to do, he had been a model customer; he reckoned if all her clients slept the entire way back she would probably make this a job for life.

The car, a large black BMW 4x4 pulled up alongside the plane, its engine idling. Martin looked out at it with a mixture of emotions; he knew who was here waiting for him and as much as he desperately wanted to see his darling wife, just how was he supposed to explain the last six months? Sighing he unbuckled his belt and slowly stood up, the muscles in his back and legs popping like corks in a fire.

There was a whir of machinery as the attendant pressed a button on the wall and the landing door opened. Pivoted slats were hidden beneath a soft veneer that pulled away as the door arched out almost a hundred and eighty degrees, making a stairwell down to the runway where it connected with the tarmac below.

Grabbing his bag from the locker to the rear of the cabin Martin made the short walk down to where the pretty young girl waited for him at the door.

"It looks like your greeting party has arrived." She said, looking down at the waiting car.

"Thank you for everything." He said pleasantly, though in truth she had done very little.

"You're welcome." She replied unperturbed. "Have a safe journey Mister Rooley."

He nodded warmly, then stepped to the top of the stairs. The sky above Gatwick was littered with arriving and departing planes, not unusual this being the second busiest airport in the UK, nor was it unusual to feel the bitter chill that greeted him as he stepped gingerly down the stairs.

As he made his descent the driver's door opened and a tall, balding man emerged. Peter Werth-Duncan looked up at Martin with a pained smile, then walked around the side of the car to the rear passenger seat. He opened the door and a well dressed woman in her early sixties stepped out, her eyes puffy, her bottom lip trembling. The businessman didn't make it to the bottom of the stairs before she was rushing forward, her dinner lady arms held open. Rose greeted him with the tightest and warmest embrace he had ever accepted, and though it hurt him physically with his numerous injuries he held on tight too, loving the feel of her back in his arms.

"Oh Martin, oh Martin, I've been so worried. When I saw the news, I just couldn't believe it."

"I know, I know." He conceded, not knowing what else to say.

"Come on, let's get off this runway." Peter said from behind them. "I think you've got some explaining to do."

"I think you're right." Martin answered, though whether he was referring to the explanation or to just getting the hell out of here he didn't make clear.

"Considering the nature of why you're here we've been allowed to clear customs away from the crowd." Peter said, holding open the door.

"Thank you Peter, as ever you're proving yourself invaluable." Martin said as he climbed into the back of the BMW.

"Yes well let me assure you my efficiency comes at a price." He replied, placing Martin's case in the boot of the car as Rose climbed in next to her husband.

"Oh?" Martin enquired with his eyebrow raised as his friend climbed back in behind the steering wheel.

"A full explanation, and I mean full, God damn it Martin just what have you been up to?"

Martin allowed himself a small chuckle.

"Now isn't that the sixty-four thousand dollar question."

Peter released the handbrake and with his foot on the accelerator the car crept along the edge of Gatwick's private runway. They were passing the side of a huge grey maintenance building, vehicles with yellow flashing lights in the entrances to huge trailer like garages. Martin relaxed back in the seat, wondering where he could possibly start.

"What have you been up to you old fool?" Rose scolded without any real upset, she was too pleased to see her man to possibly be upset. She didn't fasten her belt, instead moved to the centre seat of the 4x4 so she could wrap her arm about his arm and place her head on his shoulder; again Martin ignored the pain to allow her to do this. "I mean China, the closest you've ever been to the Orient is the Red Sun Cantonese in Battersea."

"It wasn't by choice I can assure you."

"Not by choice he says not by choice! Do you realise how long you've been gone? And with me staying with Moira, do you think her and Ken had no questions, I mean I know Ken doesn't talk much but even he found the whole situation decidedly unusual."

"Well I'm sure you managed to fill whatever silences Ken left in the conversation." Martin said in jest, though really he was only stalling for time.

"This is no jest Martin, everybody was so worried, calling me up like that and asking me to drop everything and go to my sisters. I didn't know why you were asking me to do this, I thought you must be in trouble but I didn't know what, and you refused to talk to me! I've been going out of my mind! At first I was thinking tax evasion, that the Inland Revenue had found out about some dodgy scheme or other but I told myself, not my Martin, he's as straight as an arrow.

So then I start to think about what other trouble you could be in and my mind it went around and around and the sleepless nights, if I had a one I must have had about a hundred and...."

"Ok, ok, I get the picture. I understand it was a difficult time for you, and I'm sorry for putting you through that really I am, but you have to understand, it was for your own safety."

She was about to speak again when Peter said:

"We're here."

Martin breathed a sigh of relief, after her initial joy at seeing him he had sensed Rose's temper rising, and he couldn't blame her, he really had put her through the ringer, he was very glad for the momentary reprieve.

Peter brought the BMW to a stop in a private bay next to a glass panelled door. He killed the engine and got out of the car, opening the passenger door like Martin was some kind of celebrity, which at the moment he supposed he was.

The businessman climbed out with Rose close behind, she could have stayed in the car with the special privileges they had been afforded by the airport but she wasn't ready as yet to let her husband out of her sight.

Peter walked up to the glass panelled door and pressed a button set into the wall, a couple of moments later a burly security guard in a crisp white shirt and blue blazer appeared and opened the door.

"Martin Rooley, here to clear customs." Peter said.

The security guard took a step back, closing the door slightly on the visitors so he could confirm the information with the security room. He spoke into his mic, repeating the information he had ben told and waited patiently for a response. A couple of seconds later the speaker attached to his lapel crackled and a voice on the other end said:

"Cleared. Please direct Mister Rooley to operations room four."

"Received." The security guard replied, then opened the door full again. "If you'd like to follow me please."

The three guests stepped into the security building and followed the large man down a long bleak corridor to a double security door; there he swiped his pass card against the card reader, the tiny light on top of the device turning green with a slight whirring sound, and pulled open the right hand door. They followed him through and into what looked to be a small waiting area, with several seats, a vending machine and a water cooler. A corridor ran from the left and the right hand side of the room, the man led them to the right and to a row of closed doors. When he reached the fourth door along he stopped and opened the door.

"If you'll wait in here please."

Martin and Rose stepped into the room, when Peter stepped forward the security guard addressed him personally.

"Once you've cleared customs you will not be allowed to return onto the concourse, if you give me the keys your car will be brought around to the front of the building, when the time arrives I'll take you through to the arrivals lounge and someone will show you to your car."

"Thank you for the courtesy you've extended today." Peter said, fishing in his jacket pocket and pulling out the keys.

"Of course, someone will be with you shortly." With that the security guard took the keys and turned back in the direction they had come.

The room was fairly small, with a plasma television on the wall tuned to Sky news, a small rectangular table in the centre and four plastic chairs. The rear wall was made of reflective glass; Martin was under no illusion as to what this was, he had seen enough television interrogation rooms in his time, he just hoped it would not be in use today.

"First we can't get a glimpse of your tired old face now we can't escape from it." Peter said with a small smirk.

"Huh?" Martin replied, not understanding.

Peter pointed up to the television; still feeling a little dazed from his lengthy sleep and even lengthier ordeal the white haired man looked up to the plasma screen only to see his own face staring back at him. It was a wholly unsettling experience; despite his rise to prominence he had managed to steer out of the spotlight for most of his career, so to be suddenly become of media significance was neither a pleasant nor welcome change.

This was the news conference he had given in Shandong shortly before boarding his jet back home, and despite the volume on the television being muted the subtitles at the bottom of the screen told the businessman's story clearly enough.

"You look old." Rose said wearily, sitting in one of the seats as she stared up at the screen.

"Yes." Martin agreed. He sat down in the seat next to her, rubbing at his eyes with one wrinkled hand. Peter stayed stood to the back of the room, looking up at the screen in disbelief. Martin wondered how many times the pair of them had watched this news story since his sudden rise to fame, and how many more times they would watch it still before the bizarre events of the last six months or so started to become clear to them. He supposed in a lot of ways that would be down to him and exactly what type of explanation he could give them. Luckily for him before he was forced to address this particular problem the door to operations room four opened and a tall thin man with a bald head wearing a brown suit stepped in.

"Good afternoon." He said, quickly settling into the seat opposite Martin and placing a couple of papers on the table in front of him. "I'm Ian Semen I'll be checking you back into the UK today; it seems you've become quite a celebrity on your travels."

"Not a willing one I can assure you." Martin replied with a strained smile.

"Well this shouldn't take more than a moment then we can have you on your way. Could I see your passport please?"

"Of course." Martin said, and fished in his jacket pocket; he handed over his passport and waited for it to be scrutinised. The man took a glance at the picture, checked to see it was the same man then handed the passport back. In truth Martin didn't know how he had passed the check, the man in the photo was heavier set by over thirty pounds and his jovial face wasn't blemished by a single bruise. The man in the room on the other hand looked like he had picked a fight with a mountain lion and lost.

"You'll be flying back out to the far east in the coming days?"

"In the new year." Martin answered. The thin man nodded slowly as if to confirm this was exactly as he had suspected.

"Has anybody asked you to carry anything back into the country today?"

"No."

"Have your bags been with you the entire duration of your journey?"

Martin, who had not seen his bag from the moment he boarded the plane to the moment he departed, decided this wasn't the steer of conversation that would get him home any time soon.

"They have."

"Ok, well everything appears to be in order here, I won't hold you up any longer I'm sure you're anxious to get home. I hope your new found fame doesn't dampen your celebrations, I'll get someone to guide you through to arrivals, Merry Christmas."

"And you." Martin said with a strained smile, watching as Semen stood from his seat and left the room.

A few moments later a second security guard appeared, a tall black man with biceps as thick as Martin's thighs; he led them through a maze of corridors and along several moving walkways until they were back in the main terminal building.

"There's a press presence waiting at the arrivals gate, if you want to avoid them take the door on the right, your car is parked in the disabled parking bays to the right of the exit." The large man held out the keys and Peter took them.

"Thank you, for everything." Martin replied. The security guard nodded briskly, then turned and disappeared back through the security personnel only door from which they had just appeared.

"Ok, let's get you home." Peter said with a tired smile, then led them through the door on the right. From here they could see through into the main arrivals lounge, the guard had been right, several news crews were gathered on the outside of the security perimeter, their cameras pointing towards the main passenger gate, awaiting his arrival. They hurried on past a couple of shops and a row of ATM's, but when they reached a small deserted bar Martin stopped them.

"I'm sorry for what I put you through, both of you." He said, his bottom lip trembling. "I'm sorry, but I had no other choice."

"That's ok." Peter replied, looking uncomfortable.

"No, no it's not. I can't imagine the worry I must have put you through."

Rose was looking ashen, her lined face strained about the eyes. "It's us who should be apologising to you."

"What do you mean?" Martin asked as Peter visibly stiffened.

"If only we'd never..." She replied, but was unable to finish her sentence, her face crumbling with the misery it bore.

The penny dropped for Martin and sank into his stomach like a lead weight. "You knew." He said, his eyes wide with shock.

Rose, unable to bear the weight of his stare looked up to Peter for support.

"You too!" Martin said, the shock sinking deeper.

Peter, knowing he was backed into a corner pursed his lips, his eyes becoming narrow slits. Suddenly he whipped out his hand and grabbed a glass from a table of empties at his side; he slammed it down on the edge of the table, smashing the curved edge and leaving the base in his hand with a dangerous array of shards in his hand. As Martin watched on horrified he made a lunge for Rose, grabbing he by the arm and pulling her close to him, then the hand that held the jagged shards of glass lifted to her side, the pointed edges of the glass pressing painfully into the soft layer of fat just above her right hip.

"Peter what are you doing?" Martin asked, his face stricken with horror as Rose whimpered in fear.

"Shut up!" Peter spat back fiercely. "You've brought this on yourself. Get out to the car, and I swear to God if you make one funny move I'll gut her like a pig!"

"Ok, ok," Martin said, holding his hands out in surrender, "I'll do whatever you want, just don't hurt her ok."

"Move!" Peter said.

Martin turned and head towards the exit, a few moments later he was driving the 4x4 out of the airport with Peter and Rose in the rear, and as the pieces of the puzzle slowly started slotting into place he wondered just how he could have been so naïve.

2

The BMW skidded around the corner on the wet surface, heading towards the lights at the end of the road.

"Slow it down a little we don't want to draw attention to ourselves." Peter said from the back.

"I'm sorry, I'm just nervous, do you have to hold that glass into her like that, you're hurting her!"

"Shut up!" Martin's understudy fired back. Rose was whimpering uncontrollably, fat tears rolling down her cheeks and streaking her make-up.

"Martin what's happening?" She cried miserably.

"Why don't you tell me." Martin asked. "Just how are you involved in all this Rose?"

His wife didn't reply, just let out a low guttural moan that told him as much as he really needed to know; this was no mistake, she had known about the heart.

"What did they tell you Rose? Huh? What did they say? Did they say it was the only way? Did they say I was going to die if they didn't find a heart and soon?"

"You were going to die!" She cried back miserably.

"And I would have gladly done so than be a part of this." He replied coldly.

"The two of you shut up I'm trying to think!" Peter grumbled, his eyes kept darting from window to window, as if he were on the lookout for someone or something.

"You figured this out with Purefoy didn't you Peter?" Martin said, completely ignoring his friend's request. "The two of you got together and hatched a plan to keep me alive, you used Rose as the sentiment, got her onside to talk me into an operation I knew to be flawed."

"Yeah and you couldn't have been more eager to accept the donation, you're no angel." Peter replied coldly.

"I didn't know where the heart was from!"

"No but you knew something wasn't right, still you carried on, why? Cos deep down you're no different from the rest of us, deep down when push comes to shove, you're a survivor, just like me. We aren't all that different Martin, I just have the guts to admit to what I am."

Martin made no reply, he knew there was at least some truth in what the man was saying, and knowing that truth made it difficult to claim the higher ground. Eventually he side-stepped the issue, hoping instead that he could find an answer to the question that was troubling him the most; the question of why.

"Ok," he said at last, "what are you Peter?"

"I'll tell you what I am, I'll tell you exactly what I am; I'm the man who's spent the last eight years lifting Sapient Trans-Global into the FTSE top one hundred. I'm the guy who took a business with an annual turnover of seventeen million pounds to over sixty-three million in my first two years. I'm the guy who raised net profit from 4.5 million when I arrived to nearly twenty-two million as things now stand. I'm the guy who's given hours, days, weeks, months and years of his life to ensuring the stability of a potential global super brand. I'm the guy whose blood, sweat and tears have ensured not just the survival but the prominent dominance of Sapient on the global stock exchange. You want to know who I am? Look at the name at the bottom of every sound deal; look at the name at the bottom of every crucial contract. Who am I? I am Sapient!"

"Your work has always been valued most highly, and may I add you've been justly rewarded for it too."

"Rewarded? Rewarded? There is only one reward worthy of the time and effort that I have put into building this empire and you know exactly what it is."

There was a drop in Martin's stomach like a lead weight; suddenly he understood what this was all about.

"The business, you wanted the business."

"You're God damn right I wanted the business!" Peter spat fiercely, his grip on the jagged shards of glass that were pressed into Rose's side tightening further still. "I earned it! I'm the reason Sapient is so strong in the market, I'm the reason the business keeps turning over a healthy profit, year after year when all of our competitors have struggled to stay out of the red! I earned this, it's mine, you promised it to me!"

Martin listened to this whining, the whining of a spoilt child, and wondered just how he had judged the man so wrong.

"I was going to sign the business over to you, you know that, as soon as I was ready to step down there was only one successor in my eyes, I did tell you that and I meant every word."

"Oh yeah? When Martin, huh? When exactly were you going to take that backwards step? Cos forgive me for saying, but you had a pretty good opportunity with your little health scare, but still you stalled."

The lights turned green, ahead of them the traffic started slowly creeping forwards, Martin didn't want to take his eyes from the man he had thought of as his friend, especially not when he was pressing a deadly shard of glass into his petrified wife's side, but he had no choice, he faced back forward and followed the rest of the traffic through the busy junction.

"I wasn't thinking straight at that time Peter, I had a lot on my mind remember, but we can talk now, we can work something out now, just put the glass down, please, I beg of you, put the glass down."

"You know what hurt the most Martin?" Peter asked, a pained expression on his less than spectacular face. "Even when you were putting your affairs in order, when you had no choice than to face the fact of your imminent doom, you still didn't sign the business over to me. You'd have clung on to the bitter end, and when they lay you in the ground or burned you into ashes, the shareholders would have taken what we had and floated it on the stock market. I'd have left with nothing. Eight years of valuable service and I'd have left with nothing."

"I made a mistake. Please Peter I see that now, come on, let's just talk."

The balding man carried on as though Martin had not even spoken. "I tried to convince you, God knows I did. Time and time again I tried to convince you how important it was to consider the future of the business, still, nothing."

Martin swallowed hard, was it really true? He loved Sapient, had grown the business himself from virtually nothing. Had he been so reluctant to let go that he would have allowed the business to fold rather than relinquish control? Peter was right about one thing; there had been ample opportunity to get his affairs in order, and he had squandered those chances one by one.

"That's why you had to keep me alive." He said weakly, feeling the enormity of everything that had happened over the last six or seven months bearing down on him like a prowling beast. "You needed me alive, it had nothing to do with friendship, you needed me alive."

"It was business, you were business. If your affairs had been in order sooner I'd have made sure Purefoy killed you during the procedure, but you didn't do it, you wouldn't change your fucking will before you went under the knife, you selfish cunt!"

"So you convinced the surgeon to keep me alive, to find a way, no matter how disgusting, no matter how barbaric to make sure I couldn't die before I'd served my purpose."

"He didn't need much convincing; your knight in shining armour was no saint I can assure you. There wasn't anything he wouldn't do for money."

"Is that why you killed him? Greed?"

At this Peter visibly flinched. "Oh you'd like to believe that wouldn't you."

For the first time Martin was truly astounded; if not Peter then who? Malik? He had denied it in his office, but could he be trusted to have told the truth?

"You didn't kill him?"

"Purefoy had to die, I can tell you that much for certain, if anything his blood is firmly on your hands. All those damn questions, morning, noon and night, on and on and on. Like a broken God damn record! Purefoy got spooked, wanted us to tell you what we'd done, so you see, his untimely demise can be traced directly back to your actions."

The traffic on the road was thinning out now; they were so engrossed in conversation that Martin hadn't thought to ask where he was heading, he just kept on pressing forward, heading towards the M25. If he could keep Peter embroiled in conversation long enough he may be able to somehow flag for attention on the ring road, there were always patrol vehicles out there, if he could somehow get their attention without alerting Peter...

"What's wrong? Got nothing to say all of a sudden?"

Martin hadn't realised but he had been quiet for quite some time, this wasn't the way to keep the man distracted.

"So, you had to go to quite some lengths to convince me this was all above board. First convincing Rose, the house in Tottenham, the fake donor, you really had your work cut out for you."

Peter was about to say something when suddenly there was an almighty crunch to the side of the BMW; everybody within was thrown to the left, their unbuckled bodies lifted out of their seats and thrown like rag dolls across the car, their faces stretched in surprise. The windows along the side of impact, to the front and the rear all shattered at once as the car was flung across the road towards the embankment.

They had been travelling along a quiet stretch of road, about half a mile from the trunk road that led up to the M25, completely oblivious to the imminent danger that had been closing the distance between them for the last two miles.

There could be no uncertainty about it; the second 4x4 had blindsided them on purpose, although those heavily involved in conversation within the BMW hadn't seen it the driver of the second car had traversed into the opposite lane driving so its front bumper was in line with the BMW's back passenger door. They had then slammed on the gas and pulled hard left, steering their car into the side of the BMW with devastating force.

A terrible screech of tires filled the early afternoon air and smoke rose form the surface of the still wet road as the BMW was sent skidding out of control towards the barrier at the side of the carriageway. It hit hard, buckling the far side of the 4x4 and sending the car flipping onto its side and over the obstruction towards the sloping embankment below. There was a terrible din of contorting metal and breaking glass as the BMW rolled out of control down the hill, bouncing on its roof, landing on its side and finally flipping over so it was back on its pulverised wheels in the field below.

The doors on Rose's side of the car had been completely ripped from their hinges, the roof was buckled like the crater of a comet strike and the fuel tank had been ripped from its housing, it lay in the grass about a hundred yards from the devastated vehicle emitting diesel into the earth.

Martin groaned, he lay on his side with his head on the passenger seat; he could vaguely tell that his head was bleeding but for now was too dazed to suffer any real pain. He managed to lift his body and look up the embankment in time to see the front bumper of the 4x4 that had caused the smash reverse backwards out of sight; whoever had been behind that wheel, they were now making their escape.

"Rose, Rose…" He mumbled, feeling light headed and nauseous, he didn't think he had suffered any serious injuries and considering the circumstances that was nothing short of a miracle.

There was a deep groan from the back seat, Martin turned to see his wife scrunched down in the rear foot well, her arms groping for air. Of Peter there was no sign. Martin shuffled around in his seat so he was facing backwards and used what little energy he had to grab his wife by one meaty arm and pull her up into a more comfortable position.

"Wh-what happened?" She asked, just as dazed as he.

"Someone hit us." He replied between breaths.

"An accident?"

"On purpose, come on, we have to get out of here, we may still be in danger."

Martin tried to open the driver's side door of the BMW but it was too bent out of shape, it wouldn't budge an inch. Instead he slid over into the passenger seat and placed one foot out of the empty space where the door there had resided just moments ago. Rose followed suit, sliding along the leather seat in the back of the 4x4 and pulling herself free from the wreck by way of the empty space on her side.

Martin was the first to escape the vehicle, but his attention was focused on the rise at the top of the embankment, searching for the vehicle that had caused the destruction. It was for this reason that he missed the sight of Peter Werth-Duncan lying in the grass about twenty yards from the mangled car. It was Rose who saw him first, and when her eyes laid sight on him she let out a huge, lung busting scream.

Martin wheeled around in shock, sure that his old friend had crept up on them while his attention had been averted. It was only when he saw the shoeless foot sticking out of the grass that he understood what had caused the anguish in his wife; the shoe, a very fine Abercrombie loafer was buried in the grass over a hundred yards away.

The devastating impact had thrown Martin's second in command completely free of the vehicle, though as the white haired founder of Sapient Trans-Global drew near he saw this did not mean he had been lucky. Peter lay staring up at the sky with wild, frightened eyes, his hand clutched up at his throat where two dagger-like shards of glass protruded. Blood squirted from the open wounds like water from a child's pistol, completely soaking the grass about where he lay in a pool of deepest crimson.

"My God." Martin whispered, feeling nothing but compassion for the man dying at his feet, despite everything he had learned in the last half hour. He looked down on him with pity, wondering just how greed could lead a man to such a terrible fate. He was just about to kneel down at Peter's side when the balding man fixed him with a steel filled stare.

"W-w…" He muttered, his lips coated in blood.

"What?" Martin said, assuming he was trying to ask for help.

Peter composed himself, making sure he could speak through the gargle of blood that was trying to fill his throat. "W-we were…. We were never friends, you were just a means to an end, that's all, just a means to an end."

The exertion was the last action of Peter Werth-Duncan's forty-three year stint on planet earth, and as he died in a pool of his own blood his eyes rolled up to the whites, causing Rose to turn about face and throw up her breakfast all over her Jimmy Choo's.

"Come on." Martin said, horrified at the sight of someone he still loved dearly lying dead at his feet. "We have to get out of here." Wasting no more time he grabbed his badly shaken wife by the arm and led her across the field in the direction of the bypass, he couldn't afford to be caught in a crowd of rubberneckers and do-gooder's, not now, not with a killer still on the loose and his head at the top of their hit list.

3

They were on the A217 outside of Epsom when they finally managed to flag a taxi, by this time Rose was walking with her battered designer shoes in her hand and her stockings torn about her puffy pink feet. It was a long journey home, during which Rose had to stop to use the cash machine while Martin dozed in the back; he may have slept the entire flight home but he was still exhausted, the recent collision and Peter's imminent death only adding to the fatigue.

He drifted in and out of sleep, not dreaming but seeing orange swirls behind his eyelids, leaning cradled in Rose's arms, who herself sat bolt upright, staring out of the window in a dazed stupor. She was suffering from traumatic shock, having just witnessed her first dead body, but for the time being at least her husband was not there to help her through.

The car passed through the busy Greater London streets, taking short cuts and confusing routes that only a long term cabbie could navigate. One small factor that was acting in the couples favour was that this particular black cab driver did not have the traditional cockney gift of the gab. Rather he was a quiet man who went about his business in silence, not even asking about the rather dishevelled look of his latest customers. This was a small mercy but an important one indeed, for neither would have had a single clue as to how to answer.

It took forty-five minutes to circumnavigate central London and when they pulled up outside the huge electrified gates of their suburban home the counter on the dashboard read fifty-five pounds. Rose paid it from the money she had drawn from the ATM, leaving a five as tip, money well spent indeed considering the blissful silence they had enjoyed for the duration of the journey, then woke Martin who looked about himself with confusion before reality sunk its grip into his conscious mind. He looked up at the gates and the sprawling mansion beyond them with longing; in truth it hadn't been so long since he was last here, but to him it may as well have been years. The car door opened and he stepped out into the crisp December air.

"Merry Christmas." The driver said as he backed up away from the drive.

"To you too." Rose replied with a strained smile, her shoes back on her feet now, though the straps would not fasten around her swollen calves.

"Christmas." Martin said absently, rubbing at his eyes. "I keep forgetting it's Christmas."

"Not long now til the big day itself, not that I think there'll be much cause for celebration this year."

Martin sighed. "I haven't given you a very merry Christmas have I? For the second year running."

"You're home Martin, that's the best Christmas present I could ever wish for."

Martin nodded slowly, too much had happened already this day and now he was resigned to the fact that it was Christmas day in another ten hours time and he didn't even have a gift for his wife. Merry Christmas indeed.

They entered the property via the small key locked gate to the side of the main electrified gate and crossed the large paved driveway to the front door.

"Martin!" Rose said as they neared.

The businessman , who had been deep in thought, looked up at the sound of the urgent tone to her voice, though he did not see what she saw at first.

"What?" He said, his eyebrows raised.

Rose gave him a look which advised him in no uncertain terms how utterly flabbergasted she was with him right then. "The door!"

Martin looked past her to the door, and the penny dropped into place. Though the door was closed the frame around it was splintered, jutting wood protruding from the right hand panel as though it had been forced from the outside with a crowbar.

"Do you think somebody's broken in?"

"I don't know, possibly. Probably." Martin replied.

"Well do you think they're still here?" Rose was clutching at her collar, something she always did when scared.

Martin looked from her to the door, then back to his wife again. "There's only one way to find out."

"Oh Martin no!" She pleaded, seeing what he was about to do.

"Rose, if you knew the things I've seen in the last couple of weeks you'd understand why a couple of youths hiding out in my house smoking crack or whatever it is they do doesn't faze me."

"Oh Martin." She whispered, but held no further protest.

Martin pushed on the door and without pressing the handle it opened gently, a slight creak as it came away from the splintered wood of the frame. He swallowed against the lump that was forming in his throat and stepped inside. Despite her fear Rose followed, not wanting to be left outside alone, but also not wanting to let her husband out of her sight now he had returned.

The hallway was empty and dark, no light filtering through from the overcast sky ahead. The thick carpeted stairway led up to a silent landing, directly ahead the kitchen door stood open; the white haired man could see the Christmas tree that Rose had decorated some time and day before she had been forced to flee to her sisters. There were cards on every visible surface, despite the fact that neither of them had been here for a large part of December, one thing you couldn't escape when you were in a position such as Martin's was the sheer number of well wishers at Christmastime.

Placing a finger to his lips to shush his wife who was about to speak, Martin softly closed the door and looked about himself for a weapon. There was nothing of note, but he picked up an umbrella from the stand next to the door and held it out before him like a fencing sword. Oh great, well if there are junkies hiding out in the house I'll be able to keep them dry if the roof leaks, he thought wryly as he took a step further down the hall.

Rose padded close behind him, her hand still clutching her collar, her eyes wide, darting from corner to corner like a frightened mouse. Martin couldn't help but feel sorry for her, she had been abducted, threatened, seen her first dead body and found her house broken into all in one day; this may have become the norm for him, but for any ordinary person it was a lot to comprehend.

The door to the living room was standing slightly ajar; Martin shuffled forward, switching the umbrella to his left hand and using his free right hand to push the door fully open. He had never noticed before how much the hinges needed a little oil, only now as the door creaked open, penetrating the silence that had given the house a mortuary like sensation, did he discover this.

Another Christmas tree, decorated magnificently by Rose's delicate hand but dark with its lights unseasonably dimmed, stood sentry in the corner of the room. The huge television stood in the adjacent corner, its screen a dark rectangle that seemed to suck even more light form the room. Martin's easy chair was where it had always been, next to the wall to the side of the tree, and the huge comfy sofa where he had sat and talked with Rose about life after he was gone was still pressed back to the left hand wall, its arms covered in a thin sheen of dust, the victims of too many days of neglect.

All was right in the room, and yet everything was wrong. Martin stepped a little further in, having difficulty placing what it was. It was the light, something was wrong with the light in the room, after several years it was easy to become accustomed to the altering definitions associated with each different season, each different sky-cast. After several years of sitting in his easy chair, watching as the sun broke from behind the clouds or the rain fell from a darkened sky one became accustomed to the movements of the shadows in the room, and something about the shadows in this room was wrong. There was a darkness coming from the corner of the room that was not yet visible, the corner directly behind the door. With his hand tightening on the handle of the umbrella Martin took one final step inside the room, so that he stood beyond the open panel of the living room door, and turned to look in the corner.

Martin said nothing, just stared at the man in the corner of the room with disbelieving eyes. Rose on the other hand, who had pressed up close to her husbands back in outright fear, now saw the man herself and let out a petrified shriek.

Involuntarily Martin whipped out a hand and silenced his wife, placing a palm across her mouth as her eyes stared at the thin man in horror. Martin understood the perilous situation all too well, understood that this particular man was not one to be tested, and Rose's anguish would only serve to antagonise him, and the businessman had a pretty good idea that he was already as agitated as he would be willing to get.

Haroon Malik stood in the far corner of the room, a stark juxtaposition to the feng shui the couple had created in their years in this house. His eyes, two huge white orbs that leapt from the shadows, glared at them unblinking, his hand held something that pointed in their direction and Martin had a pretty good idea that it wasn't an invite to the cheese and port society annual dinner.

The thin man stepped forward, he looked tired yet alert, as though he had spent an uncomfortable night hiding out in the house with every nerve end shooting bolts of adrenaline to his tightly wired brain, and Martin had a feeling that was exactly what had happened. His spider legs hair looked dishevelled slightly, flat on one side, as though he had been laid on one side of his head and had not the time or the care to address it. His clothes too looked rumpled and creased; sealing the deal for Martin that since the man's return to the UK he had clearly not been home.

"Silence that fat pig of a wife rich man or I'll put a bullet in her throat right here on your living room carpet."

Martin, who couldn't believe how naïve he had been in thinking it could ever have been anything as simple as junkie youths breaking into his house looked at Malik with wide open eyes. In truth he dare not blink; Malik was as dangerous as a preying mantis to its mate when he was settled, and right now he was anything but.

"Rose, do as he says, shush now."

She settled instantly, though her terrified eyes would not leave the barrel of the handgun that Malik was pointing directly at her.

"Good start." The Asian man said. "Nice place you've got here." He said looking about the room.

"What do you want Haroon?" Martin asked, not wanting to hear the answer but needing to stall for time. He needed a plan; any plan, but right now his mind was a blank.

"Well it seems I don't get what I want doesn't it rich boy." Malik replied with the curse of the Devil in his eyes. "I wanted you dead. I ordered you dead, and yet here you are, standing in front of me."

"It doesn't have to be like this." Martin said, his hand still covering his petrified wife's mouth.

"Oh I know it doesn't, don't I just fucking know it! I get on a plane back home thinking everything's hunky-dory, thinking you're in a furnace burning to ash, I land and everything's turned to shit. Your ugly fucking face all over the news. My business in ruins. Oh I know it doesn't have to be like this and yet here we are." He took a step forward, the hand holding the gun trembling slightly, not from fear, but from the uncontrollable rage that was burning inside him.

"They don't know about you; they don't know you had any involvement, not yet, there's still time for you, you can get out of here, leave the country."

"Leave the country? Leave the fucking country?" Malik raised his hands to his head in exasperation, the hand holding the gun bashing him slightly in the right temple, giving Martin if he needed it an even clearer indication of the state of the young mans mind. "I don't want to leave the country, this is my home!"

"I know, but you have to understand, you're in a corner, they're going to find out about you and when they do, they're going to be looking for you."

"They're going to be looking at me because of you!" The Asian man shrieked angrily, taking a step closer to Martin and raising the gun so the barrel was pointed right in the centre of the businessman's face.

"That may be true," Martin blurted quickly, feeling his panic increase with Malik's rising fury, "but you still have time. It's going to take time for them to conduct a full investigation in China; it could take weeks before they trace anything back to you. You can get out of here, get hold of your money, get yourself set up in a country with no extradition laws. There's still time."

"Yeah?" Malik said with a maniacal grin on his face. "If I've got as much time as you say why don't I take my time here, torturing you and your fat piggy wife before I slit your fucking throats?"

Martin could not reply, he just stared at the thin man with real growing horror. With all he had been through in the last couple of weeks this was certainly no more daunting, but having Rose with him brought a whole new and terrifying dimension to the ordeal; whatever happened, even if it meant laying down his own life in the process, he wouldn't let her get hurt. Eventually, when there was nothing from Martin but a stupefied look on his face, the black market organ trader spoke again:

"I'll tell you what you're going to do, you're going to get on the phone, and you're going to call here everybody that's been helping you. You're going to get them all here, and we're all going to sit down and have a nice little chat."

"I don't know what you mean, I've been working alone." Martin replied, feeling anxious and afraid.

"Don't you fucking lie to me old man, I know you've been working with a fucking private investigator or something, how else would you have found out about me? That's how you escaped from my office, the same people, helping you out; now get them here, every one of them."

"I'm telling you I worked alone." Martin said, taking his hand from his wife's mouth so he could hold them out before him earnestly.

Malik stepped forward quickly and pressed the barrel of the gun hard into Rose's forehead; she let out a petrified shriek and wobbled on her feet, so close to passing out from exhausted fear.

"Ok ok!" Martin said, his heartbeat doubling in an instant. "I'll call him, I'll get him here just please don't hurt her!"

"To the phone, now!" Malik said, his face an evil scowl.

Martin backed away slowly, his hands held up to show that he was no threat to the man.

"Rose, stay calm, it's going to be ok."

Together they stepped backwards towards the door that led into the huge grey and white kitchen. Rose was groaning in anguish but both men for the time being chose to ignore it. In the kitchen Martin skirted around the huge island unit to the phone nook in the corner. Once there he slowly raised his hands and grabbed the phone book from the wall. Malik stood by the island with Rose, the gun still pressing into her forehead.

"Any funny business, anything at all, you try and warn them or try to call for help, your wife's brains are gonna be decorating this worktop, you get me?"

"I understand, please, trust me."

"Trust you!" Malik scoffed, a cynical smirk on his face, but he said no more.

At last Martin dared to take his eyes from the man, and with his whole body trembling violently flicked through the contact book until he found what he was looking for. The first time he tried to dial the number he punched two of the digits in wrong and had to hang up the receiver. On the second attempt he took his time, punching each number in carefully, he waited for the connection to be made and a couple of seconds later the phone was ringing in his ear; it was answered on the third ring.

"Hi, this is Martin Rooley, I need you to listen carefully and not ask me any questions. I trust you've seen everything that's been happening in the news. I need you to come to the house, to my house, I need your help, do you think you could do that?"

There was a response from the other end of the line, then the call was ended.

"Well?" Malik asked.

"They're on their way." Martin replied, hoping in his second hand heart that he had done the right thing.

4

They sat in the living room in silence; Martin and Rose on the couch, Malik in Martin's easy chair. The exhausted woman sat with her arms wrapped around her husbands ageing bicep, her head on his shoulder and a look of abject misery on her face, Martin stared into space, worrying over whether he had made the right decision and what he was going to do to get them out of this mess. Malik sat forward in the seat, his eyes darting about the room like a smack addict, his gun rested for the time being in his lap, though his finger still itched over the trigger, tracing back and forth like the gentle caress of a lover.

The silence was unbearable, like the silence you would expect to hear inside a crypt, and the time seemed to be crawling along, with every second dragging by like a minute and every minute like an hour. There was a tension in the room that could not be described in words; you had to feel it, to live inside it, to breathe its dark odour to truly understand the depths of its foreboding. Every once in a while Malik would jump up from his seat, stomp over to the window, sneak a look outside from behind the safety of the curtains and then return, his impatience growing with every minute.

Then there were the questions: 'Where are they?' 'Why aren't they here yet?' 'What's taking them so long?' And the threats: 'If you're trying it on you're going to know about it.' 'If this is some kind of trick I'm gonna gut your wife in front of you, gonna bleed her out on the carpet.' And all the while Martin held his composure, telling the skinny man not to worry, telling him they would be here, reassuring him that it was no trick.

Still the time crept by, the shadows in the too dark room changing with the drifting of the clouds outside. One thing was for certain; there was no

Christmas spirit here. It was almost impossible to imagine that in houses up and down the street families would be preparing themselves for the festivities ahead. Children would be excitedly contemplating the presents they may receive, young people would be dressing up for a night on the town, businesses would be closing early to accommodate the needs of their staff, families would be preparing meals and laying out mince pies and sherry for the big man and a carrot for his trusty companion. All of this would be happening and yet none of it had any relevance here; in this home it was just another day in Hell, and Christmas was nothing but a dream of another life, one lived in a time of ignorant bliss.

Reflecting upon the crazy year he had endured Martin wondered upon just how much he had changed. A year ago he was the overweight, jovial chief executive officer of a global haulage company. He led a full and rich life, with enough excitement coming from his business endeavours to fulfil his needs. He had everything he could possibly hope for; from the cars, the nice house and the expensive clothes to the trophy wife, a wife who had stayed by his side despite the seemingly endless hours devoted to growing and developing the business. There was money in the bank and holidays in the sun; food on the table and the reassurance of a secure future for his fiercely loyal workforce.

Now look at him; battered and bruised, his eyes opened to a world of deceit, betrayal, torture and murder. A man who had ventured on a foolhardy quest that had taken him halfway around the world and straight into the bowels of Hell. A man that had been close to death on more occasions than he cared to remember. A man who could still die, right here, on his own living room carpet, with a bullet in his gut and the evil sneer of a deranged madman the last thing he sees. All of this was true, but he didn't regret one thing; the women, men and children of the Qingdao organ factory were free because of him, and the doors of the evil business closed. Whatever happened from here regret would not so much as cross his mind.

Malik, whose agitation was on the rise again, was rocking back and forth in Martin's easy chair, his eyes darting between the window and the open living room door. He was about to say something again, undoubtedly either a question or a threat, when yellow light flooded the forecourt at the front of the house.

The Asian man leapt to his feet, stepping into the shadows to the side of the window with the gun held up and his arm bent so the barrel was pointing at the ceiling. Martin sat forward on the sofa, his heartbeat quickening again and Rose screwed her eyes shut tight, pressing her face into her husbands arm and wishing this whole sorry affair away.

A mini cooper had pulled up in front of the electric gates, its engine idling as it waited to be allowed entry.

"Is this them?" Malik asked, staring at Martin accusingly.

The businessman rose from the couch enough so that he could look out onto the forecourt, lifting his wife with him who steadfastly refused to let go of her husband. He recognised the car right away, had seen it dozens of times over the years, but never before outside his house.

"That's them." He replied simply.

"Well let them in, and no funny business, I'm gonna be right here with your Mrs, and if I think for a second you're up to no good..."

"I know I know, you'll put a bullet in her throat."

"And don't you forget it."

Martin stood from the couch, having to forcibly remove his wife's arms from his own.

"Marty please no! Don't leave me!" She pleaded.

"It's going to be ok." He said, hoping amongst hope that he was right as he gently took her by the shoulders and placed her back down on the couch. Malik, who had no intention of offering any form of comfort, sat down beside her and shoved the barrel of the gun hard into her side. She let out a moan of misery, but that was all, allowing Martin to go about his duty. Without bothering to use the intercom that connected the house to the gate Martin stepped into the hall and pushed the button to allow access to the premises. A few seconds later the gates were slowly parting, opening up to allow the Mini to enter. It did just that, the headlights of the vehicle drowning the front of the gloomy house in light as it drove onto the forecourt.

Martin stood by the door, his heart thumping away in his chest, going over his plan again and again in his mind; at best he reckoned their chances of getting out of here alive were perhaps one in five, but any chance at all right now was better than none. Breathing deeply he stepped up to the narrow rectangular window that ran parallel to the door and took a peek outside. The car door was opening, the driver getting out; they were carrying something large and cumbersome in their hands.

"What's going on out there?" Malik asked, a new level of irritation in his voice."

"They're here." Was all Martin replied; a moment later there was a light rap at the door.

Martin drew in one last breath and opened the door, a slight creak again as it jarred against the splintered panel.

"Martin, thank God!" The caller said, the load in their arms was a bunch of carnations the size of the Chelsea flower show, and it partly obscured their face as they stood on the front stoop, the darkness of the day descending around them.

"Come in, please." Martin replied, then stepped away from the door and into the living room.

The lady followed, pushing the door closed behind her. Malik was up on his feet in an instant, the gun held out in his outstretched hand.

"Who the fuck is this?" He asked, a mixture of confusion and fury on his angular features.

"You wanted to know who else is involved, well here she is." Martin said quite simply. From the couch Rose watched on with her mouth a perfect o of shock and surprise, absolutely no idea what stunt her husband was trying to pull.

Sheila Morgan, PA to Martin at Sapient, stood behind the flowers, an equal look of hurt surprise on her own face.

"Martin, what's going on?" She asked, her eyes staring at the barrel of the gun that was now pointed at her face.

"You'd better explain yourself rich boy and explain quick!" Malik said, dancing from foot to foot on the living room carpet.

"Martin please, I came to check you were ok." Sheila persisted. "When I saw the news, my God!"

"Leave it Sheila, I know you're behind all this."

"Behind all what?" She almost shrieked.

"Behind Peter, behind my operation. I know it was you pulling the strings."

"I have absolutely no idea what you're talking about, who is this man?" She said, nodding towards the Asian man with the gun, the one whose finger kept squeezing down on the trigger of the automatic pistol, but not with quite enough pressure to release the firing mechanism.

"This is Haroon Malik, I believe from the young mans expression that the two of you have never met, though I would surmise that you Sheila know exactly who he is."

"I have no idea what you're talking about!" She replied sharply.

"Martin, what are you saying?" Rose almost pleaded from her place on the couch. "Sheila is one of your most trusted employees, and a good friend!"

"Sadly I think our true friends are a little thin on the ground right now." Martin replied steadily.

"Somebody had better tell me what the fuck is going on around here or brains are going to start hitting walls!" Malik said, the gun moving about every person in the room then steadying back on Sheila.

"When I was at the hotel in Qingdao, I got a phone call from Peter. I didn't think anything of it at the time. Then something he said just before he died got me thinking. He insinuated that he hadn't acted alone. Only one person knew of my itinerary in China; you!"

A look came across the middle aged woman's face; her expression twisted in less than a second from a look of hurt disbelief to a resigned state of acceptance, with just enough of a hint of sly mischief underneath to cement Martin's slightly shaky beliefs. Suddenly the bunch of flowers was dropping down to the living room carpet and in Sheila's own outstretched hand was also a gun; a tiny silver revolver, the perfect firearm to conceal in a purse or the waistband of your trousers.

Rose, shocked at the sudden turn of events, let out a disbelieving squeal; Martin simply stared, his cheeks slightly flushed from the confrontation.

Malik, caught suddenly off-guard at the sight of another weapon in the room, stared at the barrel of the pistol like a rabbit caught in the headlights of an oncoming truck. He had been completely in control of this situation, and now events had unexpectedly spun out of his control and he was blind with fury.

"Somebody better tell me what the fuck is going on right now!" He bellowed, his own handgun pointing at Sheila's head, his finger pale where it was gripping tightly at the trigger.

"Come now, let's not lose our heads." Sheila replied coolly, though she too was staring into the barrel of a handgun and it was easy to see that her composure was little more than a well played bluff. "Why don't we lower these guns and talk this out like reasonable people."

"I can't even tell what the fuck you're saying right now." Malik spat back angrily. "You're going to lower your gun or I'm going to shoot your tits onto the fucking wall!"

Rose let out another squeal at the exchange, looking from gunman to gunwoman and back again like an observer of a game of tennis. Martin, who had been ready for the situation to quickly spiral out of control, had already been using the diversion of attention o search the room for a weapon. He saw one now, the lengthy brass poker next to the open hearth, and he took a step closer to it, hoping it wouldn't be noticed by the pair of gun wielding crooks.

"There's really no reason for this, I'm not your enemy here." Sheila protested, though she did not support her claims by lowering her weapon.

Malik, choosing to ignore her, continued to skip from foot to foot, his gun still aimed at the middle aged woman's head. "I'm going to ask you one more time, who the fuck are you?"

"Ok, ok!" Sheila fired back quickly, she could see that the Asian man's patience was wearing thin and she didn't want to still be in his sights when it finally snapped. "I do know who you are, though we've never met."

"You'd better start talking, and if you want to get out of here alive you'd better have something good to say."

"You're Haroon Malik; you worked with a surgeon called David Purefoy and a man called Peter Werth-Duncan to source a new heart for this man here." Sheila flicked the barrel of the gun towards Martin, who until then had been contemplating another step towards the poker, then she quickly brought it back to rest on Malik.

"Go on." Malik replied, his eyes barely blinking.

"Well, I guess you could say I was the silent partner. Peter was my lover, at least when it suited me. This whole thing, it was my idea, Peter was a businessman not a crook, but he was also very easy to manipulate."

Martin, who had not expected this latest turn of events, was momentarily stunned out of motion. He had known since the journey from the airport that Sheila was involved somehow, but the mastermind behind the whole sorry affair, that he had not been expecting.

"You were a means to an end," Sheila continued, unperturbed by the shocked look on her employers face, "we needed a new heart and we needed one fast. I made some enquiries, you weren't that hard to find."

"You always were a resourceful woman." Martin said, staring in wild disbelief at the woman that was holding the gun, trying to fathom how this criminal mastermind was the same mild mannered woman who had organised his schedules and bought gifts for his wife on birthdays and Christmases. The same woman who had worked tirelessly to lighten his load through times of pressure and cried with worry when he had suffered his heart attack; or so he had believed at the time, it seemed now that the whole thing had been little more than a show.

"Yeah and wouldn't you know it!" Sheila spun slightly now and pointed the pistol directly at her employer. "Fifteen years on a shitty five figure salary while you pull in eight. Fifteen years of sorting your life out, working my fingers to the bone, doing the simplest of mindless fucking tasks like organising your meetings, answering your email and booking your appointments cos you're too fucking stupid to do it yourself. You don't even know how to use Google to book a fucking hotel room, you need me to do it for you, and somehow you come home with an eight figure salary, does that really sound fair to you?"

Martin, hurt to hear such words, looked at the woman with the short cut sandy hair in dismay. "You were my friend; at least I thought you were. I always treated you with dignity and respect. You want me to apologise for my wealth? I can't do that. I never expected Sapient to grow the way it did, but what was I supposed to do? Say no thank you? Why would I? I'm proud of what I built, and I don't owe anybody an explanation for it."

"No, what you owe me is what's rightfully mine!"

"You want money? You know I'm good for it, put the gun away and let's talk about how we make this work."

"It's too late for that, my bridges are burnt, no this ends right here and right now."

Malik, who had grown tired of being excluded from the conversation, asserted his authority once more:

"Ok ok that's enough. You think I give a fuck about who owes who what? I don't, I don't give a fuck. What I want to know is how the fuck you thought you were going to get away with pulling one over on me!"

"Please," Sheila responded with a mocking smirk on her face, "if it wasn't for this tiresome old fool you'd still be in the dark about me right now. You think you're this big hard man gangster but look at you now, running scared. You're pathetic!"

At first the Asian crime lord was so shocked to have been insulted by this wilting middle aged woman in the smart inner city business attire that he made no move, just stood with his mouth agape, looking like he had just been slapped. Then rage took over, it pulsed through every vein in his body, throbbing at his temples like the beginning of a migraine. The o of his lips curled into an ugly snarl and he crossed the room in a second, giving the woman no time to retaliate. He pressed the barrel of the gun firmly into Sheila's forehead, the force of his wrist bending her neck back slightly so she was partially looking at the ceiling, and as this was happening Martin noticed something that turned the blood in his own veins to rivers of ice.

There was a look on the woman's face, fear for sure, Martin felt certain that this was the first time she had ever truly stared down the barrel of a gun and felt the tender balance of her existence teetering so close to the edge. But there was something else as well, something underneath, beneath the surface of the natural survival instincts that anyone would encounter in such circumstances; the woman was actually enjoying this, the corners of her mouth were turned ever so slightly upwards and there was a glint in her eye the like of which the businessman had never witnessed. It was at that moment that Martin realised she was at least partially unhinged, maybe not quite outright certifiably crazy, but by all means a couple of accountants short of a board meeting.

"Do it." She said cockily, her eyes dancing with stars. "Pull the trigger; go on, if you've got the guts."

It was a risky strategy, but there was something in the woman's stare that made the black market trader hesitate. It was enough; he took a step backwards, the gun peeling from the skin of her forehead but leaving an angry looking weal, and back towards the centre of the room. Though the gun still pointed at her head it was all the confirmation Sheila needed that she had just taken control of the room.

Malik now gripped the handle of the gun in both hands, not wanting to show the slight shake that had developed in his one free hand. He had to act and act fast; this was not how the situation was supposed to pan out.

"Tell me more." He said, needing to say something, anything in a desperate bid to show it was still he who was in charge.

"What more is there to say? I used sex as a weapon to manipulate a weak man into betraying his friend. It wasn't hard to do; greed always wins through in the end."

"So the plan was to take over the business." Martin chimed in. "But when I had my heart attack and the deeds hadn't yet been signed it left you in a sticky position, you needed me alive so I could sign the business over to Peter, so together with Purefoy and Rose you hatched this disgusting plan."

On the couch Martin's wife let out a pained moan.

"A plan that saved your life, if you'd just had the decency to sign over the business none of this would have happened. Face it, you're as much to blame as anybody."

Martin wasn't going to be dragged into a petty argument over who was to blame, the who was responsible for what now was of little concern to him; getting him and his wife out of this alive was all that mattered now.

"It was you who ran us off the road wasn't it? The second car."

"Didn't work though did it, you're still here."

"Yes, and you've been trying to cover your tracks all along, that's why you killed David Purefoy."

At this Sheila's eyes gave an uncharacteristic twitch, she had clearly not expected anyone to trace the body back to her.

"Well well, maybe I underestimated you after all. David was getting nervous; all your constant phone calls, demanding answers. He was getting twitchy; he could have ruined it all; he had to go."

"You dumb bitch!" Malik almost screamed, taking a step forward again, the gun trembling in his outstretched hand. "You brought this on all of us!"

"Oh save me your blithering babble. If Purefoy had lived he would have brought the lid down on all of us for sure."

Martin took the opportunity to take another half step closer to the fireplace, his left hand was only a matter of inches now from where the heavy brass poker rested against the hearth.

"Is this what I'm dealing with? Fucking amateur hour." Malik spat back incensed. "You left a body for the police to find, what the fuck were you thinking?"

"I was thinking let them find it, I left no reason for them ever to suspect me." The devilish grin was back on the PA's face, she really was enjoying toying with the criminal.

"I should shoot you dead right here in this room."

"You could." She replied coolly. "But let's not forget we have a common enemy here."

Martin had been stretching out his hand, his fingers brushing against the cold brass of the poker, when the woman's words stopped him in his tracks, causing a cold chill to run the length of his spine. If Sheila managed to side with Malik it was over for him and Rose for sure. Then Malik spoke, and he felt there was a chance after all.

"Everybody in this room is my enemy." He replied.

Sheila sighed. "As you wish." She said, and without any note of warning pulled the trigger of her tiny silver revolver.

The report was deafening in the confines of the living room. There was a flash of fire and a tiny puff of smoke. Martin brought his hands to his ears in shock. Rose let out a terrified yelp. Haroon Malik, who had never had anybody stand up to him in his life, stared at the woman in utter disbelief. Then he noticed something new, a pain in his stomach like a hot coal, burning away at his lower intestine. He looked down and saw the red patch that was quickly becoming a pool on the lower half of his T-shirt and his hand that was holding the gun started to lose its strength. He dropped to the floor with a look of absolute shock stretched across his pointed features. He was losing consciousness quickly, but looked up just in time to see the twisted bitch grinning down at him. Then his eyes could no longer retain their focus, he saw the flowers scattered about the living room floor, and then his awareness started to slip completely. He was dying, he couldn't quite believe that it was true but it was, he was actually dying, and at the hands of a woman who looked like she spent her evenings baking cookies and reading Catherine Cookson novels.

Rose stared down at the dying man on the floor with a look that refused to believe what she was actually seeing. She was shaking from head to toe and if she had been expected to speak at that point she would have managed little more than an incoherent babble.

In shock himself Martin knew he only had seconds in which to act, but in his current state it was like walking through syrup, it was as though his brain had been dipped in molasses and every thought was clouded with stupor. He needed to lift himself out of it but all he could do was stare in shock at the dying criminal on his living room carpet.

Come on come on! Get a grip! You haven't gone through the mill and back for it all to end right here, right now. Martin scolded himself, trying to fire up the muscles in his arms and in his legs, to find the driving force to propel him into action.

All of these thoughts happened in the space of a couple of seconds, but to Martin it felt like a lifetime. Then his eye caught sight of his wife, his beautiful Rose, sat on the couch with her face contorted in terror and it struck him, if he didn't act now she was going to die!

Suddenly his body spasmed into life; his hand which had been brushing up against the cold brass of the poker until the moment the gun shot had deafened the room lashed out and grabbed for it, wrapping tightly around the shaft so the knuckles of his hand turned white. He knew what he intended to do, had known it all along, but sadly for him so had his overtly intelligent PA.

Lifting the poker from its resting place on the hearth he lashed out with his wrist, swinging his arm in an arc, propelling from his shoulder with the intention of striking the woman in the side of the head. It was no use, at the last second Sheila took a step to the right and the heavy brass poker missed her head by several inches, creating a whooshing sound as it cut through the air.

Grinning like the cat that got the cream Sheila spun her tiny frame around so she was facing her old employer; at the moment the poker completed its arc of descent she pointed her tiny silver revolver at the white haired man and pulled the trigger. Again there was a flash, a puff of smoke and a deafening roar, only this time there was something else as well, for Martin at least; this time there was a bolt of excruciating pain that exploded in his side. The force of the impact sent him toppling backwards where he struck the arm of his easy chair, collapsed over it and landed on the floor in a heap.

"Nooooo!" Rose screamed, her eyes practically bulging from their sockets. A dark patch of crimson blood had suddenly appeared on the left hand side of Martin's shirt, and a thin tendril of smoke rose up from where the bullet had scorched his wounded skin.

The businessman looked down at the wound in disbelief; even when he had been faced with dying so many times, he had never imagined how close he could actually come to the end, it wasn't until now, with the smell of his own burning skin filling his nostrils that he truly believed this could actually be it.

Sheila, the grin still stretching across her narrow face, only fiercer now, more urgent, stepped forward and lowered the gun so it was pointed directly at Martin's face.

"If I can't have what's yours, then you don't get to have it either." She said, her eyes glimmering.

Rose looked from her husband, lying soaked in the blood of his own insides, to the woman she had once considered her friend and knew that she had to act, if she didn't Martin was going to die, then it would be her turn for sure. So what of it? If Martin died she didn't want to be alive anyway.

Months of weight loss and dance classes finally served more than just an aesthetic purpose, as the sixty-four year old woman leapt from the couch and made a grab for the hand that was holding the pistol. For once Sheila was actually caught off guard; of all the moves she had anticipated any kind of action by this timid mild mannered woman wasn't one of them. But Sheila had never been in love, and didn't understand the feeling of complete abandonment in the face of love, the notion of risking ones life to save someone you loved was simply lost on her, this was to be her downfall. She turned at the last second to see the woman with the tight grey perm bearing down on her.

Rose crashed into the PA with all her force, sending the short haired woman toppling left towards the fireplace. She found her footing just in time and managed to remain on her feet but not before Rose made a grab for the hand holding the gun. She succeeded in gripping the sandy haired woman by the wrist but little more, for Sheila had regained her composure, and wasn't about to let this prissy twit spoil her fun. She batted Rose aside like a wrestler swatting a fly, the older woman crashing down to the carpet, landing hard on her bottom.

Martin watched all this in horror, unable to take his eyes from proceedings but in too much pain to be able to lift him from the floor. Instead he watched as Sheila turned and levelled the small silver pistol at his wife, intending to fire the shot that would end her life.

He wanted to scream, wanted to shout, wanted to bellow his protest in the most vulgar of ways, but all that would pass his lips was a pained wheeze; he was completely helpless, and Rose was going to suffer for his fragility.

But before she could fire a new look passed on Sheila's face; gone was the maniacal grin, replaced by a twisted look of shocked horror.

At first Martin didn't see what had caused the change in Sheila's demeanour, then he did, and he had never been as indebted to this most unlikely of saviours. Malik, who all in the room had mistakenly believed to have reached an untimely demise was still for the moment very much alive, and though he was still laid with his belly to the floor, had hunkered up onto his elbows, and with one eye squeezed shut from the tremendous pain in his belly was aiming his gun with a visibly shaking hand at Sheila's face.

The PA didn't have time to react; even with Malik in the sorry state that he was she knew she wouldn't beat him to the draw, but it didn't stop her from trying. With Rose still staring up at her from her own place on the carpet, unaware that she had just received a momentary reprieve, Sheila bucked her hips, trying to spin and lower the pistol before the shot was fired; it didn't work.

The Asian crime lord was able to focus just long enough to steady the gun, drawing in a breath and holding it between pursed lips to give him a momentarily stable grip on the handle of the gun. He squeezed the trigger and the bullet ripped from the barrel in a deafening roar. He had been aiming for her nose, and was a couple of inches north of his target, but the bullet blew away the top of Sheila Morgan's head in a fountain of blood that soaked the businessman's wife at her feet, exploding out of the back of her skull and shattering through the glass of the living room window.

The middle aged woman stood for a couple of seconds, swaying back and forth, blood dripping down a face that wore a disbelieving and rather mystified look. Then suddenly the knees buckled and she collapsed to the floor in an uncomfortable looking heap.

Rose, despite the fact that it could so easily have been her laid on the floor with a bullet in her skull, let out a scream of abject horror, that made the hairs on Martin's arms stand to attention, for his own part the millionaire looked upon his dying PA in a kind of silent wonder, unable to truly comprehend what had just happened.

Malik, the last of his energy spent on his moment of revenge flopped back down onto his face, his nose squashing into the floor, the hand that held the gun padding down with a dull flump to the living room carpet; he was dead before his body came to rest.

Martin collapsed onto his back, staring up at the living room ceiling; he held onto the open wound in his side with his crimson stained hands, hoping he was doing enough to stem the flow of blood. There was a whimpering sound from the other side of the room; his bedraggled other half. He knew that in a few moments she would be on her feet, hurrying over to check that he was ok, calling an ambulance that he hoped would arrive in time to stop him from bleeding out on the carpet, just like the two very different criminals that now lay dead in the comfort of his living room.

Before any of this happened there was relative silence, and Martin lay listening to it, feeling for the first time since this whole sorry mess began that he was finally listening to the peace that comes with closure.

5

As it turned out, the bullet that Martin feared would end his life had only done superficial damage. It had punctured the skin on the still reasonably flabby side of his belly, taking a chunk of flesh as it passed through to come to rest in the hard wood floor beneath the thick living room carpet. Not only had it passed straight through him it had also missed every vital organ, there would be a pretty nasty scar once healed but that was a small price to pay for dodging death, not just once, but several times.

Now it was December 25th; Christmas Day, and for the second year running he was laid in a sterilised bed in St. Cuthbert's hospital, only this time in the major trauma unit. He hoped that this would be the last time, that if he was lucky enough to see the next year in that the following Christmas could perhaps be spent away from these bleach smelling halls.

Since waking that morning and realising he was on a strict diet of morphine and drip fed food supplements Martin had been watching the TV news. Apart from speculation of what would be included in her Majesty's annual address and the build up to the following day's big Manchester derby the majority of the schedule was dedicated to the unravelling events in China. Impossible to be swept under the carpet after Lau's story broke and the subsequent images of the naked captives that had gone viral around the world the Chinese authorities had promised a thorough investigation; with senior minister Cheng Xiung Yau publicly demanding a transparent investigation, a bold move, and one made with political aspirations in mind for sure, but a move that had secured media coverage behind the Orient's secretive red curtain.

Video from news helicopters had shown aerial footage of the now abandoned factory, giving Martin chills as he gazed upon the red brick work that had housed both his own incarceration and torture and the death of so many innocent men, women and children, including the man who had helped him bring the whole sorry affair to an end; Young Pyo-Chang.

The guards, aware that things had gone very bad and were about to get a whole lot worse had scattered, fleeing back to whatever rock they had each crawled from under; in the days to come some would be captured, others would escape the punishment they so rightly deserved, this was real life, and in it not every villain would receive his comeuppance. The news anchors had talked of possible grisly affects being discovered within the walls of the factory, but as they were as yet not allowed entry to the facility this remained speculation. News had filtered through however of links to senior officials in both Chinese politics and the Shandong Police Department who were at present not available to support the police with their enquiries, in fact, since the exposure of the events that had occurred within the factory walls nothing had been seen of one Police Chief and two senior politicians.

Martin had finally had enough, having seen his own face appear on screen now several times as the British press scrutinised his involvement in the bizarre tragedy, he lifted the hand that was holding the control and switched off the television. Sighing he placed it back on the bedside cabinet and winced as a fresh pain stabbed into his injured side. He wished he could stay in this bed for several weeks, for as soon as he was fit to leave he had been summoned back to China as anticipated, a key witness in the unfolding saga; alas with the severity of his injuries not being as advanced as had been originally feared, this would undoubtedly be sooner rather than later. For now though, this was his Christmas; it may not have the tinsel and turkey of Christmases past, but it was a Christmas of peace and rest, something less than forty eight hours prior he would have deemed impossible. His eyes slipped closed and he waited for sleep to wrap its comforting arms about him, but before he could slip into a silent slumber there was a soft rap at the door.

Rose stood sheepishly in the open doorway, one hand clutching at her blouse the other up to the side of her mouth where she chewed absently at the nail of her index finger, a sign if any were needed that all was not well in the world of Rose Doris Rooley. Martin, who had been expecting this visit but hoping as with his impending return to China to put it off a little longer now gestured for her to come closer.

His wife looked old and tired, she had clearly not slept well and worry lines ringed her puffy red eyes.

"Martin." She said as she drew near, her bottom lip trembled but she could manage no more.

Feeling sympathy despite the situation Martin patted the side of his bed and the woman gratefully sat down, knowing that any acceptance from him was a positive step. There was silence for a few moments, neither knowing what they were to say; it was Rose who eventually broke this:

"They say you're doing well."

"I'm doing fine." Martin replied softly. "A nasty nick is all, I was very lucky."

"You don't look lucky, lying there in a hospital bed on Christmas day, in a hospital bed on Christmas day again."

"All the same, I was lucky."

She nodded absently, looking down to the floor. "Have they given any indication of how long you're going to be in this time?"

"Not so long I shouldn't think." He replied. "The injury is mostly superficial; they'll probably keep an eye on it for a couple of days then send me home with fresh dressings."

"Thank God."

"Yes, thanks to him." Martin agreed; he had never been a religious man but the last twelve months of his life had been a pretty profound experience, and more and more he found himself drawing closer to a conclusion of a higher being, someone who had watched out for him on more occasions than he cared to remember. "Rose, we need to talk."

This time his wife visibly winced, it was as though an invisible hand had stretched out and tickled her coldly on the back of her neck, but though her face was filled with dread she nodded reluctantly, knowing that the healing of the heart had to start with the truth.

"Martin," she spoke his name in a tone that was tantamount to pleading, "I didn't know, I swear to you I didn't know."

The white haired man sighed and pressed his head back into his pillow, gathering his thoughts as he looked up into the corner of the room.

"What *did* you know?"

Clutching her purse tightly in her hands his wife squeezed her lips tightly together and continued her deep scrutiny of the floor tiles.

"It was during that horrible period, that horrible period of waiting, when we didn't know if they were going to find you a new heart and we didn't yet know if you were going to pull through. Things were looking pretty bleak, in fact they were looking very bleak, well you remember, you were there.

About that time the surgeon came to me."

"David Purefoy."

"That's right, David Purefoy. He came to me saying he had an answer to our prayers, that he'd found you a new heart but it wasn't entirely...you know."

"Entirely legitimate." Martin finished for her and watched as her cheeks flushed red; good, she deserved to feel shame for her actions.

"He mentioned that he could get you the heart and that it was your only chance, he wanted me to convince you it was the right way forward, he said you were going to die Martin what was I to do? Just sit back and let that happen? You're my husband, I love you."

Martin could see how hard this was for her, but he wasn't about to let her off the hook that easily.

"Go on."

"There really isn't more to say. He told me about the heart, that it wasn't above board but that it was the only way we were going to save you, but I swear to you Martin, I swear to you, I had no idea about the terrible places these things come from, I had no idea!"

"It was a black market organ Rose, where the hell did you think it had come from? Santa Claus?"

The grey haired woman recoiled as though slapped. "I didn't think about it! I couldn't! I was thinking about you!"

"The fact that you didn't allow yourself to think about where the heart may be coming from doesn't make you any less complicit."

Rose, who for a moment had shown some true fire, now gazed back down to the floor. "I know." She said eventually, her cheeks turning an ashen grey beneath her embarrassed glow.

A deep silence filled the room, within it Martin drifted into thoughts of his own, it was nearly a whole minute before he came back into the moment, and when he did he realised his wife was in tears.

"Those poor people." She said through cracked lips. "Those poor poor people. And the children, my God the children."

Martin didn't respond; couldn't respond. His natural instinct was to comfort her but he was still too stung by her betrayal. Instead he lay in his bed watching as her shoulders shook and her tears streaked down her cheeks, dripping from the end of her chin and landing in her lap where they were making sticky wet patches on her purse.

Eventually the sobbing subsided and she turned to him with such a look of pained misery on her face that it almost broke his heart.

"How do we move on from this Martin?"

Martin was silent for a while, letting the question hang while he considered his response. Eventually, when his answer came, it was as honest as he knew how to be.

"I'm not sure we can."

The woman collapsed forward so her head was low down in her lap, a position Martin would have sworn she had not been limber enough to achieve for twenty years, wild sobs racked her body in violent spasms, but still he was completely incapable of finding it within him to comfort her. Instead he lay in silence, listening as her misery compounded, and wondering if there was any way they could ever lay to rest the things that they had done.

EPILOGUE

Somewhere outside Qingdao, Shandong Province, China, six months later.

Summer in the Orient can be a humid, muggy affair, and today was no exception, though the sky was grey and overcast the temperature was somewhere in the late thirties and the thin cotton shirt that Martin was wearing clung to the clamminess of his skin, making him feel irritable and uncomfortable. But this was a special day; he wasn't going to let minor inconveniences spoil the mood. Above everything was the desire, the need to show his respects, but he also couldn't deny an almost morbid fascination that excited him about the events that were to come.

In the last six months his already fading commitment as the Chief Executive Officer of Sapient Trans Global had sunk to new levels. With the on-going inquiry and the impending trial he had simply not had the time to commit to the business in the manner it deserved, and so in April he had hired a new officer; Susan Reid, who he had secured from Barclay's bank, and so far she was doing a damn fine job. At this moment in time it was untrue to say he had retired, but his desire to spend every waking moment in the office was no longer there, and he felt sure that if things worked out with Susan it wouldn't be long before he retired to the board for good.

It had been a difficult period of his life; at nearly sixty-nine years of age he had been required to commute regularly between the UK and China to support the on-going investigations; investigations that now stretched across three continents and implicated more than three dozen senior officials in fourteen different countries, including England, where a senior member of the Tory government was missing, wanted for questioning.

Martin was under no illusions as the man hailed as responsible for bringing an end to the whole sorry saga how valuable his input was, but some days he just felt so weary, so old. Some days he just wanted to lie in bed, close the blinds and wait out the day. On these days, when his resolve was at its lowest and his ebb had all but disappeared he thought of Chang, of the sacrifice he had made, and of his beautiful pig-tailed daughter, who had gone missing from home one day and never returned.

This last six months had also been a telling one on his health; though this time it wasn't any of his major organs that were failing, he was simply starting to feel his age. He had noticed it creeping up on him after he was discharged from hospital, with a large bag of strapping and gauze strips to redress his wounds just as he had predicted. It seemed for the last six months or so prior to the final showdown in the living room of his Greater London home he had been running mostly on adrenaline, and when he finally stopped, all of the exhaustion, all of the aches and pains, all of the things that defined you as a senior citizen finally caught up with him. His back ached pretty much all of the time now, his joints throbbed with arthritis, the lines under his eyes looked deeper, the ridges on his forehead like the inflated underside of a rubber dinghy. He was in most people's eyes an old man, and age had snuck up on him like a thief in the night and made itself known in the loudest of voices.

He wasn't complaining though, merely observing the passage of time, and if he ever caught himself sighing at his advancing years he just thought again of that little girl with the goofy smile and the pretty black pigtails and none of it seemed so bad.

Now he was here; back on the outskirts of Qingdao, only this time surrounded by news crews from around the world and a heavy police presence. The huge iron gates to the front of the factory had been closed since the investigation team had concluded its business here, and had subsequently been inundated with a sea of floral bouquets, some from as far away as Poughkeepsie New York and Alice Springs Australia, but most from right here in Qingdao, where the hurt had been felt the deepest.

At six o'clock that morning a team of demolition experts had tenderly made a path in the flowers and re-opened the gates so the cranes and the JCB's and the wrecking ball could enter the compound. Now, nearly seven hours later, work was about to begin.

Martin turned slightly and nodded to the woman on his right, who nodded her acknowledgment and then stepped forward, placing the bouquet of wild orchids down with the others to the side of the gate, the message on the greeting card quite simple, 'We will never forget.'

There was the sound like a child with a playing card in the spokes of his bicycle to accompany this; it was the sound of dozens of hand held cameras all clicking away at once. Rose, looking tired and strained kept her head low as she head back to her husband. Martin had never revealed her involvement with the terrible crime which had saved his life, and he never would, that said he took a bitter pleasure in seeing how uncomfortable she was under the scrutiny of the assembled press, she deserved to feel some discomfort for what she had done.

"Come on." Martin said when she returned.

"Where are we going?" She asked, looking pale and haunted.

"Somewhere we can get a better view."

Down below the heavy machinery had revved into life, it was the perfect moment to slip away, while the press were preoccupied with events at the factory.

Together they walked up the hill along the path to the side of the perimeter fence, the warm sun beating down on their necks and making beads of sweat dance on their ageing foreheads. The yellow grass jostled in the light breeze, the sound like the crunching of a thin sheet of paper.

As the months had been trying on the couple individually it had also been a strain on their relationship. More than once Martin had taken the decision to leave, feeling he could never look at his wife the same again, but on each of those occasions he somehow stood his ground, refusing to give in to the easy option, deciding instead to work through this difficult period, just as he had vowed to do when he had married her as a young woman so many years before. Only the years would tell if they would indeed stand the test of time, but for now it looked as though the love that had kept them together as the decades rolled on was enough to keep them together now.

He made it to the top of the hill and looked down at the hole in the fence that he had cut with Chang in what felt like another lifetime. A couple of moments later Rose appeared at his side puffing for air and wafting her hand in front of her face in that age old gesture to get cool.

Below them were the garages that had shielded him when he had made his entry into the facility, and where his friend had lost his life, taken as easily as one might swat a fly or dispose of an unsightly weed. Martin drew in a breath, knowing he had to pay due to these things, no matter how much it pained him inside.

The huge crane that held the wrecking ball was being motioned into place, two men in coveralls and hard hats gesturing for its driver to move into the space to the side of the nearest wall. Helicopters circled above, the news crews capturing the scene below just as they had done on the morning the story first broke.

"Oh Martin." Rose said, looking down on the factory with an expression of utter disbelief. "What a horrible, horrible place."

Martin only nodded, then returned his attention to the scene below. The arm of the crane was rising now and veering right, getting into place, the heavy ball attached by a chain as thick as a weight lifters arm swayed slightly with the motion. The news crews assembled at the gate preparing to give their reports, wanting to go live at the precise moment the first strike was made.

   As the crane driver readied his swing Martin stretched out his hand and took his wife's in his own. The look she gave him was one of such surprise, and such thankfulness, such utter appreciation that for a moment he thought maybe yes, it was possible to find his love for her again.

   Down in the valley where atrocities had once occurred in the pursuit of wealth the wrecking ball gave its first strike, causing an ear splitting crack in the factory wall and sending billows of dust dancing on the musky breeze. The demolition had begun.

Conceived March 2014
Laid to rest March 2016

   Thank you for reading this my fourth published novel, if you enjoyed it would you please be so kind as to leave me a review at your favourite retailer?

Thanks!

Simon Andrew Stubbs

ABOUT THE AUTHOR

Simon Andrew Stubbs was born in February 1976 in Bradford, England. He is a keen singer / song writer and avid sports fan. He is married to Vicky and has two children, Ethan and Joseph, who despite his wild imagination will always be his biggest adventure.

CONNECT WITH SIMON ANDREW STUBBS

Friend me on Facebook: https://www.facebook.com/#!/simon.stubbs.58

Follow me on Twitter: https://mobile.twitter.com/simonastubbs

JACKSON HOPE *By Simon Andrew Stubbs*

Available from all good online retailers

The young woman's eyes widened as the man approached, although the look on his face could have curdled milk it was not this that terrified her; it was the burning torch in his hand, the flame flickering brightly in the cool night air. He stopped in front of her, enjoying the moment, taunting her with the flame.

"Why are you doing this?" She asked, the tears streaking her dirty cheeks.

"Because we can." The man smiled his toothless grin, the corners of his mouth turning up into a hideous Halloween mask.

"You bastard." The woman whimpered, all around she could hear the screams and wailings of her fellow captors, their tears echoing throughout the square. She would have felt for them if she was not in the same perilous situation. Again she tugged her arms against the cruel ropes that bound her tight, but there was no give, and her fruitless effort did nothing but exhaust her.

"Oh you struggle me beauty, you just go on and keep struggling, for what good it will do ya." The man with the greasy blonde hair chuckled, then he wafted the flame in front of her face again and the woman screamed in absolute terror.

She could smell the kerosene soaked wood of the bonfire beneath her, or maybe she just imagined she did, after all her nose was badly broken. The monsters had come when it was least expected, kicking down the doors to the town's homes and rounding up their prey, their firepower too immense to defend against. Nobody was safe; they attacked without reason or remorse, their intellect too small for their evil acts to weigh on their conscience. The truth was they enjoyed their work; nothing like the smell of crackling on a brisk October's evening.

"Don't do this please." The woman pleaded. The cackle that was her reply did little to ease her concerns.

Suddenly a scream shrilled above the others; this scream was different, it was not derived from fear, it was derived from total and absolute pain; it had started.

The dirty man looked in the direction of the sound, seemingly disappointed he had not been the one to start the party.

"Fucks and curses." He muttered, spitting a huge lungful of green phlegm onto the floor of the dusty town square.

The woman tried to follow his stare but was unable from her precarious position on the wood pile. Instead she looked up to the stars, begging to the Heavens with her eyes; not like this, it couldn't end like this.

The man turned back to her, the anger unmistakable in his eyes.

"Oh no, please no!" The woman's face etched in absolute misery.

"It's fryin' time." The grin reappeared on the thugs face, happy again after his momentary lapse.

As he leant forwards and lit the foot of the kerosene soaked bonfire with the flame of his torch the young woman leant her head back, squeezed her eyes shut tight and screamed until the blood clogged in her throat.

The woodpile caught instantly, the destructive combination of fuel, heat and oxygen causing a sudden gulf of flame that tore up the wood stack in a wave of orange menace. The woman screamed in much the same vein of the screamer before her, though the flames had not yet touched her she knew it was only a matter of moments before they did and the fear was too great to subdue.

The man watched on in fascination, salivating at the mouth like a rabid dog, he could feel his penis starting to stiffen in his pants and rubbed at the bulge with his free hand.

Suddenly the woman's thin cotton dress caught fire and for the first time she felt the heat of the fire against her naked flesh. Her next scream was brought on by the all consuming pain, the only thing capable of blocking out the fear.

The smell of burning flesh filled the air as the night was torn wide open with a cacophony of screams. Those not yet burning on their stakes struggled for freedom as the smoke drifted across the square.

The woman's entire dress was alight now and her arms were rubbed raw where she had struggled against her bindings, then her pony tail caught in the flames and the hair on her head was suddenly engulfed in flame. She screamed and screamed, shaking her head from side to side; spit flying from her mouth in an unladylike fountain. The pain was like nothing she had felt before, so intense that 'pain' was not actually a strong enough word. The skin of her arms blistered in hideous yellow sores that exploded from the heat, the puss oozing down her sides, then the skin itself was alight and her flesh slipped from her bones like icing through a funnel. Her face lit up like a lantern and her eyes bulged and scorched in their sockets.

As the last humiliated and desperate wail escaped her throat her captor rubbed at himself once more and then moved on to his next victim.

Printed in Great Britain
by Amazon